MIKE GRIS

Mike Grist is the British/American author of the Chris Wren thrillers. Born and brought up in the UK, he has lived and worked in the USA, Japan and Korea as a teacher, photographer, writer and adventurer.

HAVE YOU READ EVERY CHRIS WREN THRILLER?

Saint Justice
They stole his truck. Big mistake.

No Mercy
Hackers came for his kids. There can be no mercy.

Make Them Pay
The latest reality TV show: execute the rich.

False Flag
They framed him for murder. He'll kill to clear his name.

Firestorm
Wren's father is back. The storm is coming.

Enemy of the People
Lies are drowning America. Can the country survive?

Backlash
He just wanted to go home. They got in the way...

Never Forgive
His home in ashes. Vengeance never forgives.

War of Choice
They came for his team. This time it's war.

Learn more at www.shotgunbooks.com

HAVE YOU READ EVERY GIRL 0 THRILLER?

THE CHRISTOPHER WREN SERIES

BOOKS 1-3

MIKE GRIST

SHOTGUN
BOOKS

SHOTGUN BOOKS

www.shotgunbooks.com

Paperback ISBN - 9781739951191

For Su

CONTENTS

JUSTICE WILL BE DONE

SAINT JUSTICE

A CHRISTOPHER WREN THRILLER

MIKE GRIST

1

QOTL

C hris Wren stood alone in a dried-up gully under the beating Mexican sun, thinking about how many deaths it would take until he was out of the CIA for good.

Maybe thirty. Maybe just one.

The gully's sloping banks focused the baking midday heat like a lens, and Wren shuffled his shades, scanning the sun-battered landscape. There was nothing but withered desert scrub rooting through rust-red sand to the left, a couple of long-necked ocotillo stalks rising toward splintery orange rocks on the right. Just another gouge in the epic landscape of the Sonoran Desert, one hundred miles south of the US border.

The only visibility lay dead ahead, where a few miles on the gully bled out into a desert plain beneath a chemical blue sky, broken now by a tiny plume of dust rising like a distant signal fire.

Incoming vehicles, at last.

Wren laid a hand on his SIG Sauer P320 ACP .45 pistol. Eight rounds to a mag, incredible stopping power with a powerful recoil, but nothing his solid 6' 3" frame or his conscience couldn't absorb.

"Agent Wren," came a voice in his tactical earpiece. The Kid, as Wren called him. Samuel Regis, 27 years old and son of a senator. He'd been fast-tracked into the CIA with management seniority over Wren, just as his father was warming up for a presidential run. A political appointment.

"That's Officer to you," Wren growled.

"Sure, Officer," Regis allowed in his plummy Harvard accent. "You have eyes on?"

"I see them," Wren confirmed. "Qotl cartel outriders coming up the creek. Five minutes ETA."

"Play it cool. This is a big deal."

Nothing Wren needed to say to that. With twenty years' experience, you didn't much listen to the latest newbie on the block. This was his op anyway, until the Senator had gotten involved. It was meant to be a simple back-channel anti-terror deal with Qotl leadership, headed by Don Mica. Wren knew all about Mica, had almost assassinated him once. A harsh operator, he was most famous for feeding his enemies alive to rabid dogs.

He wasn't an ideal partner, but Wren lived in the gray spaces, and had done so for twenty years. The Qotl cartel brought in drugs and destabilized the border, but they weren't waging terror wars or blowing up buildings. That made them semi-allies in Wren's book.

Then the Senator had gotten involved, his son came in, and Wren's deal was nixed.

Now he'd been sent out here for a solo mission, to restate the primacy of the War on Drugs. Put the Qotl cartel on notice. Put Don Mica on notice. It meant burning a fair chunk of his Qotl intelligence network, all on some order passed down through a silver spoon punk who'd never gotten his hands dirty.

Wren didn't buy any of it. Hadn't bought it from the start. The Senator was up to something.

Regis began talking. "In case-"

Wren cut the line. The dust plume was thicker now. Four minutes out. He'd already set certain precautions in motion. Now he brought up his phone, reset the line to his earpiece and dialed a number from memory.

"Hector," he said.

"Christopher Wren, my boy!" Hector Gutierrez crowed down the private line. Gutierrez was a fringe Qotl cartel informant, a connection Wren had made when first going undercover with the cartel fifteen years back. He was a Baja-Mexican raised half in LA and half the shanty towns of the peninsula, complete with diamond teeth grille, teardrop cheek tattoos and, bizarrely, a set of red suspenders he never went anywhere without. "What you don't know might get you killed, cuz."

Wren grunted. "You think I don't know what's coming my way?"

"Latest I heard, Santa Justicia's about to get his ticket punched." Gutierrez sounded far too happy with this prospect. And there was that nickname. 'Santa Justicia', or 'Saint Justice'. Wren gritted his teeth. It was stupid, but you couldn't pick what they called you.

"You're saying my people sold me out?" he asked, checking the incoming vehicles. They should be coming within range of the Kid's snipers now, but if this whole thing was a set-up, then the snipers weren't going to fire under any circumstances.

"Maybe I am," Gutierrez teased. "Word is you're on the outs anyway, cuz. Don Mica, you know he's got a thing for taking out the CIA's trash. Two birds with one stone, you feel me?"

"Three minutes," Wren said. "Give me something solid or stop wasting my time."

Gutierrez laughed. "Something solid, pendejo, like a knife in the ribs? What you think I know?"

Wren watched the trucks rolling closer. A Humvee. A couple of heavy black trucks, like a presidential motorcade. In back rolled a black panel van, which could be filled with starving dogs. Maybe Mica planned to watch 'Santa Justicia' get eaten alive.

"Looks like Mica's brought his dogs," Wren said. "What's he planning here, Hector?"

"Walkies?" Hector tried. "I hear the Sonoran Desert's lovely for a stroll this time of year."

Wren grimaced. Gutierrez was an idiot, but unfortunately for Wren, he was the only idiot he had in this particular pinch.

"Look at it this way, Hector. If I'm for the dogs, guess what happens when I mention your name as I go down?"

"I bet it ain't good, homes," Gutierrez cheered. The man was positively giddy, holding Wren's life in his hands. Maybe high on his own supply. "Glad I ain't there."

"You've got one minute, Hector. My lips are feeling real loose. It's now or never."

Gutierrez held out, and the Humvee entered its final approach up the gully, the trucks flanking either side. Exactly how Wren would take down a high-value target like himself, if it came to that. Maximum overkill.

"Make a decision," Wren warned. "But bear in mind, if I get out of this alive, I'm coming for you."

"Fine, ese," Gutierrez said, sounding bored, "but only 'cos you asked so nice. I got some documents."

"Documents saying what?"

"Bad stuff. That Don Mica made a deal with Regis to foment a coup in Argentina. Political crap aimed at generating some BS hit pieces? Goal was to help Regis become President by taking down his opponent." Gutierrez took a breath. "Was all good, until Regis got cold feet and pulled out. Now Mica's mad. I seen him, he's been pissed for weeks, Chris. Talking all kinds of crazy, drug war stuff, about exposing Regis as a charlatan, on the take." A brief pause. "Looks to me like you're the peace offering."

Wren snorted. Peace offering meant sacrificial lamb, just to placate the cartel. It figured. It made for an easy retirement plan for his CIA handlers, who would just look the other way. "You're lying to me, you know what happens?"

"What lie, Christopher?" Gutierrez replied. "He gonna sic them dogs on me too."

That was true. Wren killed the call and took a step forward.

The trucks pulled up. Cartel soldiers got out, solid men bristling with rifles aimed right at Wren. Don Mica followed seconds later, a thickset, vigorous man in his fifties with a bald head and a thick black beard. Wren ran the numbers. Mica was a hundred yards off. A do-able shot with the SIG .45, but not so easy if Wren was pin-cushioned by about twenty bullets from the rifles trained on him already.

"Don Mica," he called, "I hear you've come to kill me."

The Don raised a hand in greeting, spoke in low Honduras-accented tones. "Christopher Wren. I heard all about you. Looks like you're a chip in this game, now, one I'm happy to cash in."

Wren smiled, took a few steps closer. "Cash me, my team drops a bomb. Look up if you like. There's a Predator C-class drone circling at ten thousand feet, though you'll never see it. Hellfire missile, hundred-yard blast radius, this whole gulch will be a crater. You kill me, blammo, out go the lights. One less scumbag drug mule to deal with."

The Don didn't look up to the sky, though some of his men did. Instead he smiled back. "I heard about your tricks." His low, nasal voice fit perfectly with the dusty desert backdrop. "Bluffs and sleight of hand

6

bullshit for Las Vegas tourists. But there are no backcountry yokels here. There's only teeth."

He gave a signal, and the back doors of the panel van opened. Crazed barking erupted as a clutch of froth-mouthed dogs sprang into sight, yanking at their leashes.

It looked bad.

"So maybe I am bluffing," Wren said. "One way to find out. In the meantime, let me get this straight. I almost took a CIA task to assassinate you, once upon a time, but I didn't. Now Regis bailed on your coup, and you're feeling jilted. I get that, but somehow you're not trying to collect on him or his son, who's even now half a mile away. Instead you're collecting on me."

Mica raised an eyebrow. "You're well-informed. I like how resourceful men die. Always grasping for one last way out." He paused a moment, wheels turning. "But the son. You say he's here?"

Wren pointed. "That way half a mile. His team booted my standard back-up, sent me out to run point alone. If you ask me, he should never have come out here, but I guess he wanted 'battlefield experience'." Wren made air quotes. "You know how that goes."

Mica snorted. "The general on the hill. Rich men always send poorer men to fight."

"I'm as poor as they come. Born in a hole in the ground, raised by wolves. I think it's the same with you."

The dogs barked madly. Don Mica stared at Wren. Making his own calculations. "If I let you live, say I went after the son instead, I would be taking on a US senator."

Wren marked that as progress. The guy was listening, and that was half the work done. "You're either looking for payback or you aren't. No room for shades of gray, and I'm faint charcoal at best. A mile out from this coup deal. I never even took that contract on your life, and you know why? Same reason I came here. Cut a deal. You're more useful to me as an anti-terror asset. The coup idea was stupid, burning a whole country for one man's political ambition." He let a beat pass. "You know that. I know it. Civil war's great for arms traders, but not so hot for the drugs business, am I right?" Mica just stared. "The coup was Regis' deal, and he stiffed you. Not me. Place the blame where it lays."

Silence reigned for a moment.

"Or put it on me," Wren went on, "and everyone here talks about what they saw. You got bought off by an American stooge. Revenge and honor didn't mean squat to you when the big money talked. You sold yourself out for a payday."

Mica nodded slowly. "This is more like your reputation. The man who persuades. Tell me, is there really a drone overhead?"

"Let those dogs loose and find out. I figure about the time they reach me, the payload's surpassing terminal velocity, twenty seconds 'til impact. You think you can clear this gulch in time?"

Mica scratched his beard.

"The CIA's got many hands," Wren went on, "each blind to the other. I wouldn't have made it twenty years without an eye on every angle. You think I mean to die here?"

Mica took out a fat cigar, rolled it between two fingers. "You're saying I take out Regis, leave you alive." He raised the cigar, scented along its length. "I'd be doing you a favor."

"Wrong," Wren pressed. "I'm doing you the favor. You want to hold the leash, not be the dog, am I right? Deal with me here, we're equals. Deal with him, you get starved until you're rabid, he sends you after the other Dons, make more civil wars when he's ready. Chaos south of the border. Regis cheerleads a crackdown, gets your head on a pike. Looks good for his presidential run. He flipped on you once, next time will be with a bullet."

A long moment passed. Wren's life was on the line, but the equation had just shifted. Less likely it was going to be thirty dead, now. More likely it would just be one.

"Who you want for your business partner?" Wren closed.

Mica waved the cigar. "A man who'll take orders. All right. Here is my counteroffer. I leave this with you, Christopher Wren. The fabled Santa Justicia. Kill the Senator's son and make this right. Send a message for me."

Wren shook his head. "I don't take orders. I make deals. I kill him, that's my part done. Justified, because he just served me up. But you claim it. That's good for us both. Your reputation. Mine too."

Don Mica didn't blink. "It'll mean war."

"It already is war," Wren said. "Unless you want to be Regis' dog."

Mica frowned. Tucked the cigar back into his jacket pocket unsmoked. Nodded. "You have ten minutes. After that, we come for anyone left."

8

"It'll be done in five," Wren said. "Start firing. Give me cover."

He spun and started running. He crested the gully's side in seconds, already working the phone to open a line back to the Kid. Behind him a storm of rifle fire erupted.

"I'm on the run!" Wren shouted down the open line as he sprinted full tilt across the desert sands. "Don Mica came in guns blazing, something's twisted here, we need an immediate evac!"

It took seconds. Regis had to be trying to figure out what went wrong. "Agent Wren, repeat, we can hear ordinance. Are you under fire?"

"You hear gunfire, don't you?" Wren barked. "They're herding me south; I need a helo out of here right now. The guy's got wild dogs!"

Another long second. South was the opposite direction to the sniper's blind; a camouflaged hut set on a low hill in the rolling desert landscape. South wasn't the direction Wren was running, but there was no way they could know that. He'd picked the gully, even picked out the location for the blind, and left himself an alley of approach he could take unseen. Regis had let it all slide by, too arrogant or inexperienced to imagine his own double-cross might get double-crossed.

"Checking," Regis said.

Wren ran, then at just the moment he'd emerge into their sightline, he threw himself forward and began crawling through the baked dirt. He'd scoped it all out from the blind's location. There was enough scrub-brush cover to take him right up behind them without them seeing. They'd never know he was coming.

"What on Earth are you checking?" Wren shouted, keeping up the pretense. "Get me out of here!"

"Reading you," the Kid came back. "Scrambling a helicopter immediately. Hold out for ten minutes, we'll have you out of there."

"Did I mention they have dogs?" Wren called, letting his roughened breathing sound through. A quarter click covered already. He just had to sell it for the rest. He finished up the crawl then sprang back to his feet. "I shot one, but he got me pretty good. His damn tooth's stuck in my butt!"

"Stay alive, Agent Wren, that's an order!"

Bullshit. Wren had read it right from the start. The Kid was a fool. His father was a bigger fool. You didn't bet table stakes with men willing to go all-in. If Regis had wanted his stupid coup, he should have followed through.

"Working on it, sir," Wren said, throwing the 'sir' in there to be kind. The Kid didn't have long left.

He circled. More gunfire was spreading from the gully now. The dogs were running wild. Don Mica was making a good show of it.

"Wait, one of the dogs seems to be coming north," the Kid said. No doubt watching through a sniper monocular.

"You think I care about that?" Wren cried, running up the slope. The blind was just ahead. Ten men, all-in. Enough to secure the safety of a senator's son. "I've got teeth in my ass; I'm not keeping track of every mad pet on the Sonora!"

"Right, but-"

Then Wren was there. He burst through the tan camouflage strip sealing the blind and saw CIA intelligence people he'd just met a few hours earlier, each hand-picked by the senator. Now all of them were a party to betrayal: three sat clustered around a laptop, four were at the sniper's slit looking down to the gully, with twin snipers proned out side-by-side with a spotter and Regis between them.

All facing the wrong direction. All waiting on the moment Qotl cartel took out Christopher Wren.

It took a second. Wren strode over to Regis, put the SIG .45 against the back of his head, and paused for a millisecond to balance the scales. The Kid had sold him out. Worse yet, he'd sold out his country's safety for his father's political ambition, and there was no greater crime.

Half a second, and Wren pulled the trigger before the Kid knew what was happening. No need to talk. The Action Express did the job and then some. The reverberation was enormous.

Executed.

Wren turned. Let the SIG hang from his index finger. Already pistols were trained on him.

"You all wanted to hand me over, or you didn't know it was happening?" Wren asked, letting his anger burn through as he glared at their eyes one by one. Marking them all. "Either way, those dogs are coming. You want to die when Qotl cartel gets here, or you want to live?"

Nobody fired.

"That's what I thought. You crossed me here. Do it again, I'm coming for you. Now let's go."

He ran back out the way he'd come. He didn't put it past Don Mica to kill anyone he found hanging around. Not Wren's responsibility.

Twenty years' service. All it took in the end was one death. A pretty good deal.

2

OUT

A flight, sleep, shower and new suit later, Wren sat outside the Manhattan office of his boss Gerald Humphreys, Director of Special Operations at the CIA. There was lots of designer slate on the walls, chrome desks like some hip smartphone store, with blond wood flooring.

He was ready to make it happen. He'd never felt more certain of anything in his life. It was time. Twenty years of masking the truth: telling his wife he was away on business trips that lasted months; making excuses for why he couldn't call his kids every night; telling the neighbors BS stories over weekend BBQ about the state of play in Kazakh oil futures - his cover story as an international hedge fund trader.

"Come," came Director Humphreys' deep, authoritative voice.

Wren stood up. He went in. Even in a suit and minus his SIG .45, with his hair barely tamed and his scraggly black beard tied in a knot, he cut an imposing figure. Bigger than Humphreys, who rarely even bothered to stand.

This time he did. He looked pale as a cadaver straight out of his coffin, propped upright against a cream wall marked with five copper stars. Like the stars at Langley, Wren knew, each one a fallen CIA agent, though these were Humphreys' own. A wall of honor or of shame; he'd never asked.

"I can't let you go, Christopher," Humphreys said.

Wren looked at him. Late fifties but cropped sharp as a cold razor, Humphreys' only concession to personal style was his thick mustache. He was old enough that he'd be thinking of packing things in or making the next move up the ladder, to CIA Secretary or into politics.

Wren sat down unceremoniously. "Aren't you going to offer me a whisky, talk about old times?"

Humphreys stared hard and didn't sit. He was a stickler for the rule book, except when he wasn't. He'd been instrumental in Wren's last five years of deployments. He'd overlooked the chaos of Wren's psych profile, keen to get the world's pre-eminent black-ops specialist on his 'Special Operations' team; a legend in the field, more like a boogey man to America's enemies.

Saint Justice.

"I hear that maybe you killed the Senator's son," Humphreys said, like a shot across Wren's bow.

Wren waved a hand. "That was Qotl cartel. Whole thing was a set-up. Who's telling you otherwise?"

Humphreys glared, standing stock still. "I know you did it."

"So press charges. Court-martial me. Let's blow the whole thing sky high. Bring down Regis senior too. Maybe you, if you had something to do with it?"

Humphreys paled a whiter shade, nearing translucent. "How dare you accuse me?"

"Easy to dare," Wren said. "Twenty-four hours back I was in a canyon staring down a Qotl firing line. You're child's play next to that."

Humphreys' knuckles whitened. Ready to blow, maybe, and pull whatever trigger he had lined up to shut Wren up forever.

"You know this has been coming," Wren followed up. "I'm out. Dishonorable discharge me, if that's what it takes, hammer another star up on your wall. Nobody'll ever know either way. Fact is, it's time. I've got a family. My focus is them."

Humphreys laughed, deep and harsh. "It doesn't matter that you have a wife, Wren, even children. You are no family man."

Wren shrugged. Easy to take insults like that, too. He hadn't gotten this far without a plan to see it through. "So let me sweeten the deal. I walk, I give you something in exchange. Something you're going to desperately want, once you know it exists." He paused a moment, letting that sink in.

Humphreys finally sat, but remained ramrod upright. "An intelligence network I've been building for years. Off-book. It's deep, Humphreys. Loyal to me personally. Across all kinds of national lines. I call it the 'Foundation'. You let me walk, I start handing it over to you. Pending certain rules. These people aren't your standard assets."

Humphreys blinked. Hadn't seen that coming. "What are you talking about, Christopher? Across national lines? That sounds dangerously like you're courting treason."

Now Wren smiled. "Your choice. I've got hackers, all kinds of low-level criminals, some folks in intelligence. Either they're in the tent pissing out or outside the tent pissing in. Which is it to be?"

Humphreys' white cheeks flushed faintly. "Now you're threatening me with, what, a band of criminal vigilantes?"

"Ex-criminals," Wren said, then realized he'd better step that back a little, thinking about some of his members. "In most cases. White-collar at worst. But this is not a threat. It's a deal."

Humphreys shook his head. "I should never have taken you on."

Wren just met his gaze. "Really? I've cleared more open terror cases than anyone in Company history. Brought down more jihadis, cultists, cartels, gangs and domestic terrorists than you even had listed. Your star's risen because of me." He jabbed a finger. "Topple me, all that goes away too. Your stellar record. No top-of-the-heap Directorship for you. No political role at the end of the line." Wren clicked his fingers. "Done."

Humphreys fumed silently. Not much he could say to that. Piss and moan, but the facts were the facts. Best-case scenario, he black-bagged Wren and made him disappear in a secret CIA prison, with only one thing holding him back.

Fear of the Saint Justice legend. What surprises Wren had laid in store. Wren saw that fear loom large in his eyes.

"Make this easy on both of us," Wren said. "Something for me, something for you, we part ways, never cross paths again. What do you say?"

"That last part sounds ideal," Humphreys said, teeth gritted. "I never want to so much as hear your name again."

"Likewise," Wren answered. "Sign me up."

The meeting went fast after that.

Wren felt dazed on the drive home. Out of downtown Manhattan toward Great Kills, Staten Island. The end of an era. But it felt right. He couldn't keep on lying. His first duty was to his wife and kids.

They weren't expecting him home so soon. He was in Thailand, as far as they knew from his latest cover story; out there for a banking deal. He stopped at a coffee shop and bought cakes. Blue frosting for Jake, red cinnamon swirls for Quinn, and a bottle of red, a Shiraz, for Loralei.

Their place was a beautiful, spacious detached home overlooking Siedenburg Park, on the edge of Staten Island. In the winter the lake shone like a pearl, in the spring the sassafras trees erupted in yellow flowers.

Walking up the drive, his heart beat like he was going to propose again. Telling Humphreys had been one thing, it would be another entirely to tell Loralei. That he would be home more. That he'd put more time into therapy, to deal with his night terrors. She knew only the smallest part about his past, that he was an orphan who'd struggled to find his place in the world. He didn't tell anyone more than that.

At the stoop, he realized he'd forgotten his house keys somewhere, maybe left them with all his bags at LaGuardia, after the rush back from Mexico, but he couldn't stop himself from grinning as he stood at the door. Short of breath. Vision tunneling to the spy hole, wondering what she would think. He cursed softly: flowers! He'd forgotten flowers. But the cake and the wine would do.

He knocked. It wasn't late, 7 p.m. or thereabouts, so it wouldn't seem so unusual. He couldn't wait to see them and counted the seconds.

The door opened.

It wasn't her.

For a moment Wren's brain short-circuited. Maybe she'd hired a maid? Maybe this was a friend, though he didn't recognize the woman at all. Blond hair. Soft features. Cream paint splatters on her dungarees. Beyond her even the house looked different. A new oak-paneled mirror. A new potted plant.

He smiled broadly. "Hi, I'm Christopher. Loralei's husband."

The woman stared at him. "OK."

"I'm home early, forgot my keys, is she in?"

The woman's eyes narrowed uncomfortably. "I'm sorry, Loralei, you said? I think maybe you've got the wrong house?"

A sweat broke out down Wren's back. Had he somehow got the wrong address? He glanced and saw the number, saw the familiar chip in the frame's paint where Jake had dinged his tricycle. This was it. But they weren't here.

It sent him operational. They'd taken his family. It was a trap.

"Where are they?" he asked coldly. No weapon, but he wouldn't need one to deal with this woman.

"I, uh, don't know," she said, taking a step back. Reading the change in him and clutching the door, she was ready to slam it on a moment's notice.

Wren didn't give her the chance. He pushed her gently to the side and strode in. Down the hall he went, where many things looked the same, just as he remembered them, but many weren't. The same walls, floor, ceiling, but new paintings. He rounded the corner to the den and saw-

A guy standing in the middle of the room wearing white overalls, holding a paint roller. There was white sheeting on the floor, a ladder, all their old furniture gone, the smell of paint in the air, the walls half-coated in beige, half in their original warm teal.

The guy stared. Wren stared.

"Get out," came the woman's voice from behind. "I don't care who you are. I'm calling the police."

Wren tried to figure it out. This was some strange kind of trap. What foreign agency stole your family then started redecorating? This was…

His stomach sank. Something else. Something he'd never even considered, though he should have. Director Humphreys' words came back to him, 'You're no family man, Wren.'

He blinked. The guy was still standing there, but now the woman stepped in front of him, holding up a gun. Wren clocked it casually. A Glock 9mm. Overpowered for home defense. She might sprain her wrist firing it.

"The police are coming," she said. "Get out."

The bag holding the cake and the wine dropped from Wren's hand. The bottle smashed, red wine sloshed out of the bag and stained the white sheet. The woman's eyes turned to the mess, and Wren used the moment to lean off-line and take her gun. One hand swiped the barrel, the other locked her wrist, and the weapon plucked free like he was picking an apple.

She stared at him in shock. Hardly believing what had just happened. Wren clicked the magazine absently out and put it in his pocket, pulled the slide to eject the chambered round, caught it mid-air, then handed the disarmed weapon back.

Five seconds gone, and everything had changed. Now she stared at the gun, in her hands again and utterly useless.

"Get out of here right now!" she screamed.

Wren understood. She was too steamed now to answer any kind of question. Instead he focused on the guy. Deer in the headlights. "You're renting the place," he said, putting the pieces together. "From my wife. I'm sorry. How long back?"

"I don't care about that!" the woman shouted. "This is our place now. You don't just stamp in. I have more ammunition. I will use it!"

The guy cleared his throat. "A month," he managed, looking scared, guilty, uncertain. "It's our first place," he added weakly.

A month? Wren had spoken to Loralei nearly every night, even while he was undercover. If she was going to rent out their family home, surely she would have told him?

"Last warning," the woman said. Now there came the drone of sirens drawing near.

Wren didn't know what to think. Either way, he wouldn't get any answers here. He looked down at the dropped bag. "Sorry for the mess."

He strode out. He tucked the magazine and the loose shell into the mailbox at the end of the drive, lifted the flag then kept walking. Past the police cars as they raced in, he placed a call to Loralei, but she didn't pick up. After five more tries and several messages he began to worry.

Maybe everything was OK, though. If anyone knew, it would be Loralei's family, back in the UK. Pacing along the noisy street he tapped the name in his address book, waiting for the connection to land.

The call went through. A groggy voice came online. It was the middle of the night still, across the Atlantic.

"Hello?" said Loralei's dad.

"It's me," Wren answered. "Where's Loralei?"

A few seconds passed. "Christopher?"

"What's going on, Charlie? Where is she? Where are my kids?"

A low sigh followed. Wren pictured the old guy rubbing his eyes, shouldering this burden. "It's over, Chris. She found out. What you do, all this CIA nonsense? It was too much, and now you're done."

That froze him. She found out? A dozen questions burned through his head. How? Why? Who told her? Only one that mattered, though.

"Where is she?"

"I'm not going to tell you that, am I?"

The words landed like blows.

"I'm out of that life," Wren said hurriedly, like it could turn things around. "I quit the Company. It's finished, I swear."

"It is finished." The old guy heaved a heavy breath, gearing himself up. "I can't help you, son. We always got along OK. But you weren't there. You lied. I respect what you've done, protecting your country, but it's no life for them. For a family."

Silence. Wren wanted to argue, but knew it was true. There was no point repeating he'd quit. Too late.

"Where is she?"

"Not here. Come out and check, if you like. Gone, Chris. A clean break. It's been coming for years. Surely you saw it?"

He hadn't. Probably too bound up in his own lies, he hadn't seen the lie building up in her.

"Respect this. Don't try to find her, she said. She was clear about that. If you want to see your kids, you need to get yourself straight. Do that and maybe she'll reach out, get you visitation with your kids."

He didn't know what to say. Visitation? "I deserve better. This is wrong."

"So did she," said the old man. "I'm hanging up now. This is what you sowed, Chris. Reap it."

The line clicked and went dead. Wren was left standing in the middle of the road, alone.

3

VIKINGS

Wren found his truck where he'd parked it, a modified Jeep Wrangler Unlimited, and started driving. He didn't know where at first. Into the night and out of New York; he just had to keep moving to outrun his father-in-law's voice in his head.

Reap it.

By morning of the next day he was en route for North Carolina; a place they'd vacationed at together, where there was a beautiful lake and a log cabin rental. He figured Loralei's dad was telling the truth, that his days with the CIA were the cause of all this, so he wasn't searching like a CIA operator; one call to his hackers and he'd know their exact location.

Instead he was looking like a civilian.

They weren't at the log cabin, though. He hadn't expected it, but he still felt something, like the ghost of their presence in the air, and it kept him going.

There were other places to check in on.

He got back in the Jeep and hit the road. First, he went to a cousin in upstate New York whose wedding they'd attended. Next was a friend in Seattle they'd crashed with early in the relationship. Third came an alligator town in Florida where they'd talked about some far-future retirement.

She wasn't at any of them. He didn't expect her to be. This wasn't really a search. If he wanted to find her, using his Foundation and CIA resources, he could.

This was something else. Desperation, maybe. Trying to come to grips with all his chickens coming home to roost.

Beneath the weight of that, he just kept moving. For three weeks he crisscrossed the country, revisiting everywhere he could think of. Driving in a sleep-deprived frenzy over savannahs and plains, through mountains and forests, in and out of sleepy small towns and bustling metropolitan cities, searching every place she'd ever mentioned, that they'd ever been together, trying to recapture some sense of what it had been like to be together.

He only came up on dead ends.

She didn't answer any of his calls, and he called every few hours. She didn't respond to any of his emails, and he sent hundreds trying to explain.

At some point in the wilds of Utah, pulled over by the side of I-70 beneath sweeping starry skies, it finally hit him.

She really was gone. She wanted to be gone. If he ever hoped to be with her again, to be a real father to his kids, he had to accept that. Respect it.

But what did that leave? Loralei's father had told him to wait. Make a new life. But what was the point of quitting the CIA and having a life if his family weren't in it?

He didn't have an answer for that. Instead he just sat at the wheel of his Jeep, gazing out at the distant silhouettes of cragged buttes against the purplish Utah sky, looking for answers. The stars swept across the sky, and he didn't budge. The engine's cooling vents clicked until they were cold. Receding taillights on I-70 steadily melded into one seamless red tracer round in the rearview mirror.

For the first time since his childhood, he didn't know what to do or where to go.

He looked to the passenger seat next to him. Sheaves of wrinkled paper lay in a heap, covered in bright crayon scrawls. A house, a horse, a family. Drawings made by his kids, that he carried with him wherever he went. They were worth more than anything else he had. He looked at the drawings. He looked at the stars.

No answers came.

A sound did. A clank?

Wren woke from a doze, disoriented. It sounded like metal on glass, right by his ear. Maybe highway patrol?

He blinked; ahead lay bright floodlights from multiple vehicles, with more in back. Not cars, he realized, but bikes. All pointed at him, their engines grumbling low.

Not highway patrol.

Through the side window he saw a guy with face tattoos and a thick black beard, wearing a leather motorbike cap and a white wifebeater. He was in his forties and built solid. Wren recognized one tattoo on his cheek: a blue skull with blond dreads and a hammer of Thor.

His stomach ran cold.

Vikings. Dry memories from his last NSA conference rose up: the Vikings were a mid-sized biker gang based across five states, involved in drugs, illicit porn and human trafficking. They were infamously anti-government, and had been distantly linked to several failed domestic terror attacks.

Wren swiftly checked their spread in his peripheral vision. It looked like a whole cavalry, maybe a dozen of them all told; three bikes tight in front blocking his route and looked like the same in back, with more flanking to either side.

Trapped. The tap on the glass came again. It was metallic, something gleaming across the guy's fingers; a brass knuckle-duster twinkled in the white high beams.

"Open up the door, boy," the guy called through the glass. "Let's have ourselves a talk."

Wren blinked. Boy? "What's the problem?" he called back.

"You are, now step out."

Wren's brain started working again, climbing up from the depths and thinking like an operator. There was only one reason a gang like this wanted him to step out, and that was to preserve the Jeep. No need to jack the door and damage the paintwork. It'd be better to resell if Wren handed it over easy.

"The Jeep's yours," Wren said, keeping his hands on the wheel. He didn't even glance to the glove box where his SIG Sauer .45 ACP lay, eight in the mag and one in the chamber. Tempting, but he wasn't looking for trouble. "I'll walk."

"We've already got the Jeep," the guy said. Wren's mind spun faster. As the first to approach, he had to be the gang's enforcer; the muscle that did the dirtiest work. "What we want is you." The brass knuckles tapped on the window again. Enjoying this. Wren looked into his eyes and saw a deep kind of hunger. This wasn't just a carjacking. "Tell me first, though, you some kind of banker out of Salt Lake, getting high off the big money bailout?"

Wren looked into his eyes, trying to communicate the unspoken message that he was more trouble than he was worth. "Banking of a kind," he said. "I specialize in liquidations."

The guy frowned. "And a comedian? Even better. Boy, we'll all laugh ourselves sick when you're cracking jokes from a cage."

From a cage? Wren looked the guy square in his blue eyes. One direct, clear warning would be fair, he figured.

"You don't want to do this. I'm a Force Recon Marine. Until recently, I was CIA. Back up, I walk, you can have the Jeep and nobody gets hurt. That's the best you can hope for here."

Someone tried a door in back, to the right; no dice. The enforcer leaned in so close his lips almost touched the glass. "Nobody gets hurt, that's real neighborly, you looking out for us." He hawked and spat. "So let me return the favor. Go easy. You'll learn to love the collar. Failing that, we drag you behind a bike at forty for a spell, really tenderize the meat."

Somebody laughed, and the sound came muted through the glass. The enforcer grinned, revealing crooked yellow teeth. "Well, what's it to be, boy?"

Wren ran the numbers. He'd given a clear warning, and as far as he was concerned that put him in the clear.

"Don't call me boy," he said, and shoved the door out like a punch, left arm extending with all the strength of his 6' 3", two hundred fifty-pound frame. The door caught the enforcer mid-sentence in the chest, maybe cracked a rib as Wren followed through, then he was tumbling away, and Wren's hand was on the ignition.

That earned him maybe a couple seconds of shock and awe, and he was going to use every bit. His left hand yanked the key and the engine coughed, his right hand went for the glove box and curled around the SIG's snug grip just as the V6 caught. No time to pull the gun or aim; he simply fired in position, three fast rounds out through the Jeep's front fender. The sound was massive in the truck's cab, pealing out across the desert.

Enough to bank up a few more seconds of uncertainty, enough to crank the stick to first and slam the pedal.

The Jeep thrust to life, wheels spinning on the sandy highway shoulder before catching on the blacktop beneath. The bikers' mouths opened in shock, then the Jeep hit their bike blockade and plowed forward. A Triumph Bonneville lowrider clanged to the side, a thick guy with a long white beard and bandanna leaped out of the way, a Harley Fat Boy went under his chassis and stuck as he hit fifteen miles an hour, shredding sparks and dragging a screaming gouge down the hard shoulder.

The open door flapped on his left. He shifted to second and steered as best he could even as wild gunshots came from in back. One spidered his rear window, another blew out the back right tire and halved his torque.

Engines roared up all around. Wren glanced in the rearview and saw the cavalry coming online, bikers mounting up with guns training in. The crack of stray bullets continued as they gave chase along the I-70 breakdown lane, spattering the Jeep's bodywork.

Wren's mind spun fast. There was no way to outrun them, not dragging a Harley under the hood with a tire already out. Maybe he could lose them, though. He swung hard right into the wilderness, beyond the sweep of headlights and into the desert's wild dark of low creosote bushes, boulders and cacti. The tires crunched, the chassis juddered then the Harley caught on something in the undergrowth and gut-punched the Jeep to a halt.

Some three hundred yards distance into the dark. Maybe enough. Wren scrambled to the passenger side door, something they wouldn't expect, and slithered out onto the cold sand seconds before their floodlights pulled up on the driver's side.

Engines revved down and voices rose up, calling out what they were going to do when they caught him. Wren hustled on his belly like a sidewinder, snaking through the grit and desert dirt into the darkness.

"You ever been hung and quartered, boy?" someone called nearby, maybe the enforcer. "Burned on a cross for your sins?"

Wren dodged a barrel cactus to stay out of their high beams, then came up against it. A fat guy loomed right in front of him in the dark, bald head as thick as a gallon jug, bulbous gut silhouetted against the starry sky.

He saw Wren, opened his mouth and Wren surged; all the strength in his thighs thrusting him into a massive uppercut, left fist shooting square into the guy's chin. Two-hundred-fifty pounds in motion, maybe three thousand Newtons of force delivered direct; enough to snap the guy's temporal bone hinge and drive the girdle of his jaw up around his cheeks like a slipped pair of shades.

The guy's head shot back like an ejected shell and his body dropped, the scream dead on his lips as he fell unconscious.

Wren dropped to one knee, took ten seconds to palm the guy's wallet, then plunged back into the dark just as headlights wheeled across him like club strobes.

He rolled, spun and sprinted straight at a man in the dark bringing a rifle to bear. Wren hammered his trailing left elbow into the man's throat, dropping him hard, just as a chain whipped across his back, thumping the breath from his lungs.

Wren grabbed the chain and twisted, jerking the holder off balance, then tracked the chain back to sweep him into a big judo throw that pounded him into the ground. A muzzle flare sparked to his left but Wren was already darting away, right up to a guy winding up a big swing with a baseball bat. Wren scooped the bat under his left arm while evading an incoming blade aimed for his eye. Both guys dropped within seconds; one with Wren's elbow against the temple and the other with a snap kick to the balls.

Then the enforcer was right there, brass knuckle catching the light for a second before it swung into Wren's gut with a meaty whomp. Wren managed to slip some of the impact, but the metal caught his solar plexus and drove any last wind from his body, spasming the muscle. He couldn't breathe, but he didn't need to right now. He sent out a huge front kick that caught the enforcer center mass and sent him peeling away into the dark. Then he ran.

Lights wailed; bullets barked. A bike growled over the rocky ground nearby, another body flew to tackle his legs and they tumbled together through a stand of creeping cacti, both trying to bring their weapons to bear. Mid-roll Wren took a thump from a boulder in the back, the guy wrenched on his SIG and it stripped away, but Wren got in an answering haymaker punch to the guy's groin that shut him right up.

Then he was up again and running, limping, and bleeding into the night.

4

ROADSIDE

W ren woke to a deep rumbling, closing in fast. He opened bleary eyes from one of the old nightmares, flashes of his dark childhood in the Arizona desert, to see white lights rushing toward him. He rolled, and an eighteen-wheel semi-trailer truck thundered by only feet away, juddering the sandy blacktop beneath his hands.

It took him a second. Side of the highway?

More trucks followed.

He shifted further from the edge, into the shoulder amongst peeled-off rags of tire rubber and old crinkly chip packets, breathing hard. For a moment he lay flat on his back looking up at the stars, pushing the nightmare down.

Still alive.

Flashes of his flight through the desert came back to him, staggering by moonlight staunching blood from various shallow wounds, making a beeline for the whirring lights of the Interstate. At some point he'd limped up to the roadside, laid himself down and passed out.

He looked around now. There was no sign of his Jeep or the bikers. He rolled up to a sitting position, steadying a flush of dizziness with both palms on the cool blacktop. Everything hurt. He ran down a mental checklist. His jaw felt loose but he could grit his teeth. His back and sides were a blooming swell of stiffness and pain, and his breathing caught on bruised ribs. He extended his legs and arms carefully, like an infant born on the roadside shale, but there were no breaks, no bullet holes, nothing worse than soft tissue damage.

On his feet, he checked his front pockets; his wallet and phone were gone, must've been ripped clear in the fight. They'd have taken the Jeep now too, breaking it down for parts. The engine, tires and electronics would be worth a few grand. That was a blow, but the true loss only hit him a few seconds later.

The pictures from his kids on the passenger seat.

Drawings they'd sent him over many years. All the moments he'd missed while he was out fighting the exact kind of stupid, tribal violence the Vikings represented. For years Loralei had sent them on, and he'd collected them. Carried them with him. They were the purpose of all this.

Now they were gone, and it made him sick.

He checked his back pockets and came up with the wallet he'd palmed from the first guy. He opened it and looked over the contents in the strobing white light of passing cars. Some crunched-up notes. Some receipts. Social security card. A kid's prom picture behind a clear window, cute blonde with retainers. Driver's license. Address. The guy's name was Eustace. Not exactly bad ass. You couldn't make that stuff up.

Wren stuck a thumb out, started limping along the shoulder.

A few cars slowed down to check him out; a huge, bedraggled hitchhiker on the Interstate by night, but nobody stopped. Wren didn't blame them.

The gas station appeared maybe two hours later. By that time the bruising had him hunched over and walking with an ugly limp. Across the stained concrete of the well-lit forecourt, the kid behind the counter watched him approach with wide eyes.

"What happened to you, man?" he asked, after Wren pushed through the glass swing door. Tall, frizzy-haired, maybe seventeen.

"Biker gang," Wren said. It hurt to talk, so he kept it short and sweet. "You got ice?"

"I got, uh, yeah," said the kid, watching blankly as Wren started plucking products off the shelves. He craned his neck to follow. "In back, bottom of the chest freezer. Did you say a biker gang?"

"Uh-huh."

Wren picked up a box of bandages, duct tape, a bottle of disinfectant, a hand towel, a tube of superglue and a local map.

"Like, they jumped you?" The kid was peering down the aisle while Wren rustled in the ice chest. "Car-jacked you?"

Wren caught a glimpse of himself in the freezer's mirrored back. The bruising wasn't too visible yet, but the blood was. One of his eyes was shot through with red. There were scratches on his cheeks and forehead.

"You got it."

He hobbled toward the register and the kid hurried back behind the counter. "And you survived? Man, you're lucky!"

Wren said nothing, just laid out his goods and leafed through Eustace's wallet, putting fifty tatty bucks down. "Keep the change."

"Should I call the police?"

Wren looked at the kid a second. Maybe seventeen, unlikely to join a biker gang, but you never knew. Either way he'd always remember this night, when a guy walked up after an epic beatdown.

"I appreciate the concern. Really. But I know what I'm doing. Don't you worry about me, James."

"How do you know my-" the kid started, then looked down at the name tag on his chest. "Oh."

Wren held out a hand. "Restroom keys."

James gave a nervous laugh and fished them out. "Yeah. Here. You sure you don't need some help?"

"Everybody does," said Wren, and limped out the door.

The restroom was clean enough. The door didn't lock but that was no concern. He got the hot water going in both sinks then stripped and washed with the cloth. His back was a tapestry of rising purple, striped with bright welts where the chain had hit, but nothing too serious. Hard cords of muscle had absorbed most of it. His legs were much the same, bruised and cramped but basically OK.

He doused the washcloth with disinfectant and swabbed himself liberally, enjoying the clarifying sting. Rolling around on the desert floor through cacti, insects and animal spoor, infection was his main concern. Next, he used the superglue to seal up the nastier cuts, topped with bandages.

He looked in the mirror. He looked bad, dark skin that was puffy and bloated now. He'd passed for Pakistani ISIS in Afghanistan; that was sixteen months he'd never get back. He'd passed for Qotl cartel many times over the years, policing the northern border for rival coyotes and drug mules.

He wouldn't pass for much now.

His eyes drifted to the names tattooed on his broad chest, done on the day they were born. Jake. Quinn. Loralei too. They felt like testaments from an earlier life. His father-in-law's words came back to him, burned into his head after three weeks of repetition.

This is what you sowed, Chris. Reap it.

It wouldn't help to think about that now. It never did. He'd put his family to the back of his mind more times than he could remember, out there trying to beat down the tide of injustice one gang, cartel or jihadi cell at a time. Thing was, the ocean never relented. The tide kept on drawing in.

Just one more, he figured. Get his truck, then do whatever it took to win back Loralei and his kids.

He cleaned up the restroom nice and neat, dabbing up all the blood and putting the trash in the wastebasket. No sense leaving it for the kid. Back through the store, he held the ice pack to the back of his head and the kid just stared.

"You don't look any better, man."

Wren grunted and checked the clock behind the counter. After 3 a.m. "You got a number for a cab company?"

The kid frowned. "A cab? Uh, you know where we are, right? On a highway? It's not exactly downtown."

"There'll be someone."

"Yeah, maybe one out of Salt Lake? There's no cabs around here."

Wren pulled out Eustace's driver's license, peered at the tiny text. "I'm only going to, uh, Emery. Is that far?"

The kid frowned. "We're practically in Emery, man. Thirty minutes max."

"So give me the cab number. I'll wait out front."

The kid stared at Wren, rustled through a small stack of business cards beside the register, then paused. "You just bought duct tape. You gonna kill some guy?"

"Not a chance," Wren said, firm and calm, like he was handling a skittish animal. "We're just gonna have ourselves a talk."

28

The kid looked distraught. "The kind of talk where he ends up dead?"

Wren smiled. "If he was going to die, I wouldn't have told you about it, James. If anything, I'm going to save his life."

5

EUSTACE

The cab took an hour to arrive. Wren sat out front of the gas station looking over the forlorn gas pumps and the road, savoring the cold of the ice against his thumping head.

The cab was a Prius driven by a young guy, hipster mustache with an ironic T-shirt showing Mother Teresa swearing. The kid actually got out of his car to look at Wren.

"Hot dang. You get run over or something?"

"Or something," said Wren, and waved to James in the store. The kid waved back awkwardly.

Wren drifted through the ride, half-asleep on a layer of pain, until they pulled in outside Emery at the bottom of Eustace's road. He stepped out.

It was a beat-down neighborhood. Cracked blacktop with duplexes lined side-by-side like neglected herd cows, overgrown with poison oak and sprayed with desert dust. Street cleaners didn't come out here, he bet.

The cab sped away. Wren walked unevenly up the road, favoring his left side. Old trash lay in the gutters like slurry, fast food chicken wrappers bleached from long days of sun. It was coming up for dawn now and people would be rousing, headed east to the endless hay farms or north to one of the coal mines in the Wildcat Knolls. Political lawn signs sprouted from weed-clumped lawns. Big, rusted Chevy trucks were the order of the day on broken-flagged drives, trailing dark oil marks.

Eustace's house was the same as any, with a toppling telephone post at the corner, live cables trailing down around head height. The front porch had peeling white paint, showing cheap beech boards beneath. There were holes in the roof felt, dozens of dry clay wasp nests under the rotten eaves, and the porch swing hung by only three chains.

Probably Eustace's family home. A story of loss. Already the air felt hotter and drier out here. The only well-maintained item was Eustace's bike, parked on a neat cement pad by the wall. Twin heavy-duty security bolts anchored the wheels and frame to eyelets in the cement. His prized possession.

Wren walked around back. The yard was overgrown, a swing set smothered in weeds. No kids here now. The slide door was open a crack. Wren slid it further and stepped in. Kitchen, den, hall. At the bottom of the stairs Wren could hear Eustace snoring above. Each breath came with a pained catch. Up the stairs he saw family photos, Eustace with a wholesome-looking lady around the BBQ, their two cute kids playing in the yard. Hardly the standard set up for a biker gang initiate

Wren entered Eustace's room. Inside it was sparse, not even a TV. He sat on a magazine stack at Eustace's side. The big guy was blacked out on his single bed. His face had bandages, but what did a bunch of bikers know about bone chipping and temporomandibular disorders? After the knee to the chin Wren had delivered, Eustace would likely suffer stroke-like symptoms for a while, all up and down his body. Without proper care he'd go undiagnosed, and bad habits would make it worse. He'd get a hunch, twist a knee under the extra weight then never walk right again.

Wren wasn't going to need the duct tape. He probed for a gun under the pillow or down the side, but there wasn't one. There was nothing dangerous within reach. For a moment he sat there, studying the big guy. Uneven shave on his scalp, half-masking recent Viking tattoos that were red at the edges. It filled in the rest of the story.

Not a patch member. Just another lost soul, reaching out wrong.

"Hey Eustace," he said, and flicked him lightly on the jaw. "Wake up."

The big man came to with a snort. One hand went up to rub his chin, then came back with a delayed whimper of pain. His eyes rolled as he tried for focus. Wren figured they'd put him out with some generic opioid.

"Wha-?" the big guy asked, then winced.

"Where's my Jeep, Eustace?"

Eustace blinked and peered. It was dim in the room, so Wren pulled the curtains open. The sun was rising pink outside, a new day. In the fresh influx of light, the bloodstains on Eustace's pillow and sheets stood out.

Eustace's eyes grew a little sharper. Recognition came, and he started shuffling as the panic came on, trying to get the covers off and get up. Probably he hadn't done a sit-up in a decade, though, so it didn't take much to hold him down.

"Shh," Wren said. "Calm down. Your momma's in the next room. Let's not wake her."

That worked as a caution and a threat, and Eustace stopped struggling. His eyes burned through the opioid fog.

"Id's you. You tug by wallet." He winced with every word, and his eyes shone with rising tears. He probably thought he was about to die.

"I did," said Wren, and tossed the billfold onto Eustace's chest. "There you go, I brought it back. Now it's your turn. Where's my truck?"

Eustace stared defiantly. Wren chalked that up; he was ready to suffer, if not die, for his new 'family'. Wren had come across it a hundred times before. 'Don't be a snitch', that was the first thing they told you on joining any gang.

"These guys, they're opportunists, Eustace. They'll dump you the first chance they get. You're a nobody in their eyes. So what are you being loyal to?"

Anger spiked Eustace's eyes. Wren read it and adjusted. it was no good going head-on any further, the guy would just clam up, and torture was unreliable at best. Better to try a different tack.

"Why'd your wife leave you, Eustace?"

That sparked his eyes with confusion. "Whu?"

Wren gave him a second. There were many routes to breaking a man. "Your wife. I've seen the family photos, you left them up. There's no Xs over her face. Your kids are in the frame. You've got these new tattoos, Viking crap for weaker men, but there's none of that in the house. Because it would upset your wife, if she ever came back?"

Anger widened Eustace's eyes. He struggled again to get up, as if this was the final straw. "Ged tha heg out. Ged oud of by house!"

Wren just rode it. "Nice bike," he said calmly. "I know what a Triumph costs, and it's more than you or your momma has. Look at this place. When did you last dust, man? Mow the lawn? It's a pigsty in here."

"Ged out!" Eustace yelled, flailing his big arms until a call came from the next room, an old woman's wavering voice.

"Eustace? Are you all right?"

Eustace immediately stilled. The two men stared at each other. The unspoken communication was more effective than duct tape.

"I'm all righd, momma!" he said, high and thin. "Everything'th fine. Go bag to thleep."

She said something inaudible then started pottering around in her room.

"She alwayd geth up now," Eustace whispered.

Wren said nothing. Eustace didn't need to know he had no intention of hurting his mother. He could talk down the old lady easily enough, anyway. Eustace was a tougher question, but there was something there, maybe. He'd made more effort for less before.

"Your wife, Eustace. Why'd she leave?"

Again, not the question Eustace had expected. His defiant glare turned watery. Corralled in his own home, in his bed. Nobody wanted that. Wren watched and waited. So many possible answers might follow, and each would dictate his response. After maybe a minute, Eustace chose his path.

"Bitth cheaded on me. I went to du guy, and he laughed. Thaid I wath fat."

Wren tried not to laugh. Tough love, then. "You are pretty heavy, Eustace."

"I know!"

"So what happened next?"

"We had a fight. She called me a lother. She left and took the kidth."

Wren weighed that. It sounded about right. He could relate.

"So you bought the bike. Got the tattoo. Didn't shed the weight, though."

"Fug you!" Eustace's face reddened.

Wren waited for Eustace to calm down. "I was thinking about taking your bike," he said casually. "Part-exchange for my Jeep. I'd cut a mean figure on it, don't you think? Cowboy rides off into the sunset. But I think if I did, you might kill yourself. Is that about right?"

Eustace stared at him.

"You'll drink and moan, you'll make excuses, but in the end, you'll eat a gun." Wren scratched his chin. "Trust me, I've been there, and I don't want to cause that. So let's make another deal. You tell me everything you know about the Vikings, right now, and I give you a better gang to belong to. One that'll help you out and give you something to aim for, not drag you down. Good clean fun, basically. What do you say?"

Eustace stared at him. Bewildered, maybe, or more likely plotting. It didn't matter, because he was listening still.

"Either way, I'll be watching," Wren went on. "See, Eustace, I help people like you. I've got an organization called the Foundation with over a hundred members from all around the world; all people on the edges of some real bad decisions. I check in on them often, make sure they're staying on the right side of the tracks, give them a bit of help when I can. Pass your one-year with the Foundation, no bad mistakes, you get a coin, like AA. Pass your three-year, your five, your ten, all come with coins, which come with privileges and benefits." He winked. "Backslide, and you go down a coin. You're on coin zero now, because you stole my Jeep and tried to kill me, so back a step means you're into the red and I take the bike. Probably leave you in hock, but that's your choice. It's how I roll. It's on you to make better choices."

Eustace just stared. "Who de hell are you?"

"My name's Christopher Wren. I was born into a gang that makes your Vikings look like toy soldiers, so I know what I'm talking about. After that I was a Force Recon special operator, I worked for the CIA, and now…" he paused, looking around the room trying not to think about his family or the future he'd hoped for. "I guess I do this."

Eustace stared silently. It was a real moment of revelation for them both.

"So cough up," Wren went on. "Admission to the Foundation doesn't come for free. For extra credit toward your first coin, tell me where the Vikings stowed my Jeep. Don't leave a bit out, Eustace. You're complicit now, and both our lives depend on it."

6

WAREHOUSE

Eustace spilled like a split bag of meal.

There was a warehouse in the desert, he said. Wren's Jeep would be there, cooling off while the gang broke it down for parts, arranged for a fence out of state. Eustace had never been there, but he knew enough from dropped hints.

A clean hit, Wren figured. If the place was lax enough, he could walk right in, knock a few heads, get his kids' pictures, call in the sheriffs then roll out. Get back on the road, driving all day and waking up at truck stops, waiting for Loralei to call.

His second cab of the day rolled up. Dusty and gray, a Ford Taurus. The guy was old, grizzled and didn't even look in the mirror as Wren climbed in. Just the way he liked it. Eustace stood in the upstairs window, watching as the cab pulled away.

Wren slumped back in the seat.

"Here," came the cabbie's cigarette-rough voice. Maybe he'd said it twice.

Wren sat up. Maybe an hour gone. He looked out into blazing sunlight and saw the tumbled metal heaps of a junkyard. He paid the old guy and climbed out.

Orangeville. Wren sampled the air but didn't taste much other than the iron of his own blood. Out here on the fringe it looked much like Emery. Maybe a little bigger. Wider roads. Less trash.

The junkyard gate had a bell, and he rang it five times, until a ropey lady with beaded dreads came out cursing and spitting brown chaw.

"What you want?"

"A ride. Whatever you've got that'll run. Plus a thousand dollars, cash. You take Bitcoin?"

She laughed. "You trying to stick this place up?"

Wren gave a wry smile. "I lost my gun. I'll pay you double in crypto coins. Or you wanna pass up easy money?"

She huffed, spat chaw. "Wait there."

He ended up with a beat-up panel van with unsubtle branding splashed all over it. The radiator was part-fried, and the engine was on its last legs, but the plates were legit for another three months, and Wren had no intention of driving it longer than a couple of days.

It took a long few minutes for the crypto coin transaction to go through, Wren typing in the details of his wallet from memory to transfer three thousand dollars into the woman's unmarked account. It took a few minutes more as she checked and double-checked it on a scrappy rubber-bound tablet computer.

At last she looked back up at Wren. "And if the po-lice scoop you up?" she asked, holding up the van's keys in one hand, a wedge of dirty bills wrapped with a rubber band in the other. "What you gonna say about this van's provenance?"

She stretched out the word provenance like it was hillbilly French.

"Found it by the side of the road," Wren said. "Must've just bloomed there like a mushroom."

She smiled. Handed over the keys and the grubby cash. Wren pocketed the bills, climbed into the van and set off for the warehouse.

A rattling, shaky forty-minute drive followed. East along I-70, north on an unmarked dirt track through the desert scrub, buttes scrolling by in the distance, cacti blooming a riot of purple flowers. Wren almost felt good.

The warehouse lay just where Eustace had said, sitting on open scrub and circled with razor-wire fencing at a generous twenty-yard remove. Wren pulled the truck up behind a boulder on the sandstone ridge, large enough to obscure its silhouette against the hot blue sky, and studied his target.

The good feeling paled.

This place was brand new. A squarish, flat-roofed one-story warehouse with aluminum cladding, probably steel cage in the walls. There was the tang of hot, fresh tar on the air. Maybe finished within the last few months. The razor wire posts were new too, the lines glinting rust-free beneath three tall security lamps.

It didn't feel right.

Everything he'd heard from Eustace suggested the Vikings were a two-bit operation. He'd expected a busted old shed with a corroded chain-link fence, maybe a single CCTV lens slowly sweeping a sand-swept lot, his Jeep parked up by the side.

This was something else entirely.

Six bikes with Viking skull decals were parked in the lot, making for an impressive standing garrison. Too much for Wren to deal with head-on. He appraised his line of assault. In all there was a single entrance, barred with hefty plate-metal roll shutters, virtually impenetrable without substantial explosives or a tank.

He cursed under his breath.

Seemed they were snatching more than the odd Jeep left by the wayside. Maybe a meth lab inside. There wasn't much else to explain the security overkill.

Sixty miles west there was a big mall in the town of Price. Wren drove and thought through the plan. With his new cash he picked up a couple sets of fresh clothes, assorted tools, a Samsung smartphone, a couple bottles of water, a pair of field glasses, a better selection of antiseptic wipes plus a suture kit. He wolfed down fries and a couple of corn dogs in the canteen then made a beeline back to the warehouse.

This time he pulled off the track a mile out and rolled into the wilderness. Parked up a quarter mile along, screened by rocks and low cacti, changed into his new desert camo pants, jacket and boots then started to walk. Ten minutes across a flat, scrubby orange plain, then ten more crawling on his belly to settle behind a stand of creosote bushes, where he broke out the field glasses and settled in to watch.

Nothing much happened for a while. Wren lay sweating in the hot sun, sipping water, feeling his bruises sink in. Once a biker came in riding a Triumph, Viking decal on the back, bandage on his face; maybe one of the guys from last night. He parked up in the lot and entered through the roll shutter, but Wren couldn't get a glimpse inside. Within five minutes another guy came out and drove away. Changeover.

Wren drew doodles in the hot sand: an eye, a tomb, a pyramid, the same shapes he'd drawn since he was a child, until he was startled alert by another incoming vehicle.

This time his eyes widened. A patrol car, marked with the local sheriff's badge insignia, dispatched out of Price. The security gate opened. The car rolled through and pulled up to the roll-plate shutter, some four-hundred feet from Wren. Sweat beaded down his cheeks and dropped to make dark spots in the sand.

Wren crawled closer as the plate shutter began rolling up with a rusty, grinding sound. The sheriff was out of his car now; full uniform, blues and a cap, mirrored shades. He was talking to somebody inside, but Wren couldn't hear it over the squeal of the shutters.

Three-hundred feet out, the smell hit him, carried on the hot wind from the warehouse's open mouth. It took him back immediately to a field hospital for local villagers in Syria, south of Palmyra. He'd been working a psy-ops propaganda campaign with rebel Kurdish forces against the national Ba'athist Syrian Arab Army, looking for an informant.

The camp had been filthy, filled with people lying sick and exhausted in makeshift tents and on gurneys, fuming off old sweat and despair, excrement and urine. Floating over all those foul smells, though, had been the high, sweet stink of baby formula.

Wren blinked sweat out of his eyes. Baby formula in the desert? Often used in cutting heroin and ever-present in refugee camps, where UN workers tossed it out in huge bales of silvery packets for people to fight over. Adults drank it, babies drank it; the sour stench of dehydrated milk floated in the air wherever a large mass of humans were trapped together in poor conditions.

Wren's heart hammered harder. Eustace hadn't said anything about this. Maybe he didn't know, but Wren knew just from the smell.

This was human trafficking on a massive scale. Based on that smell, there were easily a hundred people locked up within the warehouse's sturdy walls, waiting to be bought and sold.

There was nothing Wren hated worse.

Now the roll shutter was all the way up. Wren couldn't see anything but some dark shelving within, but maybe he heard them. Children crying.

Women begging. Men responding with barked orders to get on your knees. The hard, flat smacks of punishment bats coming down on bare flesh; like a flashback to his childhood.

A woman staggered into view, shoved out of the warehouse's open mouth. She was dressed in filthy jeans and a stained t-shirt, hands cuffed with zip-ties at her back, browned gag in her mouth, trying to catch her footing.

The sheriff caught her, spun her, laughed at something someone said. Wren could barely hear a thing over the sudden thump of his pulse. His vision tunneled to the woman as the whites of her eyes flared. He imagined surging to his feet, covering the distance to the gate in ten seconds. He could vault it and reach the sheriff in twenty, snatch him up and rip out his throat, steal his weapon, take on the six Vikings inside and kill them all.

It could happen.

But probably not.

Then her eyes were on him.

His breath caught. His pulse ratcheted faster. No way she could actually see him, prone and wearing camo in the desert, but he saw her. She had brown eyes, frizzy black hair and an expression that was boiled down to raw terror. She didn't know what was coming, or if she was even going to survive.

The sheriff opened the trunk and hoisted her in, casual but methodical; like cargo, like he'd done it a thousand times before. Her face disappeared inside and the door slammed down. The guy laughed at something then the roll shutter crashed down to the concrete.

Wren let his rage build.

This wasn't what he'd expected at all.

The patrol car ran through the security gate. Wren crawled away fast, elbows hammering in the orange sand, head rushing with new plans. There was no use calling in the local police now, not if they were in on the game. No use calling in Humphreys, either. It wasn't a CIA matter, since it was in-country. Wren had other contacts in various agencies, the FBI and NSA, but with no evidence, none of them would touch this with a ten-foot pole.

That meant he had to use the Foundation. He couldn't just walk away now. What if that woman had been Loralei? What if the kids inside that building were his?

He'd rather die.

At the truck he revved the engine and flew south with the woman's wide eyes lodged in his head, pushing everything else aside. Flying along the rough trail he booted his new Samsung smartphone and logged into the secret Foundation website on the darknet, kept through a private server. It was one of the ways he kept in touch with his more activist members. He sent up a message pinned for his elite hackers to see.

GET ME EVERYTHING YOU CAN FIND ABOUT A WAREHOUSE AT THIS LOCATION, INCLUDING ALL VEHICLES IN/OUT. IT LOOKS LIKE MASS HUMAN TRAFFICKING. COIN REWARDS AVAILABLE. PLUS A SHERIFF'S CAR JUST LEFT. WHERE DID IT GO?

After that he focused on the road, thrumming with rage and tearing up clouds of orange dust.

7

HENRY & ABDUL

Within an hour his hackers picked up the patrol car on Interstate traffic cams, tracked it back to a roadside biker bar off I-70. The 'Brazen Hussy', it was called, an adobe block with a CCTV camera, neon sign and a small parking lot set out in the middle of nowhere.

Wren rolled up quietly and watched. There were ten Viking bikes stationed out front in the middle of the day. No way he could take them all, and that tore at him. Sitting in his truck he sketched out scenarios on the dash, stealing arms from somewhere, breaking in, shooting them all up, rescuing the woman, charging to the warehouse, running the play again.

It wasn't possible. Didn't matter how angry you were or what kind of training you had, you couldn't take out that many armed guys alone, especially if the first site got a warning out to the second, which he had to think they would.

Better to call in reinforcements.

He brought up his darknet again, sent out a second message targeted at local Foundation assets: a girl in Colorado, a couple guys in Wyoming, all past their three-year coins. The girl had hook-ups with dodgy wrecking yards, the two guys were good for muscle. Via the site's Megaphone app, emails, robocalls, texts and social media messages would pepper them every ten minutes until they dropped everything and came running. It was like being summoned to the principal's office on the school PA, he'd heard, but he'd done the same for them countless times, so…

Nothing he could do now but get some rest.

He found a Big Eastern motel back in Orangeville. The reception lady scowled at him, a dirty, bloodied drifter, but took his money and gave him a room. It was drab, with mint walls and chintzy decorative pottery on the shelves. In the petite washroom, he studied his face.

Yup, no better.

He peeled off the dirt-crusted camo gear and stepped into the shower. The hot water on his swollen back felt like heaven. On the bed he sat dripping wet with the AC cranked up to full, dabbing antiseptic on his wounds. He sutured a couple of the nastier cuts, then laid flat out on the bed and crashed, exhausted from the extended cortisol high.

An alarm jerked him awake.

Sound blared, and for a moment Wren panted in the solid dark. Beside him a clock flashed 11 p.m. Ten hours gone, two hours to go. He hit the alarm and it silenced.

Nightmares clung to him like hot chains. The woman's eyes mixing with his wife's face. He shoved them both back down, then booted the Samsung and checked into his darknet.

All three of his members had responded and were nearing position. Alli, the girl with the wrecking yard hook-up, was in transit down from her scrapyard. Henry and Abdul, both veterans Wren had met out in the Korengal Valley six years back, had already hooked up and were closing in.

'Extra credit', Wren had titled the Megaphone shout, and accordingly they'd each made their requests; points in the system, accelerating up the ranking. He approved them all. Running the Foundation was all about logistics.

He got up and hit the lights. His body ached like he'd been through a meat grinder, so he did a quick high-impact exercise routine, starting with yoga stretches and moving through push-ups, jump-squats and dips. It barely touched his reserves but was enough to get his heart pumping and blood out bathing his muscles. Some of the ache ebbed away. He dressed in dark jeans, dark t-shirt, dark boots from the Price mall, then headed out.

It was past midnight when he reached the shuttered convenience store near the Brazen Hussy, where he'd arranged to meet Henry and Abdul. He waited in the dark. Sitting quietly was the hardest. It brought back memories and let the past creep in. Good moments with Loralei, bacon and waffles with the kids, everyone laughing.

They hadn't been taken. They weren't enslaved by traffickers in some high-tech desert warehouse, but he couldn't help imagining they were. The same reason he'd had to get out of the Company. He'd seen too much.

Henry and Abdul appeared fifteen minutes later, rolling in a smooth convoy off the highway, a bland rental sedan followed by an eighteen-wheel semi-trailer truck. Wren waited as they parked and came over, padding in easy synchrony.

In Korengal they'd been a deadly sniper team; too much so. They'd acquired a taste for it, forgetting where the boundaries lay, figuring themselves as the lone line of justice operating in a chaotic, cruel world.

It was only when Wren had ambushed their unauthorized raid on a suspected Taliban-sympathizer, intending a night execution, that they stopped. Wren was there on maneuvers with ISIS as an undercover Force Recon Marine, and held out an unpinned grenade in their target's small mud-walled basement, daring them to take the shot to kill him.

They almost had. By then they'd hit a peak point where allowing any single offense seemed like a bridge too far, giving absolute punishment for even the slightest of crimes, executing potential 'terrorists' daily with no oversight at all. Wren had seen it many times before in other war zones, and understood well the only way to turn it back.

They needed to get out of the war. While he held the grenade he talked about Americana: skits from Saturday Night Live, Hershey's Kisses under the bleachers with the prom queen, reeling down the flag at summer camp, the first tailgate where you got wasted.

It was enough for that night. Through backchannels the next day he expedited their dishonorable discharge from service and set them up with jobs and extensive counseling at a VA center back home.

Now they lined up before him.

"Corporal," Henry said, throwing off a salute. His old Marine-level rank. Abdul stood at attention.

It felt damn good to see them. So good that he barely held it together. After New York, then three weeks alone going mad across the country, then the woman at the warehouse…

"This is not Company business," Wren said gruffly. The only way to get any words out. "You don't need to salute."

43

"Are you undercover, sir?"

"Something like that."

He surveyed them both, dressed in night combat fatigues and ready for war. Pulling them in like this was taking a risk with their combat sobriety, but that was the Foundation life; you couldn't stand by while another suffered.

"Thank you for coming," he said. "Did you bring everything?"

Abdul spoke up. "Yes, sir. Request the mission portfolio."

Wren stifled a smile. They were always like this with him. Full military respect, though he'd never demanded it. Abdul worked as a sous chef in a Dubois French restaurant now, while Henry rode close protection for reality show contestants on the minor celebrity security circuit. They'd both left their third tour far behind but kept up with training and drills. Henry had a kid; Abdul was just getting serious with his girlfriend.

Wren outlined the mission. In turn they shared their gear, a throat-mic and earpiece so he could stay in contact, two flashbang grenades on a bandolier, a Beretta M9 in a shoulder holster. As Wren geared up, pulling the straps tight carefully as his bruises and cuts strained, Henry tried an awkward attempt at small talk.

"How are your kids, sir?"

That hit Wren like a gut punch. Unexpected. "I haven't seen them for a while," he managed. Not a lie.

"Because of the mission?" Abdul asked.

Wren grunted. "Yeah," and let it rest there. There'd be a coin meeting for them both soon, and he'd tell them about what happened, but not in the run-up to an op. Not when he needed to focus. "Let's hit the road."

Henry nodded. "Yes, sir."

The two went over to the sedan, pulled away, leaving the semi for Wren. He watched their taillights join the stream of red pouring down the Interstate, then looked to the eighteen-wheeler.

It was big, with unbranded canvas sides. He'd driven rigs as large only a few times before. Cornering was a killer, and the rumble it made driving slow was a dead giveaway. Around the back there was a forklift, tucked in.

Perfect for what he had planned.

8

BRAZEN HUSSY

Twenty minutes later Wren, Henry and Abdul rolled down the access road to the Brazen Hussy with all the headlights out. Wren counted thirteen bikes parked out front now, one heck of a backup garrison. The CCTV's red light flashed on and off like a distant, dying lighthouse.

Wren pulled the semi to the side, while Abdul turned the sedan and parked in a culvert. Henry darted out and tossed three spike strips behind them. The tactical black devices scissored out smoothly to lay invisible across the road.

Wren gave the go signal and Henry broke to the right, Abdul broke to the left. In moments they had melted into the dark of chaparral-coated desert. Wren waited two minutes in the semi's cab, pulse running low and under control, giving them time.

"Hard lines cut," came Abdul's voice through Wren's earpiece. "No calls going out through the wires."

"Jammer in place," said Henry seconds later. "Nothing but our comms in the air."

"Good work," Wren said, and made the call; an emergency line first to the sheriff, a second call to the local newspaper. He told them a mass firefight was going down just off the Interstate, and to send everything they had. That didn't give him long.

"In position?" he asked.

"In position," said Abdul, matched a moment later by Henry.

Wren sucked in a breath, put the huge truck in gear and revved toward the Brazen Hussy. Twenty miles an hour, pushing nearly twenty tons of mass. They'd hear the grumble of the weight long before he hit; he just had one shot to get it right.

At the parking lot's edge, he swung wide and came in flush, mounting the narrow sidewalk fronting the bar. A metal STOP sign folded beneath the semi's front fender with a clang, then his wing mirror dislodged the CCTV camera. He angled tighter to grind the trailer bed against the bar's stucco, then braked.

The truck blocked the front door completely, a wall between the bar and the bikes. Shouts rose from inside as he climbed out of the cab. At the back, he deployed the forklift as the first of them hammered at the door.

"Set the clock," Wren said on throat-mic to Henry and Abdul. Completely calm, now, in the midst of an op. "Twenty minutes until reinforcements come from the warehouse."

"Roger that," came Abdul's voice.

A moment later the rear door of the bar clanged open.

"It's a guy in a wifebeater," came Henry's voice. "Coming for you. He's armed."

The enforcer, Wren figured.

"Dissuade him," he said, and steered the little forklift whirring toward the first bike. A second later Henry's first shot rang out with a tremendous bark. A 7.62mm caliber special ball buried itself in the wall of the Hussy, followed by another warning shot.

"He's not stopping," said Henry, "permission to eliminate?"

"Denied," said Wren, and stepped off the forklift. Ultimately, he needed these bikers to give testimony against each other, the cops and whoever was bankrolling the warehouse. "I'll handle this, keep the rest pinned."

He met the enforcer as he tore around the semi's back corner, not bothering to draw the Beretta. He was furious and jacked on adrenaline, eyes flaring wide, a Luger 9mm in his right fist. Wren got one hand on his pale wrist and the other on the gun. The barrel was hot, and it fired sideways as Wren shoved it away with one hand and yanked on the guy's wrist with the other, aiming to snap a finger and strip the weapon.

For a moment they wrestled, then the enforcer hissed, "You're gonna hang," and sent a headbutt at Wren's face. Wren saw it coming and tucked his chin in, flattening the guy's nose across the top of Wren's skull.

"I have shot," came Abdul's voice, as calm as if this was a company audit. "Permission?"

"Negative," Wren said through gritted teeth, and wrenched the barrel one more time, finally stripping the Luger with a finger break, sending it clattering away over the lot.

Now the guy was angry. Wren launched a high elbow, but the enforcer blocked it and sent a low answering hook into Wren's belly. It almost caught Wren's solar plexus, but he swiveled away and sent an instinctive snap kick across the guy's chest.

The enforcer staggered back; each step punctuated by more gunfire reports in back. Wren followed with a hook-jab-uppercut combination that the enforcer weaved through, throwing his own jabs in return.

"Who are you with?" he rasped, spraying blood now. "FBI?"

"I'm freelance," Wren panted, and sent another snap kick out on the 'f' of 'freelance'. The enforcer caught it on bristling elbows, knocking him briefly onto his heels, and Wren took the chance to dive at his ankles, locking them together and toppling him to the hot blacktop in a wrestler's hold. The enforcer tried to spin free, but Wren flipped and swiftly worked a heel hook lock on his left ankle, twisting it across his body and up into his armpit. He ignored the enforcer's frenzied kicks and screams and pulled until the knee hyper-extended with a meniscus-bursting pop.

Just like that the fight was over. Three months in traction and another six of physio. He'd earned it. The enforcer screamed and rolled away, and Wren let him go. He retrieved the Luger and threw it into the trailer.

"Are the rest holding position?" Wren asked into throat-mic.

"Holding at the rear," said Henry. "Time's ticking, boss."

"Took long enough," Abdul chimed in.

"He went in for the kiss," Wren smart-mouthed, and limped back into the forklift cab. "But I'm not that kind of gal."

Abdul laughed. Wren slipped back into the forklift's seat and worked the controls. He rolled to the nearest bike, a top of the range Harley Fat Boy, regular retail price around thirty-five grand, then scooped under the chassis with his forks. The forklift whined and lifted, and he spun the little truck, rolled it forward and deposited the bike in the semi trailer's open side with a thunk.

Coin zero.

"Sit rep on blue lights," said Wren.

"Sheriff from adjoining districts are inbound already," Henry answered.

Wren rolled the forklift to the next bike, began repeating the procedure. More shouts and shots came from the back of the Hussy, silenced by the deep crack of another special ball hitting the building.

Right about now the Vikings would be realizing what this was. Not just a rival gang attack or a robbery, but a total comms blackout. No way for them to warn the warehouse.

Wren worked on the third bike, then the fourth, steely control and precision with every maneuver.

"They're moving at the back," came Henry. "I don't have a visual."

"Abdul?" asked Wren.

"Looks like they're retreating into the desert, trying to flank us, looking for muzzle flashes."

There would be no muzzle flashes. Henry and Abdul were a hundred yards out and using flash cones, obscuring the tell-tale bark of flame from their munitions. The chances of the Vikings stumbling on them in the dark were incredibly unlikely.

Then an engine revved up.

"Abdul," said Wren, "engine block."

"It's an armored Humvee."

Wren cursed. That didn't fit, and he hadn't seen anything like it on his earlier reconnaissance. It seemed an awful like lot someone had warned them he was coming. Eustace? Either way, no use panicking. "Let him run. Get his tires."

"Yes, sir."

More resounding cracks rang out as Wren snatched the fifth bike.

"Got him," said Abdul, after a crack followed by a percussive blast. "Barely slowed him, but he's running rough."

A moment later the Humvee burst around the side of the semi, windows rolled down and spraying bullets wildly from patch members wielding AR-15s in the back seats. Wren rolled out of the forklift and ducked behind it as bullets zipped through the air.

"Keep their heads down," he said over the mic. "I'll deal with this."

The Humvee did a wide skid across the lot, leaving a beauty of a half-donut streak, then came on at Wren hard, wheels spinning rubber flaps and sparks into the night. Two bikers leaned wide out of the sides, firing wild as the Humvee bounced closer on its busted tires, but Wren wasn't worried. With their wheels out there was no chance they'd get a clean shot.

He bobbed out from behind the forklift just as the Humvee skidded left at the last moment, exposing its right flank and open windows. Wren hurled the flashbang grenade like a fastball straight into the back seats, then the inside of the Humvee lit up pure white.

The image of five stunned bikers burned through Wren's closed eyes and onto his retinas. The thunderclap that followed was terrible, then there was darkness again, and the growling of the Humvee's engine, and the ringing in Wren's ears.

The vehicle roared in a cloud of drifting cordite smoke. Someone inside vomited. Burst eardrums. Burned-out eyes. They wouldn't be fighting again soon.

"Sheriffs ten minutes out," came Henry's voice. "Hostiles hiding at the back of the bar still. Looks like they're beat. "

"Understood," said Wren, and turned back to the forklift. Thankfully the firefight hadn't damaged the engine or lifting mechanism. "Keep a bead on and exit in nine."

"Yes, sir."

Nine minutes of hard, nerve-jangling work followed. Wren's back throbbed as he worked the forklift's gears, punctuated by yells and intermittent gunfire. He'd loaded the eighth bike and was starting on the ninth when a roar of Harleys streamed in from the Interstate.

"Did any warning call go out?" Wren asked sharply.

"Nothing," Henry answered. "This must be some kind of redundancy, if the comms go down."

Wren grunted. He'd figured on it. When they couldn't get through to the Hussy, they'd send a squad. Looked like three bikes in all.

They came on hard, circling off the Interstate and around the access road, then hit the dark spike strips at speed. The popcorn sound of bursting tires was chased by the metallic clang and scrape of bikes going down.

"Reposition?" Wren asked.

"Already done," Henry answered. "I have you at one-eighty degrees, fair visibility on both sides."

Wren turned, wiping sweat from his temple, to see Henry had taken up residence inside the Humvee, only the spike of his flash cone poking out.

"I have eyes on the reinforcements," said Abdul. "They're headed back to the Interstate on foot, tails between their legs. They won't come in so hot again."

Wren loaded the ninth bike and started on the tenth.

"Five minutes until sheriffs," Abdul reported.

Long enough. "Get out of here, guys," Wren answered. "I appreciate you coming on short notice. There'll be a nice bonus in your next coin status check-up."

"Thank you, sir," Henry said smartly.

"It's been a pleasure," Wren said.

"The pleasure's ours," said Abdul, and sent a few final warning rounds into the sides of the Hussy.

After that there was silence, bar the whine of the forklift's motors. The sedan drew away quietly, the spike strips now cleared. Wren worked alone, sweat pouring down his face and seeping salt into fresh cuts.

The whine of sirens drew in as he loaded the thirteenth bike. A minute or two only left. He slapped away the pins holding the side canvas, let the flap fall to cover his stolen goods, then ran to the truck's cab where he came face to face with one of the bikers.

It was Eustace.

The bald, bandaged fool looked like a rabbit caught in the headlights, even as he brought up a gun to point in Wren's face.

Everything clarified. This explained the Humvee. Eustace was the rat.

Wren flung himself forward and to the right without hesitation. The gun discharged in the air to his left, then he was up and snatching the barrel and Eustace's wrist. He gave the man a sober, disappointed look, then broke his wrist.

Eustace screamed and clutched his arm. Wren wanted nothing more than to put a lights-out elbow into his dumb head. Further gone than he'd thought. Needing more effort. But still, surely not a committed slaver?

"Coin one minus," he said instead, leaning in to tilt the man's feverish, bandaged face to meet his eyes. All the information he'd gotten from him was now suspect. His coming assault on the warehouse might already be compromised. "You're not off the hook, Eustace. I guess I already took your bike, as promised. Now what did you tell them?"

Eustace mumbled something through the pain. Wren squeezed his jaw and he screamed on cue. "What did you tell them?"

"I dold them you came," Eustace panted, tongue still thick in his mouth. "I had to. I'm thorry. Pleathe."

Wren let go and stepped back, deciding on a dime. Eustace seemed sincere. He was certainly sorry. There was every chance he didn't know about the human trafficking. Too junior. Worth one more chance. "Walk away right now," Wren ordered. "Into the desert, back home on foot. The sheriffs are coming. You don't want to go down with this gang." He paused a second longer. "And I'll be back soon. I'm not leaving you a year to fester. Show me these guys are beneath you. Start shaping up tomorrow, and do not screw up again. I'll be watching."

He climbed into the semi's cab. The truck juddered to a start and picked up speed through the parking lot. The vibration of toppling bikes carried through the chassis. Stray bullets chased him but slashed uselessly into the canvas.

He pulled onto the Interstate, where the wail and lights of the sheriff's cars came in from the west. Off to the side he caught a glimpse of Eustace running awkwardly into the dark desert scrub, cradling his arm, then he hauled the semi away east into the dark.

9

ALLI

W ren drove east on I-70 for thirty minutes, then north a ways on the 6, buzzing from the strike and racing against the clock. There was a fresh sting in his left arm where someone had put a gouge the night before, and fresh regret in his head where he'd misread Eustace.

He'd learned this lesson many times, and still it caught him unawares. Change was hard, and it came on slowly. The amount of work it took to rehabilitate people was enormous.

Now the warehouse was waiting.

His Foundation member Alli was waiting for him five miles on in a broad stretch of shoulder. He pulled the big rig over behind her Ford Super Duty, hazard lights flashing. She stood at the edge, lit by the orange bead of light from a Marlboro. Her straw-blond hair sprayed in scrunchy-knotted clumps atop her head.

"What kind of time you call this, Christopher?" she asked, as he got out.

He smiled as he strode over, studying her in the semi's running lights. Full of sass, as ever. She was wearing oil-streaked dungarees, a tough young woman who spent hours at the wrecking yards, taking abuse and giving it. He'd pulled her out of a firm school-shooting plan when she was fifteen, after the FBI had flagged her record but not enough to take action. Wren had taken action for them; certain she'd have gone through with it. To get to that point, she'd survived her father's abuse for five years.

He redirected her rage into mild criminality combined with auto engineering. Like methadone, it was a good comedown drug for mass murder. She had anger and drive; she just hadn't known where to put it. Like everyone else on the coin system, she was a tinder keg that would blow if left neglected for too long.

"Nice to see you too, Alli."

She flicked the cigarette off the hood of his semi. "I hope these caged folks are worth it. Plate metal for your 'tank', and a ram cage?"

Wren smiled. He'd set her the task of building him a vehicle capable of crashing through the warehouse's plate-metal roll shutters. "It looks like you've delivered."

"Of course I have! I've been sweating over this beast all day. It's crazy. And now this?" She pointed at the semi.

"Thirteen bikes I caught," he said. "A nice batch from one watering hole. Sell them where you can, chop them for parts, take ten percent and the rest goes to the Foundation account."

"I know the deal. These idiots are going to be coming after me, now."

Wren laughed. "Yeah, right. These idiots are going to jail, and I'll mop up any leftover. Besides, when's the last time you failed to steal a vehicle effectively?"

Alli made a face. She liked to grumble, but deep down she was fiercely decent, and loyal to those who were loyal to her. "Fine," she said, sounding every bit like a grumpy teen. "I'll launder your bikes. Now I'm sure you want to take a look at your tank."

She made a weary 'ta-da!' gesture, taking in the big black Super Duty, then pointed into the pick-up's bed. "Over a ton of plate metal right there, each slab welded down. That kind of mass will give you incredible inertia, you could punch straight through a two-foot-thick concrete wall." She paused a second, as if awed by her own work. "You know how long that kind of welding takes?"

"Twenty minutes a sheet," Wren estimated, surveying the load. "Looks like ten sheets. Maybe three hours and change?"

She blew air out her lips. "Try five. You're taking the tires to their limit with this much weight. They're as hard as concrete; it'll be a rough ride."

Wren nodded. "And the ram cage?"

"Here," she pointed.

It projected off the front of the Ford by two feet, a pointed steel frame like the unpaneled nose of a ship. A battering ram that wouldn't buckle when it hit the toll shutters. This was his way in, the closest to a tank he could get on short notice.

"Welded to the chassis," she said, "bolted to your B and C columns and the trailer. It's not moving a gnat's wing."

"Perfect."

"Of course it's perfect. I did it myself. Now I expect you'll be off." She tossed him the keys and he caught them smoothly, tossed back the keys for the semi.

"Tracker scan all the bikes," he said. "They might be GPS wired."

She blew more air through her lips. That was her new thing, he figured. "I know how to steal a bike."

Wren grinned. Of course she did. He opened the Ford's door.

"When's our next coin meeting?" she asked. "There's some things I want to talk to you about."

Wren paused half-in the truck. "Urgent?"

"Not as urgent as a warehouse full of human slaves. But yeah, pretty pressing for me."

Wren hated to let his Foundation members down. "Right after this," he said, and closed the door. Every second counted now. "I promise."

"Unless you die."

She said it without a smile. Worried, maybe. Wren tried not to think about the chaos that would be unleashed on the world if he died. Hundreds of hackers, addicts, cult survivors and low-level cons let loose from the Foundation coin system. If he thought about it too much, he would never sleep, and he got precious little sleep as it was.

He laughed. Sometimes all you could do was laugh.

"I don't know what you're laughing about," Alli said. "You look like a turd warmed over. Barely warm, actually. Like you're half dead already."

"Charming," he said, then turned the key, punched the gas and started away. "I'll see you real soon, Alli," he called through the window.

"You owe me more than damn coins!" she shouted after him.

Didn't he always. But no time for that now. He focused on the job ahead.

54

10

FORD

I n twenty minutes he was creeping the low-riding Ford around the sandstone ridge, running on scant moonlight and guesswork, waiting for the warehouse to come into sight.

Except it didn't.

No security lamps on the fences. Nothing but the angular moonlit outline of the warehouse against the organic desert scrub.

They'd been warned too.

Didn't change a thing.

Wren gunned the engine and shot his lights to full flood, illuminating fresh, deep tracks in the dirt road. Something heavy had passed this way recently. The radio blasted out Springsteen's 'Born in the USA'. Nothing more fitting for a bit of shock and awe. He shifted to second gear and the Ford picked up speed on the dirt.

After ten yards he pulled off the track and onto the scrub, accelerating down a trail he'd eyeballed that morning. The ride was jolty as hell, with every pebble bouncing Wren like he was riding a mechanical bull, carrying over a ton's worth of kick. The suspension would be dead in minutes, but minutes was all he needed.

His floods lit the desert ahead, racing the quarter mile to the warehouse through knotty clusters of sage and low whipple cacti like they weren't even there. He hit a rock at forty and almost slammed headfirst into the wheel. His right hand came loose, then his floods caught the warehouse and lot; no cars that he could see, the metal shutter rolled down as expected.

He jammed the gas pedal to the deck and the engine roared mightily, tearing tracks through crusted vegetation and skating over sand, until the outer razor wire fence whipped out of nowhere and snapped across the Ford's ram cage. With thirty feet to go and racing at fifty miles an hour, Wren realized his trajectory was off; the roll shutter was two feet to the right. He was going to hit the shutter column, likely reinforced with thick rebar, and get himself splattered on the inside windshield.

He reacted fast, a switchback yank on the wheel, hard right then left, which sent the Ford screaming against its own momentum. It hydroplaned to the right on burning rubber for a giddy second, ate up the two-foot rightward dodge in a squall of burning brake fluid, then hit the roll shutters head on. The ram cage punched the plate metal clear out of its housing with a tremendous shearing bark.

Wren rocked forward on impact, the seatbelt snapped hard across his bruised ribs, then he lurched back into the seat as the shutter whiplashed away like a matador's cape and the Ford careened into pitch darkness inside. His floodlights revealed a mass of wire cages to the left and tall rows of metal shelving ahead, then he was in them. The shelves hammered off the Ford like bodies in a crowd, ripping a mangled path through four rows before the brakes finally stalled its enormous momentum, and the wrecking ball of his vehicle finally rocked to a halt.

He took a breath. Springsteen hit the chorus, suddenly unbearably loud in the contained space. He kicked the door open and slithered into darkness, running low away from the truck's island of sound and light, accompanied by the thudding waterfall of incoming gunfire, one bullet after another.

Wren kept count as he ran, four blasts that echoed maddeningly off the aluminum walls and roof. He stopped running at the end of a long row of twenty-foot-tall shelving, holding the Beretta high in his right hand.

"Born!" yelled Springsteen from fifty yards away.

Another shot came, pinged somewhere near the truck. Wren edged around the huge shelf, keeping his profile hidden by the stacked boxes, and scanned the dark interior. The plate metal shutters had fallen back across the entrance, leaving the Ford's headlights as the sole illumination; it looked like a wounded animal exhausted at the end of a rampage.

To the left lay cages.

Lit only by the red glow from the Ford's taillights, cages filled some half of the warehouse, each made of diamond-lattice steel wire and standing seven feet tall. There was only one thing you needed cages like that for.

Big enough to fit hundreds of people. Right now they were empty, bar a few mylar blankets crumpled in the darkness. Wren cursed under his breath.

He was too late. They'd shipped them all out.

Another shot zipped through the dark. Wren felt the vibration of this one, punching through boxes on the rack nearest him and trilling off the metal frame. He'd been spotted; good thing the muzzle flash had given the guy away too. Up on the cages, standing in what looked to be a guard tower, rocking some kind of long rifle, barely visible in silhouette.

Wren just had the Beretta. Not so great at a hundred yards out. Wren ran quick numbers; the guy had already fired five times now, and a standard long gun packed three to five shells in the magazine. That would make him due a reload.

Wren ran.

A shot rang and sparked just to his right. Maybe a six-shell option or a second shooter. 'Born in the USA' ended, and the radio host drawled into darkness as Wren plummeted through the open door to the cages.

A seventh shot came, closing the range now, and Wren felt the bruised air to his left. Had to be a large capacity mag. He raised the Beretta and fired up into darkness, five discharges as he ran, until he was standing near directly underneath the guy, and at last he dropped.

High ground wasn't always the best.

Wren panted, wheeled and moved.

Another shot came, skittered sparks off the cement floor where he'd been standing. His heart thumped, he ran in darkness and scanned the shelves. Now he'd locked himself in the cage. One chokepoint; the door. The guy out there would know it, if he was thinking straight.

Another shot ripped through the air, homing in on Wren in the red glow of the taillights. No time left, and Wren had to act fast. Plays ran through his head. Beretta. One more flashbang on the bandolier. Plenty in the magazine.

He locked his stance and fired three times straight through the cage wire wall. Clear muzzle barks out of the full dark, sparks spraying as

Springsteen hammered on, then he stripped the flashbang and dropped it, got off-line just as an answering hail of bullets sang out, tearing through the air where he'd been. The sniper's gaze locked on his position, straining to pick him out. Wren closed his eyes and covered his ears just as the flashbang went off.

Bright even through his squeezed eyelids. A supernova in the black. There was a scream somewhere off in the dark. The guy had been looking right at it, so his eyes would be fried, ears blasted. Wren had a window, maybe thirty seconds.

He sprinted straight through the cage entrance, made direct for the source of the cry. No need for stealth now, all that mattered was speed. The guy wouldn't hear him, wouldn't see him. Around the Ford, through the headlight beams, into the shelving where he saw the guy bent over, hands on his eyes.

Wren's blood pumped. Maybe a jump-knee, he'd take the guy conscious and get some answers, but a second too soon the guy racked back upright, trained the rifle and fired. The shot whiskered by, forcing Wren to return fire. Took the guy in the cheek, drew a red dot, and down he went like dead weight.

Wren rolled, came up low by the guy's side, hand on his throat. Dead.

He listened for a long second. The Boss was crooning for all he was worth. No more shots came. No movement. It almost added up. Six men here on sentry. Three had come to the Hussy. That left one.

It didn't take long to find him.

11

EXECUTED

Wren found him atop the cages, right next to two other bodies. He knelt beside them, amped by adrenaline, hearing now the drip of blood through the cage roof like a drum roll. One of them the guy Wren had shot; not a biker at all. Four bullets hit home, it seemed, roughly center mass, but random. He'd taken the brunt of Wren's wild charge. Fully dead, eyes staring blindly. Pale, blond hair, tall and solid in all black like a tactical strike squad member. Wren checked his pockets, but there was nothing, not even a phone.

A professional.

Bad news.

In the faint light Wren picked out faded leather jackets on the other two, Viking logo on the back. The guys were big like Eustaces, but full patch members. Wren rolled one and saw two stained holes in the chest, one through the head.

Not Wren's shots out of the dark. This was an execution up close and personal, from someone the guy had known and trusted. Possible explanations raced through his head, but none covered all the bases. He needed more data.

In an elevated office tucked in the upper northwest corner he found the lights. They blinked on musically across the warehouse, and Wren looked out through the glass to see more dead Vikings gunned down amongst the shelving.

He'd stumbled into something bigger. A cleanup operation.

The elevated office had been stripped. Cables sprayed where tower computers must have stood, monitors sat forlornly, pale marks on the walls where planners would have hung, a filing cabinet hollowed out.

In a corner, clutching a Glock and surrounded by bullet holes in the drywall, another Viking. Patch member, plenty of tats. Three random shots to the body, chased by two in the chest, one in the head.

The scale of it clunked into place. Wren had seen hits like this before, cartels mopping up their local partners after an operation went south. Dead men tell no tales. He wound back the record to the moment Eustace must have called it in. All put on their guard. When Wren hit the Hussy, they'd burned it all, thinking he had to be forward operations for some government agency.

Clean up the Vikings. Export the 'human cargo'. Leave no evidence behind.

Except.

Wren's chest went cold.

Evidence remained. The Vikings from the Hussy; they had to know about the warehouse too, and whoever was running it. The sheriff who'd been bought off would know plenty too, perhaps even where they'd gone.

Maybe all those people were in the same place right now, on duty or behind bars. His mouth went dry. Unlikely. But here were the Vikings in their own warehouse, wholly rubbed out. It was possible. If this wider organization were anything like the cartels Wren knew, they wouldn't let a little thing like a police station stand in their way of cleaning up the trail.

He brought up his phone, sent a swift darknet message on his hacker board.

FIND OUT WHERE THE SHERIFFS ARE TAKING THE VIKINGS. ALSO HUNT THROUGH SATELLITE OVERWATCH/RECORDS FOR A CARTEL-LIKE ORGANIZATION OPERATING OUT OF THIS WAREHOUSE. THIS JUST WENT LARGE, MAYBE NATIONAL

He paused a second, tapped some more.

A SEMI LEFT THIS LOCATION WITHIN THE LAST HOUR, LOADED WITH HUMAN CARGO. FIND IT.

Then he ran across the cage tops, calling Henry and Abdul via voice dial.

"I need you back on the case," he said.

"Yes, sir," said Henry smartly. "Tell us where."

"Wherever the Vikings are now. Check into the darknet, they'll let you know, likely the Price PD or nearby. Set up and watch until I get there. I'm expecting an incoming kill strike, possibly with overwhelming force."

That took a second.

"Numbers?"

"Unknown. But your job is overwatch only. Don't risk yourselves. These people are professionals with incredible resources."

"Understood," said Henry.

"Thank you," Wren said, and ended the call, clasped the cage-top ladder either side and slid down.

Professionals. Incredible resources.

It didn't add up. A conspiracy of this scale should have shown up on national intelligence a long time ago. That it hadn't meant stunning organizational capacities. An interwoven network of bribes, blackmail and loyalty spread throughout the country, capable of selling hundreds of humans in absolute secrecy.

Bigger than anything he'd yet seen, bigger than the Foundation was able to handle. He had to bring in the big guns.

Sprinting, he found his Jeep in a motor pool on the other side of the shelves. Shredded with bullets, the engine block already gone, the dash gutted for electronics. The passenger seat was empty, his kids' pictures gone.

No time to chase that up now. He found the key to a dirt-crusted GMC Sierra hung in a rack on the wall, snatched it and flung open the door, sparked the engine then punched back through the dangling plate metal shutter and out onto dark scrub, four-wheel-drive straining.

The sun would be up soon. If an attack on the Vikings in police custody was coming, it would most likely come before the dawn, and a hundred miles lay between him and the nearest police department in Price.

Already he was behind.

Racing at ninety through the wilderness along the 332, he made the call he'd been dreading for weeks, as the skies lightened ahead over the red sands of Utah.

12

HUMPHREYS

"Yes," came a male voice on the other end. You got nothing else when you called through to the switchboard of the Special Activities Center of the CIA.

"This is Christopher Wren, codeword clockjaguar3, looking for Director Gerald Humphreys."

There was a moment, then a polite, "Please hold."

The tracking on his phone line would have already begun. Doubtless his name was on blacklists up and down the nation's intelligence agencies, each one usually a walled garden desperate to hold in its own secrets. They'd make an exception for Wren.

Thirty seconds passed, then a voice came on the line. Director Humphreys, by-the-book king of his own government fiefdom, and chief oversight officer on Wren's activities for the last five years.

"Wren," he said. "We had a deal. What the hell do you want?"

There was nothing much to say to that. They'd already have his location by now, much good it would do them. Not enough cell towers to triangulate him precisely, maybe a rough of a few thousand square miles.

Basically, they knew he was in Utah.

"This is a sidebar to our deal," Wren said, dismissing so much in a few words. "I'm not calling to talk about the past. I've got a new urgent issue here, and a request."

"A request?" Humphreys snapped. "You abandoned multiple intelligence operations midway through! Worse yet, I've been looking into the cult of personality you've been building for the last twenty years, Christopher. When you told me about it three weeks back, I thought you were insane, maybe you'd gathered a handful of crazies just like you, but what I'm seeing now? It's bordering on levying some kind of personal militia!" He took a rough breath. "Who the hell are you?"

"It's not a cult," Wren answered, tightly controlling his anger, "it's a Foundation, and I told you all this. I was going to hand it over, until…" He let that hang. That had been the whole of his plan, after settling back in with his family in New York. Handing it over gradually, carefully, not compromising any of his people.

Then all that had gone to seed. He'd been driving ever since, searching for a way back that didn't seem to exist. Fair to say, the handover had slipped his mind.

"Either way," he picked up, "they're no threat to you. They're good people, and I'm going to be riding herd over them tightly going forward." A pause to take a breath. "As for the operations, I closed them all out. We went through this. I don't owe the CIA the rest of my life."

"A senator's son died!" Humphreys snapped. "Whatever you say about how that happened, you were lead on the operation! That's America's reputation and safety put at risk."

Wren gritted his teeth. Thinking back to that idiot Regis dying in the Sonoran dust. He'd brought it on himself, for self-serving purposes. The calculus hadn't changed. "We see that differently. Anyway, it's done, and you agreed. Now I'm facing a major terrorist threat here, and I'm in position to act. I need a new status to take it on."

It took Humphreys a second. "Status? Wren, you're so far out I'd be raising your profile if I dunked you in a black site for the rest of your life! There's no status."

"AWOP," said Wren, then spelled it. "A-W-O-P."

"What?" Now there was danger in Humphrey's tone. "Agent Without Portfolio? There hasn't been a freelance Company agent in fifty years!"

"Forty-five," Wren corrected. "Cold War sleepers, undercover with Russia for decades, acting on their own recognizance. It's basically what I've been doing for twenty years already. This will just formalize things. AWOP."

"I don't care if it's five damn centuries!" Humphreys raged. "I'm sending three squads for you as we speak. There's nothing left for you here, Wren. Maintaining that cult, quitting on a dime, you're beyond finished! You're a black goddamn hole."

Wren grimaced. He'd expected it to be bad, but not like this. Still, there was nothing to do but push through. "So send the squads. I'll lead them to the target location. I've got reason to believe there's going to be a major terrorist attack." While he spoke, he brought up his darknet. His hackers had worked fast. Confirmation of the holding location was in, tapped from police radio bands. "Located in Price, central Utah. Focused on the police department, where they're holding members of a biker gang known as the Vikings."

That stopped Humphreys for a moment. It was such specific intelligence that he couldn't just dismiss it. "What kind of setup is this? Is this a threat from your 'Foundation'?"

"What? Of course not, this has nothing to do with me! I'm heading there myself, trying to stop it. You'll see. There's a national organization, Director, looks bigger than anything we've yet seen. I'm expecting a paramilitary response. I found a large-scale warehouse being used for human trafficking, evacuated in the last few hours. The level of professionalism tops anything we've seen with the cartels. This could be huge. You need to contact Price PD and lock it down. They're not prepared for what's coming."

"What's coming? How can I trust any of this?" Humphreys asked. "Where's the corroboration? You're a confirmed liar, Wren, and with your pedigree?"

Pedigree. That stung. They both knew what it meant. The childhood Wren never talked about, the past he'd barely survived.

"So let this be the proof. I'll bring them down with or without your help. Easier with, though."

Silence followed, apart from the Sierra's engine roaring and wind whipping through the open window. Humphreys mulling, chewing on his mustache. Despite whatever lies Wren had told, he'd been an exemplary agent. 'Saint Justice', they'd called him, able to get in and out of any organization fast and set things right, leave it headless and toppling.

"Price," said Humphreys. "Utah."

"Right. Make it secure," Wren said. "And tell them I'm coming. Those

Vikings are witnesses to this terror group, maybe some of the cops too. We need to hear their testimony."

Humphreys chewed. "I'll talk to Price. We'll see."

He hung up.

Wren raced into the new day.

13

EN ROUTE

Wren gripped the wheel like he was throttling a snake, counting the minutes and miles as he raced west with the sun rising behind him. Dark, bare desert raced by either side, the windows down and a rain-smelling wind blowing dust into his eyes.

His mind charged ahead, running calculations. Over three hours since he'd kicked things off with his raid on the Hussy, and the adrenaline buzz was fading, leaving his body aching from the desert beating and his head churning with dark images.

Dead Vikings didn't bother Wren. Killing slavers was easy to rationalize; they got what was coming to them, and that was just fine by him.

It was the woman he couldn't shake.

Her eyes. He'd failed to retrieve her. Failed to catch the warehouse red-handed. Failed to grasp the real scale of this thing, and that burned.

He hit the wheel hard. It stung his right hand. Stupid. Also not productive, but there was no use recriminating now. He leaned half out the window, so the hot wind buffeted his cheeks, keeping him on his toes.

Price came on fast.

At ten minutes out darknet confirmation came in from his expert hackers based out of Eastern Europe: Hellion and B4cksl4cker. They were a pair he'd only brought down with a complex, interwoven sting that took three months and involved billions in cryptocurrency. They didn't always reply and only half-cared about the coin system, but when they got on the case things happened.

Except for this time. Seemed they'd found nothing on the semi-trailer carrying the slaves. There was no satellite overwatch to wind back in the desert, no sightings reported. This new terror group was long gone by now, probably out of state if they'd gone due east, well into Colorado en route for Denver.

Nothing in the records on warehouse ownership, either. It was reservation land, apparently, but never used. Nobody knew about it. Invisible.

A sign for Price whipped by. Wren called Henry and Abdul.

"Situation report."

"In position," Henry answered, and Wren was relieved to hear his voice. "Abdul's got the PD, I'm covering our rear. It's a residential dead-end, only one way in."

"Is there a cordon?"

"One went up twenty minutes ago, five squad cars across the road, six armed officers. Looks like they've brought in sheriffs from neighboring counties. There're low hills in back they aren't even looking at, though. That's where we're stationed."

Wren pictured it. "A strike force might come up behind you. Get right out, in that case. Remember, you're only there to be my eyes."

"Yes, sir."

"In fact," Wren said, imagining Blackhawk helicopters racing from the Salt Lake army base two hundred miles north, requisitioned by Humphreys. If the PD went like the warehouse, hit by a tactical strike team with war-fighting weaponry, it could become a war zone. "Get out right now."

No answer came.

"Henry, Abdul, call in."

No response.

A creeping fear rushed up his spine. He put a call through to the operator, but she couldn't get him a line to Price Police Department.

His chest went cold.

It was happening right now. An assault with jamming technology, blocking the airwaves just like he'd pulled on the Hussy. Price was incommunicado, with Henry and Abdul right in the eye of the storm.

He placed the call to Humphreys.

"The attack's happening now, sir," he said swiftly. "I'm five minutes out. Where are your squads?"

"This is too much, Wren," Humphreys stormed. Sounded like he was already burning with anger. "Who's paying you?"

Wren blinked. "What do you know, sir? Do you have eyes on?"

"You selfish, sick son of a bitch," fumed Humphreys. "It's not enough, how you left things in New York? Now you're bringing me down with you. Price just went dark, Wren. We both know what that means. Just what is your endgame here?"

Wren cursed and hit the wheel again. He tried to think of a way through. The attack was in process and Humphreys thought he was behind it, and why not? An agent with a secret 'cult' quit on a dime, lost his family then weeks later turned up ringing in an unheard-of threat?

He'd just brought a CIA Director down on his own head. His troubles of a day ago seemed positively sunny by comparison.

"This wasn't me. I swear it."

Humphreys laughed cold. "Then come in. We'll listen to what you've got to say. We know all about psychotic breaks, Christopher. They've got medicine that'll keep you high for the rest of your life."

"I'm not having a psychotic break!"

"But I know you are. You're lying even to yourself. You're not the hero here, Wren, you're the villain. Come in or I'll bring you in!"

Wren punched the gas. "I didn't invent the warehouse. You'll find it. Plus I've got two men at Price, they're in the eye of this thing."

"You've got more than two, it looks. And it's your warehouse, so we'll find whatever you left us." A second's pause. "You shouldn't have screwed with me, Wren. We're coming with everything we've got. You're going to regret this."

The line went dead.

Wren stared out the windshield.

The turnaround was dizzyingly fast. He knew he should run there and then. Break north for the border, get into Canada and take a crab boat across the Bering Strait. He could be in some tiny Inuit burg off the east coast of good old mother Russia within a few months. That could be his life.

Except he had lives on the line. Henry and Abdul. A hundred pitiful

68

souls ferried out on a truck, heading God knew where. That woman in the trunk, staring at him with such naked pain. His organization left in shambles, unleashed upon the world. His wife, somewhere, holding his kids and thinking if she was ever going to let him see them again.

It wasn't even a choice.

He pushed the pedal all the way to the metal. Screaming along at one-twenty. With any luck he'd beat Humphreys' Blackhawks in and maybe catch the cartel strike team flat-footed. If they were as plugged-in as he suspected, they'd have arrival times on all incoming reinforcements, except him.

They couldn't quantify for him.

Six miles and counting.

14

PRICE

Wren buzzed through downtown Price topping a hundred, cannoning into a neighborhood of residential streets, beyond which lay Henry's low brown hills. The sign for Price PD came up on the right and he swung so hard he almost tipped the pick-up.

Ahead the cordon lay broken, five police cars staggered across the road like tossed dominos, two officers on the ground that he could see, not moving.

Wren flew through the gap and hit the brakes only as he breasted the department's red brick fronting. The building stood alone with the hills in back, one story tall, standard metal frame with wood sidings, as easy to crack as an edamame bean. No sign of a strike team, no vehicles left over, but you could never be sure.

Wren killed the engine and sprang out of the Sierra, Beretta drawn, one in the chamber. The front entrance was shattered inward, cubic skitters of glass showing the treads of a ram vehicle. Broad wheelbase, thick and grippy tires. They'd taken Wren's trick and gone large.

A tall desk for the duty sergeant dominated the lobby like a judge's elevated pulpit. Rows of plastic seating lay splashed apart at diagonals before it, where the ram had burst through. A water fountain jug lay on the plastic floor in a puddle, magazines scattered off a plastic coffee table, doors leading away, and bodies.

Three dead police on the floor. Wren darted in with the Beretta high, saw double shots to the chest, one in the head. Rounds placed neat and tight, a professional hit despite what must have been chaos.

There was no sound but Wren's thumping heart. A hundred strikes before this, but the edge never left you. Thick wafts of cordite smoke hung like swamp gas in the air. Two doors hung open; Wren stalked left. An office spread before him, desks in rows, personalized workspaces with plush toys and family photos. A large potted fern lay on its side, spilling soil, with papers spread on the floor, bullet holes in the walls, and bodies.

Maybe another five people gunned down. In one of the office bays lay a woman Wren recognized. The woman from the warehouse, tipped into the sheriff's car.

She hadn't made it. At least the look of fear was gone from her blind, staring eyes.

Wren saw red. He backed out and ran for the second door, thick metal that hung on one hinge now, with blackened scorch marks where an explosive had chewed through the steel frame. Beyond lay a sheer concrete corridor with a few bright posters explaining the after-effects of meth. There'd be rebar in the walls, designated proof against a standard ram truck, but under explosive assault the place had crumbled.

At the end of the corridor, he found the cells, crammed full of the dead.

The bikers were easy to pick out; big guys on the floor, shot in position like beached whales. Black jackets lay in spreading pools of dark blood. The air hung heavy with cordite, the AC whirring overtime to clear it. Wren counted the bodies; eleven. Not two in the chest, one in the head here, more of an indiscriminate slaughter mowed down with automatic weapons. There was no sign of Eustace; the big guy must have gotten away.

Wren kicked through a door in back. A changing room for officers, nobody there. He ran two deadbolts loose and pushed through to the lot with a breath of relief, glad to be out of the killing ground. Too late to catch the strike team.

He ran across the lot and clambered up one of the crusty brown hills in back. Industrial off-cast of some kind. At a peak some two stories high he spun and shouted.

"Henry! Abdul!"

No sign of them. No response came. Maybe they'd lit out. It was a good place to set up, but vulnerable from behind, with countless valleys amongst the mounds. He tried their number again but got no response, scanned for footprints but saw none nearby. There were dozens of mounds and no time to search any further.

Sirens were drawing near. Reinforcements from another sheriff's station, probably Orangeville. There was also the low, deep thrum of helicopters approaching from the west, and seconds later twin Blackhawks appeared over the horizon, getting larger every second.

Wren took a deep breath. The woman was dead. The Vikings were dead. The warehouse full of people had been moved on, and possibly Henry and Abdul along with them. Stick around to explain that to Humphreys, and he'd get nowhere. The Director seemed dead set on pinning this on Wren.

It fell to him. Find these traffickers, find Henry and Abdul, find the rest of their 'cargo' and exact payback at the smoking end of a gun. They called him 'Saint Justice' for a reason, after all. No other choice.

Back in the lot the Sierra started up smooth, then he was away and speeding north, one of the Blackhawks peeling off to follow, blades roaring like thunder.

15

RUN

A call came in from Humphreys, but Wren killed it and snapped the battery out of the phone. The blades of the Blackhawk crashed down from above, a tsunami of noise. They tried their bullhorn and he ignored it. He had to hope they wouldn't fire on a civilian road.

After ten miles in six minutes he pulled through the little burg of Helper, a mid-sized desert town of some few thousand residents. He passed a couple of junk food places spinning brand logos at the top of tall poles, a car dealership, some Old-West style square-fronted craft shops along the main drag, then he found what he needed.

A big enough building, multiple exits, multiple vehicles, multiple people. Some way to launder himself like a bum hundred-dollar bill, shake the helicopters and the dragnet closing in. It came in highway signs pointing left, a middle school with an elementary school just a few blocks over.

It could work.

The Blackhawk tracked him. He gunned the Sierra sharply across the median and plunged through a low picket fence directly into the parking lot for Helper Middle School. Its single-story adobe-beige buildings made it look like a shopping mall, except with handcrafted posters for an upcoming prom in the windows, and a handful of cars in the lot. Too early for the morning rush, but hopefully enough folks to obscure his escape.

He ran the Sierra up to the entrance and braked, even as the helicopter swung back overhead. They'd overshot and lost him for a second, but he wouldn't make his escape from aerial oversight as easily as that. From the bag on the seat, he grabbed a screwdriver then bailed.

"Halt!" came the bellow of the bullhorn, then he was in through the front door. A security guard stood at the metal detector; eyes lit up with his hand on his pistol. Wren gave him a shrug, stepped to the side, and hit a fire alarm box on the wall. The glass broke easily, depressing the button inside, and out rang the alarm bell.

"School shooter," Wren called at the guard, advancing with his palms up. The guy didn't know what to think. "They think he's already in, lying in wait. How did he get past you?"

"I've been here this whole time," the guy said, flustered, still clutching the grip of his gun. "Who the hell are you?"

The first doors down the hall popped open, some kids and a teacher popped out.

"FBI," Wren said, flashing his CIA badge and walking casually through the detector. "You see my ride out there. Backup'll be here in minutes. Get the kids clear, man."

"I-" said the guy, hamstrung on where the threat lay. Wren had taken it too fast, too confidently, and the helicopter only helped. The bullhorn droned on outside as he sped down the broad hall. A few kids hurried by with a gray-haired teacher.

"Stay calm," Wren said as he passed, "it'll be OK."

At the end of the hall he ducked into a classroom. There was a mauve cardigan on the chair back; Wren shrugged it on. Too tight, but that didn't matter. He rummaged through a kid's bag, then another until he came up with a red ball cap, which he wedged onto his head. Last he picked up a chair and tossed it through the window.

The sound of crashing glass wouldn't register over the fire alarm. Probably the Blackhawk was already spitting out a few soldiers on fast rope rappels.

Wren went out the window and into a low screen of trees, paced along in the shadows for a minute heading north, then stepped out calmly across the road. Nothing untoward. He went like that east for three blocks until he came upon the Elementary School.

Double-laundered, he called it. In the absence of heavy crowds, with air support on overwatch, it was really the only way. They'd have found the broken window by now, would be winding back their aerial footage, but he should be just far enough ahead to make it work.

He entered the Elementary School, saw another guard, another metal detector, another fire alarm and pulled the same trick with his badge. This guy pulled his gun.

"FBI are raiding the Middle School," he said. "Suspected active shooter with a bomb. The whole area's getting evacuated. People are to head up to Castle Gate and convene."

"Who the hell are you, man?" the guard asked, waving his gun. A snub-nosed Colt; weapon of choice. "You ain't FBI. That's a CIA badge."

"Undercover," said Wren, then made a show of looking down the corridor and waving at people to hurry up.

"There's a bomb threat," he called, calm but intent. "Please get in your vehicles and drive to Castle Gate, where you'll be convened."

An older lady hustled by. A young guy with wavy hair ushered three little kids in matching jumpsuits along. The guard was looking at Wren, still unsure. Wren gave him a nod, as if to a fellow soldier, then stepped out of the lobby, following on the heels of the others. Before he broke from cover, he shrugged off the maroon cardigan and too-tight hat.

There were maybe twenty cars ahead in the lot; he picked an old blue Ford Escape in the middle, broke the window and boosted the ignition with the screwdriver in less than two minutes. The Blackhawk grew louder. At the same time, the guard was directing people to their cars.

"Castle Gate, you'll be convened."

Probably the strike teams were running now, covering the blocks to the Elementary School. A minute or two, maximum. Wren waited. Overhead the Blackhawk was pulling closer, shouting down that they were hunting a fugitive and ordering the evacuees to stay still, but with the threat of a bomb in their heads they kept moving.

The first vehicle drove off. Then the second. Then Wren was looking at a woman in a red sports jersey, staring at him through the windshield with her keys in her hand. He mouthed a sorry at her, then backed the Ford away.

She stared after him. He pulled out of the lot, third in a flow of other cars. In two minutes he was back on 119 headed for Castle Gate, laundered to invisibility and leaving the Blackhawk far behind.

16

DESERT

On the city limits of Helper Wren pulled into a residential zone to launder the car. At the second house along, with a rusted RV and two pickups on the drive, he pulled in, slid out of the Ford and strode to a beat-up Dodge Ram. He was in luck; the door was unlocked and the keys were in the sun visor. The engine coughed to life, and he rolled out smoothly, heading back south.

The Blackhawk raced by overhead. He got through just as they were setting up roadblocks. Even if they tracked him out of Helper in the Ford, they'd dead-end when he reached the Dodge.

Just the right amount of chaos.

He drove on, trying to puzzle through what he'd seen. Back in the warehouse the size of this organization had been a rational but distant fear; now it was real and undeniable, powerful and ruthless enough to slaughter a whole police station and execute the Vikings like fish in a barrel.

He slotted the battery back into the Samsung, tried calling Henry and Abdul again. Still nothing.

It left him reeling, seeing their faces superimposed over the bodies in Price PD every time he blinked. Utter carnage. His breathing was rapid, his heart rate elevated.

How had they pulled this off? Where had they even come from? Since the Hussy raid barely four hours had passed. He imagined a vast network spread across the country like grasping tentacles, powerful and fast-acting, all leading back to...

Where?

He had no idea. No clues. No direction. He brought up his darknet, one eye on the road, but his hackers had nothing further to report. Comms in Price had been jammed. No satellite overwatch. A highly competent strike team in and out, completely invisible. He tapped out a message for the Foundation.

THEY MAY HAVE TAKEN TWO FOUNDATION MEMBERS. HENRY & ABDUL. ALL EYES ON THIS. FIND THEM!

For a moment his finger hovered over the call button, poised to dial Director Humphreys again, but he had nothing useful to say. Humphreys would only scream at him. Blame him. Wren would end up shouting back, and that wouldn't help anyone.

He put the phone down. Pushed the pedal down harder.

By 11 a.m. he was back at the Vikings' warehouse. With the Brazen Hussy and Price PD swarmed by sheriffs and federal forces, it was the only place left to search for a lead. A prison block for trafficked humans out in the middle of the desert.

The oblong mouth leading into the warehouse's depths hung wide open, spilling out sound. The radio on Alli's 'tank' was still playing: Lynyrd Skynyrd's Free Bird. The red roll shutter lay on the bare blacktop like a severed tongue.

Wren felt drained, but he couldn't rest yet. He rolled the Dodge through the open mouth with his body hunched down in the driver's well, though no shots came this time. The place really was abandoned. He pulled up next to the tank and sat for a second.

Warm air blew in through the open side window, mixing with a gust of cold air from the building's straining AC. The place was still empty. He opened the door and stepped out, walked over to the tank and switched off the radio.

Silence reigned.

The fog of baby formula and human waste hung in the air like a pestilence. Like it was ingrained into the fabric of the walls. From somewhere in back came the hum of the air conditioners. From outside came the cricket-like buzz of desert insects. Through the open mouth lay orange earth and blue skies. It felt unreal that under this same sky some hundred-odd human slaves were currently being shunted through an invisible system.

Laundered. Now their fates rested on Wren's shoulders. Maybe the fates of Henry and Abdul too. His fingers tightened into fists. The time for shock was over.

Now it was time to get even.

He walked the warehouse shelves, opening boxes until one spilled out MRE ration microwave meals. He ripped the seal off and gulped it down cold. Chicken tarragon with mashed potatoes. He opened another and ate this more slowly, purposefully searching the warehouse for clues.

There were four vehicles in the motor pool: a sheriff's car, a white panel van, an old beater, his bullet-torn Jeep. Wren set the empty meal tray down on the beater's roof and circled wider. In one section of shelving were boxes filled with drugs. Fresh cartons of fentanyl patches, tubs of white powder, heavy bags of opioid pills in candy-colored capsules, thick swatches of weed and dark glossy blocks of resin hashish.

He popped two generic hydrocodone tablets into his mouth, tucked a few blister packs of attention-sharpening methylphenidate in his back pocket, the same kind they gave to ADHD kids, and walked on. The impact of the hydrocodone came swiftly, eradicating the pain and bringing a calming kind of looseness that bordered on light euphoria.

In other boxes he found everything a modern, large-scale human trafficking organization would need: cartons of disposable burner phones with non-consecutive SIM card numbers; box after box of MREs; stacks of vitamin pills and fish-oil capsules; bottled water, mylar heat blankets and cushions; clothing in all sizes and for all ages; thousands of tubs of baby formula; medicine and first aid gear.

He helped himself to a handful of burner phones. Further on, in a locked gray cabinet, he found his wallet sealed in a plastic bag. Vikings must have scoured it off the desert floor. Worn brown leather, inscribed with his name. A gift from Loralei. Credit cards and ID still there. Pictures of his kids in happier times, Jake and Quinn. The familiar weight in his hands, their sweet faces looking up at him.

He squeezed his eyes tightly shut and pushed back. Heart thudding. Vision tunneling. Back in the awful moment again, spinning in his old house as he realized they were really gone.

Not now. He couldn't afford to think about that now, not when Henry and Abdul needed him. It took a few moments to regain control, then straightened up. It felt like a brief reprieve only. Eye of the hurricane. He slid the wallet reverently into his back pocket and moved on.

Further along, in a chemical barrel being used as a fire pit, he found ashes: some rags of clothing, some fragments of paper, and a small, singed corner with just a fleck of bright red crayon. Wren recognized it at once. His foot from one of his kids' drawings, standing next to a giant cash register. What his kids thought he did.

His eyes stung and he rubbed them roughly, tucked the scrap carefully into his wallet and moved on.

Standing in front of the empty cages, he gazed in, haunted by the grotesque reality. Hundreds of people bought and sold like cattle. Nothing good waiting for them at the end of the line. A single trafficked human could sell for a hundred thousand dollars, given the right provenance.

The slave trade was a gold mine, and it had never gone away. It had just gotten very accomplished at hiding.

That was fine.

Wren was a very good finder.

17

FINDER

Wren walked into the enormous cage, and at once felt contained. Bad memories threatened to rise up and swamp him from his childhood.

He'd spent time in a cage. It had been one of his father's challenges to all the faithful. Wren had been a baby at the time, but nobody was excused on account of age. All had to suffer for edicts of his father's cult: the Pyramid.

Wren blinked hard, pushing the memories away. This cage was not that cage. The Pyramid was gone. The cages were gone. His father was gone, at least according to all reports...

He opened his eyes and took a step forward. Each step away from the open gate and deeper into the cage thickened the unease, but he plowed through. The difference between freedom and slavery was so simple. He'd made a lifelong study of it. Means and intent, it came down to. It began with a cage of some form, whether it was mental or physical, and the intent to treat a person as less than a person.

One moment some kid was on his way home from marching band, worrying about hitting C flat and whether to ask the girl in trig. class out, then he was in a white panel van, strapped down and lashed like a hog, no longer real. Turning people into animals was easy, once you made that leap in your head.

Wren paced the cage as if he could outrun the past, rapidly scanning the floor. The warehouse lights were bright, but his intense focus shrank the world down like a spotlight in a pitch-black cave. He scanned every scratch, indentation and blemish in the cement floor, guessing where camper beds had been laid down from the regimented outline of light scuffs, estimating the lighter-colored channels where guards had patrolled inside.

Looking for the secret places.

There were always secrets. In the Nazi concentration camps, guarded by elite SS where the slightest infraction was punished by instant death, inmates had found ways to record their experiences and hide them away. Some had even stolen cameras to capture images of the truth; not for them, not with any hope of rescue, but for posterity. They buried them, or hid them in drainpipes, or slotted them under roof tiles and into fence pipes, or secreted them in the lime of mass burial pits.

Wren walked for forty minutes until he found it, the hiding place. It wasn't by the wall, too obvious. It was out in the middle, where the raw cement flooring was broken by a power socket. Twin slots rested next to each other, embedded and flush to the cement, each offering twin holes.

It was sheer audacity to use these holes to store a message, but it could be done. On his hands and knees Wren peered into the socket. He used the flashlight on his phone to get a better angle, squinting into each pinhole of the two sockets.

No.

No.

No.

Yes.

In the last there was something, a tiny scrap that could almost be lint, rolled up, inserted then crushed down to the very bottom of the pin. There was no hope of grasping it with his fingernails, so he headed out and kicked through the motor pool until he found a toolbox of slim computer screwdrivers. He hurried back, pushed the narrowest screwdriver in carefully and tried to work the paper out.

Sweat beaded and dripped from his forehead. One splash in the pin and he'd be electrocuted. The paper rose slightly, tore slightly, and Wren slowed right down. Stilled his breathing, slowed his pulse, steadied his hand and proceeded painstakingly. Millimeter by millimeter, teasing the paper out. It was thin, like a tissue.

Minutes passed. Hairline tears slit the paper. He took a breath and tried again, until at last the white edge emerged from the pin.

It was a tight wad. Wren dried his palms and unfurled it with bated breath. It was a receipt from a convenience store, printed in faded blue ink. It had no address, but there was a phone number, and Wren recognized the area code. Chicago. One item was listed, Discount Flowers, $2.99. A two-word message had been written across it in scrawled brown, probably dried blood.

HELP WENDY

In the corner there was a date, September 27. Wren did the quick calculation.

Eleven months earlier.

He let out a breath. Eleven months meant this was most likely a dead trail. It couldn't be from the latest batch of people trafficked through. Still, it was a clear lead. He tucked it carefully into his pocket, then wrote a message to his Foundation through the darknet. He had two members in Chicago, denizens of the city's seedy underbelly, who should be able to help.

SEARCH CHICAGO RECORDS FOR SOME CONNECTION TO THESE TRAFFICKERS. POSSIBLY LARGE NUMBERS OF PEOPLE GOING MISSING. A WOMAN CALLED WENDY. REPORT BACK AS SOON AS YOU HAVE ANYTHING.

He fired off the message and continued searching, but that was it. No computers, no paper records of any kind. Laid out near the entrance he found a dozen gallon jugs of gasoline, presumably ready to burn the place down. If he'd arrived just minutes later, maybe the warehouse would have been an inferno in the night; truly bleached out of existence.

The tiny scrap of receipt weighed heavy in his pocket. At a workbench he carefully dusted the paper with pencil lead shavings, exposing a range of grubby fingerprints, which he took close-up photographs of and uploaded to the Foundation site. There should be results from his NSA mole within hours.

He bagged the receipt in plastic then strode out into the burning Utah light. Nearly noon, but already it had been a long day. Despite the hydrocodone he felt exhausted and hurting. His back, his side, his legs. He pulled up his shirt, looked at the bruises blooming across his skin.

Ugly. He dry-swallowed two antibiotics to be safe, found a black ball cap and pulled it low over his eyes, then climbed back into the Dodge Ram and barely thought at all for the two-hundred-mile drive to a taxi rank in Sterling, the far corner of Colorado.

Maybe three hours. At some point along the route he texted the warehouse location to Humphreys, then popped the Samsung's battery and flung the empty shell to the side. In the dusts of Utah it would remain.

By Sterling he was running on fumes. The hydrocodone left him aching and empty, but it was too soon to take any more. He pulled up and staggered to the taxi dispatcher's desk in a downtown bus station. Barely remembered speaking. They pointed him to a car.

Chicago was one thousand two hundred miles away, almost due east, across Colorado, Nebraska and Iowa into Illinois. Too far for one ride, so he set the destination at another bus station on the edge of Nebraska. Tag team taxis, he figured, stitched across the country.

"What's in Colorado?" the driver asked as he settled into the back. A woman, sad-eyed, looking at him in the rearview.

"A good sleep," Wren said, and climbed in the back.

"You can't lay down," she said, but Wren ignored her. Laid down and sank into blissful darkness within seconds.

18

CHICAGO

The sprawl of Chicago began twenty miles out, as the expansive fields of grain, wheat, hay and broom corn of rural Illinois intensified into an eight-lane expressway bounded by narrow green risers, boring directly into the city's heart.

The taxi place in Nebraska had been a breeze. Running ahead of whatever dragnet Humphreys had put out. Wren transferred to another cab, barely spoke to the guy for the next leg to Davenport, Iowa. Again he slept, paid in stained bills from the junk yard on arrival, then picked up a new sedan with one of his fake IDs at a rental place.

The rest had done him good, drowsing through the night, waking up to check his Foundation site on one of the burner phones. Three-hours' drive after that, now he'd arrived.

Chicago, nearly 10 a.m.

He hadn't been back to Chicago for nine years, not since breaking the Ripper Crew copycat murderers, seconded with the FBI. Five women had died by then, dumped in the city's wastelands. Wren had been called in to break the gang, and swiftly gotten to know the dark side of Chicago: the satanic gangs, the 'vampire' clubs, the S&M groups that took things too far. So Chicago had become a place of violence and cruelty for Wren.

He pulled off the Stevenson Expressway and drove deeper into the city.

The sky was a leaden gray over the Willis Tower, scarred by blurry white blemishes of lighter cloud, like burn marks on a bloated body.

His phone chimed; at a red light he brought it up. A message from Cheryl, one of the two Foundation members he'd harvested from that dark period of his life. A sex worker and dominatrix, once she'd been a major feature in the vampire clubs, before Wren brought them all down in a cascade. Still she kept her finger on the pulse of the city's sordid side.

TEDDY SEEKING A LEAD ON YOUR HUMAN TRAFFICKING GROUP, the message read. WILL BE IN TOUCH

He snorted. Teddy was an attention seeker. A wealthy once-banker, now he lived with Cheryl in a cozy platonic union. He'd been a leader in the vampire clubs, until Wren ended that era with a flood of arrests. He'd joined the Foundation in tears then done everything he could since to get out.

CONTACT ME AS SOON AS YOU HAVE SOMETHING, Wren wrote, and pulled away as the light turned green. Still nothing from the Foundation on Henry and Abdul, still no answer to his calls.

South and east, he passed through Wentworth Gardens along West Pershing Road, skirting Fuller Park. Here gangs of young men hung around at corners and on stoops. Gang signs were everywhere, evidenced in colors, bandannas and graffiti tagged on railway tunnel walls.

The gas station and convenience store sat on West Pershing, near the Dan Ryan Expressway, two blocks south of the White Sox field. Wren drove by massive empty parking lots, rail tracks running over sallow tunnels, blank-faced aluminum warehouses and construction yards heaped with mounds of gravel, then pulled into the lot.

To the left stood a Louisiana Fried Chicken place. Opposite was a dead end of new-build duplexes. Wren sat for a moment, windows down, taking in the sour Chicago air. A woman ran past in sneakers and jogging sweats, dragged by a foam-mouthed Alsatian. By the gas pumps a little boy was crying about his ice cream, splatted and steaming on the blacktop.

Wren took out the receipt encased in its plastic wallet, stained a faint charcoal gray. Wendy, it read. Had she come to this store? Lived around here, maybe?

He pulled his black hat low and opened the van door. It was hot out, late summer in Chicago, enough blocks in from Lake Michigan to not feel the breeze. The air felt dead and condensed, like the dusty stink of a stale attic, unopened for a decade.

Wren walked into the store.

Two kids on service. Wren noted the flower display in the window: wilted Calla lilies, roses, some cuttings and other flowers he didn't recognize. He studied the label on one.

Discount Flowers, it read. $2.99.

The kid at the checkout desk had a tattoo on his neck, was tapping at his phone. Wren pulled his CIA badge. A risk, with him being hunted by Humphreys, but he didn't think the kid would take note of his badge number and call it in.

"I'm looking for the person on shift eleven months back. Were you here then?"

The kid looked up, ready with some BS sarcasm maybe, then saw the badge. Peered closer. Eyes widened. "Uh, what?"

It took thirty seconds more. Authority carried you a long way. The kid placed a call.

"He says he'll meet you in the chicken place," the kid said. "The manager, that is. Felipe."

"I'll wait here," said Wren.

The kid shifted uncomfortably. Clearly not keen on Wren standing there, watching him. "The chicken's real good. You'll like it. Right, Shelley?"

He looked to the girl. She nodded. "It's delicious."

Wren gave a tight smile. Why not? He hadn't eaten since the MREs in the warehouse fourteen hundred miles earlier. "Chicken, then."

He almost heard the sighs of relief as he strode out.

Across the street he went into the Louisiana Fried Chicken. It was greasy and smelled delicious. Wren ordered a two-piece basket with fries and sat down to enjoy it. In the corner the TV clicked over to the news.

It was about him. The newscaster on CNN said something about developments in the Price, Utah murders and execution of an entire police station. Wren's picture popped up in the corner of the frame. An old shot, from far off, it didn't look too much like him now. Still he pulled his cap down. The chicken guy, some kind of Israeli-African mixture behind the counter, didn't bat an eye. Maybe he was used to wanted criminals chowing down in his shop, or maybe he just didn't care.

Wren tucked into his chicken. It was pretty good, rich and greasy. He watched the coverage on the TV; they were calling the bloodbath at Price

America's worst terrorist attack since 9/11. Thirty-two dead. Footage of the smashed PD frontage, white forensic tents swarmed with FBI lettermen, a reporter enthusiastically running up the brown hills in back, pointing out recent tracks and theorizing about the rumor of spent shell casings found by the detectives.

Spent shell casings. Wren's heart thudded. That had to be evidence of Henry and Abdul putting up some resistance.

Soon enough Felipe came in. Wren knew it was Felipe by the way he homed in on Wren; the description from the kids in the Convenience store would be easy. The big dark guy with the black cap.

He came over, combed dark hair that looked like a hairpiece but probably wasn't, just unfortunate genetics, and sat down.

"What's this about?" he asked. Mexican accent, teardrop tattoo from his left eye. No stranger to violence in the barrio himself.

Wren explained briefly, not linking it to Utah. Just a missing persons case, flowers bought at his store, a receipt.

"Let's see it then, ese," Felipe said. Not phased in the slightest. Judging from the teardrop tattoo, he'd been a gang member. In his own neighborhood, he wasn't afraid of anything.

Wren produced the receipt and laid it on the Formica table between them.

"Wendy," the guy said, reading the letters written in blood, then looked up, eyes taking on a far-off look. "Yeah, I remember selling those flowers. $2.99. I remember who I sold them to. I registered him missing eleven months back. Some homeless vet called Mason."

"You registered him missing?"

"What I said, ese. You want to see?"

19

HOMELESS

Felipe led him out of the chicken shop.

Wren followed. Felipe was a shade under six foot, which gave Wren a good view of the top of his head. Definitely not a piece, just a badly combed hairstyle. Five minutes passed as they strolled west, past the Convenience store and the open lot to the right, toward the railway line.

Felipe stopped and pointed under the railway bridge. It was narrow and dark, with tight pedestrian walkways either side bounded by railings. "There. Mason was some homeless punk, come with a whole crew. He told me his name on his first swing around the shop; he was simple, you know? My name's Forrest, Forrest Gump? Yeah." He waved a hand. "So they all came at once, some time at the start of last year; I heard they got booted from under Lake Shore Drive. You know, they put up those fences under the highway to stop them camping out?"

Wren grunted. He knew what Felipe meant.

"A whole encampment of them. I hated it. They came in the store and stank it up. Some of them high, some trying to lift whatever they could. It's not worth calling the five-oh on homeless, like calling extermination for cockroaches. You just deal with them yourself."

"Except Mason bought flowers."

Felipe sighed. "That damn kid. Twenty-something, scars all around the top of his head like some kind of crown. I reckon he was a vet living on Uncle Sam's dime, PTSD, injury in the line of duty, the whole nine yards. He'd stop by the window and just drool. Didn't matter how much I poured threats at him. Kid was too dumb to know he was being threatened. Kind of got him a free pass in the barrio."

"Looking at the flowers," Wren said. Putting the picture together.

"Like a dog for a bone. He'd beg over at the L, few blocks east, then come by. Sometimes carrying food; they give sandwiches out at the Revival Faith church on Indiana. I'd see him counting his change."

"Revival Faith?"

"Huge place. You can't miss it."

"And then?"

Felipe laughed. "Then one day he was gone. That was it, I was happy. But something was off about it. I came over here and had a look around. All their gear was left. Cardboard dens, tents, junk like that. The city cleared it away later, they're pretty good about that, but no Mason. No Wendy either." He gestured at the receipt in Wren's hand.

"So you reported it?"

"Tried. Like I said, who cares? The homeless are here, the homeless aren't here, it's like they're invisible. Of no fixed abode means you can't go missing. You already are."

Felipe sighed.

"And you don't think they just moved on again?" Wren asked. Had to be sure, despite the quickening of his pulse. "Like under Lakeshore Drive?"

"You tell me. Everything you've got in the world; would you leave that behind? It was a week before sanitation cleared it all out. Where did they go that they wouldn't still need a tent or a sleeping bag? Why didn't they come back?"

Wren didn't need much more. He could imagine the space under the bridge housing up to a hundred people. To snatch them all, presumably at night, would have taken at least one semi-truck trailer. Hit them while they were sleeping, block off the road on one side, maybe both, and they've got nowhere to go. There was nobody nearby to witness, just the empty lot, a theater supplies warehouse, empty construction yards.

He thought back to his grab on the Vikings' bikes. He'd pulled that off against thirteen armed men with just two snipers and a truck. Homeless would have had no real weapons, maybe the odd knife. Guns would have overawed them, though shots fired might have drawn some attention. That meant non-lethal weaponry, a raid completed within minutes, herding them like animals.

But what good were homeless to slavers?

That was the problem. They were hardly prime material. Malnourished, likely junkies, riddled with disabilities, each would sell for only pennies on the dollar. Not worth the cost of acquisition.

"About a hundred here, you say?" Wren asked.

"Maybe. I didn't count 'em."

"The train comes through often?"

"Every thirty minutes, maybe. And yeah, it's loud."

Wren turned and looked up, scanning the lamp posts near the bridge.

"There's nothing there," said Felipe. "I asked them to put up some cameras. This is not downtown."

Wren looked farther afield to intersections. He knew from past experience that there were plenty of cameras dotted throughout Chicago, as with any major city: traffic cams, surveillance outside banks and other high-security facilities, but how many of those would keep their footage for eleven months?

Dead-end.

"And Wendy?"

"His girl. Mason. He talked about her a few times. I mostly tuned him out. But I see that receipt now…" Felipe petered out. "Who took him, you know? For what?"

"Bad things," Wren said. "But I'm going to find him. Find them both."

"So that's it?"

Wren nodded. "That's it. Thanks. You've been a big help."

Wren walked under the tunnel. Chest thrumming. Felipe remained behind. "Will you let me know?" he called after Wren. "If you find him? I bought him his flowers. I felt sorry for him."

Wren looked back. Felipe seemed a good man. It was easy to forget, doing what he did, that there were good people out there too, people who acted right even without the coin system and the threat of Wren's wrath to stay in check. It choked him up a little.

"I'll do that. I promise."

"All right."

Felipe walked off.

Wren delved into the shadows.

20

REVIVAL FAITH

There was nothing to find. City sanitation had done a good, neat job. Not a scrap of cloth remained, not a shard of glass, no bullet tracks in the walls. Mason had been there, and Wendy, but no sign of them remained now.

Wren laid down on the sidewalk. There wasn't a lot of walking room left. The railings basically hugged the wall. A gang of kids cruised by, laughing and pointing.

He ignored them and closed his eyes, imagining how the strike might have gone. If it was him, he'd use two trucks, one either side to block off escape. Pull them up in synchrony, at night when the homeless were asleep. Using bean bag guns, Tasers or hypodermic darts, they could pacify the mass of them in minutes. Even if they shouted, what would it matter with nobody around?

A train went by overhead. It had to be freight, judging by how long it rumbled for, probably bringing in gravel and lime for mixing into concrete; building high-rises was one of Chicago's biggest growth industries. It was loud, like Felipe said. Timed right, a night train would easily cover the hit.

It suggested an MO, a modus operandi, this group's standard way of operating.

Wren knew he'd never get CCTV of the trucks that took Mason, not after eleven months. Traffic cameras held footage for thirty-one days maximum. He contemplated putting out a social media spider, an automated computer program designed to seek out specific instances matching a specific set of parameters.

In this case, his hackers could easily rig a spider to stalk video upload sites time-stamped to the nights after Mason bought his flowers, geo-locked to streets the trucks would have had to pass down, seeking trucks that didn't match up to any known shipments of goods. But that was a needle in a haystack. With the expressway only a block away, they'd be away and anonymous within minutes, fully laundered with the flow of traffic.

That suggested another MO. Again, it was how Wren would do it.

Homeless sites under freight bridges, in decrepit areas, with no CCTV and easy access to a highway. Chicago was a mass of old rail lines as well as the more modern L, with various elevated highways that would serve just as well for cover. There had to be some thousand blocks in the city on the whole, with hundreds of sites just like this one, and all of them naturally appealing to the homeless.

An endless supply. But why the homeless? Easy to snatch, easy to cover the theft, but worthless as human chattel. So what were they for?

No answers came, just the familiar hot sting of outrage.

Wren opened his eyes and brought up maps on his phone. It was simple to locate the church Felipe had mentioned, Revival Faith, along with a spread of others that most likely catered to the homeless. A quick search told him Chicago had up to sixty thousand indigents at any given time.

Sixty thousand people. Maybe if the slavers were selling them in bulk? Chicago was a bottomless font, and clearly the trafficking operation was still a going concern. Could there have been a strike somewhere in the last thirty-one days? That might leave a truck sighted on CCTV somewhere.

Hope sparked in Wren's chest. He got to his feet and strode back to his van.

The Revival Faith church filled half a block, ten blocks east on Indiana Avenue: a huge older building of corrugated red brick with a newer portion in pink cladding and glass. It looked like a sports center. Wren knew a little about the Revival Faith sect; a black church focused on community and missionary work for Jesus.

He parked in the lot and went into the lobby. Inside it was cool and white, with marble floors, a few marble plinths set with flowers, wood detailing on the walls blending into artful constellations of crosses. A security guard stood by a row of turnstiles, blocking further access. In chairs a few old-timers were sitting in their Sunday best.

One of the old ladies sprang up as Wren approached, a lady who had to be eighty years old, wearing an African pattern power suit with a fantastic slope-brimmed hat.

"Welcome to Church, go in the light of Christ, my name is Gloria," she said with the bright joy of mission in her eyes. Wren had seen it many times before and smiled back.

"And you, ma'am. I'm not of the congregation at present; I'm looking for information on your outreach to the community."

"Oh, we do many good works here," Gloria began enthusiastically, and turned to her friend seated on the nearby couch, "Anastasia, weren't you just saying to me how delicious those crumb cakes were, at the park bake sale?"

"Mighty fine," said Anastasia, a heavy lady in purple finery, eighty-three if she was a day.

"This is more about missing peoples. The homeless in particular. Could I speak to your outreach director?"

"Oh, I expect so. They have their office upstairs. Javonne over there will let you up." She motioned to the security guard. The guard just stared. Wren knew his CIA ID would get him through in seconds. Likely it would also bring Humphreys down on his head within the hour, hitting harder than a Ford Super Duty weighed down with a ton of plate metal.

"Can you call her instead?"

"Call?" asked the woman. "I suppose I have the number."

"I'd be much obliged." Wren sat down beside Anastasia. "I'd rather go through unofficial channels. It's a sensitive matter."

"Oh I see," Gloria said, then made the call and bumbled through it merrily, mangling his intent but remembering to request the outreach director, while Anastasia sized him up.

"You're not from around here," she said.

"You're right in that, ma'am. I'm from out of town."

"How far out of town?"

"Arizona on one side. God alone knows the other."

Her generous features curled into the slightest frown. "Are you a Revival Faith man? Have you been saved?"

"Once upon a time," he said, with a smile. "Now I may have lapsed somewhat."

That confused her for a minute. "Lapsed?"

"Like Saul on his Damascus Road. Like I'm waiting on a resurrection." Wren smiled, working his encyclopedic memory of names like a well-oiled slide on a Glock 19. "Like your name. Anastasia. That's from the Greek 'anastasi', it means resurrection, if I'm not mistaken. It's a beautiful sentiment."

Anastasia blushed slightly, confusion mingling into pleasure.

"She's coming," said Gloria, coming off the phone with such a satisfied expression Wren thought she must burst from the inner light. You couldn't find a more direct opposite to his old days in Chicago than that.

"The gentleman says he was saved, but waiting on a resurrection," Anastasia said, off-balance now.

"Oh, the Revival affords eternal salvation to all through the good Lord's resurrection," cooed Gloria.

Wren listened absently while she spoke. Anastasia seemed to be warming up, which was good, too. He didn't want anyone dialing in a suspicious-looking guy asking strange questions. After five minutes an attractive woman came through the turnstiles at the far end of the lobby, and Wren stood. She wore a stylish navy suit and her heels clacked across the marble. She held out one hand and beamed.

"I understand you have questions about our outreach program, Mr....?"

"Nightingale," he lied. "Thank you for seeing me."

"My name is Nkwana Mbopo. Shall we?" she gestured toward a batch of sofas a little further over.

"Thank you."

They sat down, and he told her about Mason and Wendy, and the missing encampment under the West Pershing bridge. "I'm seeking any sign that the homeless population near you has dropped considerably," he finished. "Any kind of fluctuation in numbers would help. I'm assuming you keep some records."

When he was finished, she set her hands on the clipboard laid across her knees. "May I ask in what capacity are you making this request, Mr. Nightingale? Isn't this a matter best left to the police?"

He smiled. So much easier with the badge. "I'm purely a concerned citizen," he said, "and yes, I agree that this is a matter for the police, but left to the police it will be neglected. The disappearance of some hundred people under the Pershing bridge was reported by a friend of mine, briefly investigated, then brushed aside. We're talking about invisible people, Ms. Mbopo. Nobody cares if they disappear. In some ways it's a net win for the city."

She shifted uncomfortably in her seat. "That's a callous way of describing it. I'm sure the police…"

"Are overwhelmed with other matters. But not you. This is a church. You help the least of these. So please, help me, then I can help Wendy and Mason."

She opened her mouth to respond, and Wren knew what was coming. The politest shutdown: she wasn't convinced. Time for a redirect.

"Did you know Wendy?"

She blinked, reoriented. "I don't often go to the soup kitchens myself, I-"

"Manage on the macro level," said Wren, and smiled. "I understand. But somebody keeps records. This is a mega-church. That amount of food, you treat it professionally. I'm only asking to see those records." He gave it a second. "Please."

Her eyes took on a guarded edge. "I suppose I could speak to the church director. He'll be in tomorrow. That's the best I can do."

Wren smiled. Maybe it was sad. Maybe it was just business as usual. "I don't believe that's your best."

She stood. "I think we're done talking today, Mr. Nightingale."

Wren rose as well. "By this time tomorrow, Wendy and Mason may be dead. One night can make all the difference." No dice. He could see her disengaging, thinking about calling over the security guard. Hail Mary time. "I'm also thinking about making a sizable donation. Four figures at least."

That gave her pause. Her eyes turned cold. "There's no need for bribery. I've said I'll help you. You're burning your bridges."

"Bridges are over-rated," Wren countered. "This is urgent, so I'm asking for urgent help. Besides, there's no better fire than one lit with dollar bills, am I right?"

She stared at him. He wasn't wrong. He wasn't exactly right. It was somewhere in the middle.

"I'll get the figures," she said. "I'll call our volunteers. I should have something for you tomorrow morning."

"Tonight," said Wren. "The sooner the better."

"Tonight then," she said through gritted teeth. "And a high four-figure donation."

Wren smiled as she strode away.

"Jesus' light be with you," said Gloria as Wren walked out.

"And also with you," he replied cheerfully.

21

BRIDGE

The other churches were easier.

St Thomas Episcopal. Zion Grove. Prayer Band Pentecostal. South Park Baptist. Tabernacle Baptist. There was almost one of them per block, denser than just about anywhere Wren had seen, but then this area needed a lot of faith. While he was talking to the pastor at Turner Memorial, gathering more intel on missing homeless encampments, the CNN caption flipped to news of a shooting over in North Kenwood, barely twenty blocks away.

It was late by the time he returned to Revival Faith, nearly 10 p.m. Gloria and Anastasia were long gone, though the lobby was lit up bright and white, like the glowing presence of heaven on Earth. The security guard stood inside the doors, glaring out.

Wren knocked on the glass. "Have you got something for me?"

The guy unlocked one of the doors, opened up with his hand on his weapon, then held out a manila folder. Wren took it.

"Have you been holding that this whole time?" he asked.

The guy muttered something un-Christian then closed the door again, returning to his oversight.

"Thank you," Wren called.

Back in his rental van, he opened the manila folder. It contained three sheets of paper: one with registered names of the homeless, one with head counts for the last nine months of soup kitchens, and one with stock counts from their food supplies across the same period.

None of the other churches had provided him as much. At best he'd gotten estimates. A few kept records, but the homeless were always moving from place to place as the city chased them around, like the last few crumbs of dust refusing to hop into the dustpan.

But put together with the Revival Faith data, his notes amounted to something solid. There'd been massive drop-offs in just the last two months, at various homeless soup kitchens. Hyde Park had been decimated six weeks back. Chinatown numbers had dropped in half just two weeks ago.

The pattern was there.

Wren drove to Chinatown, anticipation building, a ten-minute buzz up the expressway. If he could find an abandoned encampment, he could wind back nearby CCTV footage, tag all semi-trucks in the vicinity, and his hackers could track them onto the Interstate.

It was full night by the time he arrived, gone 11 p.m., and the streets were quiet. There weren't many bars in that part of the district, not a lot of nightlife, just residential and schools.

Wren knew what he was looking for now, the strike MO, and began a fast, weaving patrol of the night streets, looking for the needle underneath the haystack of rail lines and expressways. There were tunnels everywhere. Chicago was a city in transit.

Soon his eyelids were drooping. At one point a police car fired its sirens in back and he thought he was going to get picked up for cruising, but it fired them off just as swiftly; maybe just running a red light.

Around 2 a.m. he pulled into an all-night ramen bar on South Archer Ave, across from a strip mall with a little five-level pagoda on top. A few people were walking, a drunk lay slumped next to a trash can, drooling. Wren drank strong black coffee and wolfed down noodles, looking out the window at the traffic going by, feeling the anger turn cold and sick in his stomach.

Nobody cared about homeless people getting swept up.

The noodles were hot and salty, just the way he liked them. He left a tip. The TV on the corner played his face once in the ten minutes he was there. When he was done he checked his darknet board again for updates.

There was a message from Teddy and Cheryl, his Chicago Foundation members.

MAY HAVE NEWS SOON. WILL CALL IN A FEW HOURS.

Easy for them to say. Vampires at heart, they both still kept nighttime hours. Wren fired back a question, then moved on.

His NSA member had better news; a hit on Mason, linking him to the receipt fingerprint. He'd been a Marine, apparently, gotten his injuries along with a Purple Heart in an ambush in early Iraq. There was a picture before and after, a good-looking guy, with the crown of scars like Felipe said.

It was a huge leap forward, giving him a quick spurt of adrenaline that drove the exhaustion briefly away. He put up an All-Points Bulletin through the darknet, and a spider to crawl social media looking for recent facial matches to Mason. He was itching to call Humphreys and find out what they'd uncovered on the warehouse paper trail, but didn't want to call without something to offer. It would mean burning his present location, and he wasn't done with Chicago yet.

At the counter he asked the server about homeless people nearby.

"How's that?" the guy asked. He was Asian-American, young, with a drooping hipster mustache that made him look like the Chinese Errol Flynn. Maybe he was going for that.

"Homeless," Wren repeated. "I've got a friend said he was sleeping rough around here. Where would he go?"

The guy thought for a moment. He actually tapped his head, like it would help, then shrugged. "I'm drawing a blank. Sorry."

Wren got back in the van and drove. The whole idea began to seem like a long shot. Just because the Mason strike had left bedding behind on the street in Wentworth Gardens didn't mean they'd leave it here too, and even if they had, the city might have picked it up faster.

Then he found them.

Sometime after 3 a.m., with the city entering that fuzzy time just before dawn, with the streetlights still on and the drunk night owls crossing paths with the morning litter crews, Wren found the longest tunnel yet. It ran under a railway interchange, six tracks overhead with a whole abandoned village of sleeping bags, tents, cardboard forts and makeshift washing lines below.

But no people.

Someone honked in back of him. He drove through, parked on the shoulder then came back through at a jog. This was it. He was standing in the midst of another encampment. Well over a hundred people could have fit here, maybe two hundred. Probably they were getting moved on constantly by the city, but this was more than that. If this was the city, they'd have taken their stuff. This had to be a strike, but it could still be weeks old.

His heart hammered. Getting closer to Henry and Abdul. To Mason. Wren picked through tents and cardboard shells, upturning plastic bags and rooting through wallets of tatty documents, looking for something to give him a date.

He found a sandwich wrapper, ham and cucumber, only three days old by the sell-by date.

He ran back out onto the street. There were no cameras overlooking the tunnel, but there had to be plenty elsewhere. The onramps to the nearby expressway.

Bingo.

He put up a fresh shout on his darknet. His NSA guy was no good for this, but cracking into CCTV databases would be child's play for his genius hackers, Hellion and B4cksl4cker.

He took a breath. This was progress at last.

The city turned around him. Lights, sound, vehicles in motion. He felt dizzy. Realized how weary his legs were, barely holding him up.

Nothing else on the darknet. He was no use to anyone like this.

He walked back into the homeless camp. Under the yellow halogen lamps of the under-bridge, rocked by passing traffic and freight trains, the camp stretched ahead in a wonderland of reeking bedding. He was too tired to care, and it wasn't like he had anywhere else to sleep. No motel would be safe now, with his face on every watchlist. Worst terror attack in nearly twenty years.

This was OK. Nobody noticed the homeless.

He rolled himself up in cardboard and was asleep in seconds.

22

TEMPLE

Wren woke, and for a little while lay still under the bridge, lulled by uneasy memories of the past. The first time he'd met his wife, Loralei, in an Atlanta bar ten years back. He'd been coming down off a big sting on a Saudi prince, still in character, drinking to shake the thing she'd had to do to get there. She'd been drunk, looking down the barrel of her green card running out, and seen something in him that intrigued her.

He'd felt pretty much the same. Both at loose ends, they'd dated in a kind of joyous bubble of unreality; her waiting out her visa expiry, him using up weeks of leave he'd built up for years. Bright, uncertain days. The happiest of his life, but also dark, because he'd lied to her from the beginning.

The memory soured.

The sounds of traffic grumbled by. He hadn't meant to sleep so long and unfurled the cardboard off his face. Fake under bridge light poured in, washing away the last phantoms of the past. The homeless camp spread before him, a desert of moldy sleeping bags and trash. It presented a sobering reality; all these people were really gone, doubtless undergoing some of the worst times of their lives.

That got his pulse going. He rose to his feet, rolled stiff shoulders and walked out from the shade of the bridge.

Mid-morning sun beat down on the blacktop, releasing the pungent aroma of summer dust and tar. The city rolled on around him; cars bustling, people roaming like ants, the expressway roaring overhead. He drank a bottle of water from the back of the van and checked his darknet messages. Nothing on the traffic cams yet; the footage was compiling but it could take hours yet.

A dozen messages had come in from Teddy though, his ex-vampire club leader, sometime in the small hours. Wren scrolled through them, each growing increasingly frantic.

WE HAVE TO MEET!

I HAVE WHAT YOU NEED!

CHRISTOPHER COME NOW!

Wren typed a response then set out. Teddy lived uptown with the dominatrix Cheryl. Better to hear this in person and grab a shower at the same time.

Old Edgebrook was a few switch-backed residential streets zigzagging through the forests of Dahla Park, in the northwest of the city; baby mansions on small but expensive plots, each boasting a distinct architectural style straight out of a magazine. French shutters, round picture windows, colonial turrets.

Teddy was rich, his fortune made in investment banking, and had one of the biggest houses in the neighborhood, with a yard screened by tall fences that once had hidden their dark parties from the eyes of the world. Now, Wren knew from past visits, they mostly laid around on inflatables in the pool all day, reflecting on their glorious past.

Wren parked the van and knocked on the oak front door. Cheryl answered. Her face was as impassive as ever, giving nothing away. Beautiful, of course, incredibly pale, with thick lips, wide eyes, but cruel. She wore a tight leather bodice, amplifying a vast bosom and near inhuman curves. He must have caught her coming off an early morning shift.

"Christopher," she said, like seeing him was a terrible disappointment. "Teddy's getting desperate." She stepped out of the way to admit him, then added as an afterthought, "You stink."

Wren chuckled. "Pleasure to see you too, Cheryl."

They'd dated once in his Chicago days, inadvisably. Cheryl was anhedonic, a medical condition which meant she felt no sense of joy in anything. It had forced her to seek adrenaline thrills from the vampire groups instead. The first time Wren had seen her he'd been entranced, as she stood on the stage like a queen of the night, her generous curves heaving, burlesque with actual blood flow.

He'd seen then, it would only be a matter of time before they bled her too far. Murder. Teddy would have played it off as a sacrifice, anything to keep control of his group. Things would've only gotten darker from there.

Now Cheryl held her nose. Anhedonia did nothing to alleviate disgust. "Take a shower."

"Sounds good. Can you run a wash on these?"

Cheryl looked at his clothes. "I can throw them out. You've been sleeping in trash again."

"So throw them out. You're looking well."

"I've been spending a lot of time on social media, gaslighting people."

He frowned. She enjoyed his displeasure. Ever the vampire, now she lived off the strong emotional reactions of others, whether in person or filtered through the Internet. "That's dangerously close to breaking the terms of your coin level."

"Is this my coin meeting?" she asked sharply. "Are you here to help me, or for my help?"

Wren just stared. She swallowed the disapproval greedily. One reason they'd broken up; she did everything she could to suck the life out of those close to her. Teddy only survived thanks to his enormous self-obsession. They were two of his more challenging Foundation members, but he'd taken them on and couldn't let them slide now.

"It's not. But we will talk. Now where's Teddy? He said he has something on the traffickers."

Cheryl perked up slightly. "In his temple. He's been furious all night that you were ignoring him."

"I wasn't ignoring him, I was asleep. He can wait five more minutes. This way?"

"Sure."

He'd been in their house once before. It was beguilingly normal, and everything was spotlessly clean. The downstairs bathroom was immaculate; he expected they had maids in every day. He tossed his clothes out the bathroom door and stepped into the rejuvenating steam of their walk-in shower. Jets from the walls massaged his bruised skin.

At some point the door opened, but Wren ignored it. He cleaned his injuries, starting to scab over. He brushed his teeth. He stepped out naked and saw Teddy with a gun in his hand, pointing it at him.

Ridiculously overpowered, a Sig Sauer P226. It made Teddy look small, and Teddy was no slouch; at six feet two he was just a shade shorter than Wren and bulked up from working out. In most company he dominated. Yet here in his own bathroom, with a gun in his hand and facing a naked man, something was missing.

"Hi, Teddy," Wren said, forcing a casual tone. He picked up a towel. Had to play this carefully or he'd get his brains splashed across the beautiful slate tiles. Last time Teddy had pulled a gun, he'd fired it. Wren still had the scar in his arm.

He dried his face and chest but didn't wrap the towel around his waist. Teddy's bright eyes picked out every motion. Psy-ops was all Wren had, so he'd use it. In a dick-swinging competition, it helped to actually have your dick out.

A bead of sweat rolled down Teddy's cheek. "You ignored my messages."

"I didn't ignore them," Wren said. "I was asleep. I came as soon as I saw them."

"Too late."

"Too late for what?"

Teddy just snorted. "Christopher Wren. On the run. Naked. Needing my help. Where's your all-controlling coin system now?"

"Teddy," said Wren, part-soothing, part-chiding, then reached up and slowly tapped his temple. "It's all in here. You know that."

Teddy raised the barrel. "One shot and it's gone."

Wren gazed into the gun's black hole. Not for the first time. "Shall we sit down? Or will you execute me in your downstairs bathroom? I don't know what your maid will think of that." He looked at the walls appraisingly. "You'll never get the brain fragments out of these cracks."

Teddy trembled. He was angry, that was obvious. Wren wondered if today was the day. "Put some clothes on," he said.

"Cheryl's washing them."

Teddy made a pained face.

"They're on a hot wash," came Cheryl's voice through the door. Listening in.

Teddy sighed.

"It's nothing she hasn't seen before," Wren said. "You too."

"Use the towel. Damn it, Christopher. Take this seriously."

Wren carefully wrapped the towel around his waist. "Serious enough?"

"Come on."

Teddy backed up. Wren followed, dripping on the thick shag carpet. They went like that through the house, up the stairs, with Teddy carefully shuffling backward, holding the gun on him while Cheryl followed.

Teddy's temple lay behind a triple-bolted door. He turned each lock carefully, like a ritual. Inside it was dim, but Wren picked out the mannequins. The room was almost a hall, taking up perhaps half of the second floor's square footage. The walls were papered with newspaper clippings divided into zones, and each zone had its own diorama of figures spread in various poses, specially built to Teddy's specifications.

Re-enactments of past murder scenes. A morbid fascination, but this was Teddy's methadone, and harmless.

"No," Teddy said to Cheryl, as she tried to slip in, and closed the door in her face. Like a little sister kept out of the 'boy's den'.

They looked at each other for a moment.

"You said you had something for me." Wren said. Calm. Controlled. Like an adult to a child.

"First I want out of the coin system," Teddy said. "Out from under you. No more controls. No more rules. No more threat of getting minus coins for 'backsliding'. I want to be free again."

Wren held his gaze. "So shoot me."

Teddy shuddered. "I've tried that before."

He'd lost two years of coins because of it, setting him back to zero. Spent the days of Wren's recovery begging to be allowed back on a coin.

"So what, then? You've got me in your temple. You and Cheryl could have a grand time taking me apart."

"I've got something you're looking for," Teddy said, licking his lips. "A trade."

"Information on the traffickers?"

"Right. After your darknet messages, I put the word out in some of my more unique groups. The kind only I've got access to. Anyway, I've got a guy. He's crazy, but it's real. I'll trade you, him for the coins."

Wren leaned in. Teddy leaned back.

"Trafficker or slave?"

"Trafficker," Teddy said. "Big numbers of people, he said, moved through Chicago." A long moment passed. "Well?"

23

DIORAMA

"What does he know?" Wren pressed.

"A place," Teddy answered. "A purpose. I confirmed it from maps. There's an abandoned camp."

Wren frowned. "Like a summer camp?"

"Sure. Cabins. Cells. An archery ground."

"Records?"

"No meaningful records. A clean paper trail."

"Where?"

Teddy bared his teeth.

"Where?" Wren repeated.

"Minnesota."

"Minnesota's big."

"Huge."

Wren spread his arms. Time to swing dicks. "This big?"

"Bigger. You'll never find it."

"I'll find your guy. I know he's in your groups. You think I can't?"

"I have him somewhere. Locked up." Teddy licked his lips. Now they were getting to it, what he really wanted. "Take me off the coin system and he's yours."

"You mean coin zero?"

"I mean off!" Teddy shouted, then seemed to regret the outburst. "Not watching me. Not controlling me, scoring me, anything. You see I'm holding a gun."

"It could be a banana," Wren said, nice and calm. "I'm in your head, Teddy. If you really wanted to shoot me, you'd have done it properly the first time."

Now the gun trembled. "You're not in my head."

"I'm right in there," said Wren, leaning closer. "Every time you set up one of your dioramas, I'm on your shoulder judging its placement to the inch. Every squirt of blood is getting analyzed. I know it, you know it."

"That's not true."

Wren shook his head. Abnormal psychology was a specialty of his, but there weren't many people quite like Teddy. Leader of something like a cult himself, unfettered he would've self-imploded long ago, taking all his followers with him. Wren's intervention in his downward trajectory was really a kind of experiment.

Could a cult leader be redeemed?

"We've talked about this," Wren said. "Many times. Remember?"

Teddy stabbed the gun at the air. "Bullshit. I want out of the Foundation. I could do great things."

Wren snorted. "We both know what you'd do without me. They're not great things, Teddy. They're easy things, things that feel good that you can trick yourself into thinking are hard, when really they're just serving base, cruel needs." He paused. "But you still could matter. Look at this junk, Teddy." He gestured at the mannequins. "You think this is what I hope for you? You're a caterpillar right now, but something better is coming. A resurrection. You'll be a butterfly soon."

"When?"

Teddy's voice cracked. This was years of pain coming out.

"When you're ready. It's on you. We talked about this." Wren shifted gears, showing a little anger. "But right now I've got two Foundation members on the line, potentially thousands of human slaves getting shipped and sold, and you think I want to play games? You know what I'd do for my people. I've done it for you. You owe me already, so put the damn gun down and pay what you owe!"

Teddy's face cratered. His voice went quiet. "I dream about this sometimes."

Wren stood up. Teddy shrank back. The gun was forgotten between them, now. "Tell me who your guy is, or you're coin zero and I go find him myself. Is that how your dream goes?"

Teddy's eyes swam. "You wouldn't."

"Watch me." Wren started walking. Teddy tracked him with the gun. He reached the door, opened it, and saw Cheryl was right outside.

"He's not shot you," she said, disappointed.

"Where are my clothes?"

She frowned. "How fast do you think my washing machine is? They're still on spin."

Wren pushed past her. "I'll wear them wet."

He went down the stairs with Teddy shouting in back. Cheryl scurried at his back. "You can't open the machine mid-cycle," she said helpfully. "It has a lock."

"Then I'll just wear my towel."

He passed down the hallway, opened the front door and stepped out into the light. Teddy was shouting louder than ever now, like he was the one being tortured in his 'temple'.

"You shouldn't do this to him," Cheryl said, as Wren stalked over the lawn to his van.

"He's a grown man. He's doing it to himself."

He sat in the van and started the engine. The hot leather seats scalded his bare thighs. He started to back the van out, then Teddy appeared in the doorway. The gun was gone.

"I'll tell you," he shouted. "Just wait. I'll get you the guy."

Wren sat for a moment, then pushed open the door.

Teddy looked sad. Wren walked over.

"Two choices in life," Wren said. "You grow or you implode."

Teddy looked pained. "So do I lose coins for this?"

Wren snorted. "A gun in my face? I think it's about par for the course, don't you?"

24

MAPS

The guy was at the 'coven', a country estate Teddy kept like a memento from his glory days: more land, more walls, and a proper dungeon in the basement. He was out of Teddy's deep web forums, where he'd boasted at times about the biggest feast he'd ever seen, rooms full of people in chains, years ago.

Wren leaned in. Pulling on his damp clothes. "And you believe him?"

"I lured him in last night," Teddy answered. "I questioned him last night, while you were 'sleeping'." He made quote marks around the word with his fingers.

"I was sleeping," Wren said. "I *am* human."

Teddy narrowed his eyes like he didn't believe it. "He gave me maps. He's heard about me; he was trying to impress me. He spilled plenty." Teddy puffed his chest out a little.

Wren considered. "How many years back?"

"He says two. But then he's also covered in needle tracks, a long-term junkie, so who knows what his idea of time is?"

Wren sighed, tugged on his boots. In the coven. "In chains?"

"One chain," said Teddy, as if the accusation wounded him. "He'll barely feel it. He's comfortable."

Wren looked at Cheryl. "You're involved in this?"

She shrugged. "I use the coven for some clients. We stay out of each other's way."

Wren rubbed his temples. A lead from possibly two years ago.

"Let's go."

He drove behind Teddy and Cheryl in their hulking Grand Cherokee, drying in the rough breeze through the open windows, as Chicago bled away like a bad dream. The outskirts melded into outlying towns and golf courses. He didn't expect to come back now; the city had given up its secrets. He called Humphreys.

There were three rings, then Humphrey's deep, resonating voice on the other end.

"Chicago?"

"Leaving Chicago. That was fast tracking."

"Expedited. I've got teams coming for you already. What are you up to, Wren?"

"I'm hunting, just like you. Ready for an information exchange?"

Humphreys sounded ready to blow. "Turn yourself in, Christopher. That's the only exchange I'm interested in."

"Then I'll go first. In the warehouse I found a slip of paper, a receipt. I tracked it to Chicago, where it turns out our killers have been abducting the homeless for at least eleven months. I've got a lead on one of their trucks and I'm tracking it back. I've also got another lead on a possible old member of the group. You should look into nationwide reports of homeless encampments missing. In one instance it looks like these guys grabbed maybe two hundred people right off the street, with no witnesses."

There was silence for a moment. Wren wondered how many intelligence agency heads were now listening in on this call, to the number one most wanted man in America.

"This is elaborate even by your standards, Wren. You want us to poll the homeless? You know what a dead-end that will be. It's a time sink."

"Not a time sink. I'm not telling you to hit the streets and count them. I'm saying run a spider data search for reports in police systems. There must be reports, if the numbers are what I'm thinking."

There was silence.

"Humphreys. Give me something."

"You mean tell you if we're closing in on you?"

"You were in the warehouse, right? Somebody bought off the whole damn county to shuttle slaves through. I'm telling you where those slaves come from. I can give you a name, Mason Karitas. He was a Marine. They've got him. His fingerprints were on the receipt. They snatched him eleven months ago. Wendy, that's another name."

More silence, stretching out in long, empty seconds. Then Humphreys broke it. "I heard about what happened with your family."

That gave Wren pause.

"I said it. You're no family man. Our psychiatrists think you're having a breakdown. They say the pain of your childhood, all the lies about your cult, it came to a head when-"

"I'm not talking about that," Wren said. "Off-limits."

Humphreys pressed on. "Not off-limits. You're experiencing a psychotic break, Wren. We never knew how damaged you were. Prodigy, they called you. But you were broken from the start. That's our fault too, to give you so much authority. Now you've left me with no other choice. I'm bringing in Tandrews."

That name hit Wren like a punch, brought him out in a cold sweat. Tandrews, the man who'd found Wren wandering in the desert, right after his childhood cult had burned alive. James Tandrews. An FBI agent who'd fostered Wren, who'd made him who he was, who'd given him the chance to choose his own name.

"No."

"He's here. What did you think we were doing all this time? We're profilers too, we've got teams dedicated to breaking you, your 'Foundation'. They all say Tandrews is the key, so I'm going to put him on the line. Maybe then you'll listen."

Wren imagined the button clicking, the old guy leaning into a microphone. This was going to hurt like hell, and he couldn't afford that now. Tandrews had been nothing but good to him. After the horrors, cages and experiments of his father's cult, Wren hadn't known how to accept his kindness.

At first, he'd barely spoken at all. More like a mute animal than a boy at the onset of his teenage years. But Tandrews had been the FBI Gold Team leader who ran the cult clean-up crew, and he'd dealt with people brainwashed by charismatic leaders before. He'd seen the effect it had on children, and he'd played it right with Wren at every stage.

Gave him his space. Introduced him slowly to the real, wider world, while keeping in touch with the primal wildness Wren had learned in the Arizona desert. Together in the dark forests of Maine they would go camping and hunting for weeks at a time. Barely speaking. Slowly learning to trust, as Tandrews taught Wren how to face down a buck, bring it down with an arrow from a homemade bow, skin it, gut it, and cook it.

Away from other children. Young people. Not for fear of what they'd do to Wren, but for fear of what he'd do to them.

The years passed, and Wren's emotional wounds healed over, though the scars remained. The 'Pyramid' death cult was something Tandrews tried to talk about a few times, but Wren couldn't. The past was just too horrific to face, bringing him out in night terrors, screaming himself awake. So they simply moved on. At fifteen Wren went to high school and became valedictorian of his year. Headed up the football team.

After surviving the Pyramid, other young people were easy. It wasn't manipulation, it was just self-control. He showed them the best he could be, while bringing out the best in them too. A conscious choice, to be different from his birth father, who'd only been interested in pain.

He grew. Went to the movies. Had a girlfriend. At seventeen there was trust between him and Tandrews. Prom was coming. Graduation. Then Tandrews took the next step, a logical step as Wren was moving into adulthood and thinking about college.

He'd offered to bond them together through formal adoption. It would override the emancipation papers Wren had been granted at sixteen, legally registering him as an adult in the eyes of a county court judge.

Wren agreed, and the papers came in. Wren had nodded along through it all, not fully understanding what it meant for him until the night before the signing ceremony, and the fear hit like it hadn't in years. A terror so thick and dark he could barely breathe, like he was back in the blackness of his father's cages, back in the desert town with all those people burning alive, with the Apex whispering in his ear...

He'd fled through an open window and never looked back. All night he walked, until he hit a turning point and realized what he was going to have to do. What he'd been preparing for, really, ever since Tandrews had found him.

Face the horrors head on. Hunt down his father, if he was still alive, and any other sick men like him. It was the only way to stay sane. Despite Tandrews' best efforts, he couldn't have a normal life, after all he'd been through. Through the course of that one night, all thoughts of prom, graduation and his girlfriend were forgotten. He abandoned the idea of college. Walked straight into a Marine recruitment office in some shabby mall two towns over, handed his emancipation papers over to the guy at the desk, and asked to sign up.

HE COULDN'T BEAR to think about Tandrews for years after. At first that had been about the fear, coming on hot and visceral every time he revisited the memory. Instead he threw himself into training, first the Marines, then the special operations Force Reconnaissance group. In later years, that fear changed and mixed in with a bitter shame.

The way he'd treated Tandrews had been appalling. The fear didn't excuse it. So many times he'd tried to make the call to the man who'd saved his life, bury the hatchet and apologize for the way he'd fled, but always it was too hard. Always the shame took him up to the edge, and the fear of how it had felt to be that helpless child in Tandrews' arms again overwhelmed him. Every year it had just gotten harder.

He couldn't deal with that now. Too much was at stake to get caught up in that whirling storm of old emotion.

There was an intake of breath down the line. The old guy warming up to speak. Any second now his voice would come through, warm and kind, a decent man who'd done his very best.

Wren killed the call before anything could come through.

Abruptly he was alone in the van, though the air felt thick with swirling ghosts. He hadn't spoken to Tandrews for eighteen years. He held the wheel with his elbows and pried the phone apart, strangling an incoming call. Silence reigned, but he heard voices anyway. His wife. Tandrews. Humphreys.

The babies in their cages, calling for help.

His breathing rasped and it grew harder to think straight, making it difficult to keep Teddy and Cheryl in sight in their Jeep. He hit a pothole and almost lost control, heart racing too hard, breath coming fast.

Tandrews.

He pulled over onto the shoulder, breathing getting wilder as the past swamped him. He had all kinds of mental techniques that'd bring him back around, meditation and mindfulness, but they took time, and he didn't have time.

Rustling in the back he came up with a dose of the ADHD attention-sharpening drug, methylphenidate, and dry-swallowed it. He felt as bad now as he ever had, like a night terror hitting in the middle of the day. Memories forced their way up and tried to drag him back to when he was twelve years old in that Arizona desert town, bodies burning all around, and-

He shook his head and slapped his own face. There was no time for flashbacks. He slammed the wheel, urging the methylphenidate to flush faster into his system.

Tandrews.

After a few seconds the drug hit like a car crash, along with a flood of anger. Wren threw the phone body out of the left window, the battery out of the right and punched the gas pedal down.

25

SACRIFICE

In twenty minutes Wren veered off the highway and sped through leafy suburbs of palatial houses until Teddy's country estate appeared before him. Details popped across his vision thanks to the methylphenidate: tall iron gates, a crushed coral drive flanked by cedars, the Grand Cherokee already there in the large carport, but no sign of Teddy and Cheryl.

He skidded the van to a halt and shoved the door open, left the engine idling, and strode up the stairs to the main door feeling wired. He kicked the double doors and they burst open on the marble interior.

"Teddy!" he yelled. "Cheryl!"

No answer came.

He ran up the spiral staircase to the second floor, the world spinning like a kaleidoscope around him, and shouted again. He stalked along the hallway peering into bedrooms, each furnished like a hotel.

Nobody and nothing.

Running down the stairs felt like sliding down a helter-skelter. He hadn't been there since Teddy's party days, but he remembered the route to the basement, where the coven had met. The door hung open and Wren headed down.

The basement spread like a Nosferatu set ahead of him, all gothic archways and vaulted ceilings arrayed in a long, stone-paved nave in the shape of a crucifix. This was the belly of the beast, the altar, where the sacrifices were made.

Faux torches burned with dim orange electric light in sconces, and Wren lurched between them, past shallow alcoves where authentic devices of torture lurked in cultivated shadow: a dark metal iron maiden, tall and glinting with its inner bed of spikes; a wall-mounted scold's bridle, a head-cage designed to punish medieval women, preventing them from opening their mouths; a breaking rack with ropes and rollers for stretching bodies to breaking point, pitted with nail gouge marks.

"Teddy!" he shouted.

Then he saw him. Teddy was on his knees beside the altar, looking at Wren with an odd expression. Cheryl was there too, but she wasn't kneeling, she was lying on the floor in blood.

Then Teddy's head jerked sideways; a bullet to the skull. An incredible thunderclap of sound reverberated in the contained space. Wren dived and rolled hard left without thinking. His body flowed over the dark stones, bringing him up in the left arm of the crucifix, chased by shots cracking off the stones.

Time slowed. Out came the Beretta, a natural fit in the glove of his palm, and he started firing even before he surged around the edge of the alcove. Gunpowder blasts and bullets bounced off the faux stone walls like sparks of fire and brimstone, then there was the shooter.

Lurking in cover behind the altar; too big to be fully screened. The Beretta clicked dry. No time to reload. Wren dived and his shoulder slammed the guy in the hip. Wren lifted him sideways and they fell together.

The shooter's back cracked off the altar and Wren slammed down next to Cheryl's head. Her eyes tracked him. The gun fired again and Wren scrabbled for it. The guy was moving fast, but Wren caught his wrist with both hands and yanked.

The pistol's grip slammed down on Wren's left shoulder and he twisted, even as a shot went off that sent gunpowder stinging his cheek and a numbing shock wave bouncing around inside his ear. Another shot followed and Wren twisted and pulled. The gun skittered away over the stone, then a big fist came in and an arm swung around his neck. Wren bucked before the headlock could close, the back of his head caught the guy's chin and he twisted free.

For a second they just stared at each other.

The guy was dressed all in black like the guys from the Vikings' warehouse. Bigger than Wren at 6' 6", arms spread showing powerful deltoid muscles. Blond hair, blue eyes, steely gaze, holding a long Bowie knife.

Wren laughed. No reason. The methylphenidate made things seem funny. "Just you?" he asked, and the guy lunged. The knife stabbed out three times at a wicked pace, matched by three fast stamps forward. Wren backed up fast, sustaining one nick on his left forearm.

The guy smiled then came in again, but this time Wren was ready; he danced back for two strikes then deflected the third with his forearm, spinning into a whiplash backhand across the guy's face.

He rocked sideways, liquid blue eyes flaring in surprise.

"Where are they?" Wren asked, and shot a push kick into the guy's solar plexus. He staggered and lashed out with the knife, forcing Wren to back up.

He needed a way past the blade. The shooter charged in, and this time Wren ripped off his own T-shirt and tossed it into the guy's face. The distraction made him fumble the last step, tying to pull back. It was enough for Wren to grab his wrist and elbow, thrust with his hips and haul the big man into an arcing judo throw.

He swept up, over and slammed down hard. The knife clattered free.

Wren rolled him belly-down before he could react, dropped onto his back like it was a saddle then locked an arm around his throat, squeezing hard. The guy thrashed to get free but Wren bent his body into it.

Something creaked in the man's neck but Wren didn't let up. Not looking for a broken neck, but riding the edge. Another creak, then Wren let the guy flop down beside Cheryl's body, rattling for breath. Wren kneeled at his side, head weaving and dizzy from the impacts.

"I'll-" Wren started to say, but didn't know what he'd meant to say. The guy was going nowhere now. He found his shirt a few yards away, stumbled to Cheryl and swiftly padded the wound in her lower back. A through-and-through right by her kidney, but it should be survivable. Her pulse was firm but her breathing was shallow. Next, he inspected Teddy's head; the bullet seemed to have struck a glancing blow. He had a weak pulse and was completely loose, limbs like a dead man. Wren stripped the assassin's shirt and gently bandaged his head.

"Don't die, Teddy," Wren said. "The butterfly's coming."

The big guy hadn't moved, was still sucking for breath, so Wren moved on. In the corner by the altar a third body sat in a chair, wrapped with a single chain. Teddy's informant, the ex-trafficker. He didn't look good. He looked dead, with some torture to help him on his way.

Wren's vision spun. Too much adrenaline along with the methylphenidate was sending him into overload. Supposition spun through his mind. This all-in-black assassin had been waiting here. But how? Watching Teddy's groups, maybe? Tracking the whole Internet?

He returned to the assassin and rolled him over. The guy's eyes swirled as he sucked for air. Wren spoke in a gruff bark.

"Who sent you? Tell me anything. Tell me something. I could put you on a coin."

The guy just gasped.

"Where are you based? What are you doing with the homeless? Where are Henry and Abdul?"

The guy tried to say something. Wren leaned in.

"T…" he said.

Wren leaned in closer.

"Traitor."

26

CARNAGE

Wren called an ambulance for Teddy and Cheryl, requested a SWAT-level response, then hung up and searched the assassin's pockets. He had car keys and a phone; Wren took them. Same for Teddy. Last he stumbled to the dead trafficker in the corner. The torture was the assassin's work, no doubt. Teddy wasn't capable of this. Wallet, phone and keys; Wren took them all then ran back through the dark basement, mind spinning.

How long until another strike team came? This guy couldn't be the only one. Maybe just the advance party.

Up the stairs he emerged into the kitchen. In the cool, bright sunlight he saw the blood on his bare chest and arms. At the sink he splashed himself liberally, used a dishcloth to wipe the worst of it away. Out the window he watched the gravel drive, expecting the backup team any second.

One of the phones in his pocket rang shrilly. There were three now. He laid them on the granite counter and tried to figure out which one was ringing. The middle?

He answered it. "Yeah?"

The phone kept ringing. He looked at it stupidly then set it down and tried the one on the left.

"Yeah?"

"Is it done?" came a voice. Clipped military tones, like every word required conservation of energy. "Do you have him?"

"Sure," said Wren.

"So what is he, FBI? Where's his team?"

"I-" began Wren, then stopped himself, now in the middle of running up the stairs to the second floor. The shot beside his head had disoriented him, and he had to force himself to think clearly. "FBI."

The phone line hung silent for a moment.

"It's you."

"Sure."

"You killed him."

"He might be dead. Come find out. We're having ourselves a party."

The voice took on a different tack. "You don't sound like you're in good condition. My man, did he go down hard?"

"I guess," said Wren, stumbling into a bedroom. There was a chest of drawers, and he pulled open the middle drawer. T-shirts. "He went out happy?"

"What?"

"Doing what he loved best," said Wren, not thinking, "on his knees."

Another silence.

"We've got one of your team. Abdul. He's on his knees right now. How about we slice a few pieces off?"

Wren froze. Abdul. "Bullshit."

"Not bullshit. He's been rolling over all day."

Wren doubted that very much. Abdul was one of the toughest guys in the whole Foundation. "Did he tell you my name?"

The man said nothing.

"It's Christopher Wren." He put the phone on speaker while he wrapped a shirt tightly around the cut in his arm. "Google me, you dumb fool. Hurt Abdul and I'm coming for you personally."

There was a pause. "Too late."

Wren seethed. Anger worked strange chemistry through his brain, showing him flaring red lights.

The guy took his chance. "Now, we talk about-"

"We talk about you," Wren interrupted, shrugging a yellow Hawaiian T-shirt on. It had big print pineapples with smiles and vampire teeth. Teddy's taste? "I took down your Vikings in a day. I took down your warehouse alone, and I took out your assassin with only a T-shirt. Now I got myself a new T-shirt, a way better one, so you should look out."

"Oh, I will. Christopher Wren. We'll see you soon."

"And what's your name?" Wren asked, running for the stairs, but the line was dead.

He swept up his phone collection from the kitchen counter, stuffed them in his pockets and jogged out of the house. The drive was quiet. He fell into his van and drove around the back of the building, feeling light and breezy inside, like pieces of him were falling off. If there was time maybe he could get Teddy and Cheryl up here, drive them to the hospital himself.

The assassin's car was tucked behind the building, a maroon sedan. Wren fumbled with the keys then rifled through the side compartments, the glove box, under the seat, and came up with a license, a box of hollow-point ammo for a .45 and a slim printed booklet with the title 'The Order of the Saints'.

A noise came and Wren backed out of the sedan, stuffing the license and booklet into his waistband. The sound was getting louder. He sprinted for the van and dived behind the wheel just in time to see a large black SUV come tearing around the side of the building, sending gravel chips up like surf.

Not emergency services. Not Humphreys. The guy had said it, 'see you soon'.

The 'Order of the Saints' were already here.

Wren hit the horn and reversed, backing straight into the SUV's left headlight. The van crunched, the SUV ricocheted off to the right and Wren powered the van into a sharp turn.

In his side mirrors he saw two figures all in black leap out and shoot automatic rifles. Slugs hit the back of the van like a hailstorm, rattling around in the storage until one buzzed through the divider screen like an enraged wasp to plink off the windshield. The glass cracked and the bullet bounced onto the dash, where it sizzled into the leather.

Wren spun the wheel back around the front of the house, saw the drive leading away right there, but didn't take it. No way he was going to outrun a top-of-the-range SUV in a panel van. Likewise he couldn't just leave Teddy and Cheryl to these guys.

He slammed on the brakes, sending coral spray up ahead, and yanked the shifter into reverse just as the SUV swerved around the side of the building. Immediately the hail of fire kicked back in, two guys on foot running either side. Another bullet found a route through the back and burst his windshield outward. Two seconds out the SUV driver realized Wren's plan and tried to angle left, but Wren was ready for that.

With the accelerator punched hard down he yanked the wheel to meet him, glided for a moment up onto the lawn then hit the SUV on the right headlight. The jolt slammed Wren back into the seat as the van's low chassis undercut the SUV, forcing it to crumple through his rear paneling.

He flung the door open and surged out just as the automatic fire kicked in again. The SUV's hood was smoking and the front wheels spun uselessly in the air, with the hood jammed up through the shredded back of the van.

Wren ran, rustling through the jumble of keys and phones in his pockets, coming up with one that felt right. This whole thing had started with a Jeep. The button coaxed a beep from Teddy's Grand Cherokee, the door opened, and Wren fired it up and slammed into first.

Three men dashed around the side of the house and Wren managed to hit two of them dead-on at twenty miles an hour. One flew up and over, the other managed to grab the windscreen wiper and hang on as the Jeep bounced over a bed of flowers, automatic weapon firing madly.

Wren hit the brakes and the guy flew off, landed bad, then Wren was reversing again. The one guy left fired, shooting out the Jeep's rear window but underestimating the truck's acceleration. Too late he realized his mistake, tried to leap to the side, but Wren yanked the wheel and hit him flush with the flat back of the Cherokee.

The guy sailed like he'd been hit by a train, bounced off the wrecked van, hit the deck.

Wren's head spun. Two more guys somewhere, not in the SUV now, but he had no time and no ammo, and the cops would be here soon.

He yanked the stick to first and hit the gas, was chased halfway down the tree-lined drive by automatic fire but didn't take a single hit. At the bottom of the drive he thumped onto the residential road, spun the wheel in a sharp turn and whipped away.

His phones rang. He gasped. He ran the Cherokee up to eighty and passed a flurry of incoming emergency vehicles, blue lights flaring, then hit a freeway ten minutes later, heading west.

27

THE ORDER

W ren rang Humphreys on his burner phone. He didn't give the Director a chance to speak, just uploaded the address, the assassin, the team. It would be far better to have the massive weight of CIA Special Operations on his side rather than hunting him down.

"I found a booklet in the assassin's car," he finished. "'Order of the Saints', it's called, and that sounds like some anti-government nonsense to me." He took a breath, getting his thoughts in order. "Add to that the assassin called me a traitor as he clocked out, and the Vikings too, a well-known anti-government gang? This thing has a revolutionary component, Humphreys, for sure. See if you can dig up anything on these 'Saints'. I'll be in touch."

Wren killed the call before Humphreys could hardly splutter out a word.

Every fiber in his body felt like it was vibrating. Teddy and Cheryl on the floor of the coven. Abdul in the grip of the 'Order of the Saints'. The scale of this thing just getting bigger and bigger, and still no sign of Mason or Wendy.

He shouted and slammed the wheel. He was too wired. Twenty minutes had passed already, and he pulled off at the next services, almost wiping out a Mini on the way in.

Sitting in the lot, his hands shook. He pushed open the door, stepped out and started pacing. He'd killed plenty of people before. He'd lost team members before too, but none as visceral as this. He saw Teddy yanking sideways again as the bullet hit execution-style, his whole body tugged like a fish on the line. He saw Cheryl on the deck, dull eyes tracking him.

Abdul, in their hands.

His people. His team. He punched his own palm. The losses were too high. He had to get ahead. Quit reacting and start acting.

Two more minutes he allowed, pacing around the truck and getting control of his breathing, before he ducked back into the Cherokee and scooped out his phone. He logged into his Foundation darknet and checked the hacker board. It was buzzing with theories and research, but nothing concrete; the spider was still trawling through Chicago's many CCTV feeds, looking for the Order's semi-truck. He tapped out a message through the Megaphone app for everyone to see.

WAS JUST ATTACKED NORTH OF CHICAGO. FIVE-STRONG HIT SQUAD, ONE ASSASSIN LYING IN WAIT. A GROUP CALLED 'THE ORDER OF THE SAINTS' - COLLATE WITH KNOWN MILITIA GROUPS. CAME IN DRIVING A TOP-SPEC CHRYSLER SUV. THEY SHOT TEDDY & CHERYL - CHECK IF THEY'RE ALIVE. THEY ALSO HAVE ABDUL. FIND HIM. FIND HENRY. GET ME TARGETS.

He blinked hard and rubbed his eyes. Now the comedown from adrenaline and methylphenidate was making him sluggish. He dropped back into the driver's seat and turned to the side where three phones waited. Somebody would track them soon, but in one of those phones there was evidence, at least according to Teddy. Maps of the camp in Minnesota, maybe. A lead on this 'Order of the Saints'.

He picked up the informant's phone and thumbed the display, but it was PIN-locked. No chance he could crack that. Same for the assassin's. That left only Teddy's. He had to hope it contained the maps. PIN-locked too, but maybe this one he could guess.

Wren sat there, staring at the touchscreen keypad of nine digits, racking his mind for information about Teddy. A woman went by pushing a cart full of shopping bags, her kid in the high seat. It was strange to see normal life continuing after what he'd just been through.

Wren blinked and refocused. He knew a lot about Teddy, but there was plenty more that he didn't know. Every man had his dark hinterland, and Teddy's was darker than most.

Nothing for it but to try. He tapped in six digits: 051976, Teddy's birthday, but nothing came of it.

He tried another: 061740, the Marquis de Sade's birth month and year, Teddy's favorite writer, but no. He tried 120120, for the Marquis' infamous work '120 Days of Sodom', but still nothing. He tried various other combinations, tying Sade with Teddy and his vampire club, with Cheryl and Wren, until he tapped in the date that Wren broke the club five years back and first introduced Teddy to the coin system.

The phone opened. Wren gave a little gasp. He hadn't expected that.

He opened the maps app and watched a screen of dark green trees and grass resolve: a satellite image from above. Something like a summer camp, Teddy had described, and that was what this looked like. There were several cabins, a central building, a dirt track running up from a single-lane road. There were no vehicles, no flag at the top of the pole, and the tennis courts looked overgrown.

Abandoned. It made sense. This organization, the 'Order of the Saints', had the *modus operandi* of burning themselves completely each time they felt compromised. First they'd wiped out the Vikings and Price PD, then they'd shuttered the warehouse, and now one of their ex-members lay dead in Teddy's temple. It made sense that they would've burned this location years ago. Their MO.

Wren zoomed the map out. Northern Minnesota, near the border with Canada, a hundred miles north-east of Duluth just off Lake Superior. He studied roads leading up to it.

Would they be waiting for him there, too? It seemed possible. The assassin must have gotten that much intel via torture from Teddy's contact. Wren scanned possible routes in, keeping one eye on the road.

There was the dirt track into the camp, barely visible on the satellite image, and two roads that passed nearby, though both were miles away through dense forest. One looked to be an old lumber route, dead-ending by a small lake, while the other continued to join a larger road twenty miles north. Wren dropped four pins on the map: choke points. One at the head of the camp road, two on the through road, one on the lumber road, places they would likely hunker down and wait. Places he had to avoid.

He scanned wider and found a long straight line of grass cutting through the forest, passing within seven miles of the camp. Zoomed out, it spread more than a hundred miles in either direction, but no power lines or rail tracks in sight. Likely a disused freight line from a century earlier, bringing coal down from Canada, with the pilings now overgrown and the iron rails reclaimed.

Wren checked the Grand Cherokee's controls and found the switch he was looking for, 4-wheel drive. With his lights off he could hit the old line far away, evade any blockades they threw up, stop seven miles out from the camp and trek the rest of the way on foot.

He memorized the map and the route, then scrolled through the rest of Teddy's open apps, but there was nothing of interest. He sat a moment longer in silence, barely thinking, just breathing.

The booklet lay on the seat beside him.

THE ORDER OF THE SAINTS

He scooped it up. There was a simple design on the front beneath the title, a stylized biplane leaving a trail of spray behind it, like a crop duster. Wren knew the meaning of that well, it came from the conclusion of the Turner Diaries, a science fiction revolutionary tale, published in 1978 and set in 1999. It told the story of how a revolutionary organization called 'the Order' violently overthrew the government of the United States. The book ended with a crop-duster plane carrying a nuclear weapon to destroy the Pentagon.

Wren shuddered in his seat. The Order of the Saints. Something else came back to him. Likely the 'Saints' reference came from another fictional forbear, titled the 'Camp of the Saints'. It was likewise set in a science fiction world, and described the onset of World War III in the United States, after a large swathe of domestic terror groups turned against their own government.

Wren turned to the first page and started taking photographs. It was twenty-five pages all-told, packed in with a tight font, with no illustrations, no back or front matter and no author name; likely run off a home press.

On the darknet he sent a system shout to another Foundation member, Dr. Grayson Ferat, a seventy-one-year-old professor of psychology at Yale University. Wren had met him in an advance two-week class he'd taken on Abnormal Psychology at sixteen years old, before the CIA took him on. He uploaded the photos along with a brief summary of the case, then typed a final message, sent direct to Humphreys' number with the photos of the booklet attached.

DUST THESE PHONES FOR PRINTS. HACK THEM IF YOU CAN. HERE IS YOUR 'CULT'.

Then he got out and laid all three phones under a nearby bush. With batteries intact, Humphreys would be able to track Teddy's phone back. They were all useless to him now, better in Humphreys' hands than his.

He put his hands back on the wheel, took a breath and started the engine. There was no time to lose. The Grand Cherokee pulled smoothly back onto the highway, heading north for Minnesota.

28

SAINTS

Miles flew by and the clock on the dash advanced into the evening. Wren kept checking his phone for updates, but nothing was coming; no news on Teddy or Cheryl, nothing on Henry or Abdul.

He squeezed the wheel and glanced at the booklet on the seat beside him. He'd caught snatches of its nonsense while taking photographs, the same kind of cult dogma he'd read a thousand times before. From Charles Manson's rantings to the annals of Waco and the Jonestown 'teachings', it was all just the same thing: damaged people trying to control other damaged people. Often these texts ended in apocalyptic visions, when their leaders reached the limit of their creative vision. The only satisfying climax they could imagine was a fiery end.

An hour after passing through Madison a message finally pinged direct through the darknet. He fumbled the phone open with one hand.

CALL ME

It was Dr. Ferat.

During Wren's two-week advance class at Yale, Ferat had blown Wren's mind with his Abnormal Psychology course; the ways the human mind could be manipulated through simple neurolinguistic tricks and emotional exploits. It reminded the sixteen-year-old Wren of his father's mind-bending techniques back in the fake Arizona town.

Yet it had been the extra-curricular activity that had impacted Wren's life most.

After a seminar one afternoon Ferat had invited several standout students back to his rooms for a sherry, or in Wren's case a soda pop. At only sixteen and with little experience of the wider world, he'd thought it was just another odd occurrence on his path out of the darkness. Then the good Dr. had sat Wren down and artfully tried to pump him for the inside line on his father, the Apex.

He wanted to know what it had really been like in his father's suicide cult, the Pyramid. Ferat was, after all, one of the world's greatest practitioners of mind control. He even offered, with some modest subtlety, to cut Wren in on the book deal he envisaged, a bestseller in cult dynamics that should catapult him to head up the Yale Psychology Department.

Wren had just smiled.

It was then, perhaps more than at any other time, that he'd begun to understand that the days before he'd escaped the Pyramid and the days after were not so different. This new America was much the same as his old one in Arizona, with the same kind of powerful figures looking to exploit the vulnerable.

Except none of these predators were nearly as effective, persuasive or dangerous as his father had been. Dr. Ferat's plan to co-opt Wren was unsubtle, but still he clearly functioned at a high level in society.

That was a revelation, and it taught the young Wren how easy people were to control. For the most part, Ferat's expert academic grasp of human manipulation had served him incredibly well in life. To Wren, he wielded it like a ten-pound hammer; blunt and obvious.

He'd been disappointed when Wren had rejected his idea for a 'co-written' book. A few years later, though, when Wren returned offering Ferat a role as the architect of his Foundation, a new organization to help those who couldn't help themselves, he'd jumped at the chance.

Now Wren called Dr. Ferat back, leaving the phone hands-free on the dash. "Doctor."

"Christopher? Is that you?" Ferat had the powerful baritone of a Shakespearean actor, belying his thinning, frail frame. The last time Wren had seen him was two years earlier on the Yale campus, with Ferat standing in the rain with a fifteen-year coin in his hand, looking proud. Fifteen years he'd spent helping to build something phenomenal, taking the Foundation from three willing members to over a hundred. He'd also made Head of his Yale Department years earlier, off the strength of his own impressive research.

"It's me," Wren said.

Ferat cleared his throat, and Wren had the feeling he might at any moment break into song. Something from the Pirates of Penzance, perhaps. He'd heard Ferat's fearsome singing voice on several occasions and been impressed. But not now.

"I've scanned the whole of it," Ferat intoned, "that idolatrous screed, and Christopher, I found it very troublesome material."

That was no surprise. "Tell me."

"I know you're familiar with the author's reference points, The Camp of the Saints, The Turner Diaries. The author of this seems to be trying to underpin their ideas with a pseudoscience of natural rights versus inherited rights. It would seem his version of 'The Order' believes the current state of our governance is untenable, and the only effective remedy is to incite a national civil war."

Wren took a breath. "Civil war?"

"Quite. The details in this polemic are truly disturbing."

Wren cursed.

"Indeed. Do you believe this is a plausible outcome?"

Wren's mind raced ahead. "I don't know. Maybe. There are easily a hundred groups in the United States right now pushing for the overthrow of the government. They're largely all fantasists, without the will or the means to execute on that vision, or the FBI would have cracked down on them harder." He paused, sorting his thoughts. "This group looks to be different, though. I've never heard of them, never seen sign of them until now, but their reach is enormous. Their level of organization, and the way they've stayed hidden, are unprecedented. Plus the number of people they've snatched up?"

Fresh ramifications spun through his mind. What were all those people even for? What if they weren't just stealing the homeless from Chicago, but other large cities too? What if it was tens of thousands of people?

"Christopher?"

"Sorry, I'm thinking. What do they need the people for. Thousands of homeless, doctor. Why?"

"I hate to say execution," Ferat said, then went briefly silent. "However,

133

it seems quite possible. There are hints in this pamphlet where blame is ascribed. Many people forget that Hitler did not only persecute and slaughter the Jewish race, but also gypsies, homeless people, the disabled; anyone he considered to be a drag on the nation. This group may have taken some inspiration from that holocaust."

Wren kicked himself. Obviously. "So they're slaughtering them, just for the crime of having no home, or being sick, or just being unlucky?"

Ferat's voice sounded more brittle than ever. "It is possible. It has happened before."

Wren grunted. He knew that. "OK. So civil war. How are they going to pull it off?"

"You mentioned those hundred fantasist groups? I'd reconsider them. They may be part of the 'how'. From what I can gather, this 'Order' has been knitting disparate organizations together for years. The Vikings are a prime example. Of course, none are mentioned by name in the paper, but others can be inferred. My last research paper was on-"

"I read it," Wren interrupted, "the abnormal psychology of intra-tribal coups in tribal Malaysian societies."

"You did?" asked Ferat, sounding pleased. "Then you know it argued that mistrust of leadership is innate in human organizations, no matter how small. Sometimes the mistrust is well-founded, where corruption or incompetence is rife, but it also occurs whether those 'triggering' factors exist or not, often showing up as some form of 'fake news' conspiracy theory." He took a breath. "It's becoming a well-documented phenomenon."

"A phenomenon that can stir up extremely intense emotions," Wren added. "Sometimes intense enough for people to take violent action to overturn the status quo."

"Yes," mused Dr. Ferat. "We've seen several in recent years. Timothy McVeigh. Anders Breivik in Sweden."

Wren nodded along. "Right, but they were lone wolves with no real organization. For this, I'm thinking more like 9/11, a plot that required substantial cooperation, planning, logistics. This Order of the Saints already looks far bigger than Bin Laden's jihadis, though, bigger than ISIS or even the KKK. It's clearly well-financed. We haven't seen something this massive since the Nazis themselves."

Ferat took a moment. "The Hutu militia massacre of the Tutsis in Rwanda may be the better parallel, Christopher. A core paramilitary organization used propaganda to drive an entire population into committing atrocities against another ethnic group. The death count approached a million, and everyone in the nation was made complicit."

Wren tried to swallow that. He'd been thinking of single large-scale attacks, because that was so often the case. 9/11 followed that model, Waco, Jonestown; none of them reached far beyond a single, symbolic attack. But Ferat was right; if you really wanted to start a national civil war, you had to engage the populace at large with a sustained barrage of hate, violence and lies. Like the Hutus killing Tutsis, one attack wouldn't cut it. You'd need many.

"A range of attacks, then," said Wren, working the logistics. "Coming across many days."

There was the sound of papers riffling. "The booklet enshrines all this in quasi-religious language," Ferat said. "Here, and I quote, 'How shall we not take this burden as the burden of our very lifetimes, and carry it up not only the first hill, but the second, and the third, until the very twelfth hill is met, and there we anoint ourselves afresh in the free blood of our ancestors?'"

Wren winced. Cultists loved to reference numbers. And blood. And hills. "Does it talk explicitly about a coup against this president?"

"Constantly. There are many 'facts' about the crimes our president and his closest advisors have allegedly committed. They're dark, Christopher. Grotesque, really."

Wren could imagine. "Any dates?"

"No dates, I'm afraid."

Wren worked the numbers. He envisioned terror cells spread across the country, embedded in biker gangs and militias, armed and ready to erupt. On a given date those cells would activate, priming the pump for mass insurrection. It wouldn't be the single attack on one piece of infrastructure that the FBI and CIA and all the other intelligence agencies were preparing for, but a distributed assault on the fabric of society itself.

It painted a convincing, terrifying picture, especially with tensions already at fever pitch across the country. Mistrust in the government had been bubbling away under the surface for years, and civil society was divided. It wouldn't take a lot, just a few dozen judicious sparks in the tinder keg to set America ablaze.

Wren rubbed his temple. He had to get this all to Humphreys and fast.

"Did you do any open Internet searches on this?" Wren asked.

"What? No. Should I?"

"No," Wren said swiftly. "I think these 'Saints' are watching the Internet. I don't know how, but they tracked some of my people to a house north of Chicago. They got shot and I barely escaped alive." He paused. "I don't want that for you."

Ferat was silent for a moment. "Yes, I saw your 'Megaphone shout'." More silence. There were clearly things Ferat wanted to say, unsaid. Wren had avoided becoming too friendly with any of his Foundation members. Certainly not with Dr. Ferat, though the man perhaps viewed him as a kind of surrogate son. In the last few years, those emotions had leaked out like lightning in a bottle.

Wren waited, but none of it escaped. "Thank you for the warning, Christopher. I'll let you know if I find more, and until then, I'll be careful."

"Thank you, Doctor," Wren said, then hung up and drove on.

29

FOREST

In two hours Wren reached Duluth, where he stopped at a downtown sporting goods store and picked up a hunting knife, belt sheath and flashlight, mags for the Beretta, black camo pants and a black camo hoodie to cover the bright pineapples on his T-shirt. The guy at the register didn't bat an eye.

It was getting dark by then, just past six and he'd been driving for five hours. He ate a hamburger and fries in a greasy diner then hit the road again, tearing up the coast of Lake Superior until he hit open country. Fields of low soy plants spread into darkness as the sun set.

Wren drove with the lights out, phone GPS open on the dash, counting the intersections as they went by, little roads meandering off into the wilderness. Soon enough the road crossed the old railway line. He pulled over and looked along the line of this strange gulley cut through the forest, now filled with low brush. A little over ten miles stretched out ahead, before it reached the woods near the camp.

Once under cover of the trees, there was no way they could stop him. He'd grown into a man in the woods, survived in the woods, killed his first wolf at fourteen years old in the woods under Tandrews' watchful eye.

He shut down the telltale light of the phone's GPS, pulled off the road and rolled down the slight embankment onto the old rail line.

The undergrowth made a constant rasping sound on the vehicle's underside, but the ride was smooth. Through the open windows he breathed in the scent of crushing sap, navigating by the broad band of stars in the northern sky; the W-shaped zags of Cassiopeia, the great K of Taurus, Lyra shaped like a hot water bottle.

Driving away from the lights of civilization felt like a return to an older, wilder past. The sky brightened as his eyes adjusted, casting the gulley in silvery, monochrome relief. It was hauntingly beautiful. It took him back to his early hunts with James Tandrews in the backwoods of Maine, after escaping his father's Arizona cult; hunting deer at night, fetching back the bodies and butchering them by firelight. It was those hunts that had enlivened him, bringing him back from the darkness inside his own mind. Out there he'd been 'Wren' before he'd ever even heard of the British architect who would become his namesake.

Christopher Wren. That had been his own delightful discovery. His first steps to truly owning himself.

"There's power in a name," Tandrews had said, sitting across from him over a fire with venison steak hissing on the spit. "It's how you reclaim who you are."

Miles ticked by on the odometer. At eleven and three tenths Wren squeezed the brakes and the Jeep slowed. He killed the engine then sat in silence for a moment, listening carefully to the forest.

Life returned swiftly, no longer overawed by the engine's rumble: bats swooping and screeching, opossum and bobcats rustling, birds calling mournful nighttime dirges, an owl hooting and cicadas scratching. It wasn't the same forest, wasn't even within a thousand miles of Tandrews' Maine training ground, but it felt like home.

He stepped out of the truck, and it felt like the last step from civilization into wildness. This was unknown territory. There was no backup team to accompany him, no CIA extraction helicopter on standby, only a knife at his waist and his wits.

The forest beckoned, and he strode into it.

Trees enveloped him in earthy dark. Wren stroked their rough skins, recognizing their profiles and scents: Jack Pine, Black Spruce, Tamarack. He knew instinctively the footing around each of them, the particular gnarled fingers they turned through the earth. As he pressed deeper the darkness thickened like a velvet cloak.

Wren moved swiftly, almost at a jog. His muscles felt loose and limber, shaking off the strain of the Viking's beatdown. At times he stopped to reference the GPS; ducking his head inside the hoodie, carefully curtaining the screen so as to spill no glow, taking a reading then continuing on.

For the last thirty minutes he approached more cautiously, measuring every step, moving in near-total silence and listening for the tell-tale sounds of other humans out there in the dark, scenting the air for gasoline, cigarettes, sweat. 'Saints'. They'd been waiting at the 'coven'. They'd beaten him to the warehouse, and to Price PD. There was every chance they'd be here too.

He came upon the camp from the southwest, where a long finger lake shone like rippling mercury under a clear, cloudless sky. Wren approached the water's edge and picked out a sinking dock at the northern side some two hundred yards away. Beyond that lay a clearing and the edge of a building; the main camp hall. No sign of people, but if they were proficient, there wouldn't be.

He backtracked until he crossed a trail. It was overgrown and crunchy with years of composting leaves. A light wind blew, rustling the branches overhead.

This was the place.

His vision tunneled down. His heart thumped, a hundred beats a minute up from its resting pace of sixty. He broke off the trail and flanked through the inky forest toward the rear of the hall. If there was anything left to find, it would be there.

30

CAMP

Wren advanced wrapped in the low sounds of the forest, until the trees gave way to a low bank of ferns. The hall was a log cabin structure, more dilapidated than he'd anticipated. Char marks of deep, silvery soot ran up its sides. The roof was missing in places. Beneath the two large windows lay heaps of wreckage, as if the building had vomited its contents onto the soil. A long ventilation duct poked up in the midst of broken chairs and charred wooden desktops like a strange periscope.

Wren crept closer through the ferns. Even after years of rain and sun he could smell the fire still. Another place burned down once it had been exposed. The Saints' MO.

From the back corner he peered across the open center of the camp, looking exactly as it had in the satellite image. To the right lay a dirt track leading to the cabins, ahead was the fire circle still picked out with benches, beyond that the tennis courts, then to the left was the lake.

There was no movement, no sound, no scent other than the natural flow of the forest. Wren waited until it felt right, then stood up. If a bullet was going to come it would come now, but none did. They might be near, might even be closing in, but there was nothing he could do about that now. He stalked swiftly down the front of the building and into darkness through the open door.

The interior instantly deadened all sound. In front of him was a narrow lobby coated in a dusty mantle of moonlight. The walls were scorched through in places, revealing dark, large rooms to either side.

Wren strode deeper, sweating now. The floor creaked and shifted. Above the door to the left was a sign painted onto the wall, and he picked out the fire-scarred word, 'Office'.

He stepped through into a black, hollow space. The walls were fringed with ashy metal desk frames and chairs, with all of the wood and padding material burned away. Cinders crunched underfoot, releasing a sour ashy must. His toe struck an obstruction, and in the darkness, he knelt down to feel its contours. Some kind of metal eyelet embedded in the wood. He worked two fingers through the hole and gave a yank; screwed in tight.

He patted the floor around it. The hardwood boarding was pocked with furrows. Each no deeper than a single knuckle, no longer than his index finger. There were dozens.

Wren looked up and tried to imagine the 'Office' as it might have been. At the head would be the boss' desk, maybe, with buddy-desks spread to either side and a central aisle left down the middle.

He padded down that imaginary aisle, occasionally reaching to either side and running his fingers through the ash to find more eyelets. More furrows. In a pool of moonlight he saw stains, blotchy like spilled ink.

By the front he was breathing harder. It all meant something. He knew what he'd find by the skeleton of a larger desk frame: a single eyelet where the manager would sit, a set of furrows, a stain in the wood. He checked anyway. He was right.

His head spun as he looked back on the ravaged room. Like a microcosm of the police department in Price, filled with dead officers.

He felt ill as the picture developed in his mind.

He went back to the lobby to the other open doorway. Here the word painted on the wall was unclear, mostly stripped by the heat of the fires, but he could guess at the missing letters.

School.

The room beyond was burned just like the office, though here the metal desk and chair frames were smaller, and many remained in their original positions, laid out in rows. At the front a blackboard leaned drunkenly against the wall, warped by the heat.

There were more eyelets, and furrows and stains, offering answers

Wren didn't want to find. He felt dizzy, standing in the middle of that abandoned space.

How many people had died here?

He thought of the homeless gathered up from Chicago. One hundred in one swoop, perhaps a hit every two weeks, and that was just one city. There were countless other places where forgotten humans could be snatched up. Brought to places like this and executed.

All that remained was the how, and now he could make a pretty good guess at their procedure. He imagined the school desks filled with Mason and Wendy and all the others, yanking at chains secured to the eyelets underneath until their wrists bled, trying to escape. Then the pièce de résistance, a reason that made sense of it all.

Bullets were fired into their bodies at point-blank range: running furrows into the wood; leaving stains that the fire baked in.

The homeless were fodder for training. Everything here was a live-fire exercise for active shooters.

Wren steadied himself against the wall. He'd done scenarios much like this many times throughout his Force Recon training. There were whole schools, churches, office buildings and homes set up in the training grounds, populated with both innocents and targets, played by actors. In their training raids he'd used paint balls or beanbag guns, blanks with laser tags to record hits, so nobody was hurt.

Not here. He imagined himself walking into this, a fighter with the army of the Order of the Saints, faced with chairs full of screaming, desperate victims. Tasked with starting a civil war across the nation, and this was his moment of truth.

Wren knew that the hardest thing to do in wartime was make soldiers fire at the enemy. It took incredible discipline and intensive training to overcome the average human's desire to not kill. Nations throughout history had come up with countless ways of overcoming that resistance. Some relied on drugs, some on inciting a deep and righteous patriotism, some on threatening their own troops with death. All of them dehumanized the enemy.

The Order of the Saints had taken that training to the end of the line, by making them kill in advance. They'd simulated the stress of the moment. Wren knew well that the first kill was the hardest. After that the ball was already rolling downhill. Momentum was on your side.

He caught himself on one knee. The dizziness had spread. His left temple and ear throbbed hotly. He took slow breaths.

A slaughter was coming.

Already these Saints had killed the Vikings, their own facilitators, because they'd become a liability. They'd wiped out the Price PD in the space of minutes.

This was where all that began, churning out a stream of amoral, mentally ruptured murderers, born in blood. And this place was already two years old. Wren's mind reeled. How many camps were there like this across the country? How many graduates? How many dead?

There was a sound. Barely audible. Wren straightened at once, instantly attuned to the forest outside.

Someone was coming.

31

LAKE

He ran and dived for the open window just as the raucous bark of rifle fire chewed up the night. He flew through the frame and for a moment was airborne and falling, glimpsing the glint of silver moonlight on the finger lake, then he hit the periscope vent on his left shoulder.

The metal crumpled, dropping him crunching into the heap of wreckage. Wild bullets raked the cabin wall in back, muzzle flashes blinked from afar and Wren rolled and ran.

Bullets whipped out of the dark as he raced low into the ferns, zagging an unpredictable path that set his thighs burning in seconds. He glimpsed more flashes through the underbrush; from across the lake, from the depths of the forest, from beyond the circle of benches around the fire.

They were everywhere, tightening in like a noose.

Wren dashed into the cover of trees and swerved right toward the lake, riding a blast of adrenaline that drove him on harder, until the side of his left thigh took a hit like a red hot iron poker slicing through the skin.

He gasped, stumbled and almost fell, shifting trajectory to stay upright. His left leg barely took his weight on the next step, and his mind spun fast calculations as he lurched over knotty roots: it had to be a flesh wound only, a glancing blow; a dead shot in the hamstring would have put him on the ground bleeding out right now, femur crushed to powder.

Still, it wasn't good. Red tinged his vision as he staggered to the waterline; adrenal wrath bulling through the pain of every step. He was not just another innocent victim to be ushered to the slaughter. He too had been born in blood, killing his way out of his childhood cult at twelve years old, breaker of some of the worst evil organizations in existence.

These wannabe school shooters didn't know the wasp they'd bottled. Rounds barked out ahead and Wren hurtled toward a man who was now swinging his rifle like a club. Wren ducked the blow and sent his hunting knife in an uppercut thrust into the man's chin, driving the blade up through his jaw, through the roof of his mouth and into his brain.

He dropped dead and Wren dived. There was an instant only to suck in a deep breath, then the lake water splashed cold around him, silt got in his eyes, and he was under and swimming. Powerful strokes raked him deeper down, his fingers grabbing at thick clumps of slimy pondweed in the lake's muddy base. He kept his eyes tight shut and swam on under the surface, navigating by feel as his lungs rapidly began to burn.

Thirty seconds, and the urge to suck in brackish pond water heaved within his chest. A minute, and silver lights danced behind his eyes as he swept his arms in a broad, churning crawl. A minute thirty? He had to be close to the middle of the lake now. His left leg cried out in pain, and the panicked drive to breathe became unendurable.

Thirty seconds more, he promised himself, but from a distance, as if he was whipping some other body to further extremes. Things disconnected. Two minutes? He thought of Tandrews holding out his hands, approaching this feral child in the desert, trying to save him.

"You're safe now," Tandrews had said, as if that was a thing he could promise. Safety was something you took for yourself. You made it with strength, and you took it from others, and that was the way of the world.

Now silver was everywhere. Close to blacking out, Wren rolled onto his back and let his lips alone break the surface, gasping in breath. No bullets came. He had to be out in the middle, hopefully invisible.

Ten breaths he allowed, each one deeper than the last. Through the thin sheen of water he tracked the sky, the constellations, and re-oriented his body slightly, bearing hard on Cassiopeia above the northern tail of the lake.

He had to hope he could get out, stagger clear, and go-
Where?

One answer came to mind. The only one that mattered now, when faced with an organization of such incredible strength. He wasn't going to bring the Saints down with just the Foundation.

He submerged again and swam straight, replaying the attack in his head. Maybe eleven discreet muzzle flashes in the darkness; a huge strike team responding with phenomenal speed.

At the north bank he surfaced as smoothly and silently as possible, like a snake out of the water with his fists tight in the weeds, keeping his head low, barely breathing. A voice called nearby, but no rifle fire followed.

The dark forest opened and beckoned him in. Rising to his feet, limping and in shock, he ran on.

32

COMING IN

A few minutes in a wave of dizziness brought Wren to his knees.

He reached for his left thigh and felt the torn jeans and wound, like a slice across the side of his quadriceps muscle. The bone underneath was solid, the muscle not too badly compromised, but he was still losing blood.

He pulled off the wet hoodie, wrapped it around his thigh and knotted it tight over the wound. It hurt like hell.

Voices came from behind. Flashlights flickered through the trees, and he pushed himself back to his feet. His options were narrowing with every passing second. If they hadn't found his trail yet, they soon would, dragging one leg behind him, scratching up a path through the carpet of pine needles.

His fingers dug numbly into his pocket, prizing out the phone. Lights sparkled over his shoulder as he pushed the power button. The screen scrambled to life in a rainbow of waterlogged colors, and Wren almost laughed.

Always he'd prided himself on his strength, the umbrella of protection he offered to others, but he'd never lied to himself about how dependent he truly was. He'd survived his childhood cult, but without Tandrews' help he might have become a very different man; maybe desperate like Eustace, twisted like Teddy and Cheryl, too violent like Henry and Abdul. The coin system gave him the same thing it gave them, an anchor in a world that never wanted him.

The truth was, he needed help just like everyone else.

He squeezed the phone's screen as if he could throttle a last spark of life out of it, and somehow that did the job. The kaleidoscope of colors narrowed down to a usable band of screen. He huddled it close to his chest, hiding its light.

One bar of reception.

It wasn't swallowing pride, because what shame was there in admitting you'd been shot and were close to death? Sometimes it was just time to come in from the cold, no matter what you'd done.

With stiff fingers he dialed Humphreys' direct number. Long seconds passed and voices came closer in the dark, then there was a click.

"Hello?" he whispered.

"I'm here, Wren," came Humphreys' baritone. He sounded weary. "We're tired of this game. It won't be me answering the next time. I'll be the one slapping cuffs on you and escorting you into the darkness. You're never coming back up after this."

It took Wren a moment to catch up with what Humphreys was saying. He sounded very far away. "What?"

"The Order of the Saints? It doesn't exist, Wren. The only group we know of, with substantial membership and no known objective, is your own. You're gloating. We've run all the records on your assassin. He doesn't exist. As for Theodore Smithely III and Cheryl Derringer? They're connected to nothing, except perhaps your investigation into the Ripper Crew copycats. Is that how you recruited your 'Foundation', Wren? Piggybacking for vulnerable people on FBI investigations? It's disgusting."

Wren couldn't listen to that. "I've been shot," he managed. "You have my location? Maybe a mile north of a camp that once belonged to the Order of the Saints, seven miles west of Silver Creek, Minnesota. Do you have me, Humphreys?"

Now Humphreys sounded confused. "Yes, we have you. But what do you mean, you've been shot?"

"I'm hunting the Order. Or they're hunting me." He barely stopped a high note of laughter edging through. "I've seen what they were doing here, Humphreys. Taking homeless people and using them as live-fire training. They had one hall set up like a school, the other like an office, with the

148

victims chained down when they let their shooters in. They're training their people to kill without hesitation, and this was from two years back."

Humphreys said nothing. Perhaps the signal had gone.

"Did you hear me? It's the preparation for civil war, like in the pamphlet I sent you. They're priming the pump. They're-" he trailed off, losing his sense of the sentence in the dark of the forest. "They're trying to kill a lot of people. Lots of people. Lots of places. No one target, no one date. It's coming. I've got a-"

He stopped as a flashlight briefly shone in front of him, splashing through the trees and away. Had it seen him? He stumbled on.

"I'm working a lead on them. I'll share it. Where they've been taking the homeless, from CCTV in Chicago. My people are tracking them. It isn't me, Humphreys. Tell my wife that. Tell Tandrews. It isn't me."

Another pause, then Humphreys came back. "Are you in danger?"

Wren felt giddy. The voices were closing in. "If you could have the Army send an evac helicopter to my location right now, that would be a big help. I'd appreciate it."

"I can arrange that."

Wren laughed, feeling lightheaded as more flashlights danced around him like beams from a disco ball. He dropped to his knees then laid down flat on the pine needles. He'd be harder to see that way, buying a few more seconds.

"Thanks," said Wren. "I'll send you what I have." He rang off and tapped buttons with numb fingers, opening his Foundation darknet. The screen loaded. For a second Wren stared, not taking it in, before realizing fresh information had finally come in.

The results from his CCTV tracking out of Chicago, finally. The file was headlined 'Omaha.' He didn't have time to open it, just dumped it into an email addressed to Humphreys. There was another file, something from Ferat, and he attached that too.

Send.

Was that the sound of a helicopter coming? He looked up through the thick canopy of trees and picked out a narrow river of stars winding across the sky. He'd seen these same skies as a child when he hadn't known a thing; not who he was, not what he was heading toward, not what he'd run from.

Did he know better now?

Flashlights came closer. He pulled the phone battery out and threw the pieces as far as he could. They'd never find them in the dark.

A voice shouted.

"He's here!"

Boots stamped over. Wren watched the first of them come in as his mind drifted back over the last four weeks.

"Loralei?" he asked, reaching up to the light. "Is that you?"

Hands reached down. Had she come for him, had she finally forgiven him? Strong hands scooped him up and carried him through the darkness, to where his family would be waiting. His kids, Jake and Quinn. Then a hand closed around his throat and squeezed, ushering him through the black door into nothing.

33

BLACK SITE

Wren came back to consciousness in a chair, Loralei's name on his lips. It came out a croak, and numb.

She wasn't there. Just a dream of better days; their early dates around New York, back when he hadn't needed to lie, and she'd loved him anyway.

Now he was naked and cold in a white cell maybe fifteen feet square, surrounded by mirrors and bright light. Music pounded in and he jerked to get free, but his wrists and ankles were strapped with tight leather buckles to a bolted-down metal chair. His left leg was wrapped in bandages and there were strips of gauze taped to various wounds on his chest and arms.

He managed a snort. Not Loralei. Not Humphreys.

The Order of the Saints.

Flashes of a trip in a truck came back to him, more dream than reality. Figures in surgical masks leaning in, digging into his thigh. A drip tube into his wrist. Figures talking about someone called 'Alpha'.

The Saints had him. A cold thrill of fear ran up his bare spine and he went very still, looking into the mirrored walls where his tattoos screamed back at him. Loralei. Quinn. Jake.

No escaping the past, even here. His failures followed everywhere he went.

The music thumped hard in his ears, 80s candy pop. This was enhanced interrogation technique 101. Sleep deprivation was banned by the European Court of Human Rights in 2014, along with waterboarding, humiliation and stress positions, but what did that mean to these people?

The Order of the Saints. Cold reality settled on him. He knew what they were capable of now. Images from the camp flashed in his head: eyelets, stains and bullet furrows. He could imagine Mason and Wendy being forced through that brutal system. Victims or perpetrators? It was sickening. Same for the woman he'd seen outside the Price warehouse. All those homeless from Chicago, and God knew how many hundreds, even thousands more.

His head spun with the scale of it.

Now he was in that system too, almost certainly facing torture. He'd been tortured before, enough to know that everybody broke in the end. The only way through was to turn the tables.

Wren gazed into the mirrored glass. How was he going to turn these tables?

The pounding music made thinking hard. He needed information, but he had few clues about where he was, though the room itself was a clue: a specialized space designed for interrogations. There'd been nothing like it in the Utah warehouse. Most likely they had only one or two such facilities across the whole organization.

Did that make this the headquarters?

Wren ran the numbers; hours he'd likely been out, judging from the redness of fresh scratches on his chest and the distance he could have been transported in that time. Not long. Chicago? It was possible, but unlikely. The strike team had been waiting for him at the camp. There was no easy way they could have beaten him there in a head-to-head race north. Instead that suggested local forces, en masse.

So Minneapolis? The tracking data Wren had sent through had been headlined Omaha. That meant no help was coming to him here.

The cold seeped into him and he shuddered. The volume of the pop song ramped up, then the door opened, and intense white light flooded in, momentarily blinding him as two figures came through.

It was about the worst thing he'd feared.

34

SINCLAIR

Abdul.

He stumbled in naked and gagged with his hands bound behind him. He was ashen, with a blood-soaked bandage on his stomach and his left eye swollen with bruising, though his right eye shot Wren a fierce glare.

Not broken yet.

A woman came in beside him, tall and beautiful with pale skin, green eyes and blond hair. She wore a tight-fitting navy suit and had a neat oblong brand scar on her throat. Her outsized breasts looked to be mounted on a shelf, jutting proudly through her tight blazer. Her skirt was cut short, revealing acres of muscular thigh. Humiliation through arousal: it was right there in the intelligence handbooks. Dominate then take away the subject's manhood.

Wren only had eyes for Abdul. "You're alive."

Abdul's eye flared.

Two large men followed them in, each wearing tactical black suits and carrying rifles. Their faces were marked by more of the oblong brand scars, evidence of some kind of cult rite. They shoved Abdul roughly to his knees.

He kneeled, but still he stared at Wren defiantly, as if challenging him to find fault with his conduct. Wren couldn't find any. Where was Henry?

Something in Abdul's defiant glare told him he'd gotten away. Wren could picture a shootout on the hills in Price. Abdul laying down covering fire to save his brother in arms.

The pounding music stopped abruptly, leaving a silence broken by labored breathing. The branded men attached Abdul's bound wrists to an eyelet in the floor, just like the ones at the camp. The woman gave a signal and the soldiers jogged out, leaving her on her own.

A display of power. Standing beside Abdul, she leaned over sharply at the waist, displaying deep cleavage while she maintained eye contact, sliding a stiletto knife from an ankle holster.

"My name is Sinclair," she said in a laconic, Ivy-league-educated voice. "I'm going to ask you some questions, and you're going to answer. Simple."

Wren said nothing, adding every scrap of data to his working hypotheses. She had the look of upper management. That reinforced the idea this place was an important hub.

She leaned over and trailed the blade lightly over Abdul's bare shoulders, then passed it across to run over his scalp. He weaved in place. Thoughts of escape were clearly far from his mind. At this point he was just trying to breathe.

"Hurt him and I'll kill you," Wren said. "There'll be no mercy for you or any Saint."

Sinclair raised an eyebrow. "I've already hurt him. I've been doing it for nearly two days. But if you insist on a demonstration." She pulled the knife back then swung it in handle first, cracking Abdul in the back of the head.

He jerked then flopped forward, unconscious, only held up by his bonds cinched to the eyelet. Sinclair looked at Wren as if nothing had happened.

"We know who you are. Christopher Wren. The CIA's wild child, known as 'Saint Justice'. The most number of terrorists taken out by any agent. And a child of the Pyramid."

His eyes widened and she drank it down. He'd told them his name himself, but that she knew his CIA reputation, and his childhood in the Pyramid? He'd done everything possible to erase the paper trail linking them together.

"Yes, we know all about the Pyramid," she said dismissively. "And about your Foundation. We know he's one of yours." She nudged Abdul's thigh with her foot. "We found a three-year coin in his pocket. It's an interesting system, one we might adapt in the future. Easier than brands."

She stroked her fingers down the brand scar on her throat. By her side Abdul's labored breath wheezed in and out. Wren knew where this was going. Only one way it could possibly go, from the moment he'd seen Abdul with that gunshot wound.

It sparked a well of fury in his gut. Now he channeled that anger at Sinclair. "Kill this man, there'll be no coin system for you or your organization. I'll see every one of your Saints burn in hell, just like the Pyramid."

Sinclair smiled; impressive in itself. She must have run through their live fire exercises many times, steeling herself to violence. You only got this stone-cold with extensive practice. "That's a threat with no incentive. You're supposed to be a master of human drives. Where's my reward to let you go, or go easy on him?"

Wren saw the amusement in her eyes. She wasn't worried at all. That was either well-earned confidence or complacency. He had to make it the latter.

"What did you expect?" he asked. "I'm a traitor to the cause after all, aren't I?"

She laughed. "Are you? I think you'd have to adopt a creed to betray it, and we both know you're a lawless vigilante, working for the CIA by convenience alone. You wanted to kill people. They let you." She took a step closer. "We can use a man like that. You're a resource to be mined, and we're rather good at mining. So tell me, why have you been hunting us?"

Wren said nothing. She approached and placed the blade lightly on his chest.

"You should answer me, Christopher Wren. You're an intelligent man. With enough brands to overwrite your sins, the Order might even admit you. A fresh Saint for the war."

He snorted. "Sign me up."

She leaned closer. The scent of her was strong now, perfume and sweat. Adrenaline brought out the primitive sex pheromones more than anything. Arousal was a state tied up with so many other emotions. Wren had no interest in her but couldn't help his body's automatic responses.

"We can do that," she said, lowering her voice to a husky burr. "Save Abdul. Save Alli too."

He tried to keep himself from flinching at Alli's name, but couldn't stop his eyes bugging. Sinclair saw it, then pressed the blade firmly against his throat and leaned in to lick his cheek. A long, wet streak. Her tongue was hot. He forced himself not to flinch this time.

With sinuous ease she slotted her long legs through the chair's arm loops, sinking down to sit astride his naked thighs. Her skirt rode up and her heat blushed against his bare skin as she leaned in closer, whispering in his ear as the knife dug into his neck.

"We haven't started on her yet. But we will. Abdul first, then Alli."

She pressed so closer her bulging chest crushed against his, her hot stomach touching his bare ribs. He flushed, unable to stop it. She was hot and lithe. She had all the power. Their faces were an inch apart now, generating their own heat. She gazed into his eyes like a lover.

"I find you disgusting," she said softly. "Your desperate desire to please your masters, your wife, your past. The way you prostrate yourself before them all. A man of your talents should fell the King and take his place, not crawl on his belly like a snake. See."

She leaned her head back, showing her vulnerability. In any other setting he would headbutt her trachea, but the knife between them prevented that. Power. Instead he looked at her neck where the single oblong brand flickered with every beat of her carotid artery. It showed three words marked in raised white lines.

SIC SEMPER TYRANNIS

The famous words John Wilkes Booth shouted after he shot Lincoln; a rallying cry to tear down tyrants and install something better in their place.

"Kiss it," she whispered, and squirmed forward like a cheap stripper, pressing her neck to his lips as the knife dug into his throat. He felt his life hanging in the balance; a quarter-inch deep and she'd sever his jugular.

It was a textbook tactic. Threaten extreme but ask for the smallest act of betrayal, an act the victim might even want to do. She was a beautiful woman, why wouldn't he want to kiss her throat? Why wouldn't he want to save himself, for just this tiny price?

"Kiss it," she repeated, her left hand now tightening painfully in his hair, drawing him against the knife, his face pressing hard into the supple flesh of her throat. With one bite he could kill her now, but then he'd be dead too. A queen for a king, and he would lose. His organization would lose.

Better to cede the pawn.

He kissed. She pulled back at once and slapped him hard.

His head spun to the side. In that moment of disorientation, she climbed off his lap and moved to stand behind Abdul, holding his head back to bare his throat. His eyes were open again and he was looking at Wren with a faint kind of wonder. Yes, Wren thought, probably that was the real purpose here. Doubtless they were filming this. They would show this betrayal to Alli, trying to break his organization right now, to show him as a craven man and shatter their loyalty.

Sinclair put her knife to Abdul's throat and Wren's mind raced. This was a game he couldn't win. Sinclair controlled the frame, and he couldn't compete with the rules she'd laid out.

"Tell me who you're working with at your Foundation," she said. The blade drew a slim line of blood. "Tell me now, their names, their stations, and how much they know, or you're killing another follower."

Abdul stared at Wren, jutting his chin out. That showed he understood the choice Wren faced. Sacrifice Abdul or give up the Foundation. A wrenching decision, but Abdul had already made it, and Wren had only one thing left to offer him as thanks.

"Coin ten," he said.

The smallest smile quirked at the edge of Abdul's mouth.

"What did you just tell him?" Sinclair demanded.

Wren turned his attention to her. "I just told him he's safe. You'll never get anything from me if you kill him."

She frowned. "So you think that makes him safe?"

Wren just looked at her. She was so sure she had all the power, but nothing changed the game faster than a man with nothing to lose. When you couldn't win, you stuck the blade in their eye as far as you could, and Abdul understood that. Brazen it out like a hussy and try to break the frame.

"You don't get it," he said. "Safe from me."

The frown deepened. "You're serious. What can you possibly do to him?"

Now it was his turn to smile. Now she was asking the questions that would help him switch this thing around. "You're not the leader of this two-bit cult, are you? A leader would know. This man already told me everything I needed to know the minute he walked in. He made his choice on that hilltop on Price; a sacrifice to save his brother. How do you think he'd like me now if I threw that sacrifice away?"

There was the light of pride in Abdul's eyes. Wren went on faster. "This is what you people don't get. It's not about loyalty to some rabid tyrant. It's loyalty to decency. To good people. I'm proud of him, and I hope he's proud of me, and there's nothing you can do to take that away. I'll not forsake his choices."

Sinclair just stared. Maybe starting to understand. Gone completely cold.

"Consider him forsaken," she said, and slit the knife sideways across Abdul's throat. His eyes widened. His blood poured out.

Wren felt it like a knife in his guts, but he still glared at Sinclair, because this was all part of the war. It was a defeat for him and a victory for her, but it was hollow. One man was dead, but Wren's Foundation still stood. He hadn't answered her questions. Any videotape of this exchange designed to break Alli would now do the opposite.

"I love this man," Wren said, hoping Abdul would hear before he died. "I love him because he wanted to be better than the man he was. Every member of my Foundation is the same, including me. There's no tyrant. We're all trying to get better, and I couldn't think of a braver, more selfless way to die than protecting that. I'm proud of him. I think I'm going to name a coin reward after him."

Sinclair stared, then dropped the knife. "We'll see," she said, and strode out.

Wren was left alone with Abdul, staring up at him from empty eyes.

35

PYRAMID

It stayed cold. The music came back on. The lights began to flash in unpredictable, maddening patterns.

Abdul lay dead on the floor.

Wren felt sick.

Abdul had made his choice, but it was on Wren's orders. He'd sent him to that hilltop in Price. He'd underestimated the power of the Saints from the start, and now Alli was next. On top of all that, they knew about his childhood cult, the Pyramid.

He shuddered in the cold, but closed his eyes and worked to regulate his breathing and enter a meditative state. Steadily he brought his heart rate down and calmed the shivering, until the pounding beat and flashing lights seemed very far away.

He had to think, had to turn the tables before anyone else died.

Minneapolis.

That was a starting point. A guess, but solid enough. Near the camp, about as close as the Utah warehouse was to Salt Lake City was for. A training/storage warehouse within a few hours range of a major city. He thought back on all those boxes in the warehouse, stuffed full of food and baby formula, implying plenty of homeless grabs still ahead. Seemed the Order were still months if not years away from the start of their civil war. If anything they were undergoing expansion, enlarging their base of Saints and the scale of their war.

He barely noticed when the flashing lights and music stopped.

The first punch took him square on the forehead. He opened his eyes and did his best to roll with the second blow as it cracked into his jaw.

The strikes hurt but he put that aside. Now a large golden-skinned man stood by the door, watching with a curious expression. He wore a white button-down shirt open at the neck, dark slacks and wingtip black shoes. Every inch of him was perfectly coiffed, with a rakish side-part in his dense blond hair, a slender nose, strange blue eyes and a square jaw. His skin was a deep, burnished bronze. There was no brand scar on his face or neck. He had to be early thirties, still carrying the effortless vigor of youth in thick arms and a broad chest.

The guy punching Wren was younger, and there was something familiar about him. His mottled face was a mass of scar tissue from SIC SEMPER TYRANNIS brands, peaking in a crown of thorny white knots in the skin around his scalp. Images of a similar image ran through his mind, a young Marine with scars from shrapnel and surgery, and he almost laughed.

Could it be?

Mason?

Another punch came in that flipped his head back. The golden-skinned man took a step forward.

"It will go poorly for you now," he said in a rich, confident baritone. It was the kind of voice you expected to hear headlining a self-help seminar: in control, intelligent, throbbing with confidence. "We'll take you apart, Christopher Wren, like we've done many times before. It's a process. You understand."

Wren hawked and spat blood, struggling not to gasp for breath. "I understand *you*."

"Do you?" The man sounded curious. "Tell me."

Wren's mind thrummed. This man had the look of a cult leader, and the best cult executions began at the top. Time to swing for the fences. "I know you're from here. Minneapolis. It's a poor choice for a headquarters: too far north, too few cities to snatch from and nothing to the west but the sprawling Dakotas. You'd have been better off choosing Chicago or Indianapolis for your base. Too damn cold. But you didn't, because this is home."

The man's odd blue eyes flickered for a moment. A hit.

"Guesswork," he said. "And wrong."

"Not wrong," Wren sped on. "I've got you all mapped out. Your lieutenant Sinclair wanted to know about my Foundation? They're coming as we speak, rolling your organization up, along with the CIA and all the King's horses. You should run while you can, maybe emigrate to Canada. We're close to the border up here. But we do have extradition." He sucked air through his teeth. "Tough break. They'll follow you there. I'll follow too."

The golden man gave a nod, and the boxer hit Wren hard in the gut. He coasted for seconds on the edge of choking.

"Empty threats," the man said. "Parlor tricks. I know you're not operating under CIA direction or with CIA information. They're hunting you, not me. Your director, Gerald Humphreys, has had an inter-agency alert on you for three weeks, ever since you went AWOL after your 'resignation' in New York. They don't know where you are or where we are. They are blind. And as for your Foundation?" He gestured to Abdul by his feet.

Now Wren smiled, getting control of his breathing. "So you Googled me after all."

"What a record you have."

"I'll bet it's nothing compared to yours," Wren went on. He'd opened a crack in the man's façade and now needed to lever it wide. "'Lead a civil war' makes for interesting work experience."

"Who said I'm leading it?" the man asked, but there was amusement in his eyes, and that confirmed it for Wren. The pleasure. All cult leaders got high on power. Even if it wasn't what they'd sought at the start, they soon became addicted to it.

"I say you are." Wren flashed on a throwaway snatch of dialogue from the strike. "You're the Alpha, exercising control over life and death. The brands are just one sign of that. I see them on your boy here, I guess he resisted?" He nodded at the mutilated boxer. Mason. "Even Sinclair had one. I notice you don't, though."

"Not on my face."

Wren laughed mockingly. "That's solidarity. You wanted to feel the pain but without the drawbacks. Difficult to find gainful employment with a face brand."

The Alpha's expression smoothed out, showing no pleasure now. That was better. That was a defensive position, which gave Wren the advantage. "In truth you're just another junkie," he pressed, "like all the cult leaders who went before you. More power, more adulation, more love." He spat another mouthful of blood. "Are you having sex with them all yet?" He looked at the boxer, maybe Mason, and nodded to the 'Alpha'. "Is he? It'll come. And the civil war? You can't gratify a junkie better than that. People dying on your command is one hell of a trip. People killing for you? That's the greatest thrill there is."

The Alpha's face remained flat and unimpressed.

"You never thought it would grow this large," Wren went on, "I understand that, but things got out of control and you couldn't back down. So let's talk about what happens after the war. Say you overthrow the government and rewrite the Constitution. You get your glowing picture in every schoolhouse, post office, police station. Last comes indoctrination, gulags for protesters, re-education and a war of global expansion. Is that about right?"

Still nothing. The guy had a great poker face, impossible to cold read. "It's a well-worn track," Wren said. "But at some point, you start to lose them, and you can't bear that. You break out the poison Kool Aid, like in Jonestown." He smiled. "It always goes that way in the end. Junkies can't help themselves. Once you've killed your first million, how can you settle for less? You need the obedience, you need the proof of selfless love, and there's no better proof than mass suicide." He took a breath. "Seems you know I was with the Pyramid, so you know I'm speaking from experience. My suggestion is, why not jump straight to the big finale, with you at the front of the line?"

The Alpha's jaw set tight. "Pop psychology. I could go to a fortune teller in the street and get much the same. I'd expected more from the great Christopher Wren. Surely the Pyramid taught you better?"

Wren snorted. There he went with the Pyramid again. "So you asked around, figured out something about my past."

The Alpha leaned in. On the attack now. "I didn't need to, Christopher. Imagine my surprise. I already had the inside line."

Wren frowned. "Bullshit. There is no inside line to the Pyramid. There were no survivors; they all burned themselves alive with home-brew napalm. The town's a wreck; there's nothing left."

Except perhaps that wasn't completely true. There'd been one body never accounted for…

The Alpha grinned. "Not bullshit. Your father survived, Apex of the Pyramid. And yes, before you ask, I've met him, though you needn't take my word for it. I've sent him the news that you're here. He was very interested; I can tell you that."

"You're lying," Wren spat, heart rate instantly spiking above a hundred beats a minute. The old terror never went away. "He's dead. You never met him."

The grin faded from the Apex's face, and he grew ominously sincere. "No? You think I don't know you, Christopher Wren? Or should I call you by your Pyramid name, Pequeño 3?" He paused for a moment, drinking in Wren's reaction. "It doesn't quite trip off the tongue. And the things he did to you, the things he made you do? I read everything I could find on the Federal record, not much I agree, but the truth was so much better, heard direct from your father. He's quite the storyteller." He paused again, blue eyes digging into Wren. "Where does that put your profile of me now?"

It left Wren reeling. Inside he came unmoored.

Pequeño 3.

Not even James Tandrews had known his Pyramid name. He hadn't heard it spoken anywhere for twenty-five years, hadn't told a soul since he was that twelve-year-old in his father's desert death cult, but he'd never stopped searching for the man who gave it to him.

The Apex.

Now the Alpha's eyes gleamed. Wren could feel he was losing the exchange. It didn't matter that no questions had been asked, that he'd spilled nothing of value; he'd just spilled everything with his silence. It showed his weakness, the key to who he was. This man knew him better than he knew himself.

"It appears I've given you something to think about. Let's see if we can't drum that in."

The Alpha turned to leave, and the boxer's next blow his Wren in the belly again, blowing the air out of his lungs.

36

BEATING

The beating came and went in stages. Sometimes a disorienting slap across the ear. A punch to the sternum. A kick into his thigh. The young man with the scars moved around him constantly, looking for weakness.

Just when Wren thought he had the tempo of it, that tempo changed, sometimes interspersed with long minutes of agonizing tension. Wren tried to push thoughts of the Pyramid and his father to one side, studying the young man when he could.

Oblong brand marks had ruined his fair face. They all said the same thing. SIC SEMPER TYRANNIS. Through stamping the message in, they transformed the man. More blows came, but Wren barely noticed. The words stinging inside his head were far worse.

Pequeño 3.

There'd been dozens of Pequeños in the Pyramid's heyday. In beat-down cabins in the desert wilds of Arizona, isolated from the world, completely at his father's mercy.

Apex of the Pyramid. Wren's father. Leader of America's worst death cult in history. He'd considered all his followers to be his personal possessions. If ever there'd been a tyrant, it was him.

Little Christopher Wren, then known as Pequeño 3, had been born into that tyrant's brutal domain. Born into a cage and raised to believe, alongside his brothers and sisters and the Pyramid one thousand.

With each punch and slap more memories shook loose. They'd all done terrible things, at the Apex's command: dunking disobedient followers in the boiling vats; digging pits in the desert to test the belief of the faithful; framing the cages that served as gibbets for those who'd failed to appease their father's whims...

Another hit dragged Wren back into the moment. It wasn't the strength of the blow, this time, but something else. If anything, it was the weakness.

The hits were coming softer. He blinked back sweat, blood and memories to focus on the boxer. He was stalking and staring at Wren with such intense eyes from that wreck of a face.

So why pull his punches? He didn't look tired, wasn't even short of breath. Something else was going on behind those furious eyes.

Time to play the trick card.

"Mason?" Wren said.

The next punch came with some sting behind it.

Wren righted himself. That seemed like confirmation. It wasn't just the man's face that was different from his Marine ID, though. It was his eyes and his whole bearing. Felipe back in the Chicago convenience store had described him as a simple man lit only by love for his girl, Wendy.

Now there was the light of a different purpose in his eyes, much like the madness of the Pyramid faithful.

Another hit came, harder still, and Wren tried to picture what he'd been through; enough to make a loyal Marine flip on his creed and his country, escape the homeless fodder line and become a Saint himself. The brands went some way to explain it, but not enough. That kind of torture could break even a Marine, but twist his loyalty so completely?

Wren didn't think so. If he was the Alpha, he'd have used something else, and it didn't take him long to land on it.

"Where's Wendy?" he asked.

The effect was immediate. Mason froze.

That answered the question and raised a dozen more.

"She's here, isn't she?" Wren tried. "They've got her chained up somewhere. They're blackmailing you."

Another hit came then, spinning his head and splashing stars across his vision. Full strength, maybe the hardest yet. Wren couldn't take too many more of those. He blinked and refocused. Mason's eyes were furious, but why? Because he'd guessed right, or because he hadn't?

"Not chained up," Wren guessed, reading Mason's eyes like an open book. "But she was here, wasn't she? Is she even alive?"

Another hard hit, and Wren glimpsed the shape of it. The live-fire exercises. How he'd do it, if he wanted not only to break a Marine, but to shift his whole system of loyalty and belief. Shared guilt formed some of the strongest, sickest bonds.

"You killed her."

Mason shook once, like a ghost had run icy fingers up his spine. And there it was. To really break a man, you had to make him complicit.

Wren's mind whirred. There was the urban myth about Hitler's SS, given a puppy to raise which they then had to kill to become an elite soldier. Not true, but the psychology was real. Make someone commit to an ideology far enough to kill, and they were yours. After that they'd do everything they could to make that ideology real, because if it wasn't real, then they were actually an evil person and nothing they'd done could be justified. It became self-protection.

Wren gamed it out. The Saints would have framed it all wrong. Brainwashed Mason. Tortured him. Kept on working on him until he was thinking along dark new lines of loyalty that made him believe his only choice was to kill Wendy.

Make her into a traitor. Make him into a hero.

That could have this effect. Break a Marine all the way. Strip him of everything. The dozens of SIC SEMPER TYRANNIS brands proved it. Mason had resisted them for as long as he could.

So Wendy was dead.

"They made you do it," Wren said. "Brainwashed you. And you killed her."

Now Mason unloaded a flurry of blows. Wren rolled them easily, the fury too predictable. Mason kept on until he was panting hard, chest heaving.

"You don't know me," he said at last, the words coming slow and thick, then he stamped out before Wren could say anything more.

He was left alone. Blood drooled through his lips. His own battered visage mocked him in the mirror, throwing back his own failures echoed in the names tattooed on his chest, not so unlike the brands covering Mason's face.

37

ALLI

Wren surfed the pain like a man drowning, seeking some firm place to grasp. Memories from three weeks earlier tumbled through his head: quitting the CIA, surrendering his Foundation, heading home full of hope about putting his family first.

It had all gone wrong.

Now he glimpsed those moments stretching back through time like links in a chain. His dreams were crushed under the weight of his choices, and his choices were determined by the trials of his past. He couldn't escape it.

Flashes of those days in the desert cult rose up around him, twelve years old and doing awful things to survive, back when he'd gone by only 'Pequeño 3'. He could still feel the sting of his father's lash on his back, the cries of his brothers and sisters all around, the hot Arizona sun scalding his cheeks, the hard leather lash handle placed in his own palm...

All links in the chain of who he was. You couldn't escape the past. Everybody needed help. Mason. Wendy.

Christopher Wren.

At some point the door opened. The Alpha, Sinclair, Mason and one other came in. Wren saw her face and wanted to die. Things could always get worse.

Alli.

The last time he'd seen her had been by the roadside in Utah, handing off the Viking bikes. Now she stared at Wren with the same defiance Abdul had shown. One of her tight blond topknots had come undone, trailing straggling hairs across her face that only made her more fearsome to behold. She saw the body on the floor and spat.

"I'll sell this bastard out," she snapped, nodding toward Wren. "Just tell me what you want, I'll cough it all up. Coin three my ass."

Wren couldn't help a smile creeping through the pain. In the mirror it was near invisible, but Alli saw it. She was stubborn and would be a tough nut to crack.

Mason kicked out her knees, hooked her wrists into an eyelet beside Abdul's slack body, then circled behind Wren. Their eyes connected briefly, and something flashed between them. The Alpha took up position beside Abdul, watching everything. Sinclair stood behind Alli; knife drawn.

The Alpha spoke, but Wren ignored him. Something was different. Even in the depths of his despair, he could feel it in the air. Any torture handbook would suggest he be left to stew for long hours, deprived of sleep, food and water, but not that much time had passed, an hour or two at most. Something had happened to shift the calculus and bring this on early.

With their stern faces and show of force they were giving him the play.

"The first raid came," he guessed, interrupting the Alpha. The hit landed, as the Alpha's eyes sharpened at once. Sinclair drew her knife. "The CIA hit one of your training centers."

"More guesswork," the Alpha dismissed, recovering quickly, but Wren had seen it. "P. T. Barnum would be proud. But you don't know anything."

"Then why torture me anymore?" Wren countered. His lips and tongue were numb, but his brain felt like it had been jump-started by the possibility he was right. Maybe Humphreys really was coming. He'd got the message Wren had sent from the woods. Omaha. "If I know nothing, why waste your time?"

The Alpha showed a brief glint of annoyance, then inclined his head, and Sinclair pressed her knife to the top of Alli's right ear.

"Bitch, you do not want to try cutting off my ear!" Alli snapped.

"Hurt her and I won't tell you where they're hitting next," Wren said quickly. Alli's eyes blazed at his betrayal, as if he doubted her ability to handle a little pain, but he ignored that.

"Will you tell me if I don't?" the Alpha asked casually. "I killed one of your men already, you knew I had this girl, and still you haven't said a worthwhile thing."

"Sinclair killed him," Wren corrected.

"You're parsing a nothing. Sinclair is an extension of my will. Whomever she kills, they were killed by me."

Wren snorted. Here was another opening. Cult leaders were ridiculous figures, if you dared to point it out. Their self-importance was a ball of hot gas. "And the brands, are they an extension too? Is that why you don't have any on display? So Mason's face is an extension of your own?"

Another chink of annoyance shone through, not least because Wren knew Mason's name. The Alpha would have to assume Mason had told him, and that started tearing a gulf. He responded the only way he knew, and nodded to Sinclair, who began to saw the knife down through the cartilage of Alli's ear. Alli sucked in a sharp breath.

"Omaha," Wren said.

The cutting stopped at once. Sinclair looked up as blood rolled onto Alli's shoulder. The Alpha's gaze bored into him.

"How do you know that?" he asked, cold now.

Wren had been holding onto it. Abdul had died because the information then wouldn't have saved him. Only now, after the raid had come and the Saints were spooked, did it give Wren any authority, and put the rightful fear of Uncle Sam into the Alpha.

"I told you earlier, they're rolling you up," Wren said, feigning confidence. "It's a pattern at my direction, because I've got a Foundation mole in your Saints, loyal to me." A gasp came from Sinclair. Buying the bluff wholesale. "They've been feeding me information for months. Why do you think I started in Utah? So I could take as much as possible where you were just starting to expand, before the CIA took the rest. I promise you; more hits are coming."

All of that struck hard, but he knew it wouldn't be enough. At this point everything he'd said could still be a guess. There was no guarantee the CIA had further leads, or that any more strikes would come, so he couldn't just wait to be saved. He needed something more to convince the Alpha.

He spun a map of the States in his head, trying to sketch out an expansion plan the Order might have followed. From Minneapolis it was natural to head west and south, away from the east coast and its diverse cities. Ferat had said something about this, an organization knitting together

170

existing gangs. The Utah expansion suggested a more refined MO: using biker gangs to grease the wheels of local law enforcement and keep the Saints invisible.

So Chicago to Omaha to Salt Lake City made up one western arm. Along that route there was the processing warehouse Wren had busted open near Emery, plus some kind of troop center near the Price PD. He could throw out Salt Lake as the likely next CIA strike site, but that wouldn't impress the Alpha; probably the Saints there had already scrambled out.

He swung his focus to the south, where there were deep resentments to tap into, instilled since the first Civil War and ripe for reopening. He tried to get into the Alpha's head; cities sprang up and dropped out of his searchlight beam. Interstate human trafficking made perfect sense, as missing persons cases rarely made it to the Federal level. Once you'd crossed one state line you were mostly home free, once you'd crossed two your new slaves were basically anonymous. Omaha was two states over from Chicago, and Salt Lake City was two states over from Omaha. After that the cargo was fully laundered and could be transported anywhere with relative ease.

All of it was MO.

Wren played it out to the south, a second gone now, all eyes on him. Two states from Minneapolis took him to Missouri, and a modest-sized city comparable to Omaha might be Nashville. That looked like a whole-cloth guess, so Wren leapfrogged it. Two states further lay Alabama, Mississippi, Louisiana and Texas. He delved deeper into the MO, thinking through his internal register of biker gangs.

The Warlocks had chapters across many Southern states, but not the ones on Wren's list. The Hell's Angels were too big, along with the Outlaws, Black Pistons and Bandidos; if they heard of a new organization with assets and plans trying to co-opt them, they would throttle or absorb it. That left the Corpse Knights, started from 1979 with three chapters across Mississippi and Louisiana. They were focused around the coast, in particular Lafayette, where they infamously owned the local police. Even better, they were aligned with the Saints' revolutionary ideology. There were lots of records of dead government workers in their vicinity, lynched and left to be found, but no convictions yet.

They would make the perfect partners for the Saints. It was a gamble, but all he had left.

"Lafayette," Wren said.

The Alpha jerked. Direct hit.

"They're going for your troop centers," Wren went on, working the guess for all he could. "Salt Lake, Minneapolis, Lafayette, but that's not all. The whole organization is poised to break wide open. I can guide you on an escape route out where the CIA won't be looking, but you don't hurt my people anymore. You let them go."

The Alpha stared, his jaw now clamped, his mind doubtless racing as fast as Wren's. Sinclair looked to her boss then back to Wren. If he bought this, then it would seem like his whole Order hung by a thread. Everything would have to accelerate.

"He's guessing," Sinclair attempted, but the words fell flat.

The Alpha's casual bravado was gone. Wren saw the end of the Order playing out in his eyes. The best cult executions started at the top, break the leader and you broke the spell. Wren took a chance and craned his neck back as far as he could, to where he could just see Mason.

He only had a second. He could have said anything, whispered any message.

He winked.

Then he swung back and pressed on. "You'll never see them coming. They'll mass in plain clothes and bring your centers down in synchrony. They're probably coming here this minute. Ask your sources in intelligence; hefty logistics are being put into play." He was freewheeling now, feeling the room bend before him and leaning in. "Believe it or not, they value me. You know I have my own Foundation, over a hundred operators around the States and the world, but what you won't know is I was in the process of handing that network over to the CIA. Honestly, that's their big goal here. Your little civil war hardly matters. They're after me."

He could see the words registering in the Alpha's head. It didn't matter that they were all bullshit, inflated with forced arrogance and bad logic. The Alpha was in a moment of weakness, doubting the security of his own Order and he was amenable to bad ideas, especially thrown out from a fellow alpha male.

I'm bigger than you, Wren was saying. I matter more. Your 'little' civil war will hardly scratch the surface.

"When the FBI rolls in," Wren plunged on, "it'll be to raise me into their inner circle. You they'll execute on the spot. Your Saints around the nation will roll belly up and flake out on their targets. When the rubber hits the road, your live-fire exercises won't mean a thing in the face of an armed response. Let's be honest, when you go recruiting for domestic terrorists, you're not going to get America's finest." He turned again to Mason. "No offense."

At last the spell broke.

"It's a wonderful story," the Alpha said, his face finally calming. "And you tell it so well. But a story's all it is. There is no mole in the Saints. Everything you've said you inferred while-"

"So kill me," Wren interrupted. "If it's just a story, kill Alli. See how far that gets you, when I'm your only shot out of this. You'll have no collateral, nothing to trade when your flea-speck 'war' goes down the tubes. Take it from me, 'Alpha', you're going to want us when the end comes. Even Hitler had his newlywed in the bunker at the end."

That last bit made no sense. It didn't need to. It put a picture in people's minds; one of the most successful tyrannical organizations in history had ended in ignominious suicide in a bunker with the lights out.

"Imagine those feverish moments," Wren urged, painting the picture for them in full color. "Herr Adolf freaking out like you're doing right now, hugging his dear Eva to his chest and trying to decide if he shoots her first, or himself." He looked at Sinclair. "Do you think you'll go before he does? I know suicide cults, ma'am. My father killed all his wives, all his husbands, all his children and all his slaves, all as an 'extension of his will'. He gave the order and they did it for him, and where was he? He disappeared, just like your Alpha here will. A dollar takes ten this guy's already got a one-man escape route set up. No face brand? That makes it easy. He'll disappear while the rest of you are forever marked. I've seen it a thousand times. You're nothing special, and he never really committed."

The Alpha was seething now, the veneer of calm he'd just summoned stripped away again, and Wren kept staring at him, goading him on, until the Alpha pulled Sinclair's pistol from her belt and trained it on Wren. He held it that way for a long moment, his hand steady.

"Do it," Wren said. "See what happens. When the dice shake out, it's your own death warrant."

The barrel held rock steady, but Wren felt the Order of the Saints begin to crack. The smart thing to do now was for the Alpha to either execute

Wren, or keep Wren alive as a bargaining chip and kill Sinclair and Mason to prevent the infection of doubt spreading. Lose or gain everything.

The moment stretched out. His face rippled with flashes of emotion until he mastered himself once more, let the gun swing loose, and laughed. It was a good pretense.

"You talk a great deal, Christopher Wren," he said. "I am interested to hear what your father will make of it. He's coming right now. A truly great man. I'm sure he'll be pleased to have the last Pyramid member delivered to him on a plate. His own misbegotten son, Pequeño 3. Now, I thank you for your candor. Next time we speak, it'll be with your father at my side."

It was Wren's turn to be stunned. His father was coming here? It had to be a bluff. The Apex hadn't been seen since the Pyramid burned.

The Alpha saw his confusion, gave a sunny grin and strode out.

38

BREAK

They were left in silence. Seconds passed. Sinclair stared at Wren.

"Get this knife out of my ear," Alli said into the silence, "you bitch."

Sinclair took a step, thought for a moment, then removed the blade. Alli yelped. Another few seconds passed. Wren jolted himself away from thoughts of his father and back to the moment.

"Go after him," he said. "Before he kills all your collateral."

Sinclair's eyes focused on him. She looked confused and angry. "What are you talking about?"

Perfect. She was asking him for direction now. The question was mocking, maybe, but she was still asking. This was why the Alpha should have killed her. Wren didn't need to turn around to know that Mason would be feeling the same thing. The uncertainty.

"You saw that light in his eyes," Wren said. "He believes me. He's going to burn it all down and activate his escape plan. I'd wager he's about to activate all your terror cells right now. The civil war begins today, and he's just hoping it'll cover him slinking out the back door. You think he'll take you with him?" He let a frown slip through. "It didn't look like that to me. And I'm sure you're not ready to bring the country to the boil. What have you got, a few thousand shooters? I'm thinking ninety percent of them will falter at the last step or get stopped in the act." He pulled the numbers out of thin air, aiming to overwhelm her. "That leaves one or two hundred Saints who get through; maybe they kill a handful of people each? But now the authorities are on it. They'll get their narrative out before you can; it won't appear like a grassroots thing anymore. The country will stand against you, the President will send in the National Guard, and they'll smother your revolution in the crib. The element of surprise was the only thing you had going. Now that's gone."

Sinclair's eyes widened. On some level she believed it too. Wren's bluff had gotten through to her just like with the Alpha.

"He wouldn't," she said, not really to him but to the air. "It's too important. This matters."

Wren just laughed. She twitched, as if only now realizing who she was speaking to. Half of what he'd said had just gone into her head unfiltered, and now she was trying to figure out where she stood. Her hand went to her waist, but the gun was gone; taken by the Alpha. It took her a moment to remember the bloody knife in her hand, and she pointed it toward him.

"I should kill you."

Wren met her gaze dead-on. No smiling now and no beating around the bush. "Mason, what would the Alpha want?"

Sinclair looked at Mason, then back to Wren. "What are you doing? He works for me."

"He works for the Alpha," Wren corrected. "An extension of his will, right? And it seems like the Alpha wants to make a present of me for my father. Are you going to stand in the way of that?"

She was angry. She was uncertain. She held the knife out like a gun, as if all it would take was a gentle squeeze and it would shoot through Wren's skull.

"I know him. I know what's right for him."

Wren nodded. "I see that. I'm getting the picture, Sinclair. You made this thing together. He was nothing when you met him, right? But you built him up. One question, though. Where's your title? He's Alpha, so what are you, Beta? Maybe you were equal, once, but you know that's not been true for some time. You know what humans usually put a brand on, right?" He paused a beat, but she offered no answer. "Animals, Sinclair. Property. You're like a cow, and a cow means riches, and he gets high off being a rich man." Another brief pause. "Was it your idea or his to get you dressed up for my interrogation?"

She said nothing.

"His," Wren confirmed. 'They call that brainwashing. My man Mason here knows what I'm talking about, don't you, Mason?"

Again Sinclair looked to Mason, then back to Wren.

"Seriously," he went on "if you think he shouldn't trigger the Order right now, that it's too soon, you should go after him. If you think he should, shouldn't you be there to help him do it right?"

She stared, then straightened up and stabbed the knife toward Mason.

"Watch this traitor. Gag him if you have to. It's all poison."

Then she left, leaving them in temporary silence.

"This is so messed up," Alli said, weaving woozily. Blood still trickled down her neck, and she gazed into the mirror at her own reflection. "Like, extreme body modification."

"Can you help her please, Mason?" Wren asked, looking at him in the mirror.

Mason didn't move. He just stood there like he had throughout, frozen, as if he'd dropped into a catatonic trance. Wren remembered reading about that on his profile; one effect of the brain damage from his war injury.

Alli weaved in place. "This is some nonsense," she mumbled.

"Mason!" Wren said sharply, and that woke him up. "Please help Alli. Nobody ordered her dead. That means she shouldn't die, don't you agree?" He gave that a second to sink in. "They'll hold you responsible if she does. Plus, I know you want to help her. The Marines didn't teach you to be a sadist."

Mason blinked, then stepped hesitantly forward until he was standing next to Alli. He seemed lost. "What should I-"

"Bandage her head," Wren said gently. "Use your jacket. It's OK. You know how to do this. You've had the training."

Mason began. Ripping his jacket. Bandaging. Occasionally he looked to Wren then away swiftly, as if stung. It all helped to re-activate the man he'd used to be.

"I can't see," Alli grumbled, and Mason mumbled a soft apology and shifted the angle of the bandage. "Better."

"Now let her go," said Wren.

Mason turned to him.

"I don't mean out of the room," Wren went on. "I don't expect that. The Alpha is going to trade us, remember, when the war fails? No, I mean untie her wrists. That's an unnatural position, and it's cutting off her blood flow. She might die from that alone. You've done this much to follow the Alpha's wishes and keep her alive. Go the whole way."

It took Mason a moment longer, but he took out a knife and went to cut Alli free, then stopped. He turned and looked at Wren square on, with the light of thinking intelligence was back in his eyes.

"There you are," said Wren. "Good to see you."

"I don't do what you say," Mason said. "It's the other way around."

Wren nodded. "Precisely. So tell me what you want. Ask me."

Mason frowned. "Ask what?"

"What you've wanted to ask since you were pulling those punches. How I know about Wendy."

That sparked the same anger; a clear desire to rush over and punch Wren again for even saying her name. It took a long moment for Mason to chew it back. "You guessed," he said. "Like the Alpha said."

"Her name? How would I, I'm not a telepath. Try again."

Mason chewed on his lip. "Maybe I told you. Sometimes I forget things that I said."

"Ding ding, no. Third time lucky?"

Mason stared. On top of the rest of it, and underlying it too, there was this. The final lever Wren could pull. "I don't know. How?"

"I found your note," Wren said. "In the warehouse in Utah. I'm sure you didn't know where you were at the time. After they snatched you from Chicago, under the West Pershing bridge. After they took Wendy." Mason flinched. "Her name was written on a receipt for flowers, in blood. You screwed it up and put it in a socket in the floor, and I found it. Those days must have been hard, almost a year ago now."

"I don't remember," Mason said reflexively, but Wren could see that he did.

"I went to Chicago looking for you, Mason," he pushed on. "I found where you lived under that bridge. I talked to the man in the convenience store where you bought the flowers, Felipe? He was worried about you; said he called the police several times to find you. I went to the church where Wendy volunteered and I found your trail. They told me about her; how kind she was to others. How kind she was to you. She must have been a special woman."

Mason's eyes shone. It didn't matter that half of it was lies, and the Revival Faith outreach director had never even met Wendy.

"She sounds wonderful," Wren pressed, charging right up to the edge. "So why did you have to kill her?"

The first tear fled down Mason's cheek. It worked a path through the crevices and ridges of his many scars.

It was always the same with the breaking of a cult member. The scales came away from their eyes, and all that remained was pain; pain at being fooled, at committing atrocities for a lie, at wanting to belong so much. It broke many people, and there was no one who could help; you were alone with what you'd done. Wren knew all about that, and saw Mason was almost over the edge.

Except now something different came into his eyes. "I didn't kill her," he said in a small voice.

That stopped Wren cold, rewriting the story of what must have happened. If Mason hadn't killed her, then why had he grown so angry when Wren had mentioned her?

"But she is dead."

"No," Mason said, but his voice was even quieter now, and Wren leaped into that gap.

"She's alive?"

"I-" Mason began, then faltered, hinting at the shame. Wren adjusted his approach.

"Are they holding her for you? Do they let you see her sometimes, Mason? Maybe when you're good, when you please the Alpha?"

Mason said nothing, but his eyes swam with tears.

"Like she's an animal. Like you're an animal. But Mason, you're not. She's not. You don't deserve any of this, and neither does she."

Mason was shaking now. Trying to throw off the shackles in his mind. Wren didn't want to think about how they'd clamped those shackles in place. If they hadn't made Mason kill her, then they must have come close.

"Where is she?" he asked. "Where's Wendy?"

Mason lips moved but no sound came out.

"Is she here?"

A sound escaped Mason, more of a whimper than a word. Wren took it for confirmation, and it broke his heart.

"You can free her. Whatever they said about her, that she was a traitor, that she was dangerous, they were lies. You know Wendy, Mason. She was good. She loaned you crayons to make your signs. She worked with the churches to feed your people. Wendy is good."

Now the tears broke down Mason's cheeks. "She was killing them," he whispered. "In the training site. She had a gun and she was just killing people. Innocent people! I had to do something."

At that, Wren saw it all. They'd brainwashed her first and set her loose on victims in one of the active shooter training sites. They'd let him see the results, then left Mason to do the 'right thing'.

"Why was she killing them?"

"I don't-"

"Think about why, Mason," Wren insisted. "Think about all the horrors they could have done to her, the ways the Alpha might have wound her up like he's wound you up, and Sinclair, and all these Saints. you're a Marine. I know you don't want to be beating me. You don't want to kill me, and Wendy didn't want to kill anyone either. Wendy was good, Mason, and she deserves far better than this."

More tears followed the first. The pain was coming. Nothing would help Mason when the dam broke.

"The Alpha said-"

"The Alpha has been lying to you since the start. Think back to where he found you. Did you go willingly? Did Wendy go willingly?"

"I-"

"He stole both of you, Mason, from underneath a bridge! You were hurting nobody. You were innocent. And he put a brand into your face countless times, and a gun in Wendy's hands, and he smashed you together to see what would happen. You didn't deserve any of it! Look at me, Mason."

Mason glanced up, away, then down to Wren.

"You didn't deserve this. I don't deserve this. Abdul didn't deserve to die, and neither does Alli or Wendy."

Mason thick hands went to his head. "I don't know. I can't think."

"I need you to think," Wren urged. "The Alpha never asked you to think, did he? He just gave orders. Do you think I would ever do that to you?"

Mason's mouth opened but no words came out.

"Ask Alli. She's right behind you. She's been with me for years. She was a meth addict heading toward school shooter, she made threats all over social media, and I was there when the court system spat her out. She hasn't shot anyone. Ask her."

Mason's gaze flickered like a skittish animal. He wanted to trust Wren, but it didn't come easily. He stepped away, turning his body so he could keep both Wren and Alli in his sight at the same time.

"He's a real regular Joe," Alli slurred, woozy from the blood loss. "A stand-up guy. It's true, he forgot when my coin-three check-up is, and he's not always there when you want to talk, but I understand that. He's got a lot of people to help. Like you, Mason. In fact, I've been meaning to talk to him about that." She leaned toward Wren. "You have to open this thing out. Foundation, support group, whatever it is. I want to know these guys." She nodded to the body on the floor. "This dead guy, before he was dead. We can do great things together."

Wren grunted, looked back to Mason. "She'll die if you don't let her go. Cut the ties. You know that's right."

Mason's whole body vibrated, then he leaned in and cut through the zip tie in one smooth motion. Alli sagged forward onto the floor, but Wren couldn't let up now.

"That's good. Now you've got to take the next step, Mason. Any moment someone's going to come through that door. It might be the Alpha, or Sinclair, or a Saint sent to kill us all. You saw that in the Alpha's eyes, didn't you? He was on the edge of turning this room into another live fire 'simulation'. Even you, even Sinclair, especially Wendy. He's a dangerous animal and he needs to be put down. You're the only one that can do that, the only one who can save Wendy, just like a Marine should."

Mason stared. He looked lost, a child in the body of a full-grown Marine, but still he sheathed the knife and drew his gun. All eyes turned to the door.

39

BROKEN

Wren's breath came in short pants. There was nothing more to say. Now they waited, until the sound of distant shots carried from outside, starting slow and intermittent then bunching together like corn popping on a fire.

Mason's gaze flickered to Wren. "What's that?"

"Depends," Wren said, "who's left in the building?"

Mason stared at him, eyes boiling with suspicion. He wouldn't want to give that kind of information over.

"Whatever you tell me, I'm still tied up," Wren said. "Letting me go, that's a whole different decision. Tell me this much, we all get wiser."

Mason's brow worked hard as thoughts rippled under the mottled surface. He reached a decision with a tight nod. "My strike team. Hounds of the Saints, Acker calls them. Forty elite soldiers, all ex-special forces like me." He paused a moment, thinking. "And the Core. They're inner converts, the Alpha uses them for logistics, support." A pause. "They run the Order, really. Down the corridor."

Wren grunted. It figured. "How many?"

"I don't know. Thirty?"

"That's thirty-three gunfire reports so far," Wren said. The shooting had stopped. "Best guess, your Alpha just cleaned up his tracks, starting with the Core. Thirty-three for thirty tells me they let him. Execution-style, die for the cult leader. Does that sound about right, from a guy who used your Wendy just to make a point?"

Mason flinched at her name, looked at the door then looked down at Alli. She lay on the floor by Wren's side now, too weak from blood loss to do anything more than track the conversation back and forth.

"This is your boy's MO," Wren pressed. "He did it in Emery, in Price too; his Order gets found out, he kills anyone who knows anything. Police. Bikers. His own people. Now he kills the Core, that makes him good for a getaway. Everyone here who saw his face, who knows him, will be rubbed out."

Mason glared. "You're twisting it. You want me to think I'm next."

Wren softened his face. Sympathy could do so much with a person starved of it. "Mason, it's not me making you think that."

The silence after that was deep, broken only by Alli sucking in breaths, then by footsteps stamping closer, until the door slammed open and Sinclair strode in.

She was sprayed with blood. She lifted her gun and aimed it at Wren, until a click came from her left, and she turned to see Mason training his gun at her heart.

Hope rushed up in Wren's chest. A moment passed.

"If I could negotiate," he offered, but Mason held out a hand.

"Stay out of this."

"Stay out of what?" Sinclair asked, looking between them. "What is 'this'?"

"Who've you been shooting?" Mason asked.

"What has he been saying to you?"

A silent moment passed as they gazed at each other.

"We talked about Wendy," Mason said. "You remember her."

Sinclair frowned. "Wendy?" She thought for a moment. "Your bitch traitor pet?"

"Don't call her that."

Now Sinclair laughed. "Mason. You moron. Are you really defying the Alpha for some woman who killed your own brother Saints?" That hung for a moment between them, receiving no answer. "You idiot! Do you know how ungrateful that is, do you know how much I did for you? I plucked you off the street. I gave you a home, a place to belong, an important role in the new Order of America, and here at the edge of all our dreams you're turning on us over some useless dreg bitch?"

Mason inched the gun closer. "Not my dreams. And I said don't call her that."

"Mason, wake up! Think about all that the Alpha gave you. Now you're throwing all that away for lies spewed by a professional con-man?" She waved at Wren.

"You branded me, I know that," Mason said. "You hurt Wendy, too. You made her do those things, like you just killed the Core."

Sinclair's face darkened. "I haven't got time for this, so listen to me very carefully, Mason. Wendy's dead, or she soon will be. The Core are dead. This facility is undergoing purification, the Great War has already begun, and it isn't too late to get back on the right side. I can forget what I'm seeing here if you turn that gun on him right now." She pointed at Wren. "Place the blame where it lies. It's liars like him who have ruined this country. His lies drew you to the Marines where they put this loyalty to the State BS in your head. They put it in and I took it out, just like I'll pull out the lies he's fed you with. This is your last chance, Mason. There's no going back from this. The Alpha's already starting the righteous work. Will you ride at his right hand or fall beneath his feet?"

Mason's hand trembled. "I don't care about the work. I want Wendy back."

"She's as good as dead," Sinclair spat. "And you will be too, along with ten million traitors just like her. What I've given I will take away. The Alpha has empowered me."

"The Alpha's a liar."

"You're such a child," Sinclair said, and fired.

Mason's chest absorbed the first slug with a flat meat-smacking sound, but he was already moving, and her second shot skimmed his side. His first shot entered her shoulder and tore out through her back, his second entered her stomach as he fell, at which point her third powdered through his thigh.

They both dropped.

"Hot dang," Alli muttered, as the gunfire echoed around the room.

Sinclair slumped awkwardly on her knees and chest, her trigger finger twitching slackly by her side though the gun had fallen away. Her bright eyes darted side to side as if looking for a way out. Mason gasped and rolled onto his back on the white floor. The sound of their gurgling breaths filled the room.

"Where's the Alpha, Mason?" Wren asked.

Mason's head lolled toward the sound. He was pale already. His lips framed words and his eyes throbbed with some aching need.

"Where is he?"

"Why didn't you-" Mason began, speaking in barely a croak. "Why didn't you come help me earlier?"

He slumped on his back, his breathing growing shallower.

"I'm sorry," Wren said, maybe the last words Mason would ever hear, then he looked down at Alli. "Can you get his knife?"

Her head bobbed, drowsy and numb. "I'll have to crawl."

"So crawl. We're not proud in the Foundation."

She gave a half-laugh, then lolled forward onto her hands and knees and started to crawl. It took her three attempts to catch the clasp of Mason's knife, then she crawled back to Wren. She cut his right hand free, then he took the knife and did the rest.

He hadn't moved from the chair for many hours, so he stood up slowly, worried his legs wouldn't hold his weight. The back of his left thigh seared, gave once, twice, then just about held. Standing upright, everything hurt. Beating upon beating.

Just the way he liked it.

He dropped carefully to one knee at Mason's side. The man was barely breathing, and Wren tore more strips off his jacket to bind the wounds in his chest and leg as best he could.

"Hold this," he said to Alli. "Please."

"I think I'm dead," Alli answered woozily, gazing up at the ceiling. "Is this hell?"

"Just hold this, Alli."

She rolled over and put her hands on the makeshift bandages.

"Hard as you can," Wren said. "Don't let go. Promise me."

"Promise."

Wren crawled over to Sinclair, feeling the urgency building now. The Saints' Great War was beginning. He rooted through her pockets, and she mouthed a word that began with the letter T. Maybe 'traitor'. He yanked out her phone.

"PIN number," he said.

She stared, maybe seconds away from dying.

"PIN," he repeated, and pressed the bullet wound in her chest. She groaned. He woke the phone to the lock screen and held it up before her eyes. "Tell me and I won't kill your Alpha. I'll try to save him. Tell me the PIN."

She turned her eyes away.

"So die then," Wren said, reached to retrieve her weapon, a Sig Sauer P320, then pushed himself agonizingly up. "And the Alpha along with you."

He made three hobbling steps toward the door before her whispered voice rose up.

"Swear."

He turned.

"Swear to it," she rasped. "On something real. Swear he'll live."

Wren stared at her. She loved the Alpha, that much was obvious. She'd do anything for him. "On my wife," he said, and dropped back to one beside her, started plugging her wounds. "On my kids. I swear I'll try."

She gulped hard, clearly distraught, Eva looking for her Adolf as the bombs rained down. Then she gave him the PIN.

Wren tapped them in. The phone unlocked.

"Where's the Alpha gone?"

"Don't ... know," she mouthed.

Wren wrapped a final makeshift bandage over her wounds then grunted to his feet and dialed a number from memory, limping out the door.

40

JIB-JAB

The corridor outside had white walls smudged with bloody palm and foot prints; Sinclair's trail leading away. Cold vinyl stung Wren's bare feet but he lurched on as the phone rang, bringing up the GPS app.

"Yes," came a voice on the other end as Wren turned a corner.

"Christopher Wren," he said, "codeword clockjaguar3 for Director Humphreys, he'll take it direct."

"Yes." There was a beep, then a few seconds later Humphreys was on the line speaking guardedly.

"Wren, we've been waiting, where the hell are you?"

He'd never thought he'd feel so happy to hear the Director's voice. He lined up everything he needed to say and pushed it out in a rush. "I'm in Minneapolis. I was shot, captured, tortured and now I'm free. Humphreys, the Saints' civil war just began. Multiple shots fired here; dozens are likely dead."

He sucked in a breath, leaned against the wall and zoomed in on the GPS app as it localized to a large office block. "Looks like, north-west of the city, near St. Michael, a complex marked as 'Jib-Jab'. Send armed response and ambulances immediately; two grossly injured females and a male in a room on the-" he reached a window and peered out, seeing rinsed-out blue skies, the sun a low crescent on the horizon to the left, orienting himself. "South-east corner, third floor."

A second passed. "What are we walking into, Christopher? Do you have any evidence for any of this?"

"Yeah," Wren said, and flipped the phone, activated the camera and began a livestream that showed himself as he starting staggering again along the blood-smeared corridor. "You need to mobilize the whole country, Humphreys. Evacuate every government office, town hall, school and wherever else federal workers might be. The Saints have been activated; I don't know how many, but I'm guessing thousands." He almost fell down a flight of steps, barely catching himself on the handrail.

"Christopher-" Humphreys said, but Wren cut him off.

"You need to get the President on the airwaves right now, addressing a national emergency so people are forewarned. This is a nationwide attack, planned for many years. They want it to look like a grassroots uprising, but we cannot allow that notion to spread. It's a coordinated attack by domestic terrorists. You need to get that immunization in."

A moment passed as Humphreys processed that. "OK. I'm dispatching emergency units to your location. We found the camp where you left the phone, Christopher. Schools and offices, is that what that was? Training for active shooters?"

"Exactly. The whole country, Humphreys, right now."

"And if this is a distraction from whatever attack you've been planning?"

Wren barked a laugh. "I'm not planning anything! Look at me, Humphreys, is this a good look to run a war?"

He held the phone away so the camera saw his whole blood-spattered, bruised and bandaged appearance.

"Possibly," allowed Humphreys. "It could be an elaborate ruse."

Wren laughed again. "Elaborate, yeah. I resigned to be with my family, not to start a civil war. I was going to hand the Foundation over. That wasn't a lie. It just got messed up." He turned a corner and passed down another flight of stairs to a heavy-looking black door. There were red boot prints stamped brightly around the entrance. "I thought I'd be free, but I was wrong. My wife figured it all out somehow. She took the kids. I'm not a family man, like you said. I just started driving. Ask Loralei."

"We did." A pause, then he went on in a slightly softer tone. "Wren."

"Watch this," Wren said, then shoulder barged the black doors and stumbled through into a slaughterhouse.

Sinclair hadn't been lying.

Bodies were everywhere; slumped at three ranks of desks looking toward a large central screen, like a flight control deck. There were around thirty of them, like Mason had said. All were dead where they sat, tipped over their keyboards, lying on the floor by the wheeled legs of their ergonomic office chairs, blood slashed across their monitors.

Wren took in the gory details. There were no eyelets or chains to hold them in place here, just like he'd thought. This was an execution they'd accepted, just like the Pyramid, and his gorge rose.

Humphreys cursed.

"Yeah," said Wren, panning the phone across.

The large screen at the front showed what seemed to be a list of some twenty text messages and emails, along with phone numbers and emails. Each one said, 'Go!' followed by an address.

Government offices. Schools.

Targets.

"Start with these," Wren said, taking a photo with his cell phone camera. He lumbered closer. On individual monitors there were more lists: hundreds of targets, sent to thousands of operatives. He took photos rapidly, then held the phone up again.

"The Alpha's on the run. Get the President on the line. Stop this, Humphreys."

He hung up.

A big man slumped by the door looked about Wren's size. He quickly stripped the man's jeans, check shirt, brown leather boots and pulled them on. The wound in his thigh burned with the exertion, but there was nothing he could do about that right now.

The phone rang as Humphreys called him back, but he ignored it and tapped out a darknet Megaphone message for his Foundation.

HAVE BEEN HELD CAPTIVE APPROX 18 HOURS BY THE SAINTS – THE CIVIL WAR HAS BEGUN. POLICE AND CIA NOTIFIED. PULL ANY AND ALL KNOWN GOVERNMENT WORKERS FROM OFFICES, SCHOOLS, HOSPITALS IMMEDIATELY – THEY ARE TARGETS. RING FIRE ALARMS. SHOUT 'BOMB' TO GET THEM OUT. IF LAW ENFORCEMENT NOT PRESENT AND YOU

ARE ARMED, STAND GUARD UNTIL THEY ARRIVE. ALSO PLANT NOTION IN NATIONAL PSYCHE THRU SOCIAL MEDIA THAT A MASS TERROR ATTACK IS UNDERWAY – GOAL IS INOCULATE AGAINST GRASSROOTS FEVER SPREADING. THANK YOU. WREN.

He sent it and thought for a moment, coming up on a large-ceilinged lobby to the building.

ALSO TRACK DOWN RECORDS FOR ME ASAP. AM IN PURSUIT OF THE SAINTS' LEADER, THE ALPHA, AND NEED A TARGET DESTINATION. A MALE 6FT 3, 220LBS, APPROX 38-42, CAUCASIAN, BLUE EYES BLOND HAIR, LIKELY NO CRIMINAL RECORD, RAISED IN MINNEAPOLIS AREA, LIKELY ATTENDED A SUMMER CAMP NEAR TWO HARBORS OFF LAKE SUPERIOR DATE RANGE OF - he did a quick calculation - 1980 - 1986.

He sent. It wasn't much to go off.

Ahead lay another security gate and he clambered awkwardly over it, to find himself in a large lobby marked as the nexus of 'Jib-Jab', some kind of Internet shopping firm. Not a bad cover operation, he figured; space for a large standing stock of weapons in a concealed location on the verge of the city, with constant incoming and outgoing deliveries, a big motor pool, many freelancers rolling in and out every day, and a whirlwind of financial transactions, many of them invisible to state auditors due to their international status. Likely there was a website to go along with it, maybe they even made a little money toward funding the war from sales of baby formula.

The glass doors were open and Wren stepped out into the light. The lot held several cars, but where was he going? He needed to give his Foundation more on the Alpha, a history they could build out for likely targets, but what else could he add?

The man didn't have any visible branding, but there was that unnatural golden sheen. His eyes were strange too, maybe contacts, and his nose too slim. He was clearly vain, like most cult leaders, but unlike most of them this guy actually looked the part.

THE ALPHA'S HAD POTENTIAL MAJOR PLASTIC SURGERY. NOSE, JAW, CHEEKBONES MUSCLE IMPLANTS. He sent the message and racked his mind for more as he limped toward the nearest vehicle in the lot. It might be enough, but there was something missing.

A final piece clicked into place. Something the Alpha had said in a throwaway boast about the Pyramid; that he'd read everything on the federal record. But Wren had pulled in a lot of favors to expunge all publicly available federal records on his childhood cult. There was only one place in the world to access the record that remained, one single room which kept a meticulous record of all attendees, but allowed no material out: the reading room at the Library of Congress. Wren had tried to get that record wiped multiple times and failed.

ALSO, HE VISITED THE READING ROOM IN THE LIBRARY OF CONGRESS AT LEAST ONCE. THAT SHOULD NARROW IT DOWN.

The nearest vehicle was a Porsche. He elbowed through the window with a sharp crash, already feeling the buzz of messages coming back through the phone as the Foundation activated. Even now his more robust members would be gathering arms and heading out to lead evacuations. His hackers would be sending alerts to government offices, as well as seeding social media with the notion of a terrorist attack in progress.

Wren slumped into the driver's seat. He had no keys, no screwdriver, but the car had a wireless ignition, so he downloaded a skeleton key near-field radio frequency app off the Foundation darknet. It downloaded in minutes, paired with the car then fired up the engine.

GET ME A TARGET LOCATION, LIKELY SOMEWHERE DOWNTOWN, RIGHT NOW he tapped and sent, then cranked the car into gear and tore away.

41

MINNEAPOLIS

Wren raced southeast at almost twice the speed limit, weaving madly through midday traffic, heading for downtown. The broad Highway 10 ushered him through flat Minneapolis suburbs as the green floodplain of the Mississippi River swung in and out on his right like a Yoyo.

Exits whipped by but he stayed on the 10 like a tracer round on an unstoppable trajectory. What was the price of failure here? His head barely worked. One more attack amongst thousands, the Alpha's crowning glory, but surely it didn't matter that much?

Except Wren knew it would. This guy had planned meticulously for years; he had to have a bigger strike in mind for his hometown. Something to clearly announce him as the leader of this Great War.

The 10 swerved to become the 47 headed downtown, almost to the city center and he still had no destination. The phone rang and he snatched it up, tapping for speaker.

"Talk to me."

"Christopher," came the wizened, genteel voice of Professor Ferat. "I volunteered to bring the consensus. I'm afraid we don't have anything."

Wren slammed the gas pedal harder, nearly ramming into the back of a silver Lexus. Dr. Ferat? He hadn't expected to hear from him; maybe his NSA guy in LA or one of his Eastern European hacker team. His head spun with the chain of events that must have led to Ferat being chosen. It seemed off; he wasn't a hacker and didn't know a thing about forensic data analysis.

But he could read a message board. Wren cursed under his breath. Ferat had always been excellent at pattern analysis. For the moment, Wren forced aside the concern of Ferat co-opting his Foundation.

"Not possible. He's got to be in the record somewhere. Explain."

"Maybe he's in there, but we can't find him," Ferat said. "There's no single cross-correlation across the data points you shared. It'll take time to sift through all the possible candidates. I'm sorry, Christopher, I know this is not what you-"

Wren smacked the wheel and the horn blared. A guy in a red Toyota gave him the finger but Wren sped by in seconds, closing in on downtown and about to butt into a winding tail of traffic.

He pulled right across three lanes and shot onto the off-ramp for the city circular. "You're saying they found candidates," Wren said, "but no standout."

"Exactly."

"How many candidates?"

"Who attended that summer camp across those years? Thousands. Who might have had plastic surgery? Hard to say, but fewer. Who also went to the Library of Congress? None, Christopher."

Wren pulled over onto the narrow shoulder and started scrolling rapidly through the conversation thread on his open board. Already there were in excess of three hundred messages with more pouring in; some fresh intelligence, some partially correlated databases, some attempts to draw conclusions. To Wren's fuzzy brain it was like drinking from a fire hose.

Thousands of candidates, but not one who'd attended the Library of Congress. Wren felt his brain jamming. There was no other lead, so where did that leave him?

"I can imagine how you're feeling, Christopher," Ferat said, his voice coming smooth and clear. "Now I hope you will listen to me, because-"

Wren hit the red button to kill the call. It flashed and the hiss of audio died, taking away the ambient noise of Ferat's college office.

He was panting and his heart pounded. A semi thundered past on his left. This outcome didn't seem right. He'd been certain there was enough information. It felt like a dizzy crevasse opening before him. The attack was about to happen, people were going to die, and he had no idea where or how to stop it.

The phone rang and he ignored it. Nothing to say. Listening to Ferat now could be dangerous for him. Like Teddy, like Cheryl, he couldn't fully trust the good doctor either. Ferat had been a social predator, and if he saw how weak Wren was right now, he'd pounce. People didn't change that much, they just waited for their chance to stab you in the back, take control, turn the Foundation to their own ends.

Or maybe not? Wren couldn't tell. He wasn't thinking clearly. He was back in the weeks after Loralei had gone, driving aimlessly with no way forward, no way back. He envisaged himself in Humphreys' promised black site and the Foundation turning against him, taking this chance to escape the coin system and become something dark and cruel.

He sagged on the wheel, feeling every ache and pain in his body. Maybe the Saints really were going to break America and take his Foundation along with them. What kind of authoritarian government would rise up in the revolution's wake?

The phone kept ringing. Text messages buzzed in and he ignored them. There were no more leads. No brilliant leaps of deduction. When you didn't have the data, you didn't have the data, and that was all she wrote.

42

SHOULDER

PICK UP, CHRISTOPHER.

Wren watched messages scroll by on his phone screen; each one coming too fast too read. He couldn't trust any of them now. It was Tandrews all over again.

All those years ago James Tandrews had become like a father to him, and Wren had leaned into it. He'd enjoyed having a 'normal' family, and a normal life at school, and a girlfriend and career prospects and...

Then it had all just become too much.

He remembered the moment it happened. It was the day before his seventeenth birthday, with Tandrews' family all around him, in readiness for the formal adoption proceedings the next day. The papers were in front of him, and his new life as one of the Tandrews' clan stretched ahead.

James Tandrews had only ever been good to Wren. His family had accepted this strange, wayward boy who didn't act like anyone else they'd met. Wren should've been happy, should've been grateful, but instead all he felt was the cold sweat running down his back, and the sensation that he was walking into the worst trap yet, of his own free will.

He'd smiled and nodded his way through the evening, thinking the crushing sense of doubt would pass, but it only grew stronger, until in the middle of the night, he acted.

He went out his bedroom window, leaving only the briefest note to apologize; barely an explanation. Now that choice twisted in his stomach like a knife.

Sitting at the roadside while semis and trucks rushed by inches away, he thought back on how it must have been for Tandrews, to come to Wren's room and find him gone on the day of the adoption.

The thought broke his heart. He'd never trusted anyone, even when he should have. He'd never let go of control for a moment, and where had that brought him?

To here. It couldn't get any worse. People needed help. Even Wren needed help. He couldn't do any more alone. Maybe sometimes you had to just trust and jump.

He answered the incoming call from Dr. Ferat.

"Christopher, thank heavens," came Ferat's voice, bordering panic, "there's new intelligence coming down just now."

Wren blinked. He hadn't expected that. "From where?"

"A girl called Alli, through an FBI connection I'm hearing, straight into the Foundation darknet. People are all over it, a name: Richard Acker."

Wren's mind swam. Alli? How could Alli know anything? She was half-dead.

"But how-"

"It just came into the boards," Ferat interrupted, his usually staid tones sparkling now with the thrill of the hunt. "Someone called Mason provided it; they say you saved his life. Both Mason and Alli are in an ambulance now. We're cross-referencing this Acker, your hackers are digging deep, and-"

Wren tuned out for a moment. "Mason was shot twice. I didn't think he was going to make it."

"Well, apparently he did. And there's something more, we're getting it now. Oh sweet mercy! Look at the boards, Christopher."

Wren flicked to speaker and fumbled with the phone. His hands suddenly felt hot and clumsy. He tapped through the hundred or so posts since he'd hung up, scrolling with increasing disbelief as the life track of one Richard Acker unraveled like a social media stream in fast forward, pieced together from city census records, IP logs, financial tracking, international travel and hospital admission data.

Richard Acker.

He was everything Wren was searching for, yet different at the same time. He was rooted in Minneapolis, but not in the way Wren had imagined. He had received plastic surgery, but not the kind Wren had expected. He had attended the summer camp off Two Harbors, but not in any recognizable way. He had been to the Library of Congress, but under an assumed name and with a different face, before plastic surgery changed it forever.

The pieces spun together. A photograph of Richard Acker appeared in the feed, and Wren just stared. In it he was maybe eighteen, wearing graduation robes with a forced smile. The forehead was the same. The broad shoulders, the build, the set of the eyes, even the chin and some aspect to the cheekbones, but everything else was different.

Richard Acker was black.

Or at least his skin was, in certain parts; a dark cherrywood. Wren peered closer at the picture. Wispy blond hair straggled down over brown eyes and a face with the hawkish nose and thin lips of a Caucasian, but with blotchy dark skin, as if the melanin had been applied unevenly in round blobs.

Records of surgical alteration followed in an avalanche, from trips to Thailand, Vietnam, Singapore, all medical tourism to get skin bleaching treatments illegal in the US, along with numerous attempts at beautification; cheekbone enhancement, nose-bump reduction, chin contouring.

More photos cataloged the transformation as Richard Acker changed himself from a black-and-white-skinned man with desperation in his eyes to a golden-skinned surgical creation. There were hair implants to thicken his scalp to a lustrous mane; muscle implants in his arms, back and thighs. A technique called 'distraction osteogenesis' had been used, which involved repeated breaking and resetting of the leg bones to increase height by up to six inches.

Wren would have laughed if it weren't so horrifically sad. Last of all, the blotches on Acker's face came into sharp focus as he read the childhood diagnosis: N1 neurofibromatosis, causing scoliosis, skin lumps, hearing loss and café-au-lait spots.

That shook Wren. Café-au-lait were birthmarks that grew; a skin condition where white skin turned dark and blotchy over time. There was an accompanying picture of Acker as a child, maybe five years old and mostly white-skinned, with only four café-au-lait blotches on his face, round stains no darker than spilled tea. But they'd spread.

Wren sped through more photos recording the transformation, watching those spilled tea spots spread and darken, colonizing his cheeks, his nose, his forehead until his entire face was an uneven blur of black.

"We were never going to find him," Wren muttered.

"Exactly," Ferat said, audibly leafing through the fresh flood of accounts. "The Library of Congress recorded his visit before all of these changes. He looks like a different man."

Wren brought that image up. In the CCTV picture, Acker looked more like a black man than a white one. "It's incredible."

"It is. It also made his life a misery." Ferat summarized Acker's troubled adolescence in the municipal system of foster homes, after being abandoned by drug-addict parents. His unusual skin saw him ostracized and bullied by the other children. Accusations of child abuse against his various foster parents were leveled but no action was taken, except to shuttle him on to the next set. As he hit his mid-teens he began acting out violently, leading to several stints in youth detention.

"We have his earliest Internet record," Ferat went on, breaking through the buzz in Wren's head with his clear tones. "Posts on numerous anti-government sites advocating sabotage of the foster care system. It only takes a few years for him to widen his target to the whole federal government and start demanding blood."

Wren knew just what this young Richard Acker wanted. He could see it burning in his eyes, in his arrest record, in his steady transformation.

"And the abuse?"

"Never substantiated," Ferat answered. "But I'm inclined to believe he was telling the truth. His current rage could be the outcome of a large-scale cover-up, Christopher. His changing skin made him isolated and weak; easy to target by sick adults. He had no friends, no advocates, no one to take his side."

Wren's knuckles tightened. In another situation, he'd be fighting on the same side as Richard Acker. He'd felt the call to revenge every day of his life since the Pyramid fell; a shapeless fury that needed to be fed.

If it weren't for James Tandrews, he might have become every bit as vengeful as Richard Acker. He would have sought any means possible to make somebody pay, becoming a destructive force to rival the Saints, and he wouldn't have cared who he hurt.

Tandrews had just steered that rage in a better direction. The Foundation had helped. Maybe it could help Acker, too.

"The Internet allowed it," Ferat went on, his keyboard clicking frantically as he sped through pages. "The conspiracy theory believers found him and fed him, and he grew to become their hero. He developed the Saints into an organization with hundreds of devoted members, but he didn't get off the Internet and take it into the real world for several years, at least not until-"

"Sinclair," Wren whispered, finally seeing the connection.

"Precisely. It looks like she set him up with the reconstructive plastic surgeons."

Wren thought back on the fake-looking golden glow of the man. That had to be some off-shoot of the surgeries.

"No wonder we didn't find him," he breathed.

"We were looking for a Caucasian male," Ferat said. "Acker was ruled out by default."

Wren stared. Traffic slashed by. The civil war was still on, but now he had a better sense of what Acker's main goal was. Revenge. He wanted to inflict pain on the federal government for the crimes he'd suffered when he was too small to fight back.

Wren scrolled through Acker's records rapidly, finding what he was looking for within a minute. The pieces fell into position. It made sense. The first shots in the Alpha's great civil war would be fired against his earliest tormentors.

He knew where Acker was going.

43

BISHOP HENRY WHIPPLE

W ren cranked the Porsche into gear and took off, hitting a hundred miles an hour plus in ten seconds flat. Exits flew by in a blizzard as he called Humphreys, and the line connected after one ring.

"The Bishop Henry Whipple federal building," Wren shouted over the churn of the engine. "That's where Acker's going, I'm certain, along with at least forty of his most elite Saints. It's where the Minneapolis Fostering Authority's based, the place that let him be abused for years as a child. I need-"

"There's no one to spare," Humphreys interrupted. "All FBI field agents along with police, fire, ambulance; they're all engaged where you told us to post them, securing hospitals, schools and offices. If this Henry Whipple Building is lost, it means he already broke through our cordon. There's no one else to send."

"So activate the National Guard," Wren fired off, making a hard right heading south. Ahead a thick black pall of smoke was already rising over the Mississippi delta like a shadow on the sky, a grisly confirmation. "Army, Coast Guard, Boy Scouts, whatever it takes, Humphreys. The building's already on fire!"

"It's not the only place on fire, Christopher," Humphreys snapped back.

"The country's in uproar. There's not a free team in a hundred miles that can tackle an army of forty fanatics!"

Wren cursed. He wished he'd seen it coming earlier. "There's got to be a thousand people in that building, Humphreys."

"So get them out! You're the only one in the vicinity, Wren. Figure it out."

The line went dead. Wren dropped the phone and focused on the road ahead. Humphreys wasn't wrong; he had a nation to help secure. A thousand lives in Minneapolis mattered, but there were thousands of lives everywhere at risk.

Wren pushed the pedal down harder, heading directly for the smoky cloud of the Whipple Building, the place that had authored so much of Richard Acker's pain. He didn't even have a gun; but maybe he could change that.

The off-ramp was coming and he sped onto a bridge over the Mississippi. The Whipple Building peeled into sight to the right as he shot out over the water, a large standalone office block that was two-tiered like a wedding cake, with a broad lower level only one story tall and a narrower tower jutting another five stories up from the center, encircled by an expansive parking lot.

It was an inferno. The fire was up over the first-floor roof in places, orange tongues bursting through the windows. Smoke rose in a thick charcoal column. Saints in black strike suits ringed it, firing automatic rifles at the roof where hundreds of people were clustered.

Wren brought up his phone and tapped out a frantic message.

GET FORCES TO THE HENRY WHIPPLE BUILDING NOW. USE ANYONE YOU CAN. STEAL WHAT YOU CAN. THE BUILDING'S ON FIRE. THE ALPHA'S HERE WITH 40 ARMED SAINTS. IF WE STOP HIM HERE, WE BLUNT THE WAR.

He fired off the message to his open board then wrenched the wheel right, cutting in front of a large cruising semi. The trailer had metal sides and looked to be a refrigerated unit; both should help.

He slammed on the horn and the brakes. The semi responded quickly, swinging over to the next lane to avoid hitting him, answering with its own roaring horn. Wren pulled left with it, staying in front with his horn blaring and one arm out the window signaling frantically.

The semi finally braked.

At a dead stop in the middle lane, Wren climbed out into traffic, holding one hand authoritatively up at the driver, an older woman in jean jacket and red cap. She looked down at him in surprise; a bloodied, staggering man on the Interstate. He climbed up to her door and spoke through the window.

"I need this truck for a federal emergency, ma'am. You see the burning building behind me? I'm going to rescue those people. No one else is coming for them."

She stared a moment longer, then clicked the lock release. "Get in."

He opened the door and slid in. "I need you to get out, ma'am."

She sneered at him. "You think you can drive this beast?" She had a loose Boston accent and tight lines around her mouth, pushing sixty. There were pictures of kids on her sun flaps; tow-haired grandchildren with her sharp eyes. "I saw you in that tin can. You won't get across the median."

Wren lined up arguments and dismissed them. Everyone was a soldier now. The radio played in the background; breaking reports on shootings across the country.

"I'm a patriot," she said, and punched the gas without waiting for his approval. The semi started forward with a jolt.

"We need to hit the government building," Wren said. "Dead-on, without getting shot up."

"Been dying to hit that place. My alimony's a bitch."

Wren snorted.

"Lacy Demille," the woman said, extending a hand to him as the semi thundered around the curve of the Interstate. Wren took her calloused hand and shook.

"Christopher Wren."

"Like the architect. What are the chances we get shot in this, Chris?"

Vehicles screamed by on either side, their horns jammed down hard as Lacy picked up speed. The exit for the Federal Building was half a mile away.

"High," he said. "Or the fire will get us."

"We're good for fire. Gas tank is under the trailer and I'm full of iced meat; you picked the right truck to hit a burning building with."

Wren laughed. "I'm selective."

"Shouldn't have picked that toy car then. You've got a gun?"

"Sure, have you?"

"Under the seat," she said, and shuffled over.

Wren reached across and hunted under her seat, pulling out an old, well-oiled Colt .45.

"Personal protection at nights is a son of a whore," Lacy said, and winked.

Wren ejected the magazine and checked the breech: all smooth. He slid it back into place and cranked the slide to push a bullet into position. Properly maintained. He tucked it into the glove box.

"Try to stay out of the firefight until I'm back."

"You're back? Where are you going?"

"Into that building. Now, can I climb back into the trailer from here?" he asked, checking on the Sig Sauer stowed in his waistband.

Lacy laughed. "Are you crazy, into a refrigerated unit? Of course not."

"Of course not." Wren grinned back. This felt more like it. "Don't corner too hard while I'm out there, OK?"

"What?"

He flung open the door and pointed off to the side. "You're going to throw me onto the roof of that building. Just think of it like I'm surfing, only you're the wave. Hunker low as we come in, aim for the least burned-up section, then get out. The smoke should cover you."

She stared at him.

"Thank you, Lacy," he said, then pulled himself out of the cab and up onto the roof, using the wing mirror as a foothold. Off to the left lay a fantastic view of the Whipple Building, angry fires sparking through its shroud of smoke.

"Hang on!" Lacy called from below, and Wren just managed to snatch hold of the trailer's metal rim as the cab swung sharply right. The trailer's momentum yanked against the truck's coupling, metal screaming high before obeying Lacy's command, cornering onto the exit at an outlandish speed.

44

HELTER-SKELTER

Lacy's truck raced helter-skelter through clutches of new development apartment blocks, shot out on a short bridge over the Mississippi then crashed hard into another screaming turn on the far bank. Smoke was thick in the air.

Wren's left leg throbbed but held, and he stood tall on the cab scanning their approach. Acker's Saints encircled the Henry Whipple Building about fifty yards apart; several of them tracked the semi with their rifle muzzles as it rocketed into the last hundred yards.

The Henry Whipple was a two-tier building: the single-story bottom tier was a wide and low oblong like the base of a sheet cake; the second-tier had a much smaller footprint, rising five square stories from the lower tier's eastern side.

Now it lay directly ahead; the bottom floor was engulfed in tearing flames while the upper five five stories were a fuming black smokestack. As they pulled with a hundred yards through the parking lot, Wren spotted some kind of rock-strewn defensive moat around the base.

He threw himself flat to the cab's roof and ducked his head in through the window.

"Swerve, Lacy, now!"

Lacy raked the wheel left. Wren was sent tumbling as the huge vehicle cornered hard, brakes screeching and metal shearing. His body slid off the cab roof and into open air, but his right hand on the rim and held. He fell through the air like a closing hinge to slap against the cab's door, smacking the wind out of his lungs.

For a second he hung there, legs dangling above the front wheel, then the truck swerved right to circle the parking lot. Wren used the shift in impetus to get his chest against the door and his feet on the running boards.

"I thought we was gonna ram it?" Lacy shouted through the window.

Wren snatched a breath. "Security moat," he managed, "they started digging them after Oklahoma City. I didn't think-"

"Didn't think? How we gonna hit the building now?"

Wren's mind raced. The moat was maybe only five feet deep, a shallow incline filled with large shale rocks, but there was no way a semi could traverse it. He scanned the building's layout as the Saints' automatic gunfire sprayed in the semi's wake. There were only moments left until they were out of the lot and back onto the highway on-ramp.

Then he saw it.

"There, northwest corner," he shouted, making the bet, "there'll be access."

"What? I don't see anything but them idiots with guns." Lacy shouted back.

"That's a guard tower. Trust me, we'll make it." He hauled himself back up onto the cab. A long block of low outbuildings flew by then Lacy cornered hard again; this time Wren was ready for it and held on. Rifle fire raked the back of the trailer, then they were steaming down a narrow aisle of parked cars, headed directly for the intermittent line of Saints.

"Get down!" Wren shouted, and laid flat on the cab as incoming fire punched through the windshield and smacked off the grille. Bullets filled the air, then they were through the line and Wren saw it up ahead: access to a service courtyard in back of the building. There was a narrow gap where vehicles could pull up for delivery, screened by the raised arm of a security gate.

He stamped on the cab's ceiling and shouted. "Hit it, Lacy, then get out!"

The truck sped up, crumpling the fenders of parked cars and smashing a path over a low separating verge of bushes. At the building's fringe the trailer released a massive crack as it went over over the brick curb, signaling one of the axles splitting. An instant later they slammed down into the narrow courtyard beyond and raced straight for the raging building.

Smoke wreathed the roof ahead like a dark cocoon, making the edge hard to pick out. In the five seconds before impact Wren climbed to the top of the trailer and took up a surfer's stance facing dead ahead. The height should be about equal. The speed wasn't too bad, about thirty miles per hour. If he rolled well on landing, he should be fine.

Two seconds, one, then the cab hit the wall with an immense crash; forty tons of mass hammering into the Whipple Building's rebar-reinforced concrete, launching Wren like a bullet from a gun.

His feet plucked off the trailer and he was in the air flying through smoke, until maybe two seconds later his right leg caught the roof, he ran a single step then his left leg gave out and he folded into a commando shoulder roll. His pelvis cracked on the hot felt roof, his elbow took a glancing hit then he came to a halt on his side.

He coughed; smoke was everywhere. His left side felt raw with the impact even through his clothes; he'd come off a motorcycle once before in full leathers and this felt like that. Par for the course, he thought, as he grunted against the pain and lurched to his feet.

The fire's heat was already rising up through the roof and pouring out from the gathering blaze at the base of the second tier. Wren blinked and started toward it, staggering on his left leg. Gunfire carried from behind, but the Saints couldn't pick him out through the smoke. The fire popped and whined as if in answer.

He checked Sinclair's Sig Sauer P320 in his waistband, still there, then drew Sinclair's phone and rattled off a quick message to his Foundation.

NORTHWEST SIDE - SAINTS ARE EVERYWHERE - CLEAR ME AN EXIT ROUTE

He picked a spot in the second tier's windward side, where the smoke was thinnest, and shot out the window with the P320, releasing a blast wave of heat. He kicked through the shards of glass and stepped down into a long office of desks, chairs and cubicle dividers obscured by leaping orange flames.

His skin baked in the sweltering air. Suddenly it hurt to breathe, and each gasp carried too little oxygen. His eyes watered and he could barely see. A fine rain of sprinkler water played down from the nozzles above, not nearly enough to extinguish the fire. He held his shirt to his mouth with one hand and lurched in, limping between desks and trailers of flame as best he could, letting intuition lead him toward the cooler central core.

To the left there were banks of elevators opening and closing crazily, ahead on the leeward side a wall of fire shot up outside the windows, then he pushed through a door to the central stairwell.

It offered momentary relief from the raw heat; there was no fire here yet, but thin drifts of toxic black smoke were already wafting up through the vertical chute. He squeezed his eyes half-shut, slammed the door behind him to keep the smoke out as much as possible, then clamped his shirt tighter to his mouth and began to climb.

His left leg screamed with every hopping step up, barely taking any weight. His right leg burned with the strain. Thank God he'd doubled down on his CrossFit training. Working the railing hard, using his upper body to pull and his right leg to push, he counted the steps passing underfoot, turning at each landing and circling back. Thirty-three steps in all for one floor, eighteen north, fifteen south to the third floor. He'd have to remember that split or he'd be sending these people down to die in the basement. He reached the third floor, fourth floor, and by then he was running on willpower alone, panting at the thickening air until finally he reached the top.

People were screaming nearby. Wren scanned the corridors branching off and watched smoke rolling like a river, then followed it for the final stretch to the roof.

45

ROOF

The roar of the fire below grew tremendous as Wren emerged onto the smoke-encircled roof, sounding like a ravening beast ripping chunks out of the building's innards. Rifle fire skittered haphazardly nearby, masked by swirling sooty updrafts flecked with orange tongues of flame.

People loomed in the hazy gray, shouting, shoving, terrified, and Wren plunged into their midst, passing tight throngs locked in heated arguments, people sobbing and pleading desperately into unresponsive cell phones. Some screamed in pain from blackened burns, others lay still or slumped coughing from the smoke, all blinking madly as their red eyes ran tear trails down soot-stained cheeks.

Panic and fear were everywhere he looked. Wren had dealt with crowds in similar situations before; they didn't understand what was happening to them and didn't know what to do. No past drill had prepared them for a building-engulfing fire while armed troops prevented escape. Logic dictated the roof as the safest place to wait for emergency services to arrive and save them, but the only emergency service now was Wren.

He lurched deeper through the crowd, looking for the center of their shifting mass and steeling himself to be calm. People in this state could be counted on to act against their own interests, and panic and fear combined to a lethal cocktail where logic no longer operated. They would trample themselves to death if he wasn't incredibly clear and careful with any directions he gave. A panicking spirit of mass exodus could send them all over the roof's smoke-fogged lip in less than a minute.

Survival required order and control, and control required authority, and authority was his specialty.

That meant getting their attention.

At something like the whirling center he stopped and turned, taking in the people nearest him, making guesses about what their capability.

His first target was a slender man, mid-thirties maybe, wearing a purple shirt smeared with soot in handprint shapes and a skewed tie, with red, flickering eyes.

Better than a vacant gaze. He was still trying to process this, hadn't succumbed to the chaos and grown numb. Wren grasped him by the shoulders to stop him wandering, clasped his face firmly to still his gaze and looked dead into his eyes.

"My name is Christopher Wren. I'm going to get you out. You will survive this. First, I need you on your knees and silent. Do you understand me?"

The man just stared. The direction made no sense, but Wren just pushed him gently down to his knees. "Like that," he said, leaning close to his ear. He patted his shoulder. "Stay like that and I'll get you out."

He moved on to the next. A young woman was screaming and beating at her skirt though the fire was long out. He batted her wild arms away and repeated the same trick, compelling her with a firm, calming touch.

She went pliantly and fell silent, staring at him as if he wasn't real. Now there were two. He pointed at a third person, a thickset man in his fifties who had watched him work on the first two, and the man stared. Wren pulled his gun and the man swiftly dropped to his knees. Wren nodded approval and moved on, radiating outwards.

In less than five minutes he had some thirty people kneeling silently; the effect beginning to spread organically as people recognized what was happening. The hubbub of motion and noise at the center of the throng dropped sharply away. In ten minutes the rooftop was silent but for the sounds of the fire and rattling coughs.

"Some of you saw me ram the building in a semi," Wren called over them in a deep, controlled voice, letting his words hang for a moment, encouraging their rational minds to switch back on. He needed them as thinking individuals for what would come, not a mindless mob. "I came in from the northwest side. That means there's a route out. We can get out."

One person rose and ran. Wren fired the P320 without thinking; the shot went over the man's head and he flattened to the hot roof with a cry. A man running was a leader whom others would follow, creating a wild crush that would certainly kill them all.

The crowd gasped.

"I can lead you out," Wren said, "but you need to follow my orders to the letter. You must not panic. The stairwell is filling with smoke, and we'll be climbing down half-blind. Panic there and you'll kill everyone. Do you really want to survive alone with a thousand deaths on your conscience?" He left that for a moment. Get them thinking about the days and weeks to come. Get them believing survival was not only possible, but likely, if they followed the rules. "I don't think you do. So we go in single file. We go in a line. We use our brains and we'll all survive."

They stared at him with glossy red eyes, hope shining through the desperation. He wasn't done yet though.

"Once we're out they'll be shooting at us. The northwest lot is narrow, they can get maybe ten of their shooters in there. They have automatic rifles, they'll spray us wildly, and we need to face the possibility we will be shot. But there is no retreat here. The fire is at your back, ready to kill you if you won't charge. There's no choice and no bravery to this, just necessity. With sheer mass of numbers we will bring these bastards down. I promise. Charge and have a chance. Stay here and certainly die. Who's with me?"

They stared. He didn't expect anything else. They had nothing left to give.

He pointed at a woman nearby, someone who'd seemed resilient and aware on his first triage assessment. "Lead the first fifty. Pick them by touch, guide them on. If any of your people try to get ahead, you're responsible for bringing them down. They're a threat to all of us."

He pointed at others swiftly, twenty more lieutenants he'd assessed on the way in, though the thickening smoke was getting difficult to see through. The heat was intolerable. Had he taken too long?

"Three stories down," he shouted, binding them with his voice. "We want the second-floor exit to the lower roof. It's around thirty steps per floor, split into two flights each. That's six flights, around ninety steps total; count them. Do not go too far, do not go too few. Enter the ground floor and you'll die. Get off on the third and you'll die. Follow the trail and we'll get out. Cover your mouth with whatever you can. Now stay on your knees until you are chosen, or you will be shot."

He tapped the woman then started back through the masses, and she followed behind him, tapping people along their path. They rose up in near-silence and followed. He had to hope it would stay this civilized through the end, because he couldn't stay with them. Not even he could survive in that smoky stairwell for long, and once they hit the ground?

None of them would survive on their own against Acker's Saints. Against automatic rifle fire they'd all be dead as they emerged, contrary to what he'd just said about a brave last charge. The chances of that succeeding were vanishingly small, and Wren had only one gun, with limited bullets.

Now he was counting on the Foundation. On help coming through at the last minute.

Sometimes you just had to hope.

46

OUT

The fifth floor was rife with smoke and flames, visibility was foggy but for bright licks of fire. Wren ran unevenly, left leg giving out as he lurched over blazing patches, until at last he reached the elevators and the stairwell.

"Cover your mouth with your shirt," he said to the person nearest him, briefly holding their arm. He couldn't tell if it was a woman or a man. "Close your eyes, count ninety steps, then get out. Pass it back."

He covered his mouth then plunged first into the swirling haze of the stairwell. It was slightly cooler here than the open floor, but visibility was terrible. He stumbled at the edge but caught the railing, painfully hot to the touch now, then started down fast, counting every step and feeling the billows of heat rising from below.

The chute soon filled with the sound of clattering feet, and someone behind him fell. He thought about going back to help but didn't. It would only clutter the stairwell further, and he didn't have time. There wasn't enough air. Every gasp in through his wadded shirt forced him to cough and splutter. If he stopped, he would die, his body would block the route and then they'd all die.

Thirty-five steps, the fourth floor, and there was a rush of fresh heat raw on his cheeks. The corridor outside the fire doors had to be ablaze: the linoleum, the paint, the insulation inside the walls. He sped deeper down.

Fifty-three steps and the mist from the sprinklers no longer reached him at all, swept up in the inferno. He was dizzy with lack of oxygen, back under the lake with every step further feeling like a stroke closer to boiling alive.

He risked a glance through cracked eyelids but saw little other than the red glow of the metal railing through the smoke. On the second floor he punched through the door and stepped directly into fire, opened his eyes and saw a lick of flame running up his jeans. He slapped at his leg with his bare hands as he staggered onward, back past the dead elevators and through the office. It was a hellscape; the walls roaring, the ceilings, the floor, making a long tunnel of fire to the windward window.

His feet thudded on the burning vinyl, left leg barely holding his weight, acrid smoke filling his lungs, then he reached the open window and burst out onto the first-floor roof.

On his back on the scalding concrete he coughed black phlegm and rolled, groaning. His left leg smoldered, and he patted the embers out. More bodies came shooting after him, splaying onto the roof. Here the smoke was thinner and drifted with fresh air. They could see the sky. Escape seemed so close and hope pumped fresh adrenaline into Wren's muscles.

He slapped out fires on those nearest to him. A woman's hair was scorched. A man's shirt was cinders, stuck to his chest and back.

"Help the others as they come out," he shouted, too loud after the roar of the fires, "then follow me. Wait at the roof edge if you have to. I'll find a way down."

He staggered on with the P320 in his hand, the grip so hot it scalded his palm. To either side he picked out black flecks through the smoke; Saints still standing sentry around the building's moat. Acker hadn't deployed them all to the semi, which meant he was overconfident, and there was a chance.

At the edge of the roof Wren flung himself blind through a rising wall of flame, trusting the semi would still be there. For a second, he fell, then hit the flexing metal of the trailer's roof with a hollow bong and rolled. The surface warped beneath him, and a welter of rifle fire rang out in response.

Only the smoke saved him; he flattened himself and rolled to the trailer's edge, grabbing the rim just as his body tipped over the side. Bullets pierced the trailer's far side and thudded into the cargo of frozen meat.

Wren dropped down to the blacktop and his wounded left leg collapsed beneath him. He grunted and crawled to the shelter of a huge melting tire.

There was no sign of Lacy anywhere. God willing, she'd gotten away before the Saints had closed in.

Wren lay flat, pressed his cheek to the cold ground and edged his left arm around the curve of the half-gelatinous tire, squinting for a target. The Saints were standing out in the open unleashing fire on the trailer; looked like twelve of them. They couldn't see Wren wrapped in smoke at the base.

A metallic bang came from above, followed by others as the first of his refugees dropped from the roof. There was no time to waste, and Wren fired. One of the Saints went down, shot in the chest, but the others kept up a steady rain of bullets. Wren sighted and fired again, taking one of them in the gut, another in the shoulder, one in the leg, then they swept their fire toward him behind the wheel, just as a refugee fell beside him.

"Stay back!" Wren cried, as bullets hammered the tire's heavy frame and the nearby blacktop, ricocheting in sparks and stinging shrapnel spray. There was no way he could take any more of them pinned down like this.

"Lay down by the wall," Wren called to the four refugees squatting in the shadow of the wheel. "Charge on my signal!"

He didn't wait for a response and forced himself to his feet, loping in awkward jolts to the semi's cab, half-buried in the wall and choked in thick black smoke. Operating largely by feel, Wren clambered up into the cab and ducked low in the footwell, scrabbling for the gearstick. The engine was still grinding. He found the clutch, cranked the huge machine's gears into reverse, sent a swift prayer up to whoever was listening and punched the gas.

The semi rumbled to life, extricating itself from the building and pulling away backward. It meant the route down for the other refugees would be gone, but Wren couldn't think about that now, as the remaining eight Saints concentrated their fire on the trailer now beeping noisily as it reversed toward them.

Bullets smashed atonally into the trailer's back and sides, some even rattled through the load of frozen meat to plink musically off the wall behind Wren's head, but the Saints were fighting a few tons of near-solid metal. The speedometer crept up to five as the truck reached the edge of the smoke, then Wren cranked the stick to neutral and rolled his body out of the cab.

The Saints tracked the semi with a hail of bullets. Wren limped along behind the retreating cab, shielded within the foul black fumes gushing from the grill. It was time to turn this thing around. He took a deep breath then stepped up onto the cab's grille, completely immersed in the black, and waited.

The truck rolled through the line of eight Saints in seconds, then muzzle flashes popped through the black to his left. Wren fired back, then shot another on the right. In the chaos of gunfire and motion the other Saints kept on shooting, even as more ghostly bodies gathered at the roof's edge, looking for a way down.

The truck's reverse slowed as the rear wheels climbed a sidewalk. Wren picked off a nearby Saint on the right, then hopped down and hobbled over to the body, snatching up his automatic rifle. He hefted the stock, slapped the slide and let rip against the others.

He took out three of them to the left before they knew what was happening, completely clearing the near side of the trailer.

"Come on!" he shouted, and into the breach came a handful of refugees from the fire. A woman in a power suit snatched up a rifle. She turned it this way and that in the low smoke, checked the safety then started firing.

Wren loped around the rumbling semi, flanking the remaining few Saints from behind. They were caught up in events, trying to figure out the location of their enemy; no 'live-fire' training exercise with victims chained up at desks could have prepared them for this.

Wren opened up on them. Two dropped instantly, and the others broke into a sudden retreat. Wren tottered in pursuit, bursting through the thinning veils of smoke to see a bizarre scene in the parking lot beyond.

Vehicles were pouring in off the expressway, but not fire trucks or ambulances, squad cars or riot police; these were civilian. A blue SUV, another semi, a white Ford panel van, a Prius with a guy standing up through the sunroof. Citizens within brandished handguns and hunting rifles with muzzles flashing, trained in on the Saints.

The bark of gunfire retorted across the blacktop. The Saints on the perimeter were totally exposed, and broke for cover under this incoming attack.

Wren's heart swelled, pumping fresh energy into his battered legs. Not only had the Foundation come through for him, but regular citizens had too. People off the street, out of their homes, the real grassroots. He didn't know any of these people and they didn't know him, but still they'd come in defense of their country.

He dropped the spent rifle and stumbled toward the lead vehicle, a blue SUV, with his arms up. It pulled up with twin rifles trained in his direction.

"People are coming down from the roof," he shouted, his voice rough and dry. "Northwest side, pull up so they can jump down on your vehicle, then get them away from the smoke. Thank you."

The driver, a steely-faced man with a handlebar mustache, nodded sharply and drove directly toward the fire.

Wren lumbered out into the middle of the lot, surrounded now by gleaming cars. It was so different out here, as if the fire wasn't even happening. He rubbed grit from his eyes and spun, taking in the lay of the lot and searching for Richard Acker. He pulled out his phone to check a building plan but found it already ringing.

"Wren," he growled.

Dr. Ferat's voice answered, coming clipped and cool. "Your hackers have us watching via camera drone above, Christopher."

"Where's Acker?" he rasped.

"We don't see him," Ferat answered coolly. He made a bizarre operator to have in the midst of a firefight. "The Fostering Authority is on the southeast corner, so perhaps he's there. No vehicles are getting out. There's a flood inbound and they've blocked the route, which means he's trapped in here with you."

Wren scanned the spot where the off-ramp pulled into the Whipple Building's grounds. There was a barricade of mismatched vehicles in a wide range of colors, only letting traffic flow through in one direction.

"Thanks," he grunted, then let the phone drop by his side and shambled on at a half-run.

Acker was here somewhere.

47

IN

Wren's breath came in rasping wheezes. Each stride felt like a hot dagger in his injured thigh. He was singed and bruised, lightheaded from smoke inhalation, but he was still Christopher Wren.

A squad of Saints ran to intercept him, firing rapidly. Wren took cover behind a Tesla, firing over the trunk until his magazine ran dry, taking out two, three, until several of the vehicles racing around the exterior road took out the remaining two. Wren raised a hand in thanks and shuffled on. The nearest driver blasted her horn.

Acker.

His eyes worked the outer ridge beyond the moat as he cleared the southern side of the building, but there was no sign of the Alpha. Perhaps he'd gone into the Mississippi and taken his chances with the current, but Wren didn't think so.

He had to be here. This was the beginning and the end for him.

Wren turned back to the building. Across the shallow moat, the glass entrance doors hung open now, cracked in the maelstrom of flame. Wren thought he saw movement and squinted. A figure was standing before them, some fifty yards away and haloed by fire; a large golden man with a bloody face and a gun in his hand, pointing it right at Wren.

Richard Acker.

"Christopher!" Acker called. "Come die for me."

He fired; the bullet struck a vehicle somewhere behind Wren, starting the alarm caterwauling.

Wren broke into a zig-zagging run. At fifty yards out, Acker would have to be an incredible marksman to pick him out with a handgun, and Wren didn't believe he was.

Acker was a talker. He was all noise and fury; fake face, fake muscles, fake tan. Wren figured he'd never taken the months on a range required to clear a kill under these kind of conditions: flames at his back, his team of Saints in retreat, the adrenal surge of combat likely setting his nerve endings on fire for the first time ever.

There was almost no chance Wren would be hit.

But Wren had that training. He raised his rifle as Saints wearing tactical black ran nearby, fleeing from the civilian vehicles now thronging the lot.

Acker fired again and again, but all the bullets sailed harmlessly by. At thirty yards out Wren judged the distance dangerous, and dropped to one knee, butted the rifle against his shoulder, and took aim.

Acker was on the bridge above the moat now, advancing toward Wren. His face was a mask of blood welling from a wound in his forehead, while flames framed him on all sides.

Wren remembered his promise to Sinclair back at the Jib-Jab complex, to save Acker's life if he could. If at all possible, he'd keep that promise. Better for this man to face judgment for his many crimes in a court of law, where all his victims could see true justice done.

He fired once.

The slug took Acker in the shoulder and spun him. The gun dropped from his hand, the whole arm now incapacitated.

"It's over, Richard," Wren called, letting the rifle hang and advancing slowly but steadily now toward the bridge, like he was approaching a wounded animal. "Time to come in. I'll see you're treated fairly."

"Fairly?" Acker boomed, clutching at his wounded shoulder, with the light of true madness shining now in his eyes. "Do you think anything in my life was fair, Christopher Wren? You'll put me on display, a monster for the masses to poke and prod. Better to die a martyr here as the spark that ignites America!"

He ducked toward the gun with his left hand.

Wren shot him in that shoulder too. Acker was spun and roared again.

He had no hope of using the gun now, but the threat was clearer than ever to Wren. Martyrship was incredibly powerful. There would always be those to follow in the footsteps of man with such incredible faith, no matter how misguided. Many people still lionized Wilkes Booth.

Better by far to take Acker alive.

Wren dropped the rifle, raised both hands with the palms out and kept advancing. Acker was a talker, so Wren would have to talk him down.

"It won't be like that, Richard," he called, closing the gap to twenty yards already. "I promise."

"You promise!" Acker retorted, both arms hanging uselessly now as he staggered back toward the flames. "You're nothing, Christopher. You're nothing!"

Wren discarded a friendly approach. It wasn't going to work; he needed to get Acker's attention until he could close the gap and physically shut him down.

Maybe he had just the thing: the fresh wound in Acker's forehead. It looked familiar, the same rough shape as Mason's many face brands, but this was deeper still. As if the branding iron had been held in position too long, burning the letters into his skull.

SIC SEMPER TYRANNIS, they read.

"I see you finally got your brand," Wren called.

Acker laughed and turned, just yards from the shattered doors and the flames. "Yes. You were right about me; I wasn't willing to sacrifice everything for the cause. I am now."

"What cause?" Wren pressed, stepping closer with every word. "You're killing innocents here, Richard. They didn't all abuse you."

"They covered it up!" Acker roared back at him, stepping back again. "They're all complicit. You talk about justice? These people took advantage of me when I couldn't fight back! I'd think you would understand, after all you've been through. We're brothers now, Christopher, though I've walked where you would not dare."

Wren snorted and pointed at the building. "I've walked in there while it was on fire. Have you?"

Acker snarled. "I will walk in the fire soon, brother, and will you try to stop me? Would you save a fellow suffering soul?"

Wren kept closing the distance. Keeping him talking was everything. "Yes. I put two bullets in you already, but I didn't kill you, did I? I agree;

219

what was done to you by the people in this building was abhorrent, Richard. It was evil, and those responsible should be punished. You want to burn those people alive? I'll light the match. But not like this. Every one of those responsible should pay with their lives, but that's no excuse for killing the innocent along with them."

"None of them are innocent!" Acker raged. "They all looked away, until I became this." He tried to point at his face, but his right arm only flopped helplessly. "Tell me, could I make it in your collection of freaks, Christopher? Your wannabe vampires and hackers, your bikers and broken souls? What would it take to put me on a coin?"

"A little less plastic surgery," Wren countered.

Acker laughed. "If not a coin, then what will you do with me, Christopher, when I'm in your grasp? Will you learn new and wonderful things?"

"I learned all I needed to know in the Pyramid. Some people are broken, and that makes them dangerous. You're both. You need professional help."

Acker's lips split in a grin. "Ah yes, the Pyramid. Your father is a very great man, Pequeño 3."

There was less than eight yards between them, now. "Not 'is', Acker, 'was'. He's dead."

Acker's grin spread. "If you're so sure of that, then tell me where your wife and children are. Are they truly safe from his reach?"

Wren's heart skipped a beat. "You don't know what you're talking about. You're bluffing."

"What bluff, that I sent my Saints to kill them? Look at my works, brother, am I a man who bluffs?"

Five yards, now. Wren was ready to charge and grab Acker, but abruptly he leaped backward, through the shattered frame of the doorway and into the shooting flames of the lobby.

"It's like the Pyramid in here," he shouted over the fire's roar, as red and orange tongues lapped at his clothes. "You should know that more than anyone, after walking the streets as the bodies burned. Do you remember how that felt, Christopher?"

Wren had to squint against the punishing heat of the fire as he edged closer still. "I remember I escaped. I survived. You can too."

He lunged.

Acker was too fast again, skipping three sharp steps deeper into the lobby. Now the inferno churned all around him. "Nobody escaped the Pyramid, Christopher Wren! Your father told me every delicious moment. About how you killed all those people."

Wren blinked and had to hold both hands up to shield his eyes against the fierce heat. "What are you talking about?"

"I know you were his favorite," Acker cried as the fires licked up into his golden hair. "How you painted every one of the thousand with napalm and lit the match. Together you burned every soul of the Pyramid, and he was so proud. Do you remember how that felt, Christopher?"

Images suddenly flashed before Wren's eyes; fire everywhere both in the past and the present.

"Never happened," he shouted, then plunged three blind strides into the inferno, hands outstretched and grasping.

They closed on empty air.

The Alpha of the Saints stood in the center of the lobby now, arms miraculously spread and engulfed in flames.

"Someday you'll see the beauty!" he cried as the fire swallowed him. "Do you know these people put a mark on my record, Christopher, to show that I was weak? They passed me around like a thing. Where were you then?"

Wren sprang back as Acker's body became a yellow pillar of flame. Was he laughing or wailing?

"Make sure they write songs about me," his voice screamed out of the hellscape. "Bigger than Manson!"

Then he was gone.

The fire swallowed him completely, licking up his bronzed head and into his golden hair, melting him like a pillar of wax.

Wren backed away with his eyes burning, and kept backing up until he almost fell at the edge of the steps.

Sweat drenched him. Both legs shook. Old ghosts danced in the flames where Richard Acker had disappeared; memories long buried.

Had he been the one to burn the Pyramid? Had his hands truly set the blaze?

He grasped the railing and turned in a daze.

Now the lot sang with vehicles. Smoke-blackened people streamed away from the building, while others rushed to offer them water and bandages. They weren't from the Foundation. They were just people.

The phone rang in his hand. Wren looked at it numbly: Dr. Ferat. At the same time a message flared in from Director Humphreys.

COME IN, CHRISTOPHER. THERE'S A PLACE FOR YOU HERE.

It sounded like what he'd just said to Acker. He stared at it for a long moment, then dialed in a number from memory. Mid-afternoon Central time, that had to be late evening in the UK. Skirting the edge of the lot, he limped away as the line rang.

48

REAP IT

The line answered. Wren's father-in-law sounded gruff and angry.

"Chris? Is that you?"

"It's me," he answered, cupping the receiver against the receding wail of sirens. "Tell me she's safe, Charlie. Tell me the kids are safe. If you won't do that, I'm going straight to her."

A long moment passed. The old guy had to be thinking it through, sat on his bed back on the edge of London, living a totally different life. A sigh came down the line. "I'm watching the attacks over there. It's on every news channel. Are you mixed up in all that?"

"Are they safe, Charlie?" Wren insisted.

"Yes," the older guy spat out. "She's safe. I just spoke to Jake. They're all fine."

The relief rushed through Wren and almost knocked him out. Like a tidal wave breaking over his head, it sent silver specks swamping his vision, but he gritted his teeth and bulled through.

"The things that are happening over there," the old guy went on, before Wren could speak, "it speaks well of you, Chris. I can see your fingerprints all over this. I can see you fought it."

"But you still won't tell me where she is?"

Silence hung for a long moment. "That's two different things, isn't it? On the one hand, I'm proud. You've saved a lot of people today, haven't you? I expect she's proud, too. But after this, you'll be more of a target now than ever. For the government, for enemies of your country, whoever. That means Loralei and the kids are targets too, because of you. Nothing's changed, really. If anything, it just got worse."

Got worse.

"I'll find her. My hackers can have her location in half an hour. She's my wife, damn it, Charlie!"

"Don't do that," Charlie cautioned. "No CIA tricks. Like I said before, if she wants to talk to you, she knows how to do it. You wait for that, son. It's best for everyone."

Best for everyone.

Reap it.

He hung up, then sat down on a railing by the river's side and tapped out a message for his Foundation.

COME GET ME

Many hours later, Wren woke in a quiet and still apartment. He had only the vaguest memories of Foundation members coming to collect him in an unmarked family saloon.

Now he looked up at the cracked white plaster ceiling and listened to the calm sound of a fan ticking over. By his side sat Alli. She had bandages wrapped around her head, but otherwise she seemed OK.

"Hey," she said.

Wren almost laughed. His wrist was clamped in her fingers. She was counting his pulse quietly to herself, like it was a rocket about to launch.

"Hey yourself," he croaked.

She smiled. "That was a close one, Chris. Wild, really."

He pushed himself upright on the bed, feeling nauseous. There were a lot of pieces jumbling around in his head still. "Are you OK, Alli? Where are we?"

Alli smiled. "I'm fine. My ear's been sutured; they say you won't even see the scars. We're in a safe house on the edge of Minneapolis. Dr. Ferat set it up. Foundation members have been coming and going. There was a surgeon, a nurse. They sewed you up. You're in pretty good shape now, they said. It's just me left."

Wren tried to take that on board.

"And Mason?"

"He's OK. In a big government hospital somewhere. I thought that sucker was dead, too, but you know what they say about Marines." She shrugged.

Wren smiled along. "I'm sorry about this. I shouldn't have dragged you into it. Abdul..." He trailed off.

"Bullshit," Alli said. "This is exactly why I'm in the Foundation. Broken people, right? We need each other. And you're king of the freaks, you know?"

He chuckled. "I guess."

"You guess? You never told me all that death cult stuff, Chris. Your past. It's heavy. We should talk about you more in our coin meetings."

Wren had no answer to that. Dr. Ferat must have told her. It wasn't the kind of thing he told anyone, but he didn't feel so bad that Alli knew. Maybe it felt OK. "Yeah."

"Yeah, he says. Well, listen. They found Henry, did you hear that? He was unconscious in some hospital in Utah. He's OK too. Dr. Ferat said you'd want an update, and I volunteered. Cheryl's fine, he said, and Teddy, or Theodore Smithely III, he's in a coma, but the doctors are hopeful he'll make a full recovery, if he ever wakes up."

All that sounded good. Better than Wren could have hoped for. "How long have I been out?"

She did quick sums in her head. "Sixty-seven hours, I'd say? Long enough. You had sepsis coming on, apparently, but they beat it back. Saved your leg, too."

He pushed off the bed. His right leg held him, his left crumpled and he cursed.

"Yeah," she said. "They said that'll last for a while. It'll be a month or two before you walk properly again. Lots of tissue damage, but they said the muscle fibers should heal nicely." She beamed.

"Thanks," Wren said, then held out a hand. "Keys."

She laughed. "To what, the Promised Land?"

"I appreciate this, Alli. All this, you waiting. Really. But I have to go."

"To see your kids?"

His eyes widened.

"It's OK. You've been talking about them in your sleep for days. I get it. So I'll make you a deal. I give you some car keys, you do something for me."

He smiled and leaned in. "What?"

"Bring this thing together more. More coin meetings where we really talk, not just about me and my problems, but you too. More crossover in the Foundation. Also, I want you to come meet this guy. Maybe my boyfriend?" She blushed slightly.

Wren smiled. "Boyfriend?"

"Maybe. Who knows. Would you?"

"I'd love to. And the rest, sure. I'll work on it. I promise, Alli."

She nodded solemnly. "Good man. Here's your keys. I'll see you soon, Chris. Breakfast's a burger and fries in the fridge; I figured you'd want to roll out fast."

The car was a Jeep Wrangler; a nice touch by his Foundation. He pulled into traffic on the edge of Minneapolis, chewing on the cold burger. His head was still a swamp of clamoring thoughts; about Loralei, his kids, the Foundation.

He'd promised Charlie to stay away, but he had to see them. He had to talk to her at least once.

Within a few hours he crossed the state line into Wisconsin, figuring he'd head back to New York and pick up her trail there. Maybe call in his hackers, like he'd threatened; finally use all his CIA skillset for something good.

His mind churned hard as he drove. Memories drifted up with each hot pulse in the side of his thigh. Sometimes he was back in the flames with the Alpha, as the man called out madness from the depths. The heat was vivid on his skin still, the desperation in Acker's eyes, his last words echoing again and again...

Wren cranked up the radio and tuned through stations. All anyone was talking about was the Saint's terrorist attack on the United States. He drove and listened. It seemed around three hundred people had died in total, scattered across the country. Many of them had been the Saints themselves, as good people everywhere had risen up to protect their fellow Americans.

Over five hundred additional Saints had been arrested. A mass trial before federal court was being posited, with links to the International Criminal Court for war crimes.

Wren followed the story distantly as he drove south and east. That first day, he covered only a few hundred miles before pulling over at a motel. He ate well and slept better than he had in years, as if a burden had been lifted.

The next day he got back in the Jeep and drove on, down through Wisconsin, across Indiana. As the hours passed, he watched the Foundation's darknet board, waiting for Dr. Ferat or someone else to rise up and take control. After they'd seen him so weak, he expected that moment was coming. His members would break cover and announce their locations to each other, start meeting in real life and changing the rules of the organization.

To his surprise, they didn't.

Instead they discussed the Order and the cleanup. They talked about their coins and their progress. They shared stories about past addictions and current temptations. Most of all, though, they talked about Christopher Wren. The real 'Saint Justice', bringing justice to the Saints.

Dr. Ferat reached out regularly, but Wren ignored him, until at some point while driving on his third day through Ohio, he finally answered.

"Doctor," he said.

"Christopher!" Ferat said, clearly surprised. "I'm so glad you answered."

"I owe you, Doctor. Without you, I never could've saved those people. I also heard you arranged for my urgent care."

"It was my honor. Now, how are you, my boy?"

A tough question. Lots of possible answers. "Fine," he settled on. "A lot of thinking."

"About what?"

Wren considered how much he wanted to share. The old Wren would say nothing, but maybe Alli had a point about opening things up. Everybody needed help, after all.

"Something Acker said before he walked into the fire."

"Yes?"

Wren gritted his teeth. Saying it made it real, but it was already real in his head. "That I was there for the final burning of the Pyramid. Acker said my father told him all about it. That he's alive still and coming for my kids."

There was a long silence. "Yes. Well, about that. I found something, Christopher, that may be relevant. In Acker's records, salvaged from the Whipple Building."

Wren squeezed the wheel tight. There was something in the way Ferat was speaking. "What did you find?"

"There was a symbol drawn on his profile. An infamous symbol used by child abuse circles to signal a weak target."

Wren felt the world tunnelling down and his pulse climbing. "What symbol?"

"A blue fairy. Like the character from the Pinocchio tale? It's a symbol your father also used, apparently, during his Pyramid days. To mark out his favored children."

That pushed Wren right back into the past. He pulled the truck over and had to sit by the wayside and just breathe, staring out at blue skies as a cold sweat ran down his back.

Did he remember that? A blue fairy symbol chalked onto the bunks of his brothers and sisters. Maybe he did. Maybe he'd doodled it himself in the sands of Arizona, never really knowing what it meant.

"You're saying the Apex really was linked to Acker? Was even one of his abusers?"

"It could be, Christopher. We don't know anything for sure, but-"

It grew hard to hear anything after that. Not over Wren's thumping heart and rasping breath, as old fears surged to the surface. The same horrors that had kept him with the CIA for so long, righting wrongs for weeks and months at a time. The same drive for justice that had kept him from his own wife and kids, trying to wipe out the legacy of his father.

"… need to reckon with this," Ferat was saying. "I believe your father is alive, and out there somewhere. Further, I fear he may have influenced the Saints to take their terror attack national." Another pause. "Sinclair's been talking, Christopher. It turns out the scale of Acker's ideas, they were out of character. He was angry and vengeful, but not on that kind of scale. Sinclair thinks he might have been brainwashed, or at least manipulated, into taking things to the next level. If so, then I believe this could be your father's influence. If it was, you must find him before he pushes someone else to do something worse."

Wren squeezed the wheel so hard it hurt. Worse than the Saints? "Like what?"

"I don't know. We only have the blue fairy as a clue, but there's a myth about that symbol on the dark Internet. Apparently, it represents a cabal of the world's richest, most depraved men. I have no idea if this is true, but it's possible this 'Blue Fairy' serves as a rallying point for such sick individuals.

In theory, they could mobilize for a Saints-level attack, if they wanted to, or perhaps something bigger still."

Wren gritted his teeth, kept listening.

"I've taken the liberty of speaking with Director Humphreys at the CIA on your behalf. I know you wouldn't want me to, so now I'm asking for forgiveness rather than permission. I believe you have an essential role to play in what comes next, Christopher, and Humphreys agrees. He's willing to extend you AWOP status, Agent Without Portfolio. You'll have the full resources of the CIA to hunt down the Blue Fairy and end whatever conspiracy your father may be trying to build. They'll give you a crack team. With them and Foundation resources, maybe we can bring him down once and for all."

There was nothing Wren wanted more. Except for one thing.

"I can't. You'll have to do it without me."

Ferat paused. "What? Christopher. You-"

"I owe it to my family. I'm out, Doctor. Of the CIA, the Foundation, whatever I have to do. My kids matter most. I have to-"

"He knows about your children," Ferat interrupted sharply. "We found records embedded in Acker's files. Their names. Photographs of them, their ages, even their current address." A beat passed. "Not even you know where they are yet, do you? But Acker did. Maybe your father does, right now. They're somewhere in Delaware. Loralei, Jake and Quinn, staying in a duplex with her new boyfriend." A pause. "I'm sorry, Christopher. Both your children have been marked with the blue fairy brand."

That hit Wren like a sledgehammer to the head. It shifted everything. A sudden rush of adrenaline pumped the bellows on his heart, leaving no time to think. The effect of shock peeled back. The sweat dried down his back. He'd use the CIA, Ferat, the Foundation, whatever it took to keep his kids safe.

"Tell me everything you've got," he said, and punched down on the gas.

NO MERCY FOR THE WICKED

NO MERCY

A CHRISTOPHER WREN THRILLER

MIKE GRIST

1

MINSK

Christopher Wren laid out flat atop a snow-capped roof somewhere on the outskirts of Minsk, Belarus, targeting a building three hundred yards away with a Barrett M82 sniper rifle.

The Blue Fairy, in his sights at last. He prayed this would be the raid that finally made his family safe

In the tawny dusk light, the building looked like nothing special. Just another communist-era construction, a brutalist block of thin concrete slabs half held together with propaganda postings, like the gravestone for a dying ideology. Wren picked out scraps of communist-red clenched fist posters, overlaid atop Lenin's jutting arm and the old and gold hammer and sickle. Breaking their torn wallpaper effect were a few tinted, metal-barred windows on each of the building's seven floors, with a single steel door at the front opening onto the snow-frosted sidewalk.

Wren switched to his Thor infrared scope. Heat-mapped, the building was alive with processing power. The outlines of hundreds of computer server racks across all seven stories blazed like a hellish scaffold, glowing brightest at the top. Thick data lines burned hot down the building's exterior, venting heat before they plunged through holes drilled to the sewers, each laundering vast quantities of dark Internet data out to the open digital ocean.

An international data trafficking operation. Men Wren had been hunting for three months, ever since the Blue Fairy had placed the crosshairs on his children's heads. In those months he'd leveraged his new Agent WithOut Portfolio status with the CIA to track the Fairy's trail ten times around the world already, coming up every time with smoke and mirrors.

The Blue Fairy was a myth. She flitted through the darknet's hidden trunk lines like a ghost, leaving only her stylized, child-like image as a calling card on forums and chat boards, a signal to the world's most depraved men.

Drugs. Sex. Weapons. Children.

Five bright orange figures were on guard on the ground floor near the entrance. A few stood scattered across the levels, two patrolled the roof, and three were seated on the seventh floor, their faint haloes outlined within the white-hot heat of the servers, searing through the thin walls.

These were the traffickers themselves, hard at work managing the ceaseless flow of data. Maybe Blue Fairy operatives. It would be better to take them alive if he could, gather every possible shred of evidence, but the real prize was the building itself. The data flowing through its hundreds of servers, kept invisible by Belarus' dictator-sanctioned haven status, should be enough to bring the Blue Fairy crashing to the ground.

"In position, Commander," came a voice in Wren's earpiece. His Interpol captain, name of Isa Rashidi, a 6' 5" ex-GRU Russian special forces soldier.

Wren swung the scope over and down to a dark alley at the building's side. Rashidi stood in front of the glowing yellow engine of their bullet-shaped UAZ-452 insertion van; a Russian Military Police vehicle that looked like a VW camper van. Plenty of them around in Belarus, easy to blend in. Around it stood Rashidi's five-strong Interpol IRT Incident Report Troop.

Rashidi was a man Wren trusted implicitly. He'd been instrumental in one of Wren's biggest black-ops stings on the Belarusian regime, toppling an underground railroad in trafficked humans. Wren pulled back from the scope to bare-eye the alley, but the troop were wholly invisible in their gray urban camo gear.

"You have eyes on the power line?" Wren asked, switching back to the scope.

"Da, Commander." Rashidi opened the rear doors of the van. "Under the chassis, beneath a grating. It looks like two-inch reinforced copper sheaths. We will burn the grate, then my team blow the lines on a ten-second fuse. All the lights will go out."

Not all the lights. Wren swept his gaze up to the seventh floor, where the lone dark block in the superheated space marked out the building's backup generator. Taking that out fell to Wren. He scanned up to the roof, where the guards patrolled. They didn't seem to have noticed a thing. Wren's overwatch team had already digitally looped their CCTV remotely. If only it was as simple a thing to hack their darknet.

"You're screened from above?"

"Da, under the UAZ. We are ready to cut the grating for access. Two blowtorches, two minutes."

Two minutes. Three months of prep.

"Cut it."

Wren caught the flare of the blowtorches igniting underneath the van. He checked again on the two men on the rooftop through the scope, but there was no response. No line of sight, with the van in the way. He shuffled his grip on the M82's stock, then checked his chamber; loaded with .50 caliber Browning Machine Gun rounds, able to make mincemeat of a wall even ten inches thick. With the rifle on semi-automatic, he could put a dozen shots from the box magazine through the wall in ten seconds flat.

He'd need them all. Turn the backup generator to slag, and no one else Wren trusted to make the shot. Miss it, or the traffickers if they ran, and the warning signal would go out. The darknet would know a hit was underway, and any trace of the Blue Fairy would flush from their servers as if they'd never been there at all.

Three months' worth of intelligence capture and asset risk lost in a flash.

"Explosives placed," came Rashidi's voice in Wren's headset. "Standing ready."

Wren took one last breath, looking out over the city. The faintest glow of a cold, dreary day died out in a rust-red line across the western horizon. Some four thousand miles further on, his kids would still be asleep in their Delaware duplex, no idea of the threat hanging over their heads.

A wind gusted, pulling Wren back to the moment. Maybe minus ten degrees out now, and seemed fresh snow was in the offing. He adjusted the scope's reticle to the wind, took a steadying breath. The air tasted of diesel fumes and raw onion, stinging down his lungs.

He wasn't a fan of Minsk.

"Blow it."

"Fuse is lit," answered Rashidi. Wren refocused his scope on the backup generator, nestled between two of the traffickers on the seventh floor. At the same time he watched with his off-eye as Rashidi led his IRT troops toward the building's front, readying a portable ram. Five seconds, three, then came the firework flash from under the van, the firecracker snap as the blast reached Wren, and he was firing.

The first shot burrowed dust from the wall dead-on, the second hit three inches over, the third tore a divot and the next five .50 cal slugs tunneled wider through crumbling concrete to rupture anything on the other side. Metal, plastic, wiring, bodies.

"Power's out on the ground floor," came Rashidi's voice in his ear, accompanied by the muted barks of rifle fire. "Two down so far. We're seeing heavy-gauge server stacks, computers are all dark."

Exactly as planned. Wren scanned the guys on the seventh floor. One of them was down and motionless already, might have caught a ricochet or shrapnel, another was balled-up under his desk, but then Wren caught a shadow of the third, running west toward the core server racks.

Either making a break to escape, or toward a kill switch to fry every computer on the grid. Every darknet hub he'd come across had a self-destruct plan of some kind: one pull to self-combust the servers, sending the evidence Wren needed up in digital smoke.

He couldn't take that chance, and fired three times through the wall. The guy's orange silhouette collapsed. Maybe going for the door, but equal chance he was going for a

He swung back to the two other guys, saw the one lying flat was now moving at a crawl. Wren put a shot through his chest to be sure. No loss. The balled-up one hadn't budged. All the better to keep at least one alive. He could help them open Pandora's Box.

"Ground floor clear," Rashidi said in his earpiece. "Five hostiles down. We're heading up."

"Proceed with caution," Wren said, and reached out a hand to his loader, who dropped a fresh box of BMGs into it. Took three seconds to eject the old box and insert the new, then he swung the scope up to the roof.

The two guys there looked to be panicking, dithering at the edge. Their heat signatures came in crystal-clear compared to the diffused blue of the others, seen through the building's tissue-thin walls. Wren pinged them both with chest shots then strafed the scope down to scan Rashidi's path, catching movement on the third floor. It didn't look like armed response, someone running in the wrong direction to flee, but maybe headed for the trip switch.

Wren fired five times, and the figure collapsed.

"Second floor looks clear," Rashidi said.

"Two down on the seventh, two on the roof, one on the third," Wren answered. "Entering overwatch."

"Appreciate it, Commander."

Wren scrolled the building, tracking ahead of the IRT as Rashidi led them higher. In back of the squad a figure silhouetted itself briefly, maybe bobbing out of the elevator shaft before dropping back in.

Wren fired without thinking, the rest of the mag and clipped the guy's arm through concrete as he ducked back into shelter.

"Your floor, man winged behind the elevator," he reported.

"I see him," said Rashidi, sent his troops flanking. More rifle fire erupted then died away.

"Second floor clear, continuing the ascent."

Wren's heart pounded. He reached out a hand and received another reload, another three seconds to switch out. It took his eye off the scope for a heartbeat, and when he looked again the trafficker on the seventh floor was in motion. Heading the same way as the first, west to the server racks.

Wren cursed and fired every round from the box, sawing a line through the wall to cut the guy down like a felled tree. He dropped.

Wren let a breath. "All three on the seventh are down."

"I heard that. They ran?"

"They ran."

"It's a pity. Third floor's clear. Anything else in store?"

Wren reloaded again, sweating now despite the cold. "I think you're clear."

The building looked quiet except for the IRT methodically clearing room by room. The building didn't have a big footprint. He swept the building again, saw nothing, then pulled out from the scope and blinked once long and slow before casting his eyes over the street.

Hot afterimages popped across the dark road. About time reinforcements appeared.

"We have incoming," came another voice in his ear, this one belonging to Sally Rogers, his CIA lieutenant poached from a rival department, and a brilliant field analyst. She was operating remotely out of Texas, with eyes in the sky via a LUNA surveillance drone at ten thousand feet. "Looks like two trucks inbound, they're big, eight-wheelers, maybe MKZT-6002 by the profiles. Military bearing, five men apiece."

Wren cursed under his breath. The MKZT-6002 was a beast, looked like the flatbed for a tower construction crane, but no crane attached. Squat and solid as a double-length Humvee, and not commonplace on the streets at all.

They were ready for this.

"Activate the second squad."

Somewhere below a second IRT squad fired up their UAZ van, ready to ram the inbound trucks. It'd barely make a dent on the eight-wheelers, though.

"Coming out of the northeast, boss," Rogers said.

Wren swung the scope over the building one more time, saw Rashidi on the fourth floor and advancing unopposed, then trained in on the road coming in from the north. No sign of the massive MKZTs yet.

"Estimate fifteen seconds 'til you have visibility."

They'd prepared for something like this. Not coming so fast, or with as much mass behind them, but he had redundancies in place. A Lada saloon below waiting to ferry Wren closer to any action, a second UAZ van weighted down with plate metal, ready to act as a ram or blockade a road.

"I'll take their engine blocks if I can," he said. "Get the ram vehicle ready to intercept."

"Boss."

Three seconds left, then the first of the squared-off MKZT-6002s came into sight, as big as a squashed garbage truck and racing at forty miles an hour. Easily three times the mass of his UAZ backup van, even loaded down with metal. Most likely it would be shredded by the bigger MKZTs.

Wren unloaded with the M82 rifle. He hit the glass windshield but sparked off, had to be triple-layer reinforced. He tagged the front grille but it was armored and didn't do a thing to slow the truck's momentum.

"Unable," he barked, reloading as the truck plowed on, chased by the second. "Hit it with the UAZ!"

Two blocks over, the UAZ rocketed out of a side street at the perfect ninety-degree vector, making up with velocity what it lacked in mass. The hit came with a delayed crunch, just enough mass to jog the massive military vehicle to the side and send it careening up the curb to bury itself in a shuttered storefront.

Wren drilled twelve more shots through the windshield, digging enough holes to take out the driver and passenger and maybe coring the engine from above.

"Boss!" called Rogers.

He swung as he reloaded, watched the second MKZT-6002 closing on the building. He didn't have the angle now, it was almost directly below his vantage point. He fired shots that sparked off its roof anf bodywork, then it stopped at the front of the server building, shielding the entrance with its bulk.

"You have incoming, Rashidi!" He shouted down the line. "Rogers, give us a count of how many enter the building."

A second passed, and Wren stood, lifting the M82 off its tripod prongs to a shoulder lock, trying to get an angle. Via the thermal scope he picked out six figures inside the truck, but they weren't moving.

"I'm seeing no movement," Rogers said. "Boss, do you think-"

The truck started up. Wren's eyes flared. Not a single man had exited.

He scanned the building again, saw Rashidi on the sixth floor, almost to the core servers, and made the only leap possible as the MKZT raced away.

"Bomb, Rashidi! Get your men out!"

He barely heard the response. Dropped his M82 and snatched up the waiting fast rope, tossed it off the roof then threw himself after it.

Three big bounces carried him down six stories in seven seconds flat, then he was on the frosted sidewalk and unclipping. The Lada was right there as planned, door open, and he dropped into the passenger side.

"Go!" The car took off. Up ahead came the clanging crash of gunfire, the moonlight splash of glass breaking as the IRT squad broke a way through and tossed fast ropes of their own.

"Exiting," came Rashidi's urgent voice as the Lada strained for velocity. Only two blocks away now and the driver breezed through a red light.

Maybe there were figures rappelling fast down the building's side now, hard to tell.

Wren drew his Sig Sauer P320, .45 ACP eight-shell mag at the ready. There were barely two hundred yards left to cover with the MKZT charging west.

"Get out!" he shouted, looking up at the foreboding building as figures raced down the side like evacuating data trails. Nothing came back but whistling wind and the urgency of movement until-

"Team clearing the building, Commander," shouted Rashidi, with Wren maybe a hundred yards out. "I have-"

Then the building exploded.

Blasts rippled up from its base to its tip like a shockwave, dozens of fiery eruptions ripping through the structure like a vertical field of flowers blooming in dizzying fast-forward, each blowing out jets of cement dust and shrapnel.

The Lada skidded. The feed in Wren's earpiece roared to static. A second of crazy weightlessness followed as gravity took charge of the building, then it began to collapse, some two-hundred-fifty standing feet of ancient Russian engineering crashing down into a falling storm of masonry debris.

The Lada braked hard into a sudden bank of brick dust, striking the windshield like a tidal wave as the building vented its insides out. Shrapnel smashed spidery trails across the glass, a chunk of rock punched through and knocked out the rearview mirror. Dust puffed through the busted ventilation system, the brakes backwashed burning rubber, the Lada's momentum died out and Wren rocked back against the seat.

"Rashidi!" he shouted, already kicking his door open and charging ahead.

No answer came.

The earth shook like it had been hit by Lucifer's hammer, smoke and tumbling debris spinning through the dark. Ten yards on Wren stumbled on a chunk of concrete twisted with rebar but kept on, entering an avalanche of sloping rubble as the destroyed building found its new equilibrium.

"Rashidi!" he called, reached what had to be the curb, now buried some ten feet deep beneath the fresh flow of wreckage. A gusting wind pulled ribbony openings through the dust, giving Wren interlacing sightlines across the block where the building had stood.

All gone. A giant, groaning heap of broken concrete, hissing with ruptured gas lines and spurting water mains, all muted by the swaddling dust. Sirens pierced the shifting stillness, but distantly. Wren's heart pounded. He spun, trying to get a sense of where the team had exited, where they might have reached.

"Rogers!" he shouted. "Give me something."

"Winding back the footage," she answered. "Here, looks like they all made it out but got swallowed up by the rubble wave. Your five o'clock boss."

He staggered backward down the ruins. "Tell me!"

"Ten yards," she answered.

He reached the point, picked up a chunk of masonry and tossed it away, calling Rashidi's name.

Maybe some of them were alive. Some of them had to be alive.

Into the night he worked. Barely thinking about what had happened, about how the Blue Fairy had been more ready than he'd imagined, with a trip switch big enough to bring the entire building down. Scale, size, intensity, resources. The darknet was a trillion-dollar industry.

He kept working as fire crews filed up, police secured the area, earth-moving equipment was brought in to clear the roads and allow better access. Right alongside the emergency services he labored, accepting gloves and a mask when they were handed to him, swinging a pick when it was given, periodically calling Rashidi's name.

By the dawn it was done.

Five members of the IRT were alive. Dug out bleeding at the fringe of the wreckage, suffering from smoke inhalation and a dozen other injuries. Bloodshot eyes, dust plastered to their skin with cold sweat, but alive.

All except Rashidi. They found him last, closest to the building, where he'd been ensuring the safety of his team. His cold gaze burned into Wren's heart.

The Blue Fairy was going to pay for this.

Rashidi was laid on a gurney and carried away. Wren was left standing as they unearthed the dead traffickers. There was nothing to say. Smoke steadily rose, bulging out in a column that blocked the dawn light, and Wren's rage only grew with it.

They'd known. They'd been waiting for him.

His phone chimed in his pocket. He brought it up, found dozens of messages were waiting, all come in while he'd been digging. All of them images. He tapped one and it full-screened.

A stylized image of the Blue Fairy, black silhouette on a blue background, with twin children standing either side of her, holding her hands. Above their heads were his children's names.

Jake. Quinn.

Text ran along the bottom in block capitals.

SUFFER THE LITTLE CHILDREN, CHRISTOPHER WREN

2

LORALEI

Thirteen hours, two flights and a dozen calls later, Wren stood on a suburban Delaware street in mid-afternoon, striding toward the duplex where his wife and kids had started their new life without him.

For three months he'd let his wife go. Loralei. She had cause to be angry with him. He'd kept his double life as a black-ops Force Recon agent for the CIA secret from her. He'd quit the CIA to spend more time with his family, but it had come too late.

She'd found out. Taken the kids and fled their New York apartment, leaving him out in the cold. She'd wanted to get away, and he'd respected her wishes.

This was different.

This was a genuine threat against her, Jake and Quinn. He'd already sent Sally Rogers out to find and secure them, set up some kind of witness protection, and Loralei's response had been clear and absolute.

No.

Now he strode up the drive, muscles working under his jaw. He saw his son Jake's bike by the garage, a small red BMX with the training wheels on, and it broke his heart. Knocked on the door and stood with his pulse thumping upward. Instantly he was transported back to their New York apartment, when he'd been carrying a bottle of wine and cakes for the kids, freshly out of the CIA and hoping everything was going to change.

How wrong he'd been.

Footsteps sounded closer. The door unlatched and swung open.

It was a guy.

Wren blinked.

He was almost half Wren's size, wore glasses, a sweater vest, khaki pants and loafers. He looked like the kind of guy who came out to fix your cables when the Wi-Fi was down. Maybe he was.

"Yes?"

"I'm here to see Loralei Wren. My name's Christopher Wren. I'm her husband."

It took a second, then the guy's expression soured slightly. Not to fear, surprisingly, but to anger. To Wren's surprise, the guy actually stepped forward, pulling the door ajar behind him.

"You shouldn't be here. She doesn't want to see you."

If Wren weren't so wired, he would have laughed. One slap and the guy would go cartwheeling down the yard. But he wasn't here for that. Rather, Wren lifted him gently under the arms the same way you'd lift a toddler, and deposited him to the side.

Pushed through the door.

Hall in cream. Nice hardwoods. The guy barked something behind him, but Wren paid him no mind, then he was in the kitchen, and so was she.

Loralei. She was standing at the counter chopping cucumbers. The smell of bacon sizzled in the air, smoke rising from a griddle, two plates laid out with bread, tomatoes, salsa. Loralei's infamous 'Mexican' BLTs. Not bad for a Brit from East London. There was a jar of mayonnaise with a butter knife sticking out. The guy jogged around to stand in front of Wren.

"I tried to stop him," he started, but Wren just laid a hand on his shoulder, barely even needed to squeeze to shut him up.

Loralei stared daggers. Wren tried to read her. It had been five months since he'd seen her, and she was as beautiful as ever. Dark strands of hair hanging down from a slack ponytail, dressed in snug jeans and a check shirt. Sweet lips spreading to an angry O, those wide-set green eyes flaring, her hairpin brows glowering like tiny thunderheads.

"Chris," she said.

"Loralei."

A heavy moment passed, then she pointed the kitchen knife at him. "You can't be here. I said that to your people. I'm saying it to you. Witness protection? I'm not interested. This afternoon I applied for a restraining order."

That was news to him. "What? Why?"

She laughed. "Why? You're kidding me, right?"

Nothing to say to that. He looked around, saw pictures drawn by his kids on the fridge, toys strewn in the den, signs of a normal family life. Everything he'd lost. "Where are Jake and Quinn?"

"With their aunt. Now let James go."

Wren looked at 'James'. He looked to be in pain, wincing away from Wren's glove-like hand on his shoulder. He hadn't realized he was squeezing so hard, and let go. The guy whimpered.

"Give us a minute, James."

Loralei snorted, reached for a phone. "You haven't changed. This is his house, Chris. You need to get out or I'm calling the police."

He hadn't expected that either. "His house?"

Loralei just stared. Holding up the phone, ready to dial.

"Listen," he said. "I'm sorry, Loralei. For everything. Maybe sometime soon we can talk about all that, but it's not why I'm here now. I'm here about the credible threat to our family. Our kids." He paused a second. He'd called from the plane, asked Sally Rogers to come over and secure his family. She'd done it. Explained everything. Loralei had shown her the door. "You know this. Why are you rejecting protection?"

Her eyes flickered slightly, a hint of tenderness, though that was swiftly replaced by anger.

"You don't get it, Chris. Any threat to the kids, it's because of you. Because of choices you made. Now you just pull us back into your orbit, into your 'protection', like our lives don't matter at all?"

"I'm trying to keep you alive."

Loralei laughed. "You really don't get it. There's more to life than just being alive. Chris. Try to understand, we-"

"So I'll have nothing to do with it," he interrupted. "It's why I didn't come myself. I can't live with the kids in danger, Lor. I don't even need to know where you are. I-"

"Like you didn't know where we are now?" That shut him up. Loralei pressed on. "I didn't tell anyone. Only my Dad and my sister, and I know they didn't tell you. So you used some shady back channels to find us. I know that can't be legal. Now you want us even closer, in the palm of your hand?"

Wren flinched. "It's not like that. I-"

Now her eyes burned. "It's exactly like that. You want to protect us, you do it the way you always did. Somewhere far away, CIA bullshit, keep it out of our lives. I am not moving the kids again. I will not make them into refugees. You want to be their father? Clean up the mess you made!"

She was almost shouting. Wren recalculated fast. If she wasn't on board, witness protection wouldn't work.

"At least let us have a presence here. Rotate security, keep eyes on, we can-"

"No." She came around the counter. Holding the knife up now, eyes flaming. "I want you gone. The 'Executioner' they call you, right? Department of Defense 'black-ops'. Once I found out, did you really think there was any coming back from that?"

Only one thing to say to that. "I hoped so."

She snorted. "Hope'll kill you slow, Chris. Truth is, I don't know you. The man I loved, the man I married, it's not you."

"I quit the job," he said. "I gave it up. I wanted to-"

"You don't look quit to me."

Nothing to say to that. She was right.

"I don't think you're going to try and abduct me, or kidnap our kids. So I'm telling you to leave. You may be a killer out there," she waved a hand vaguely, "but right here you've not got a leg to stand on. Ask any court in the land. They're going to find in my favor."

He opened his mouth. Closed it. There were ways to surveil his family without being seen. Keep them safe from a distance. It wasn't ideal, but...

Something struck him. Something he'd never really thought about.

"You called me the 'Executioner'. How did you know about that?"

She smiled, set the knife down on the counter. "True to form. That's what you want to talk about. How your cover was breached?"

Abruptly, it was the only thing that mattered. He'd always assumed she'd just suspected him as a liar and decided she'd had enough. But knowing his CIA nickname? It sent him instantly operational. Sizing up the windows, the house, even the guy. James.

"Yes," he said, intently now. "Nobody knows that. Tell me, Loralei."

She laughed again. Gave him *that* look, like she was humoring him, but brought up her phone. Spent a few moments scrolling, then held it out. "You want to know, have at it."

He took the phone, looked at the screen, an email message. Every word came like a shot in the head.

Your husband, Christopher Wren, is a CIA agent known as the 'Executioner'. He has been involved in the following operations:

A long list followed, complete with dates coinciding with his every 'business trip' away. There were photographs too, of him in far-flung locations, overseeing cartel arms deals in Mexico, meeting with princes in Saudi Arabia, exchanging briefcases in dank Swiss parking lots.

The email scrolled on and on. His CIA record, beyond Top Secret designation. His kills listed out in graphic detail. Strangulation. Hanging. Gunshot. Knife. Photographs of the victims. All memories he'd put to one side, but seen like this, in this setting, they were horrifying. The things he'd done to protect his country.

He looked up, already planning what he'd say.

"Don't," Loralei said. Tears welled in her eyes now, one hand out. "Don't try to explain. I didn't just believe some random email, like a wide-eyed yokel. But I did check. I went back through some of your contacts. Your trips. The hotels you stayed at. You always brought so many mementos, Chris." Her voice cracked. "Stationery from every place you 'stayed'. Gifts for the kids. In the end I spent days tracking and calling them up. Not one remembered you." A tear ran down her cheek, and she wiped it angrily away. "Not one record anywhere. Your 'colleagues' in the hedge fund? Their cover never went deep. I asked far enough and they'd clam up. Your favorite restaurant. What your folks did for a job. To say more than one thing about your kids. We had these people over for BBQ, Chris, but they were all lying. You were lying. You're a liar."

He felt gut shot. Spiraling now, eyes roving for unseen threats.

"You said you were in Thailand, the last trip?" Loralei went on. "Chris, I flew out there."

His heart drummed and plummeted.

"You'd talked about the hotel, all the beautiful nature, the people you were meeting. I guess they gave you an information packet, details to repeat? I found hardly any of it. Not the people. Not the places, at least not the way you said. Not you."

The world spun. His fake life finally coming untethered.

"I'm sorry."

"Too late, Chris. The decision's been made. This is it, and we are over. You'll get divorce papers, as soon as there's a place to send them. Now you need to leave, before the kids come back.

His eyes swam. He didn't know where to look. The threat from the Blue Fairy felt very nearby. He looked at the phone again, scrolling through the list of his atrocities like there might be an answer there.

Then he found it.

The signoff was the last name he'd expected. A man twenty-five years dead, America's most famous cult leader, and Wren's own father.

The Apex.

3

FAKE TOWN

Wren fled the Delaware duplex without another word. Mind buzzing, heart racing. He called Sally Rogers. Sent messages to his team. There was barely a word back on the Minsk raid. They'd left the country via a hard exfiltration after the wreckage was surrounded by government forces, and everything since then had been covered up by the dictatorship.

Wren was left with nothing but the Blue Fairy's image dancing in the darknet. Nothing but some jackass pretending to be Wren's dead father, trying to rip his life apart.

Looked like they were succeeding.

WATCH MY FAMILY

Wren tapped out in a furious message to his Foundation group of petty ex-cons, grifters, disgraced marines and hackers, sent and resent via the Megaphone app to every member until they acknowledged receipt.

KEEP THEM SAFE.

"I can arrange them plain clothes agents on surveillance," Rogers said later, when he called from his Jeep, racing through the fields of apple orchards west of Frederica, no real clue where he was going. "Where are you going, boss?"

He wasn't going to give the answer for that. Instead, he drove west, using the miles covered to try and unpick his broken memories of the past.

The Apex. Leader of the Pyramid death cult. Maybe the first man to use the blue fairy symbol some twenty years ago, to mark out his own children. He had to be dead now, had been dead for twenty-some years, and not one of Wren's many investigations had turned up a single clue as to his whereabouts.

If anything, this had to be another copycat. Pyramid wannabes chasing the Apex's tail, hoping to recreate the 'glory days' of his Arizona death cult. Wren knew precisely the place to go hunting for men like that.

A flight and five hours drive later, he arrived. Parked up in the desert emptiness of Arizona, some wild time after midnight, and stood looking out over the fake town.

Heat radiated up from the cracked, sand-covered blacktop, carrying wafts of tarry creosote sap, though the sun had dropped six hours earlier. The sky was so black it seemed blue, overhung by a wicked sickle moon.

Wren ran his eyes along the fake town's silhouette, like a thumb along a blunted knife. Moonlight dappled the last few buildings in place, once a set for a Western movie that was never made. The saloon stood to his right, but only just. The front façade was badly bowed by decades of rain, its boards bleached gray by the sun. Next to it lay a bare cement base; that had been the hardware store, before fire claimed it. Beyond that it was just bare cement bases stretching away into the desert like toppled tombstones, keeping their secrets in the shifting sands.

The fake town had taken on a second life when the Pyramid had bought it and sealed off all access. His father's cult. The cult he'd grown up in, that had burned itself alive in an act of mass suicide right here, an act that Wren may or may not have witnessed as a twelve-year-old child. Official records stated he was the sole survivor, though of course they'd never found his father's body…

Now there were fresh tire tracks in the sand. Wren toed them with his boot. Wide wheelbase, cutting deep. Carrying something heavy.

Copycats.

Wren had cleaned out half a dozen groups come to pay their respects before. Putting kids in cages again, setting them to scream. There was no other reason to be out here in the desert wilds.

It made him sick with rage. The Pyramid. The Blue Fairy. The Apex. They were all connected, and he could sense them watching him now. There were CCTV cameras perched on the corners of the few structures still standing. He knew the outline of those decrepit buildings by heart, had imagined their sagging, bulbous frames going up in flames many times over.

Now several stood bolt upright. Last time he'd been here, the townhouse off Main Street had been only a drooping, faded front piece. The film hadn't required many interiors. Now the structure had been repainted and rebuilt. Wren had only vague memories of the atrocities that had taken place there, back when the 'rooms' had been caravans towed and staked into place.

A movement came from the end of Main Street.

Wren advanced slowly toward the townhouse, SIG Sauer .45 shifting in its holster against his hip. They had CCTV eyes on him, but Wren didn't need cameras to track them. This place belonged to him more than any. The rustlings it made as figures passed over its sighing sand felt branded into his skin.

There came a muffled clank of metal. The greased slide on a rifle, filling the breech.

Wren stopped ten yards from the townhouse. Up close it looked much as before, restored to its former glory. He'd read the script of the movie it was built for, Sam Peckinpah's 'The Texans', written toward the end of his life. It was incredibly violent. The funding had dried up, Peckinpah died, and the fake town was abandoned.

It was quiet, now. In the Pyramid days, used to be there was crying and weeping all the time. Cage children for any period of time, and you tapped a keg of raw human misery. The Pyramid had thrived on that kind of thing. Wren's fists tightened.

As if timed to that reaction, a security floodlamp switched on in back, casting his shadow large across the newly-painted boards. He didn't move. Let them get a good look at him just standing. I know you're there, those seconds said. I'm waiting.

He turned.

They stood at the Main Street crossroad, cutting off his route back. Five dark figures, rifles held at the ready.

"Who in hell are you?" one of the five called. The lead guy, on the right, with an upright bearing. "What are you doing here?" Wren caught the faint twang of a Boston accent. Long-distance transplants weren't unusual out here. The Pyramid had gotten under the nation's skin back in the day, and there were always sick people looking to come pay homage. They didn't often rebuild buildings, though.

"I used to live here," Wren called. "I drop by sometimes."

"You don't live here now," Boston said. "You have to go."

Wren let that hang. Thought about picking these guys off where they stood. Long-range with a handgun against hunting rifles, though. He could maybe ping a few, but not before they'd fired a few shots back. Hundreds, if the rifles were automatic, and most of the buildings here were flimsy. He wouldn't get much cover.

He worked a route back to his Jeep through his head. He had a Mossberg tactical shotgun and an M27 infantry automatic rifle in the trunk, and those would help some. A tight sprint down the side of the townhouse, then he'd be in the dark desert beyond. His eyes would adjust before theirs, and they'd have to come at him through the security light. A few might branch right immediately, try to cut him off on an angle, but they wouldn't know where to intersect.

Wren knew. He'd pivot sharply and hit them first, by the saloon. Say two guys go that way, two chase him around the loop, the leader stays still. Gut-kick the first into the wall, swipe his rifle and blast the second.

It could work. He'd exit through the saloon then circle around in the dark. He knew the rugged terrain back there by heart, every minor dip and rise in the gritty, packed sand. He had the lighter and kerosene too, that would make for an effective distraction, the work of seconds only. The saloon goes up in flames. Hit the others from cover while the blaze blinds them. Draw the rest out on his terms.

It would be a bloodbath in the streets. No problem, if they deserved it. But he had to be sure.

"I'm looking for the Blue Fairy," he called. "You know anything about that?"

Boston frowned. His face wasn't clear at this distance, more a shadowy emoji. "You're looking for what?"

Wren stared. "The Blue Fairy. Maybe this is where it started. I heard the Apex, he carved that symbol into the cots of his children. Marked them out for abuse. I burned that place down years back, though. Every year I come out here, I pick one of the buildings, they're just props really, it's amazing they're still standing, and I burn it down. It takes me back to old times."

Boston was just staring now. "The hell?" he mouthed to the others with him.

"I was with the Pyramid," Wren went on, "I suppose that's why you're here too. Drafting behind a famous brand. Really, that's copyright infringement."

"What on Earth are you talking about?" Boston asked. "Fact is, you're trespassing. I got five armed men here telling you to get. You go on and get."

Wren considered. If they were Pyramid or even Blue Fairy, they'd never let him leave. There were plenty of the Apex's followers buried in the shallow sand graves all around, who'd gotten that way by underestimating the leader of the Pyramid.

"Are you with the Blue Fairy?" he asked. "Better to tell me now, I'll go easy."

"Man, what are you even talking about? This is private property, and-"

"Bullshit. This is Federal land, designated persona non grata, in perpetuity. If it belongs to anyone, it belongs to me. So actually, you're trespassing on my land."

It was a stretch. Wren was just looking to see what shook out.

Boston said something into his radio. Wren read his lips, something about a whack job in the street. A crackle came back, then the guy gave instructions to the others. Three of them advanced. One came head-on while the others spread out in a pincer to left and right. The one on the right had his rifle up now, the stock butted hard into his shoulder.

"We're asking nicely now," Boston said. He came a few steps forward, far enough into the light for Wren to pick out details. He was older than Wren, with a scraggly salt and pepper beard, wearing a check shirt, jeans and cowboy boots. "We'll start shooting soon."

Wren switched his attention to the lead man in the pincer. He was ugly; a busted ear from college wrestling, eyes too far apart, a scar on his cheek. He didn't blink.

"What's your name, hoss?" Wren asked.

The guy spat in the sand. "Don't you mind. You been told to go."

Wren counted the yards between them. It would be six big bounds and an elbow to the trachea. The guy slacked off on his aim when he spoke, and that opened a window. Wren could ask another question then charge while he was distracted, maybe make it. Dance by a few bullets then bat the

253

muzzle aside, hold him like a shield and absorb fire from the other two, leveling the rifle. Seven seconds, maybe, before the two in back got their weapons up. Do-able, but foolhardy. High casualty count before he could end it, and a good chance he'd take a few hits.

Not ideal. They were closing in now. Wren switched back to Boston. "Last chance. Clear your people out. Walk away from this town and never come back. I'll even give you a running start before I come looking."

The pincer movement finished. Now there were two guys to his back left and right, one in front.

"You're leaving now," called Boston. "This can go easy or hard, so start marching."

"I've never gone easy in my life, and that's because-"

Wren moved, back and to the left. The guy there had his rifle barrel pointing down. Four strides was three seconds for Wren, the move slotted in and executed while the guy's brain was still jammed up with that 'because'.

Reasons always followed a 'because'. You got yourself set waiting for the sentence to close, a little logic loop you couldn't escape, because all your life logic loops like that had closed. So maybe a second to forget that and register the big guy coming right at him, another second to remember the rifle, a second more to lift it up, and by that time Wren hit him with a clothesline. Full pelt, arm rock hard across his throat, lifting the guy and spinning him horizontal in the air. Sky up above, then back slamming hard on the sand with a forced wheeze.

Wren wheeled, ducked behind him and snatched up the rifle, an AR-15 strapped tight around the guy's back. Shoot now and they'd tear their own man up.

He held the guy in a tight headlock, aiming the rifle. The others were log-jammed on the street, staring. It had happened too fast. They stared down their barrels. Boston's mouth was wide. His radio crackled.

"Now you put down your weapons," Wren said, not showing any exertion, no panting or uncertainty. "We get some coffee, if you like, and we talk about what in hell you're doing here."

4

MAGGIE

Stalemate. Nobody moved. Seconds ticked by with weapons aimed. The guy on the right had the best angle on Wren. If he was a fair marksman, he could pick off Wren without touching his hostage.

"This joker to my right backs up now," Wren said, "or I start pinging kneecaps. I'm a good shot. You won't be getting those back."

The guy on the right didn't budge. Wren scanned him in peripheral vision. Rifle up, waiting for orders from Boston. Wren racked the slide on his stolen rifle and glared at Boston too.

"Glenn," called Boston. He had one hand out now, the other still firm on his rifle. "You back up now. It's OK."

The guy moved. Wren breathed easier. Now would be the perfect time for them to jump him from behind. He listened to the town, to the wind and the sand, but this seemed to be it. They'd committed all their forces in one go.

"I'm not putting my rifle down, though," Boston said. "None of us are. If it comes to shooting, so be it. We'll not be driven off. We've children here."

Wren squeezed the trigger, instantly seeing red. Children? Boston would go first. "How many?"

"I'm not telling you that."

"In cages?"

The guy made his frown emoji face again. He had it down to a tee. "Cages? Man, who do you think we are?"

"Where do you think you are?" Wren countered, letting his anger show. Last time he'd busted a Pyramid clone, they'd been experimenting with parboiling apostates. Big iron cauldron atop a raw fire. Wren had dropped three explosive charges around the perimeter then walked in firing. "To my left the Pyramid had their main torture halls, for children. All day and all night the screaming went on. Did you really think I'd let it happen again?"

Boston was all out of frowns. Now he was into full shock. "Wait. Again? Are you saying you were in the Pyramid? In the cages?"

Wren stood up. Screw the cover; the guy wouldn't move far if he knew what was good for him. He trained his rifle on Boston's face. "I already said I was in the Pyramid. Now put your weapon down."

It was already slack. Shock was getting the better of Boston. An unstoppable force meets a soft plaster wall, it busts right on through. He let it slip to the ground.

"You need to understand," Boston said, "that's why we're here. The crimes of the Pyramid-"

"Stay in the past," Wren interrupted. "Everyone puts their weapons down, steps away, and you get your boss out here now. Are we clear?"

Boston didn't know what to say. He clearly wanted to argue. His radio crackled. On the other hand, the guy at Wren's feet was a hostage.

"Yeah," he said. "Clear. Weapons down, fellas. It'll be OK."

They stared at each other through a humming silence, until a few moments later the door of the townhouse opened. Wren swung his rifle over. In the doorway was a woman dressed like a Shaker schoolmarm, with a plain tan smock, white blouse and dress, tawny ringlet hair tied back loosely.

"Christopher Wren," she said, with a hint of a question. Her voice was powerful, like she was used to projecting to the back of an auditorium. She was around his age, a handsome and sturdy woman, looking frontier rugged in the Shaker gear.

She knew his name. Of course she did. "You're trespassing on hallowed ground," he said. "Explain."

She strode out of the townhouse unarmed. Wren caught a glimpse of the hallway beyond; candlelit, with no sign of cages. Two kids stood either side of the door, peering out afraid in their long cotton pajamas.

256

"Can I check the man you hit?" she asked.

Wren shrugged, backed away a few strides and she advanced, kneeled by the man, said his name and touched his throat lightly.

"He's fine," Wren said. "I barely touched him."

She ignored him, helped the man up, sent him back toward the others. Then she stood and looked at him. She didn't have a weapon, but she didn't seem intimidated by him in the slightest. He imagined her facing down a charge of Sioux warriors with that steady gaze.

"It is Christopher Wren, isn't it?" she asked. "Sole survivor of the Pyramid."

Wren cursed under his breath. This could still go bad. He had the gun, but maybe they'd radioed for reinforcements. Any Pyramid clone that could get their hands on Christopher Wren, last son of the Apex left alive, would have a field day putting him in a cage.

"Sure. And you are?"

"Margaret. Maggie. None of this is what you think it is, Christopher. I apologize for you finding us this way. I tried to contact you, to seek your blessing, but never found a way. The Order of the Saints raised your profile, and I thought..." she trailed off. "You're here now. Good. May we talk?"

"We're talking."

She allowed for that with a slight incline of her head, like a teacher brushing off the smart alec at the back of class. "Walk with me. My men will stay here. They won't pick up their weapons, I promise."

Wren scanned the five of them. Aberly in particular looked sullen. "Tell them that."

"I just did. Christopher, please. We have children here. Vulnerable people. If you don't like what I've got to say, then I'm a better hostage than they are."

"Maggie," said Wren, tasting the syllables. Weighing what he'd seen. "You're the leader of this cult."

She smiled. "I prefer to call it a commune. But yes, I'm the leader. Now shall we?"

She gestured toward the darkness. Wren felt like bowing, inviting her out to waltz. "After you."

5

PYRAMID CLONE

Into darkness they walked, and Wren thought about what she'd said.

Female cult leaders, or commune leaders, were rare. The vast majority were male, and usually followed the same old drives, seeking greater fulfillment of their own whims. With women it could be different. They were more unpredictable. Some of them had harems, like the men. Some of them were serial killers. Others just liked the idea of a big, happy family.

It didn't seem like a profile for the Blue Fairy

Maggie walked alongside him. She seemed to know the rough terrain underfoot well. She didn't stumble once. She didn't say anything, but it didn't feel combative, as it might with a man. It felt generous, like she was giving him time to process.

"You're not a Pyramid clone," he said at last.

"We're not."

Their pace slowed. "What are you?"

"The opposite, in fact. We're a refuge, really. Cult survivors come to this place. We focus on rehabilitation."

Wren gritted his teeth. "I'll need to see it. I'll need to look inside all your buildings. I'll need to interview your people."

"Because you're the governing body on cults?"

He looked over at her. She wasn't angry. If anything, her confidence was infectious. Was she teasing him?

"When it comes to this place? I am." He felt a spike of anger hen, at how close he'd come to hurting those men. "Whatever you're doing here, it's dangerous. You've got no signs up. Nothing on the Internet. This place, it's…" He trailed off, moderating what he wanted to say. "You shouldn't be here. No one should."

She didn't say anything for a long moment. They walked in silence.

"I read about your work with the Saints," she said. "Thank you for that. I know you lost people."

He grimaced. The Saints had waged their attack five months ago. Wren had stopped the bulk of it, but he hadn't protected everyone. "Nearly a hundred people died."

"And one person from your organization. The Foundation. Yes, I've researched you." She looked in his eyes. Now there was something shy about her gaze. "Your work. It's hard to find much concrete. You don't take credit. It's the same for us."

He didn't say anything. Waiting.

"There's no signs because we don't want to put out a flag for other Pyramid devotees to see." She looked at him. "I know they're out there. I know they're dangerous. That's why there's no website, no online presence at all. At least not until we're strong enough to rebuff them, if they come. Not when we have children."

Nothing to say to that.

"I'm sorry, for what it's worth," Maggie went on. "To put you in that position. We reached out, but we could have done more. I think I was afraid, on some level, you'd say no. Block the work we're doing here. But it's good, Christopher. Please, give us a chance."

He didn't know to think about that. Let her steer him in a gentle circle, around the tip of the cement foundations, back toward Main Street and his truck. A single text to his Foundation through the darknet would bring up answers about this Maggie and her 'work'.

Then he stumbled over something that shouldn't have been there.

In a second he had the rifle up, pointing at Maggie. She didn't move. The night was still around them, filled with the rustlings of marmots and prairie rats.

"You didn't know that was there," she said. Offering an explanation for the sudden panic he felt. "It's OK. It's part of our work. I have a flashlight. I can show you."

He looked down; now he could see the thing he'd stumbled over dimly in the moonlight. A flat oblong block of stone set on the sand, like a miniature of the building foundations.

"So show me."

She took the flashlight out slowly, clicked it on and aimed the beam. It took Wren a second to realize what he was looking at. A flat oblong of gray stone laid down in the sand, a name inscribed, some dates, a line of description.

"It's a grave."

"It's how I got started here," Maggie said, and ran the flashlight beam sideways, over more of the flat oblongs stretching away in a squarish plot. "We scour the desert for them. Victims of the Pyramid. Animals have dug many of them up and scattered the bones, so we do what we can. Metal detecting helps with fillings in jaws, with heart fittings and such. We have several contacts on staff at nearby universities, for radiocarbon dating, DNA checks. We're not high on the priority list, but we push it through."

Wren's head spun. This was not what he'd expected. It thrust him back into the past. "You're digging up the Pyramid?"

"Less digging, more hunter-gathering," said Maggie. He looked at her, but there was no mockery now. "You'll know these numbers better than any. Your father's cult, Christopher, killed far more people than those that died in the final firestorm. Many hundreds, by anyone's best guess. Many of them are buried in the desert around here. We've found approximately forty-three so far. We've been doing this for over a year."

Wren blinked. Over a year. "You're burying them," he said.

"What we can find. We notify the families, and arrange for re-consecration in line with their wishes. Set up headstones. They come out here and pay their respects. It's why we've built the place up, why cult survivors come to stay. They meet with the families, they come with their own children, and they all move closer to some kind of forgiveness."

Wren studied her. He didn't know if he was angry or happy about that. "Why?"

She shrugged lightly. "It's a good thing. I don't like to think of those bones scattered throughout the desert, alone. Unmourned."

He shook his head. "No. Why you? You said you're the leader. Why are you doing this?"

"Let's just say I'm a concerned citizen."

Wren looked at her. She looked back defiantly. There had to be an angle. "Bullshit. No one's that concerned."

"Then how about this? I grew up watching the Pyramid on TV. The day it broke open was huge news in my little town. Your father took dozens of people from us. It's been a hole in me ever since. I never stopped thinking about the bodies in the streets, burned by napalm they'd brewed themselves. I imagined all the lost souls who'd tried to stop your father on his path to destruction. I dreamed of them. They called me here."

"Not good enough."

She went cold. "It has to be."

Wren let the anger through. "It's not. I don't buy it. It's bullshit empathy, and people don't just do that. If I believed you, then all these graves would sicken me. You'd be an emotional parasite like all the other Pyramid clones, just coming at it from another angle, living off the pain of the families. It's just as sick. I'll burn the whole place down and break you six ways from Sunday, if that's true. So tell me why."

Now her eyes bored into him, catching the moonlight.

"You've researched me," he said. "You think you know me. Now I'm researching you."

She looked away. For a moment Wren thought she would walk off, but when she spun back her eyes swam with anger.

"The Apex took my mother," she said. "Or she went willingly. I'm not sure there's much difference. My aunt followed, then two uncles. They all went willingly, and it ruined us. Emotionally. Financially. A year later my dad killed himself. I was put into foster care. I bounced around the system and I came out angry. Like you. I followed you up as best I could. I hated you, maybe. Why did you get to survive when all my family died? But I never forgot." She took a breath. "When the Pyramid fell, they didn't find my family. Not burned up, not anywhere. So I started hunting. I'd come out alone and walk in the wilds. I got my doctorate at the same time. I thought about starting a family, but this place was in my bones. I had to come back. Now I'm back. We've got Federal approval, we're a listed NGO with rights to identify and consecrate any remains we find. Does that answer your question?"

She let out a breath. She was furious.

Wren sagged a little. Bullshit empathy, he'd said. "You kept coming back."

"Yes."

"So you saw the buildings burning down."

"I saw it."

"That was me."

She said nothing.

"I came every year. I burned another one down. That was my way of dealing with it."

"You destroyed his legacy."

"I did. I used to worry about the day I ran out of buildings to torch. I never once thought to do what you're doing."

She stared. "So do we have your permission?"

Wren met her gaze. So much had changed in the last few months. His Foundation had opened up in new ways, but it hadn't turned on him. His family had run from him, no knowing if he'd ever see them again, but he had to remain hopeful there was a way back. If he could just find the Apex, the man who'd started it all, then he could rest.

Try to reach out again, be a father.

Now this.

"You've got it the wrong way around," he said. "This is your place now. I see that. I'm the one who needs your permission."

A single tear beaded down her cheek. Wren rubbed his own eyes. The bottle of kerosene and the lighter felt heavy in his back pocket. He should've thought about this earlier, but he'd only ever had anger. It was better to build.

"Thank you for what you've done," he said. "I hope you find your family. I'm sorry I scared your guys. I'll make a donation, you can get better security, start putting up signs and properly own the place."

She started to say something, but he was already walking away, back into the desert.

"Come back, Christopher," Maggie called out, but made no move to follow, and that wasn't what she meant anyway. It was something else. "Whenever you want. Whenever you're ready. This is your home, after all."

Wren strode on and the darkness swallowed him.

6

HUMPHREYS

His Jeep was waiting. He got in and pulled away, along the old road headed for I-40.

No answers from the desert. No Blue Fairy. Just another dead end.

At some point his phone rang. Coming back into signal range. Wren killed it without looking, battery squeezed out on the seat, but another phone began chiming as message after message poured in. Wren ignored them. When they were done, it rang, and judging by the blaring ring tone he couldn't ignore this one.

Humphreys' direct line. Wren rustled in the glove box and looked at the display, saw seven missed messages telling him to pick up. Choice insults. Asking him where in hell he was. Reminders that despite his new 'AWOP' Agent WithOut Portfolio status, he still had to file constant progress reports.

He hadn't filed once since Minsk nearly two days back. Hadn't told anyone where he was going; not his team, not Rogers, not the Foundation. The Pyramid was his mess to clean up.

The phone kept ringing.

He answered.

"Not a good time, Humphreys."

"Not a good time?" Humphreys snapped. His voice was deep and pissed off-sounding. "I've been calling since midnight. That's five hours, Wren! What the hell were you doing?"

Five hours. "I was off-grid."

Humphreys laughed, shot through with anger. "You asked for this, Wren! You've got a team and right now they're on red alert. How you think it looks for me when you go off the grid and they can't contact you, and every second the trail's getting colder."

"What trail?"

"Especially after the Minsk screw-up!" Humphreys blustered. Clearly not done with this. "You broke faith with the Company once before, you think you get to do it twice? I will retract your AWOP status so fast you'll bleed out from hydrostatic shock. Do not toy with me on this, Wren. I don't want these calls coming to me."

Wren grunted.

"Did you just grunt? I could have you up on court-martial charges, you ungrateful b-"

"I get it. It won't happen again."

"You bet it won't happen again. When your team calls you, what are you going to do?"

"I'll answer."

"Will you turn your phone off?"

"No."

"Will you take out the battery and leave it on the passenger seat of your stupid Jeep?"

He couldn't resist a smile at that. "No."

"Don't make me regret this, Wren. I already regret it. Don't make me eat it."

"Humphreys, get to the point. What is it? Tell me what it is, you think I'm not out here busting my balls to get a lead?"

It took Humphreys a moment to calm down. As the CIA Director of US Special Operations Command he had considerable reach and power, and wouldn't usually get himself worked up like that. Wren thought he enjoyed it.

"Well, I've got a juicy one here. Six hours back we got a big hit on the Blue Fairy, action taken in the real world. These people just made a huge leap, Wren. One dead catfisher, two kidnapped. An anonymous strike in downtown Detroit like nothing we've seen before."

Wren's blood ran cold. All traces of good humor fled him.

"What strike?"

"Call your damn team, I'm not your go-between. And consider yourself seconded to the FBI as of this moment, since this attack's inside the continental USA."

Humphreys rang off.

Wren sat very still, heart pounding as the truck plummeted headlong into the night. Action taken in the real world? It was out of character. Something wholly new.

He checked the dashboard clock. Albuquerque Airport was four hours' drive, with Detroit a three-hour red-eye flight away. He could be there mid-afternoon. He picked up his other phone and fumbled the battery back into place. More messages spun up from Sally Rogers, heading up his thirteen-strong team back in Washington. He scanned them.

There was CCTV footage. Wren pulled over to the side of the dark road, brought it up and hit play.

The camera angle was high, the footage grainy black and white, looking down on some kind of paved triangular forecourt, narrowing to an intersection between two busy roads. Looked like middle of central Detroit city, people flowing in and out below the camera, circling a large round planter with a weary-looking tree in the center.

Wren checked the timestamp in the bottom right. 19:07, tail-end of rush hour, marked with the letters MCH AVE PPL MVR. He paused the feed to check a map. Michigan Avenue People Mover station, a one-track monorail around the city center. He'd ridden it before. It was slow. He checked the triangle forecourt from above. Michigan Avenue one side, Cass Avenue another. Tuned back into the CCTV.

People moved in and out of the station. A guy stood off to the left, smart-casual suit and jacket but low-slung ball cap that shaded his face, holding a clipboard and asking questions. People weren't stopping. A trio stood almost out of the camera's angle, a big guy holding a fat binder, the other two holding camera rigs, a man and a woman. Watching the guy with the clipboard asking his questions.

These were the catfishers, Wren figured; citizen vigilantes who took it upon themselves to stalk the Internet stalkers. Wren was running a bunch of them through the Foundation himself, trying to get an in to the Blue Fairy. They pretended to be underage kids online, gathered evidence and built relationships with perps until they could lure them out into the real world, where they hit them with the evidence, tried to record a confession, then brought in the cops.

Wren followed their gaze back over to clipboard guy. He looked nervous, constantly adjusting his cap down over his face, like he was aware of the CCTV, looking around for something and not seeing it, letting people pass him by, questions unasked.

A clear profile. This guy was a perp getting catfished, and for all his glancing around, he didn't see them coming.

The big catfisher with the binder circling in from behind, while the other two flanked with their cameras lifted, one coming in close, the other staying further out for the wide angle. The big guy laid a hand on the perp's shoulder, and he about crapped his pants. Jumped, flinched, spun. Both side-on to the CCTV now, in the midst of the People Mover's outward flow. There was no sound, but Wren leaned in, puzzling out the gist from reading the big guy's lips and the perp's body language.

'Are you …?' the big guy was asking, though Wren couldn't catch the name.

The perp rocked back slightly. 'What?'

'Is your name …? Are you waiting here for …?'

The perp freaked out. Started looking side to side, like there might be some way out. He saw the cameras watching him and flinched. 'No, that's not me.'

The big guy opened his binder. Pointed to evidence, talked a little. Catching the guy in an obvious lie. Wren couldn't see, but guessed these were chat records with a minor, inappropriate photographs sent both ways, an arrangement to meet. I'll be the guy in a ball cap asking questions about laundry detergent. You be the kid looking for an adventure.

The perp's pixelated face blanched white. Spluttered, hands flailing. 'You've got the wrong guy.' Starting to make excuses.

Wren had seen it before countless times, both in person and online. Catfishers uploaded their videos to the social media site WeScreen, and every time it was the same: portraits of twisted men watching their worlds crumble, capturing that teetering moment when they realized they'd just lost everything.

They'd taken their depravity into reality, and now it was all gone. Their freedom. Their family, if they had one. Their job, their reputation, everything. The catfishers posted these videos as both a boast and a warning. This could be you too, they said. Better not try it. Wren cheered them every step of the way.

Now the woman to the right lifted her phone, made a call. Bringing in the police, no doubt. The perp saw it, eyes weeping now like fresh oysters, gaze darting. Probably trying to plot his escape, make a run for it, somehow slip this noose that was coming-

The hit came out of nowhere. Wren saw them but didn't register the approach, too engrossed in the perp.

Three guys came out of a white panel van pulled up by the curb, wearing hoodies, jeans and pale-faced Pinocchio masks. The masks had long noses with eyes flashing. The lead guy swung a baseball bat which smashed into the back of the big catfisher's head.

Wren almost felt the jolt. The big guy's head jerked forward and his body shook like he'd been hit with a thousand volts. He dropped the binder then dropped to his knees. The perp's jaw fell open and he dropped his clipboard.

The second blow came fast, a big wind-up and a T-ball homerun to the catfisher's head, flattening him to the paving. Now people were screaming and running. The two filming catfishers tried to flee, but the other two Pinocchio guys were already on them. The woman took a bat to the shoulder and went down, the camera smashing. The guy tried to throw a punch but missed, took a hard swing into the ribcage which felled him.

Wren switched gaze back to the lead Pinocchio. The big guy was down and out for the count, but still the Pinocchio kept hitting him. Four times, now. Five, the bat rising and falling. The perp stared, too terrified to move. It was vicious. Four minutes into the tape, twenty seconds into the attack, and already it was ending.

The lead Pinocchio rallied the other two. The woman fought and scratched while another Pinocchio dragged her by the hair back to the van. The second guy was barely staggering, yanked along by the scruff of his jacket and dumped into the back of the panel van.

The lead guy got in front, fired it up, and took one last moment to roll down the window. Wren couldn't see for the mask, but seemed he shouted something at the perp, just standing there like a mushroom sprouted in the empty forecourt, standing over the still catfisher.

Then the van peeled out into traffic. The perp watched them go, looked down at the dead catfisher, then jerked into a run too.

The video ended.

Wren looked up, sucking in a breath. The night desert closed in and his heart beat hard. Two different worlds, and he'd never seen anything quite like this. A brutal hit dressed up in cosplay. It was murder in plain sight, and double abduction with no fear of repercussion.

And the Pinocchios. Pinocchio was a thing on some of the darker boards, a fringe part of the Blue Fairy's mythos. It was all tied up in Carlo Collodi's tale of the little wooden boy, just like the sick notion of 'Pleasure Island', a legendary real-world graceland for abusers, and the Fairy's fabled headquarters.

Little kids liked Pinocchio. He made a great lure for these sick men to drop in the Internet's unmonitored deeps. Hook them in, make them promises, talk up the magic of the Blue Fairy and Pleasure Island to get them on board with sending pictures; just like Pinocchio was sucked in to a wonderland of ice cream, booze and cigars where gradually he turned into a donkey.

Bad stuff. All in the Blue Fairy's name.

But all of that was online. Now Wren was looking at three Pinocchios in a coordinated real-world attack. It suggested an infrastructure capable of moving fast, an intelligence operation that could uncover the catfishers' plans, as well as the will and the funding to pull it off.

Something far bigger than he'd expected. Something big enough to prep for his raid on the Minsk data hub. His heart skipped a beat. This was the lead. Maybe even a possible route to Pleasure Island.

Wren put the past behind him. The graves through the desert and Maggie's mission to heal. There was no room for mercy now, to let his softer side and forgiveness bloom. Not with his kids at stake, not with all of America's kids at stake.

Now it was time to bring the hammer down.

7

ROGERS

Albuquerque airport was a blocky mesa-like structure in clay-colored stucco, all modern angular lines housing the huge Departures concourse. It was already bustling in the hot dawn sun. Wren pulled into long stay parking, fed the meter one of his credit cards and shouldered his bag. It was light; one change of clothes, various documents and IDs, his netbook and a small clutch of phones. In the past five months he'd adapted well to his Agent Without Portfolio status.

At the walk-up counter he bought one-way to Detroit, got a piping hot Americano from a coffee shop and sipped it into security. His CIA ID got him through and boarded early. He took the mid-wing seat for the legroom, logged into Wi-Fi and called Sally Rogers.

She answered on the third ring; probably he'd woken her up, if she'd gotten any sleep at all. Maybe in a backroom somewhere, crashed in a chair, after wasting no time racing from Washington to Detroit.

She was a hard-charger, aiming for Director-level before she was forty. Brought up as a military brat, dragged halfway around the world by two Army parents until her mom was killed in Afghanistan, she burned with a need for revenge.

Wren liked that about her. You couldn't fake drive. In their set-up phase Humphreys had given him choices, cyber-ops experts who were between missions, and she'd not been amongst them. Too mission-critical to her

269

current assignment. He'd gone direct, got her to request a transfer and snapped her up before anyone else registered her potential.

"Boss," she answered, her choice of address, though he'd asked her several times to call him Wren. "You're in Detroit?"

"Three hours yet. Sorry it's taken me so long. How you holding up?"

She took a breath. She'd never show weakness, though she sounded worn out. In the last few months they'd fallen into an easy relationship, plenty of respect, a little bit of teasing too, but now wasn't the time for that.

"Fine," she said. "At a dead end here, honestly. Waiting on your input."

"You'll get it. For now, give me the sit-rep, starting with CCTV on their escape route, facial recognition on the perp."

It took her a second, scooching up in the seat, Wren figured, stretching out the crick in her neck. "What I can tell so far, there's no footage anywhere else. Not where they went after the People Mover station, not on any routes to or from. They must have planned in advance, scouting for overwatch. I looked at the map; there are plenty of blind corridors leading west into Corkdale, Warrendale, and then you're into the heavily blighted areas. It would've been easy to disappear after that. A panel van there is basically invisible."

Wren nodded, pretty much what he'd already figured. He'd worked a hybrid mescaline drugs sting through Herman Gardens seven years back, before the city had seriously started tackling the urban blight.

"Throw out a search spider on social media. I bet somebody was filming at that moment, somewhere along their route. We need to map and rule out all traffic. Where did the van go, where did the perp go."

"It was rush hour," she protested. "That's a huge endeavor."

"Farm it out."

Rogers snorted. None of his team really knew what Wren's limits with Humphreys were, especially after the failed Minsk sting. Bringing the Saints down had earned him a lot of capital. The way he'd done it had clawed most of that back. Still, he was in the black.

"What about facial recognition? Can you pin down the perp?"

"Nothing there, boss. That camera's ancient, resolution's garbage and too far out to sharpen, plus the ball cap? All we've got are broken snatches of two blurry eyes and a mouth, way too imprecise."

Wren grunted. Also what he'd feared. "What about cyber?"

"Nothing yet." Creaking sounds from the chair as she got to her feet.

"No claims on any of the known boards, no chatter at all. We've already put it to three of the darknet admins we flipped last month, but they don't know anything. This thing is new."

Wren chewed on that. "Talk to me about the catfishers."

There was a faint click; a light switch going on, then shuffling papers. "Affiliated with the 'Marcy's Heroes' group, seventy members nationwide, out of Nebraska somewhere. They have their own message boards, good encryption. We're requesting details now. They're cooperating, but we only have ID on the dead guy. Malton Bruce, he's a lawyer by day, catfisher by night. Coached Little League on weekends. A big guy, but he didn't stand a chance."

Wren grimaced. "A baseball bat to the head will do that. We need all their chat logs. Who they were stalking."

"Already on it."

"The Pinocchio masks. Have we got a match through the e-fit system?"

"Local PD is merging eye-witness reports now, working on colors. The CCTV's good for the shape. I did some preliminary searches; I'm seeing up to a dozen Pinocchio mask models available commercially, widely shipped. We're requesting the data from the big online markets using Freedom of Information laws, setting up a correlation spreadsheet."

Wren ran the footage through his head again. Three people get out of a van with masks and bats. The attack came out of nowhere.

"Vehicle rental on the van?"

"In the spreadsheet."

"Eyewitnesses?"

"Three useful; commuters headed home after a long day at the office. PD already released them, it was late, but we can call them in today."

Wren checked the time on his phone. "Call them for evening, same time, outside the People Mover station. Michigan Avenue. I want to jog their memories."

"Together?"

"All together." Wren thought a second. Took a leap, because there was so little to go on. "We're going to re-enact it. Get a van and masks, fake blood, rehearse the hit just like it went down, like a rolling e-fit. We'll spring it on them."

Rogers paused, analyzing what he'd just said. "Rolling e-fit? Like a suspect line-up?"

"Not for their faces. We haven't even got two facial descriptions to rub together. And not static. This'll be for the event itself, a full-on re-enactment, see if we can shake some memories lose by putting the witnesses back into the thick of it."

There was another pause. "A re-enactment? Boss, that's hardly procedure. If anything, we're likely to pollute their testimony."

Wren was scrolling through a batch of masks available online. Some Pinocchios were sweet while others were darker, closer to Carlo Collodi's original vision of the wicked little wooden boy. Some had long noses, some short.

"Yeah," he said, "but there's nothing useful in that testimony right now, is there? Did the bat guy have a deep voice or a high voice? Was there an unusual smell? What did they say to each other? We can't ask all the questions, and the witnesses don't know what they know." He looked out the window, the plane was moving toward the runway. "I'm hoping they'll see something that feels off, and figure out how to verbalize it." A pause. "There's research backing this methodology up."

Rogers brightened at that. "What research? I'd like to see it."

Wren didn't want to reference Dr. Grayson Ferat, functioning now as his Foundation's acting-COO, a one-man bureaucracy. His groundbreaking research into the bystander effect on witness testimony was set to reinvigorate the field, if it panned out. "It's at an early stage."

"Early stage research is my favorite."

Wren smiled. He'd hired Rogers for her bulldog curiosity. "There's a lot to it, but basically it says if you take a math exam in a blue room, you'll perform better if you also studied math in a blue room."

A beat passed. "A blue room?"

He was ready for that. "The research claims the effect is broad-based."

"What does the research say about witnessing a murder?"

He almost laughed. "I'd imagine it uses the same functions of memory. Recall is aided when it takes place in the same conditions and circumstances as the first memory was laid down."

"It is? You're saying these witnesses will have better recall if we re-expose them to the intensity, violence and emotion of the attack that already traumatized them."

It didn't sound so great when expressed like that. "Basically, yes."

"Because some researcher found blue was the key to taking a math test."

"Like I said, there's more to it than that. Sound, emotion, mental state, they all play a role in recall. Match the state closer, you get better results." Rogers didn't say anything. "I'll send you the research. For justification, we just call it a hunch and move too fast for anyone to stop us."

"That's one hell of a hunch, Boss. And expensive to set everything up for what you're requesting."

He knew what she was thinking. "If we get nothing, it's on me. I'll write the reports and take the heat."

She clucked low. "It's not that. After Minsk, Director Humphreys told me to keep an eye on your 'unusual methods'. He's looking for any excuse to shut us down."

Wren could think of a few choice words for Director Humphreys, but swallowed them down. "I'll deal with Humphreys. Just get the assets in place."

She coughed; he thought maybe covering laughter. "OK. Anything else we're missing?"

There was plenty, but none of it could go through CIA hands. "That's enough for now. I'll see you in a few hours."

He killed the call.

The woman next to him was trying not to stare. Wren set the phone down, gave her a smile. "Work," he said, like that explained anything. She nodded and busied herself looking at the in-flight magazine.

The plane took off. Wren opened his darknet to surf the Foundation boards, but they were quiet. Probably they hadn't heard about the hit yet. That meant his own catfisher teams were still out there, setting up stings of their own.

He wrote a message through the Megaphone app and sent it to them all, especially flagged for the attention of his elite hackers.

BLUE FAIRY JUST STRUCK IN REAL-LIFE, THREE GUYS IN PINOCCHIO MASKS KILLED A MAN IN DETROIT - ABDUCTED A MAN AND A WOMAN. I'M BOUND FOR DETROIT NOW. NEW DIRECTIVE – NO MORE IN-PERSON GRABS UNTIL WE KNOW WHAT THIS IS. FIND ME WHAT YOU CAN. THE PERP. THE CATFISHERS. THE PINOCCHIOS. BE CAREFUL.

He hit send, settled back and closed his eyes. He'd barely slept since Minsk, and this might be his last chance for quite some time.

8

PEOPLE MOVER

S eemed he'd barely blinked when the pilot's voice came over the PA, announcing they were starting their approach into Detroit. Wren looked out the window, saw the city passing like a broken circuit board below.

He traced its familiar patterns through neighborhoods with components missing. There were green patches spotted throughout, where abandoned homes had become blight, and blight had been burned and wrecked by bored kids, then demolished by the city. It made Wren think of a cancer metastasizing, dots here and there blasted by the chemotherapy, but always reseeding itself and spreading wider.

The plane touched down. Wren was first off, pre-approved with his CIA clearance, down the ladder to the waiting apron. The airport buildings looked natty and clean. He walked through still hazy from the snatched sleep, thinking about the Pinocchio strike. For a moment he stood at the railing of the airport's shopping concourse, looking down on the bustling crowds, feeling trapped in a thought he couldn't quite finish or express. Sometimes cities did this to him. Out West, in the fake town or in the desert, you knew exactly who you were. In the city, things felt different.

So many people. Maybe four thousand filling the concourse. Odds said that maybe twenty of them were abusers. Some worse than others. Some active, some passive. The vast majority men, all of them making the same sick choices again and again. There was no room for men like that in the Foundation. They'd poisoned themselves to the bone.

He took a cab. Forty minutes, give or take, to reach downtown. Out the window Detroit thickened like a broth, broad streets and residential zones giving way to big malls and parking lots. The roads narrowed, the green blips of blight melted away and the city's few skyscrapers grew larger in the distance: the glassy Detroit Marriott, the clay-red Guardian, the gray Ally Detroit. The abandoned Michigan Central Train Depot appeared on his right, empty windows gazing across the bare grass of Roosevelt Park. It made him think of Maggie's graves in the desert. Here was a tombstone for the scattered bones of a city.

Michigan Avenue station was waiting for him. Around 3 p.m. on a Tuesday, he got out of the car. A People Mover train hummed into the station on its elevated line overhead. Cars bustled through midday traffic. People hurried this way and that. Lots of ways in and out.

The station was a slim two-floor block, really just walls around a flight of stairs. In front of it lay the same triangular forecourt, familiar from the CCTV, though it looked different from ground-level. Like the narrowing prow of a ship, pinched off by the intersection of Michigan and Cass Avenues. Not much bigger than the floor plan of a fair-sized house, broken only by the low tree in the central brick planter. Buildings loomed either side.

Wren circled the narrow triangle, taking the air. It smelled of the city at the end of winter: diesel fumes, frost in the air, a hint of wafting coffee. Sixteen hours ago, the Pinocchios had killed a man here, but there was no sign of that now. The police tent and tape had been removed. The blood had been bleached and cleaned. Cities didn't stop.

Traffic hummed by on Michigan Avenue to his right, four lanes wide. Cass Avenue rumbled with a passing garbage truck, a mirror image of Michigan. Across the intersection stood the McNamara Federal Building, a grid-iron cement block some thirty stories tall. Another People Mover train rolled into sight and stopped at the station. A few miles of elevated track circling the city center on long cement stalks.

He thought back on the attack. Paced out the distance to the curb, where the van pulled up. A guy with a clipboard facing off with another, bigger guy with a binder. The perp and the catfisher. He stood where the catfisher stood, Malton Bruce, then the perp.

Where had he come from? No answer, but probably not public transport. A perp picking up a girl for a first time would want to show off. He'd seen it before. Splash out on a fancy ride. Not ask her to get on a bus.

It ruled out the People Mover.

He scanned the area for more CCTV cameras, calculating lines of sight, trying to figure a route through blind spots. Cass Avenue was well covered; anyone fleeing the station south would be caught on the station's security camera. Anyone running north would soon cross in front of the Rosa Parks Transit Center nearby, which had three cameras mounted in its sweeping white tensile canopy. Add to that the imposing glare of the Federal Building, and any escape along Cass became unlikely.

Michigan was a different story. To the west a Second Federal bank narrowed the field; they'd have footage of the sidewalk and road. Rogers had said no useful footage existed, so Wren ruled that out as an escape route too, leaving only Michigan heading east, toward the Campus Martius Center and the Detroit River a few blocks over.

Wren walked that way. The air was brisk and fresh, the sky a painful wintry blue, though it wasn't very cold. Behind the station was a slim parking lot, past that lay shuttered buildings either side of Michigan: a closed law office on the right, graffiti on large boarded panels to the left. It was a broad street, four lanes, with beautiful old wrought-iron lamps. Largely unobserved, with parking at the curb.

Wren picked a spot, standing at the edge of the sidewalk, nearside to the station and a sightline around the law office's corner. You could feel safe parked here, he thought. A good view of the station's forecourt, waiting in case the girl showed herself first. Parked on the south side of the street, you had a clean run east. It matched the CCTV too; the Pinocchios had driven off this way. The perp had to have come this way too, evading oversight.

Did they know each other? Were they working together? The perp's shock at their arrival suggested otherwise, but then there'd been that final moment, the lead Pinocchio shouting something through his open window.

It was a beginning, but there was still so much missing.

He called Rogers.

"Have you cracked the catfishers' database yet? We need to see those chat logs."

"Boss." Rogers sounded harried, like she in the middle of something. "I'm on it, but they're stonewalling. Claiming right to privacy.

My guess is, they're worried they crossed boundaries. Verged into entrapment with some of these guys. They're demanding we go through the courts. I'm trying to get a warrant but the judge is slow-walking me."

Wren sucked air through his teeth. "During which time they could clean the record."

"Or erase it."

Frustrating. This was what happened when you tried to play vigilante. The law came for you as often as it came for the real bad guys. "Send me the catfishers' number. And come over to the People Mover. Let's have coffee."

"On it," she said, and ended the call. A moment later the number for Marcy's Heroes pinged through as a text, along with a contact for its president. Reince Jeffries.

Wren leaned against the law office and dialed. Seven rings in, Jeffries answered. "Hello."

"Reince Jeffries?"

"Yes." An older gentleman. Professional. A lot to lose. "Who is this?"

"You've been speaking with my colleague, agent Sally Rogers in the CIA. My name is Christopher Wren, I'm leading the investigation of the death of one of your volunteers."

He let that hang.

"Yes," said Jeffries cautiously.

"Yes," said Wren. "She tells me you're blocking our request. I'm calling to ask you to reconsider. This is an issue of national security, and your cooperation would be appreciated, noted, and passed along."

An uncomfortable second, filled with the elder man's light, wheezy breathing. "I'm afraid that won't be possible, Mr. Wren. Our records are of a highly sensitive nature."

Wren took a breath. One more try, the civilized way. "Mr. Jeffries, I'm enabled to offer rewards, if this information pans out. I can also assure you that this is not a fishing expedition for flaws in your record-keeping. You've seen the news. I'm after a hardcore group of killers. Not your organization."

Jeffries barely paused this time. "As I said to your colleague, I'm afraid that won't be possible at this time."

Wren cursed. Jeffries was on the right side of the issue, one of the heroes taking down abusers, so why wouldn't he offer up his records when it could help his own catfishers?

Only one reason Wren could think of; something in Jeffries' records was rotten, and only one way to winkle that out: the uncivilized way.

"Mr. Jeffries, it falls to me then to notify you that we have a team outside your office this moment, another team outside your home, and I'm ready to pull the trigger. You just fell into the Twilight Zone, sir. Due process does not apply today. I don't need a court order or a warrant. Send your full, unredacted files immediately, to this number, or things become very unpleasant for you."

A long silence followed. Jeffries breathed. A professional man, a lawyer or a professor, not easily cowed. Trying to figure out if it was a bluff or not. "You can't threaten me like that."

Wren steeled himself. "I can and I am. This is a tiresome obstruction for me, Mr. Jeffries. Please understand, I really don't care how you hunted abusers. More power to you, I'm a kindred spirit in bending the rules. You send it to my phone, we'll bend the rules together. In order to rescue your people who were taken and get justice for the one they already murdered, I need to know what kind of man this perpetrator was. Was he working with the attackers, was he even aware of them, did he drop clues to his location? This is really the first step in a hundred-meter sprint. We're just getting started. Imagine how unhappy I'll be if you trip me up here."

A long pause. Maybe moving to the window, looking out for signs of a strike team. "I think you should contact my lawyer."

"Reconsider that, Mr. Jeffries. When we have all your records in the next one hundred twenty seconds, after busting in the door and traipsing through your happy home, you think I'll stop at Malton Bruce? I'll be pissed off by then, and I'll steamroll you completely. How many times have you entrapped perps then doctored the record, because what you had wasn't quite enough to put them away? I don't blame you, I've done worse myself, but in the eyes of the law that's a crime. If you've done it, we'll find every instance. I'll rig a team just to bring you down out of vindictiveness. Ninety seconds now. Quit pissing in the doorway and come out of the cold, or I'll toss in obstruction of justice charges, aiding and abetting murder, kidnap and child abuse, whatever I can think of. I'll strap Malton Bruce to your forehead and parade you in front of the press. Is that what you want?"

"I..."

"Sixty seconds, Mr. Jeffries. You're already bending. Bend further. A little yoga will do you good."

Silence but for raspy breathing.

"Thirty seconds. That's it. We're coming through the door."

"Wait!" Wren imagined the old fellow at his desk, reaching out to grasp at the air. "I'll send it. My family is here. I'll send the files."

"Good man. You're on the clock. Don't tamper with a damn thing."

"Yes," said Jeffries. "Thank you."

Wren rang off. Thank you. That was nice and civilized.

He went to get a coffee. Two blocks east, checking out sight lines as he went, he found a nice artisan spot at a key intersection, the Orange Pip, promising a pure Columbian blend. He got one Americano and one soymilk Latte.

"Were you on duty last night, around 9 p.m.?" he asked the lady behind the counter. Early thirties with a sarcastic look in her eye, a pin pierced through her cheek and a weird bowl-cut hairstyle.

"Yes," she said, almost biting off the word. Like she was angry. "Why?"

"I'm investigating the attack at the People Mover. You heard about that?" He held out his CIA badge; she gave it a good long look, like she would know if it was a fake or not. "A white panel van fled the scene and likely made a turn here." Wren pointed through the glass. "Did you see it?"

The woman frowned. "CIA. You're not supposed to operate in the USA, right?"

"I'm with the FBI right now. Waiting on the badge. Now about the van, did you see it?"

She was miking this. "A van, on the road?"

"On the road." He pointed again, just to be clear. "Out there."

"Why would I notice that?"

"It's not a trick question," he said, like he was talking to a difficult toddler. "You either did or you didn't. Which is it?"

She looked annoyed. That made two of them. "Then I didn't. I make coffee."

Wren took a steadying breath. No use going around riling up witnesses. "The coffee smells great, by the way," he tried, but his smile didn't make any impression on her. "My colleague's especially keen to try the soymilk. Now, last question, was anyone else on duty then?"

Her frown deepened. "Monday night? I close at 9:30. It's dead in here. It's just me."

Wren nodded. He'd have to get a team crawling the sidewalk, asking questions at every business. "Thank you, you've been very helpful."

He headed for the door. Her voice stopped him before he opened it. "There was something though."

He turned. "Yes?"

"I didn't notice it myself. A couple of customers did, they were taking pictures as I was closing up, posting them online somewhere. Maybe just after 9? A Firebird, I think they said."

Wren took a step closer. "A Pontiac Firebird?"

"Is there any other kind?" Wren almost laughed at the sarcasm. She couldn't help herself. "Anyway, it's unusual. There's plenty of supercars out here, Ferraris, Porsche, like that. Rich schmucks. But not something old like that."

Wren thanked her and left, juggling the coffees with his phone. Dialed straight through to his team in Washington.

"Let's look into ownership or rental of a Pontiac Firebird in the Detroit area." He paused a second. It was a rare car, easy to check. Also one hell of a trip to impress your 'girl'. "Scratch that. Widen it out. Give me a two-state radius and an APB, all emergency units looking out. And send some police officers to canvass Michigan Avenue between the People Mover and the Campus Martius. There's not much, a couple offices. Asking after the Firebird and the panel van."

He ended the call. That felt like progress.

Sally Rogers was waiting at the triangle forecourt for him, looking at her phone. She was 5' 9" and thick in the shoulder; a prize-winning weightlifter in her college days, she'd clearly kept it up. Wren wondered if she could squat as much as him. He was out of practice, after the Saints put a bullet in his thigh. Maybe. She had a sweet, earnest face, leafy blond hair and the wicked mouth of a trooper.

"Boss," she said, looking up as he approached. "Firebird?"

"It's a lead. Perps want to impress." He handed her the coffee. "Soymilk latte, just as you like it."

She made a face. "Soy? When did I ever say I liked soy?"

Wren hid his grin and took a long, satisfying pull on his Americano as she took a tentative sip.

"This is disgusting," she said flatly.

Wren sat on the planter, shrugged. "When life hands you lemons."

"This is not lemons, this is soy," she protested, pried off the sippy-cup top and eyed the foamy drink beneath. "You know soy's a bean, right? It's not even close to milk."

Wren chuckled. She took another sip, sat down beside him.

"Oh, man. This is not fit for human consumption. This is the kind of thing they feed to cows to make milk. You'd need five stomachs to properly process it."

Wren laughed. For a few minutes they sat there, sipping and watching people flow through the People Mover. The trains came and went. Traffic bustled by on Michigan and Cass. No Pinocchios. No murders.

"On the plus side, it'll help with your Spanish," Wren said.

Rogers frowned at him. "What?"

"Soy milk? Yo soy milk?"

She stared, got it, groaned. "Dad jokes? Are you kidding me?"

He grinned. Hadn't busted out a Dad joke since New York. Thinking about that flattened the good humor somewhat. Happily, his phone pinged just then, and he brought it up.

The records from Reince Jeffries.

9

CHAT LOG

Wren airdropped the records to Rogers. In a zip file titled 'Sophie - Ravenous6' there was an untitled pdf and a document titled 'Notes'.

"His handle's Ravenous," Rogers pointed out. "Like he can't stop himself."

It wasn't lost on Wren. "You take the pdf," he said, "I've got the Notes."

They both tapped at their phones.

"There's offices we can use for this," Rogers said helpfully.

"Drink your soy."

"Bigger screens," she went on, "access to printers. What the normal people do."

"I like the fresh air. What are you seeing?"

Rogers took a second, scrolling down. "Looks like their full chat log. Hundreds of pages, the transcript of every communication. Photos too. Yours?"

"Highlights from the log," Wren said, scanning the 'Notes' file. It was a neat document with four columns: the date, catfisher's name, page reference to the full log and a comment for follow-up. Malton Bruce's first name appeared frequently, interspersed with others. A Tom. A Clara. "Have you got names of the ones they took?"

Rogers answered without looking up. "Tom Solent. Clara Baxter. They've both been in Marcy's Heroes for around a year. Two and three perps arrested respectively; Solent lives in the metro area, seems Baxter flew in special."

Wren scrolled on. The comment column held key quotes lifted from the full log: promises, boasts, sexual innuendo. Wren whipped the document down; it extended for fifty-three pages. More photos loaded the further he went. The catfishers had invented an identity, a girl named Sophie, fifteen years old, a cheerleader by the looks of things.

Ravenous6 had basic tradecraft, it seemed. He requested pictures in specific poses, and sent the 'girl' links that passed as online games but implanted spyware, designed to test if she was for real. Sophie, or Marcy's Heroes, seemed to pass all Ravenous6's tests; at least as far as Wren could see. He recognized some of the spyware games but not others. The field was rapidly evolving. As the perps cooked up new means of verifying their targets, the catfishers came up with new workarounds. The CIA, FBI, NSA and other agencies occasionally dipped their clunking, massive feet in the waters and shut down a whole strain of code, but the waters always returned to a kind of furiously churning balance after.

"Do you know all of these testing links?" Wren asked.

Rogers looked up. "Not all. Some are new."

"Our database is out of date."

"It's always out of date," Rogers said. "It's a digital arms race, boss."

Wren grunted. She was the expert, why he'd picked her. "What about digital forensics? Can we lock into the coding style and narrow it to known hackers?"

Rogers made a face. "Difficult. The field changes fast, and the tests are easy to design. Anyone with basic coding can dash one off." She pointed at the screen. "Many of the ones listed here are already outdated. Look, I know this one, two months ago?" She tapped the link for a ball-bouncing game. "It got nerfed." Wren frowned. "I mean, defanged, made useless, by a simple workaround. All the catfishers know about it, so the perps don't use it anymore."

Wren considered. Back and forth the Blue Fairy and catfishers went, using bigger weapons every time, executing better attacks, causing greater collateral damage. Now they were acting in the real world.

"This real-world attack is the logical next step," he said.

Rogers set her phone on her lap, looking at Wren. The soy latte sat forgotten by her side. "In the arms race? You think it's an expansion of the battlefield?"

Wren looked at her. She was sharp.

"We know they've been organizing," he said. "The Blue Fairy know we can't crack them, and they're getting confident. We don't even know how many members they have. It could be tens of thousands worldwide. We could be talking accomplished figures, with wealth, ability, power. Now seems they figured out a way to catfish the catfishers. My guess is it's in these test links." He tapped his phone. "They hid malignant code and smoked out Marcy's Heroes." Wren paused. "But they didn't warn the perp. Ravenous6. They let him walk right into it. Why is that?"

Rogers' eyes lit up. "They needed a patsy. A guy as bait for the catfishers."

Wren nodded along. These thoughts had been forming on the plane, on the drive, throughout the afternoon; that this Pinocchio strike was just the beginning.

"We call it an arms race. What happened here was a declaration of war."

Rogers' eyes widened. "You think there'll be more?"

Wren churned through the last twelve hours of data, projected the connections going forward. Malton Bruce was dead, but they'd taken Clara Baxter and Tom Solent alive; warriors at the forefront of their digital war. They had passwords and inside knowledge, likely not only for Marcy's Heroes but for others too. They could potentially bring large swathes of catfish community down with them.

Wren stood, coffee forgotten. "Get Humphreys on the line. Tell him to send a warning to every known catfish organization: pull their sites down, retract any information they've got on the web, change their passwords, warn their people. The Blue Fairy is coming for them."

"On it," Rogers said.

Wren opened his darknet and ordered a total lockdown of the Foundation. No new member admissions. Password changes for every user. He double-locked his inner files in the cloud, where he stored names, addresses and coin status on a dedicated server. He sent a warning messages out in another Megaphone blast.

When he finished Rogers was looking at him, her call to Humphreys abandoned. He could see what was coming in her eyes.

"There've been more attacks."

10

ATTACKS

"Looks like four hours back," Rogers went on. "We're just putting the pieces together now. A sister network to Marcy's, they've not been responding to our calls since midnight. I'm seeing," she scrolled, "two anti-abuse volunteers dead. Their children missing. Mutilations." She winced. "And that's just so far. In their home. No evidence yet, no trace."

Wren stared ahead, feeling the scale of the Blue Fairy swell around them. Bigger than Detroit. Faster than he'd expected. "Where?"

"Sacramento," Rogers said, then turned pale as more notifications pinged into her phone. "Also Seattle. And Orlando."

"Three cities?"

"Three cities," Rogers confirmed. "Three different corners of the country."

Wren just stared.

"Four dead," Rogers said, her voice flattening out under the barrage. "Sacramento was the family, Seattle and Orlando were single victims, left at the scene."

Four dead. Two children taken. All in the last four hours. Potentially acting on information extracted from Clara Baxter and Tom Solent. It meant Pinocchio teams ready to go on the moment, spanning the nation.

"Get Humphreys back," he said, then brought up his phone.

Intelligence reports were shaky and brief. Photographs, initial impressions, scraps of video. Wren burned through screen after screen, drinking from the fire hose. No witnesses at any of the hits. Each was done in the middle of the night or with the dawn. It looked like proficient work, with no fingerprints, no 911 calls made, very little on CCTV but for the Sacramento hit, which was caught on a neighbor's hidden security cam.

It was another team of three Pinocchio masks, dressed in jeans and hoodies, armed with bats and knives. Wren watched them break in fast and easy. The security video showed they were inside for an hour, long enough to extract more information before the kills were made. He gritted his teeth. Now this thing was a snowball rolling downhill, gathering mass and speed.

He looked at the pictures of the victims. Clean slices. No hesitation. Blood loss was the cause of death. Fresh beachheads in the Blue Fairy's new war.

Wren rubbed his temples. Rogers held out her phone. "Humphreys."

"Start spinning up switchboards," Wren said, taking the phone. "Exhaust our budget getting the message out to every catfisher we can reach. They need to run."

Rogers nodded. Wren raised the phone to his ear.

"I need all the agents you've got on this right now, Humphreys," he said. "We're looking at a massive terrorist assault, across the whole country."

"All the agents?" Humphreys said. He sounded annoyed, like he'd been disturbed in the midst of something more important.

"Enough to secure all the catfishers." Wren started pacing around the forecourt. "Our agents plus police, other agencies if you can. Overwatch on them all right now."

A moment passed as Humphreys digested this. "That's thousands. It's not possible, Wren."

"It's necessary. We're talking about incredible coordination: three teams, Humphreys, four including the hit team that struck here, spread across the country. Professional, smooth, no hesitation, no trail left behind. God knows how many hits there've been that we don't yet know about. More hits are coming and we need to be ready."

Humphreys' tone was exasperated. "So narrow it down! That's what we have you for. Don't ask me for thousands of agents. I might as well order the army in to defend every single citizen. It's not feasible."

Wren gritted his teeth. "The army's a good idea. This is an existential threat against the citizenry. Have you seen these pictures?"

"The mutilations?"

Wren sucked in a breath. He'd seen few things worse. "Yes. They're ruthless and prepared. They wouldn't be doing these attacks if there isn't more to follow; they're too smart to not have an endgame in mind."

"What? What endgame?"

"I'm working on that. That's another reason we need the catfishers protected, they're our front line in intel against the Blue Fairy. If anyone knows what's going on, it's them. I have switchboards spinning up to make contact, but it's not going to be enough, especially with many of the catfish groups running dark right now. We have to save the ones we can."

Humphreys took a slow, steadying breath. "I think you're over-reacting. Christopher."

"Was I over-reacting with the Saints?"

A pause. "That was different. That was a war. What's this but a few freaks clubbing together?"

Wren paced in circles, forcing himself to be calm. Shouting wasn't always the best way. You caught more flies with honey. "This is more than a few freaks. They're trying to bring something awful into the light here, Director, something we don't want to come out."

"Something half-baked," Humphreys said. "Where you see professionalism, I see rank amateurs. They'll slip up, Christopher."

That was enough with the honey. Humphreys always brought out the worst in him. "Have you even seen the mutilations?"

"I've seen them!" Humphreys answered. A few harsh breaths. "They're ugly, but it's not enough for what you're asking. You want agents, which means I have to take them off other areas. There's no huge reservoir of them just sitting around waiting for your call, Wren! You know that. Everyone's out there with their finger in the dam already. The world doesn't stop just because you broke a nail." He paused, perhaps regretting that last. Wren gave him time to climb down. "Look, I'll free up some people in major cities; you can advise them of a select few target locations. A select few, Wren. If it goes bigger, the response will get bigger. That's all I can say."

The phone line went dead. Wren felt like throwing the phone into traffic. Instead, he checked his feeds, but nothing was in from the

288

Foundation, or his Washington CIA team yet. Hundreds of Firebird rental companies. Dozens of owners. Countless white panel vans. Teams were headed out to knock on doors, but that'd take hours.

Another People Mover go by overhead. More attacks could be happening right then, anywhere across the country, and he was powerless to stop them. He turned to Rogers, interrupted her mid-call.

"Get those witnesses in. The rolling e-fit I asked for? We're doing it. It's getting dark. I want to see what this strike really looked like."

Rogers blinked. It took her a second to refocus from whatever logistics she'd been engaged in. "The re-enactment. You still want it?"

"Right now. Police escort to get them here, whatever. Maybe we'll smoke out a few more witnesses. Let's have big signs up in front of the People Mover, where they can see it from the train."

"Understood," said Rogers and got back on the line.

Wren strode to the tip of the triangular forecourt. It felt like standing at the prow of the ship, looking out into an ocean of traffic. Down Michigan police teams were going from business to business already, knocking on doors, but he didn't expect much. Half the places had been closed for years.

Five dead, he thought. Two children and two adults taken. The ship was sinking, and Wren was sinking with it.

11

LIVE E-FIT

I t grew dark, and the live e-fit came together.

"The actors are an improvisation group," Rogers said, standing at Wren's side as a rented white van was parked at the curb. The People Mover triangle wasn't taped off. The street wasn't blockaded. The whole thing was guerrilla, unauthorized by the city but with the knowledge of local police, just the way Wren wanted it. "The best I could get on short notice."

Wren said nothing. Three of the actors were sitting in the panel van now, waiting for their first take. They had on the Pinocchio masks Rogers had bought, hoodies and jeans, and just looking at them made Wren want to stride over and start breaking jaws. They were actors only, he told himself. He'd dressed them that way. They weren't the real Pinocchios.

Traffic rolled on behind him. The People Mover came in overhead, emptied and re-filled, and a fresh flow of people came out of the ticket gates.

Their three witnesses stood at the side, with the best view. A woman and two men, all apologetic that they couldn't remember more, still stressed from what they'd seen the previous night. Wren hadn't pressed them.

The actor playing the perp, Ravenous6, was in position, matching the description as best they could gather from the grainy CCTV; a middle-aged, medium-height, white male wearing a suit, ball cap and carrying a clipboard. The three catfish actors were in waiting; a big guy with a binder as Malton Bruce, a blond woman with a camera as Clara Baxter, a slimmer guy with another camera as Tom Solent. At the edge there were signs up requesting information. Police and agents stood on the periphery, ready to harvest testimony.

6 p.m. on a Tuesday.

"Go," Wren said into the radio.

The catfishers heard the order and sprang into action, following the script. Malton Bruce approached the perp. Tom Solent lingered by the ticket gates with his clipboard. Clara Baxter occupied a middle distance with her camera, tracking the action.

Seconds passed as Bruce confronted the perp, and angry improvisation led to raised voices and a real tension. The perp did a good job of looking terrified. Then the Pinocchios came on. The van doors opened and they walked swiftly up the triangle. In seconds one of them was behind Bruce. He brought the bat around, faked the hit well, and the catfisher went down on cue. Four more mock hits followed.

People nearby screamed; fresh bystanders who didn't understand it was a mock-up. Wren was traumatizing a fresh load of citizens, but he couldn't think about that. Instead, he watched his three witnesses intently, looking for signs of recognition or confusion.

It was there, but he wasn't sure what. Something didn't feel right; about the e-fit, about the reactions, and Wren tried to pin it down as the Pinocchios ran back to their van. The perp was standing there shocked, commuters were running and shouting and making emergency calls, everyone was in the right positions; just as they should. So what was wrong?

"Run, you idiot," the lead Pinocchio shouted through the window, a guess at what the guy had actually said, then mimed hauling ass back into traffic, though the van didn't move. A big reverse U-turn, Wren figured. Sweep out, stay out of surveillance, and beeline east along Michigan. Hit the Orange Pip intersection then disappear into thin air.

The perp would follow in the Firebird from its perch around the corner. Witnessed, maybe, from the Orange Pip, but there was no social media confirmation on that yet.

The scene ended.

The cries of terrified Detroiters stilled as the dead catfisher, Malton

Bruce, stood up sheepishly, rubbing the back of his head. People ebbed out then back in, like a wave, curious then angry. Were they filming a movie? What the hell was this? Wren let his team handle the explanations and studied the witnesses. The two guys looked nauseated. That made sense. Seeing it all over again would bring it back.

But the woman? For a time in the middle there'd been faint confusion on her face. Now she just looked blank. Not nauseated. Wren had seen her profile, an office worker in the Guardian building a few blocks over. There was no sign she had psychopathic tendencies or anything to evidence a lack of empathy. She should be nauseated like the others, thrown back into the trauma, but she wasn't.

Something about the performance hadn't rung true.

Wren strode over. She was a tall woman, dark hair and brown eyes, summer freckles across her cheeks, mid-thirties.

"Mrs. Reveille," he said, reading her name from his clipboard. "Janet, if I may?" She nodded. "You saw something after the victim was struck with the baseball bat, something that didn't seem right to you. What was it?"

Her lips pursed. She wasn't sure. It wasn't something she really remembered, lost in the stress of the moment. "I don't think so. I think…" she paused. Questioning herself, now. Exactly the sort of thing he'd rigged this whole thing to avoid. She gave up. "It was horrible. It seemed right."

"No," Wren shook his head. Sticking with the feeling, with what he'd seen. "In the middle, I saw your reaction. You weren't even looking at the bat. You were watching the other one. The Pinocchio with the female victim. What happened there?"

"Oh. Well, I don't… I mean…" she paused, trying to get a grip on her memory. "Maybe it was louder?" Her dark eyes now shone. Tears suggested she was heading back into the memory. "The clown, the Pinocchio, I don't know. I was nearer to him. Over there." She pointed. "There was so much shouting. They were right beside me. I was worried it would be me next, but I just froze. I wanted to run but I couldn't move."

Wren cursed inwardly. Of course. He'd set the witnesses aside like they were neutral observers, like they were watching a movie, but that wasn't right. When it had happened they'd been in the thick of it. The Pinocchios had waged a disciplined attack designed to maximize shock and awe, and the fear in the midst of that would have been intense.

He needed to replicate the original conditions as closely as possible.

Ferat's theory applied directly. Sensory details were key right alongside emotional state, and he'd muted both by setting the witnesses aside.

"We'll re-run it," he said.

"That's not necessary-" she began, but Wren held up a hand.

"Help me here, Janet. Please. There are other attacks happening right now. Other people dying. I need your help. I need you to be brave. One more time, standing where you stood last night. Can you do that for me?"

Now her pupils dilated. The fear was coming back. It was obvious now, the first re-run had been too safe. Even she'd seen that. Too quiet, too distant, and that was the problem.

"Janet?" he said softly. "I can't force you here. But the things you know? I need that information. Can we try again?"

She gave a tiny nod. Mustered herself as much as she could. "Yes."

He touched her shoulder. "Thank you."

Rogers followed after him as he strode away, moved into his path. Her eyes were wide and bright.

"What are the hell we doing here, boss? That woman has been traumatized enough already! Doesn't matter if she gives consent, it was harassment to put her through it once, but again? Not to mention that her testimony will be muddied irreparably. You're going to insert yourself into any sense memories she comes up with."

There wasn't much Wren could say to that. "She knows something, Rogers. I can see it. We need to get it out. I'll apologize when it's over."

"Apologize? We're causing damage right now." She gestured around at the re-enactment. "Everything we're trained to do in witness testimony is about minimizing the trauma to the victim. They're victims, not toys. You can't use terror as a tool for recall."

Wren looked over Roger's shoulder, to the woman. She was walking now, back to the position she'd been in for the strike. Turning pale, like she was heading back into the memory. But was something still missing? Something she'd said about the real strike being louder?

Rogers was talking. Wren looked at her but barely heard a thing, like he'd dialed the volume way down to the silent fuzz of CCTV. He fast-forwarded through the strike in his head again: the van, the attack, the escape. He'd had the actors arguing, improvising angry dialog, but that wouldn't have been the only sound. There was one more, maybe the most traumatizing of them all.

It hit him like a bat to the head, and he refocused on Rogers. "What does a head sound like, when it's hit by a baseball bat?"

Rogers blinked. "What?"

Wren tried to guess. He didn't have long. He'd pushed the witness into the right mental state, now she'd hold that for maybe ten minutes, but afterward she'd be too exhausted to do it again. He'd set the fuse burning; now he was on the clock and had to get it right. "Not a ham," he mused. "And it's not good enough just to hit the ground. Or a tree."

Rogers stared at him, beginning to glimpse the logic. "You're talking about hitting a skull? Malton Bruce's skull?"

"A thin bone globe with soft meat inside. A thunk, kind of hollow. What sounds like that?"

Rogers frowned, her anger fading already in the thrust of this new angle. "It depends on the bat, I suppose. One of those metal bats, it's going to ping. A wooden bat, more of a thunk and a crunch."

Wren thought back to the CCTV. Too low resolution, you couldn't tell. He looked back at the witnesses. An agent stood by them, filling out forms. Wren strode over. Young guys, suit and tie, desk warriors who'd never experienced anything like this before, each in their own state of heightened emotion.

"What did the bat sound like?" he asked. "Hitting the guy's head? Was it metallic or wooden?"

They stared at him. They looked at each other.

"The bat hitting his head," Wren prompted. "How did it sound?"

Their eyes rolled up and to the left; accessing memory. "Wooden," said one. The other nodded. "It was loud."

Wren sucked through his teeth. Of course it was.

"The actors are using a wiffle bat," Rogers said, getting into the spirit of it. Maybe she'd read Ferat's research after all. "They're not even hitting anything. The blows are pulled."

"That's it," Wren said. And it wasn't only the bat. Aside from the Pinocchio and the perp, there'd been hardly any noise through the whole re-enactment. Almost like a silent movie. No impact of the bat on Malton's skull, no groans as Malton died, no screams from the bystanders.

Nine minutes. He brought up his phone and clicked into the maps app.

"Does it matter that much?" Rogers asked.

"It might," Wren said, scrolling the map as he talked, thinking back on

Ferat's research. "Blue rooms and math, Rogers. Emotional state, auditory input, anything could be a keystone memory that'll trigger greater recall." He looked up. "We have to get it right. Something will come out of it."

Rogers stared. "I really need to read this research. But I'm worried about the witness. The trauma you're going to cause her, by putting her through it all over again."

Wren took a breath. "I know. That's not what I want, either. You know my expertise in psychological operations. I'm confident I can reframe this experience as a positive. She'll come out of it stronger."

Rogers didn't look convinced.

"Either way, I can't do it alone," Wren went on. "We've got less than nine minutes to pull it off. Are you in?"

Rogers gritted her teeth, jaw clenched. Some anger, maybe, but putting that aside. "I'm in. What do you need?"

Wren held up the map on his phone, pointed east along Michigan. "There's an athletics store on Woodward. Get me a wooden baseball bat."

12

SKULL

Wren ran, hit the ticket gates for the People Mover in seconds and vaulted over them. People CIAged either way and he sprinted up the stairs, onto the long narrow platform and dropped down onto the track.

Somebody shouted, then he was away and sprinting north. The track was shallow, two rails for the People Mover, the electrified third rail in the middle, low cement walls at either side. A human aqueduct flowing through the city, cutting corners and shooting over the tops of buildings. He'd worked the angles already. If he took Cass north on foot and busted east, he'd reach the grocery store in five minutes, probably slower if he took the van, thanks to traffic. Call it a minute to select what he needed, five to come back the same way, and the witness would be out of state.

The People Mover track was his only shot. A train ahead was pulling into the next station: Times Square Grand River Avenue, less than a mile away. Wren pumped his elbows hard, his left thigh twinged from the old injury, but he bulled through, far too fast for security in the station ahead to react. Two minutes sprinting there, two back, two to get a skull, that gave him a rough two minutes to play with.

The train ahead pushed through the station, clearing his route in, and now faces were leaning down from the platform looking back at him, trying to explain this bizarre sight away. Twenty seconds later he was there.

He hauled himself off the track and bustled through the waiting crowds before they could raise the alarm, driving down the stairs to hurdle the ticket gates out onto Grand River Avenue, two blocks north of Michigan.

Before him stood a tall multistory parking lot fading into offices six floors up, with more graffitied panels at ground level, and no store where the map had said there should be. Wren sprinted around the corner onto Washington Boulevard, ran a hundred yards north and there it was: Adam's Market.

Organic produce, it looked like, farmer's market-style, minimum food miles, all very ethically responsible. He dashed in and scanned the aisles: Fruit, Household, Seafood, Meat.

Seafood was in back, an artistic display of fish, crabs and shrimp on a bed of ice chips and kale. Wren vaulted over the glass display counter, snatched the prize King Crab from its place in the center, then rolled back across.

"Sorry," he called over his shoulder, tucking the crab under his arm.

In Meat a big guy was coming up the aisle already, store security. Short hair, thick tight beard, hand going to his waist for a taser. Wren charged him like a tight end, thrusting with his shoulder. The guy wasn't expecting it, was high on his feet not hunkered down, and took the charge below center mass. Wren sent him bowling through the air to crash into a pyramid of cans.

Wren scanned the pork products in the refrigerator bay and scooped the largest ham joint they had, packaged in plastic with a thick fatty rind. On the way out the security guy was getting up.

Wren jumped over him. By the registers he grabbed a roll of duct tape and sped outside. People were staring now: a huge man running at full speed, carrying a giant crab under one arm and a huge ham under the other. Late for the dinner party of a lifetime, perhaps.

A transit worker stood in front of the People Mover, looking this way and that, trying to figure out what had happened, whether he needed to call the police or not. Wren breezed by him, jumped the gates and ascended back to the platform.

"It was him," somebody shouted as he dropped down to the track. "Now he's got a crab!"

He ran, five minutes and counting. A train came directly toward him, the driver open-mouthed. Wren jumped up and sideways at the last moment, onto the track's thin outer wall, as the train rolled by inches to his left. People inside pointed and started. Somebody shouted, "Crab!" like they'd sighted a rare bird.

The train rolled by and he fell into its wake, hitting the Michigan Avenue platform a minute later. Seven minutes gone. Down the stairs he went, out onto the triangle, where his witness had drying tears on her cheeks and Rogers was already standing by the tree, panting, a baseball bat in her hands.

"You went for groceries?" she asked.

"What they had," he said, dropping to his knees. He stripped the plastic packaging off the pork and slapped it on the ground. "Get them all ready. Tell the guy with the bat to hit this with everything he's got. Hard. Five times."

Rogers stared. "Yes, boss."

Wren dug his fingers under the flap of fat covering the pork joint. It was slippery but he dug his nails in and yanked. Fat skinned away with a ropey tearing sound, until it was almost entirely separated, like a combover blowing in the wind.

Wren picked up the crab and smashed it on the concrete. People stared. The case cracked and Wren tore the creature apart. Top shell, bottom shell, pink and gray meat. He snapped dangling legs off the upper shell, pressed the shell on top of the pork, then swung the flap of fat over the top.

Brain, skull, skin.

With the duct tape he bundled it into a tight, compact package, rapped the top twice with his knuckles, and it gave a solid, boney thunk. He looked up; they were all in position. Rogers was staring at him, a look that said he was either a genius or a madman. That would depend entirely on what happened next.

He got to his feet and strode over to Malton Bruce. The guy looked scared. Wren set the bundle down on the floor.

"As soon as this gets hit, you grunt and go down," he said softly. "Each hit, you grunt. Then you die."

The guy's eyes widened and he nodded jerkily. Probably he'd never taken a director's note so fully to heart before.

Wren checked on the witness, Janet. She was in position, standing near where the female catfisher was lurking, glancing around like she didn't know quite what was happening, like she wasn't sure it was really a re-enactment. Wren went on to the van and leaned through the open window. Three Pinocchios leered back at him, their noses obscenely long.

"You hit that piece of meat with everything you've got," he told the lead guy. "Don't screw around. Pull a muscle in your back if you have to. Five times. Hit it like you hate it." He looked to the others. "The rest of you go in hard. Shout. Improvise. Throw some punches. You hate these people. This is your big break."

He stepped back. Out of the fray, to the roadside where he could watch his witness. There was silence across the triangle now, all eyes on him, even the pedestrians coming out of the station were muted, as if they knew something important was about to happen. Waiting.

"Action," Wren shouted.

13

RECALL

The re-enactment began again. The catfishers swooped and things got heated fast, more heated than the first time, louder, more desperate. Emotions were running high after Wren's frantic disappearance onto the People Mover and his frantic reappearance with the meat. Permissions had been granted. The air felt charged and everybody breathed it in.

Commuters stopped in their tracks to watch, as the catfisher and the perp yelled. It hadn't happened that way; Wren knew they hadn't raised their voices from their body language in the CCTV. The perp had buckled, not resisted, but Wren didn't care. He wanted high emotions, and Janet Reveille was clearly feeling them. She looked terrified. She knew what was coming, more real than the first time, and she didn't want it to come.

The door of the white van opened and the Pinocchios flooded out. They came up the triangle like a tide, bats swinging, pushing regular people out of their way. Better. The atmosphere was thick with fear.

The male catfisher played it beautifully. Malton Bruce. Caught in his own moment of righteousness, making this pitiful perp squeal. Moment of glory, but all the time listening for his cue. The bat went up. The bat came down.

The thunk on the crab and pork was gruesome, sounding out across the triangle. It didn't matter that the Pinocchio was only hitting a piece of meat on the ground. The deep thunk of it went right through Wren, married to the sudden violence of the strike. That was a person dying, right there.

Malton dropped to his knees with a well-considered grunt. The Pinocchio struck again. Just meat and crab shell bundled on the floor, but people stared in horror, too stunned now to scream. They couldn't compute what was happening. Violence was violence, and with each blow Malton cried out and jerked like he'd been hit.

Had he been hit? They weren't sure. It sounded real. It felt real.

Three more hits and Malton lay on the floor convulsing, and the screaming was now well underway. A second batch of commuters for whom all this was fresh.

Wren swept the scene. The other two Pinocchios were rough-housing their catfishers, as per the CCTV footage, and the catfishers were doing their best not to get actually hurt. Barely-pulled punches to the stomach. Slaps around the head. Shouts. Wren had orchestrated the thing, and still, he couldn't take it all in. Trauma narrowed the brain's focus.

People screamed and ran. None stepped in to help. The Pinocchios had carte blanche to drag their two remaining victims toward the van. The back doors of the van clanked open and they were hurled inside. It hadn't been like this in the first re-enactment. That had been a walk in the park compared to this.

Through the midst of that chaos Wren strode toward his witness. Janet Reveille. She had turned ash-white, right back in the moment. He stepped in front of her like he was popping into her personal nightmare. It took her a moment to register him, too caught up in her private terror.

"Janet," he said, firmly now, because softly wouldn't cut it. "Tell me. What did you see?"

"I-" she began, but couldn't get it out. He saw something moving behind her eyes, like a shark swimming in the depths of the unconscious.

Wren leaned in, pointing without looking. "That man broke his head open. The others were beaten and stolen away. You've never seen anything like that before, and God forbid you never will again. Now help me make that true. What did you see?"

Her eyes flickered: Wren, the duct-tape package, the van, a space in the air.

"There," she said, pointing.

Wren looked. It was empty space, but Wren rewound the action. It was where one of the Pinocchios had grabbed the female catfisher. Janet's finger trembled.

"Tell me."

Her body shook. Wren thought she might vomit. "Shouting. He was shouting. She was screaming. He elbowed her in the face. There was blood."

Wren leaned in. "Go on."

"He said something."

"What did he say?"

"I couldn't hear clearly. The mask." Janet's face was locked now, seeing it happen again. Feeling it. "He was so angry. I've never... I've never seen anything like that." Her eyes flickered to Wren and away again, like she couldn't hold focus. "I couldn't see his face, but the way he moved, the way he held her? He hated her. He wanted to rub her out."

That was all new. Until now, Wren had assumed Malton Bruce was the main target of the attack, with the other catfishers taken as collateral. But maybe there was more to it than that.

"He hated her generally, as a catfisher, or her personally?"

Janet's eyes ran cold. "Personally. Definitely."

"What did he say?"

She twitched. "A name. I think."

"What name?"

"I can't- I don't know. I don't know."

Now Wren soothed. She couldn't take much more before the stress overloaded her system. "Give me a letter. Just one letter."

She strained at the air, her vision wavering like she was trying to pin down a mosquito with her eyes. "L? I think, L."

"Keep going."

"Maybe Lance?"

"Lance," affirmed Wren, "good, Janet. Now give me the rest. Give me a last name."

She stared. She weaved. Then she went still. Wren had seen this before. She was about to pass out. It happened when people drove their bodies to the extremes, in faith healer churches, in exorcisms, at rock concerts. Their

302

emotions went up to the edge of what their minds could take, and found there was nothing to hold them back, no safety railing before overload. Without someone to pull them back, they tipped over into unconsciousness.

"Hepbert," she said, staring right at him. Through him. "Hebbert. Heppert."

Wren nodded. That was it.

Janet's gaze was stone cold now. She was lost. She was speaking from the fall on the other side. "This is for Lance Hebbert", she said weakly. "That's what he said. Like a vendetta."

Wren took hold of her hands; they were ice cold. He had to get the reframing of this experience in before she collapsed. The nightmare had to end better than this, or she would suffer for it. Wren knew all about PTSD, panic attacks and night terrors.

"Thank you for what you've done here today, Janet," he said, speaking clearly and making sure her wide eyes saw him, saw his lips moving. "This shouldn't have happened to you, and I'm sorry for my part in it, but you've been incredibly brave. You have definitely saved lives tonight, and that makes you a hero in my book. You should be very proud."

She nodded vaguely. Wren felt he could see right into her heart. Then her eyes rolled back in her head, her body went limp, and Wren caught her. He guided her gently to the ground as a medical team came rushing in.

The world rushed back in with them. There was a sense of people gravitating toward them at the center. In the seconds before the wave of attention crested, Wren took out his phone and sent a message to his Washington team and the elite hacker board on the Foundation darknet.

ONE OF THE PINOCCHIOS SAID 'THIS IS FOR LANCE HEBBERT' OR HEPBERT OR OTHER DERIVATIONS. SEEMS HE TARGETED THE FEMALE CATFISHER PERSONALLY. FIND ME THAT MAN, AND FIND ME WHY HE HATED HER SO MUCH.

Then Rogers was there. She was staring at him in disbelief. What she'd just seen probably looked like magic. Wren felt about the same. A witness who'd known nothing suddenly gave hard testimony. The first time he'd seen his father fundamentally manipulate people from the inside out, rewriting the way they thought about the world, it had been the same.

"What did you get?" she asked.

"A name," Wren said, straightening up. "This wasn't just a random hit to start their war. They were after these catfishers in particular. Maybe the female catfisher above all."

Rogers' eyes lit up, spooling through the possibilities. "This was revenge?"

"This was revenge," Wren confirmed. "And I think they're just getting started."

14

CIRCLES

Wren paced north up Cass, away from the cleanup at the triangle, away from the constant low bustle of Federal agents interviewing potential witnesses, away from Rogers glancing up at him after every call made.

He walked and scrolled on his phone. The boards of his darknet were abuzz with security advice: how to bleach-scan a hard drive in case the Fairy had gotten in; how to set and track unhackable passwords; how to break your habits and get out of town without leaving an obvious onward trail. His Foundation were in flight.

His elite hacker board was quiet by contrast. A few posts about Lance Hebbert or Hephart or whatever it was. Speculation mostly. Various national intelligence service directory searches turned up nothing solid, neither did a cursory scan through international police databases, prison records, army files, airport customs logs. Thus far the man was a ghost.

Cornering west toward a small park, he tapped re-dial for Reince Jeffries, head of Marcy's Heroes. Trying to get a better sense of the overall picture, and squeezing an old informant for more. After three rings Jeffries answered.

"I'm recording this call," the older man said. His tone was angry. "I have spoken with my lawyer, and-"

"Mr. Jeffries," Wren interrupted, "that's all fine, do as you like, but please just answer one more question. Have you ever catfished a man named Lance Hebbert?"

There was a moment of silence. Wren pictured him Jeffries stewing, wondering if there was a team outside his house this time, wondering if he should expose himself to more legal jeopardy. Wren expected prevarications and delay in reply, requiring another push to crack through Jeffries' resistance, but what he got was unequivocal.

"I have never heard that name, Mr. Wren. Be assured I know the details of every evil man my organization has incarcerated. I cannot help you. Do not call this number again."

He hung up.

Wren reached the park. A big circle of parched grass lit by floodlights lay ahead, with smaller circles around the outside. He started pacing along one of the paths. Each one linked to the next. It was a perfect metaphor for going around in circles.

Jeffries said he didn't know Hebbert, and Wren believed him. That meant Marcy's Heroes hadn't captured him, which meant, what?

Circling. Wren's phone buzzed but he ignored it for the moment, working the facts in hand. All this was a set-up by the Blue Fairy. A sting on these catfishers in particular, seeking revenge for some as-yet-unknown crime, but against who?

Not Malton Bruce, he figured. If they'd wanted real revenge, they wouldn't just kill him. So, that suggested Clara Baxter the target? She was the one the Pinocchio had been shouting at. Interlinking lines stretched out from her name, taking shape in Wren's head. A cloud. Connections. What did he really know about any of these catfishers?

Who was Clara Baxter?

He thought back. Rogers had said she'd flown in specially for this hit. What kind of catfisher did that? He imagined a woman with resources, probably hiding her true wealth. Far more than a hobbyist predator of predators, maybe even a full-time operative. How else would she have earned such hate? Bringing abusers down could be her vocation.

If that was true, then the Blue Fairy had struck paydirt when they'd taken her. He dialed Jeffries again and didn't wait for the old man to make any more protests.

"Mr. Jeffries, I need everything you have on Clara Baxter, sent to this phone right now. Let's start with how long have you known her?"

Reince Jeffries said nothing. Wren waited, pressed the phone closer to his ear, and heard someone breathing. He stopped pacing. It wasn't Reince's breath. It didn't have the same light wheeze. This was someone else. An echoey sound. Like the phone was being held inside a mask. Wren's mind whirred.

"Pinocchio," he said.

"Is this Christopher Wren?"

Wren's heart skipped a beat. The voice was refined, calm, in control. The opposite of how he felt. He stamped control atop that uncertainty.

"Where's Clara Baxter?"

A long silence. Wren's heart thudded.

"Where are your children, Christopher?"

It stunned him. Too much. His children? He instantly saw red. The Alpha of the Saints had threatened them. He'd checked up on them after that, knew they were OK through talking to his father-in-law. But now?

"Touch them and you'll die."

Another long silence, then an answer came in clipped sentences. "Too late."

The phone went dead. Wren stared at it for a moment, barely able to breathe.

His kids.

They weren't talking to him. He didn't know anything. With shaking fingers he stamped out a message to his Foundation, Megaphone blast to everyone on repeat, serious coin rewards for success.

THE BLUE FAIRY JUST THREATENED MY KIDS. FIND THEM. SECURE THEM.

Already striding out of the park, he called Rogers.

"Boss," she answered, "we've been trying to contact you-"

"Get a squad to Reince Jeffries' home right now," he barked, "along with drone recon overwatch, heat-tracking equipped, plus two tactical helicopters inbound. The Blue Fairy have him, and they may have my kids."

A moment of silence passed as she digested that, then she answered. "On it. Meet you on Cass."

Wren rang off and ran onto Cass, head spinning as he stabbed a message for the Megaphone.

WE FIND THESE BASTARDS NOW. SEARCH FOR CLARA BAXTER ALONGSIDE HEBBERT. MAY BE CONNECTED.

In moments a detective's car sped up toward him, siren and light blaring. Wren flagged it, saw Rogers in the front passenger seat. It pulled over and Wren ordered the officer out of the driver's seat, then dropped in his place and punched the gas, revving hard into traffic.

"Boss," said Rogers, giving him a look, "I'm sorry about your kids, I-"

"Do you know where they are?"

"I don't, sorry, I-"

"Direct me to Jeffries' address," he said, no time to waste. "I just talked to a Pinocchio there. He threatened my kids." He squeezed the wheel, took the car up to seventy in seconds. Trying to get a handle on all this, through the tunneling effect of adrenaline and the riotous thump of his pulse. He glanced at Rogers, who looked as overwhelmed as he felt. "What were you trying to contact me about?"

She stared for a second, getting a grip, then nodded. "Right. They've got a color on the Firebird. Spider picked it up from that coffee shop, witness testimony off the People Mover backed it."

"Red?" asked Wren.

Rogers looked disappointed. "Yes. How did you... left here!" Wren ran a red light at forty and skidded hard onto West Fisher, rising to fifty alongside the freeway. Five seconds passed in acceleration, then he pulled a hard right going the wrong way onto the exit ramp. Rogers braced against the dash as exiting traffic sped toward them. Wren pushed the pedal down and swung over to the shoulder.

"Unh," Rogers said, as the stream of oncoming vehicles honked and peeled left, missing them by inches. Three seconds later they merged into oncoming traffic; Wren spun a hard handbrake turn into the middle of the three-lane expressway, stopping two lanes of traffic and nearly getting reamed by a speeding semi. He cranked the gear stick, the tires squealed and burning rubber backwashed into the car, then they were accelerating like a cannonball. Past the semi, past everyone, up to ninety in twenty seconds and wailing west.

Rogers took a breath. "Hot damn, Boss. I drive next time."

"The Pinocchios have Jeffries," Wren said, willing the road ahead to empty out so he could go over a hundred, forcing himself not to think about Jake and Quinn. "Only Jeffries so far knows anything about Clara Baxter.

Did she have any next of kin? I didn't see it in the report. Do we even have her address?"

"I, uh, no," said Rogers, and brought up her phone, started scrolling. "I don't think so. Catfishers are cagey, in case they get doxxed."

Wren sucked breath through his teeth. Doxxed: having all your vital docs, or documents, exposed to the world on the Internet. Address, phone number, social security. Now the Fairy had doxxed Jeffries; was that because of Clara? How much did she know, and how many other catfishers had she already handed over?

"Baxter's the key," Wren said. "She did something to Lance Hebbert. Off books, I'm thinking." He swerved to the middle lane, around some knucklehead in a Ferrari thinking he could outrace the cops. "Jeffries had no record of it. I've got people digging into her now."

Rogers grunted. Wren overtook a long Lincoln Navigator limousine too fast. Already they were out of central Detroit and rushing northwest toward Redford Township, where Jeffries lived.

"How'd you know the Pontiac was red?" Rogers asked.

Wren flashed her a quick grin. "Firebird. It's in the name, these idiots wanna look cool. Just a lucky guess. Does it narrow it down any?"

"Barely. We have twelve teams out right now canvassing: seven Firebird owners near Detroit, a few possibles further out, one we like out of state."

"Out of state?"

"Cryptography on his Internet traffic through the roof. VPN, IP masking. Could be peer-to-peer piracy, or…" she trailed off.

"Yeah. Any crossed off?"

"A couple. Teams moving in. We'll get the bastard."

Wren tightened his grip on the wheel. There were teams all across the country now, closing in on catfishers and suspects alike. Dozens of specialist agents, along with many more local police and some FBI assists. The Detroit perp could be a lead, but he was a patsy only. What really mattered was Jeffries, and Clara, and finding just one crack in the Blue Fairy's façade to jam a lever into.

Catching a single Pinocchio ought to do it. In Wren's hands, the guy would spill it all.

15

REDFORD

Wren dragged the patrol car off the freeway and into Redford Township at seventy, barely letting up as the off-ramp veered right. Gyroscopic force pushed Rogers against Wren and made the vehicle's grip on the road seem a tenuous thing, then they slammed into a straight and tore through one, two intersections, cutting up traffic with sirens wailing.

"Turn right here," Rogers barked.

Wren cranked the handbrake and pulled hard onto Inkster Drive, leaving burned rubber trails behind as he accelerated into nighttime traffic, past the Tim Horton's and the Dollar General and into an all-American suburb of wide streets, spreading lawns and porch swings.

"Who's with him?" Wren asked. "Jeffries."

Rogers had the information ready. "He lives with his daughter, her husband, and their two kids. We don't have their confirmed locations right now."

Wren looked ahead. The skies were empty. "Where's overwatch?"

Rogers pressed her phone harder to her ear. "Choppers are thirty minutes out, but I'm wired into a Redford PD drone up on heat seek."

"If we've got one the Fairy could too. What does it see?"

Rogers tapped through to the live footage. "Vehicle in the driveway with a cold engine, a saloon belonging to Jeffries. Five people clustered in the house, that could be the family or Pinocchios. Nobody running, nobody hiding, nothing telling."

Wren cursed under his breath. "How are they clustered?"

"Have a look." Rogers held up her phone showing the drone's dark heatmap.

Wren scanned the screen: Jeffries' home was marked in red crosshairs at the far right, on the north side of the street, with five figures clustered closely together near the front window. Not panicking, not escaping, not fighting off the Pinocchios, just uniformly spread and stationary.

"This a photograph?" he asked.

"It's streaming video. Why?"

"Heat signature says they're still alive?"

"Yes. What is it, boss?"

Wren chewed at his lip and blew through another intersection, thinking about the Blue Fairy catfishing the catfishers with a patsy, about Internet games that doubled as traps, about an MO he'd already seen play out once in the real world and now…

"Jeffries' house, is it steel frame or brick?"

Rogers frowned, but fed the question and got a reply. "Brick, why?"

"No eyes on the windows?"

"Officers in attendance but all curtains are drawn."

Wren's mind raced: five people not moving meant one Pinocchio with a gun trained on four family members, or five Pinocchios lying in wait with the family removed, or the family themselves, somehow compelled to sit perfectly still like…

Bait in a trap.

Wren pushed the pedal down harder, blowing past Bell County Park at sixty. "How long's the drone been up?"

"Ten minutes, local PD are sitting outside. Our end advised them to hold back on any strike."

"Good. How many officers in the street?"

Rogers listened to the answer. "Seems like the whole station turned out. We've got five patrol cars blocking the street in either direction, and eleven officers in attendance. Armed response coming via helicopter, ETA unknown. We're it for now."

"They'll have a mobile weapons locker with them," said Wren, flying through another intersection with horns blaring in his slipstream. "I want two loaded shotguns in the yard waiting, and three officers in flak jackets set to breach."

Rogers frowned. "Will you have fries with that?"

Wren bulled on. "Two EMTs waiting in the back would be nice, and paramedics on standby in the road."

Rogers transferred the orders then turned to Wren. "What about weapons for us?"

"There won't be time for that."

Rogers frowned. "Why not?"

Now they could see the flashing police lights ahead: five patrol cars sealing off the block, with neighbors out on their porches rubbernecking.

"I think it's a trap. Some kind of bomb rigged to blow as soon as we breach, take out our strike team, take out Jeffries. They're the patsies, just like our perp, another darknet tactic carried into the real world."

Rogers turned to stare at him. "You're serious."

"Buckle up."

Her eyes went wide. "Don't tell me you're going to do what I think-"

"It's the only way to spring the trap fast," Wren said, and flew through the final intersection. "If there is a bomb, we need to force the trigger on our schedule or everyone in that house is pink mist. Show me the map again and put the officers on speaker."

Rogers cursed then cinched her seatbelt tight, tapped her phone and held it up, showing the drone's feed. Wren spoke loud as the patrol car roared closer. "Shoot two slugs through the bay windows now, we need to get their heads down! Chase with more shots as soon as we're in, no hesitation, and watch out for an explosion."

He didn't wait for a reply, shooting through the gap between the barricade of police cars like a heat-seeking missile. Their vehicle appeared like a red bullet in the cell phone's frame, the hot engine five seconds out. The house was on the left, Victorian style with large bay windows up a sloped front yard set to grass. Twin shotgun blasts took out the windows just as Wren yanked left, whipping the car hard to mount the curb with a chassis-cracking jolt.

"Daaamn!" Rogers shouted as they passed two officers at forty miles an hour, grabbed the back of her neck and braced, then they hit.

The fender struck brick just beneath the two-story structure's bay windows and crumpled instantly, followed by the grill which squashed flat, then the safety roll cage which sheared back on itself but didn't buckle, stripping a bolt in the undercarriage. Beneath it the building's outer layer of brick powdered with a terrific bang, sending fracture lines shooting out too fast for the structure to settle onto, opening a cavitated hole that the roll cage blew through in an explosion of bricks. The headlights ruptured as they hit the crumbling wall, then the indicator lights, sending glass sprinkling with brick dust and mortar as the car fed itself into the wall. The bodywork scraped and tore as the roll cage piledrived into an inner layer of breezeblocks like a hammer splitting a coconut husk. A run of electrical cabling tangled on the front axle, then the flat front fender punched through the interior wall. Pillows and throws flew through the air from the bay window seats, along with an airborne avalanche of masonry, timber and glass. The three-paned window above shattered under the warping stress, blowing back across the flashing siren lights. The front wheels tore off like pencil erasers on jagged brick ends, the wing mirrors clipped neatly away and the windshield smashed inward as the A-pillars hit the base of the wooden window frame and plowed through.

As the car slowed in a burst of heat, sound and motion, Wren and Rogers flew on at fifty miles an hour; the seat belts caught their bodies but their heads jolted onward despite the brace positions, stretching the nerves and muscles in their necks toward hyper-extension, until the airbags deployed with a double blast of air that was masked in the overall crash. Hard canvas balloons punched them both in the face, bruising their eyes, noses, lips, but halting the neck-snapping whiplash and pushing them back into the soft recesses of their seats.

The patrol car buried its momentum halfway into the Jeffries' dining room then rocked to a stop in a cloud of dust and tumbling debris, less than a second all told. Wren blinked and craned his clicking neck over the airbag as it deflated. The car hummed and the structure above them teetered, the engine still growled but the front end was buried too deeply in masonry to push any further.

Wren saw them, five people with Jeffries in their midst, lying face down where the shotgun blasts had dropped them to the floor. Dust clouded the air. An older man dressed in rumpled tweed, Jeffries, was already trying to push himself to his knees when the next round of shotgun blasts went off.

Jeffries flattened like a pinned butterfly to the floor, and Wren scanned the dusty interior. There were no Pinocchios, but amongst the detritus flung to the far side of the room he picked out a low coffee table on its side, and beside it the silver glint of a suitcase, resting open.

Just like in Minsk.

Bomb.

"Down," Wren had time to say, then squeezed his eyes shut and slapped his hands over his ears just before all hell broke loose.

16

BOMB

A tsunami wave of force smacked Wren down into the footwell and left him bent double in a kind of suspended state, not certain where or who he was. Heat, blast wind and noise poured through the open windshield above, shredding the driver's seat and scraping shrapnel down his back.

Then it ended and he reared up. The world ahead was black and dizzy. The Jeffries' dining room, only moments ago wrecked but recognizable, was now a dark cave filled with smoke and fire. Wren stared but couldn't figure out what he was seeing. He couldn't hear a thing, except the muted popcorn rattle of gunfire. Pop pop pop.

Gunfire?

He turned to Rogers, lit in the sickly light of the dashboard display. She was looking back at him, eyes blasted red by the shockwave, pinkish tears running down her cheeks, face pale, mouth open like she couldn't get a breath in.

"Holy crap, boss," she croaked.

Wren turned and shoved at the car door. It opened two inches, buried in rubble. Rogers laughed, then clicked her seatbelt and fell out of her side. Wren poured himself through the shattered window, the car's hot metal frame scalding him on the way out. On his knees amid rubble, he peered into the blast zone.

The ceiling lights had blown out. The floor was scoured clear of furniture and cratered. The walls were peppered with fracture lines and shrapnel holes, and smoldering fires were springing up in the thick carpet, lending toxic smoke to the miasma.

A substantial explosive, his muddled mind calculated. Several pounds of Semtex or the equivalent, kept in the silver case. The Blue Fairy. Like their booby-trapped tools scattered on testing sites, catfishing the catfishers. How long had they been watching Jeffries? At least since they'd taken Clara and Tom, but probably earlier. They'd set him and his family up as bait to take out emergency services, just like they'd set up Ravenous6.

Wren lurched to his feet. Springing the trap had been a huge risk. Now he needed that risk to pay off, with Jeffries alive and sharing information. He took a step forward, stumbling over crushed brick and scorched carpet, felt like he was floating in water.

"Wren!" came Rogers' voice.

He moved toward the sound. Light from the hallway chandelier spilled through hot black updrafts like angelic rays. He dropped to his knees and scanned the sparking carpet for the old man.

Rogers was right there, scooping up a child. In the chaos looked like his own kid, seven-year-old Jake. It wasn't him, though. Jeffries' grandson. There was another by Wren's side, granddaughter, lying under the protective embrace of her mother.

Wren scooped them both, a deep squat and fireman's lift that twinged his left thigh and almost toppled him. Silver lights flashed and he staggered through smoke, glimpsed Rogers starting back toward the car, away from the rising walls of flame.

Pop pop, pop pop in the distance.

"Not that way," Wren called, lurching forward, throat feeling raw. "We're taking fire. Pinocchios out front. Through the back." He half-ran, half-stumbled by Jeffries then his son-in-law, both laid flat out unconscious. No time. He skirted the blast crater, two-foot deep through parquet oak flooring, burst through a curtain of flame rising up the blown-open hole into the yard and into the chill evening air, where twin EMTs were already helping Rogers with the boy.

Wren set the mom and daughter down gently, spun to face the Jeffries' home and saw an inferno. Antique furniture going up like a tinderbox. Rogers' hand came on his arm but he ran anyway.

Leaped through the halo of flame, ten big steps in without sucking a breath, found the son-in-law hacking on his knees, turning in the chaotic black. "That way, go!" Wren pointed, gave him a shove, then turned to Jeffries.

The old man lay still, his face pale and shrouded with shrapnel. Wren seized him by the lapels and lifted fast and careful, his frail body lolling over Wren's shoulder. The squat almost toppled him into fire, but he pushed up and ran back toward the crater. The son-in-law had fallen in, was screaming on his hands and knees. Wren dropped in heavily, seized his arm and pulled. The guy fell and Wren dragged him, five more steps out through the fires and finally back into blessed cold.

Wren lay flat, rolled Jeffries clear, called for an EMT.

Pop pop, went gunfire, louder now. Pop pop.

Wren sucked in air, scanning the yard: enclosed by tall hedges and trees. That should buy them some time. One of the EMTs started chest compressions on Jeffries. Wren rolled onto his side, saw the wide eyes of the kids, the mom, the dad laid out and clutching a burn on his arm.

"There's shooting out front," Rogers shouted somewhere nearby.

Wren rubbed his stinging eyes, then his left ear popped painfully and sound came pouring in: the roar of flames, sirens and shouting, the barking of weapons fire out front.

More Pinocchios. It made a terrible sense. Everything was bait.

"The whole neighborhood's a trap," he barked, pushing himself to his knees. "Pinocchios'll be on us soon. Warn the helicopters."

Rogers looked distraught, soot-stricken and horrified as he sucked in an ashy breath, but she pulled her phone and made a call. The EMT pumped Jeffries' chest. Wren's mind reeled with what it all might mean. The scale of it.

"I can't get through," Rogers shouted. "There's no signal."

Wren reared to his feet. Jamming tech. One EMT was working on Jeffries, the other on the mother. Wren padded two steps and laid a hand on the nearest one shoulder.

"Get under cover," he slurred, "wait for the helicopter to land, call this in, and give us your weapons." He held out his hand. The EMT passed her service revolver to Wren wordlessly. A snub Beretta M9, standard issue. She seemed relieved to hand it over.

"Come on," Wren said to Rogers, and turned back toward the flames.

317

17

PINOCCHIOS

Three steps and he almost fell, still dizzy from smoke and the blast. He racked the Beretta's slide and clicked the safety, then stood still in the firelight for maybe five seconds, listening. Focusing. His one good ear heard the fire, and beyond that a steady hail of gunfire, and perhaps, yes, the approaching thrum of the first helicopter.

She stumbled to stand at his side, her blood-red eyes ablaze.

"Pincer," she said with a lisp, pointing left then right, either side of the house. No way could they go through it now. Blood ran down her jaw; tongue bitten in the blast. Wren nodded. The fence around the Jeffries yard was low and easy to scale.

"Come out slow," he said, catching his breath. "Pick them off where you can, don't give away your position."

She grunted and broke right. Wren broke left, turning the neighborhood heat map in his head and coming to the only possible conclusion. Pinocchios had been there the whole time. Stood in gowns and pajamas watching while the police closed in, rubbernecking for the bomb to blow. Totally overlooked when the blast went down. An easy thing to start picking off the police in the aftermath.

He rolled over the fence, came down hard on rooty soil, was up again and running low through fire-speckled Douglas Firs.

At the front he dropped flat in a bank of tall lavenders, looking down on the suburban street in chaos. A few police were pinned behind their vehicles, taking fire from Pinocchios. Wren tracked muzzle flashes to at least three locations, a perfect crossfire. Streetlights lit the carnage: burning blast debris scattered across the blacktop, cops lying still in the road, tracer rounds lancing out like lasers.

Wren slithered through the lavenders, keeping his head low so his bright eyes didn't give him away. The sound of thumping helicopter blades grew closer. Near the bottom of the yard, he shielded his eyes to watch the chopper coming in. An N29FX two-door, single-rotor SWAT helicopter with tactical officers leaning out the open sides cradling rifles, already letting rip. Floodlights swept across the street from above, and a terrible thought struck Wren's mind.

Were the Pinocchios ready for this too?

He rolled to the bottom edge of the yard and into a low culvert beside the sidewalk, waving frantically, just in time to see the rocket launch from cover toward the helicopter. Like a firework shot along a string, it beelined directly to the chopper's undercarriage and impacted. They had a millisecond only, Wren figured, between hearing that clank in the cab and then being obliterated by the blast.

It erupted in the sky.

Wren curled into a ball as metal wreckage spun out in a terrible burst of light. Cars parked below took hits and their alarms rose into a caterwauling chorus with the sirens. Street lamps blew out in the frenzied rain, casting the neighborhood into deeper darkness. Fragments rained down on the blacktop like hail and Wren turned, rose and ran into it.

A glowing metal shard skittered over the road's asphalt toward him like a skipped stone. He pulled his foot back as fast as he could; the shard missed by an inch and embedded in a tire with a melting hiss. The helicopter's fireball chassis crashed down, broken rotor blades still spinning.

Wren dashed around it to hunker behind a huge Escalade, peeking ahead. A train of figures were crossing the road now, firing toward the Jeffries home and Rogers, somewhere in the dark of the yard. To his right the firework trail of the rocket's propellant still hung in the air, tracing back to a two-man team kneeling on a clapboard porch. One holding the launcher, another sliding a second rocket in. Already prepping for the second helicopter.

They knew. That meant an inside man, maybe more than one. The CIA had been infiltrated.

Wren ran up the yard beside a low row of dwarf lemon trees, yellow fruits gleaming obscenely in the firelight. The deep whup-whup of the second chopper approached as he took cover against the raised porch boards. No way to warn them now.

The rocket team took aim, and Wren broke from cover. Two paces to get the angle, two silhouettes in the darkness. He locked his stance and the Beretta sang out, four bullets discharged in two tight clusters, two into center mass of one, two into the other, but still the rocket whistled out.

It flew horizontally, bounced once in the road then erupted in a yard on the other side, throwing up gouts of vegetation and dirt.

Wren was already on the Pinocchios. They both wore masks; he tore them off. One was still breathing. Wren planted an elbow in his forehead, putting out his lights, then snatched the launcher and scanned their gear: a black tray holding more rockets. He grabbed a rocket, fed it into the launcher tube then ran.

Emerging around a topiary hedge he shot the Beretta's last eleven bullets into four Pinocchios charging toward the fallen rocket team. Large builds, holding rifles pointing the wrong way; their mistake. Two went down and the last dropped to his knees, still raising his rifle to fire.

Wren felt the whistle of the bullets and leaped, meeting the guy with a knee smashed up into his chin. The Pinocchio mask buckled inward and so did the guy's jaw. He squealed and went down. Wren drove an elbow into the back of his neck, planting him hard into the sidewalk.

Bullets pinged off a nearby car from across the street. Rogers had been overawed. Wren rolled to the vehicle's rear, sighted a team of four more Pinocchios backlit by the burning Jeffries house, then fired.

The rocket flew out as if on a string and erupted in their midst. For a moment their bodies lit up like jack-o-lanterns, then they were pink mist descending in the darkness.

"Wren?" called Rogers' voice from across the way.

"It's me," he answered. The helicopter circling overhead made it hard to be heard.

"There's four more patrolling on your side."

"Got them."

The helicopter's beams scoured the street and yards. Ropes tossed out and figures came rappelling down. Wren let the launcher tube fall and dropped to his knees, abruptly dizzy. Warzone in the suburbs. Monsters coming out into the light.

18

JEFFRIES

Wren roused back to full alertness with torchlight in his eyes. A figure kneeling beside him, inspecting his pupils.

"Have you been shot?"

Wren made a sound he didn't recognize, flailed for a moment like a tortoise tipped on its back, found his balance.

"It was a bomb," he managed. "I'm fine."

His own voice sounded like it was coming from deep underwater. His back throbbed. Scraped up in the explosion. He was dizzy but leaning on a blackened truck, he stood.

The helicopter's lights filled the street. A squad of SWAT officers were running from body to body, taking pulses and moving on. Rogers was sitting on a curb talking intently on her phone. Fires raged in the Jeffries' living room across the way, casting strange shadows down the torn-up lawn, in concert with the flashing lights of the squad car buried in the wall.

Maybe a minute, he'd been half-conscious.

He looked at the SWAT officer who'd roused him. Full tactical gear, belt of ammunition and equipment.

"Do you have adrenaline doses?"

The SWAT officer frowned. He was young, clean-cut, careful. "For what?"

Wren looked at his shoulder: three chevrons, a sergeant. There wasn't time to explain. "Wrong answer. You know who I am in your chain of command. Hand it over." He held out a hand.

"Sir," said the officer smartly, and unclipped a slim black box from his belt, placed it in Wren's hand. Wren held no police rank, but his CIA status carried the weight of a Deputy Chief.

"Who's commanding you?"

"Commander Grimes, out of Detroit Fifth.

Wren nodded. He knew her from his designer drug days. "How many of the Pinocchios survived the assault?"

"Pinocchios, sir?"

"Masked terrorists."

"Sir, it looks like," the officer turned, spoke into his shoulder mic, received an answer, "three alive. Two of those are unconscious and unlikely to survive long. One is conscious but had to be sedated, he took shrapnel to the head."

Wren cursed. The whole batch was spoiled. "Try and keep them alive, and get them out of here. Their intelligence is vital." He scanned the street. "And get three teams going door to door on every house within a hundred-yard radius. The terrorists must have taken up residence hours ago. The genuine occupants may need help. Get this block secure."

"Yes, sir," said the officer.

"And get that under control," he pointed at the Jeffries' fire. "There may be evidence inside."

"Right away, sir."

Wren gave him a nod of thanks then strode across the road to where his lieutenant was pacing, phone glued to her ear.

"Rogers!"

She spun "Boss."

Her voice was hoarse. Smoke-damaged. That was to be expected, his own throat felt stripped inside.

"Are you all right?"

"Not really, but I'm operational."

He grunted. About the best he could have hoped for. "Good. I need you for this. What's the sit-rep?"

She hobbled to meet him on the sidewalk. "It's chaos in Washington,

Humphreys is apoplectic. We're still getting tallies of agent numbers lost but-"

"What?"

Rogers took a breath, steeling herself. "First up, I've got nothing on your family yet. I'm sorry, but in all this chaos…"

Wren grunted. He knew a thing or two about chaos. His Foundation were looking out for his family as well; nothing he could do about that right now. "Go on."

"The Blue Fairy, they're not only attacking here, boss. Seems Humphreys had his FBI counterpart expedite multiple arrest actions on known abusers, while we had our teams out looking for catfishers and the Firebird. They're all getting hit." She surveyed the street. "Like this. Ambushes with war-fighting weaponry. Bombs and rockets in the hands of Pinocchios. They're crawling out of the woodwork, and we weren't prepared for it. Losses are, well, there's no count but it sounds…"

"Catastrophic," Wren finished. He gazed into the burning house, seeing the shape of things unspooling. The Blue Fairy was catfishing them all. First Clara Baxter, then Jeffries, now every location where the government had extended force. Countless traps, and they'd walked into them all.

"We've been underestimating them from the start."

Rogers just stared at him. Entering shock, it seemed, locked in by the scale of the attack. There was shock enough for them all, but they couldn't afford it now. They had to keep moving.

"The Blue Fairy knows where our strikes are landing," he went on, "even that we had two helicopters inbound, which means they've got inside information. They rigged this whole block." He gestured around, trying to bring Rogers back into the moment. Her red eyes tracked the gesture. In moments like this it was easy to feel beaten. That was the desired effect. The attack had come when they weren't looking, in a place they hadn't expected, and caught them completely by surprise.

The wrong end of shock and awe.

"They've been planning this for a long time. We're looking at months of prep here, investments, training. Still, they got lucky here. They're clearly not amateurs, but they won't get lucky like this again."

Rogers' phone chimed and she brought it up, her eyes widened slightly. "The tally's climbed to fifteen strikes. Dozens dead, boss. There are countless more arrest actions in progress already, too late to pull back, and-"

"Don't think about that now. Come with me."

He started up along the fence beside the burning Jeffries' house, into the back yard where firelight cast red shadows across the Jeffries' family, clustered in shadow on the perfectly manicured grass. The kids were hugging their dad and crying. The mom was on supplemental oxygen. He couldn't help but think of his own kids.

Block that out. Jeffries lay flat out in the middle, eyes shut.

"What's his condition?" he asked the female EMT.

"Bad," she answered. "Not responsive. Weak pulse, fragile breathing. He's in shock."

Wren held out the adrenaline box. "Will this kill him?"

She leaned in to read the label and her eyes bugged. "An Epipen? It could drive him into cardiac arrest. What's so-"

"Can you bring him back, if it does?"

"I, uh... I don't know. He's old. Frail. He might die from the smoke anyway, or the shock. Can't this wait?"

Wren looked up at Jeffries' burning home. Nothing was going to survive that conflagration. No evidence, no records, nothing to lead him back to Clara Baxter, and from her to the Blue Fairy.

Only Reince Jeffries knew who Clara Baxter was. Only Reince could help save her, and stop the incoming flood of Pinocchio attacks.

"Get a crash cart on standby," Wren said to the EMT, then kneeled beside Jeffries and popped the clasp on the adrenaline box. It was foam-packed inside, cushioning a narrow tube filled with yellow liquid. Wren slid it out and pulled the plastic lid off, exposing the thick silver syringe.

"Boss," Rogers cautioned, "you might kill him."

He knew it. Knew all the arguments and didn't like any of them, but couldn't afford to wait. Not with so much on the line. "I'm the one doing this," he said, "not you. I'll swing alone if it goes south." The EMT dropped in by his side, started opening a bright yellow cardiac crash kit. "On this, please," Wren said. "Get ready for defib."

She stared at the syringe. "Wait, there's no medical reason to-"

Wren didn't wait, instead just stabbed Jeffries in the chest and depressed the plunger.

The old man bolted upright at once, gasping hard. His eyes flashed wide and his neck quivered like it was under tension from some hidden inner spring. He looked jerkily at his burning house, at Wren and Rogers, and it was clear panic was only seconds away.

Wren put a hand on his shoulder, another on his chest beside the syringe and spoke in a soft, soothing tone.

"Mr. Jeffries, I'm sorry to ask this right now, but I need to know everything you know about Clara Baxter."

19

CLARA

The old man's eyes fixed on Wren. Dark processes turned behind his pupils, trying to come to grips with the things that had happened, that were still happening.

"My house is on fire," he said. His voice sounded strange, too high. Now his eyes were roaming. He'd see the grandchildren on the grass any moment now. They were fine, but Clara Baxter would be buried beneath an avalanche of worries.

"Mr. Jeffries," Wren said, and clicked his fingers in front of Jeffries' eyes. It worked as a distraction for the moment; Rogers rose and silently began to move the children out of the old man's sightline. "The house is burning but your family are fine, and that's what matters. You'll see them very soon. What I need to know about is Clara Baxter, one of your catfishers who was taken in Detroit last night."

Jeffries' eyes steadily focused on Wren. His breathing remained high and whistling, though some of the deep, commanding timbre returned to his voice. "You."

"Me. I am sorry for all this. I'm trying to stop the men that did it, before they can do it again. The attacks tonight stretch far beyond Detroit. Now I need to know about Clara."

"Clara?"

"Clara Baxter or Lance Hebbert. Whatever it is you're not telling me. I need to know it right now."

More deep processes turned, like cogs in an ancient machine. Reaching a calculation. "Not her real name." He paused to wheeze. "Clara."

"So what's her real name? Why did they take her?"

Jeffries drew a shuddery breath. "She came … five years ago. Before I started … the Heroes. Encouraged me."

"You mean she got you started?"

Jeffries nodded. He was paling further. Wren worried he'd lapse back unconscious before he got the information out. "She emailed. Many times. Different addresses, different names. She knew I had money." Long pause. "She wanted me to work with her."

"So she ran your group?"

Jeffries coughed. Wren saw the EMT in the corner of his eye, readying to step in and push him away, but he held out a stalling hand.

"Ran it. Designed it. Coded it. Enlisted the people. I just…" Coughing.

"You bankrolled it?"

Nodding.

"So who is she?"

"Emily," said Jeffries. "Mona. Gloria. Lots of names. She'd done … this before. Made groups. To catfish them."

Wren felt like he was teetering on the edge of a huge cliff. Answers lay on the other side. "How many groups? Which ones?"

Jeffries gave a weak shrug. "Dozens, I think. Across the country."

Dozens. Wren reeled. "Give me something more. Where's she from?"

"Idaho?" Jeffries asked. His eyes rolled up in his head, only rolling back when Wren gave him a light shake. "Maybe Idaho, the accent. A farm. She gave hints. I think … she was lonely."

"Why would she be lonely?"

"This was her whole life. Hunting them."

"And Hebbert?"

"Hebbert," said Jeffries, and his eyes roamed. "Where's my daughter? Have you seen her?"

"She's fine, right by your side, everyone's OK, you'll see them in a second. Now, Lance Hebbert, Jeffries. Who is he?"

Jeffries sucked at the air once, twice, perhaps straining to answer, or to ask about his daughter again, then his eyes rolled up and didn't come back down.

The EMT jumped in, took the old guy's pulse, looked up.

"Pulse is thready, but he's there. Just about. Nothing more."

Wren felt a wave of relief wash over him. Five for five, scooped out of the fire. Plus names, and a place.

Rogers cursed low. "Boss."

Wren didn't say anything, wheels already spinning up in his head.

Idaho.

It wasn't much to go off. An entire state, but perhaps it would give them a lead on Hebbert, which perhaps would lead them to…

He had no idea. Hopefully the Blue Fairy and Pleasure Island. He brought up his phone and tapped out a message on the darknet, sent via Megaphone to his elite hackers.

CLARA BAXTER POSSIBLE ALIAS EMILY/MONA/GLORIA. A FARM IN IDAHO? HEBBERT.

He wrote another for the Foundation at large.

KEEP HEADS DOWN – THE BLUE FAIRY ARE ATTACKING MULTIPLE GOVERNMENT FORCES. HIGH FATALITIES. DO NOT RISK YOURSELF.

Last he scrolled to speed dial and hovered his finger over the icons for Humphreys and his Washington team. But he didn't press.

"You think we're compromised?" Rogers asked, watching his screen.

"It's the only answer, after that attack. Someone high in command at the CIA. There's no telling who."

"Likely more than one," Rogers said. Now her red eyes were focused and alert, recovered from the immediate shock. "We can't go through Humphreys. Or our team."

Wren let his hand holding the phone drop by his side, playing the possibilities forward like a chess game. It left him, and Rogers, and the Foundation.

"Idaho," he said.

Rogers nodded. "Idaho."

"What we really need is for one of these Pinocchios to flip, but they're all done. Two almost dead, one brain-damaged." He thought a second. "Did any of the other strikes go our way?"

Rogers shook her head. "Not that I heard. Nobody else rammed a residential building with a car to spring the trap." She gave a light smile that became a grimace. "They took us by surprise, almost simultaneously across the country. The scale of this thing… Boss, I don't see how…" She trailed off.

Wren didn't see how either. They'd stumbled into something huge. Something months or years in the planning. The Blue Fairy had the initiative, were dictating all the plays. He had to break that frame, and fast.

"Anything else coming in? A lead on the panel van? Any group taking credit? Fresh witnesses at the People Mover?"

Rogers just stared. She didn't need to say what they were both thinking. Anything that came through the chain of command now was suspect. Even their team in Washington. Even Humphreys. That left few options.

"Your red Firebirds," Wren said, switching midstream, "which do you like best for Ravenous6?"

Rogers blinked; making the switch along with him. "Best? The out-of-state guy, probably. Lot of downstream bandwidth on his Internet line, strong cryptography that we can't break through. Makes sense for him to fish outside his own pond, in another atate."

Wren grunted. It did. Across the state line, it would be easier to evade any accountability. Ravenous6 was careful, they knew that from the chat logs.

"And you sent teams inbound?"

"Twenty minutes back. Last I checked they were thirty minutes out."

Twenty minutes felt like a lifetime.

"Call them and redirect. Don't let them anywhere near him. Make up some bullshit reason, forces needed elsewhere. I don't want any Pinocchio there tipped off. I want them still in play."

She lifted her phone to make the call, and Wren started moving, over the fence and back down toward the street. The fire baked the air. His mind buzzed with ideas.

Out front bright white floodlights illuminated the scene like it was day. There was a fire crew attaching hoses to a hydrant. They wouldn't put out the blaze now, but they could stop it spreading. Squad cars swarmed in an orchestra of flashing lights. Police and SWAT moved from the wreckage of the first chopper to the bodies of the dead Pinocchios, while paramedics worked on the injured.

Wren stopped on the sidewalk. A moment later Rogers stepped alongside him.

"Done. Are we going there? This guy's three hours out. Canton, Ohio. That's a lot of time on a hunch."

Wren smiled, settled his gaze on the helicopter in the middle of the street. "I'm not going to drive."

20

HELICOPTER

Wren and the pilot flew southeast at two hundred miles an hour. No rockets launched out to meet them. The fiery tableau of devastation in Redford quickly faded into twinkling suburbs. Detroit shone briefly like a setting sun then sank below the horizon, until soon they were hammering blindly over dark, empty wilderness.

Every part of Wren hurt. The seat did nothing to cushion the explosive drumbeat of the chopper's blades, sending daggers up his spine and neck. There was no escaping whiplash. His shoulder ached. His back throbbed from the pummeling it had taken in the blast.

Canton, Ohio.

Earlier he'd dismissed the Firebird perp as a nothing: unaware, unknowing, incidental to the snatch of Clara Baxter. Now he could be Wren's way into the Blue Fairy. Seemed they had a mole in US Intelligence. About time Wren had one with them.

If it was the guy. If he wasn't too far gone.

Wren rubbed his jaw, lulled by the pain and the thrumming blades, thinking about his kids. Where they were, now, and if they were OK.

So many people had died already. All the Pinocchios Wren had killed, hunting for some sign of his father, just trying to keep his family safe. Even now he didn't know if they were, and that thought drained him. Couldn't think about it, though, or he'd just freeze up and stop moving.

The only was was forward. Try to save as many people as he could along the way. Clara Baxter, maybe. Too late for Malton Bruce. Get to the root and dig it out like a cancer. He remembered what Maggie at the fake town had said. This is your home, Christopher. She'd taken a different approach to him all along. Not trying to punish the bad guys, but trying to rescue the good. It took both sorts, maybe.

He blinked up from a brief reverie, chopper blades hammering. Not long left, and he had to get things ready. There was every chance this perp was sitting as bait in another Pinocchio trap; a trap he couldn't afford to spring. What he needed was a way to turn the trap around.

He lifted a headset from the clasp on the helicopter's column wall. The heavy mufflers slid over his ears, muting the hammering of the blades. He pulled the mic down and squeezed the button to go live with the pilot.

"How long?"

The pilot answered without looking. "Twenty-five minutes, sir."

Wren killed that line and plucked a second phone from his jacket. He always carried two on him, along with a clear wallet of five spare SIMs. The phone booted. He jacked the headset cord out of the wall and plugged it into the phone, then worked the screen and tapped to dial.

"Fifth District, Operations," came a woman's crisp response through the headset. Detroit PD, Wednesday at 8:30 p.m.

"Get me Grimes," said Wren, "this is Christopher Wren, I'm heading up the Redford mess."

"Hold please."

The line went silent and Wren waited. Thirty seconds, a minute, then a voice boomed down the line.

"Wren!" Wren knew Grimes from his days shutting down designer drug lines in the blight. They'd gone for drinks once. She was a woman who could handle her liquor, and they'd compared war stories until the dawn, a bottle of Jameson's the wiser. "Word is you've stolen one of my birds."

He trusted Grimes. She was too far removed from anything to make her a useful tool to the Pinocchios. "That's a rumor I'd like to see quashed. For your ears only, I'm en route to Canton, Ohio. Do you have any contacts in the station there?"

The silence on the line stretched. When she came back, it was quieter, like she'd stepped into a side office. "Wren, what are you up to?"

"Above your pay grade. Call it taking down the bad guys. I need an insertion, some gear, a distraction."

She didn't sound convinced. "You've got my pilot on that helicopter with you. That's right on my pay grade. I've already lost police tonight, and I won't lose another for nothing."

"Then rest easy, he's well out of this. My chauffeur, that's all. He won't go near any action."

"Bullshit. I'm turning him around."

Wren cursed. "Wait, Grimes. Damn it. I've got a lead on a perp in the sticks. I need your help to set up a sting."

"What kind of sting?"

"A complex one. If I don't play it right, it'll blow it up like Redford."

"Redford? So don't run it. Send SWAT in."

He grimaced. "The guy could be an asset. I need him on our side. It's going to be delicate."

Another pause. Thinking it over, weighing her duty, maybe calculating how much she trusted Wren. "I'm hearing reports about hits across the country," she said tentatively. "Dozens, it looks. The casualties are unbelievable. Tied up with your 'Pinocchios'. Is it about that?"

It wasn't good to let operational details out. She had him over a barrel though, and a few bottles of whisky weren't going to bridge that gap. "Yes. This guy may be an eyewitness. Better yet, I can use him to-"

"Enough, don't compromise yourself," she interrupted. "Just tell me you can stop this bullshit."

He took a breath. Thank God for professional respect. "I can stop it."

"Then all right." More certain now. "Yes, I have a contact. We get together and smoke Cubans after the quarterly conferences. What do you need?"

Wren glimpsed a brief mental picture of Grimes drinking whiskey with him, smoking Cubans with a district judge, maybe pulling out the bong for a state senator. He snapped himself out of it and told her what he needed. They'd have to improvise. They'd all have to move, right away, to pull it off. They'd have to keep it quiet, and none of them could know who or what it was for.

It took three minutes to explain. Some specialist equipment. Some specialist roles, not without risk. She was up to it.

"Good luck," Grimes said at the end, and closed down the call.

Another minute to transmit that to Canton. Call it two total. Nineteen minutes or so left. Already it was getting late. Wren peered at the pilot's dashboard. 8:42 p.m. If the Pinocchios were laying in wait around Ravenous6, they'd be getting antsy now. The other strikes had gone down in near synchrony. Too late and Wren would drop on an empty house, an empty neighborhood, with all the Pinocchios spooked. He had to hope they were hungry for their taste of blood. To prove themselves.

He logged into his darknet and downloaded some tools. Data hackers. Cryptoworms. Programs his elite hackers had put together for just such purposes. Then he dialed Rogers. She answered swiftly.

"Boss?"

"Give me the address and everything else we have on this guy. Red Firebird. Out of state. Ravenous6."

She was ready for it, had the information to hand. "Wife, two girls aged seven and nine. South side of town, off Cleveland Avenue. He's an accountant, the Firebird looks to be some kind of hobby. Medium height, forty-five years old. His name's Charles DeVore."

21

CANTON

Wren had the chopper land in a dark, barren field near the Speedway on the Lincoln Highway, east of Canton and six miles distant from Charles DeVore.

He loped away from the thwacking blades, stamping through old stalks of hay sticking up in the stubbly field. The highway ahead was four lanes wide and desolate. The Speedway had a handful of cars parked in front of its halogen white windows. Products inside cheered their brands on, competitors in a different kind of race.

The chopper took off in back. Headed for a holding pattern. Wren picked the waiting car out with ease; an unmarked Toyota sedan. Dark green. The keys were on the rear tire, the fob warm to the touch. Whose car was this? He figured something from the impound lot.

He clicked the button and got into the driver's seat. The glove box held the gear he'd asked, and a spare magazine for the Beretta. He put the stick in gear and reversed out, following the map he'd memorized. Through the town center, ten minutes or less. Canton was asleep already. Wednesday night, 9 p.m., and mostly residential plots lined the route. A small ballpark. A few patches of industry. A long strip with junk-food eateries. His heart began to beat harder as he pulled into 34th Street southwest, one street south of DeVore.

He'd already picked his ingress point. Street view was a wonder. The yards backed onto each other with no fences but plenty of trees for cover. He cruised slow along 34th like he was making a considerate run home, looking out for kids in the road, nothing untoward. If the Pinocchios were here, if they were watching him even now, he couldn't put a foot wrong. They might be amateurs, but if they suspected a thing his cover would be blown, and so would Charles DeVore's.

He ran the Toyota along the street for two hundred yards, scanning porches and windows, looking for curtains peeled back, blinds askew, but saw nothing. It didn't mean a thing. DeVore's house was number 46 on 33rd Street. He went a hundred yards past that, still one street north, then pulled into an empty drive. Outside the range they'd be watching, he figured. He killed the engine, the lights died, and he gathered up his gear, holstered the reloaded Beretta in his waistband, then opened the door.

Canton was quiet. Across the street somebody was watching TV; fuzzing light played through their thin lace curtains. The night was cold and his breath plumed frosty. Maybe it would snow; winter was still in the air. He clicked the fob and the car beeped, then he strolled up the drive, around the side of the house and out of sight from the street.

He stopped by the door and stood quietly, all senses humming.

The TV across the street buzzed. A radio played muted pop, Lady GaGa, coming from the house backing this one on 34th. A plane droned far overhead, air conditioning whirred nearby. Wren slipped away from the door and into the shadow of an oak tree. Screened by bushes, ducking low, he snuck east until ten steps on he faced a gap.

The front lawn of number 82 was empty. Wren cursed under his breath. On the streetview photographs there'd been a tall stand of bushes right here, stretching from edge to edge. Excellent cover, allowing him access to a run of houses thickly planted with trees leading up to 46, an easy route through shadow. But now?

Now the bushes were only stumps. A new owner, maybe. Commercial satellite maps updated infrequently. He peered around the side of his cover, wondering if all this was for nothing. There was no guarantee DeVore was the perp, no guarantee any Pinocchios were even watching. All this could be an elaborate trespassing dance across ten lawns.

But still. He hadn't come this far to go half-ass now, and it felt right. The air hummed with invisible tension. He studied nearby houses. It seemed unlikely the Pinocchios would be in any of the south-side streets on

34th; too far away to usefully see DeVore's place on 33rd. Most likely they were staked out closer. Right on the edge of where Wren was hunkered, hovering in shadow.

He ducked deeper into shade, lifted his phone and fired off a message.

DRIVE-BY 34th STREET, SIRENS ON

All part of the plan. Within seconds a squad car from the local precinct, waiting at the nearby Dairy Queen, fired up its sirens. Wren heard them and waited. A drive-by was a huge risk; a gamble that any waiting Pinocchios wouldn't get trigger happy and spring their trap early.

Nothing he could do about that now. The siren grew louder, until he felt the tone shift as it turned onto 33rd. Wren hunkered low and waited for his moment. The wail grew louder, then he saw the flashing blue lights rippling down the street. Everything here looked a lot like Jeffries' home. Maybe that was going to happen again; another 9/11 right here, erupting in the fabric of the suburbs and burning a hole in the heartland. It would be on him, if it did.

The car came on, almost there. At the moment it passed in front of DeVore's house Wren broke from cover and sprinted across the front of number 82's lawn in three seconds, plunging into darkness on the other side. For a long few moments he stood still, listening and breathing as the siren wailed away.

Nothing followed. No movement anywhere, though that didn't tell him much. If they'd seen him, they'd be waiting for him now. The trap would be closing in.

There was no choice but to take the risk. From here to DeVore's place there was cover. He took a breath and moved on; slow, steady, low, nothing to draw a watching eye. Like a stalking fox, skills he'd learned so far back in the Pyramid, when his father had punished him harder for every failure.

Wren pushed the memories away and moved on instinct, drifting on the cold January air like a light breeze. More TVs whispering behind windows. Maybe a curtain twitching there, though it could be the wind.

They hadn't seen him. He felt sure of it. Treading stealthily through yards he closed the distance.

Number 50 on 34th street. Wren hugged a stunted sycamore. Now the moment of truth. He took out his phone and sent a second text. It took longer this time. The helicopter was farther out, working a holding pattern with the last of its fuel.

Air support. Two minutes, waiting in the cold. The thrumming of blades crescendoed like artillery homing in, as the machine raced low from the east. Wren held his breath. It came in like it was on a bombing run, suspicious in itself, even more so after the squad car, but hopefully not enough to spring the trap just yet. He'd promised Grimes she wouldn't lose another pilot.

The noise grew unbearable, and Wren ran. Down the back of number 46 on 34th street onto the grass of DeVore's house on 33rd. There were no lights on inside; that didn't bode well. He hit the back porch and tried the back door; sliding glass that didn't slide. Now the chopper was right overhead, unleashing a hurricane of sound. No gunshots or rockets answered it.

Wren hit the glass by the handle with his gun. It broke, and the sound was swallowed by the roar of the helicopter, though already it was pulling away. Any eyes it had drawn would be returning to their target. Wren slipped his hand through the gap, worked the lock and slid the glass open. He kicked the tell-tale shards of broken glass into the grass, strode in and shut it behind him.

Twenty seconds, all-in. No shots taken at the helicopter. The trap was still poised, waiting. Wren stepped deeper into shadow, away from the window and alongside a heavy oak dining room table, surveying the darkness ahead. To the right lay a breakfast nook, stools, a kitchen still laid with cups and bowls. Ahead lay a sunken den, with a long L-shaped sofa and a reclining armchair at one end; the man of the house's seat.

It was occupied.

Wren saw a flash of reflected light in wide, staring eyes. Charles DeVore, looking right back at him.

22

CRICKET

S econds passed, eye contact in the darkness. Wren worked through the possibilities and realized two things at once.

First, Charles DeVore was guilty.

He was sitting alone in his den with the lights off at night, not even alarmed when a stranger broke in. Not shouting, not standing to fight, not calling the police. Just sitting and staring.

Rogers' hunch had been right. This was their guy.

Second, he was holding a gun pointed at Wren's face.

A long moment stretched out.

"Charles," Wren said, breaking the silence gently, but DeVore cut him off.

"I know who you are."

His voice was high and fraught, like his lungs were too full of air and he could only manage clipped sentences. On the edge. Wren's eyes adjusted to the gloom. The gun trembled in DeVore's delicate, desk worker's fingers. A Remington 380, a hell of a piece of punctuation.

Wren took a sliding step forward, barely perceptible. "So, who am I?"

"You're with the Blue Fairy. This is a test." DeVore's tone was high and emotionless, but Wren felt the tension humming underneath. The moment heightened. Wren imagined his trigger finger squeezing. Even if he missed, the real Pinocchios would be alerted and the house would be flooded in seconds. Wren had no doubts they were watching now, waiting like spiders for the fly.

"I'm not from the Fairy," Wren said calmly. He'd done hostage negotiation many times before. The key was to offer a way out. No insurmountable boundaries had been crossed. There was still a way back. "I'm here to help."

DeVore stared. "Help?"

"Help," Wren confirmed, sliding subtly to the end of the table. "I've been looking for you, Charles. I was there at the People Mover. I know what happened to you, what you witnessed. I know that you weren't involved." He paused, weighing the moment, trying to play into the guy's delusions. "I've seen your chat logs. I know Sophie was barely underage."

Charles twitched. His shaking gun-arm extended. A hint of anger, now. "Sophie wasn't real."

"I know that. They entrapped you. They broke their own rules, Charles. A case against you would never stand up in court. You could sue for damages. They'd have to pay."

Charles leaned forward slightly. Some of the tension rang through in his voice now, trembling somewhere between hope and fear. Glimpsing the old world, if only briefly. "You're a lawyer?"

"No. With me, you won't need one. I can see what they've done to you, what kind of man you are, how this isn't fair. The catfishers got you first, now the Blue Fairy wants dessert."

Charles stared. "You don't know."

Wren slid to the steps leading down into the den. "I can wager a guess. The Fairy gave you that gun, didn't they? Along with a Pinocchio mask and instructions to wait for the police. Is that about right?" Silence. "I've just come from another Blue Fairy trap in Detroit, where everybody died. Pinocchios, the police, good people and bad. They even tried to blow me up." The first step down. "I blew them up instead. I killed four Pinocchios with their own rockets. You don't want that to be you." The second step. "But you are holding a gun on me. I wish you'd stop that, for both our sakes."

Charles shuddered.

Wren's eyes adjusted to the gloom, and the den revealed itself in stages, etched in silvery moonlight like an old-style photograph, taking on texture and depth. The sofa, the TV, the coffee table, the recliner. He'd half-expected to see DeVore's wife laid out on the floor. Bound and gagged, perhaps dead. Used up as Ravenous6 fell off the dark side of the crimes he'd already committed; a murder-suicide in the offing. His daughters on the sofa, dead too, but they weren't there. That could be good or bad.

"Stop moving," DeVore said. "Who are you?"

Wren countered with a question. "Where are your girls, Charles? Where are Agatha and Veronica?"

The gun wavered. Wren weighed the moment again. He could charge. In the darkness, in his current state DeVore might fumble the gun, but it was a poor gamble. Even if no shots rang out, he'd be visible from outside, charging across the den. DeVore's cover would still be blown.

The gun steadied. "Tell me who you are."

"My name is Christopher Wren. Sometimes I'm with the Central Intelligence Agency. Sometimes I'm on my own. Today could be one of those days. I want to get you out of this, Charles. Out of the trap."

DeVore rocked up in the seat. Finding some measure of confidence. "You're lying."

Silence. Staring. Wren wondered how long it could stretch out for. How long had DeVore been sitting there, just waiting? Wren had seen men like that before. Men who'd committed atrocities, or who were considering them. Men coming to terms with a new world. Men deciding whether to eat their own gun.

"What did they tell you to do, Charles?" he pressed. No answer came. Wren could pick out the contours of his face now, matching the image Rogers had sent through. Weak chin, but good cheekbones. Warm, watery eyes. Slightly balding, but handsome enough.

The gun shook. It would take a second only; raise it to his own temple and pull the trigger. Wren would be powerless to stop him.

"She was almost sixteen," DeVore said. It came curiously flat, like it was a sentence he'd been repeating for hours, so many times that any sense of meaning had long evaporated away.

Wren could use that.

"She was a trap," he pressed. "You didn't mean for any of this to happen, it just spiraled out of control. Whatever you did since, you did it under duress. You weren't in your right mind; not a jury in the land would convict."

He took the third step. Charles blinked, like he was coming back to himself. "I told you to stop moving."

"You know I can't do that," Wren said, and took another step. Only three long strides from Charles now. The air smelled of hickory and wood smoke; an open fire, reduced to cold ashes now.

DeVore's eyes widened in panic. He sucked back into his chair like a snail in its shell. "Stop."

"No," Wren continued forward. "I've come too far to stop, just like you. Tell me, where are your girls, Charles? Where's your wife?"

"Not here."

"Now you're lying. They're in this house. Are they upstairs? In the basement? Are they even alive, Charles?"

DeVore squirmed, one arm wrapped protectively around himself now, the gun twisting like a snake's head in his hand. "I didn't do anything!"

"Shh," Wren said, as he drew closer. Barely a stride now. "Almost sixteen, Charles. Keep thinking that. That's how I'm going to help you. She was almost sixteen."

"I'll shoot." Now his voice cracked. "Stop, please…"

"Cut it out," Wren said, still soft but with an edge of iron. "We're both adults here. Both fathers." It hurt to say it. "You're in trouble and you need a way out, and that's me. I'm your Jiminy Cricket, here to tell you what's right and what's wrong. You want that, don't you?"

Wren reached out. DeVore was blinking furiously, his knees coiled up before him now, the gun trembling. A shot could go off accidentally.

"Please," he said.

Wren laid a hand on the gun. He guided it to the side, then gently lifted it from Charles' palm, who pulled back like his hand had been burned. His eyes flared wide, and Wren had seen this too; in the imagery these men enjoyed. The terror of being powerless. There was no pleasure in it for Wren. There never had been, no matter how cruel his father had tried to make him.

He tucked the gun carefully in his waistband, then knelt down and put his hands on Charles' knees. A calming move, and a move to dominate. Charles tried to pull away but Wren was firm.

"Where are your girls, Charles?" he asked.

It took Charles a long moment. He gulped and stared at Wren. He gagged and almost vomited.

"Where!?"

"Basement." The word slithered out wet with shame. "In the basement."

Wren leaned back. He listened, but heard nothing. No muffled screaming. No small-voiced cries for help, rising through the floorboards.

"Are they alive?"

Charles blinked, eyes like a mollusk shell, sobbing in self-pity. Wren wanted nothing more than to reach in and rip out his heart. You should've been better, he'd say. You were supposed to protect them.

Charles spoke in a whisper. "I don't know."

23

PICS

Devore wept, and Wren stood.

This was a problem. His mole was broken. The Pinocchios would never accept DeVore like this. He would never get to Pleasure Island, which meant Wren wouldn't either, and the Blue Fairy's plans would roll on.

He had to turn Charles DeVore around, and that all came down to one basic question.

How far had he gone?

"Where's your phone?" Wren asked. Charles' gaze darted up briefly to Wren, flashed to the sofa, then back down again. Too pathetic to speak anymore.

Wren found the phone shoved down the sofa's back. "PIN?" he demanded.

Charles flinched.

"I need your PIN, Charles. If I'm going to help you, I need it. Here."

He pressed the phone into Charles' hand. He looked at it for a long moment then responded, tapping at the screen tentatively. Six digits. Wren memorized them and lifted the phone away. Charles reached one hand after it, then let it drop. Already beaten.

Wren scanned the incoming-calls log. There were several, all unanswered, scattered over the last twelve hours. JOE WORK. WORK

AMANDA. MOM. Nothing Wren was looking for. He tapped over to messages and found the motherlode. A long train of unanswered texts, each a word long, repeated every thirty minutes and stretching back through the whole day.

PICS?

GIFS?

VIDEO?

Wren scrolled further back and found the instructions. They were specific. Detailed. Exactly where the camera should be placed, the scenes of abuse they wanted to see DeVore carrying out. It was all spelled out; not quite the Pinocchio trap he'd expected, but a different one. Using DeVore like bait, while breaking his family for entertainment. Two birds with one stone, and why not?

It was a test, just like DeVore had said, maybe for all the low-level Pinocchios across the country. Burn down their old families, their old lives, in a rush of violence and abuse. Taking pictures and sending them on. Proving themselves worthy to enter Pleasure Island.

Wren scrolled back; DeVore hadn't sent them anything yet. No PICS, GIFS, or VIDEO, but it was clear what was required.

Wren looked down and spoke in a low growl. "Don't move an inch. Don't say a damn word. Do you understand me?"

DeVore looked up at him like a child. So miserable, so sad. He nodded.

Wren strode away, back across the den and into the kitchen. A shadowy Pinocchio mask lay on the table next to two bowls of cereal, half-eaten, and a half-drunk cup of coffee. The smell of stale milk curdled in the air. This was where it had begun. The Blue Fairy had been clear in her instructions.

The basement door stood in back of the kitchen. Things were going to speed up now, and Wren paused to tap out a message to his contact in Canton PD. He airdropped an app from his phone into DeVore's, then opened the basement door.

The smell hit him first; the ammonia tang of urine, the rich stink of human waste rising from the deep black. The low hum of a dehumidifier burred up. He flicked a wall switch and white lights buzzed to life, illuminating walls hung with family portraits. Happy as a foursome at a beach. Charles DeVore smiling like a real person. At the bottom lay the bare cement floor and a wall filled with mildewed boxes on shelves.

Wren went down; swiftly, smoothly, no sound but his footfalls. If they were alive, they were holding their breath. A small pool table lay to the right, a desk with computer in the left corner, silver pipes in the ceiling, just a basement like any other.

At the bottom he turned, and it was what he'd expected. The camera stood between him and them; on a tripod, with the tiny fat tails of a Wi-Fi transmitter attached. Ready to stream video. Beyond that lay three pink deflated air mattresses, with three people huddled upon them; the mother in the middle, the girls curled to either side.

They were motionless, like flies trapped in the bright light's amber, eyes wide in the sudden light and fixed on him. Alive. Pale faces staring back. Who knew what DeVore had done.

"It's OK," Wren said softly, holding his hands out. "My name's Christopher Wren, I'm from the FBI and I'm here to help."

They stared at him in terror. Dirty, wet gags in their mouths prevented them from answering. He circled away from the stairs slowly. No sudden movements. The smell was worse here. Waste stained their sparse bedding and pajamas. Their arms were zip-tied at the wrist to metal wall pipes, their wrists red and bruised. They'd been here all day.

"I'm going to release you," he said, padding toward the camera. "I promise. Very soon."

He hit the camera's power button to wake the screen, and the mother began screaming into her gag at once. The sound was horrible; like a wounded animal trying to escape a trap. She understood what the camera meant, what the blinking red light stood for, and yanked at her zip ties, thrashing her body like a jackhammer on the floor, trying to get free. Her girls screamed too.

There was nothing Wren could do except go faster.

"I swear I'm not here to hurt you," he said, while swiftly scrolling through the memory card on the camera's LCD screen, afraid of what he might find, what DeVore had done to his wife and his girls: still shots of the basement wall, of the set-up, a few practice runs of footage with DeVore's fingers fumbling over the lens, his family unconscious on the mattresses, and then…

Nothing.

No more stills, no video, no PICS. Wren let out a breath.

Good, but bad.

Good because DeVore hadn't done it. He'd brought them down here and left them, but ultimately been unable to go through with it. All day gagged and bound in the basement, filled with terror of what might come, but nothing worse yet.

Bad because the scene wasn't there. The PIC. And Wren needed the PIC. The Pinocchios wanted it and Charles DeVore had to supply it, or there'd be no acceptance, no mole, no way into the Blue Fairy.

Wren cursed quietly. There was no choice. He'd have to set it up himself.

He pushed the camera to the floor. It smashed noisily on the hard cement, drawing the mother's gaze and halting her screams for a moment. "I'm sorry this is happening to you," he said, raising his voice to be heard over her muffled screams. "I'll set you free very soon, I promise, but I need to take a picture first. I'm not going to hurt you. I'm sorry."

She roared at him, cheeks puffing madly, eyes flaring so hard Wren thought they might bug out, tugging on her bloody wrist. A mother trying to protect her children but not knowing how. She looked from the fallen camera to him and back, not knowing what to think.

"I need to make a scene here," Wren explained, trying to calm her. "All fake, for the audience who put this camera here." He pointed. "I'm not with them, but I need to give them something. So they'll go away. It won't be real. Please tell your girls to close their eyes."

The woman kept screaming. She'd hyperventilate soon. Maybe if he took the gag off, she'd listen. He could set her free, but then he'd never get her to stay for the PIC. She'd be gone with her girls, they'd run right out into the Pinocchios' hands and Charles DeVore's cover would be blown."

"Tell them now," Wren pressed, putting some authority into his voice. He didn't want to scare her, but would if he had to. "You can keep your eyes open. Just don't let them."

He stood, waiting for her to register what he'd said. She wasn't thinking clearly now. It wasn't possible, given what she'd been through. But steadily, she stopped screaming. Instead she made a low, keening whine, broken by sobs. She didn't know. Maybe this was the moment she died. Nothing Wren said could persuade her.

Still, she curled closer into her girls and mumbled soft sounds.

Her girls closed their eyes.

"Keep them closed," Wren said. "You're going to feel a warm rain, but it won't hurt you, I swear."

He drew his knife.

The mother gasped, sucking in the gag and ready to scream again, but Wren moved the knife too fast, slashing into his own left forearm. The cut ran deep and blood began to flow at once. Her screams were swallowed in confusion. Wren sheathed the knife and strode into that uncertainty, holding his arm out above them so blood splattered down on their bodies.

The girls flinched but the mother squeezed them closer, mumbling soft sounds while staring at Wren. Maybe she understood. Wren hoped so. More blood rained down. The girls began to cry and shifted under the hot rain, but that was good; his blood would smear with the other stains, building the scene he needed.

He swayed his arm back and forth and counted: ten seconds, twenty. At thirty seconds the first wave of dizziness hit. Already he'd dumped maybe a quart, but the scene wasn't there yet. Now his blood pressure would slow, his heart rate dropping off. Lose thirty percent of your blood and you died.

How much now?

The girls sobbed, but it felt distant. The scene looked better, like a pig had been bled out, so red in the white light. Fifteen percent? His left knee gave way, startling him back to full consciousness. How long? He looked at his arm, clamped his left hand over the wound. Too much.

"That's it," he said fuzzily, staggering backward. He snatched up a towel from the back of the torn sofa and wrapped it tightly around the wound, then lifted DeVore's phone.

In the clinical white strip lights, the scene looked like a slaughterhouse. Blood covered them, like a madman had been let loose with a hatchet. Exactly what he needed.

He took the PIC.

24

DEVORE

Upstairs again, Wren staggered into the kitchen. For some reason he had to be quiet, but he couldn't remember why. At the kitchen table he pulled a bottle and a lighter from his pockets; his fake town arson gear. A plastic pellet followed, then his phone, DeVore's phone. He tapped at the screens...

He stirred up from another blackout, leaning against the kitchen table and looking down at the face rising in the middle. Pinocchio. He picked up the mask and handled it, spreading blood across its cheery cheeks. It was authentic. The rubber flexed smoothly. He thought about putting it on.

He put it on. The edges scraped his ears. It was a snug fit, and dark. Immediately the sound of his own breathing grew loud and raspy. He tugged it and the wide-cut eyeholes aligned. His breath boomed in his ears. He'd read a paper once, maybe Ferat's, on the anonymizing effects of wearing a mask. The paper hadn't mentioned the immediate impact of hearing your own breathing.

It felt wrong, like he was breaking unwritten rules. He turned and saw DeVore in the den, staring back at him in terror. Finally the Pinocchios had come for him.

Wren lumbered across the den and dropped to his knees in front DeVore, trying to straighten things out in his mind. In his hand was a phone.

"Are they alive?" DeVore asked. Hungry. So desperate.

Wren's world swirled. He was close to collapsing, now. He knew it. Maybe DeVore knew it, and now could be his chance to escape. Not without a leash, though.

"Yes," Wren slurred. His lips and tongue were thick and slow. "They're terrified. All day, you left them Charles. All day."

It was a lot to say. Speaking made him dizzier. Emotions played across DeVore's pudgy face in turn. Good. He had to wake up now. Absently Wren slapped him, not hard. Once, twice, three times. On the third DeVore caught his hand and shoved it away. Wren laughed.

Good. Everyone had to be angry.

"So get us out," DeVore said. "Please. Help us."

Wren laughed harder. Us. Everything seemed funny now. Inside the mask it sounded so loud. He felt drunk. He knew it was the blood loss talking, but he was just a passenger now on this particular ride.

He slapped DeVore again, harder this time. Almost a punch. His round head reeled to the side, and anger became shock became fear again.

"Do you like this?" Wren asked, and hit him once more. DeVore threw up his arms. A good strike off his temple. Smearing him with blood. Bruising him up. He pulled back and punched Charles hard in the chest, in the shoulder, in the thighs. He raked his fingernails down DeVore's cheeks, his chest. All the evidence a triple rapist would carry.

By the end DeVore was sobbing. Not just for the pain but because he understood. "What do you want?" he hissed.

Wren climbed up onto his elbows on DeVore's knees, pushing the Pinocchio mask into his face, digging the long nose into his cheek. "You think you get to leave, now?" he whispered, drilling into the truth. "With your family? After what you did?"

DeVore went paler. He'd forgotten, perhaps, in the rush of blows. He sank back into himself. A little hope was a potent thing. A little despair went a long way. Wren had to strike the right balance.

"You said-"

"I'm your Jiminy Cricket. You do this right, Charles, and you will get what you need."

"I didn't hurt them! I swear I didn't-" He was back on his excuses. Like all the men like him, bouncing back and forth from reality to their needs to their justifications, with every step further a step faster, speeding the boulder down the hill.

"You did plenty." Wren dug his elbows into DeVore's thighs. Bleeding, smudging. It hurt and DeVore tried to weasel out from under, but Wren didn't let him. It was nothing compared to what his family had been through. "You did hurt them. You tied them up. You left them. You sat here dreaming about what you'd do."

"I didn't!" DeVore gasped, CIAging his legs side to side, "I just, I couldn't, they told me to-"

"I'm telling you now," Wren whispered. Leaning closer still, eye to eye through the mask's rubber holes. "I'm worse than the Blue Fairy, Charles. You don't want to screw with me. You think this is bad? We're at one percent right now. This train goes all the way up to eleven." That was the threat. Time for the reward. "But do what I say? You'll see your girls again. They'll never need to know it was you."

DeVore's terror and hope reached a peak at the same time. Wren smelled urine release. That was good. The stink should be on him too. It didn't matter that it wasn't true, and Wren would never allow DeVore near his family again.

"I-" Devore could barely speak. Probably he'd never been this scared in his life

"Don't think," Wren said, "just do. You belong to me now." He smeared his fingers up the mask. "You wear your mask. You find the Blue Fairy, you find Pleasure Island, and you tell me where."

"I- I-"

Broken still. Wren had to turn that around. Hope followed fear.

"You lie about all this. About this place. Your wife and girls, the things you did. They'll ask. You say it was personal. Repeat after me. It was personal."

DeVore squeezed it out. "It was personal."

"The best time of your life," Wren hissed. "You keep that in your head. I'm in there too, listening. Watching. You don't forget it."

DeVore nodded, barely breathing, close to passing out.

"Good. Now." Wren pulled the mask off; the rush of air made him feel like vomiting. The dark room spun. He tugged it roughly over DeVore's head, like a dunce's cap on a misbehaving child. "Find Pleasure Island. Tell me tonight. One chance, Charles." Wren brought up DeVore's phone and clicked through the tabs. "Any news site, you leave a comment. For Attention Of Christopher Wren. That's important. Nod your head." Devore nodded. "FAO Christopher Wren. Where Pleasure Island is. I'll come get you. Repeat it."

"Christopher Wren," DeVore said through his sobs, "Pleasure Island, tonight."

Wren tapped out a message on DeVore's phone. Things were getting faster now. Time slipped by like greasy bacon on a big platter.

IT'S DONE, he wrote, then waited in dizzy silence. The phone buzzed in his hands as a new message came in.

PICS

"Stand up," he grunted at DeVore. DeVore stood. "Get your car keys."

"Where am I going?"

"You're going to drive."

DeVore moved like a sleepwalker through his own den. Wren tapped out a new message. Was there a light in the yard now? Was that an engine rumbling in the road outside? He attached the image and sent.

THIS WAS PERSONAL

Now DeVore was standing before him, trembling. Wren didn't envy him what was coming. He held out the phone but DeVore just stood there. Second thoughts.

"Take it now," Wren said. "Get in your car. Drive. Your new life begins, Charles."

"I don't think I can-"

Wren grabbed him before he could finish. The sudden motion sent white waves crashing across his vision, but he dragged DeVore down. His fingers wormed up inside the mask and plunged into DeVore's mouth, wriggling with a life of their own. He pushed them knuckle deep, until the sad man's jaw began to creak and he screamed. Wren grabbed his tongue and yanked.

"Don't think," Wren hissed. "It can always get worse. Think about me. Think about this. Now go outside, get in the car, and drive."

He let go. He wiped his hand on DeVore's chest.

"Go!"

Devore swallowed and panted, staggered backward, not really knowing what had just happened. No longer thinking, just obeying. The door opened and slammed shut behind him. The Firebird's engine revved.

Wren slumped to his knees, looking out the window while the world swirled. Too much blood lost. Had he done everything correctly? He didn't remember. The engine sound pulled away. Meanwhile, were there figures in the yard? Approaching the window. Scarecrows in the dark.

Pinocchios.

He tipped on his side. Took the bottle from his pocket. Fake town arson kit. He opened the top and splashed it toward the door, on the curtains, on the sofa, into the thick shag carpet in the den. There was a heady, acrid stink.

A sharp, splintering bang came at the door. They were breaking in. Checking DeVore's work. Wren sparked the lighter and pressed it to the nearest patch. The carpet rushed into flame, then the curtain and the sofa, until in seconds he was surrounded by flames. Smoke rushed up to shroud him. The fire spread with phenomenal speed. Already he couldn't breathe.

The door cracked inward. The Pinocchios came in but stopped, staring at the flames. There was shock on their rubber faces. Surprise in their cutout eyes. They didn't see Wren. Wren was at home in the fire. Wren was invisible, Jiminy Cricket in the air.

The story here was clear. Charles DeVore had eaten his fill and left nothing behind for them. This was personal, like he'd said.

They left.

Wren bolted up into dizziness, smoke and pain. The heat was everywhere and he couldn't breathe. The thick, lighter-soaked carpet threw up sheets of flame. He ran through them as light-footed as a drunk, striding until-

The steps to the basement jumped up at him. He barely managed to catch them as he ran downward. DeVore's family lay where he'd left them. He drew the knife and stumbled in, drawing screams in a chorus, but he barely heard them. He slit the first zip-tie. The mother sprang on him but he shrugged her off and moved to the next.

Then they were running, up the stairs and away. Wren fell to his side. Smoke poured down the stairs, thick and black. It wouldn't be the fire that got him, it would be the smoke. He tried to lift his body, but it was too heavy. A laugh came out strangled. The smoke rolled over him like a tsunami tide. If only his father could see him now...

25

OUT

W ren came up from the depths to creamy warm light, a ceiling that curved and twin rails of compartments running overhead like train tracks. He blinked, then a face loomed out of the fuzz. Blond hair, red eyes, freckles that he hadn't noticed before, brought out by the blast.

"Rogers?" he asked.

"It's me, boss," she confirmed. "What the hell happened to you?"

He tried to get up, but an ache in the back of his head pulled him down. Still dizzy. "Nightmares. You came for me."

She smiled. It made her look pretty. "That's right, Sherlock."

He smiled back. Teasing him. "So that makes you Watson? Where's your bowler hat?"

She laughed. "Where's your deerstalker? We're both letting ourselves down."

It would hurt too much to laugh, so he held it in. "After this, we'll go shopping. And thank you. Glad you came."

Rogers just nodded.

In his peripheral vision he saw a metal stand with three drained blood bags on it and a dark red tube leading into his right forearm.

"AB positive," Rogers mused, following his gaze. "Universal recipient.

Useless as a donor. I could transfuse into you directly, and you couldn't give me a damn thing."

Wren tried for a grunt and failed. His body felt very weak. His breath had no punch behind it; that was smoke damage to his lungs. "You don't want to tube into this," he croaked out. "I'm full of bad stuff."

Rogers looked at him deadpan. "How do you know I'm not, too?"

Wren gave a slight snort. Covering for the faintness he felt at speaking so much, and the disorientation. Rogers gave him the moment, adjusting to the change. From asphyxiating in the basement to this.

He tracked the ceiling down to the door at the end of the corridor. Not a corridor, of course, or a train track. A fuselage. A private jet, in the air already, judging by the drone of engines. He'd requested it before entering the basement. Along with blood bags and a field surgeon on board. He hadn't expected Rogers to come. She must have been on a helicopter less than an hour after he'd left Detroit. Already well in the air before he'd sent the request.

He looked at his left forearm. Bandaged neatly. No doubt there were some staples underneath that. A new scar and another story he'd never want to tell.

"My back?" he asked, looking at her.

"All taped up," Rogers said. "Doc did it in the ambulance. Flesh wounds all, some remnant shrapnel from the blast, and you lost a lot of blood. I don't think I need to tell you that." She looked at his arm. "I saw the scene you put on. Pretty grotesque, but I'm assuming to a purpose?"

She looked at him patiently. She'd already have figured most of it out. She must have spoken to the mother, DeVore's wife, and that would have given her the broad strokes.

"He's in with the Blue Fairy," Wren confirmed. "Devore. He's our guy, Ravenous6. I put the fear of God in him."

"The fear of Wren."

He went for a grunt again, just about landed it. "I wore the Pinocchio mask. You were right about the model type."

"It's the little things. Listen, boss. There's been developments."

Of course there had. Pretty soon he'd have to get up again and start moving. A private jet over America, with three blood bags down, meant they'd been flying for at least an hour. That was a range of five hundred miles plus, which left maybe three hours until they arrived, if they were headed where he'd asked. Lots to do in that time. "What time is it?"

"Past eleven. We're somewhere over Illinois."

Illinois sounded about right. He'd need to check his phone. They didn't even have a precise destination yet. Unless…

"What have you got?" he asked.

"Plenty. First up, DeVore's family. They're all in shock, of course, dehydrated and on edge, but I spoke to the wife. She didn't know anything. Hadn't seen anything unusual in his behavior. No clue at all. She didn't even know it was DeVore that tied them up."

Wren nodded. "You told her."

"She has every right to know."

"But not the kids."

"No. I hope they never know. Maybe someday, when they're old enough."

Wren sighed. Everyone made their choices, and always it was the kids who got hurt, soaking up the pain and getting ready to recycle it somewhere down the line.

"Yeah."

Rogers cocked her head. "Yeah. But are you sure he's working for us? He locked his own family up. You've sent him direct to where he wants to go."

"He's a boulder at the top of the hill," Wren said, then took a breath. "But he's rolling now. He's getting a taste, and maybe he likes it, right. He'll want more."

"So you think he'll report back?"

Wren shuffled up in the reclined seat. "You don't send a boy scout into the lion's den. It's better this way. But I think he'll come back in from the cold. He hates me enough for that."

Rogers frowned. "If he hates you, he might turn. They can trace you back."

"We'll deal with that when it happens. Either way, he'll lead us closer to the Blue Fairy."

"That's optimistic," said Rogers, looking into his eyes, "but I guess we'll take it. Onto the other news, our social media spider found hits on the panel van after it crossed into Dearborn. One came from some kids shooting up a

STOP sign pulled off Snapchat, another from a wake BBQ two blocks over, passing in the background. We got it signaling a left turn."

"Good driving etiquette."

"Probably trying to evade a routine stop. We flooded the zone with police and found the van."

Wren closed his eyes, pictured the scene. Blooms of red rose behind his eyes. "In a ruin."

"Yes," Rogers confirmed. "I was there, it was a mess. Baby mansion derelict for three years, no apparent ties to the previous owner. Just a good, anonymous shell with no residents nearby." She paused. "There was no sign of Clara Baxter. The other guy was there, though, Tom Solent. Mutilated like the rest." She took a moment. "He didn't die of blood loss though. They tied him off after the cuts. Then they cut some more. A lot of pieces, boss. Not much of him left by the end. Probably the shock did him in."

"Torture," Wren said. He was starting to feel a little better. The blood bags they'd poured into him doubtless had some pick-me-up in them, a clotting agent, painkiller and maybe antibiotics to stave off any infection. He'd take anything he could get. "Fun for them."

"Fun, right. Who knows what information they got out of him. Jeffries is still out for the count, but we pulled some of his records out of the fire. Tom Solent was no Clara Baxter; he's just a regular guy. I don't think he had any idea what he was mixed up in."

Wren looked at the ceiling, as if he was afraid the sudden surge of anger he felt would slosh out of his eyes and be lost. Torture for fun. You had to keep it all in, every drop. Anger was useful. You tamped it down deep and used it as fuel. The deeper you tamped it, the longer it lasted. Rage like that could go for years. It could become a part of you. Wren was an expert, and never ran empty.

"Poor bastard. Anything else?"

"No DNA except for him. The van was there, burned out in the yard. The masks were gone. No further leads. They had a vehicle or vehicles waiting, and you know there's no way to track them through footage."

"Into the wind."

"Called back by the Blue Fairy." Rogers took a breath. "There've been more attacks, too. The same kinds of traps, before we sent word out to pull them back. Something like thirty now. It seems Humphreys really listened to you, the first time. News keeps coming in; scenes getting reported up the chain. No Pinocchios captured anywhere, which is hard to believe. The rate of new attacks has dropped right off, but that's just because we've pulled back. They've got us on the defensive, afraid any strike will blunder into another trap. There's plenty of targets we should be acting on, but we're not. Suspects to grab up. Catfishers to protect. We're not doing either now."

Wren took a long breath, testing his lungs. Better, but not full capacity. Suck any more and he'd start coughing, probably do more damage. "We're running scared."

"Exactly. Humphreys is in meetings with the big boss. The President's in a briefing right now, I believe. We're being held hostage, basically. The criminals own the streets, for now at least."

Wren cursed softly. "Coming out into the light."

"What's that?"

"Something I just figured out." He pushed himself the rest of the way to a sitting position. The blood bag was empty now, all sucked into his body. Still there was dizziness, but it was fading. His body was repairing itself. Cuts sealed over with extra clotting. Bruises bathed in healing fluids. Oxygen carried to places starved for hours. He held to the seat sidearms and pulled the lever to rack the backrest up. Rogers leaned back a little to give him room.

"It's what the Blue Fairy wants," he added.

"Coming out into the light?"

Wren shifted his feet off the leg rest and put them on the floor. His toes hurt. He remembered seeing them on fire, maybe two hours ago now.

"All this is for something," Wren said, thinking it through as he spoke. Projecting it forward. "Part of a grander plan."

"But what? There is no end game here."

"There is. We just can't see it yet." Wren rubbed his cheeks, speckled with stubble and dried blood. The patterns were lining up. "These attacks are just the beginning. A message. It's in the news cycle now and everyone's seen it. It's a message for us to back off, sure. But not only that. It's also for all the potential Pinocchios out there." Wren turned the idea over, looking into Rogers' red eyes. The place it led was very dark. "They're trying to radicalize all the abusers in America."

"What?"

It made sense. Wren took it further. "Push them to the extremes, make it personal and get their boulders rolling; you're with us or you're against us. Look at the mutilations. It's not only our agents, is it?"

Rogers frowned. "I'm not sure-"

"I checked en route to Canton. They're leaving a trail of mutilations behind, including 'moderate' abusers. Those who won't sign on to the Blue Fairy's way of doing things; they mutilate them. It's a purge for purity."

"Driving moderates to the extremes."

"Exactly. And the news media is spreading the message for them. There's no escaping that it's a call to arms. This is a war, Rogers, and so far they're winning."

Rogers frowned. "It's a good theory, but how can you be sure that's their goal?"

"From DeVore," Wren said, more confidently now. "And just their initial goal. The way he was acting today, compared to his chat logs. Two days ago he was a nobody, absolute soft-belly fringe, a moderate peruser of middling teens on his first real-world meet. They'll find tamer imagery on his computer, I guarantee it. Then the Fairy gives him the push and starts his boulder rolling faster. Threatens him enough to make him tie up his family. He sat there all day, Rogers, and did nothing, because he was paralyzed; he couldn't take the step they wanted him to take."

"Filming it," Rogers said. Her tone was dead. "The wife said as much. The camera gear, all set up. They wanted him to do that."

"And the Pinocchios sat outside all day, waiting for him to make the decision, because they're hungry for soldiers. Yes, it was an ambush for us, but it was also a war for another conscript's loyalty. Recruitment. Join us and go to Pleasure Island, or die by our hand, in the worst way possible. They're weaponizing the middle and killing off any who resist. It sends a signal to the whole community. It promotes unity. They'll all be jacking off to the dream of Pleasure Island now."

Rogers paled further, so her freckles stood in painfully sharp relief. "And you think it's real? Pleasure Island, that it's a real place, not just a website?"

Wren turned that over. He thought a lot of things. He suspected others. Now wasn't the time for his wilder speculations. "I think there are answers in Idaho."

"Idaho," Rogers repeated. "Looking for Clara Baxter, based on a fragment Jeffries maybe remembered."

"It's all fragments," Wren said. "We stitch them into a quilt."

"All right. Well, it's a big state. So where?"

"I'm working on it. In the meantime, get me Humphreys on the phone. There's things we need to start doing right now."

26

CRYPTOWORM

Rogers worked her phone, chewing a path through multiple layers of staff in Humphreys' retinue, while Wren brought up his darknet. A host of VPNs bounced his signal around the world. Reinforced password protection. The best cryptography his elite team could build.

He logged in and tapped through to the open boards. They were empty, as he'd expected. No one posting since he'd given them the last warning. He thought of all his people out there now, some on the road, some staying in motels, trying not to be found. If the Blue Fairy had hacked them and doxxed their addresses to their Pinocchio army…

Better not to think about that. Still he did, with Alli in Wyoming, and Jay in Utah, and Cheryl and Teddy in hospital in Chicago, and countless others across the country and the world, all willing to put themselves at risk on his word. For coins, for influence, just because it was something good to do and Wren was there asking them to do it. Almost four hundred people total.

He rubbed his eyes and logged into the elite hacker board. These people couldn't be doxxed because they were the world's best, led by Wren's prize jewels.

Hellion and B4cksl4cker.

He'd scooped them both at the same time, in his legendary break of the

362

Huggintime anti-government virus. Huggintime was a ransomware cryptoworm; a program designed to replicate itself across networks, take up residence in as many computers as possible, and lock them down with cryptography. It would then demand payments to unlock the data. Knowing that MO, along with several lines of the worm's source code generated after meticulous reverse engineering, Wren had narrowed his targets down based on coding signatures.

Arrogance often felled hackers. It wasn't enough for them to break into CNN or the Federal Reserve. To really 'own' the man they had to leave their graffiti tags behind: their handles, memes they favored, taunts that gave away grammatical and lexical clues.

Wren's team had followed that trail in an epic hacking slog that lasted weeks and put more than one member of his team into the hospital for exhaustion, but ultimately resulted in clear lines of data leading out.

One went to B4cksl4cker.

B4cksl4cker was then a twenty-three-year-old Armenian who ran an elite hacker collective, waging crypto-currency attacks through several enormous botnets. The numbers involved had been dizzying; half-a-billion compromised devices across the globe, including computers, phones, watches, tablets, all compelled by B4cksl4cker's directives to phish, keylog and data-mine for cash.

His operation was worth millions. Wren set forensic data analysts to track that flow of cash across the darknet, but still B4cksl4cker proved impossible to pin down. He took an un-doxxable approach to hacking, by never having a home to doxx. He and his team lived in multiple coach convoys that were constantly moving, through Europe, Africa, Asia, wherever. He wielded his teams, his botnet and all the hacking techniques like a virtuoso conductor, leaving a trail of legendary exploits behind and amassing a net worth close to four billion dollars.

Then Hellion broke him.

Hellion was a fourteen-year-old Belgian wunderkind who'd cut her teeth on the e-sports strategy game StarCraft. There APM, or Actions Per Minute, were a vital determiner of success. Speed on the keys mattered just as much as tactics and strategy; the best players at pro-levels were capable of 300+ distinct actions per minute, equating to at least five keystroke decisions per second.

In StarCraft the player used those staggering APMs to control a squad of fighters in pitted, top-down open warfare against another squad. At her peak at the age of twelve, Hellion had averaged a stunning 400 APM, with an armada of strategies that saw her undefeated on the semi-pro boards. She could have gone pro, but that hadn't seemed like fun. More fun were the amazing opportunities her APM offered as a professional hacker.

At thirteen she initiated open warfare on B4cksl4cker. He counter-attacked, and for three days they fought to bring each other's virtual identities down. Hellion on her own, at home, going deep on single techniques with her phenomenal tactics and speed on the keys, and B4cksl4cker in his convoy using all his resources at once.

Hellion won. A simple but original hash attack disrupted B4cksl4cker's network of control, peeling off his teams coach by coach until he was left steering his vast web of infrastructure alone. Hellion ran rings around him, too agile by far, ultimately locking him out with a repurposed version of one of his own cryptoworms.

When it was done, she sent him the unlock code and message.

THAT WAS FUN LET'S DO AGAIN SOMETIME

There was no ransom; she didn't take his money, only his reputation.

B4cksl4cker could have gone after her in the real world. His hack had worked, just more slowly. He had her docs by then, and knew how unprotected she was. He could have handed her to her own government, or the Russians, the Chinese. They all would have been glad to have her.

Instead he went to see her. Outside her school one day he introduced himself. She laughed at how old he was, then offered to teach him a thing or two.

It became a friendship. They saw something in each other that they couldn't get in any other way: the understanding and respect of a peer. He taught her about cryptoworms and botnets. She worked on his APM and strategy. From that blooming platonic partnership came the Huggintime cryptoworm, which dealt billions in damage globally. It also offered Wren a way to bring them down, through a catfishing operation of his own.

Posing as Hellion to B4cksl4cker, posing as B4cksl4cker to Hellion, he cracked into their trusted comms feed and logged an emergency. They had to get out and meet at a hut in the Belgian Blue Forest.

They both came. Wren was waiting, and offered them something better than either could envision alone. She'd had her 'lulz' by then, troll-like 'lol' or 'laugh-out-loud' moments in hacking through firewalls, now seventeen and lapsing into uncertainty about what the future held. He'd made his billions and wasn't sure what came next; Hellion had wrecked his reputation, his collective had largely disbanded, but now he was hanging out with her whenever he could.

"More than hacktivism," Wren said to them in the hut, holding them only with the brazen magnetism of his bold approach, "no more coin theft, no more cheap kicks. I'm talking about a new Internet order. I want you to build a darknet police."

They scoffed. They thought he wanted a lever of control over government, or a way to scoop up big data and exploit it, or some other awful scheme to manipulate 'the people'. They weren't interested. Even if they actually built what he wanted, a darknet police service to trawl the depths and dig out the sickest, why would they need him involved at all?

"Because I'll know what to do with it," he answered. "Look me up. Talk to the people in my Foundation."

"Foundation?" they asked.

He smiled. "Make your own judgments. Just know, for the first time in your lives, you'll be doing something better than ransoming data for dictators. That feeling you're both missing? That thing you glimpse in each other? I can help you live there all the time. You want to pass into hacker legend, then let's transform the web tonight."

He left.

By that night all his social media feeds went down. By the morning his bank accounts were drained, even the hidden ones. By the afternoon the Foundation had been scrubbed out of digital existence.

He didn't do anything. Didn't go after them, though they had to know he could. Even when they started posting stupid meme images with his face attached, and sending them viral across the Internet, he did nothing.

Let them have their fun. Get it out of their systems. He'd seen something in them by then, and believed they wanted what he was offering. So he waited. A week passed, and he got by without access to his Foundation or funds. Figured they were auditing him. Watched the viral games go by with something like amusement.

Then it went away.

He got access to his accounts back, his Foundation, along with a report card. Pink paper, waiting in a manila envelope at his home.

B-

The next time he heard from them was three months later, when he opened his darknet to find new security protocols in place. The Foundation had been transformed into a digital fortress. Impregnable, unbreakable, unlike anything he'd seen before.

Inside there were barriers everywhere. New apps he had admin access to, including the megaphone. Rooms he hadn't built. In one, a chat board under the name 'B-', he found them waiting. They spoke with one voice under the handle H3llsl4cker.

LOOK ON MY WORKS YE MIGHTY AND KNOW DESPAIR

Wren responded. "You'll be the police."

A long moment.

WE ALREADY ARE

They'd warmed up somewhat since then, two years ago. Wren knew from B4cksl4cker that Hellion, now 19, had a girlfriend. B4cksl4cker had a rotating harem of his own. They traveled in their own convoys, undoxxable, and spent much of each day and most of every night working together to build, maintain and fine-tune their policing over-structure. It was a big job and far from complete.

On the elite board now, Wren expected to see their fingerprints everywhere; a stream of data points building to the answers he wanted. With Clara's name and a farm in Idaho he was certain they could weave a rich tapestry of compelling interconnections. He expected a great mash of folders crammed with pertinent details lifted from government records, social media accounts, credit card spreadsheets, networked surveillance, web service provider logs and more; entire lives stuffed into digital format, cross-referenced and arranged by relevance.

Instead there was nothing. The board was empty but for a single message.

CALL ME

DR. FERAT

Ferat?

Wren felt his insides churn. What the hell was the doctor playing at?

He drilled Ferat's number into the screen. The phone rang.

27

CLIFF

Ferat answered after only one ring. "Christopher. I was hoping you'd call."

He sounded out of breath. Wren tried to place that. Ferat liked marathons; once he'd confessed it helped to suppress unwanted desires. Was he running now?

"Doctor, what the hell is going on? What are you doing on the elite board?"

"Ah, yes," said the Doctor awkwardly, as if this was a source of some embarrassment. There'd been a certain discomfort between the two of them ever since Ferat had taken over the day-to-day running of Wren's Foundation. Wren had allowed it, since he was no longer able to dedicate the time the Foundation required, but still he hadn't grown comfortable with it.

He'd kept Ferat's hands off the wheel of the Foundation for fifteen years, for fear he'd exploit its members like lab-rats for the furtherance of his career as Head of Psychology at Yale University. Ferat hadn't shown any signs of doing that yet, though, so maybe Wren's concerns were misplaced.

"I assure you, Christopher, I had no intention of appearing there. I understand how this might be a shock, but allow me to explain. Hellion and B4cksl4cker brought me in." Ferat spoke swiftly, reading Wren's frustration. "I've been speaking to them for some time. They're very polite young people. They reached out after you took your, ah, sabbatical. Looking for guidance, and-"

"And they invited you into the elite hacker board?"

"Well," began Ferat, even more embarrassed-sounding now, "it's more a therapeutic relationship, I suppose. They were looking for guidance. They may be world-class hackers, Christopher, but they aren't especially emotionally mature. They spend a lot of time alone. And their lifestyles, well, they're not exactly wholesome…"

Wren ground his knuckles against his forehead. "So you're counseling my elite hackers?"

"Ah, yes? I suppose I am. That's how it started. But Christopher, you must see it from their point of view. They needed help. You weren't there."

Wren squeezed his eyes shut. It hurt, mostly because it was true. "So they came to you." He caught up with his own thinking. "And they found something?"

"Well, not just something. This is big, Christopher."

"Big. OK. First thing's first, where are you? Are you safe now?"

"Safe's a relative term. I'm on the move, as you suggested. I couldn't stay at the university."

A chill worked up Wren's spine. They were all hunted now. "So what did they find?"

"It's less what they found and more how they felt, Christopher." Ferat took a moment, and Wren didn't press him. Sometimes the old fellow just couldn't be rushed. "To show you what I mean, consider this. Hellion called me via video chat. She never does that. She had B4cksl4cker networked and we all talked together." The chills worsened. Not once had Wren seen his hackers faces since that hut in the Belgian forest.

"So?"

"So they are terrified. They have uncovered something that is beyond their expertise to defend against. You've seen their latest reports on the over-structure, their second layer Internet?"

"Yes."

"Not the most recent, I wager. In building this structure, which I do not claim to understand, they say they have found another that already exists. Like a second skin atop the digital world, but not serving any clear purpose.

Not a policing structure, with search and destroy tendencies. Something else. They probed it and it lashed out."

Ferat went silent.

Wren remained silent, listening and thinking. Ferat's breath rasped like it was coming from inside a Pinocchio mask. Hackers who were better than Hellion and B4cksl4cker? He'd never seen any. Never heard of any. But…

"Within hours their over-structure was disintegrated by this 'second skin'. I can't explain it any more clearly than that; I don't think they really know what happened. For years they've been building it, and suddenly it was gone. Now they are functionally blind. They're running, and I told them not to look back."

"But-"

"That's not all," Ferat went on. "The Foundation has undoubtedly been compromised by this second skin. I had the two of them overwrite the whole database, including everything on the Blue Fairy investigation, along with all member records and the coin system."

It took Wren a moment to register that. "You're saying you erased my site?"

"Yes. They backed it up first and I downloaded it to a storage disk. I sent that disk into a holding pattern through the postal system. Not even I know where it's going to end up. But you will."

"What?"

"You need to deal with this, Christopher," Ferat said sternly, taking control of the conversation. "I've been picking up the slack for you these last six months, since the events with your family. Now you need to take the reins. The Foundation needs you; it's why these people joined up to begin with. I'm no replacement for that."

Wren took a breath. The records he could deal with. He made regular backups of core files himself, and carried them with him at all times on extra SIM cards, though when was the last time he'd backed up the coin system? Too long. Before the Saints. Now all that coin information could be lost. For some of his members, it was the only thing keeping their darker drives in check. The Foundation could lapse into disarray.

"I-" he began, but Ferat interrupted.

"It is really that bad. It's where we are. We need to deal with it and move on."

Silence for a few moments as Wren swallowed that. Ferat being right and taking the lead. "OK." He redirected his attention. "You said you're running now. Where are you?"

"I can't tell you on a hacked phone. You know that."

"You think they're tracking your phone?"

"I know it. Hellion told me before we cut ties. It's quite likely they're listening to us. I advise you to destroy your phone after this. Not just the SIM, Christopher, also-"

"I know something about hacked phones," Wren interrupted. "It means they'll have both of our positions now. You're going to change direction after this call."

Ferat didn't answer. In the silence Wren glimpsed things going unsaid. He listened to the older man's heavy breathing and the chill in his spine intensified.

"You're going to change direction, aren't you?"

A beat passed, then Ferat chuckled, but there was a catch of something pained in the sound. "I'm no operative, Christopher. You see right through me. Part of me hoped to just let the moment pass."

The chill in Wren's spine shot up to take a stranglehold of his throat. "What moment?"

"It has been the great honor of my life, working with you to build the Foundation all these years. I expected to-"

"Grayson," Wren interrupted, growing urgent. Ferat's first name. He never used it. "Tell me what's happening."

Now there was both pleasure and pain in Ferat's voice. "I am glad you called, my boy. I wanted to contact you myself, but I couldn't risk it. Too much is at stake, and I could never endanger you or the Foundation that way."

Wren's heart skipped a beat. His mind leaped ahead, to the only place left to go. "They're on you now." It came out dead and flat.

Ferat chuckled again, and again there was a pained edge. "They are indeed following me. They have been for hours. I knew that as long as I kept driving, they'd follow. Waiting for me to lead them somewhere. I am leading them somewhere, Christopher, but not where they expect."

"Where?"

"It's better off a secret," Ferat said, calmly now, as if he was just making conversation and not speeding down a highway somewhere.

Wren's mind raced through his options. Ferat was on the East Coast,

Yale University, well out of Wren's operational range. He could call through to Humphreys and demand help but knew nothing would come. In the midst of the worst stream of terrorist attacks in American history, where every effort to fight back was being met with overwhelming force, no help was going to come for Dr. Grayson Ferat. He was on his own.

Wren swallowed hard. "Get to a military base. I'll set up your access. They can protect you."

"I don't think so, Christopher. The Fairy's got cars in front and behind me. They're wearing their masks openly. There can't be long left. Really, we're all just running down the clock now."

The world's focus tightened around Wren. He wasn't in a plane anymore; he was back in the fake town with his father forcing him to witness terrible things done to living men and women in the tanks while the victims begged for more, forcing him to film them as the end approached and they pretended panic and pain were pleasure.

Had they really believed? His father had kept records of every disturbing second, and played those seconds back on a loop as they died, or almost died, so they could know what their lives and deaths amounted to; absolute, unapologetic subversion of reality, in the name of the Pyramid. In the name of the Apex.

"Christopher," came Ferat's voice, sternly again, professorial. "I know what you're thinking, that they will torture me, but I won't allow it. I know this area well; I've been coming here for years." A pause. "It's a cliffside road. They can't stop me now. I'll hit the barrier and I'll be free."

"But-"

"No buts. I owe these last fifteen years to you, Christopher. You have changed me in ways I never imagined possible. I am a better man because of you. You didn't give up on me, when I tried to use your painful past to further my own ambitions. I want to thank you for that. When you came back to me with such disappointment in your eyes, but also hope..." He trailed off, battling the catch in his voice. "I want you to remember this for the future, Christopher. Not all selfish men are fated to become evil. This is the message we have built into our Foundation. Continue saving those you can and use them like you used me, to help the weak."

"Doctor-"

"The Blue Fairy is vast," Ferat went on, sounding very distant now. Climbing a mountain, maybe, weaving in and out of cell tower reception.

Maybe there were only seconds left. "And it's never static. Your hackers found that much. It moves ceaselessly, Christopher. Their websites. Their center of control. Pleasure Island." A pause. "Think kindly of me, Christopher, will you?"

Wren didn't know what to say. Nothing else mattered now. "Of course I will. Grayson."

Ferat said something in answer, but his voice phased out as the signal dropped.

"Dr. Ferat," Wren called. "Grayson!"

"...believe that most people can change, Christopher," came Ferat's voice, squirling back in like a tuning ham radio. "Even you." A pause. "Now I'm sending the final findings Hellion and B4cksl4cker gave to me. You know the state in question. It may be that the Pinocchios don't know it, and you will be ahead of them. Now, let me see." He went silent for a moment, and Wren hung on every second. "Ah, yes, closing arguments. Christopher, you must go see your father. Not that fool from the Pyramid, though his time will come. I mean the man who rescued you. Tandrews. You owe it to him and to yourself. I believe it will help resolve the pain within your own family. These are wounds you must find a way to bind. You must be with your children again. Find a way."

"Grayson, if you-"

"None of that. They're closing in now. I'm about to-" there was a distant crash, "go through the fence!" He sounded giddy. Probably he was, high on adrenaline. "They're all wearing their masks, Christopher, and don't they look ridiculous! Maybe I can lead them over the edge. Do you think…."

He phased out. Wren pressed the phone tight against his ear, straining for the smallest sound, but there was nothing more except perhaps the faint whistling of wind. Wren couldn't breathe. His whole body thrummed. He imagined Ferat's car falling from a very great height. The Pinocchios behind.

Then there was a crash, so loud that Wren jerked, then nothing, then a dial tone.

The phone dropped from his hand.

Doctor Ferat was dead.

28

FARMER

W ren leaned forward with his head in his hands, in shock. His phone buzzed on the thin gray carpet before him. A message. He saw it but didn't see it.

Grayson Ferat was dead.

It hit him like a sucker punch. The last thing he'd expected. Since he'd been seventeen in Ferat's 101 Pyschology class the old man had become an odd, unexpected pillar of Wren's world. The things he'd taught in class had started formalizing Wren's understanding of the human mind. The lesson he'd taught back at his apartment, following an invite for a special tutelage session, when he placed one hand on Wren's knee with the clear hope of raising it higher, had been even more valuable.

Namely, that there was nothing for Wren to be scared of. There was little worse in the world than the Pyramid. There were few people as dangerous as that, few predators as cruel or persuasive, and in turn that meant Wren was strong. He'd never fully realized until then just how strong he was. Everything that followed had been built on that foundation.

Now Ferat was gone, and his Foundation was crumbling.

He felt sick and dizzy. It wasn't blood loss but something else. His own roots coming unstuck. His Foundation was in the wind, its records winging their way through the postal system. The Blue Fairy knew who he was and had already dug out Ferat. Maybe it could dig out others. He saw again the pictures of mutilation in his mind. He imagined that done to his members.

His family.

He shuddered.

"Boss," came a voice, but he barely heard it. A hand rested on his shoulder and he looked up.

"Oh," he said. It felt strange that he could even talk. "Rogers."

She looked scared. "Your phone, boss. I'm sorry for whatever just happened, but we need to destroy it. If they were watching the doctor, if they really have some kind of second skin on the Internet, then they're watching us now."

Wren looked at the phone. Black plastic and metal resting on a gray carpet, on a plane somewhere over Illinois. Maybe Iowa now. He reached toward it and saw a hand stretch before him, like it wasn't his own. A stranger's fingers picked it up, and he felt nothing. There was an edge of red on the rim near the speaker. Blood, he realized, from his ear. He'd pressed it too hard against his head.

"Boss," urged Rogers, and Wren opened the lock screen automatically, not thinking. A message hung down in his notifications and he swiped it open.

MY BOY

LANCE GEBHART, NOT HEBBERT, WAS A PIG FARMER, ONE DAUGHTER - MONA GEBHART

SHE DISAPPEARED 15 YEARS AGO AT AGE 11, NEVER SEEN AGAIN

FACIAL AGING SOFTWARE PROJECTS A MATCH TO CLARA BAXTER

LANCE PRESUMED DEAD 9 YEARS AGO, ALONG WITH HIS WIFE CINDY GEBHART, WHEN THEIR FARMSTEAD BURNED DOWN

NO IDENTIFIABLE REMAINS WERE FOUND

THE PROPERTY AND LAND WERE ALL UNCLAIMED INTESTATE AND REMAIN FIFTY ACRES NORTH OF RIRIE

YOURS IN BELIEF,

GRAYSON FERAT, PROUD MEMBER OF THE FOUNDATION

Wren read the words, but they didn't seem to make sense. Clara Baxter was Lance Gebhart's daughter? That revelation was lost in the enormity of it being Dr. Ferat's final message. Something splashed off the screen, and it took him a moment to realize it was a tear. He wiped it away. A moment later the screen warped. Bright bands of color rolled right to left, as if the screen were being bent. Then it went dark.

"Boss!"

He flipped the phone and popped off the back. The battery came out, then the SIM card, killing any connection. They'd gotten into his phone that fast, slicing through his defenses like they weren't there. Better even than Hellion and B4cksl4cker, Ferat had said. A second skin atop the Internet, destroying their policing over-structure in hours.

His mind reeled. Who had he already called on that phone? What sites had he searched, what messages had he sent? All were compromised now.

He looked up at Rogers. Her bruised and sooty face seemed torn between a storm of emotions: urgency, fear, sympathy, anger. Wren registered them and cataloged them. Only one of those was useful, an old friend. He knew it well. He just had to get there too.

"They killed him," he said flatly. "The Pinocchios."

"He was in your Foundation." She didn't ask it as a question. She didn't need to. "I'm sorry."

Wren let out a long, shuddery breath. It was a lot to lose, but that was enough grieving for now. There'd be an accounting later. Always later. Every bill came due at some point. Now he had to tamp this feeling down and use it as fuel.

"They'll know we're coming," Rogers said.

"Let them," said Wren, feeling the process begin. Burn the sadness into rage, then focus that rage to a gas-jet torch and sear out their eyes. He looked up at Rogers. "We'll be ready. Did you get me Humphreys?"

"He's on a secure line. Can we trust him?"

"Let's find out."

29

THE PRICE

"Wren, what have you got for me?"

Humphreys at peak intensity. In the White House while the crap rained down, dealing with strikes all across the country. Angry, focused, intense. If you couldn't trust that, what did you have left?

"I'm chasing a lead on the origins of the Blue Fairy," Wren said, "a man named Gebhart, and I need a strike team to fend off a potential Pinocchio assault."

"*Potential* assault?" Humphreys asked. He sounded disgusted. "And you're going after, what, the origins? I need actionable intelligence right now, and that sounds-"

"We need the source code," Wren interrupted, "and that comes at the beginning. We need to know what these bastards really want."

"Listen to me, Wren-"

"No, you listen! I've been hunting the Fairy for months and this is the closest we've ever been. I understand why you're pulling back, but this is our best shot at bringing the whole thing down."

A pause. "Are you done?"

"Get me a team, Humphreys."

"It's not so simple. We're on lockdown nationwide; orders straight from the Joint Chiefs. I can't green-light anything now." His voice became quieter. "Call on your cult."

"It's not a cult. And anyway, they've been compromised. Pinocchios just ran my lead guy off a cliff. The rest are in the wind."

Humphreys cursed. "I'm sorry. I can't do it, Wren. There's too much at stake. You're not seeing what I'm seeing."

"You're talking about the hack on the Internet," Wren guessed. "The second skin on top of everything?" A pause. "Tell me essential services are exempted."

Humphreys sucked in a sharp breath, continued in a whisper. "How the hell do you know about that? I'm briefing the President on it in five." There was the sound of a door clicking; he was off in a side room. "A second skin, you're calling it? My engineers say it's a crypto-matrix, and I have no idea what that is, or what's exempted; only that they can take control of us whenever they want. It's all happening right now."

Wren didn't have to think. There was only one response to blackmail. "So take the country offline. Reboot it all right now on clean servers."

"What? Do you have any idea how destructive that would be?" A pause, probably calculating how much to share. "It doesn't look good, Wren. Signs indicate these bastards are in Wall Street already, power, communications. Even a partial shutdown in any of those areas would be incredibly damaging, with potentially millions of computers locked up in cryptography. We would be bankrupted and blind at the same time."

"So better we do it now, on our schedule, than they do it to us later."

Humphreys laughed. "And what if that's exactly what they want? Shut down the power and we'll be blind, deaf and dumb. Maybe Russia takes this chance to bomb us back to the Stone Age. We can't take that chance. One misstep here and God knows what damage we've done to ourselves, for nothing."

Wren didn't need to weigh that. You cut off a dead limb before it began to rot. "So kill the Internet wholesale and go low tech. Cut the wires and keep all services siloed; I know there are systems in place for that. Start rebooting the country state by state. We may black out for a while, but we'll be up again within twenty-four hours."

Humphreys' tone went cold. "Partially up. There are countless unknowns in what you're describing. And I'm not having this conversation with you,

Wren. If they're in even one of our nuclear power stations, we're talking about tens of thousands dead and millions affected. The fallout would devastate us for generations. We can't just act without learning more."

"That's what I'm doing out here," Wren countered, surfing the anger from Ferat's death like a wave. "I need backup and that's what you're there for, in the White House, to get me what I need, so do your job and set me up with some protection!"

Humphreys grew louder. "You're not listening. Even without the reactors they could lock up Wall Street in code and all our financial records are gone in a second. We'll drop into anarchy before the night's out. I can't make a move without the President's OK, and do you think she's going to take a chance with all that on the line?" Angrier. "We're pulling back, Wren. They've as good as ordered us to stop."

A pause as Wren absorbed that. "The Blue Fairy's giving us orders?"

"We don't have any choice! Unless you've got something actionable now, some magic trick to strip the second skin from our systems, this is it! I'm about to go in with the President and Joint Chiefs and I'm going to advise them to negotiate."

Wren was dumbfounded. Negotiate with terrorists? "You're not."

"Believe it, it's happening."

Wren tried to comprehend. "Negotiate for what? How many laws we're going to scrub off the books so they can breathe easy?"

"They have us by the balls, Wren," Humphreys spat. "We're talking about the survival of our nation. We can afford some minor adjustments. We already halted all actions against them. Now they're making proposals."

Wren seethed. Of course they were making proposals. Incentive and punishment, just like with DeVore. A baseball bat on the one hand, Pleasure Island on the other. The American people wouldn't just hand their children over for free.

"What are they promising?"

"Promising? We're lucky they haven't pulled the country apart already! They don't need to offer us anything more."

"Bullshit," said Wren, detecting a shift in Humphreys' tone. The shame, already building. "There's more at stake here than financial records and nuclear fallout. We're talking about the founding ideals of this Republic, the moral integrity of the United States. I'd rather have ten years of chaos with

378

half the population dead than compromise on that. You can't give them a damn inch!"

A silence passed; calculations spinning in the distance between them.

"Nothing's been decided," Humphreys said, "we haven't-"

"Don't lie to me. It's already gone down; I can hear it in your voice. What did they promise you?"

A long moment passed, followed by a clicking sound. Humphreys pushing through another door, probably, into an access corridor. Hoping not to be overheard.

"A process." A whisper. "No more attacks. A trust-building process where they'll give us control back of our infrastructure one step at a time, provided we stop looking for them."

Wren laughed. "You'll never sell that to the American people. There's no way that's all you got."

Silence.

"Humphreys!"

"No. It's not everything."

"So tell me the rest! I'm out here at the edge. I've got irons in the fire. I need to know."

"I'm supposed to be shutting you down. Your Washington team are already on remand." A pause. "What irons?"

"Big things, Humphreys. You don't want to be on the wrong side of this when I rip the Blue Fairy to shreds. You know I'm not stopping; it's why you took the call. You want me to convince you, but I can't do that unless I know. What have they promised us?"

Humphreys took a breath and let out a shuddery sigh. Wren felt the shame weighing on him. Now he was taking the fate of the country in his hands, and he wasn't sure. He'd pay for this moment no matter what.

"No more abuse on American children," he said. "I mean, completely. Never again, anywhere, by anyone."

That didn't make sense. Wren twitched, trying to resolve it. "Explain."

"Just that. It's protection money. We give them safe harbor in international waters off our coast and some measure of protection and they use their second skin to keep our children safe. They'll snatch up any US-based abusers breaking the rules and deal with them. They'll protect us." His voice grew small. "Think of it, Wren. No more of our children facing that horror; we can sell that. The people will buy it, at least as long as they don't know the full cost. We-"

"So whose children will they be abusing?"

Humphreys said nothing. He didn't need to; the answer was obvious. The wide spread of the darknet allowed it. Increasing trends of nationalism would excuse it. Demographic shifts from zones of violent civil war would fuel it. Most people would be glad to accept the shift as long as their own lot in life improved.

Children from other countries. Children snatched from war zones. Children lost in the immigration system. Orphans, lost souls, prostituted sons and daughters brought to America's coastal fringes for abuse. They'd hush it up like never before. There'd be no official sanction of any of it, but it would happen.

Wren reeled at the scope of the Blue Fairy's ambition. This was just where it began. Next thing they'd go for constitutional change. New laws. They were looking at the moral corruption of a whole country. The Blue Fairy would own their souls.

Wren looked up at Rogers in the silence. She was staring at him aghast.

"Coming into the light," she said weakly.

"Coming into the light," Wren repeated, then tuned back into the call. Humphreys was talking now; low and fast words to cover up the shame.

"Do not negotiate," Wren said, over-riding the Director. "I'm warning you. I don't care what they offer, what promises they make. Do not give an inch or I'll be coming for you myself."

A moment passed. Time to choose sides.

"Where are you, Wren?"

There was the answer. Humphreys already starting to police for his new overlords.

"You'll never see me coming," Wren answered. "Think about that. If there's a decent bone in your body, you'll slow this thing down. Do whatever you can. Sacrifice yourself on this hill if you have to. Buy me some time."

He killed the call.

Rogers was staring at him. They'd wondered if they could trust Humphreys. Now they had their answer. Wren looked into her eyes, trying to get a read. Play it safe? Take a gamble? She was probably teetering right now, but turning on the CIA, the President and all the Joint Chiefs at once was a bold play.

"You've got nephews," he said. The hit landed. "Do you want to see them grow up on the Blue Fairy's terms?"

A moment passed. It was enough. Rogers took the phone from his hand and pinched the battery out, snapped the SIM card in half.

"They're going to throw everything at you," she said.

"At us," he said, "and they've tried that before."

Just then a clanking sound came from the head of the fuselage. It took Wren a moment to place it, but once he realized what it was it made perfect sense. Not his jet. Not his pilot.

The door to the cockpit had closed, the security bolts run home.

"They've already started."

His weight shifted subtly on the seat as the jet's vector changed. Rogers felt it too.

"They're turning the plane around."

30

AILERON

Wren drew his gun and strode up the aisle, only a few paces to the cockpit door. It was a light jet, maybe a Cessna Citation, with six porthole windows either side showing blipping red lights on the wings against a murky ocean of clouds. The turn accelerated and their altitude began to drop; the pilot had seen them on the internal security camera.

"You are under arrest, Christopher Wren," came a voice over the PA. Not Humphreys' voice; someone higher up, maybe. They must have been listening in on the call. "Special Agent Rogers, this is a direct command from the Director of USSOCOM; pacify Christopher Wren."

Wren didn't even turn to look at her. There was no time. The pilot knew their approximate flight plan; Wren had given a seven-state westbound corridor. Now the CIA knew that too, and if the CIA knew then so would the Blue Fairy.

Wren kicked the door to the cabin but the thick sheet metal didn't so much as flex. Standard cabin locks were triple bolted with recessed hinges, all baked into the superstructure of the plane.

The door wasn't going to open. The gun was useless against it.

He turned. The voice was saying something more, doubling down on his order to Rogers, and already she was torn. Wren had no cards at all, and this was a lost cause. They were prisoners on a flying tin can, and her career was vanishing before her eyes.

Wren raised his gun and dealt himself fresh cards, firing four rounds rapidly at the nearest porthole. The first shattered the inner plastic plate and ricocheted like a mad bee around the cabin, the second and third put cracks into the outer glass seal then chased the first, burying themselves in the upholstery and hand luggage holds, and the fourth blew through the glass with a resounding crash.

Instantly the thunderous roar of the engine flooded the fuselage, matched by a whipping hurricane wind that tore their air out into the upper atmosphere.

Forty thousand feet high, air pressure eighteen percent of ground level; in maybe a minute the fuselage would be drained completely of oxygen. Three minutes after that Wren and Rogers would be dead.

Rogers stared at him aghast, rocking against the gale-force pull of the wind. Only a second already and it was getting hard to breathe.

Wren kicked the door and shouted. "Open the door or I take out the aileron flaps. You'll lose control, maybe we all spiral out of the sky. You've got five seconds."

"Wren, give it up, he's-"

Wren didn't bother to count, he just turned and fired through the open window. The flashing tips on the wing provided a clear line of sight. He hit the nearest wing-flap and it buckled visibly.

"Try your ailerons now," Wren shouted. The voice called something over the speaker but Wren ignored it, watching the flaps through the window with the gun raised, ready to fire again. His breath grew ragged in the sucking rush as the seconds ticked down, waiting for-

The flaps moved; all down the left wing they waggled an inch, all except the panel Wren had pinged. It was jammed. At once the plane banked to the right. Rogers was thrown into a seat. Wren's head slammed off the luggage compartment, dropping him to his knees seeing stars. The air filled with noise and shouts through the PA, and Wren listened for only one thing, until finally it came.

The clunk of deadbolts sliding open.

He caught the door as it swung outward. The pilot on the other side had her hands up. No heroics. She knew that enough damaged flaps would bring the plane down just as surely as a bomb.

Wren took Rogers' arm and guided her into the cockpit. He was feeling light-headed. Now the air was being sucked from here too. Hopefully there'd be enough reserve in the tanks. That seemed a funny thought. He remembered children drowning in the backlots of the Pyramid's fake town. Not enough air for them all. Starting to die as the Apex watched. His father's eyes alight. There were some people you couldn't negotiate with. Your pain was their oxygen.

Rogers tugged him in, the security door slammed shut and the roar of sucking air faded, leaving just the hiss of oxygen replenishing the spent supply. Wren stood in the narrow, cooped entryway. The pilot was young, late twenties maybe, with cute freckles and auburn hair, wearing an FBI badge. Borrowed assets. The voice came from her headset in a thin, reedy stream.

"Take it off," he said, pointing. She removed the headset, held it out, then let it fall to the floor when Wren didn't take it. The voice squawked uselessly from within. "Move."

She moved. Rogers shuffled sideways. It was tight. Wren slid past her into the pilot's seat. The cockpit dash was an array of dials, lights and levers, most of which he didn't recognize. It was some time since he'd flown a plane. Never with a jammed aileron, of course, but there was a first time for everything.

He looked out through the windshield, to darkness and the odd faint contour of cloud tinged with moonlight. It was beautiful and unreal. He leaned closer to the instrument array, ignoring the dizziness and studying his dials and GPS. Off course now by easily ninety degrees.

"He ordered you to Offutt Air Force Base?"

"Yes," said the pilot.

"Sit down," he said, and she did it right there on the floor, by the door.

"I was following orders."

"New orders just came in. Rogers, take a seat."

Rogers slipped into the co-pilot's seat beside him.

"Settle in," he said, taking hold of the yoke and pulling it gently back and to the right. The jet responded sharply, banking right and up. "We're in for a bumpy ride."

31

MICROJET

On course again, Wren watched the dials and GPS scroll back to position, thinking. Rogers sat beside him, dealing with her own issues. They'd just hijacked an FBI jet. She'd ignored a direct order from her boss' boss. Best case scenario, her career in Defense was over. Worst case, she went to jail for treason after a humiliating court-martial.

"It'll be OK," Wren said, but it sounded like cold comfort even to his ears.

"How?"

"When we bring the Fairy down." He tried a smile but it didn't take. Rogers wasn't in the mood. He wasn't either. The odds ahead were bleak.

Three hours flight time lay before them, and the CIA knew their westward corridor. Humphreys didn't have enough to pinpoint a final destination, but he had easily enough time to mount a mid-air interception. Fighter jets could be scrambling even then from Offutt. Would he go that far?

Wren thought so.

"We need to go wholly dark," he said. "That means finding and neutralizing any location transponders on board."

Rogers just looked at him. Entering shock again. She was highly capable, but all this was a huge amount to take in. Most people didn't turn against US Intelligence in the midst of a national emergency. For Wren that was old hat. He softened his tone while sharpening his message.

"The alternative is Humphreys shoots us down. Intercept could be twenty minutes out. We don't want that, do we?"

She blinked, registering the threat. She hadn't thought that far ahead. That was why Wren got paid the big bucks. Now her brain started to work again.

"The black box transmits location," she said, and turned to the pilot. "Where is it?"

An uncomfortable silence.

"If they blow us up," Rogers went on, adopting Wren's softer tone, harsher message style, "you'll probably die too."

Wren smiled. Probably. That was a nice touch, and it worked. "It's in the back," the pilot said quickly, "under the gantry, above the rear wheel. You won't be able to get it out without serious cutting equipment, though, not while we're in flight."

"I'm not going to cut it." She looked at Wren. "I need your gun."

He handed it to her. She looked at the pilot.

"Pliers?"

"Uh, what? I, in the…" the pilot pointed at a compartment.

"Pipe?"

"What?"

"Never mind," said Rogers, scanning the cockpit now, looking for materials. Wren guessed what was coming; he knew she'd taken an advanced course in improvised explosives. With pliers she could crack the bullets, pour the powder into a narrow pipe, seal it with a crimp and a makeshift fuse, attach it to the black box's outer shell and fire a shaped charge directly through its GPS brain.

It would be humane, like captive-bolting a cow. All within the next twenty minutes before jets intercepted them, and limited by the airless environment in back.

"Do it," Wren said.

Rogers nodded. No time to worry about setting off an explosive in the undercarriage of a small jet. If she blew off the rear wheel then landing would be a real drag. If she hit a fuel line or the tail controls, they probably wouldn't even make it that far.

Probably. Wren's smile widened. Those were all problems for later.

"There'll be pinging software in the console as well," Rogers said, already stripping the magazine from Wren's gun and clicking the rounds out into her lap. "I can fry the box, but we need a software solution for the console."

"I'll handle it," said Wren. "Call it nineteen minutes."

She bent to work, enlisting the pilot in prizing off a console casing in search of a length of pipe. Wren picked up the headset and slipped it on. The voice was no longer bleating into the other end, so the headphones transmitted only white noise.

He found the radio dial and cranked it over, tapping in a password on the screen. It would be an ugly patched-up comms job, but that was the best he could do from here. The CIA would hear it. So be it.

He pressed to transmit. A signal shot out of the belly of the plane and pulsed down, recorded by local towers and converted into broadcast radio; one of the off-Internet systems he'd mentioned to Humphreys. He'd picked an old ham radio frequency that was barely policed; terrorists didn't use them because they were too easy to hack. Wren kept a few operational at all times; when linked to the Internet they offered an unexpected backdoor to the cyber world.

The CIA would track it and block it, but that would take time and Wren didn't need long. He listened to ancient whining and chittering as his signal passed through the internal circuits of an open-stream radio in a Minnesota apartment, then slipped on into the web. His password activated an existing protocol, opening a fresh re-routed channel that bounced perhaps three times around the world before hitting its destination.

Somewhere far off, a digital phone rang. The signal was picked up. A voice came back, excellent English slanted with an Eastern European accent.

"Christopher?"

"Hellion," Wren said, relieved. She was on the run, but never truly dark from the Internet. How could she be? "I'll be brief. You'll need B4cksl4cker for what's coming. I'm in a small FBI jet model number," he turned to the pilot. She stared back at him for a moment, midway in the process of hacksawing a metal pipe out of the wall, then blinked and answered.

"Cessna Citation M2."

Wren repeated that down the line. "I need a full hack of the software so no tracking signal is going out. I recommend you tunnel directly through the microwave spectrum; don't worry about the legality. We're looking at being shot down in," he checked the console, "seventeen minutes."

"Cessna Citation M2," Hellion answered, instantly focused on a new task. "Microwave tunnel, working." A pause. "Routing B4cksl4cker in." A pause. "You spoke to Dr. Ferat, then." Another pause. "We're worried about him. How is he?"

Wren gulped. No time to tell the truth right now, especially if he was basically their therapist. "He's fine. ETA on that hack?"

"I'm not with my main gear," Hellion answered through the scratchy connection. Wren could hear her fingers flying over the keyboard. Activating old data packets. Bringing up the specs. Probably stealing access to a red-wave cannon somewhere in their upcoming flight path. "And you're not supposed to contact us. Your Blue Fairy has burned our infrastructure to the ground. B4cksl4cker is very upset. It's years of work."

"He'll get over it. Whatever their second skin is, we'll co-opt it for you. The work's already been done."

More furious tapping. "That is one way to think of it. Christopher, tell me, did the doctor die well?"

For a moment he thought he'd heard her wrong, then realized he hadn't. It shook him. She'd just asked how Ferat was, but she'd already known. It was a test, and he'd failed.

She went on. "We were piggybacking the hack on his phone, so we heard it all. We watched the explosion from above on a stolen drone feed. You don't need to lie to us. The doctor was a great man and you used him like a butler." Her voice hummed with cold anger. "He valued you immensely, and that is why I answered this call. This is something we will speak about more."

Wren opened his mouth but didn't know what to say, or what to feel. Chastised, perhaps. "You're right. Thank you. We will."

"Good. Now B4cksl4cker has something to say."

The line clicked. B4cksl4cker's deep voice rolled in, heavy with his rolling Armenian intonation. "There are three jets coming your way, Christopher Wren. Weapons systems armed. Hellion has routed your Cessna's feed on a false route; the transmission will begin on our signal. I am killing low-range radar for you; splitting the time signature. You need to dive below ten thousand feet, and you will be invisible."

Wren didn't waste time marveling at how swiftly they worked. Midwest

American air security was probably as sturdy as cream cheese to them. "I will. There's the black box yet. We have to kill it too."

B4cksl4cker cursed in florid Armenian. "I will adjust my blackout timing. How long until it is dead?"

Wren turned to Rogers. She gave a thumbs up. On the floor lay empty shells and duct tape. In her hand was a slim pipe with a spike of magnesium ribbon sticking up through a crimped and duct-taped seal.

"Improvised," she said. Beside her lay a stripped panel and assorted flight controls. "Take-off circuits," she said, by way of explanation. She almost looked to be enjoying herself now. "We won't be needing them."

"Get it done."

"Yes, sir." She stood up. "And take a deep breath."

"Christopher?" B4cksl4cker prompted.

"Call it three minutes," Wren said into the headset, then took a deep breath just before Rogers clanked the internal deadbolts and opened the cockpit door. Immediately the near-vacuum of the fuselage ripped all the air away. The roar of the engines and buffeting wind came so loud he could barely hear B4cksl4cker.

Rogers and the pilot were already halfway to the back of the jet, holding on to seat backs against the sucking wind.

"Remember I am doing this for Dr. Ferat," said B4cksl4cker. "Not for you."

"Good," Wren said, croaking to conserve oxygen. "Honor him."

A moment passed. There was nothing more to say. They'd decided to answer, for whatever honor-among-hackers reason.

"We will help you in Idaho. Hellion has an idea. After this is finished, we will talk again about our relationship."

"That's more than fair," Wren croaked. Thirty seconds had passed and he was already feeling the pressure in his lungs. He looked back down the jet. The rush had stopped now, with the cabin equalized to the external pressure, but the roar of wind chopping past the open window was still cacophonous. Rogers and the pilot were kneeling in the aisle, hoisting up a metal panel.

Maybe a minute until they all began to asphyxiate. Already their fine motor control would be failing. One slip on the direction of the shaped charge, and…

He caught his mind wandering. No.

"What idea?" he croaked to B4cksl4cker.

"It involves drones. You will like it."

He hummed an answer. Thought about getting up and going back to help them, but knew a third body in that contained space would only snarl things up. A minute, just waiting now.

"I'm sorry about Dr. Ferat. I really am."

"We are too," answered B4cksl4cker. "The jets are within ten minutes range. You need to dive now, Christopher, or they will find you no matter what."

He looked around. Rogers and the pilot were just stumbling up into the cockpit. Two minutes? The pilot was on her knees already. Rogers was barely conscious, pale-faced and mouthing something he couldn't hear. In the airless environment sound traveled poorly. He read her lips as the door slammed shut.

"Brace."

He remembered what that meant just in time, and braced.

The back of the plane exploded.

32

BREATHE

The blast kicked like a bull and the little jet bucked; the back end driven down several inches, the front end thrown at a diagonal. The yoke wrenched from Wren's failing grip and he rocked out of his brace position into alarms and sudden smoke.

Smoke?

There was barely any oxygen still. The thin high hiss of air replenishing the cockpit came slow. Wren's vision blurred and he glimpsed Rogers vomiting to the side, the pilot pale on the floor, then a second hit came that smacked his head off the upper console as the jet entered a roll. An accidental explosion, or a missile...

No seatbelts, and they all rolled like rag dolls in an industrial drier. The pilot hit the wall then the ceiling then the other wall as the cabin spun, unconscious. Rogers took the hits like a cannonball. Wren clenched the yoke but it didn't stop the jet spinning him like a yo-yo; his thighs smacked the console, his knees dinged the ceiling, his hips came crashing down on the co-pilot's seat.

Screaming and spinning together, the roll became a corkscrew. They'd wanted him to dive. Distantly he heard B4cksl4cker's voice coming to him through the headset. "Christopher, this is too fast."

Too fast; that was funny. His hips hit the pilot, then hit the wall. A slap in the face came from Rogers' arm as it waved unconsciously in the tumble, then the jet bucked again; another explosion? The smoke thickened and he coughed as he rolled; oxygen mingling with fire was a bad combination aboard a jet.

"Too fast," came B4cksl4cker again, then he was gone as the headset came loose and the cable cinched tight around Wren's throat. He didn't need oxygen for the minute, and ignored the tightness around his windpipe to focus on pulling back on the yoke.

He got his legs under the console and pushed hard backward, wedging himself into the seat. The jet rolled crazily but he kept pulling. They were spinning faster now, multiple Gs, enough to knock out an astronaut as the structure of the jet wailed under the spiraling pressure. He eased up on the yoke; too much pressure now could shred the flaps or break off the back of the plane. God knew what damage they'd done with that blast.

He pulled slow but firm as bodies tumbled around him, ripping the cable off his neck before he could choke. The compass, altimeter, and artificial horizon spun madly in their sockets. Blood smeared the front windshield, but maybe, perhaps, the spin was slowing.

A corkscrew dive. Twenty thousand feet and dropping. He judged the spin and pulled right, countering the turn and pulling the jet into a steep dive. The pilot's body slapped the front glass and rolled down the console, switching buttons on or off. Somewhere in back various plane systems engaged and disengaged.

"Come on," Wren grunted, pulling on the yoke. "Come on!"

The fuselage shrieked under the pressure; a high metallic whine. Metal under incredible torsion, bending. He imagined the cabin cracking apart like an egg and bleeding seats and microwaveable meals into the atmosphere. What a strange rain.

"Aaarrgh!" he screamed and pulled, arms and shoulders straining, legs braced either side against the underdeck, until finally-

The jet leveled. Wren sat panting. Rogers lay tumbled with her face in the co-pilot's foot well, her hips balanced precariously on the seat, her feet in the air. The pilot was contorted in back. Maybe they were breathing, Wren couldn't tell, but they wouldn't be soon if he didn't do something. Fire and oxygen meant another explosion. Something in the back had ruptured, probably an air line.

He'd have to risk it again.

He stood and accidentally garroted himself as the headset cord pulled tight. He caught a displeased-sounding B4cksl4cker saying, "...take this seriously, please, Christopher. Bear southwest, telemetry-"

Wren grabbed the cord and wrenched it over his head like a too-tight sweater, then barked into the mic. "Fly the damn plane!"

He didn't wait for a reply. He hit the door release and shoved the metal door open. The air sucked out for the third time, along with the smoke. Wren strode over the pilot and looked back down the cabin.

Smoke gushed from the place Rogers had blown the black box, pouring up and heading straight through the broken window like a floating river. An electrical fire. Already he wanted to breathe, but all the oxygen was getting burned up before it reached him. In the tiny crew galley, he snapped open three cabinets flush to the wall; in the last was a small fire extinguisher. He pulled it out and tore the restraining plastic strip free even as he advanced down the aisle and into the flow of smoke.

The black fumes blinded him, but he kept moving forward, counting his paces and feeling his way until his feet hit the gap where they'd lifted the panel. He leaned in, getting a geysering face full of hot smoke, and fired the extinguisher.

White powder rushed out to quench the black. For ten seconds Wren held it tight, spraying evenly until the black smoke stopped and sucked away and the white smoke sucked away as well and he was left on his back sucking at the thin air.

Probably now he would die?

Too late. He tried to get up but silvery lights flashed and he couldn't move. His muscles had no fuel. What a way to go.

But he didn't go anywhere.

He lay there breathing. The air was good?

He rubbed his eyes. His arms worked. His brain was slow to fathom it. Seven thousand feet, had the altimeter said? Air at approx. eighteen percent oxygen, only three percent less than ground. Only half as high as Everest. That was fine...

He pushed himself up. He felt like he'd been battered and deep-fried. He staggered back to the cockpit. He knelt by the pilot, checked her pulse. It was weak but stable. He laid her out in the recovery position and moved to Rogers.

She was breathing with shallow pants, lying on the floor. He set her in the co-pilot's chair and strapped her in. Superficial wounds on her arms and scalp, and a broken left arm.

"I'll be all right," she croaked.

Wren hoped it was true, and patted her good arm gently. "Just hang in, OK?" His throat was raw from the cable garrote and smoke. He put on the headset again.

"B4cksl4cker."

"Christopher. What is happening there?"

"We're fine," he said. The details didn't matter. B4cksl4cker only really cared for three people in the world; himself, his mother, and Hellion. Maybe he had cared for Dr. Ferat, but that was done now. "Tell me about this idea with drones."

33

BLUE FIST

The Cessna's fuel ran out a hundred miles from the planned airstrip.

"There's more air friction at these lower altitudes," Rogers said. "Slowing us down."

Wren grunted and ran adjustments. Rogers was looking better, and that was good. She'd made a makeshift sling for her arm with her jacket, and a quick check of her pupils had shown no obvious signs of concussion.

"We're lucky we got this far," Wren said.

"Lucky," Rogers repeated.

It had been a strange flight, controlled by Hellion's autopilot program remotely. Three hours together with the unconscious pilot and the chop chop of air smacking across the broken window in back, like an endlessly racing pulse. Talking about what was to come, and what lay ahead.

They didn't make any calls out. Wren didn't check his darknet. Only the microwave tunnel to Hellion and B4cksl4cker remained open, offering their flat-toned updates on the world beyond. At one point Rogers got up, opened the door to the back cabin, and went into the fuselage.

The air grew thinner with the door open, but not desperately so. Wren didn't question it. She had the right. She came back after a distinctive ping rang out, carrying two piping hot microwave meals. Wren hadn't eaten since the plane to Detroit twenty-four hours earlier, and wolfed down his Beef Strips in Red Wine Sauce.

"I looked for a soy latte for you," Rogers said, cracking a smile. "Couldn't find one. Here's the next best thing." She held out a sealed plastic cup containing jelly-like cubes, some kind of tofu dessert. Wren knocked them back in one gulp.

At some point he drowsed, letting B4cksl4cker's jury-rigged autopilot take control. Hellion occasionally reported to them on movements across the country.

"National Guard standing down in Sacramento, Phoenix, Gatlinburg, Orlando," she said, her voice a monotone drone. "Police forces reported pulling off the streets in New York, Las Vegas, Philadelphia, Dallas. No news of further Pinocchio strikes. Fewer stories are getting through on social media before deletion. There's no public statement on any of this. Just algorithms shuffling through a catch and kill routine for certain keywords."

The words washed over Wren as he tossed and turned in the pilot's seat. Too many bruises and cuts to stay in any one position for long. Too much uncertainty in the country down below, as the United States entered an uneasy night of détente.

Negotiating.

Wren drifted.

More reports of the media clamping down followed, puncturing his fitful sleep. Field agencies closed their doors. Washington hunkered down in a warlike pose, Congress was called to an emergency session, the Joint Chiefs were meeting with the President and heads of major intelligence agencies.

Humphreys was there still, apparently, in the White House and determining national policy. That meant the CIA would be out hunting for Wren everywhere. His Foundation, his contacts. There was no going back.

"What do they want?" Rogers asked at one point. Maybe ninety minutes in, with some color back in her cheeks. After the food, before the fuel began to run dry. Somewhere over South Dakota. Wren stirred from uncomfortable, chilly slumber. The blast to the black box must have damaged the heating systems.

He looked at her. Still bloodshot eyes. Maybe she'd been crying. He didn't have an answer though. Maybe in Idaho they'd find one. He closed his eyes and dreamed of a new America overshadowed by a great blue fist.

"Boss," Rogers said, waking him again. "The fuel."

The fuel. He looked at the gauge, then at maps and judged the distance.

B4cksl4cker and Hellion made their reports through the microwave tunnel while he checked. It seemed like they hadn't stopped talking all through the night. 4 a.m. now. It would be light in three hours.

"I'll put us down on the Interstate," Wren said, rubbing grit from his eyes. I-15 was the target. They would come in on an arc north of Ririe, heading to Gebhart's abandoned farm in a broad valley sandwiched between Yellowstone and the Salmon-Challis National Forest.

"You can fly a jet?" Rogers asked.

"Land, yes. At least, I've done it in smaller propeller planes. How much difference can there be?"

Rogers laughed. "About three times the speed and ten times the mass. How about that?"

Wren felt like laughing too. Looked at the pilot, deep into unconsciousness. "You have a better idea?"

Rogers said nothing for a moment, then nodded. "So we brace hard."

"Brace hard and think of apple pie. Strap in."

She did. Wren looked out over the landscape ahead as the plane began to rattle, running on fumes. Countless tight constellations of light sparked into the distance; tiny towns like nodes in a nervous system, connected by a network of interweaving roads. I-15 swooped to the west, flatlining against the massive darkness of Yellowstone Park. The Cessna seemed so small next to all that.

His eyes welled up. The dry air, he told himself. The lights far below seemed to throb with a slowing, sickened pulse. America looked so innocent from above. Its people had no idea what kind of black dawn was coming. The Blue Fairy was ascendant and Wren could feel it in the air, drawing down over the Internet and the world like a blinding, gagging mask.

How strange it was, to go to sleep in one country and wake in another, with the monsters walking freely in their midst.

Pinocchios following their whims. They would all be complicit.

The plane rattled. Wren held the yoke and gritted his teeth.

"I'm taking us down."

Rogers clutched the belt across her chest and gave him a nod. It came to this. Wren guided the yoke down and the Cessna tipped into a dive.

34

GOOD PEOPLE

The glide path stretched ahead, I-15 swerved and Wren tracked it. Three thousand feet already, and both engines were slowing.

"My team's almost in position," came Hellion on the microwave tunnel. "Within an hour. We see nothing there now. No movement at the farm. We'll talk to you-"

The signal cut out. At three thousand feet there was too much domestic interference on the spectrum. Wren clicked the send/receive button a few times but nothing followed. They were on their own now, moving forward on faith alone, watched over by a pair of hacker gods.

"It feels like we're going underwater," Rogers said.

Wren knew just what she meant; descending through the Blue Fairy's 'second skin' on the Internet. Into a world soon to fall under their total control. Two thousand five hundred feet. Their airspeed slowed; dragged by increasing friction and flagging engines. Much longer and the engines would cut out, leaving them to glide, then to drop.

Two thousand feet. The stepped woodlands of the Salmon-Challis National Forest lay dark to the west, while the glories of Yellowstone were lost in shadow to the east. Just the two of them.

"Go to ground," Wren said without looking at her. "Don't go to a hospital. They'll be monitoring every check-in. Every camera. The world just turned against us."

"I'm coming with you," Rogers answered, offering no argument, only a fact. "You mentioned my nephews? I didn't think you knew they existed. Either way, you'll know I'm dying on this hill too."

Wren glanced over, saw that hard-charging certainty in her eyes. "Dominic and Tom," he said. "Six and nine, your sister's boys. Last summer you all went fishing together."

Rogers snorted. "You're a weird guy, boss. We never talked about them once."

"Usual order of business, I never would. But you're on my team, you better believe I know everything I need to."

"Good," said Rogers. "Same here. Your kids; Jake and Quinn. You had any word?"

That was painful, like a hypodermic dart in his side, but not unexpected. "Foundation has eyes on. They're home. That's all I can do, for now."

Rogers nodded. "Good enough. The things we do for the next generation, huh?"

Wren grinned.

The left engine cut out. Abruptly the terrible chopping sound of air through the broken window became a high, haunting wail; like breath blown across an open bottle top. It sounded to Wren like a funeral dirge.

One thousand feet. He braced his feet and they sank. The altimeter spun like the dials in a Vegas fruit machine. Down, down. Looking for a chance to merge into sparse traffic below. There was no window in the floor and soon he'd lose sight of the road.

He pulled back on the yoke, coaxing a few extra miles out of their momentum, waiting on a straight section of I-15.

"We're going to kill them all," Rogers said. Almost to herself. She was right there beside him, but Wren felt lonely still, with the funeral note wailing out from behind them, with his hackers cut off and his Foundation dispersed, with the FBI turned against them and the country on a precipice preparing to jump.

"Final descent," Wren said, and leveled the yoke as the right engine went out. The low roar of combustion fled, leaving only the desperate pulse of wailing wind as they entered a glide. Intermittent lights on the highway raced toward them, cars streaming red and white, five hundred feet left to fall. Trees sped up toward them, the landscape opened to swallow them. At three hundred feet Wren engaged the landing gear and the front wheels clunked into position, though he didn't expect the rear wheel to deploy.

It was going to be a rough landing. If he'd misjudged the road ahead. If he'd made any one of a number of mistakes. Two hundred feet now, and treetops whipped by, seconds only and always the most dangerous part. One hundred feet, dropping far faster than they should, coming in hard and he pulled back on the yoke until-

The back hit blacktop with another explosive kick, then the front gear touched down and the wheels stripped away in a few violent, juddering seconds. The cabin wrenched and metal tore then the cockpit dropped the final three feet to the road as the gear splintered, slamming down to skid along on its belly. Sparks flared up across the front glass and a terrible grinding filled Wren's ears, then the cockpit veered toward the edge, tilting so far that the right wing clipped the ground and jerked the vehicle into a dizzying spin.

Round, round, heading for the trees far too fast, skidding and sparking and screaming until finally-

It stopped.

Wren breathed out. They were tilted but motionless. The air was good, if charged with the noxious smells of burning rubber and melting metal. The thin carpet underfoot smoked. Hot through his shoes. He looked at Rogers and she looked at him.

"That counts as a good landing," she said. "Under the circumstances."

"We're alive. Come on."

He unbuckled. A car honked its way past them on the highway outside. Red taillights disappeared into the darkness. What kind of person honked at a plane after an emergency landing? Someone soon enough would call it in, and it wouldn't take long for Humphreys to hear about it. How many busted-up Cessnas were landing across the country at any given time?

He'd get teams in the air. They had an hour or less, a scant lead.

Wren stood, shoulder-charged the jammed cockpit door and stepped over the pilot's prone body. The back of the jet was a jumbled wreck, with the spine of the plane broken in the middle. Through the windows he saw that the right wing had shredded, leaving it spiky with threadbare metal feathers. The ground was only a few feet away, with no landing gear to raise them up. He walked along the tilted aisle, leaning on the baggage cupboards. The exit door opened with a swift twist and shove, and he dropped down onto the dusty verge.

The underside of the plane was scored with deep weals that glowed an angry red. The asphalt underneath it glistened; melted by the heat. A slug-like trail ran behind them, scored in shining black tar. It was good there was no fuel left; that kind of instant heat could have caused the pressurized tanks to explode.

Rogers followed behind him swiftly, holding her broken arm close.

"Is that all right?" he asked. She had to be in a lot of pain.

"Fine," she said.

Wren nodded, and strode into the middle of the highway to flag a vehicle. In thirty seconds, an SUV stopped. A young family were aboard. Wren wanted to let them go, but couldn't afford it. They pulled over, goggling at the wreck of the jet, and rolled the window down.

"My God," the driver said, a young woman. "Are you folks all right?"

A young man sat in the passenger seat with two kids in the back, looking up with surprised, scared faces. Six and seven, maybe. Holding their tablets, watching movies or playing games.

"I'm sorry," said Wren, holding his badge out. "I'm with the Central Intelligence Agency, and we're in the middle of a pursuit. I need to requisition this vehicle."

The woman stared at him. It wouldn't take much to push her over the edge, he figured, to hit the gas and race away. He'd given her no reason to trust him.

"Please," he said. "You see our plane. My partner's injured. We've come a long way to stop some very bad people, and we need to get there now."

"What people?" she asked. Southern accent. A Texan, with her family on a trip to the National Parks. It seemed like, in that dark and uninhabited place, she had a right to know.

"Monsters," said Wren. "Trying to take our country from us. Tomorrow things will be very different in America, if we can't get where we're going. The lives of your children won't be the same."

She didn't know him. Still, something in his eyes gave her pause. Maybe the spattered blood, maybe the badge, maybe Rogers with her sling. She killed the engine. Her husband nodded, and in an orderly fashion with very little trouble, they began to rouse the kids.

"And I need a phone," Wren said, as she climbed out and passed him the keys. "I'll find you when all this is over and get it back to you, I promise."

The young man handed his phone over in silence. It was strange and surreal in the dark. The kids got out carrying their tablets and a few blankets. Bleary-eyed, confused, but ready to give what they had for this strange man and woman who'd landed a plane on the highway, who looked so desperate.

"Thank you," Wren said. His eyes welled again but he brushed it away. No time for that. He climbed in and Rogers followed. There were good people in America still.

He hit the gas and raced north, while Rogers made the 911 call for the family and the pilot.

35

IDAHO

The SUV plunged into darkness. The roads were empty and the woods either side were black and impenetrable. Every little sound seemed amplified: Wren's hand rustling on the wheel; the tiny squeak of the gas pedal moving up a fraction, down a fraction. It was made worse by tinnitus from the blast at Jeffries' house. From all the blasts.

Wren switched on the radio. A sad country song faded into the news, but there was nothing real in it. Talks in Brussels going well for the EU's new religious liberty law. Three dead in a school shooting. A new tunnel discovered under the Mexican border wall. The usual, and nothing about the Blue Fairy strikes. As if they hadn't even happened.

Wren clicked it off. Silence and the ringing in his ears were better.

"How can they silence the media so completely?" Rogers asked. She didn't look at him. She didn't even really want an answer. It was just a way to fill the awful, resonating silence.

"They've done it before," Wren said, not really answering for her. More just to fill the emptiness. "Lincoln did it."

Rogers looked over. Her eyes asked the question.

"In the Civil War, alongside suspension of habeas corpus," Wren went on. He'd studied all of this once. Memorized it. There were countless routes to an American dystopia, and he'd measured them all. "He seized the telegraphs. Destroyed newspapers. Made disloyalty to the Cabinet a crime.

404

People were imprisoned for speaking against the war. For speaking against him personally." A silence. "They called him King Lincoln. We don't talk about that much."

Rogers looked away. Not the answer she wanted to hear. But she was no child. Working in the CIA, you knew what fail-safes the government had built into every means of communication. They owned the infrastructure. The words. The enforcement. With habeas corpus they owned every citizens' body too.

Now the world was changing.

Minutes ticked by and the darkness grew thicker around them, closing in like an oppressive force. Wren imagined Humphreys and the others around a table, hammering out possibilities. Just men and women, deciding the fates of other men and women. They had no more right than him to make these decisions.

An hour passed, 5 a.m. Trees grew tall around them; Ponderosa pine needling the stars. Wren made the turn off the Interstate onto 287, past the silent town of Three Forks. Now the only light came from their headlights, sending cones out over the dusty blacktop. The vehicle climbed into barren clay mountains scarred by centuries of acid run-off from copper mining.

"What if there's nothing there?" Rogers asked. Her voice was stark after such complete silence.

"Then we keep looking."

"Looking where?"

"Wherever we can."

Ten miles on they descended into a sparse valley, like a crater of rugged life amidst the dead red rock. Another turn followed, west before Toston. Wren killed the lights and drove by starlight. The pig farm lay ahead somewhere. Gebhart's farm. Burned alive with his wife and daughter. Only ruins left behind.

Wren thought of Ferat. His truck would have stopped burning now. Crushed at the base of a cliff. His body charred and broken.

"Boss," said Rogers, pointing.

To the left ran a ramshackle wooden fence, broken in places. Wren slowed, and they came upon a gate standing at the head of a drive, buckled on its hinges, seesawed at an angle. Give it a few more years of rust, rain and freeze-thaw cycles and it would collapse. The pig farm. Dead intestate, Ferat had said. No will, and no heirs left to carry it on. Probably the paperwork was still grinding its way through the bowels of a government building somewhere.

Not a place he'd aspire to. Wren pulled off the road onto a narrow earth bridge over the encircling drainage ditch. Starlight illuminated the empty pig enclosures. Small fenced sections, gradually collapsing through neglect. Dark expanses of empty boxes. In the distance, at the end of a long and weedy gravel drive, sat the fire-bitten husk of the farmhouse.

A shudder passed up Wren's spine.

On the day Gebhart had died his pigs must have begun to starve. Wren imagined them frantic in their cages, like the Pyramid's captives in the fake town. Ramming their bodies against the wood, against their brothers and sisters. Thinning out, eating mud and drinking rain, biting each other in desperation. The first would die and the others would eat, until there was only one left. Lying in the mud, looking up at the sky and wondering if this was all there was…

"Boss," prompted Rogers.

Wren killed the engine, opened the door and strode out. The air was cold. Good. He touched his holster; a gun but no bullets. Rogers had used them all for her shaped charge. He was unarmed. If the Pinocchios came now he'd be defenseless.

The gate hung on a simple chain lock. He didn't have bolt cutters.

"We go through," he said, getting back in the SUV. It would leave an obvious trail, but the vehicle was an obvious sign anyway. He rolled the truck forward, pressing against the gate. It gave no resistance; screw plugs sucked out of the rotten fencepost like cores from a lump of cheese. The gate half-collapsed then splintered under the wheels. What would have taken Nature years took the SUV seconds.

The gravel crunched under the wheels. Wren rolled all the windows down, listening to the wind. Smelling the air. There wasn't a hint left of the corruption that must have been everywhere after the die-off began. Flies would have buzzed thickly for months. All gone.

Barren cells passed either side. The farmhouse drew nearer: a swing set out front with the chains rusted away; an old Chevy up on blocks. Graffiti covered it thickly. A woodpile, outbuildings that had been broken apart by local vandals. The porch was intact, the swing still hung, though there were scattered cans and bottles littered around.

The ground floor windows were shattered and the frames blackened.

Flyscreens lay pierced on the floor; around the side a pile of tires had been melted into a jelly-like mound, half-absorbing a stack of wooden pallets. The dirt in front was dry and scrubby, with patches of stubborn pampas grass pushing through.

Wren pulled up. The first floor had been cut away at a diagonal on the northeast corner, leaving a few roof rafters poking through like desiccated ribs. White boards on the front stopped abruptly where the fire had chewed down. The master bedroom, perhaps, completely gone. There was no place to hide the SUV. He pulled around to face the drive, in the event of a swift exit.

"There can't be anything left here," Rogers said, gazing at the ravaged structure. Graffiti coated its face like tawdry makeup. Basic tags. A hangout for local youth. Their DNA would be everywhere, polluting fingerprints. Rot would have set in throughout. There'd be no evidence of any kind left; looted or burned after nine years. Anything electronic would have long ago degraded. "There's nothing."

Wren got out, stood in front of the building and felt another shiver. Not just the cold. This was it, he felt certain. No neighbors within miles. Pigs to dispose of any organic evidence. In the back, a satellite dish big enough to wash a hog in. He pointed.

"Could just be for TV," Rogers said, stepping out alongside him. Shivering too in the chill. No snow on the ground, but the melt wasn't long past. "There's no easy signal out here."

"That's a satellite scoop," Wren said. "Gebhart could pull down gigabits a second with that. The mountains would scramble any attempt at detection. It's a perfect hiding place."

Rogers frowned. The dish was a tarnished, graffiti-tagged moon on a metal frame. Clearly swung out of place by vandals, but too well-secured to rip free. Precision controlled to the millimeter. Anchored deep.

"Pull data down or send it back up," Rogers said.

Wren started forward. The porch boards creaked under his weight. The nearest beer cans were cracked and rusted. Nobody had been by for years. The place was cursed, anyone could feel that. The fog of all those dead pigs still hung in the air.

The door stood ajar. Wren pushed and it swung in on groaning hinges.

36

GEBHART

hat was a house but walls and a roof?

Wren wondered this as he advanced into the smoke-blackened darkness. Once a hallway; here a place to shake off boots muddy with pig filth, there a plaque on the wall serenading Home Sweet Home. Shriveled photos in cracked frames lay broken underfoot. A homestead from the 19th century. Wooden walls that bent and flexed. A roof that collapsed more each year as the wind swayed through the gaping windows. Gradually dissolving, turning a home into a ruin, into a heap, into dust. Like the fake town. Like the Pyramid.

Wren turned right through an open doorframe and Rogers followed. The air was musty here. Damp had gotten into everything. There was a thick fur of moss on the walls where rainwater had run down. The den was obliterated, with holes bashed through the outer shell. The broken wooden frame of a sofa lay crumpled like a carcass at the edge, bones mummified by their own upholstered leather skin. The TV was shattered glass and wood in the corner. A coffee table was kindling, the floor was strewn with papers and weeds grew up in a damp patch in the central boards.

"Cozy," said Rogers.

There was no ceiling here, only stars above. Wren stood in the middle looking out through large holes to the desolate yard outside. Pipes and cables dangled in the gaps. Vandals had done much of this, not the fire. It gave the lie to the official story.

"They didn't burn to death," he said.

Rogers grunted.

"Smoke might have killed one of them, but not both. Coughing would have woken the husband or the wife. Upstairs was most likely the master. The girl's bedroom would be down the hall. She could have roused them. This is the only part of the house that burned badly."

Rogers looked up, imagining the contours of the missing room above. Maybe the sky was lightening already, as dawn set in. It felt like a hard deadline. They had to be done by daybreak, or what, the Pinocchios would come? In and out of the tomb before the vampires came.

"You think the master was above us?"

"No doubt of it," Wren said. "The biggest room in an old house like this, looking out over the pigs? It's what any farmer would want. Last thing at night, first thing in the morning."

"OK. So let's say they didn't burn. What happened?"

Wren shrugged. He had his theories. Nothing in this room would confirm them. Through one of the wall holes he saw the twisted satellite dish. Fifteen paces away, maybe.

He strode into the adjoining dining room. A rustic farmhouse tabletop lay on its belly with its legs splayed. The back door was missing, so an open rectangle led down steps into an overgrown yard. Spikes of plastic toys lay in the long grass. There'd been children here once. How old had the daughter been?

He did the quick math: Mona Gebhart would have been sixteen when they died. Ten years ago. She hadn't been the one playing with those toys.

Wren passed through the kitchen. Getting a feel for the place. Studying the walls, the floor. Thin here. Thick here.

"She did this," he said, standing at the bottom of the stairs looking up. "Clara."

Rogers made a face. "You mean Mona? Records say the Gebhart daughter died in the fire. There's no solid evidence that was our Clara."

Wren shook his head, seeing the pieces. "She set the fire. A cover story. But sheriffs never found her parents' bodies. Whatever fire burned here, it was far from hot enough to incinerate bone. The wind blew it out, kept it from taking the back of the house."

"Supposition. So where are the bodies?"

"Here."

He went upstairs. The boards creaked. It was getting lighter now, illuminating his path by tiny fractions. The top landing was bare and black. Walls shimmered silver where rain had glossed the soot, stretching away into empty air. A doorframe alone stood, last remnant of the master bedroom, with the walls and roof burned away. Graffiti cans lay at the edges of the hall. Wren paced the other way.

A room on the right had a bedframe and tangled bedding, sprouting with weeds. A little girl's room, with faded cartoons from the Pinocchio story on the walls. Pinocchio himself, the Blue Fairy, Geppetto, the children turned to donkeys on Pleasure Island. There were also crude graffiti messages.

DEATH LIVES HERE

Wren pointed.

"Doesn't mean much," Rogers said, but her tone was shifting.

In the family bathroom there was a metal frame embedded in the wall, peeking through holes torn by vandals. Looked like braces for a heavy load, suggesting an unusually large water tank. Another sign.

"What?" Rogers asked, looking from Wren to the braces. "That's structural."

"In a nineteenth-century homestead? Come on."

Rogers followed him back down. Into the living room again, Wren imagined Gebhart's routine. Keep his eyes on the pigs at all times, and his prisoners too. Wren reached into one of the sledge-hammered holes in the wall, touching the pipes. They were clad in relatively new insulating foam. He envisaged the plumbing map, coming down from the water tank in the attic.

At the wall he kicked away the remains of the sofa. It shouldn't be too hard to find what he was looking for. They'd want to get regular access. Mr. and Mrs. Gebhart both. It couldn't be hidden too well. Like the pigs, there'd be regular feeding. Regular slaughters.

"Here," he said, looking at a stretch of plain pine floorboards.

"Here what?" Rogers sounded doubtful. "You think we'll find a trapdoor?"

"We will." He pointed at the hole in the wall. "See the pipes and cabling? There's no need for those here, but here they are. To what? New wires too. One of those outbuildings probably covers a sump pump, ventilation."

Rogers frowned, studying the boards as if they might give up their secrets by deeper contemplation. Her face was purplish in the new light, shadowed with bruises. "You're serious. You think there was some kind of bunker down here?"

"There still is," Wren said, and knelt. It seemed obvious. Clara had been careful not to burn this spot. This was a memorial for her, a way of stamping back control, just like the fake town was for him.

He dug his fingernails into a crack in the boards. Closely seamed. He prized, but there was no give. Good workmanship. He scanned the skirting board. Neat and flush. He tapped it; even all round. No signs at all, but the pipes wouldn't lie. Not out here on the edge of civilization, where efficiency was everything. Conserving heat. You didn't run hot water all around the walls for nothing.

He looked wider, to the corners. He took out his phone and tapped the flashlight on. Rogers winced, but they were in this now. The SUV was out front. If Pinocchios were coming, they were already on their way.

Wren turned in a circle, casting light around the living room. On the second pass he saw it, a small divot by the baseboard in the corner. Recessed in a natural knothole in the wood. He strode over and stuck his finger into the hole. His fingernail tickled metal.

"What?" Rogers asked.

"Give me your belt."

Rogers stared, then unspooled her belt. The buckle was narrow. Wren inserted it into the gap. It caught on the catch inside, like a hook. He stepped back and pulled, but it wasn't long enough. He was still standing on the trapdoor cover. He unspooled his belt, buckled it into hers, then stepped back and pulled. Still not long enough. He cast about, snatched up a piece of wood with a nail in it, punched it through his belt, stepped back then tried again.

Rogers watched like an audience waiting for the magician to pull off the trick. Wren pulled harder. There was a crack like a gunshot, startling them both, then a large patch of the floor shifted. Heat and cold had wedged the trapdoor into place. Wren pulled harder, another crack came, then the trapdoor rose. Easily five feet on a side, itself as big as a small room, the hinge just in front of Wren's feet.

Rogers gasped. It kept coming. It rose and rose, half the floor.

Wren moved to the side and caught the wooden cover. A metal frame supported the boards on a squealing hinge. Six inches beneath that lay a broad oblong of raw concrete, with a metal hatch tucked flush inside it as big as a refrigerator door.

"Gebhart," Wren said. Now the trapdoor stood open like the lid of a grand piano. Rogers kicked it further, breaking the hinge backward so the wood slammed to the floor. There was no way they'd get caught inside.

Wren's heart began to pound. He looked in Rogers' eyes and reached for the hatch's handle.

37

PRISON

Wren's mouth was dry. The hatch cover lifted easily, on some kind of spring-release. Light spilled up from within, white and harsh, illuminating cement steps leading down.

Rogers cursed under her breath.

For a second they both stared. Working lights? Wren counted the steps. Ten. Dribbles of oil stained them. Maybe blood. Ten feet underground. The light came from industrial strip lights on the sides. That explained the cabling. Pipes ran above the wires. There was also a strange mechanical sound, like an air conditioner whirring in the distance.

"There's power," Rogers added.

Wren said nothing. Working things out.

"How is that possible?"

"It means she was coming back."

Rogers looked at him.

"Clara," he went on. "Mona. Back to the source. It's common behavior for survivors of childhood trauma. Revisit the scene, like she can overcome it somehow." He didn't mention his visits to the fake town, gasoline and lighter in tow. He didn't need to. Everyone on his team knew his history.

"So she comes here," Rogers said. "Regularly. I get that. But she keeps the power running at all times, too? For what?"

"Do you hear that sound?"

They both fell silent. Leaned in. A chugging sound. Perhaps more like a steam train than an air conditioner.

"What the hell is it?"

"Let's find out."

Wren started down. The opening was big enough. The stairs dropped sharply. It would be easy to descend with a burden, like a child over the shoulder. A slight duck, leaning back as he hit the seventh step to avoid his head grazing the opening, then he was at the bottom.

Raw, dry concrete walls stretched to the west for maybe eight yards. A narrow passageway, barely tall enough for him to stand, sealed with a metal door at the far end. There was no smell at all, except maybe the dry fuzz of ozone, electrical equipment drying out the air.

"Come on down."

Rogers followed. The sound was louder here. A piston, maybe, pumping endlessly. This was Clara's handiwork, Wren felt certain. He was beginning to understand her. She was like him, really. Darkness as a child followed by vengeance as an adult. She'd picked up catfishing, he'd become a special ops Marine. He'd built the Foundation, she'd single-handedly maneuvered people like Reince Jeffries into action. They weren't so different.

"I don't want to know what's on the other side of that door."

"Let's hope she left it open," Wren said, and advanced. Eight paces only, out from under the footprint of the house and into the dirt of the yard. Gebhart must have used an earthmover to clear all this. Working alone, including drainage canals, foundational rebars and concrete pours, it must have taken months of work and thousands of dollars.

But who would have known? Out here in rural Idaho, surrounded by the pigs, it was only visible from above. Call it a wine cellar and he was fine. No permissions required. A dungeon in your backyard.

The door was metal, with three large pneumatic bolts. On the wall to the right was a screen showing white static, a keypad with nine digits. No way to know how many numbers in the passcode. No way to guess. Would she have left it open?

He pushed the door. It moved. He said a silent prayer to Clara Baxter and pushed it the rest of the way. Eight more yards of concrete corridor lay beyond, ending in a dark wooden board with glints of silver. The back of a mirror? It was narrower here. Wren had seen similar designs before, in homemade dungeons. The plans circulated on the darknet. The narrow, long corridor offered no room for the captive to struggle, no place to lay in wait, no way to charge or swing back a makeshift weapon.

A camera hung overhead. Gebhart would order his captives to retreat to the end of the corridor if they wanted food. It made escape attempts impossible. One way in, one way out, with the camera to confirm, all planned out meticulously.

The piston-like sound was much louder now. Wren could feel the vibrations through the floor. Like a dentist's drill.

"This place is sick," Rogers said. Calmly. Wren knew she'd seen things like it before, raided staged sets in CIA training, but nothing really prepared you for the reality.

Wren grabbed a chunk of rotten wood fallen down from the trapdoor and wedged the heavy metal door open, then advanced up to push on the wooden board. It opened outward on oiled hinges, and the sound from beyond grew abruptly cacophonous, hitting Wren like a jackhammer as he gazed into the space beyond.

Clara had arranged a tableau. It took Wren a moment to take it in. The room was a square space maybe eight yards by eight, with rich mahogany boards on the floor and lush orange light glowing from subtle wall sconces. It was warm, perhaps underfloor heating. Mirrors covered several walls, while others were decked with padded red leather.

Equipment was spread around the sides. Frames. Tools. Several large wooden chests no doubt contained more, but none of that was what drew his eye.

There were cameras in the middle of the space. Red lights blinked. Wren stared. Transmitting now? Six cameras stood in a clutch of power lines, two of them in operation, pointing at two figures in the tableau. Slightly to the left sat a mangy, withered corpse in a chair bolted to the floor. Dressed in a white nightgown, yellowed in places, with skeletal arms lashed to the chair. White hair cascaded down a sunken, mottled face.

"Oh no," said Rogers, pushing past Wren. She covered her ears against the terrible hammering.

"Mrs. Gebhart," Wren said.

Rogers gagged. Mrs. Gebhart had decayed in an air-conditioned, clinical environment; more of an evaporation. Moisture had sucked out of her pores, tightening her skin like a mummy. Still, she'd watched. Her chair was angled to face the companion piece in this dark performance art installation.

Mr. Gebhart. The sound drilled in Wren's ears.

Lance Gebhart's desiccated corpse was held upright in a metal frame, like a gibbet, draped in a kind of white ceremonial tunic. His lips were curled back tight in a silent, permanent scream.

Before him lay the machine making all the noise: a single long slim piston that pumped backwards and forwards with powerful force. A blade on the end, stabbing a well-worn groove through his chest, into the place his heart should have been.

Wren felt his own gorge rise.

Three motors sat neatly on the floor, attached to the piston mechanism. Each had some kind of breaker switch. Redundancies, Wren figured, just like the cameras. If a fuse blew, if part of one mechanism failed, the next in line would pick up the slack. Endlessly filming. Endlessly stabbing.

So Gebhart had died in his own dungeon. Nine years now and counting. All being filmed.

This was why the Blue Fairy hated Clara so much. Why the Pinocchio had whispered Lance Gebhart's name in her ear. It was payback. Gebhart must have been a major player on the darknet boards. Nine years ago, with a setup like this, with the will to lock his own daughter in place and who knew how many more…

He would have been their idol. One of the first to run a livestream, delivering foul delights to a growing cabal of monstrous men. Maybe he was looking at the birthplace of the Blue Fairy. They'd worshipped him for it.

Then, somehow, Mona had gotten free and strapped her father down. Clara, now. She'd made her mother watch. She'd turned the cameras on and made them all watch.

The cameras blinked. No doubt the satellite uplink was live.

She was making them all watch, still.

38

FUEL

R ogers was first to stride over. It was only a handful of paces to the machine, but Wren held her arm before she could reach it, holding up a silencing finger to his lips.

Her face was a blotchy red with outrage: at this room, at what it meant, and now at him for stopping her. The sound was intolerable, Wren understood that, but there were dangers here they hadn't yet fully understood.

He knelt and unplugged the cameras. The red lights died.

"Now go ahead," he said.

Rogers shook free, a tear spilling down her cheek, and ripped out the plug for the motor. The machine slowed, the racket stilled and the chamber fell into an uneasy silence, perhaps for the first time in nine years. Rogers turned back and nodded, unashamed by the tears running down her cheeks.

"Thank you."

Neither needed to voice what he'd just saved her from. Her face on the Gebhart livestream. Transmitted into the darknet, recorded for posterity, logged by every Pinocchio in existence. Even if they managed to break the Fairy, would they get them all?

"This is what Clara survived," Rogers said.

Wren just nodded. "This is what she might be surviving right now."

Rogers bit her lip so hard the skin went white. Wren felt the same way, tamped down inside. You could use anger, he told himself. You could burn it like fuel. You had to.

"We're going to bring these sick bastards down," Rogers said. Not a question. Not quite yet a statement. "Every last one."

"We need to know where," Wren said. His voice sounded strange after the barrage of the machine, almost shallow and insufficient to fill the space. Clara's revenge still owned these four walls more than anything he could say or do. "I think Gebhart was the Blue Fairy's architect. They're following his blueprint still. There has to be something here about his plans. About Pleasure Island."

Rogers nodded, smearing tears away with her sleeves. "Agreed. There's more to it than this room. Where did Clara sleep?"

It plainly wasn't here. Wren scanned the walls again. More mirrors, one behind the tableau, one to either side. He strode over the tangle of camera wires, passed between the frail cadavers of Mr. and Mrs. Gebhart and threw out a snapping front kick.

The ball of his foot struck and smashed the mirror, buckling the board behind it and carrying through into empty space beyond. Wren stepped up and tore it away at the hinges.

Another narrow tunnel lay beyond, fading swiftly into darkness. There was a switch on the wall and Wren hit it. Harsh lights down the length chugged to life, ending some eight yards away at a metal grille door. Wren pushed his broad shoulders into the slim corridor and advanced. From behind came more sounds of crashing glass as Rogers took out another mirror.

The grille door was unlocked and opened easily, revealing a room barely three yards by three. A single bed lay on one side, a small tunnel TV on a nightstand, a range of books lined neatly on a desk along with papers and pens. A toilet, a sink, a bucket to wash in, a towel on a rack.

There were faded dolls on the threadbare bed, one of them blue with fairy wings. More faded Pinocchio characters on the walls. It knocked Wren sick. He leaned to the right and vomited in the grimy toilet.

There were no words to express the disgust he felt. The betrayal. The rage.

He flushed the toilet. A flop sweat coated his face. He looked around, but there was no reprieve here. A few worn board games on top of the cupboard, documenting moments of play snatched from the horror. A small

418

refrigerator, a gas hob. Books on a shelf, amongst them a well-thumbed copy of Pinocchio. Canned food in a stack, long past its sell-by date. Barely enough room to stand in. A toothbrush and paste.

All preserved just as it had been, like a museum exhibit. Like his fake town. A place for Clara Baxter to come back and listen to the machine in the room next door as her revenge endlessly played itself out.

Relief. Rage. Fuel for what was to come.

Wren staggered out and squeezed back down the corridor like he was escaping his own prison, only to find himself back in the red room, cameras pointing directly in his direction.

The Pyramid had been bad, but never like this. Before he could stop himself, he charged the cameras. He hurled one across the room so hard it shattered in three places. One he smashed into bits on the floor. One beat off the ceiling, one flew into the corpses and knocked Mrs. Gebhart askew in her chair, one he tore apart with his bare hands, prizing the extendable viewscreen away, until he had the last in his hands and Rogers was there, one hand restraining him now.

"Boss," she shouted. Not for the first time, he realized. He blinked and focused on her.

"Boss," she said again. Giving him a moment to come back. "You have to see this."

He snapped out of it, let her lead him toward the sidewall, where another broken mirror opened into a room covered on every surface with papers. Schematics. Line diagrams. Maps. There were computers stacked on the desks and floors, all humming. The air was hot, dry and smelled of ozone. All working.

"Oh man," Wren said.

"Better than that," Rogers said. "I think we're looking at the center of Clara Baxter's resistance against the Blue Fairy."

Wren turned and took in the walls. There looked to be enough intelligence to keep a twenty-strong squad of forensic data analysts busy for a year.

This was it.

39

FLARE

Wren stared in wonder. Aladdin's cave, the motherlode. Three screens sat arrayed at the center of the desk, each flashing an old-school DOS command line prompt.

Six computer towers networked in? He turned. Seven; there was a big one in the corner half-buried under papers. Clara had co-opted her father's center of operations. The power it was sucking down to this day had to be phenomenal. How had they concealed that draw, letting the house above pass for vacant?

There were skills here he hadn't accounted for. Gebhart had been far more than a pig farmer. His livestream had never been detected by law enforcement. For the last nine years Clara had kept it running presumably non-stop, and the Blue Fairy still hadn't found it.

How?

It meant Gebhart had been a data wizard better than Hellion, B4cksl4cker or anyone in the Blue Fairy. His daughter had simply followed in his footsteps.

Had he taught her? Wren blinked. He imagined Gebhart on the rack begging for it to end, and Clara offering him the chance that it might. Draining the knowledge from him in pieces. Weeks, maybe. Months, to pass all this along.

His network broken from within.

But it hadn't been enough. The Pinocchios were still live. The Blue Fairy had risen still, even after Gebhart died. All Clara's efforts to gather together a vigilante group of her own, to support and defend the mission to bring them down, had stalled when coming up against the combined weight of her enemy.

They'd organized first. They were bound together tight. She'd never had a chance.

"Get us in," Wren said, barking himself out of a fugue state. Clara's sad room was forgotten now. This was a data issue. "If we can piggyback it to my hackers, they can tear this old gear apart like wet tissue paper." He gestured to the flashing command prompt. "Hack it any way you can."

Rogers nodded and bent over the keyboard, starting to run the first of many password exploits. Wren let her, taking in the walls. It couldn't be long now. If the Pinocchios hadn't known already he was in Gebhart's dungeon, they'd learned it when Wren turned the cameras off.

They were coming.

His gaze scrolled the walls; not searching for the details yet, but the pattern. The system at work. It had always been his gift, from his earliest days at the bottom of the Pyramid when he'd had to model the constantly-shifting power dynamics around the Apex just to survive.

One day the Apex wanted this, then the next day he'd change with the suddenness of a lightning strike. Those who'd been praised were punished. Those he'd raised up were humiliated. Every day was a lesson in the Apex's changing moods, and Wren had survived by becoming an expert, reading the climate rather than the changing weather.

What Wren saw now was the map. It seemed to be the sun at the heart of this room. It was large, five feet by two in curling old paper, pinned to the wall above the computers. It showed a flattened globe with hundreds of fine lines arcing across the oceans in a scratchy, riotous rainbow; shipping routes.

Wren re-calculated.

He imagined freight ships trafficking containers full of children. Refugees from war-torn nations. Families displaced by escalating gang violence. Youths fleeing religious persecution. He envisaged all the weak places in the world torn apart by the shifting flows of globalizing power, leaving the weakest people to spill out like juice from a crushed grapefruit. Unseen, unrecorded, unmissed.

So the Blue Fairy network scooped them up. The Saints were nothing compared to this. Wren imagined the tens of thousands of abusers out there being activated and radicalized further by Gebhart's system of blackmail; all-in or lose it all. Like DeVore. Pleasure Island on one hand. Complete humiliation, destruction and jail on the other.

Slip on the mask. Become a Pinocchio. Do as you're told.

The system was an unstoppable juggernaut. Who even held the reins anymore? It clearly hadn't needed Gebhart alive to continue growing. It was an ever-hungry, self-reinforcing idea: more pics, more film, more pleasure, more pain. It would keep going until it had steam-rolled America and the Constitution and every moral value good people held dear.

That was Gebhart's real vision. Bring his people into the light and cast their darkness across the world. The scale was awesome and terrifying, and it was working. Humphreys had already bowed down. The President was negotiating. National self-interest and personal survival mattered more than what was right.

Wren's fists tightened. He'd made decisions like that himself before, in the dark times at the fake town. Do whatever it takes to survive until tomorrow. That time was in the past, though.

"He's shipping them in," he said.

Rogers looked up.

"War zones," Wren said, pointing at the map. "Unrest. Drought. Tsunami. Every one is a flow of human resources to be tapped, and Clara was tracking them. Pinocchios activated all around the world. They bring them in, they ship them to us, to America, where the laws will soon protect them if they stay offshore. It's why it'll work."

Rogers bit her lip again. "So where do we hit them?"

Wren tried to find it in the map, but couldn't see a clear hub. Maybe Hellion and B4cksl4cker would find it in the Blue Fairy's flitting code trail, but now he didn't think so. It was the core secret of the Blue Fairy, and they hadn't hacked it yet, not the website or the real-world location.

Where was Pleasure Island?

He didn't know. He looked back to her and gestured to the computers. "Can you get in?" He didn't need to ask. The screen still flashed with its DOS prompt.

"It's unresponsive. Pegged to a password from her or from him. I don't have the gear to try and bypass it. My phone has some tools, but nothing here is wireless enabled. We need a backdoor, but I don't see one."

She cast around her despondently.

Wren stopped listening. A backdoor. What they needed most was to transmit on Gebhart's uplink somehow, to run a flag up that pole and signal to Hellion and B4cksl4cker. Only they could make sense of the trove of data on the computers, but how?

He needed a way in, but without a password lock. He needed…

Abruptly he turned and pushed back into the corridor. Through the broken mirror he surveyed the wreckage he'd caused in the torture chamber; broken camera parts scattered on the floor, Mrs. Gebhart leaning into her bindings ready to topple, and in the midst of it, one camera left.

He'd almost smashed it too. They needed a backdoor, and here it was. A livestream going up for years, but undetected. It had to jack directly into Pleasure Island; the website his team had never been able to find. His mind raced. If he could somehow hijack it enough to transmit a message of his own along with the stream, then maybe he could force the Island to be visible. Hellion and B4cksl4cker could dive right in.

He studied the camera. Bluetooth-enabled, an off-the-shelf model. It seemed neither Gebhart nor his daughter had considered it a weak point, but it was.

Rogers appeared beside him. "What is it?"

He pulled his phone out of his pocket. For most purposes it was inert; Rogers had destroyed the SIM card. He slipped the battery back in.

Rogers blinked. Maybe getting some sense of what he had planned. "They can still track it."

"We're beyond that now."

He turned the camera on. The red light blinked to life and he scrolled through menus on his phone. Blue tooth pairing, followed by several tools he'd downloaded before he went to DeVore: scraps of digital skeleton-key code for hacking the radio frequency key log-ins of different makes of car, plus a handheld version of the megaphone app he used to mass-message his Foundation.

The skeleton key code made short work of the camera's non-existent local defenses. Through the darknet Clara was secure from hack, but up close and personal via near-field communications? There'd be no need to even put a password on the line.

Wren was into the video uplink.

He wrote a message to Hellion and B4cksl4cker, encrypted it so only they would be able to track it back, then piggy-backed it onto the live video feed. If everything worked according to plan, the message would trigger his Megaphone app and his hackers would get whacked over the head ten times a second until they sat up and paid attention.

Started pulling on the thread leading back.

"What did you do?" Rogers demanded.

Wren couldn't help but track the camera cable back down the concrete corridor to the data room, where it would pass innocently through the password-locked computers and blast up into the atmosphere through the satellite dish.

Using Gebhart's own system against him.

"I just put up a flare," Wren said.

40

HACK

Wren and Rogers stood in the data room and watched the DOS command line prompt flash.

There was no immediate way to know if it had worked. Anything could have gone wrong, and even if everything went right, there was no guarantee Hellion and B4cksl4cker would even see his Megaphone shout. Maybe they were dead. The Fairy was hunting them. The Pinocchios were everywhere.

The command line flashed and Wren's heart beat in time. Seconds stretched into minutes and neither of them spoke as his message stretched out through the secret alleys of the darknet.

FOLLOW ME BACK

The Blue Fairy had to be closing in; not only through the airwaves and data tunnels but in the real world. It would be getting light now above ground, as a wintry sun rose over the barren pig enclosures, the burned-out husk of the Gebhart's forever home, the weedy gravel drive. Pinocchios creeping up to his stolen SUV. Pinocchios creeping past the satellite dish.

Then the command line flashed and didn't come back.

Rogers gave a little gasp. Wren felt his eyes bugging. He leaned in, waiting for something more to happen. His heart seemed to hold back on every beat. Sweat beaded on his temples.

Still nothing.

"What does it-" Rogers began, then there was a sound. A tinny, half-heard scrap of spoken audio calling from afar, like an animal trapped inside the walls, scratching to get out. Wren stopped breathing and listened to the tiny voices, then understood.

He ran back down the tunnel to the red room. The sounds were coming from the video camera. Voices calling his name via the playback facility. There was nothing on the flip-out screen, but still Hellion's familiar voice came through the tiny speakers.

"Christopher, can you hear us, give some sign that-"

"I'm here," Wren said directly into the camera microphone; three little holes in the front corner. It would be poor quality, a scratchy audio profile, but it should be clear enough. "Hellion, B4cksl4cker, what are you doing?"

Silence passed for a moment as the signal went up and down, through whatever loops Gebhart had set up and Clara Baxter had reinforced, to his two-person hacker collective currently fleeing in their separate convoys through the wilds of Europe.

"I'm in his computer," Hellion's voice followed, a thin and reedy whine. "The scale is immense and protection is cutting edge, but don't think about that now. You have to get out."

Rogers stood beside him, eyes widening. Wren had expected it.

"Where are they?"

"They are everywhere," Hellion answered, "it looks like forty of them, dozen vehicles, broad range of weaponry. They have you surrounded; you need to - oh no. B4cksl4cker!"

The signal cut out.

"What's my route out?" Wren demanded.

Static played through the camera. The image showed only dead Mr. and Mrs. Gebhart in their death poses, like one of Chicago Teddy's dioramas.

A burst of garbled noise followed, then Hellion came back in again with a loud curse in Belgian. "… was close, they are trying to kill this line, but B4cksl4cker is fighting, it's…" she trailed off. "Christopher, I don't know if I can take them all. Maybe twenty, enough to dig corridor, if you move quickly."

"What route?" Wren persisted.

"Not SUV," Hellion said, and Wren imagined her hunched over a monitor, watching a top-down feed like just another StarCraft level. If anyone could guide them through a tactical battle map filled with enemies, it was Hellion. "South is blocked, west you've got nothing, north is the mountains, which leaves east and open prairie."

"And the drones?"

"Under my control. About to launch. I will not have long, and there should be-"

She cut out. Wren and Rogers looked at each other.

"Move now!" Hellion crashed back in, louder than before. "They are up to porch, you will take incoming fire. I will do what I can, but you must-"

The signal died.

Wren nodded at Rogers and then ran. Three steps out of the red room and he plunged into the corridor, darting along sideways through the plate metal door to the stairs leading up.

"Head down," Wren barked, "follow me," then ran up the concrete stairs, emerging back into the silence of the Gebhart's living room as the first watery light of dawn crept in through a frosty mist over the pig enclosures. He caught a glimpse of muzzle flashes out on the drive before the sound rolled over them both like a hurricane.

The Pinocchios let rip.

Munitions smacked off and through the remnant shell of the farmstead like a barrage of hail. Wren and Rogers ducked and ran, shielding their eyes against splintery ricochet spray; into the dining room and through to the kitchen, past the steps leading down to the back where a team of masked Pinocchios were already advancing through the long grass with rifles in their hands.

Jeans, hoodies, Pinocchio masks.

East was the rear of the house, largely undamaged by fire but warped by neglect. There was a high whining sound in the air, like a nest of hornets had been stirred up and were raging closer. The back corner of the house held a wet room with boots on the floor and dungarees caked in dry mud hung on the walls, dancing now with the furious rattle of bullets passing through. A single faded door stood in the east wall, already punctuated with a dozen fresh holes.

Rogers huddled close to Wren by the doorframe as the thunder of bullets and the buzzing of wasps climbed toward a crescendo.

"We run and don't stop," Wren shouted over the noise. "Due east."

Rogers nodded. Maybe one of them would make it through the storm of incoming fire, with Hellion's help. What followed after that was another question.

Wren surged up, kicked the door through with a terrific crunch, and raced out into the frosted, pinching air, directly toward a five-strong troop of Pinocchios.

41

HORNETS

J eans. Hoodies. Pinocchio masks.

Wren and Rogers stood on the gravel just outside the door, staring at the masked men as the sky buzzed like a ripsaw. Five of them were right there, with others spread further to either side in the lightening gloom. They were everywhere, and their rifles were leveled. There was nowhere to go.

A dozen thoughts ran through Wren's mind; what they'd do to him and Rogers, what they'd do to his country once the government buckled. He imagined his children, his wife, his Foundation and his hackers all gathered up in the Blue Fairy's embrace. Its corruption would poison the heart of America and from there the world, because if you didn't stand for others when they were weak and at risk, who would ever stand for you?

Morality would fracture. The boot would stamp down on the face of the innocent and weak, as it always had before, but this time with the full weight of Uncle Sam on board.

No shipments of children would be intercepted. No abusers would be arrested. Laws globally would bend to accommodate the bending of laws off the USA's coast. The Blue Fairy would rise like a Third Reich for the modern age.

Wren raised his arms slowly, and Hellion acted. At once the buzz from the sky grew louder, crescendoing like Gebhart's piston until something large, whirring and black crunched into the head of the middle Pinocchio with a terrible, bat-to-the-skull thunk.

For a moment there was only buzzing and disbelief; the man crumpled, blood pouring from a gash in his forehead, then more followed and the dark sky fell. Black and whirring hornet-like machines plummeted from the misty sky with a tremendous chainsaw roar, striking and encircling the Pinocchios in seconds.

Drones.

Wren stared for a moment as a swarm of the machines flattened the four remaining Pinocchios in a buzzing black flood, then swept outward to flank the others; batting their rotor blades off masks, arms and bodies in a sickening chorus of meaty blows, dropping some and starting the rest shouting, shooting and fleeing in a mad, stunted panic.

Wren took Rogers by her good arm and ran. Everywhere now was the waterfall roar of swooping drones, burying the sound of screams and gunfire. Black hornets whizzed in all directions, chasing and regrouping, clustering and striking Pinocchios in kamikaze attacks that stripped their rotors or smashed their housings, leaving them shattered on the ground and the enemy in flight, all under Hellion's steely command.

The two of them ran into the chaos over hard-packed Idaho dirt. A clutch of drones dropped in front of them and shot forward in an arrow formation, digging an opening through the Pinocchio cordon. Wren charged into that tunnel chased by a symphony of thunking metal-to-bone impacts. They hit a crumbling fence at the yard's edge and Wren vaulted it easily, helping Rogers over.

"How?" she gasped as she dropped to the other side.

"B4cksl4cker's idea," Wren called as they picked up running again, "networked drones stolen from a wedding display in Bozeman, but they won't last long,"

The arrow of drones spun off northeast, leading the way. Together they ran into dawn's half-light over the sparse prairie even as the storm raged on the Gebhart farm behind them. Dry clay dirt broke into dust underfoot and more rounds whined in the air. A stray Pinocchio emerged out of the gray gloom, rifle aimed, but three drones spun out like jabbing fists, striking his face, chest and the side of his head before he could get off a shot, breaking their rotor blades on his bones.

He fell and Wren and Rogers ran on with the diminished arrow leading them sharply east. The cries of the Pinocchios grew distant, until at a rise some four hundred yards away Wren risked a glance back and saw chaos boiling over the farm. A one-hundred strong performance fleet, B4cksl4cker had promised, set to dance in the air at the wedding that night. Easy enough to steal; one post on a darknet gig economy forum and his team had assembled within an hour: a specialist thief, a driver for the transport truck and an engineer to disable the drones' hard-wired safeties. The rest fell to Hellion, expert in top-down strategy with more Actions Per Minute than a hummingbird's wings.

Only scattershot gunfire rang out now, with the Pinocchio ranks temporarily broken. Shock and awe, Wren figured. The sense of panic would be overwhelming, engulfed by a forest of flying blades.

They deserved every bit. Wren ran on, feet beating the frosted dirt, until their arrow peeled away and flew back. A few more hornets to die with the pack. He scanned the field ahead; the sun was peeking over the mountains, but the air was thick and gray with mist still. Maybe there was movement there. Now the drones were gone he could make out the sound of an engine.

A long dark semi was waiting on a two-lane road, its back shutters open. Two figures stood in the opening with their arms out, beckoning them in. B4cksl4cker's darknet mercenaries. Wren kicked a path through mounds of plastic drone cases, helped Rogers up then climbed in after. The shutter rolled down, the engine revved up and they were away.

42

HACKERS

The interior of the semi was brightly-lit and strewn with pieces of shaped foam from the drone cases. On one canvas wall was a desk kitted with a laptop.

"He said we go north," said one of the two mercenaries by the shutter, but Wren cut her off with a glance. A middle-aged woman with a scar across her lips. Not in the Foundation, but maybe she should be.

"Do what he said."

He strode to the laptop and sat down. Rogers dropped in at Wren's side as the semi picked up pace. He scanned the desktop screen, picked out the coded chat icon B4cksl4cker had remote-loaded and clicked. There were a few taut, tenuous seconds as the signal connected; Wren had no clue what combination of satellite, cell phone and hard-wired patches his hackers had rigged together to make this uplink work.

Then audio kicked in, with B4cksl4cker's voice barking from the tower's crude speakers.

"Wren, I'm busy. Talk to Hellion."

"Hellion, give me a report," Wren answered, even as he tapped out codes to tunnel him back along their uplink to his darknet site.

"The fight at the farm's over," she said, sounding energized. Orchestrating a battle like that had to be one hell of an adrenaline shot.

"Estimate a handful of fatalities, a dozen seriously wounded, while the bulk of them are now spread across a half-mile radius."

That made sense. "Are any of them on our tail?"

"None. My first wave took out their vehicles. The swarm is depleted, but it did its job."

Wren let out a breath. "And this signal? I thought they had the Internet clamped down. Are they tracking us?"

A pause followed. Wren figured she was talking to B4cksl4cker, conferring on how much to share. How much they could trust him, still, after Ferat. At the same time Wren opened his darknet and found his site empty, just as before, though his admin tools were still available to him. He started writing a message for the megaphone function to blast out.

Hellion clicked back in, the clacking of keys rattling by underneath her voice. Hacking still. "We took leaf from Gebhart's book. Or his daughter's. Details are sketchy, but it looks like fifteen years back he hacked weather satellite with backdoor to the Internet. Very high level of sophistication. I do not believe he could do this himself. This data signature, access required, it looks like he had institutional help."

"Helped by who? What institution?"

"Impossible to say. If I guess, based on code we found used in the Order of the Saints, you will jump to conclusions."

Wren's stomach went cold. "You're suggesting Gebhart knew my father. Apex of the Pyramid?"

Silence for a moment. "Or they used same hackers. Very professional, many assets in place. Many millions spent to achieve this."

Wren stared at the wall, struggling to grasp this. The same hackers? "My father's infrastructure. If he's alive."

"Yes," Hellion answered. "Or could be nation-state. Many have resources to fund this. Dark money and dark skills."

Wren grunted.

"Yes," Hellion went on, "it looks like fourteen years ago your government separated weathernet systems with hard firewall; physical break in cables. But Gebhart's hack survived. It should have been discovered in one of numerous updates since, or the Blue Fairy would have found it, but I think your Mona has taken responsibility. She has been upgrading. So it remains functionally invisible, zeroed out and code-locked in every way imaginable. There is no way anyone could find a route in, until you opened the door. We are using that same link now."

Wren filed all that away for later consideration. "And the Blue Fairy?"

"They can't see us. This is less darknet link and more whole 'weathernet' of its own, up in the clouds where they wouldn't think to look. Already I am hacking into…"

She trailed off again.

"What?" Wren prompted.

"There," said Hellion, distracted. "Things are happening fast. I am going to-"

"Don't cut me off. Tell me everything you see."

Another silence, then Hellion began a disjointed running commentary over the racing of keys. "Gebhart's computers just cracked; we are in. At same time…" A pause. "The Pinocchios are entering the farm basement, but I have hands on his stored content. Uplifting it now…" A pause. Wren imagined terabytes of data sucking up through Gebhart's dish and into the 'weathernet'. "It's fast. Shutting down backlinks." Another pause. "They'll never find us. But maybe…"

Wren finished typing his own Megaphone message and pressed send; shooting out to his Foundation wherever they were, contacting them again and again until they registered receipt.

THE BLUE FAIRY WANTS TO USE AMERICA'S INTERNATIONAL WATERS AS A DUNGEON FOR ORPHAN CHILDREN SOURCED FROM GLOBAL WAR ZONES & FAILED STATES.

YOUR PRESIDENT AND INTELLIGENCE SERVICES ARE IN COLLABORATION TO WRITE NEW OFF-BOOK LAWS THAT BEND THE CONSTITUTION TO PROTECT THEM. AMERICAN CHILDREN WILL BE SAFE, BUT NOT ANY OTHERS. GET THIS MESSAGE OUT. GET GOVERNMENTS AROUND THE WORLD UP IN ARMS NOW.

Hellion clicked back in. "I ran analysis on Gebhart's data stream, and I have something. B4cksl4cker thinks it is first piece in Pleasure Island re-routing algorithm." A pause as keys rattled manically, prosecuting invisible espionage. "We could never find them before. This is why; they learned tricks from Gebhart, but it looks like he did not give them his weathernet. Instead…"

She trailed off again, and now Wren spun through websites checking on news reports. There was still nothing about the meetings at the White House, nothing about a Constitutional change coming down the pike, nothing about suspension of habeas corpus.

Had Humphreys delayed them? He could only hope. Just as likely, it was all happening now under cover of media blackout: writs going out with judge approval, gagging orders to muzzle free speech, Coast Guard orders activating a twenty-mile border zone off the coasts, in which the Blue Fairy would be protected while operating their freight ships.

Pleasure Islands. One at first, Wren figured, but dozens to follow. All the Pinocchios of the world would come. The flow of globally trafficked humans would swell like never before, flooding into an outlaw zone off the American fringe, protected by American might. A hostage situation on the scale of nations.

Wren blinked the image away. "Hellion, talk to me."

"Christopher," she answered, "Lance Gebhart's underlying code is extremely complex. It is elegant. We are scanning the remnants of our second skin for matching pieces of code. Looking for his signature in the Blue Fairy's hands. If we get that then we can..." Pause. "Here!" Talking to B4cksl4cker. Hammering the keys. "OK, I am seeing ... there are countless information streams ... they should not be able to carry this kind of data. Webs ... like weathernet: I see earthquake warning systems ... networked buoys ... GPS satellites ... even piggy-backed signals on radio and television. We never thought to look for it before because..."

She trailed off again. Wren swiftly downloaded and brought up several apps he kept parked on a neutral domain.

"The routing's astounding," Hellion barked, interrupting his preparations. "We've never seen it like this. I'm getting the outline of the Blue Fairy's organization ... self-reinforcing authority systems... democratic gamification before it was popular ... this looks like Gebhart's major innovation. He had it years ago ... I think he was a genius, Christopher, to create this system! He's been dead nine years and it's still in operation.

Wren tried to make sense of that. Self-reinforcing authority? Democratic gamification? "What does any of that mean?"

"It is crowd-sourced," Hellion cheered, clearly delighted with the discovery. "Like social media algorithm. People enter his system and vote with their likes and clicks. These votes raise up influencers, powerful people in his system. These influencers then carry more weight than others; they get deeper access and greater powers. So the system builds a leadership cabal based on contribution and voting." A pause. "It means there is no single or fixed leader for the Blue Fairy! Just individual users vying for influence, with all decisions crowd-sourced to the masses. A kind of meritocracy."

Wren blinked. He was familiar with such structures, primarily from social media. Absent editors, there had to be a means of deciding what content was shown to users, so the users decided themselves by up- and down-voting. In the case of the Blue Fairy, those votes likely came from producing 'good' PICS; the material these Pinocchios lived for.

It was a lot to take in. Such systems rarely operated well, or consistently, without regulation. The moods of the crowd constantly changed.

"So how did they pull all this off?" he asked. "We're looking at years of planning, an enormous infrastructure, millions spent to make it work."

"That is genius part," Hellion said. "There are multiple rings of command, like layers in a pyramid. It takes many valuable contributions over time, or phenomenal popularity in the moment, to rise up to the top. Ultimate goals remain fixed, however. Gebhart's goals."

Wren felt ill. All those thousands of men across the world, harnessing their energy to make Gebhart's dream come true. "What goals?"

"I cannot read this. Only guess."

Wren didn't need her guess. They were seeing the effect of that goal playing out now. A world safe for Pinocchios, the Blue Fairy and for Pleasure Island. Gebhart's ghost was haunting them still, in the systems he'd built.

"So anyone putting forward practical plans to achieve his goals had their profile weighted upward?"

"Exactly. We cannot read data, but patterns are familiar, much like any social media algorithm."

"Are you inside?"

"On the fringes. They don't see us!" She was exhilarated. "Like with the drones, we're coming from above, and-"

"Break them," Wren snapped. "All the rest will follow. Break them, blind them and rip them apart."

"What?"

She sounded dismayed, but Wren had to be hard now. Too much was at stake. "I don't care how beautiful the system is, Hellion. B4cksl4cker, I know you're listening too. I appreciate the elegance, but this is not the time to fangirl over nice code. Ferat is dead, countless children are at risk and more are on the way. You burn those bastards to the ground right now."

A pause.

"We know Dr. Ferat is dead," Hellion said. Her voice had turned deadly calm, with anger bubbling beneath the surface. "You killed him."

Wren knew where this was going. Anger that had been building for a long time, married with fresh grief and the victory of this long-sought hack. It could make her do something crazy. He figured she was seconds away from pulling the plug on him forever. He had to push back now.

"Me? Hellion, did I invite him onto the elite hacker board? Did I make him the point person while the two of you jetted off in your convoys? Do you think he had an escape plan the way you do? Do you think he had any chance at all against the Pinocchios, alone?"

Silence.

"You brought this on his head just as much as I did," Wren pressed. "You may be gods on the darknet, but you don't have the first clue about your impact on the real world!" He thought about stopping there, but didn't. Better to win all the wars at once. "I said it at the start; what good is power if you don't know how to use it? That's why you've always needed me, to show you how. I get it that Dr. Ferat helped you, but you have to remember that the only reason he was any use to you at all was because of me! Because my Foundation helped him reform his life. The same goes for you; you're on the coin system not just because I need you, but because you need me." A pause to breathe. "Do you have any idea how many lives you ruined with your cryptoworms, B4cksl4cker? How many people died in miserable gulags when your hacks inadvertently helped dictatorships like North Korea, Hellion? Children are suffering in the worst way possible, right now, and you want to talk about code?" Another breath. "You're on *my* coin system. That means sometimes you do exactly what I say. There's no debate here. Coin zero is always a possibility, and trust me, you don't want that. Now I'm telling you, shred Gebhart's code at the first opportunity! Get the stranglehold off the USA. That's an order."

A long silence. Crackling; the sound of Hellion and B4cksl4cker talking on a private channel. Probably they were stunned. Wren was too. Rogers at

437

his side was stunned. Normally you coddled hackers, even feared them, but that wouldn't wash now. They needed a wake-up call and accountability. They needed boundaries. It was the reason they'd accepted Wren into their lives at the start, and the reason they would listen to him now.

The silence and crackling stretched out, then B4cksl4cker's voice came onto the line. "Hellion won't speak to you."

Wren felt like laughing. Sulking, now? Like he'd sent her to her room? He felt giddy with the adrenaline comedown of the Pinocchio attack. "So you speak for her."

A sigh. B4cksl4cker was twenty-seven now, but trapped in the endless youth of the millionaire. Instant gratification in everything became boring. Only Hellion had ever presented him with a meaningful challenge. "We will do what you ask. Shred it all, if we can."

"And can you?"

"Perhaps. I don't know. We are trying. Don't reduce us to coin zero. Dr. Ferat spoke highly of the coins. I think…"

He trailed off. Hackers and their social skills.

"Tell Hellion I'm sorry," Wren said. "I don't think you're to blame. This is on the Blue Fairy. We're all doing our best."

"She knows that," B4cksl4cker said, "and we are working. You can rely on us."

"Thank you," said Wren.

The line went dead.

Beside him Rogers let out a breath. "Hot dang. Hackers."

Wren laughed. It wasn't funny, but you had to laugh. He took a moment to scan through his open apps, then hit the button to send the next call through, to Humphreys.

43

DELAY

I t took five minutes. Ringing, ringing off. Wren kept trying. Humphreys in a meeting, maybe, in the midst of negotiations. Sneaking out, Wren hoped. Setting up surveillance was a possibility too. Rigging the call to hack backward.

Wren was on Gebhart's weathernet now, though, protected with Hellion's best cryptography. There would be no easy hack back.

Ringing.

His mind turned to Charles DeVore, out there somewhere in the darkness of America. A new dawn was already rising up for him and his people, 7 a.m. on a Thursday, a new day across a new world. Wren thought about the Blue Fairy, and Gebhart's code that drove it deeper into the darkness like an unstoppable machine, and all the Pinocchios getting swept up in its wake like dolphins fished by a seafloor trawler.

Would Charles DeVore alone have ever graduated to the kind of scene Wren had made in his basement? Maybe. Maybe not. He couldn't help thinking of Ferat, and what he'd said in their last conversation. Save those you can. What did that mean now? The Pinocchios made their choices. DeVore had made his choices. He'd gone to meet Sophia. He'd tied his family up.

The call answered, though no voice came through. It made sense. This was Wren's direct line to Humphreys, but Humphreys had no way of knowing who the call was from. It could be a test from the Blue Fairy, or even his own government.

"It's me, Humphreys," Wren said. "I need to know what's happening there."

That was nondescript enough. If anyone was listening in, there was nothing to go on. The last thing Wren wanted was to get Humphreys tossed out of the room if he actually was acting as an effective brake on negotiations.

"You're out of the Company," came Humphreys' voice. Flat, professional, giving nothing away. "Hand yourself in."

"Not going to happen. Irons in the fire, Humphreys. Can you talk?"

No response. It gave Wren no choice. If Humphreys was truly compromised by the Blue Fairy, or disempowered within the CIA, that was the end, probably. He had to hope that wasn't the case.

"The line is secure at my end," Wren said. "I can tell you where I am and what I have; I found Lance Gebhart, he looks to be the Blue Fairy originator, nine years dead on his farm in Idaho. He was sitting on a data goldmine; seems his daughter Mona Gebhart, AKA Clara Baxter the catfisher, turned the tables and used his network and his code to attack his organization, but she couldn't bring it down. The Blue Fairy was too well distributed, and-"

"Wren," Humphreys whispered. Holding a hand over the phone. In a bathroom somewhere, maybe. "You can't tell me this. Anyone could track it, you-"

"Shut up and listen. What comes next trumps everything. We're working on Gebhart's source code now; I have a clear picture of how it works. Multiple connections that through data networks not designed to carry traffic. That's how the Pleasure Island site bobs in and out of view so easily. It's not hosted on anything like a normal server, but we're cracking it. Don't tell me to stop, you know I won't. Just buy us some time. Don't let them sign anything. Things are happening in the next few hours, it's-"

"Wren, listen to me!" Barely audible now. "It's already been done. I got kicked out of the room. The deal's in the air, new Internet protocols instituting a media firewall. Any mention of last night's events, of the Blue Fairy or Pinocchios or the deal, will be exed-out like Tiananmen Square. It'll be like it never happened, along with anyone who opposed these changes. The President has selectively suspended habeas corpus while they draw up a border zone-"

"Along the coasts," Wren finished. "Dammit, Humphreys. I need more time."

"There is no time! I've been blinding our own networks as best I can, but I'm not Secretary of CIA, and if I was they'd have replaced me by now. I'm already on the way out. This thing is wholly transactional, and we don't have any choice. We're coming for you with everything we've got."

Wren took a breath. He'd been chased by the CIA before, but not like this, in a media environment that made America a dystopian state. His face would be everywhere. Public Enemy Number 1. He'd have no freedom to operate, no way to push back.

"So get the word out. I've taken steps to publicize this in other countries. The rest of the world will know what's happening here, and they're not going to take it lightly."

"They'll take it any way we tell them to!" An angry hiss. "We're America, dammit, and we rule this world. Our military outnumbers the next ten countries combined. Our nukes can decimate them all. When we go all-in, I guarantee you every country will back down."

"Not every country. The Blue Fairy wants their children, Humphreys. They'll resist."

Humphreys laughed. "You think they'd rather see their capital city a smoking hole than lose a few already-forsaken children? There have always been sacrifices, Wren. There's a price to pay for existence, and the world's a brutal place. We won't even need to use the nukes, because our economic weapons are just as destructive. Trade embargoes and blockades combined with unceasing cyber attacks? We could break the back of any country in the world without firing a shot. They'll be starving and rioting in a week. The people will beg us for protection. Mobs will run the streets grabbing random kids to send our way. The Blue Fairy will be appeased, and it'll only take one example to make all the others sit up and beg."

Wren cursed. He might be right. "You're talking about weeks. I need hours. If I can't do this by the end of business today, then it's over. Until then I need you to prevent radar overwatch on the coasts. I need to get a team in."

"Get a team in?" Humphreys' voice almost went falsetto. "There's no way that can happen now. They'll trigger a nuclear plant the minute they see you."

"Not if you stop them from seeing. Blind the radar. Muddy the water. Get them to hold back on enforcement."

A pause. "You're talking about mass insubordination. When they find out, I won't just lose my job. They'll kill me and everyone I involve."

"They're killing us already! If this goes through, we won't be the United States of America anymore. There'll be no shining city on a hill. We'll be the Great Satan they always called us, devouring the world's innocents and asking them to like it. I'd rather be dead than see that happen, wouldn't you?"

A second passed. "Yes."

"Yes. Others will feel the same way. Get yourself together, Humphreys. I'll try to be in touch. If this thing fails, then thank you for trying and goodbye. If it succeeds, I'll be wanting a little more leeway on my freelance deal."

Humphreys gave a bitter laugh. "You're making mutineers of us all. Goodbye, Christopher."

"Yeah."

He hung up.

Rogers was there at his side. Her lips set in a grim line. "You really think all of that will happen?"

"It's already happening. The US is not a rules-based moral democracy by accident. People died so it could be this way. They're going to have to die again."

She winced. "So what now? You said you're going to insert a team, but how? Where? We don't have anything and we don't have a target."

Wren hit refresh on his battery of apps. Still nothing on the alert he hoped for from DeVore, but there were other ways too, other irons in the fire…

"We'll get it. Whatever it takes."

44

SYSTEM

The semi reeled through the darkness of rural Idaho, bearing east and south, and for thirty minutes Wren hadn't taken his eyes off the weathernet connection. Still there was no alert from DeVore, but there was something else maybe bigger: the photo of DeVore's 'dead' family had gone viral.

It was everywhere. Wren scanned through a dozen darknet feeder boards, the kind of places Pinocchio-wannabes gathered hoping for their invite to the Blue Fairy, and it was on them all. Discussion swirled around it frantically. The wannabe Pinocchios of America knew something was happening, and they were on board.

"Get some tracking on these IPs," he said to B4cksl4cker on the open line. "I want to know where they're going."

"How do you know they're going anywhere?"

"Because they're celebrating. The Blue Fairy won and they all want in."

"Correlating now … I don't see any clear flows, Christopher. We are looking at lowest levels here. They don't have access or authority. They don't know more than we do."

Wren grunted. Access and authority had always been the issue.

"Are you in Pleasure Island yet?"

"In a way."

"What does that mean?"

A long pause. Probably B4cksl4cker talking to Hellion. "We see the shape of it. I can see the flows of data, the function of the algorithms, but no more. I cannot shred them like this."

It was one step closer to the Fairy's core, but still not enough. "You don't have the key."

"Yes, exactly. Their cryptography remains strong."

"But you hacked Gebhart's computers."

"From inside, from access node you provided. We are looking for weakness, open port somewhere, but..."

Wren gritted his teeth. Yes. That was going to be the next step. "I may have the key."

A pause. "What?"

"A way in. I don't know for sure. It may amount to nothing."

B4cksl4cker sounded frustrated. "So give it to us."

"I don't have it yet. I need to be there in person."

"What are you talking about?"

Wren committed. One of his last irons in the fire, putting it all on the line and trusting them to the hilt. "You're seeing that photo circulating the darknet. DeVore's murdered family. What you don't know is that I took it. I-"

"You did what?"

Hellion's voice came swiftly, instantly outraged. Looking for an excuse.

"It's not what you think, I promise. I mocked it up; those people weren't dead, the blood was my own. I just used it to inject my own Pinocchio 'mole', Charles DeVore, into the Blue Fairy bloodstream. That photo was his meal ticket in, and it was mine too. Before I fired it off, I tagged it with one of the cryptoworms you wrote for me, a back-tracking contact logger. I hoped-"

"They don't work," B4cksl4cker interjected. "We tried that many times, Christopher, trying to get photos and video with cryptoworms through. The Blue Fairy's firewall is too strong; our code always was blocked."

"I know, but I think this photo has broken through in all the chaos." He paused, bringing up metadata on the photo. His cryptoworm code looked to be there still. "This image is everywhere. Some Pinocchio with authority must have posted it through the firewall himself. Now it's everywhere, in every Fairy computer and phone and device that shares it, self-replicating like Huggintime, and reporting that data back. It must have logged a map of the entire active Fairy net by now. But I can't get to it inside their firewall."

A pause.

"So you're saying you have key," Hellion said caustically, letting her anger slip out in little bursts, "but it is locked in house?"

"That's right," Wren said. Letting her have this, bringing them on board step-by-step.

"What good is that to us?"

"What's good is that I can get it. If I can find Charles DeVore I can take his phone right out of his hands."

Another silence. This time B4cksl4cker spoke. "So you are saying you must get inside Blue Fairy, in order to get inside Blue Fairy? Through DeVore's phone. Is that right?"

"Exactly."

"But how?" Hellion bleated. "We need key to find Pleasure Island. This is paradox, Christopher!"

"That's almost right." Nearly at the final iron now. "And it's true, I don't have the key yet, but I'll get it. DeVore's going to tell me via an Internet drop."

"But-" Hellion began, then paused. "He is Pinocchio. Why would he help you?"

"Because I've got his family. He didn't kill them when he had the chance, so I believe he wants them back."

A silence. "OK," Hellion went on, "but even if this is true, he is bottom rank Pinocchio, yes? What does he know about Pleasure Island?"

"Not bottom rank anymore," Wren said. "You've been telling me how the Blue Fairy system works. Popular pics means upvotes which means power, and now his pic is everywhere. For the next few hours at least, he's a top-level influencer. He'll be wherever the influencers go. If Pleasure Island's a real place, that's where he'll go."

Silence.

Now Rogers spoke up. Beginning to see it. "We got lucky. The system's helping us."

"Exactly."

B4cksl4cker rapped his keys; it sounded angry.

Rogers broke the silence. "So we prep for an insertion. But where? When's DeVore going to check in with you?"

445

"He's hours overdue."

"There!" said Hellion, like she'd just won the argument. "He is Pinocchio. He will not help us."

Wren hesitated a moment. He'd played his cards close to his chest on this one from the start. He trusted his team; but with moles in the CIA, he hadn't wanted to take the risk. Now there was no choice.

"I've got a backup," he said. "High risk. Maybe high reward."

His hackers said nothing. Rogers only stared.

He spilled it all.

45

PING

The message came in through Wren's alert program an hour into their onward flight.

The jet was a Gulfstream G280, capable of three and a half thousand nautical miles on one fuelling. Bigger than the Cessna and decked out for luxury. The owners had apparently planned a day trip to Niagara Falls; some nice romance if you could afford it. Hellion had taken control of the booking system remotely and rerouted the jet for Wren.

Easy.

Now he sat in the co-pilot's seat, unwilling to allow a repeat of what had happened on their last flight. The pilot insisted he sit in back, but Wren had insisted harder. Rogers and the mercenaries were in the fuselage along with a crate full of gear he'd requisitioned, preparing a 'distraction'.

They'd agreed a frontal assault on Pleasure Island would never work; even if Humphreys managed to blind all radar overwatch, Wren had no doubt that Pleasure Island was armed to the teeth.

But one man, coming in on a fast drop from the air?

Then Charles DeVore's message came in.

FOR ATTENTION OF CHRISTOPHER WREN

GO SCREW YOURSELF

Wren stared at it for a long moment. As he'd feared, DeVore had flipped. There was now just one way to locate him.

The transponder.

Wren had inserted dozens of moles before. He'd gone undercover himself with Honduran drug cartels, with ISIS in Afghanistan, with cults up and down the United States, and he knew the odds. Sixty percent of moles failed. Some gave themselves away and died under torture. Some quit; they couldn't handle the pressure of living a double life. And some turned.

Wren always took those moles out himself. It hurt every time. But he'd learned ways to extract value from them still. Reconnoiter them like they were the enemy. Use them to plant false information. The risk of detection increased, but you were already burned by then.

He'd been burned with Charles DeVore from the start. Wren knew his type, boulders hungry for the shove to get them rolling downhill, men out there in the vast darkness of the soul looking for answers they knew they shouldn't find.

Wren had requisitioned Grimes of Canton PD for a small, silicone-coated GPS transponder. Every time they'd used them before, the Blue Fairy had detected them after one 'ping' to grab their location. It was a last-ditch move he'd intended to use when he was on Pleasure Island and needed DeVore's precise location, before the man could think to destroy his phone.

He'd forced it down Charles DeVore's throat in his living room. Grabbed his tongue and waggled it while the smaller man swallowed, not realizing he'd just made himself into a homing beacon.

But a one-shot deal. One ping and that was all he got.

Now he brought up the tracking app. Sweat broke out on his forehead. Ping it now or later? Later, and maybe he'd get Pleasure Island itself, but they'd be forewarned he was coming. Ping it now and maybe he'd get a vector. His finger hovered over the button. One shot at this.

"DeVore gave his answer," he said on the open line.

"We see it," B4cksl4cker answered swiftly. They all understood what was at stake.

"I'm going to send the ping now."

"Standing ready to record."

He hit the button.

The location request went out through the airwaves. The transponder responded. In seconds data poured in. Cell towers triangulated it to the side

448

of I-76, fifty miles east of Harrisburg, Pennsylvania. Immobile for the last forty minutes, after moving steadily east for hours.

Immobile?

"B4cksl4cker," Wren said.

"Checking," the hacker replied. "I'm seeing reports, mixed up … there was a man firing shots on the highway around then."

Wren's heart thumped. Something had happened. Immobile for forty minutes made no sense. Either DeVore was dead, or he'd vomited up the tracker. But why the shots? Wren couldn't guess what had happened. He stared at the dot on the map, flashing gently.

"Are there bodies? A vehicle?"

"Checking. Hold."

Wren held. Piecing together what they could through the scrambled police frequencies, live satellite footage.

"There's no vehicle."

Wren swore softly.

"Two bodies, stripped naked on the roadside. Police tried to respond but were warned off. The embargo in effect."

Two bodies? That didn't make sense. Either way, all it left them with was a vector; east through Pittsburgh.

"Is DeVore one of the bodies?"

"Zooming. It looks… one is black, so no. The other, it's difficult to tell, but he's thicker than DeVore. Facedown. Unlikely."

Facedown. "Dead?"

"Almost certainly. Fading heat signature. Headshots would be hard to see through the hair, but they're not moving."

Wren tried to play that out. Imagine the Charles DeVore that he'd sent off into the night like a live hand grenade, under cover of a fake PIC. Maybe he'd blown that cover. Maybe the Pinocchios had seen through him, leaving only one option for a desperate man.

Execute them before they could reveal him as a charlatan. Heave up his guts after doing it, plunking the transponder right there on the roadside. The first time you kill a man, it sticks.

But going where? It had to be Pleasure Island.

"DeVore's alone," Wren said.

"That seems likely, yes," B4cksl4cker agreed.

"Can you backtrack ID on the vehicle these men came in?"

"Nothing yet. It may come, but it's no use if he's dumped it already. Assume we can't track it."

"Then all we know is he's heading east." Wren's mind spun up to speed. "He's almost to Philadelphia, a major port. Remember all those shipping routes in Gebhart's farm? Plenty passed through Philadelphia. One of those ships has to be Pleasure Island." He paused a second, gaming it out. "How many container ships are in the vicinity of Philadelphia?"

Keys clacked while Hellion and B4cksl4cker worked. Drawing a radius on the map, double-checking with satellites and shipping records.

"Fifteen large container ships on approach or exiting. Another twenty in port currently."

"The fifteen," Wren said swiftly. "Give me them. Cross-reference everything we've got. Double down on data use through the second skin. I guarantee the Pinocchios are going to livestream what's coming."

A pause. "What's coming?"

"The end of America as we know it. And their Independence Day."

46

FALL

Wren stood at the open door of the Gulfstream, fifteen thousand feet above the border shallows of the Atlantic Ocean, scouring for glimpses of the surface far below, fleetingly visible through drifting mists.

Weather fronts had collided east of Philadelphia; hot from the south, cold from the north, thickening into a wet fog that hung over the ocean and coast, obscuring the line where land met sea and making any kind of visual identification impossible. As ever, Pleasure Island sailed in a sea of uncertainty.

A guess based on a guess, and fifteen thousand feet to fall. Water was like cement, if you hit it from more than two hundred feet high. It didn't compress. It shattered anything coming in hard.

11 am on a Thursday. Wren squeezed the walls of the plane, leaning out to graze the buffeting, freezing jet stream. Wind ripped at his clothing and tried to tug the air from his lungs. Freefall for a minute thirty. The chute deployed for five seconds, ten at the outside, then release. He'd have to judge the height by eye; too low and he'd die on impact, too high and every second longer increased the chances of his deployed chute being seen, if anyone was there to see it.

Call it seven seconds under the parachute, followed by icy cold water.

His mouth was dry. He'd skydived many times before, tactical insertions with his Force Recon squad out of USSOCOM. Each time he'd come through unharmed, but never in mist, never with a mere seven-second deployment, never from fifteen thousand feet, without oxygen, into water.

He'd already checked his waterproof pack and gear three times, all scavenged by B4cksl4cker; tactical knife, twin Sig Sauer P226 handguns with spare magazines, Twaron bulletproof vest, sat phone linked direct to the weathernet, magnetic clamp boots, dart gun, front and back body cams, throat-mic. One-man insertion was notoriously challenging. Only one pair of eyes on board had to raise the alarm for his chance to be lost.

A deep breath. Behind him Rogers and the mercenaries were waiting.

"This is it," came Hellion's voice in his ear. She'd asked to be his operator. Wren wasn't sure if that was because she genuinely wanted to help or because she wanted to hear him die. Still, there was no one better he could ask for. Her phenomenal reactions and tactical genius could save him, if she chose to.

Wren chose to trust her.

"I can't see anything," he said.

"Neither can satellites, but the tanker was there two hours ago, the last time the mist cleared."

"Pleasure Island."

"Our best guess. Or a ship full of soybeans, iron ore and raw sugar."

Wren snorted. Major exports from Brazil on this shipping line.

"Check your chest cam."

He gave the middle finger to his own torso.

"Perfect signal," Hellion said. "I wish you the same sentiment."

Wren turned and gave a thumbs up to Rogers in back. She nodded.

He leaned further out into the biting wind. Fifteen minutes in icy water and he'd be dead. If there was no ship down there, he'd hit that boundary fast. If the chute deployed a second out of place. If the Pinocchios saw him coming down. If Charles DeVore wasn't even there…

The engines roared to his left. After ten or so seconds he'd hit terminal velocity and gain maneuverability, be able to cover a mile or two horizontally in the minute remaining. Hopefully put down close to the ship, if there was anything to aim for.

A hand came on his back. "You've got this, boss." Rogers, shouting over the wind.

He didn't turn. She was right. There was nothing more to say, now, just to do. He pulled on a set of goggles, stepped out into air, and the wind yanked him away like a kite in a storm.

He tumbled and soared, counting the seconds as mist streamed over his cheeks, cutting and chilling. Nine seconds, ten, then he hit terminal velocity. He threw his arms back and his legs out and felt the wind catch him like he'd hit a steep slope on a sled, stabilizing his fall and propelling him forward like a loosed arrow.

Still there was nothing below.

"Fifteen seconds," came Hellion's voice in his ear.

"Nothing yet."

"Scanning thermals. It's too thick. Get a bit closer."

Wren couldn't laugh for the wind.

"Twenty seconds."

Still nothing. Falling out of the sky like an angel. A memory came to him; a girl he'd played with as a child in the Pyramid. Maybe eight years old behind the fake town, dancing together in the dust. A few captured pure moments of joy from all of that.

"Thirty seconds."

She'd been so pretty to him then. Not because of her face, but because of her smile. The way she'd laughed; to think that any kind of true, joyful happiness could exist in that place. The Apex had put her in a pit soon afterward. She hadn't come back up again.

He hadn't thought of her for a long time. His eyes streamed in the goggles. What had her name been? Grace, that was it. Just a child, trying to be a child. Maybe Maggie in the fake town had found her bird-like bones by now. Laid them to rest, trying to build something good from her death.

Wren couldn't feel anything but terrible rage.

"Forty seconds. Christopher, I think I see something."

His body felt like it was being guided by the hand of God. If only vengeance brought justice and peace. It had never brought either to Wren. Better to build than to burn, Maggie would say, but how did you let go?

"It's there, Christopher!"

He saw nothing. He yanked at the goggles, rubbing his eyes to clear them. The movement sent him into a slight roll but he corrected quickly.

"Where?"

"On thermals, northeast at a mile distant, the container ship."

Wren lowered his right arm slightly, lifted his left and felt the wind

453

resistance drag him in a sweeping, neat arc. Still he could see nothing. Fifty seconds? Almost there. Somewhere far off he heard the first explosions ring out.

IEDs, blowing low in the mist. Tossed out of the jet on a fuse, several nautical miles away, loud enough to drag all eyes in that direction.

"How far now?"

No answer came.

"Hellion?"

The wind roared. The signal must have cut out. Wren had forgotten the count. How high was he? How far before the ship? His hand swept to the parachute release; a modified sky dive chute, cut for a more explosive deployment.

He had to be at more than a minute now, but still there was nothing. Still he coasted the fog like a skipped stone, soaring into gray with nothing to see but-

The mist split abruptly like a cracked egg, unveiling everything in one sudden blast of information: the container ship ahead hulking low in the water, faded red and black hull, stacked ten tall with container boxes, while around it the choppy gray Atlantic breakers frothed with white. Toy figures at the railing were looking up right at him.

Just a few thousand feet, thirty seconds until he hit; cut off ten for the chute to deploy, five to ride it, two more to drop, and he had thirteen seconds to work with.

One second gone already.

They couldn't be looking at him. It had to be the IEDs, which meant the jet had gotten turned around. More of a highlight than a distraction.

Two seconds.

He threw his body into a sharp, arching twist. Ailerons out of whack, bent like a boomerang, and the wind responded, spinning him into a back-breaking arc. He had to get around the ship and out of the sightline of the airburst bombs.

Five seconds more and the wind raked at his belly and arms, threatening to toss him any second into a roll. The turn was too sharp. To tumble at this altitude was a death sentence; he'd deploy his chute in a tangle, get caught up in the lines and splatter across the water below.

But there were white breakers on the wave tips. Frothy water could compress better than flat; maybe enough to buy him a higher entry speed.

He cut seconds off the chute deployment. The ship soared closer and he plummeted down in a dizzying corkscrew, around the stern where the great engines frothed the water, arching until his spine creaked under the pressure. He let out a scream, hit thirteen seconds, swept into the blind side of the ship's aft corner and ripped the release cord.

The chute ejected, caught the wind with an enormous whomp on its shortened lines, and nearly yanked Wren's shoulders out of joint. The ship was so close now; he saw the spinning radar vanes, the satellite array and a huge upstreaming dish.

Six seconds of float time, no eyes on him that he could see, then he pulled the release to cut the chute's left tether. It yanked away and the wind fell out of his chute, then there were two seconds left with the ocean charging up toward him and his legs slightly bent, toes tilted down, aiming his body like a pro diver at the frothy tip of those breakers, until-

The ocean hit him like a truck; straight up into the bowl of his gut, a heavyweight uppercut in the chin and off the pack on his back, then he was under and blacking out.

"Christopher."

A voice in the agony. Trampled by the herd.

"Christopher."

He blinked in the black. He felt loose and disconnected, like a broken Pinocchio doll with its strings cut. Damage, his mind told him. Ankles. He kicked gently and felt one of them go. Left. He needed to breathe. He couldn't breathe, but the air had all been blasted out of him by the impact. A third of terminal velocity, perhaps.

Too fast. Too hard. He'd be lucky if the ankle wasn't shattered. How would he walk? His groin felt pulverized; a welling, incapacitating sickness. Punch a man in the balls and he could be down for days. Wren had just taken an ocean to the nuts.

He blinked and turned. Blue black. Up above the ocean surface was so far away, twenty feet or more. The cords of the parachute were around him. He pulled the second release but missed two times, three, only scratching at his left breast where the release should be. Blue sky psychology, they called it; panic. He was looking but not seeing.

Training kicked in. He forced himself to slow down and found the release hanging over his shoulder, then yanked it and the strap drifted free. He kicked away to the side. Five feet, ten, ignoring the pain in his left ankle; better to get clear of the chute than risk surfacing through it in a strangling tangle. His lungs burned and he started up. Hellion was chattering away in his ear, or was that static?

At the surface he let only his mouth break through, obscured within the waves, sucking in a gulp of air.

A minute spent like that, waiting for the cold-water shock to pass, waiting for Hellion to reconnect.

"You're clear," she said, sounding distant. "I've reviewed the footage from your back-cam. None of them saw you enter the water."

That was a relief. Already the cold was spreading; he had thirteen minutes yet before hypothermia. The sound of the ship's engine drilled dully through the water, but not too loud. Holding position against the tides only. Anchored for the celebrations to come, under the protection of their new lapdog nation.

Wren broke the surface and peered across a distance of some four hundred feet to the sheer metal wall of the ship. Pleasure Island. At last.

47

PLEASURE ISLAND

After three minutes of front crawl, he hit the ship's flank. Up close it loomed like an overhanging cliff face, towering and sheer. Touching the rough, barnacle-scarred metal, he felt the low thrum of the engine reverberating like a pulse.

From his pack he dug out the first clamp; an oblong high-powered magnet fixed at the end of a wrist-mounted frame, specialist oil rig-repair equipment B4cksl4cker had been extremely proud to source and deliver in time. He touched it to the hull and it clamped on hard. He tethered a cable, linked himself in, then leaned back in the freezing water to get the foot braces on.

They looked like strange black snowboard boots, with large magnetic plates mounted vertically in front of the toes. He tightened the plastic catch on his right foot then tried to slide his left foot in. The pain of his ankle almost blacked him out.

"What's taking so long?" Hellion asked in his ear.

Wren grunted as he tugged the boot on. "I might have broken my ankle."

Hellion said nothing. Not shocked, Wren figured, but re-working, compensating for this in his route through the ship. Footage from his spiral descent should have given her a clear view of the guards; now she'd be mapping them atop the tanker's schematic.

"Can you walk at all?"

"Let's find out," Wren said, and heaved at the boot again. His left foot slid in and the blackness rose up, but he gritted his teeth and willed it back. Pain was just weakness leaving the body. He tightened the plastic strap; it hurt, but the boot functioned like a splint. He touched the front-plate to the hull and it clamped noisily.

He leaned in and stood up, lifting his body out of the water. The pain came like a mantrap around is ankle. Stars spun before his eyes and he felt nauseous; his left foot trembled and chilled, but the clamps held.

"Well?" Hellion asked.

It took Wren a second. "Maybe a stress fracture, could be just an ankle sprain. I'll manage."

"Then manage. I'll talk you through the route."

He attached the right hand-clamp then began to climb, shifting his hands up one at a time, shifting the foot clamps, bracing his weight on his right leg and arms. Every step on his ankle stung, but it worked so he worked it.

"We're looking at ten guards on the walkway," Hellion said, doubtless working from a 3D model built from his footage. "They're spread three hundred feet apart, with four high on the container stacks. On the walkway it looks like they patrol their section, one fore and aft, four down the sides. On the stacks they circle. The best spot for insertion remains aft-port corner, where you are."

Wren worked through what he knew. The ship swelled at the middle and tapered sharply at the rear, confusing sightlines for the guards on the outer walkway. There was no overwatch possible from the five-story castle to back here, thanks to the six-high stacks of twenty-foot metal containers. The men on the stacks had limited visibility straight down; really they were lookouts for incoming ships.

"Also looks like two on a circling perimeter patrol," Hellion added. "They'll notice when you take somebody out."

Wren cursed. Sweating already, a third of the way up the hull. The pain in his heel bit but he ignored it. "How long between sweeps?"

"Working ... calculating pace from your twenty seconds of eyes-on ... looks like three-hundred feet per minute, two of them, which would give you five minutes lead time on a three-thousand-foot perimeter."

Wren ran his own calculations. Halfway up now, he focused on the climb, carefully unpeeling each clamp off sideways, careful not to jostle the others. Trying not to think about what lay on the other side of the hull: four deep cargo bays down to the ship's spine, containers stacked eight deep below the deck and seven above it, in excess of ten thousand twenty-foot boxes in total, filled with soybeans, iron ore, raw sugar and children.

And children.

He squeezed the grips and hauled himself up. Three quarters. They could be anywhere on board, hidden in more floor space than a dozen city blocks, but Hellion had leads; original plans recovered from Gebhart's computer. His old designs called for secret compartments carved into the depths of the stacks, an interchangeable system of boxes that allowed for rooms, corridors, even huge hollow arenas.

The belly of the whale.

Hellion had mocked up some 3D models; access provided by makeshift industrial elevators, containers assembled like blocks in an Egyptian pyramid, with the internal chambers already formed, offering a straight shot down to the cages where the slaves labored. All day and all night. Remnants tossed to sea. A movable feast.

Wren felt his face burning. The cold of the ocean was forgotten. Almost to the top now.

"Christopher?"

"In position," he whispered back. Under the railing, squatting on his magnet clamps. The ship groaned, and the engine was a dull, ever-present throb. The sour tang of cigarette smoke curled in the misty air.

"Give me eyes," Hellion said. Wren unlatched the front bodycam from his chest and lifted it slowly above the rim.

"Angle left," Hellion said. He heard keys clacking; the sound of her marking targets and re-assessing her map. "Now right."

He waited.

"Static guard is thirty feet to your right," she said. "The nearest to the left is over five hundred feet, almost beyond the curve. No sign of the patrol. Hold fast."

Wren held. The sea lapped below. He played out the strike ahead: onto the narrow railing encircling the cargo, take out the static guard, get into the castle and find the access point to the elevator shaft down.

"Christopher!"

Hellion's voice was cold. He hung still, barely breathing. Easing his dart gun out, checking the action, unstrapping his feet from the boots. Over the thump of waves there came the clank of footfalls. The guard on patrol.

"There's two of them," Hellion hissed. Wren recognized it now; the double beat of footsteps in tandem. "Fifty yards apart."

Wren said nothing. There was no need to. Two at once meant three men in his vicinity; two on patrol and the static guard. Three times the chance of the alarm going up.

"Wait for the first to pass," Hellion said, "shoot from the middle, hope the static guard is near."

Wren dismissed it. In a game it might work; you could always try again, but he had no second chance. He peeled his right foot off the hull, pulled it back, waited, waited, then kicked it hard into metal.

A deep, ringing bong thrummed out.

The footfalls stopped. Wren aimed. Guessing. To his right at the railing, twenty yards away. Not a good angle for them to use their rifles. Not an easy angle to see him. For him a straight shot into their eyes.

The first leaned over. Wren saw only his silhouette, like a paper target on the range, and loosed three darts with three fizzing whips of air. Two thunked home, eye and cheek. The man's mouth opened wide, and then he slowly, agonizingly tipped...

Wren didn't wait.

A second face appeared, too soon after the first to react well, almost directly above Wren. He fired three more fizzing darts and they all hit, face face neck, and the man, a ruddy-cheeked giant, sagged instantly, bouncing off the railing.

"What the-" came a voice from above, but Wren was already moving. Springing up and vaulting the railing, landing awkwardly and tipping on his bad ankle, but turning that tip into positive momentum.

The third man was wide-eyed and terrified, scrabbling to grip his rifle slung low across his belly. It was right there but he wasn't ready. His finger couldn't find the trigger. Fifteen yards, and Wren fired. Two darts remaining, one hit in his left arm and it sagged, but not enough. His mouth was opening, signals getting to his brain and back again with the message to raise the alarm.

Wren buried the cry with his knife, a sweeping cross body toss from the holster on his left hip like he was sending a Frisbee for the distance. The knife shot out, end over end closing the gap in half a second, took the guard in his open mouth.

He sagged without a further sound.

Wren stood unevenly, looking left and right.

Two bodies. The railing, the stacks at his back, containers rising in rust-patched red and yellow and blue. No sight line to the aft, the castle, or the nearest guard to the left.

"Three down," he said, and retrieved his knife. Two bodies went over the rail. A clean sweep, and no time to waste. Ten minutes lead time, maybe. He was going to need every second.

48

PYRAMID

The castle door swung open. Inside was the guards' quarters: dimly lit, two desks at the side with old tower computers, several beds along the far wall behind a partially-drawn curtain, a rec area, kitchen, but no stairs up or down and no secret door through to the containers.

"It's not this," Hellion said, watching through his body cam. "You're only seeing half the width of the castle. Access must be on the other side."

Wren strode further in.

"Where are you going?"

Near the desk he looked up. A hatch in the ceiling, one in the floor; welded over. There had been stairs here. Now the guards were on their own loop, completely separated from the Pinocchios within. Layers within layers, like multiple VPNs built into reality. Gebhart's MO.

"You'll have to go around," Hellion said, whispering now. "Two more guards on the walkway, maybe. It eats into our lead, but…"

"No," Wren whispered back, and strode toward the curtain, hung from rivet holes in the deck beams above. He stepped through into the dark rear section. It smelled of stale sweat and musty clothes, like a locker room. Standing in the hot, humid dark, Wren's eyes adjusted. The false partition wall didn't match the sides; not metal, more like plasterboard painted to look like metal. He scanned the beds; four of them, two figures asleep.

Pinocchio wannabes, Wren figured. Hoping to prove themselves and one day be admitted.

Their bad luck.

"What is it?" Hellion whispered.

Wren strode to the first man. There was no time to be kind. Every Pinocchio left here was a man he'd have to fight later. He leaned in gently, cradled the man's head in his hands, then twisted.

His neck broke with a crack, like a dry stick. Dead in his sleep, instantly. No thrashing, no mess. The second went just the same.

"Oh, Christopher," said Hellion.

"It's a false wall," Wren said, already moving on. "Plasterboard. It'll come away."

He moved to the edge of the rear wall, where damp had turned the plaster black, pushed against it, and the softened material gave way. He pushed harder, tearing the boards away from a few bolts fastened to the bulkhead.

On the other side lay a dark, cold cavity space, five feet wide and bordered to the right with another wall; this one was inset with wide windows and a door. Cameras were set up in the darkness, blinking red and pointed through the glass to a very different world.

Dark wood flooring, red leather panels, sconces releasing an orange glow. Like the lobby of a five-star hotel, modeled after Gebhart's dungeon. Lush-looking armchairs were set out with ashtrays, potted jungle plants bloomed in the corners, fresh flowers sprayed outward on a central table, and a reception desk was manned by a young blond woman in a pert blue cap. On the left an ornate gilt door was built into a marble-effect wall, leading into the containers.

"Bingo," whispered Hellion. "But why the cameras?"

Wren didn't need to answer. Given their gamified system of control, the Pinocchios would be constantly vying with each other. This was the elites keeping tabs on each other, stacking up blackmail. How much trust could there be in a society shaped by daily votes for popularity?

Wren strode past the cameras, switched off the last on the left that overlooked the marble wall, then opened the door.

Instantly the atmosphere was different. Underfoot the wood flexed like ancient boards in a grand Southern home. The warm air smelled of jasmine and lemongrass. To the right the girl at the reception desk stared.

"Don't you move," Wren said.

She didn't move. There was no way she was a Pinocchio, not with those eyes. Maybe she was someone's favorite, graduated to an above decks role.

"Keep quiet and you'll be free soon," Wren said, then opened the door through the marble wall. Beyond it lay a corridor that passed through the outer skin of the castle and into where the containers should be. Wren couldn't help but admire the workmanship to cover up the welds. Fifteen yards the corridor extended: carpeted in red and gold, framed with elegant dark baseboards, wallpapered in taupe and hung with scenes of ancient Greek temples. In reality it was a tunnel bored through containers, a metal tube hanging in carved hollows, but it didn't look like that.

Gebhart would have loved it. The idea of stepping through the cracks in the normal world and into a secret realm that belonged only to him. Like the darknet, like the dancing web portal for Pleasure Island, like his dungeon hidden beneath the Idaho dirt.

Wren turned at the corner. Ten yards further stood the elevator; classic brass frame, safety grille concertina, with a guard either side. Not the same as the men outside; these were clearly Pinocchio elites, with better gear, greater alertness, their hands already on their weapons.

Wren fired, dual-wielding his twin P226s, four shots ringing out in fast succession. One each in the head and chest. Two enormous combined blasts. Echoes rang around Wren as he advanced; the sound trapped within the metal echo chamber.

"Couldn't have done it better myself," Hellion said.

The guards dropped and Wren strode into the elevator, feeling the flow state descend upon him. Gold, mirrors, carvings of depraved sexual deeds. The pain in his heel was very far away. He tugged the concertina grille across and pulled the brass lever set in its attractive casement.

Finally.

49

BELLY OF THE WHALE

The elevator stopped some four stories down, the door opened, and a luxurious corridor extended ahead through the concertina grille. Wren took it all in. Plush beige carpeting, soft-glow wall-sconce lamps, wood-paneled walls, and men in cream terrycloth gowns walking, talking, smoking. Attendants in blue tunics pushed cleaning carts full of mounded laundry. Children stood here and there, leashed like animals, dressed in costumes as if for Halloween Trick-or-Treating.

The belly of the whale. Wren saw them but they didn't see him. Tactics went out of the window and strategy failed him. For a second, two, he just stood behind the grille and stared.

Children. The warm, balmy smell of vanilla cigar smoke on the air, barely masking the earthy undercurrent of sweat and the tang of blood. Wren's skin crawled. Three seconds. Maybe one of them had seen him now, was looking. A guard leaned out from the side, peering in through the concertina.

Both Wren's guns fired at once, and the man's head flew back.

Every eye spun to him now. Silence fell in the corridor for a moment, the calm before the storm. Then it began.

Wren shoved the concertina aside and strode through, shooting the guard to his left then firing ahead into the rich hunting ground; twelve bullets from each pistol in less than ten seconds, striking twelve targets each. Heads rocked back, bullets tumbled through to targets beyond, high above the height of the children and slaughtering their masters. A blood mist rose and Wren glided into it in a transcendent haze, like a god yanked in on the machine, bringing holy retribution for crimes against humanity.

No mercy for these men. No sympathy, no help, only the cold certainty of the grave.

He reloaded and fired while the screams and the chaos became a scrabbling, desperate roar. He shot a fat man with yellowish skin and a large liverwort exposed on his chest. He shot a tall man as thin as a cadaver, standing in a cluster with a short round-faced man, a man with an Elvis hairdo, a man with a tasseled beard.

Dead dead dead.

Reloading again, in the screams that followed.

His arms moved independently of his mind, finding targets one after another as he flowed over freshly-fallen corpses, dropping bodies like stringless dolls, all Pinocchios here. The hail of gunfire built into a storm in the corridor, thunderous with the pealing of screams, the terrible ricochet of bullets.

They screamed and died. Children stared as he passed, unable to fully comprehend his arrival. A middle-aged man on the floor, dark-haired, handsome, tried to shield himself with one pale palm, and Wren shot through his fingers.

Doors slammed to all sides. Pinocchios taking refuge. Wren didn't care. They couldn't hide from this.

"Christopher!" came a voice in his ear, but he didn't hear it. It didn't matter.

He kicked in a door on the left. A five-star hotel room, bed, furniture, lights, trimmings; two glass-eyed little girls with a powerfully muscled man holding them as a human shield, trying to shout out some kind of negotiation. Wren fired through a gap into his groin. He shrieked, his blood spumed out over the sheets like a burst catheter. Wren shot him in the head then moved on.

In one room a tall man swung a lamp as a weapon, then died. In one room a man all in leathers died. In one room a man, then a man, then another man.

Dead dead dead.

His guns clicked.

Standing in the corridor, wreathed by gun smoke, the smell of cordite was everywhere. Bodies draped the floor.

"Christopher!"

He looked at the P226s in his hands. Hot. Smoking. What were these? A trail of bodies lay behind him and a trail of bodies lay in front, like the streets of the fake town, back when he'd burned them all. They were burning still, and it was all his work. He felt his father's hand at his back even now, guiding him on, gleeful with his dedication to devastation, but this was not his father's work.

This belonged to him alone.

"Christopher, this is not what we-"

A shot rang out. He looked at his guns, perplexed. Tinnitus? An echo, a bad dream? Then another came, and this one he felt. It hit his lower back, left side, and reeled him sideways. He lurched into the wall, staggering on his bad ankle. His back bloomed cold; hopefully the vest had taken the worst of it.

He spun. A man stood in the middle of the corridor.

"Charles?" Wren asked.

The man fired in a frenzy, spraying the walls and floor. Wren dropped his empty guns and advanced, pulling his knife.

"Shh," he said, "Charles."

It was DeVore in his chair again, sitting in the den and waiting for permission. The gun in his hand wasn't a gun at all. He fired only once more, arm shaking so bad he hit the ceiling, then dropped the weapon as if it had bit him. He turned to run and saw only bodies. He dropped to his knees.

Wren caught him.

"Shh, Charles," he said, and brought the knife around, pushed it into his throat in one smooth movement. The man pawed up at him. Begging for mercy, but Wren had nothing to give.

He sagged. Wren picked up his gun and looked at his face. Realized it wasn't Charles, just another man. He touched his lower back and his hand came back clean. The vest had done its job.

"Christopher Wren, get on point right now!"

He blinked and turned. The voice was familiar. Coming from very far away, nearly tuned out by the mass of metal above. Probably she'd found a way into the Fairy's wireless network. His very own Jiminy Cricket.

"Hellion."

"Yes, Hellion! What happened, you went crazy."

"I-"

"There's no time. They are already sending signals, Christopher, doubling security. We can see enough to fend off the walls they're throwing up, B4cksl4cker's doing all he can, but not for long. We need that key!"

It came back to him. He wasn't here just to kill these people. He needed Charles DeVore. His phone was the key to a more total devastation of the Blue Fairy than this.

He looked to the elevator. The concertina grille still hung open, perhaps the only unsullied part of the corridor. The mirrors within reflected the world back at him, all the dead. Children moved amongst them now, some escaping, some taking their revenge. Here a girl punched a dead man in the face, again and again.

Good. Anger was the only bandage that had ever helped Wren.

He found an attendant amidst the dying, struggling to breathe in his blue tunic, and knelt beside him. Gasping, eyes rolling, wondering, 'Why me?' Wren descended across his field of vision and he tried to jerk away, limbs reeling.

"Where is Charles DeVore?"

The man sucked at the air like a bellows. Blowing himself up like a balloon.

"I- I-"

Wren pressed the muzzle of the gun against his forehead. "Charles DeVore, where is he?"

"I don't know!"

"The guy from the photo. The guy who caught Mona Gebhart."

"I-"

Wren put a foot on the wound in his thigh.

"Arrghh! In the temple."

"Where's the temple?"

"All the way along!" The guy pointed with one flapping hand. Wren wondered what his level of guilt was. Another wannabe, maybe not a full-blood Pinocchio yet, but aspiring to join them one day. Wren put the knife in his throat and moved on.

"Mapping," said Hellion, but Wren didn't need it. The corridor went in only one direction.

50

TEMPLE

W ren burst through the doors at the end of the corridor into the Blue Fairy's true heart.

The temple.

It was a grand hall of iron stretched into cavernous space, thirty feet tall and held up with great sloping girders. Wren's mind boggled at the mechanics of the space, dug out from within the boxes deep inside the container ship, decked all in raw, corroded metal. The fake, bullshit luxury of Pleasure Island ended here.

This was grimy and harsh, the brutal, primitive heart of Gebhart's Blue Fairy, beating with the thrum of the engine.

A metal block stood in the center as an altar, surrounded by concentric rings of tiered metal seating. Cameras were spotted everywhere, blinking red, but no Pinocchios left except the naked male rearing back on the altar, knife held high, straddling the thrashing figure of Clara Baxter.

Charles DeVore.

Wren fired.

The bullet hit Charles in the shoulder and punched him off the altar, crunching to the metal floor. Wren ran down the stairs. He saw the fear on Clara's face and understood that this was Charles' endgame, his boulder hitting the bottom of the slope, and it pushed Wren beyond the edge.

He fell on Charles in a frenzy. Hellion's voice in his ear meant nothing as he drove punches into DeVore's fleshy face, body convulsing on the unforgiving metal.

Then he stopped. The voice in his ear was screaming.

He looked down at Charles. His face was a mess but his eyes were the same, looking up from within. The same man he'd been some twelve hours earlier, before any of this, but so much further along. Broken, bitter, and full of unforgivable drives.

"You can't do that, Charles," Wren said, softly now, like Charles might somehow understand. Charles struggled to breathe. His hands patted Wren's face feebly, seeking something. "You just can't do it."

Wren looked around, as if seeing the space for the first time. The cameras that were watching. He staring down their lenses one by one. Every one of them, marked. The voice in his ear became clearer.

"The phone, Christopher! Before he passes out!"

Wren looked at Charles, then he stood, his heel grating painfully, and scanned the floor. A shirt there on the floor. Pants. He picked them up, fished in the pockets and came up with Charles' phone. He tapped in the PIN, six digits he'd memorized twelve hours ago in the family den, and the phone opened. Wren pulled out his satellite phone and tapped Hellion's app, beginning forced pairing.

A second passed.

"I am in," Hellion said sharply, "I see it, beginning uplift." She was triumphant now, playing her game, hacking another system. Wren was just another avatar.

"Get ready to kill the cameras," Wren whispered. Looking down at Charles DeVore. A bitter, twisted man. A man who'd corrupted himself. After the fear and the horror, all that remained now was the waste.

"Ready," said Hellion.

Wren stood. The red lights watched.

"I'm coming for you all," Wren said. To Pinocchios around the world. "You will never be this free again. Turn yourselves in or die. There will be no mercy from me."

"Now?" Hellion asked.

Wren grunted.

The red lights started winking out around him. He stared the last of them down. Cutting them off. Left to live in fear. Awaiting the day Christopher Wren would come for them too.

He turned to Clara Baxter on the altar and cut her free, smiling as gently as he could. "I'm a fan of your work."

As he cut the last tie she rolled off the altar, scooped up a pistol where it lay and trained it on Wren. She was naked, but didn't seem to care. Tougher than any of these small men. Battered but unbowed.

A survivor.

"Who the hell are you?" she asked.

"Christopher Wren," he said, arms out with palms up now, not daring to budge an inch. "I've got an organization you may want to join. We can help with all of this. The catfishing, the Pinocchios, with anything you need."

She stared at him, cool and untrusting. That was fine, as long as she didn't shoot. When all this was over, she'd make her decisions. The offer would stand. He thought of Maggie in the fake town. It could be a good thing for them all.

"Here," Wren said, and bent down to scoop up Charles DeVore. His ankle almost betrayed him, but just about held. For a moment there was hope in DeVore's watery eyes. Maybe he thought it was compassion. Then Wren set him down on the altar. Devore began screaming like a wounded animal.

Wren strapped his legs in, then his arms, like he was buckling the seatbelt of an unruly child. DeVore tried to resist but was too weak to stop it. Now he lay naked on the altar, completely vulnerable, just like Lance Gebhart before him.

Clara watched all this without blinking, without moving the gun off Wren's chest. "Turn the cameras back on," she said.

Wren looked at her, saw the anger in her eyes and recognized a fellow traveler on the road out of pain. This was what she needed to survive.

"You heard her," he said to Hellion.

The red lights started to blink back to life.

"He's all yours."

51

DEPTHS

Wren found the Pinocchios in the deck below.

Trudging down the empty corridor with his heel grinding on every step, Hellion spoke in his ear.

"It's all here, Christopher ... we are breaking Pleasure Island right now ... I am seeing whole map: addresses, code, cryptography. B4cksl4cker is relaying it live, Interpol are moving in, Germans, British, Japanese, Chinese, French ... locations all around the world."

She was excited. She'd earned it.

He found the open stairwell halfway down the corridor, a gap in the containers filled with scaffolding stairs that led down into the sound of children crying, like a well of human suffering.

"Belgium, China, now Philadelphia! ... There is Interpol envoy closing on your position, looks like ... requisitioned UN troops from nearby diplomatic mission ... the US government is calling back into session. The media ban's been lifted already. I think that's your Humphreys' doing, and ... the nuclear threat's gone! We have full control of all nuclear facilities."

"Give it back," Wren said, starting down the stairs. Holding the railing, watching blood spots drip from his hands. The back of his leg ran slick and hot and already he felt weak.

"Of course, Christopher."

"All of it. You'll get the second skin, Hellion. The rest is theirs. No backdoors."

"Of course."

"Promise me."

"I promise."

He hit the bottom, feeling lightheaded. Round the corner lay another corridor, very different from the one above. The floor was metal grille. The walls were all container boxes. Built from the ground up, the Pinocchios had assembled their paradise with the children bricked in as the foundation. There was wailing, now, and so much fear.

The stables.

Wren could feel them stretching ahead of him: children stolen from Syria, Lebanon, Yemen; children bought from Thailand, Malaysia, Vietnam; children snatched from Ethiopia, Somalia, Eritrea.

He went to the first box and looked through the window lattice. There were children inside, maybe fifty of them wearing rags, clustered together at the back with eyes that kept darting right.

Everything he needed to know. Wren swung the door open and plunged in with the knife. It buried in the neck of a Pinocchio to the left, hidden against the wall. He looked surprised. There were two more behind him, half-naked in their robes, and Wren shot them through with one bullet. They gasped in harmony, like a pair of whistling reeds, and dropped.

"They're all yours," he mumbled at the children, echoing what he'd said to Clara.

Probably they didn't speak English, but it didn't matter. They would know what to do.

He moved on.

The next container. The Pinocchios hadn't thought clearly, hiding in the cells of their slaves. Every time the eyes of the children gave them away. The door opened, the gun fired, the knife rose and fell. Some tried to fight, but they were weak even if they were strong. Their conviction was broken, their gym muscles meant nothing against Wren. He killed them one after another, box after box.

There were labels printed on each, categorized like animals, by skin tone, gender, age. Wren killed his way down the cells. Children ran in his wake. Children followed him. Children darted in each time he made a kill, teaching the others how to get their revenge.

Wren led them on. Suffer the little children to come to me. His people.

His Foundation. Killing after killing. Soon all the Pinocchios were on their knees, begging him, but there could be no quarter given. He executed them and left their bodies for the children.

"I traced all the camera feeds back," Hellion said in his ear, "we have international forces moving everywhere, making arrests. You should know that the Interpol boats are closing on Pleasure Island now, with a Coast Guard fleet in back. They'll be boarding soon. You can stop killing them."

"Hold them off," Wren mumbled, "we're not finished."

"Holding," Hellion answered.

He killed them until they were all dead. It was a job to be done, some thirty containers swarming with children and hidden Pinocchios. Little angels taking something back for themselves. There was no need to speak now. In every box the children were waiting, staring at him with round, wondrous eyes, starting to understand that somebody good had finally come.

Cheering.

He drifted. He walked back along the corridor above. From the temple came Charles DeVore's muffled screams. Wren didn't want to see. Clara's revenge was personal. Rage would take you a long way. He trailed the knife along the walls while his army of children rampaged in back, tearing open doors and flooding in like a tide, scratching, biting, finishing any men within. His children, now.

He weaved. The elevator was there and he rode it up.

Through the lobby, out of the hidden door to the deck, he stood again at the railing. All the guards were long gone. There were lights through the mist, now. Interpol. Coast Guard. Voices calling on megaphones, announcing they were boarding.

A fine rain fell. Wren felt dreamlike, different. Not healed, but not broken. Nothing, really. Floating perhaps. It would be good to go over the railing, drop into the cold water and sink, not come up again. What could be better than that?

"Report," he said.

"I have your exit coming," Hellion said. "It's Rogers."

Wren laughed. Rogers. That seemed like a lifetime ago.

"Port side. Just her and one of your Foundation. Her name's Cheryl."

Wren laughed again. Cheryl, the dominatrix from Chicago? She'd been shot on Foundation business dealing with the Saints, had a liver transplant, and made a surprising recovery. He imagined her in leathers, sneering at the filthy state he was in. Called in, he supposed, answering a request he hadn't even placed. Hellion and B4cksl4cker understood more than he did. Looking after him. Thinking through to the endgame when he only had eyes for the present.

Cheryl didn't have a motherly bone in her body, but she was a kind of friend. It would be good to see her, to talk to someone who'd known Dr. Ferat. Maybe he could visit Chicago Teddy too, in his coma, in his hospital bed. That would be nice. Tears ran down his cheeks. He thought about the look in Clara's eyes when he'd strapped DeVore down. He thought about how it had felt to just keep killing them all. He thought about all the children whose lives would be forever scarred by what had happened to them here.

There had to be a better way. Such a damn waste.

Still he felt something like joy. Maybe relief mingling with sadness. It was always like this. A catharsis, and a weariness, and wondering what came next.

"Get Clara out."

"She's finding her own way. I'm in the cameras; she's finished with him."

"He's dead."

"Not dead," Hellion said. Wren could hear the distaste. "Mutilated, though. He'll live, and serve his time. Everybody will get to see the trial."

Wren grunted. Everybody had already seen, and perhaps that was right.

"Humphreys sends his best," Hellion added.

Wren thought about the jet he'd had to steal, and the pilot who'd been injured. Maybe it wasn't Humphreys' fault, not exactly, but Wren wasn't yet able to forgive. You had to be ready to fight right at the start, just as soon as the boulder started to roll. You had to be ready all the time.

"They're ahead of you," Hellion said.

Wren looked out, and saw them through the mist. A small fishing boat approaching without any lights. From behind him, on the other side of the tanker, the clank of boarding gear rang against the hull. Lights and megaphones. Wren didn't want to be here for that. He leaned over the railing and smiled. Less than two hundred feet. It would be fine.

He dropped, splashed into the deep, smothering cold, and let himself sink.

52

HOME

W ren stood at the edge of the fake town at night, Arizona, looking out at the fires.

Kids were clustered around them, toasting s'mores. Kids from the ship, from around the world, who had probably never had a s'more before, who might not even know what a graham cracker was. They seemed to be having a good time. Only a small group of them, for now, but more would follow.

His back throbbed still. The bullet had dug through the Twaron vest and bumped against his hip; a flesh wound and a bruised bone, extracted and sewn up by a doctor in his Foundation two weeks ago.

A lot of things had changed in that time. The darknet site was sturdier than ever. Hellion and B4cksl4cker had agreed to limits, but the possibilities of their new second skin, along with Gebhart's weathernet, still had them hopping with excitement at all hours.

His foot was in a cast. Sprained ankle. He'd probably broken records for that sky dive, but he wasn't shouting it from the rooftops. Rogers and Cheryl had been happy to see him on the boat, fishing him out of the cold water, but he didn't really remember much after that. Now Rogers had been promoted, and was leading her own freelance team at CIA. He'd called her to offer his congratulations, but she hadn't taken the call.

Humphreys had reached out several times. Wren hadn't answered.

"I'm sorry," the Director said in a voice message. "I can't say any more. I'll do whatever you ask."

Wren wasn't sure that was enough. Still, he always spent capital. On his demand, every child brought to the United States by the Blue Fairy would become a citizen immediately, with a substantial trust fund set up in their name. No questions about it, no delays, ram it through in a week.

Humphreys made it happen. On every one of their papers was Wren's name, and Mona Gebhart's too, enshrined as legal guardians. He'd been proud to see the first of the certificates, scanned through and sent on by Rogers. Something good from something so bad. It was an enormous expansion to his Foundation, and a substantial shift of focus. The Foundation had the funds to provide care, but it required a phenomenal degree of management.

Maggie volunteered. Wren barely even had to ask.

Now millions in donations were pouring in. The breaking of the Blue Fairy had energized the world. Maggie had set up a website and Hellion and B4cksl4cker ensured it was visible everywhere. The fake town was coming back to life with a huge amount of new construction; dormitories, a library, a school, a gym and pool, a new oasis of life in the desert. That made Wren happy in the most complex way. One thousand one hundred and twenty-three children, ages three to seventeen, very few of whom spoke English, most of them orphaned, deeply damaged and angry, but containing still so much potential. Wren saw it every time he looked at them.

Stars tumbled overhead. His leased Jeep stood ticking at his side, fuelled for a long drive. For the kids there'd be a hayride soon, and a hand-held tour of the desert without flashlights, and the children would cackle, and squeal, and be children again for a time. He'd wanted to burn all this down before, but now he was glad he hadn't. Things could change. Things could heal, maybe, even while crimes were still happening.

At least the crimes were not happening here. Here life could go on.

Out there, Mona Gebhart was still hunting somewhere. Thanks to her, Charles DeVore was passing through the judicial system for all to see. He'd wanted to be a big man in the Blue Fairy, and now he was the biggest. Reviled by all. His family had gone into witness protection, changing their names. They hadn't told his daughters yet. One day, perhaps, they would find out. On that day, maybe they'd like to come see the fake town, to come and understand what good things had come from their hardest pain. There could be healing for them, too.

He looked down at his hands, at the flash drive twined in his fingers. Sent to him by Dr. Ferat through a postal back-and-forth that saw members of the Foundation constantly posting it on. It contained more than backups of the Foundation's latest records, the coin system, and the forum boards. There was a message from Dr. Ferat in there too. Several times he'd almost opened it, but each time he'd pulled back.

They'd found Ferat's body near Woodstock in the Catskills, on rocks at the bottom of a lakeside cliff. He was cinders, really, but the autopsy showed his neck had broken on impact. It would have been painless. The fires that followed had been cleansing. Now he had a tomb at the edge of the fake town that was no longer so fake. It was becoming a home.

Wren squeezed the flash drive. He was angry at Ferat for dying, for being the hero and pushing himself into the crosshairs, but there was nothing to do with that anger now but add it to the pile. He'd read Ferat's last words sometime in the future, but not now. He wasn't ready. He knew what he was going to say anyway; words about Tandrews, about seeing his wife, his kids. He wanted to be with his family more than anything, but how could he, with the Apex still out there?

He slipped the drive back in his pocket.

The sound of laughter rose from below. Bobbing for apples, it looked like, while some played with sparklers. A Roman Candle fizzed yellow and green. The smell of s'mores carried on the wind, along with hotdogs sizzling on a charcoal griddle.

He'd been right here, watching from a distance, when the first school bus of children had driven in. They had so many needs. Maggie had bent admirably to helping them, hiring experts in post-trauma childcare, physiotherapists, a dozen different translators, a diverse range of summer camp counselors and more. She'd bustled and hustled them all in, clucking like a mother hen, though at the end, when the children were all in, she'd looked around quizzically.

Looking for him, he'd figured.

"You're leaving."

The voice took him by surprise. She knew the desert better than him, now.

He turned to face her. Maggie. Just standing by his truck, a sad smile on her warm, ringlet-framed face. Now she wore a long, flowing gown in comforting shades of brown, with a tan sash hanging down, wrapped up like a desert rose seed husk.

Wren smiled. "You got me."

She just looked at him. He didn't like the way her eyes seemed to peel through his defenses. She took a few steps forward to stand beside him, so they were looking out at the town together

"They look happy now," she said, "but they still cry at night."

Wren didn't know what to say. That was too close to his own experience. At night was when the memories came. The nightmares. He opened his mouth to say something, but nothing came out.

Now she was looking at him. Her eyes were deep like the Atlantic, like cold water he wanted to fall into and be smothered. She was just a person, but the things she'd dedicated herself to… He didn't know what to do with that. What to say, where to put it.

"You're like a ghost, haunting this place," she said. "I've felt you watching us. I know you've been out here."

He gulped. His throat felt dry. "I try to be invisible. I don't want to scare them."

She looked into his eyes. It disturbed him, to think what she saw within. Not afraid of her, exactly but afraid of the things she could do, if he ever let her in.

"That wasn't me telling you not to come," she said. "I can see it's not easy for you. I tried to catch you a few times, but you're fast." She smiled. "I'm glad I caught you now."

He nodded. Normally he'd have plenty of words. Something charming. An easy way to shrug off the moment, to make it not real, but this was completely real. Real like Dr. Ferat being dead, real like all those children finding a new start in life.

He looked up, and she put a hand on his arm. A moment passed, and neither of them moved.

"You're a good kind of ghost," she said. "A kind, generous man. I feel it. The children feel it too. They feel protected. You stay out here as long as you need to, just as long as you know there's a place at the head of the table when you're ready to take it. You were right before, when we first met. This is your town, Christopher Wren. It belongs to you, and we are just guests

479

within it. Thank you for letting us stay. I'm sorry our presence here is so hard for you."

She squeezed his arm. "I've seen pain. I've felt echoes of it all my life. The Pyramid scarred me, and now those echoes are in the ground. But you're not an echo. You're a ghost who will come back to the living, one day. I know it. I'm looking forward to it."

Then she walked away. Across the darkness, moving smoothly over the rough desert grass, her nimble feet making no sound at all.

Home.

More than anything, Wren wanted to follow her. To go play with those children, to laugh with them, then to go home and see his own children, Jake and Quinn.

He couldn't do either.

Loralei's words echoed in his head. Back in Delaware, with her new guy standing by Wren's side. That he didn't get it. That she didn't want to see him. That he was bad for his own kids.

Seemed she was right. How could he be anything to them, a father, maybe even a husband, while his children were targets still, of Pinocchios out there in the darkness, supported by an ingrained infrastructure of power and money. While the Apex was out there too, or someone trying to pick up where he'd left off.

They all had to die. The Blue Fairy. The Apex. Every last one.

Wren climbed into his truck, feeling the rage surging anew. Turned the radio up high and punched the vehicle into gear, then peeled away from the fake town, from the lights and laughter, and flew out into the dark of the hunt.

CLAIM YOUR REPARATION

MAKE THEM PAY

A CHRISTOPHER WREN THRILLER

MIKE GRIST

1

DEADHORSE

C hris Wren sat in his truck in Deadhorse, Alaska, lit only by the glimmering green tendrils of the Northern Lights above, planning his next kill.

Pythagoras.

On the Blue Fairy's dark Internet of abusers, he was one of the worst. Active since the beginning. His track record was phenomenal, with hundreds of children destroyed in his wake. Maybe he would have some answers.

Wren rubbed his bleary eyes. He was worn out, hadn't been sleeping well recently. His hands shook like an alcoholic's coming down, smeared with blood still.

Whose blood?

He couldn't remember. The last three months were a blur of Blue Fairy interrogations. He'd been in Florida for one, then California, then New Mexico, hunting the 'Pinocchios' who'd targeted his children, who might know something about his father.

Apex of the Pyramid death cult. The man who'd ruined Wren's young life, and even now hung over his children's' lives like some sword of Damocles.

His phone started buzzing in the glove box.

Wren ignored it, looking out at the rippling green aurora as it danced across the deep Arctic sky. It was almost painfully beautiful. So much beauty in such a dark place. 1 a.m., and the sun had only gone down an hour back, with sunrise coming in three. The company town of Deadhorse on the northwest coast of Alaska in mid-January, a place for oilfield workers, ice road truckers, the occasional coach full of Japanese tourists and now Christopher Wren.

He'd pulled up five hours earlier after a long-haul drive up from the States, shown his fake passport and special permit at the town limits. The guard had been chatty, said he was the only tourist in town this deep into the winter, boasting that the rivers were so frozen even the fish were hibernating. Wren hadn't known if that was a joke or not.

The phone kept on vibrating.

Wren popped the glove box and picked it up, a burner bought a few weeks ago. He thumbed the screen and the vibrations stopped. An alarm, the same time he'd set night after night. He tapped in the phone number on the glass for the hundredth time and stared at it. 4 a.m. here, 7 a.m. back east in the Delaware duplex, where his wife Loralei would just be waking up, laying out her yoga mat for a morning routine. Their kids Jake and Quinn would be asleep still, almost as if nothing had changed.

Except everything had changed. They weren't in their family home in New York anymore. His wife and kids had fled when Loralei found out what Wren did for a living, the CIA's international assassin of cults, gangs and cartels. 'Saint Justice', they called him.

Already Loralei had found a new man. She didn't want Wren's protection, despite or perhaps because of the threat he brought to hang over their heads. She didn't even want to let him see his kids, at least not until the threat had passed. Until Wren found his father and put him down like a rabid dog.

So Wren was out here, hunting leads.

He squeezed the delete key and the Delaware phone number disappeared, just like every night before. To see his kids again, he first had to make them safe, and that path lead right through Pythagoras.

A top-level Pinocchio in the Blue Fairy organization. One of the founding members, even, Wren's interrogations so far had unearthed. If anyone had the link back to Wren's father, it was this man.

Wren reached into the backseat of the truck, began pulling on his cold weather gear: thick boots, a Twaron-fiber bulletproof vest under a heavy red parka, a big toboggan hat, goose down gloves. In the belly flap of the parka he put his SIG Sauer P320 .45 ACP, then opened the truck door and stepped out.

Freezing air blasted his face. Fresh snowfall crunched under his feet.

He stood for a moment, taking in the green-tinted scene. To the south lay snow-coated mountains like shaved ice confections, sauced with thick veins of melt water. To the north lay the empty expanse of the gray Arctic Ocean. The sky above was a dappled wash of aurora, and beneath it lay Deadhorse, just a cluster of boxy modular structures constructed atop gravel pads staked into the tundra bog.

Wren strode forward. The supply depot lay at the rough center of town, a few hundred yards past an iced-over lake. Industrial structures hugged the road as if for warmth, a mechanic's yard, a field of towering electrical transformers, a heavy vehicles pool.

A few people were out early: a guy scraping ice off the windshield of his pick-up in rough, raspy strokes; drunk pipeline workers heading back to their company lodgings, all bundled up in bright jackets. It was a dry county, but the locals always had their ways to source booze. The air smelled impossibly fresh and stung his throat. A few cars lined the road, big country trucks with all-wheel drive and snow chains.

The depot was a blue box in their midst, airdropped into position on a corner overlooking the lake. 24HRS, the sign said. Company workers sending scrips down the Pan-American Highway back home; requests for mis-crated booze, moonshine stills, letters from loved ones, and laptops.

Wren had a lead on one particular laptop, its precise address encrypted six ways from Sunday and unreadable, but the metadata remained. It had last been used by Pythagoras to access the Blue Fairy's dark Internet. He'd been online and watching the feed when Wren tore down Pleasure Island. Records showed the IP address was routed through the central company hub, offering no better geographic location than the whole of Deadhorse. Standing population of fifty, transient workers hitting three thousand.

Time to whittle that down.

2

DEPOT

The depot's door swung open smoothly, revealing a ten by eight waiting space with a few rows of plastic seats, a black vinyl floor puddled with melt water, a desk running from wall-to-wall and shielded with glass. Beyond the glass lay the dark warehouse; crates, boxes, shelves stacked with consumables, machinery, tech. Easily four hundred square feet, plenty of space to smuggle booze, cigars, an illegal chipset...

The clerk behind the glass was in his sixties, grizzled and hard-bitten with deep crevasse wrinkles in a wind-whipped face, buzz-cut gray hair and a heavy black raincoat. A rig-worker or pipeline man too broken to brave the ice anymore, Wren figured. His breath made puffs of steam in the cold air as he stared ahead.

"Good morning," Wren said brightly.

"It's midnight," the guy answered flatly. "You're the tourist. What do you want?"

Wren smiled. He knew tourist names were listed on a town-wide bulletin. Permits were required for the whole area; too close to the Alaskan pipeline for unsecured access.

"I'm here for the natural beauty," he said, striding over. The guy's ice didn't crack. "This is the only place open. Which do you recommend for sightseeing, midnight sun or northern lights?"

The guy frowned. "Aurora's burning outside right now, last I checked. Nothing to see in here."

"But there are other kinds of beauty," Wren allowed, and let a beat pass. "I heard you take special deliveries."

The guy gave him a long, bored look, then held up one hand and started counting off fingers, like this was a checklist he'd long ago tired of repeating. "We don't run hookers. We don't smuggle. We don't traffick. This is a depot for company men. Shampoo, toothpaste, luxuries. Whatever you heard otherwise is wrong."

Wren let that slide off him. He'd run contraband through similar frontier depots for years. He knew the temptations men on the fringes faced, each a point of leverage.

"What about computers?"

The guy didn't blink. "You want a computer at midnight? Go on to the Best Buy over in Prudhoe Bay. Better rates. They open at nine."

Wren smiled and leaned in. "Prudhoe Bay's smaller than Deadhorse. There's no Best Buy. Besides, this is a custom order. A laptop with powerful encryption capacity." Wren let that hang for a moment. "I have a referral."

The guy's eyes narrowed. "Like I said, we don't smuggle; women, drugs or computers. I don't care about your referral. Go out look at the sky, son, before you get in trouble."

That wasn't enough for Wren. There was something familiar in the guy's eyes. Smugness, maybe. Maybe fear. "This particular laptop's not illegal. Not in itself, anyway. Cryptographic software baked onto the board, I hear it's nearly undetectable. I also heard you took delivery of one seven months back. My friend said I could get another here."

The guy stared. "What friend?"

Wren smiled, pulled off his gloves and set them on the counter, then pulled out his wallet. It was fat with bills. He fanned through them. "Pull the record of receipt. You tell me. That's all I want, then I'm gone. No mention of the whisky crates I saw down the side. It's a dry county, last I heard. That's one count in the smuggling column. So get out your books. Slide a finger down. Five hundred says it never happened."

He eased the bills out of his wallet, laid them on the counter. Five hundred. A week's work, maybe. Consider it overtime. He pushed them closer.

"There's blood on your hands," the old guy said. It didn't seem to faze him.

Wren noticed it too. "It's not mine," he answered, like that made it all right.

A long moment passed. Wren's breath steamed the glass. One more corrupt official to bribe, or threaten, or whatever it took, and he was already thinking ahead to his plan for Pythagoras. Active for decades, with dozens of children destroyed in his wake.

The guy would talk, he could feel it. The link back to his father was achingly close. The route back to seeing his kids.

Then he heard a siren.

It was far off, but growing closer. More than one. He refocused.

The smug glint in the old guy's eyes had come to the fore, now. When had that change happened? Wren cursed silently. He'd let himself get distracted by the big picture.

"You hit the panic button," Wren said. "Under the counter."

"Company security," the old guy answered, offering the slightest shrug. Montanan accent, maybe? Wren wondered. Moderated by long years away. It took all sorts to populate a pipeline station. Loners, largely, men drawn to the verges of society, to the allure of the maddening wild.

The sirens drew in.

Wren didn't react. Didn't run. "I can give you the order number," he said, smiling now like it was funny. "I have the signature of the receiving agent, one William Hartright. Would that be you?"

"Man before me."

"Care to show me some ID?"

The guy almost cracked a smile. "Wouldn't care to, friend. But you'll be needing yours. Last fella came in asking about shipments, he left with two rounds in his chest and a bag over his head. Helicopter, FBI lettermen, the full contingent. We shoot first out here. Terrorism demands it, this close to the pipe-head. Tourists come on our good graces, and you just blew right through."

"I made threats?" Wren asked. "You'll testify at my trial?"

"It'll be a write-in." The guy let his smile through now. Feeling his own power reaching out. This was what happened when you asked about laptops in Deadhorse. "And if you're carrying a weapon, like the pistol weighing down your belly pouch, on federal land like this? That's a straight up terror charge, ten to fifteen years in solitary, if they don't shoot you outright."

Wren nodded, thinking through his position. The FBI threat was empty, at least in the short term; there wasn't a field station any closer than Anchorage, which was a. two-hour flight away. Maybe the local cops, enough to secure a remote pipehead and keep three thousand rowdy pipe workers in line, but that'd be a handful only, ten at the most, say three or four on duty at any one time.

It didn't worry Wren overly. On the other side of it, this guy had punched the alarm button to call them out, on the strength of what, a couple of insistent questions and some old blood on his hand?

Something else was going on here, and Wren decided to lay his cards on the table. "The laptop guy, how much is he paying you?"

The old guy smiled. Showing his hand too. "More than you can afford."

That was a tell, and it made things easier. This guy knew about Pythagoras. He was loyal to Pythagoras. The sound of sirens wafted in like a bugle call, growing louder.

"Usually they run now," the clerk observed.

"Nowhere to run," Wren answered. "We both know that. Not for me, not for you."

The guy frowned. Wren almost laughed. Sometimes he felt sorry for the people who crossed his path. "What is he, Pythagoras? A foreman on the pipeline, maybe a director of the company?"

The guy leered at the name. "I wouldn't worry about him. Think about yourself, son. Get your story straight. Explain that blood to the feds."

That was all the confirmation he needed. The guy knew who Pythagoras was, and the meant only one thing: he was in the Blue Fairy too. Wren felt the world flip around him as permission was granted. It always felt like that, when a civilian became a target.

"Explaining the blood's easy. I've been killing my way across America." He said it flat, knew from experience it would come off intimidating. "Pinocchios, like the man you're protecting." A flicker of annoyance. "You saw the Blue Fairy livestream off Pleasure Island, I'm thinking. That means you saw me, Christopher Wren, by the altar, shackling in one of your boys?"

The guy paled noticeably. His eyes widened. "Wait, what?"

Now it was Wren's turn to grin. "I look different in real life, right? Ever since then, I've been cleaning up the mess." He placed both his stained hands palm-up on the counter. "Maybe this was from Des Moines? Or Cincinnati? I thought I washed all the blood off, but it sticks, you know? It gets in the grain. I drove straight north afterward. Slept in the car. Three days driving just to see you. William Hartright. That's you, right? You've got what I want. Give me Pythagoras, maybe you get off easy. A man like me, Hartright, you sure you want to go hard?"

The guy blanched a little but forced a laugh. "Bullshit. You ain't him."

Him. The boogey man who brought the Blue Fairy down.

"Let's find out. Your toy town cops'll be here soon, no way you've got FBI lettermen on standby, and maybe they'll try to bag me." He reached into the belly flap of his jacket and pulled out the SIG .45, laid it on the counter. Hartright's eyes flashed to the door. The sirens were getting real close. Coming around the lake. Not far to go. Maybe on snowmobiles, blue lights flashing? Wren would like to see that.

"The glass is bulletproof," Hartright said.

Wren snorted. "Not against hollow point bullets. Three shots and I'm through, then the fourth finds your heart. Probably you should run." He pointed back into the warehouse. "You've got two exits plus the loading bays back there, but what if they don't open? Those locks are easy to jam with a heating filament. You can do it with an industrial light-bulb in seconds, and who's to say I didn't?" He paused, charting the guy's sharpening breath. A bluff, but the guy wouldn't know that. "Now you're really thinking. What kind of crazy fish you hooked. Hartright, you don't want this. Roll belly up now and I'll let the feds have you. Otherwise you're dealing with me, and I'm not that big on forgiveness."

Hartright gulped, took a step back. Wren could almost see the thoughts flying in his head; too much to take in, narrowing reality down to an immediate calculation. It had been a normal, quiet night in Deadhorse, and now everything had changed. Things were life and death, and who was ready for that kind of decision?

Wren always tried to make the math easy for perps, and tossed his wallet on the counter, like lead on the scale. The sirens sounded to be right outside.

"Take it all. Must be three thousand in there. Give me what I want, I'll give you a day's head start before I call you in."

Hartright wilted like an orchid under studio lights. Events were compounding and jamming him up. Wren fixed him with a steady gaze. It was all in the pitch, all in the delivery.

One of the sirens bleeped and cut out at the door.

"Your call," Wren said. "Either way, I'm getting what I want, but how angry do you think I'll be if I have to kill these guys? Their blood'll be on your hands. Pretty soon after, yours will be on mine. You won't like that."

Footfalls on the steps outside.

"It's on your word now. You pushed the button. Better decide."

Wren slipped the gun back into his belly flap as the door opened.

3

TOYTOWN COPS

A kick; the door swung wide and a gun came in first, left hand clamped underneath, finger already squeezed to the trigger. Two in the doorway, a young white guy in front and a black older guy in back, both wearing navy security outfits with golden badges.

Company cops.

"I need you on your knees right now, sir, with your hands up," said the lead guy. Twenty-five at a push, with rough stubble, swollen shoulders and a rounded back from unbalanced powerlifting. He shuffled in through a meltwater puddle, making room for his colleague; mid-fifties, maybe a family up here.

"This is all an accident," Wren said. "Right, Mr. Hartright?"

The cops looked to Hartright in back.

"It's him," Hartright said, his tone dead cold. Wren glanced over his shoulder and saw Hartright was now holding a gun. "Christopher Wren. The guy who brought down the Fairy."

That was unexpected. Wren turned back. The lead cop's eyes immediately flared wide and now his knuckle bruised white, riding the trigger hard. So they all knew him. In a second the world flipped once more, changing Wren's calculations. These weren't just toy town cops anymore, responding to an alarm. He'd stumbled upon a Pinocchio nest.

"He's what?" the cop in back asked.

"The guy from Pleasure Island," Hartright went on. "I didn't recognize him at first, but he says he's been killing Pinocchios up and down the country. Bastard boasted he's got their blood on his hands."

This revelation stunned the room further. The older cop kicked the door closed behind him, gun beaded now on Wren's face too.

"Fellas," Wren said, with a slight nod. "I didn't recognize you without your masks."

"You're sure?" the older cop asked. The young one's brows beetled hard together and his lips curdled to a sneer. Maybe Wren had killed some of his idols.

"It's me," Wren confirmed, "and you're all screwed."

This made for another odd moment; Wren stood with three guns pointing at his face, making threats.

"It's a bluff," Hartright said in back. Empowered by the layer of glass between them. "He's alone, here under a fake name. He's got a SIG .45 in his belly flap but that's it."

"That's not it," Wren said, keeping it cool and calm. The lead cop made a step forward. His face had turned blotchy red, like a parboiled sausage. "I have got a SIG, but I'm not going for it as long we all go easy."

The guy blurted a laugh and stabbed with the gun. "Easy? Wait until Pythagoras gets here. The things you did! You mother-"

"Be quiet," Wren snapped, and strangely the cop did. They all did. Afraid of his reputation, maybe. He worked the angles swiftly. "If you want to live through this, you need to stay calm and think, before this depot becomes another oil lake crater in the ice. You take me out, and fire rains down from the skies like a Biblical plague. I've got two MQ-1 Predator drones circling at twenty thousand feet, it'll be a minute or so before their missiles hit; you think you can clear the blast radius before that happens?"

He eyed the men. Didn't matter that there were no drones. It was a cozy fall back bluff he'd used many times before; deliver it confidently enough, it gave everyone pause. It helped that plenty of times it hadn't been a bluff. "Maybe not, and we're all pink mist. This block becomes a crater, Deadhorse's latest dark tourist attraction."

Silence. The front guy licked his trembling lips, eyes darting to Hartright.

"Bullshit. He's bluffing."

"We're in a hostage situation now," Wren went on, "whether you like it or not. I want Pythagoras. You want to survive the day. I could be convinced to let you go, if you give him up easy." He paused on that a second. "Well, not go. Like I said to Hartright here, I'll give you a day before I call down the FBI. I think my boy here would like that." He nodded at the lead cop. "Am I right?"

"Like it?" the guy blurted. His eyes burned with rage. Wren figured pushing him to the limit was his next move, get him hot enough to break the logjam, and smiled as patronizingly as he could. "I'm going to tear your damn head off."

"Figures," Wren said dismissively, and looked to the older cop in back. "Get this joker out of here. He's going to get you all killed."

"We need to see the proof you've got the drones," the guy in back replied.

Wren gave a short, sharp laugh. "I'm proof. The fact that I'm here. So get him out, he's a liability. Then we talk."

"Simon," said Hartright, behind the glass to Wren's left. A cautionary voice now, telling a kid to calm down and put his toys away, to let the adults deal. "Take it easy, OK?"

"Now he knows my name?" the young guy hissed. Winding himself up like a pressure cooker, ready to pop. "He doesn't just walk away from this. Not on some bullshit threat he can't even back up."

Wren eyed him head-on. "You going to be the hero, son? Die for your right to wear the Pinocchio mask, is that it, and take all these fine gentlemen with you?"

"You don't know what we've done here. The things we've built-"

"Are you serious?" Wren snapped, winding him up tighter. "The things you've built? I pulled Pleasure Island down in an hour. Whatever two-bit BS you've propped up here is just sad. It makes me sick, how pathetic your infrastructure is. Look where I am. One step away from your leader on my first try! A crypto laptop sourced through the depot, with records on the net for all to see? You're all children here playing at being big men."

The young cop's hand trembled with adrenaline. More humiliation than he could bear.

"Don't listen to him, Simon," pleaded the cop in back, "he couldn't understand-"

"Children?" Simon shouted. Like an eruption. "You don't know a damn thing-"

"I know cowards when I see them," Wren said, getting louder. "You'll squeal and roll over like every other Pinocchio on that ship when the moment comes. At least they were ambitious, but what are you here? Lice under the rock I just flipped over, belly-up and begging to be stomped. I think-"

"Don't listen to him," Hartright called, but Wren had a head of steam going now.

"I think secretly you're terrified, all you mask-wearing man-children, the biggest cucks of the darknet, so frail you can't face anything but a child. I'll show you what it means to be a man, Simon-"

Simon flipped. Eyes so wide open they were white all the way around. He forgot about Wren's drones and any sense of his own superior position and fired.

4

SIMON

Wren was already moving; a single sharp step to the right blocked the line of fire from the cop in back and saw Simon's first shot hit the glass where he'd been standing. The impact came with a sharp crump, chased by the resounding blast of the cordite discharge. His second shot zipped wide to Wren's right; young muscles bathed in corticosteroids overcompensated wildly, not expecting Wren to stop moving so sharply.

Two seconds gone, long enough for Wren's right hand to find the SIG .45 in his belly flap. Without pulling it out he fired three muffled blasts directly through the fabric and into Simon.

Every one hit. Simon's body jerked with each impact, his own bullets spraying wildly. The cop in back staggered as one of Wren's .50 caliber hollow points punched straight through into his chest. He squeezed off one shot that Simon took in the back, then they both dropped.

Double thuds. Ten seconds or less.

A silent second passed, echoes ringing around the small box and out into the Arctic wastes. Simon breathed his last, muttering words into a dirty melt water puddle. The cop in back dropped to his knees like he was in slow motion, wheezing hard, gun forgotten, both hands to his chest. He wouldn't last much longer.

Wren turned to Hartright. Unhurried. Like he had all the time in the world.

Hartright was holding a gun up to the glass. A black metal Colt Python with a walnut stock, Magnum .357 caliber. Cool looking, but not nearly as much bang as Wren's SIG .45. His crevassed face was white. A second passed, then he started firing. White starbursts broke across the plate glass, each chased by another sharp crump.

Bulletproof glass.

Hartright emptied his cylinder. Six shots. The thunder of the blasts filled the warehouse and echoed back in tidal waves of sound, until there was just the clicking of the hammer on metal. The glass was a spiderweb pattern of fractures. Hartright was barely visible through the sharp-cut lines of white, his once-smug eyes gone wide.

Wren knew exactly what he was feeling. Red tunneled vision, pounding heart, hyperventilation, diffused thoughts, time dilation. Everything Simon had just felt. The mind could be a weapon, turning people's own bodies against them.

"I bet you wish you'd taken the money now," Wren said.

"I-" began the older man, but had nothing left to say. His rational mind had deserted him in the throes of the strongest fight or flight reaction he'd ever felt.

"You messed up," Wren said companionably. "But let's be honest, the mistake wasn't today. Maybe it dates back sixty years, to the day you were born, so it's not even really your fault. Maybe it was the day you met Pythagoras. Nature or nurture, Hartright, and I don't really care. I've heard all the sob stories. You've seen what I am and what I mean; no excuses stand up to that. Tell me what I want to know, and maybe you get to go to jail. There's no other option here."

Hartright jawed at the air. Looking for an avenue to argue his way out of. Ten minutes ago his life was normal. Good, maybe.

"Where's Pythagoras?" Wren asked.

"He shot you!" Hartright insisted, paling further.

"He missed," Wren answered. "Now decide."

Hartright's eyes flickered, then he ran.

Wren didn't wait to see if the back doors would open. He knew they would; the heating filament story was all part of his bluff. Instead he strode through the main door and looked out over Deadhorse and Colleen Lake.

The cold air was bracing on his ungloved hands. The SIG instantly absorbed the cold and bit into his palm. He put it back in the torn belly flap.

The lake stretched on forever. It looked like fresh snow was in the offing. Out here, you wouldn't know. A deep breath brought a sharp pain in his lungs. So cold it hurt. He listened out and heard the slam of the rear door go, then advanced down to the snow-coated road, where one patrol car, a sedan with its blue lights still spinning, and a snowmobile with lights of its own were waiting.

No other blue lights spun up across the little town. Maybe just two guys on duty at a time. Someone might place an emergency call, muster them out, but Wren figured he had time.

He took the snowmobile and caught up to Hartright in thirty seconds. The machine ate up the distance, the snow making every surface navigable; off the road, over the sidewalk, up a low embankment. Around the back of the depot he went, down a fence encircling a heavy vehicles pool, where he ran down the older man beside a heaped pile of glinting gray sand.

He hit Hartright with the snowmobile's nose. Enough to send him reeling. Killed the engine and dismounted. Hartright scrabbled at the snow, crazed now and babbling like them all, desperate to survive.

"Please, listen, I can help you! I'll tell you whatever you want to know."

Wren already knew that. He had just one question, and it didn't take long to get the answer.

5

LOCKBOX

Wren retrieved his gloves. The depot was a wreck. He went in through the back door, wrote up a sign and duct-taped it to the front. Decent behavior, but it wasn't like it mattered much. There were no kids up here to stumble on such a horrific scene.

At least no kids that were stumbling around, free.

Wren pulled on a pair of heavy-duty goggles, maybe Simon's. He killed the blue lights on the patrol car and listened, but still no other sirens were inbound. Why should there be? A couple of gunshots wouldn't be that unusual up here; this was true wilderness, and hungry Arctic foxes or polar bears wouldn't respect the Deadhorse permit system in their search for food.

As for the two dead cops in the depot, Wren guessed he'd exhausted the local PD's graveyard shift. Maybe there was no one left to come until the dawn changeover revealed Simon and his friend were out of commission. That should give him hours of clearance yet; but in that time he had to find Pythagoras, extract the information he needed, then get back and out of Deadhorse before hard security walls shut the airport down.

The snowmobile revved and he gave it its head.

According to Hartright, Pythagoras was a global shipping magnate tangentially involved in the pipeline; a Thai national named Somchai Theeravit. A multi-millionaire, he had secretly retired three years back onto a thousand-acre property twenty miles west of Deadhorse, hunkered in a fifty-room mansion that was part research station, part hotel, part torture garden.

Nobody knew he was up there, officially. There were no records. Exactly the kind of man his father would look to recruit.

Wren gunned the throttle off the road at the edge of Deadhorse, beyond which lay only scrub and tundra. No roads, no routes, only access via boat, helicopter and snowmobile. It seemed a joke that a shipping magnate had been undone by such a simple thing as a laptop imported up the Pan-American Highway, but everybody made mistakes under stress.

Icy tundra flew by, interspersed by the vacant eyes of oil lakes and patches of thaw showing dark wet sedge and gray tundra moss, past old cement foundation blocks spraying abandoned pipes upward. Tattered shrubs broke ground cover in places, studded with withered red winter berries.

Pythagoras.

Thirty minutes ripped by in Arctic winds and powder spray. It began to snow and the route ahead quickly fogged; any sign of the lakes, the tundra, the vegetation faded under a fresh blanket of white. His goggles crusted over. West two-ninety degrees, Hartright had said, twenty miles out.

When the complex appeared, it came fast out of the heavy snow. Three blocky mesas of concrete hollowed out by dark windows, like a giant wind chime laid flat. Apparently the design had won awards for its architect. Shipped out here in secret along with a construction crew. Hartright had turned out to be as chatty as the guard at the Deadhorse town limits, at the end.

Wren pulled past a helicopter on its pad, onto the faint outline of a long drive leading up to the raw cement structure. To the right lay a large, crane-equipped jetty, with the Arctic Ocean flat and gray beyond. No boats, but one hell of a view. Was Somchai even here? Hartright said he hadn't seen him for days.

Wren killed the snowmobile's engine and stood, studying the building's façade. It was impressive; three floors of stacked cement boxes that were heavy and brutalist but also somehow graceful, with large floor-to-ceiling windows revealing dark inner depths. He didn't want to imagine the secret cruelties hidden within those walls.

He strode closer. The front door was sunken below ground level and heavily reinforced, controlled by an electronic lock. The garage was sunken too, with blast shields that opened side to side. No way to crack that short of a C-4 cocktail. He circled the compound on the snowmobile. No pipes affixed to the exterior, no visible vents, no back door, no route to the roof. By now he'd almost certainly been spotted on a dozen heat and movement cameras.

Somchai had to know he was here; maybe busy destroying the 'evidence', which meant children could be dying right now. Wren had to get in fast. Part of him longed for a semi-truck to smash into the building, but there was nothing like that. Maybe he could shoot out some of the windows, though they were all too high to reach, and the concrete walls were sheer and unclimbable.

He pulled out his SIG .45 to test the theory anyway. The nearest window was ten feet up; he trained in and fired, a full mag's worth of seven bullets with one in the chamber. Eight plinking ricochets chased eight .50 cal booms. The snow deadened the echo, leaving Wren with his ears ringing, looking up at the window.

Unmarked. Maybe a couple of divots bitten through the outer polycarbonate layer. He laughed. Triple-layer plate glass, no doubt, incredible for insulation out here, and helpfully bulletproof even against his hollow point rounds.

Wren looked around the concrete and barren snow. An idea came to him, but it was crazy. Still, what choice was there now? He could hardly lay siege to the place for weeks until Somchai gave out.

The helicopter.

It was probably a vanity exercise on Somchai's part, another display of conspicuous wealth, something to enjoy looking at out of his window. Still. The impact force on a helicopter rotor blade had to massively outrank the percussive inertia of his hollow point rounds.

Crazy, but possible.

Wren ran the snowmobile over to the pad. The helicopter was a Dhruv Advanced Light, one of the fastest single-rotor civilian vehicles in existence, worth some five million and capable of hauling two thousand pounds of gear.

Wren climbed up the side and tried the door; locked. He smashed through the cockpit side glass with the SIG .45 and jiggled the door controls until the cab opened. The key for the electrical system was in a slot between the seats; likely standard procedure out here, where helicopter thieves were few and far between. Wren turned it and the dash lit up.

Bingo.

It had been years since he'd flown a helicopter. Unlike riding a bike, it was a skill you could easily lose. He'd never flown a Dhruv, to boot, but that was OK; the maneuver he was about to try wasn't on any training scheme he'd ever seen anyway.

His pulse flashed at him from the smart watch, pushing eighty. Any time kids were on the line. He looked over the controls, took the cyclic, set his feet on the anti-torque pedals and pushed the engine start. The rotors engaged and spun up fast, straightening out and chopping the falling snow into a downward cyclone that frothed like whipped cream off the pad.

He cycled it up and the machine lifted hard, bucking wildly in the wind. Wren adjusted the cyclic, sweat beading on his forehead, trying to control the machine before it splattered him across the pad. Take-off and landing were always the hardest parts, when dealing with the backwash of your own downdraft.

It was only going to get harder. Finally stable, he turned the machine toward the house. Ramming speed could be fun, but there was little chance he'd be able to jump clear safely. No. Instead he approached slowly, winging the finer controls and working calculations. The rotational diameter of the blades was about forty feet. That was the kind of thing he could judge by eye. Hit solid reinforced cement and the blades would snap. The bird would roll, crash, and if he didn't burn up in the resulting fireball, he'd get chopped to pieces as he tried to flee it.

He'd just have to avoid hitting cement.

He hovered in low over the snow-covered gardens. Here a statue. There the replica of a Japanese pagoda. He brought the helicopter up to the top floor of the three stacked concrete boxes, to the biggest floor-to-ceiling window overlooking the Arctic Ocean. Through the tinted glass he picked out a richly appointed office; a stately desk, shelves stacked with leather-bound books, tall Ficus plants framing the window.

The helicopter roared in a sound chamber of its own making; the echo of its rotors bouncing back off the glass. He pulled in close, the edge of his rotor blades only yards from the window. Snow whipped madly down then up, caught in complex crosswinds dictated by the angular shape of the building. Wren bit his lip and edged closer still. It would be tight; the turning circle of the blades versus the width of the window.

No time to play patty cake. He worked the cyclic and the helicopter jogged left, hovering within inches, leaning in until-

The blades struck the window and screamed, and spun, and glass crashed and sheared and metal whined and the whole machine juddered away, blades rattling madly.

Wren fought for control as the Dhruv reeled, hit autorotation after thirty seconds of heart-stopping battle, then peered through whirling snow at the window. There was an ugly gouge where the tips of his rotors had smashed clear through the glass, but only a gouge. Shatterproof triple-layer glass backed with polycarbonate, he figured, as if he'd raked a serrated knife down a pat of cold butter; all he'd done was leave a scar. He laughed out loud, imagined trying to work the Dhruv on another horizontal and two more verticals to cut out a square. It wouldn't be possible.

Better to go with what already worked, now the first cut had been made. He edged in close again, pulled the SIG .45, aimed near the gouge at an angle that wouldn't see ricochets bouncing right back at him, and fired.

Eight bullets drained the mag, each impact shredding the gouge wider and deeper as if he was swinging a ten-pound hammer into a concrete wall, until at last the window hit some tensile inflection point.

Glass screamed, metal crashed, and the whole shatterproof array finally gave out, calving into three great plates which toppled inward, thumping down hard on the fine Persian rug. The Dhruv bucked and whined in the snow. Likely he'd warped the blades and done permanent damage to the transmission knuckle with that stunt, and every second in the air moved it closer to a fatal malfunction.

He steered sideways as close as he dared then let the machine coast into autorotation, even as he kicked open the passenger door and flung himself through. The downdraft flattened him hard across the gap to land half-in and half-out of the building, chest on the toppled pane of glass and legs dangling. He kicked and slid, scrabbled for purchase and managed to pull himself in as the Dhruv rotated away, blown back by its own backdraft with no hand at the cyclic.

Wren rolled to the side. The Dhruv rolled like a leaping whale, lost purchase on the air as it toppled then slammed to its side on the snowy ground with a clattering shriek.

The rotor blades tore themselves away in the frozen soil and the transmission knuckle screamed; for a few seconds the whole machine danced like a jitterbug. Wren tucked in tight at the side of the office with snow whipping in around him, waiting for the blast he knew would come, but none did. The engine just whined down to silence.

He stood up and retrieved the SIG .45 from his belly flap.

6

SOMCHAI

Wren kicked open the office door, SIG .45 locked in a two-hand grip.

A corridor-walkway led away, strung above a steep drop to a grand lobby below, all winter-lit by the white tinge of Arctic sun. Teak flooring, Persian rugs and chrome railings stretched along the walkway for ten yards. A stunning modernist chandelier hung to his right five tiers deep, made with the life-size alabaster casts of cherub-like children.

He looked down to the lobby below. It was minimalist, massive and open-plan, with a sunken den and sofas, a dining table and a kitchen bar. The air was warm, climate controlled despite the gale whipping snow in behind him

No sign of Somchai.

Wren advanced along the walkway into a bedroom; a four-poster in the middle of a circular space suspended on tensile cables, like a giant hammock. It swayed slightly as he entered; bed, cabinets, empty. He pushed through to another walkway which led into a rec room of some kind, kitted with cameras in the four corners, then onto a circular staircase of rough corrugated iron. Halfway down Wren stopped to listen, but there was no sound at all. No whoosh of recycled air, no faint cries, not a thing.

The open plan kitchen was empty and pristine as a show home; granite worktops, chrome-fronted appliances. The entrance area spiraled brightly with snow shadows through the reinforced glass, heavyset metal door lodged with triple inch-thick bolt locks. A real fortress. Wren scanned the windows, sunken dining area with twelve-foot table laid for a feast, through the glossy black-tiled lounge with a three-sided chaise longue, until finally he saw Somchai.

His heart rate leaped to ninety easily. Obscured from above by the thick tiers of plaster cast children, there'd been a recent addition to the chandelier. Suspended beneath the cherubs hung an adult male body. Naked, the light tan skin of a wintering Thai, strung from a black metal crossbar. Arms stretched forward as if begging, threaded with taut cables that ended in strapped him to the crossbar. His elbows were threaded the same way, as were his feet and his knees.

Somchai Theeravit. Pythagoras. Left like a Pinocchio puppet, hanging on his strings.

Wren stared.

Dried blood below him. Looked like death by blood loss. No sign of anyone else. No sign of a fight.

It didn't make any sense. Somchai was a Pinocchio leader, right at the top of the Blue Fairy. His local team had been loyal to the last, willing to die to keep his existence a secret. So who had done this? And when?

They could still be here.

Wren moved on without thinking, SIG .45 up and fully operational. Back through the open kitchen he went, found stairs leading down and took them fast. A concrete corridor stretched away and Wren cleared it quickly, past open cells in Pythagoras' gaudy hell: bright yellow walls, padded flooring, oversized soft toys, murals painted with colorful trains and teddy bears.

At the end of the corridor lay a room all in black, cameras studding the ceilings and mounted on tripods, ready for livestreaming to the Blue Fairy, but no people. No Pinocchios. No children.

He swept back up, from the bowels to the lobby to the dizzy heights of floating offices and bedrooms, but found nothing. No sign of the killers. He stood on the smashed window in Theeravit's office looking out into a thickening snowstorm. The jetty onto the Arctic Ocean was obscured by whipping walls of snow.

Most likely they'd come by ship, docked in the jetty and walked right over. Wren doubted they'd come up through Deadhorse. The record would be too easy to track back. But the record here?

Just a snow-coated jetty with no evidence of their passage. No sign of anything in this ice-blasted wilderness.

Standing in the lobby before Theeravit again, Wren gazed at the strange diorama. The dried blood from his threading wounds suggested he'd died more than twelve hours ago. The killers had at least a twelve-hour start on Wren, maybe more.

A dead Pinocchio. The man deserved no better, Wren had no doubt about that, but who would have done this? Not the Blue Fairy, surely. Not to one of their own. Yet all signs pointed to this murder being committed by someone Somchai had known, even trusted. There were no signs of forced entry. Whoever it was, Theeravit had let them in.

Wren stepped closer, looking up into Somchai's blindly staring eyes, and noticed a thin leather cord pulled tight around his neck. He walked around and saw something dangling down Theeravit's back, a glint of metal like a pendulum. Wren jumped up and grabbed it, snapping the leather cord with a sharp snick.

It was an aluminum flash memory drive. Words had been engraved into the shell, words that flipped everything on its head.

I THINK YOU'LL ENJOY THIS ONE, PEQUEÑO 3

The world narrowed down. Wren's heart began to race.

Only one person had ever called him Pequeño 3. The reason he'd been hunting the Blue Fairy to begin with. The man he'd been hunting for twenty years since the Pyramid burned, whose existence was a threat to everything Wren held dear.

His long-dead father, the Apex.

7

ENJOY

A drenaline dumped into Wren's system, preparing him for a fight or flight reaction; but there was no place to run and no one to fight. Instead the chemicals left him trembling with an emotion he'd barely felt for twenty-plus years.

Fear.

Fear turned into a weapon, bending his own mind upon itself. The same way Simon must have felt at the end, and Hartright, and countless other Pinocchios when Wren found them. Not since the end days of the Pyramid had Wren felt anything quite like it, but you never really forgot.

How it made you small. Made you weak.

He hadn't forgotten how to fight it either. Fear was a fuel you could burn, and he was working on that already. Pumping his fists in the cold air. Tensing every muscle in his body to fight back the chills. The anger came surging like an old friend, swamping the cold fear with red hot rage.

This wasn't just a message. This was the sign he'd been searching for.

He read the words engraved on the flash drive again, so clearly designed as a provocation.

I THINK YOU'LL ENJOY THIS ONE, PEQUEÑO 3

It sounded like something his father would have said, right before beginning another one of his life and death 'experiments'; maybe Pyramid members pitted against each other in the deserts of Arizona, testing their faith in grand battles of stamina beneath the hot sun, waiting for the first to surrender and beg for water.

Sometimes nobody surrendered, their faith won out, and they all died. The Pyramid had cheered extra hard whenever that happened.

Wren had survived every one of the Apex's games as a child, learning to judge just how far to go to appease his father, without dying. He'd even survived the final 'experiment', where all thousand members of the Pyramid had burned themselves alive.

He'd survive this one too.

He uncapped the drive and plugged its micro-port into his phone. A screen popped up showing one icon in a menu, an mpeg file titled REPARATION. It didn't mean anything to him. He tapped it to open.

The video full-screened across his phone, darkness resolving to a high, fish-eye view of a shadowy, dank prison of some kind. Long narrow pens of wire mesh stretched away, barely two yards across, maybe ten long, with raw concrete floors. Naked men paced inside them and close-ups danced across their faces. It took Wren a second to recognize them.

All famous billionaires.

Dead ahead of the camera was Handel Quanse, CEO of a top finance company, well-known for the enormous profits he'd wrung from the housing crisis. While every other financier had still been buying into the bubble, he'd jumped the gun and spiked it with a crack needle, dumping hundreds of billions in garbage investments everywhere he could. Those companies failed. He came out richer than ever. Now he was striding up and down the confined space, unashamed in his nakedness, a silver fox in his fifties looking toned, tanned and tall.

Merriot Raine, the inheritor of the Raine diamond fortune, was next to him, though he cut a very different picture. A trust-fund inheritor in his mid-twenties, he didn't have the killer gaze of Quanse or Joes, rather he was huddled limp and terrified in the corner of his cell. All he'd done with his life, as far as Wren was aware of him from the occasional news story, was gamble in the world's top casinos, date the world's top glamor models and open high-end restaurant after restaurant that all went belly up within months.

Wren scanned the rest, six more in total arrayed to the left of Handel Quanse's cell. Wren didn't recognize them all, couldn't pick some out for the distance, but there was Cem Babak the arms trader; an Iranian mob boss in his thirties who'd made an art form of inciting African inter-tribal wars. Next to him was Inigo De Luca, the Italian social media maven who'd sold all his user data to the Russian government in a multi-billion dollar windfall, then turned himself around as a champion of green energy. It was thanks to him that Wren was seeing countless electric charging stations popping up across the country.

Others lay beyond De Luca; one looked like Geert Fothers, another Saul-to-Paul Damascus Road conversion. Until he was fifty years old Fothers had been a tobacco man; to Wren's knowledge he'd played a pivotal role in pushing for fake medical assessments claiming certain cigarettes were not harmful, and perhaps even healthful. In his fifties though, after he was struck down by lung cancer, he'd had a complete change of heart; and lungs too, with implanted organs that kept him alive.

He'd turned his prodigious fortune to the fight against cancer, and that involved battling the industry he'd helped to grow. He'd already spent hundreds of millions on the fight.

Wren watched the group of billionaires as they paced. All men, he noted. He wondered what it meant, whether any of this was real or just some deepfake computer graphics fantasy, concocted to serve as propaganda. He was about to scroll the video forward when the camera panned to the right, revealing one more billionaire, taking the total number to ten.

The breath in Wren's throat stopped.

In the cell to Handel Quanse's right was the enormously fat Damalin Joes III, naked belly jutting out and proud a good two feet. He stood in the middle of his cell, so pale and immense he almost filled it side-to-side, staring up at the camera as if he knew what all this was. The look in his eyes made Wren think this wasn't a deepfake. This looked like the real Damalin Joes III.

Once a successful corporate raider, he'd infamously bought up the debts of thousands of Midwest family farmers during the '08 housing crisis, then bankrupted and evicted them all in one swelling roll of human misery that, by some accounts, had set the national economic recovery back by six months.

He was one of the most hated men in America, for the way he'd profited off the pain of the common man. At least he had been.

Now he was a Foundation member.

Wren's jaw dropped open. He thought of the message on the flash drive.

I THINK YOU'LL ENJOY THIS ONE, PEQUEÑO 3

Bullshit, he thought. No way these people, whoever had jailed Damalin Joes, could have known Joes was in the Foundation. Nobody but Wren knew that. He had records, sure, but they were secured. But then here was Joes staring up at the camera, like he knew who the intended audience was.

Wren.

Like some half of the other billionaires present, Joes had experienced his come-to-Jesus moment. Unlike them, his had come at Wren's hands.

8

DAMALIN JOES III

Wren hadn't meant for any of it to happen. Damalin Joes III wasn't even a blip on his radar when he'd gone into the mission; black-ops for the DoD's US Special Operations Command in Cuba. The mission had entailed complete deniability, only Wren and a small insertion team two years back.

They'd set up as darknet drug dealers for La eMe, the Mexican Mafia. Their surface 'goal' had been to score a new Atlantic 'Silk Road' for shipping raw Afghan opium to Cuba, the Pearl of the Antilles. Their deep goal was to uncover and destroy a suspected underworld of opium processing factories somewhere on the island, preventing the forward transit of lab-grade opiates up through Mexico into the US.

He'd had a full work-up done on his cover story, using his Qotl cartel hookups to build out his new identity; a crooked CIA agent looking to cash in on some dark connections after twenty years on the job. It was a story almost too close to reality for comfort.

Damalin Joes III had come into the picture entirely by accident. Turned out he was holidaymaking in Cuba aboard his luxury 400-foot superyacht, hunting an infamous painting by the Uruguayan artist, Joaquín Torres-García. It was pure coincidence that Wren's black-ops mission ended on a superyacht docked in Havana Harbor directly next to Joes'.

The entrepreneurial criminal who'd set up the heroin labs, Herman de

Guz, closed out his career with a black bag over his head, looking forward to a five-hundred-mile aerial commute to Guantanamo Bay on the other side of the island. Wren oversaw it all, from the gung-ho clearance of seven private security operators on the yacht to cracking de Guz' panic room to pulling down the black bag over his head, walking the hollering man off his yacht and into the secret flatbed of a waiting pick up truck.

Mission accomplished.

Wren had taken one last look around before climbing into the truck with his squad, rifle poised, all in tactical black gear splashed with enemy blood, and that's when he saw Damalin Joes III.

An enormously fat man standing high up on the upper deck of his neighboring superyacht. 'In Excelsis' was the yacht's name, written in curlicued gold leaf on the side. Bigger than de Guz' ship. It had a bowling alley, two swimming pools, a helipad and a total of 24 bathrooms, Wren would later learn.

Joes looked down at him, dressed in only a white terrycloth dressing gown, and raised a cocktail glass as if in a toast. As if to say, 'Nice job.'

Wren slapped the side of the pickup truck, sending his team on. The engine started and the truck rolled away. Wren stood there for a long moment, looking up at Damalin Joes. An American billionaire, far out of his comfort zone.

"Are you not riding with your team?" he called down. His deep voice carried over the distance easily, but casually, like this was small talk at a cocktail party, not the tail end of a noisy, violent rendition.

Wren debated swiftly. There'd been no mention of an American involved in the drug labs. Certainly not a high-profile billionaire. At the same time, it seemed too much of a coincidence to overlook. He raised his rifle.

"Lower the gangway," he commanded. "I'm coming aboard."

If anything, Joes seemed rather pleased about the prospect. He gave a signal, and within seconds a hatch in the side of the yacht opened.

"I do hope you like a mojito," Joes called as Wren stalked toward the entrance. His second yacht infiltration of the night. "The rum's Havana Maximo 25 Anos, Special Blend. It costs ten thousand a bottle."

Wren ignored him and entered the yacht with his rifle raised. An astonished young man in service whites raised his hands and backed away.

Wren ascended up a set of stairs to the top deck, where Damalin Joes was waiting.

For a long moment the two looked at each other. Joes in his fluffy white gown, cocktail held high, Wren in his coarse black strike suit with the rifle.

"Can I tempt you to a drink?" Joes asked. As if a guest like Wren was perfectly commonplace.

Wren almost laughed. Kept his rifle at the ready throughout. "Two things," he said. "With a foreword. Foreword is, you get this yacht moving right now. Out of the harbor. On the way back to the good old USA."

Joes looked at him a long moment. "I haven't retrieved my painting yet."

Later on, Wren would laugh about that phrasing with his team. 'Retrieved', like finding and purchasing a famous painting was not a question of reaching an agreement with the current owner. No, it was more a question of prizing free something that had always belonged to him, with money as the crowbar.

"First thing then," Wren went on smoothly. "You just witnessed a hit that's going to bring half of Havana down on our heads within the hour. There's no covering that up. They see you here, you're going to get tangled up in it. Bad for you, bad for the USA, bad for me. That's reason one."

Joes seemed unphased. Like he dealt with this kind of thing all the time, and it mostly bored him. He took a sip of his mojito. Wren became aware of armed men behind him from the click of a safety switching over. Sounded like two of them, making noises they didn't have to make, but they clearly wanted him to hear. One to his right, one to his left, pretty close judging the layout of the yacht.

"And reason two?" Joes asked. Same easy confidence.

"You were here next to him. That makes you a suspect in my book. So, if you don't order this yacht to move right now, I'll take that as resistance and put a black bag on your head too, requisition your ship and steer it out of the harbor myself."

Joes took another sip, seemed to think about this for a moment. Made a show of looking over to the yacht Wren had busted, to the pier below where his pick-up truck had left from, then back up at Wren. "What do you weigh, maybe two hundred pounds?"

"Two-fifty."

"Then I'm twice the man you are. Put the gun down and let's see how you wrestle."

"Not going to happen," Wren said. "Easy way or hard way, Sir, and-"

"Boring," Joes said, then in one beguilingly smooth movement tossed his drink over the side, slid out of his gown and started at a run toward Wren.

Wren barely restrained his laughter. With the robe gone Joes' pasty white body looked like an uncooked turducken, a chicken stuffed inside a duck stuffed inside a turkey, ready to be basted. But massive. Not the kind of man you'd want to get crushed beneath, same way Wren felt about giant redwoods. When timber was called, you got out of the way.

Ten steps across the deck, maybe, for Joes to reach him.

Wren spun, jogging his right elbow up and out. Far and fast enough to catch the rifle barrel of the guy standing to his right. He wasn't ready, and Wren followed through with a fast step, managed to shoulder barge him square in the sternum. The guy, no slouch himself, maybe two hundred pounds of meat and bone at six foot even, was lifted off his feet and sent backward, leaving his rifle behind.

Wren spun and flung the weapon hard to the right, straight into the face of another security guy in a blue uniform, pistol raised. It took him a second to deal with the incoming rifle, still log-jammed on Wren's sudden attack, then Wren hit him with a flying dropkick in the upper chest.

The guy somersaulted on the spot like a little man on a foosball table, rotating around some hidden axis, almost a full three-sixty before he came down on his face, knees slamming into the deck like the trailing edge of a whip.

Then Damalin Joes hit Wren like a wrecking ball.

Wren was swept immediately off his feet and driven hard into a wall, blasting the wind from his lungs. Before he could get his feet underneath him, Joes swept one meatball hand up between his legs, hoisted Wren bodily by the crotch and hurled him like a human javelin.

Wren flew, saw the bright lights of Havana from the air, then hit the pure white deck and slid on his chest. Already there was the thunder of Damalin Joes charging; each mighty footfall beating the deck like it was a big bass drum. He thought about barking some kind of order, a warning about interfering with the work of a CIA operative about his country's business, but decided to save his wind.

Instead, he rolled and opened his arms wide for what he anticipated next. Joes didn't disappoint. He flung himself right at Wren, likely hoping to crush the smaller man beneath his immense weight, too high or drunk or arrogant to really think through what he was doing.

Wren braced and Joes hit like a falling redwood, crushing his ribs between a rock and hard place so powerfully Wren almost blacked out.

But he didn't.

As Joes hit, Wren wrapped his hands around Joes' neck, trapping his thick right arm upright beside his face. Joes huffed and tried to tumble free, but Wren had him then. Didn't matter how much mass the big man had; everybody's carotid artery beat near the surface, and Wren squeezed, using Damalin Joes' own arm to block the flow of blood to his brain.

"Don't…" Joes murmured as unconsciousness crept over him, "drink all my rum."

Then he was out.

Wren stood up. His crotch hurt like the devil. Ribs too. He pulled four zip-ties from his belt and hog-tied Joes before he could wake up. Then he looked over at Joes' security contingent, now beading their rifles on his head.

"He's a rich idiot," Wren said. Staring them down. "What's your excuse?"

They put their rifles down.

After that it was just a matter of time.

9

ARENA

Wren refocused on his phone screen, strange memories of his time with Damalin Joes on the yacht blending uneasily with the vision of the man on the screen before him. During their one-week trip back to the USA, they'd become something like friends. After close interrogation, Wren concluded that Joes was guilty of nothing more heinous than coincidentally being alongside a criminal's yacht, and the colossal arrogance that he could take down a Force Recon operator with impunity.

They'd talked. At some point Wren mentioned the Foundation, and Joes asked to join on a dime. Not as a financier, but as a member.

Wren had thought about that hard. By then Joes was an ultra-billionaire, but bored and acting out. The world had opened up for him, and he still wasn't satisfied. In Wren he thought maybe he saw a way to scratch an unseen itch.

Wren made one condition of Joes' acceptance to the Foundation; that he find a way to do something good to make up for the way he'd hoovered up his enormous wealth. He'd steadfastly refused to engage with any of Joes' pointblank arguments about the ultimate benefits of capitalism. Wren was no politician and didn't care either way. For him the calculation was much simpler.

"You want some meaning in this life? You help people."

In the years since, Wren watched Joes take that simple creed further than he'd ever expected. He bought out several entire counties along with great swathes of farming land, then suspended all rent payments from the tenants, while also providing them with a universal basic income.

He called these areas his 'Damalin Incubation Zones'. The idea was to foster local development and fuel ingenuity by freeing up people's time. No more endless exhaustion from working three minimum wage jobs, no more farming dawn 'til dusk just to pay for the rented equipment that pushed conglomerates to ask for more acreage to be covered by a single farmer.

He'd just gotten started in all that, though, and it was only some fifty thousand people affected so far. A pilot program. Not the hundreds of thousands he'd hurt. The renovation of his image, not that he cared too much about that, was a long time coming.

As if to reflect that, Damalin Joes III's name was currently at the top of a game show-like ranking bar down the screen's side. All the billionaires' names were listed there, along with their industry and their net worth, and what looked like a shifting vote tally. The vote numbers were in the tens of thousands already and rising constantly. As far as Wren could tell, it looked like a hate-vote situation, with the worst of the worst at the top.

That was Damalin Joes. Handel Quanse came in second.

Wren watched the phone screen, rapt. Apart from a few guesses, he didn't know what he was looking at. Some kind of reality TV show? But why would any of these men agree to be trapped naked in a cell? So was it a deepfake, imagery created in a computer and rendered to look ultra-realistic? Or was it exactly what it looked like; ten men who'd been kidnapped and imprisoned?

After several minutes of the ten men pacing in their cells, a montage followed. It seemed as if many days had been compressed in the editing suite: the billionaires being fed in their cages; being hosed down with jet spray like animals in a pen; being herded into corners by figures in white haz-mat suits wielding long sparking cattle prods.

The cattle prods changed Wren's calculation significantly. This didn't look like any reality TV show he'd ever seen. That left incredibly realistic deepfake or genuine kidnap scenario. Both would have cost millions to prepare.

After the montage the screen brightened abruptly, and Wren found himself looking down from above at some kind of arena. At first he thought he was looking at a close-up of a strange, unblinking golden eye. Then he realized what it actually was; an oval of sand surrounded by five full tiers of stadium seating. An arena.

Wren's heart skipped a beat and he peered closer at the screen. It looked like stone walls, like a Roman amphitheater where gladiators would fight, skirted outside by a hint of more sand and green scrub. The tiers of seating looked to be full, with brightly colored figures packed in tight. Judging from the scale of their bodies, the arena had to be some two hundred feet on the long axis, around half as big as a football field.

The image sharply crosscut to a close-up in the midst of the tiered seating. A diverse, modern-looking American audience filled up the stands, drinking beer, eating popcorn, waving foam hands like they'd come to watch a football game. Big screens around the walls rose up ten feet high, showing the current ranking of billionaires. Many of the spectators were holding phones with that same ranking on their screens.

The camera briefly closed in. On each phone was the ranking bar with the ten billionaire's names, ten buttons by each of their names. A finger came into the shot, hit a button, and the vote tally shifted. They were voting right now. But voting for what?

The camera zoomed back out, way out like the camera operator was standing on the building's walls, and Wren found himself wowed by the scale of it, even seen on his small phone screen in the dark of Somchai's house. There were men, women, children in face paint. Thousands of them. Wren felt a sickness building in his gut. Something awful was coming.

It came.

Doors around the top of the stands opened, and the billionaires were brought out. They were naked still, steered by the guards in their white haz-mats with their cattle prods. Camera-wielding film crews tracked each one of them, and the big screens on the walls shifted to showing close-ups of their faces. Some were terrified and sobbing, like Merriot Raine, needing to be dragged every step of the way. Others were defiant, heads held high, like Handel Quanse and Damalin Joes III. Joes in particular looked arrogant, walking proud as a bride down the stone steps, his giant naked belly bulging; much as he had when he'd charged Wren on his yacht.

Wren's pulse raced. If this was an anti-popularity contest, Damalin Joes wasn't helping himself. The thought crossed Wren's mind that whatever this was, it wasn't live. The outcome was on a flash stick and had already happened. He could scroll ahead to find out what happened, but he couldn't bring himself to touch the screen.

Joes was on a coin wo. He'd made incredible progress on himself and his footprint in the world, since he'd started with the Foundation. Wren gave him no more attention than anyone else, didn't coddle him, and if anything Joes had responded positively. He was turning his life around. To look at him now, you'd never know it.

"Cut the act," Wren muttered to himself, reading the audience as they cheered or booed accordingly as each billionaire's face appeared on the big screens. They booed loudest for Quanse, Joes and Merriot Raine. They cheered for Geert Fothers; his turnaround had been well in place for a decade now, and his expression was not one of arrogance. If anything, he looked contrite. The crowd loved it.

The ranking bar on the side spun up to a frenzy as the billionaires descended toward the oval arena, names swapping positions rapidly as the audience bent over their phones, tapping the app to cast their votes. Some kind of violent game show, Wren wondered, though the production values were through the roof.

Handel Quanse was first to step out onto the sand, head up and spine erect. This was met with a resounding boo. One of the haz-mats pointed at a mark in the sand and Quanse strode confidently toward it, taking up a position near the center. The others followed suit, Joes arriving second to flank Quanse. Staring out at the crowd.

"Read the room, Damalin," Wren urged, but it was no use. Joes was an arrogant man, not about to kowtow to a rabble like this. Swiftly the billionaires formed up in a neat circle at the center of the arena, maybe thirty yards across.

Abruptly wooden gates in the arena wall opened and the camera crews swarmed. Nine horses were led out, beautiful dark mustangs, easily sixteen hands tall and built like tanks. Their handlers brought them up one to a billionaire, positioned facing away from the center of the circle. The handlers hooked long leather ropes into harnesses mounted around the horses' powerful shoulders.

Maybe some kind of race? Wren scanned the arena, picturing the stampeding chariots of Ben-Hur, but there hardly seemed enough space. He imagined the billionaires getting strapped in armor and given a sword to fight from horseback, but that made no sense; who amongst these pampered men knew how to fight like that? It would be an amateurish, drawn-out joke.

The feed switched back to the shot from above, showing the haz-mat attendants stretched the rope from each horse's harness toward the center of the circle, like spokes in a wheel. There was a damp patch under Merriot Raine where he'd pissed himself. The crowd loved it. On big screens atop the fifth tier Raine's tear-stricken face was blown up large.

Only Handel Quanse didn't have a horse. Wren scanned the ranking; Quanse's name was locked at the top of the vote tally now, his name highlighted in red. Quanse looked around, trying to figure out what this meant, but still he didn't see it coming.

Four haz-mats peeled away from the horses and closed in on Quanse from behind. The camera cut with a crash back to ground level, on the sand and watching Quanse's figure from behind as the haz-mats approached. They leveled their cattle prods and hit him with an almighty electric shock.

Handel Quanse stiffened, his nervous system instantly and overwhelmingly overridden. Not all the money in the world could do a thing to protect him. One of the haz-mats gave him a shove and he toppled, hitting the sand with a thud.

The crowd fell silent.

The four haz-mats dropped their rods and descended on Quanse's jerking body, dragging him to the center of the circle of horses, where they strapped him wrist and ankle with the long harness ropes. Damalin Joes and the eight other billionaires were being guided up into their saddles. Joes was red-faced now, eyes bugging on Quanse, shouting and battling with four haz-mats of his own until they cattle-prodded to rigid silence atop his horse.

Nothing anyone could do about this now. Wren stared mutely, already seeing ahead to where this was going.

The crowd fell silent. Soon the only sound was of Handel Quanse's limbs thrashing out the aftershocks, and the herky-jerky suck of his breathing. One camera operator pushed in on his face and splashed it across the big screen. His eyes were wide and staring, locked within a body temporarily out of his control.

A voice boomed out across the arena. It was female, accented slightly, the words so loud that even Quanse seemed to comprehend them, his eyes twitching.

"Finish him and live!"

The camera feed switched to a split screen of the other billionaires; their faces blown up large. Wren focused on Damalin Joes. Waiting for him to grasp what was required, for the calculation to take place just like it had atop his yacht. Arrogance bordering on mania. An ability to take advantage of the temporary weakness of others. It was a skillset he'd taken from rags to the billionaire rich list.

It didn't take long now. Wren watched the shift in his eyes, the fresh set of his jaw as the decision was made. Grasping that there were no rules anymore. That survival was everything.

Damalin Joes kicked his horse hard in the flanks, yanked on the reins and shouted, "Yaaa!"

His Mustang took off.

The camera tracked him as he tore away. In the background the other billionaires responded, whipping their reins and geeing their horses to run, but they were out of focus and unimportant. Joes' harness rope leading back to Handel Quanse's right arm was first to pull taut; briefly dragging him after Quanse's horse across the sand. Then he hit tension as the other horses bolted away and was pulled apart.

The rope whiplashed clear.

The cameras didn't show the catastrophic damage done, at least not until Joes' horse neared the wall and veered left, leading a frantic spiral of all nine horses galloping around the oval arena, each trailing pieces of Handel Quanse behind them.

Torn to pieces by wild horses.

Wren let out a horrified breath. The crowd roared their approval. After maybe a minute Damalin Joes slowed his horse, fighting for breath and composure. Someone pushed a microphone into his face.

"How does it feel?" they asked. "How does it feel to finally do something good?"

Joes had no answer. Neither did Wren. The screen flashed to black, and a single line of block-capital text appeared that brought some measure of clarity.

YOU ARE OWED REPARATIONS

A moment passed, then another line replaced it.

CLAIM THEM IN BLOOD

10

EVERY LAST DROP

Wren stared as the video ended. The phone returned to just being a phone. He turned the flash drive over and read the inscription again.

I THINK YOU'LL ENJOY THIS ONE, PEQUEÑO 3

Handel Quanse was either dead, executed in the most gruesome display Wren had ever seen, or that was an incredibly persuasive deepfake video. He didn't know what to feel. Stunned. Confused. Enraged.

He brought up his phone and ran an Internet search, looking for instances of the arena film online. He found none. That cleared up nothing. He ran another search for stories publicizing the kidnap of Joes or Quanse or the other billionaires and found nothing either.

What the...?

He rubbed his weary eyes, trying to put Damalin Joes' sickened final expression out of his mind and jumpstart the search for answers. Neither search result made any sense. These 'Reparations', the people who'd gone to all the trouble of making this video, hadn't done it just for Wren's benefit.

So what was it for?

He tried to imagine the effect the death of medieval-level death of Handel Quanse would have, if released to the public through a streaming app like WeStream. Destructive, was the word that came to mind. After the Saints and the Blue Fairy had caused such chaos, America stood at a precipice. There was anger out there in spades, and fear, and people were primed to turn on each other. Now a billionaire was dead, and the audience had cheered themselves red in the face.

They wouldn't be the only ones.

But the video wasn't online. At least not yet. Which could mean only one thing: the Reparations wanted Wren to see the video first. They wanted this to be personal. They wanted him to think his father was involved.

That pissed him off.

Wren jerked to action, striding back through the grotesque home; now just a set with Somchai Theeravit's dead body as a prop. Stamping up the stairs, he spun up a spider search algorithm to ping him when the Reparations video appeared online, then tapped out a swift message to his top-level Foundation members via Megaphone app: calling, texting and messaging them every minute until they acknowledged receipt.

JUST RECEIVED THE ATTACHED SNUFF FILM, STRAPPED TO PYTHAGORAS' CORPSE. COULD BE A DEEPFAKE, CHECK THAT, BUT I DON'T THINK SO. DAMALIN JOES IS A FOUNDATION MEMBER, TURNING HIS LIFE AROUND. NOW HE'S A CAPTIVE IN A REPUGNANT REALITY TV SHOW. THIS IS PERSONAL.

Wren sent the message, thought for a moment, tapped out more.

FIND OUT WHO CAME TO DEADHORSE BEFORE ME TO KILL PYTHAGORAS, AND WHERE THEY WENT AFTER. FIND OUT WHERE THEY FILMED THIS ARENA. FIND OUT HOW THE BILLIONAIRES WERE TAKEN, IF THEY WERE TAKEN. FIND OUT WHO THE AUDIENCE ARE, EVERYTHING YOU CAN. LINE UP SOME SUSPECTS WITH THE MEANS, MOTIVE AND OPPORTUNITY TO PULL OFF SOMETHING OF THIS SCALE.

He sent that, wrote one more line, deleted it, then wrote it again and sent.

MY FATHER MAY OR MAY NOT BE INVOLVED. BE CAREFUL.

Standing in an incoming gale of snow blowing through the shattered window of Theeravit's third-floor office, Wren dialed a number from memory. 4:45 a.m. in Alaska, that was 8:45 in New York, and his old boss Gerald Humphreys, Director of US Special Operations Command, answered in moments. In his mid-fifties, Humphreys' deep voice was measured, careful, emotionless.

"Christopher. I've been trying to contact you. Where are you?"

Wren was surprised how little anger he felt upon hearing Humphreys' voice. The man had played both sides in the battle with the Blue Fairy, even trying to have Wren's plane shot out of the sky, but right now Wren didn't care. They weren't friends. The man was an asset to be exploited.

He stopped at the top of the stairs. "I'm out hunting Pinocchios, Gerald. There are some dead ones here. I'll let you know the location soon, but that's not why I'm calling now. There's-"

"The killing, Christopher," Humphreys interrupted, a hint of anger showing now. "You have to stop. You-"

"Damalin Joes III," Wren said, cutting straight to the chase. "Handel Quanse. Merriot Raine. Some of the richest billionaires there are. Tell me they're safe and sound on their superyachts, they haven't been kidnapped, there have been no demands."

There was a long silence on Humphreys' end. There was only one reason for that.

"I can neither confirm or deny the pre-"

"That's a yes then," Wren interrupted, feeling his heart plummet in his chest. The video wasn't a deepfake. Handel Quanse was really dead. Damalin Joes' life was on the line.

"… changes here, Christopher," Humphreys was saying, though Wren barely heard. "We have new protocols, new systems to better protect us. Fact is, you're not just a wanted person anymore, you're on a catch/kill list, emphasis on the kill."

He left that hanging. It took a second for Wren to re-engage, putting Quanse's actual death to the side. "What?"

"You've been executing American citizens, man! Pinocchios, but with no due process. We've got hit teams ready to go across the country, waiting for you to show up. Agent Sally Rogers is leading them. You killed," he took a moment, "one in Seattle, one in Idaho, one in Cincinnati, one in Las Vegas, and at least a dozen more. I don't even know where you got their data."

Now Wren's anger began to stir. "I got it from Pleasure Island. I shared it with you. You didn't do anything with it!"

"You mean we didn't swoop in extra-legally and assassinate them? Christopher, you're on a killing spree unlike anything in American history. It places you up there with Dahmer and Bundy. Right now we're focused on catching or killing *you*, not some missing billionaires."

Wren gritted his teeth. It figured, but he'd deal with that later. "Listen to me very carefully, Gerald. I've just come into possession of a snuff film like nothing I've seen before, with all your missing billionaires in it, and one of them's dead already. Handel Quanse, executed through some Dark Age torture, in front of a crowd of roaring Americans who voted for him to die." He took a breath. "Maybe it's the French revolution redux, the beginning of some anti-rich pogrom in the name of income equality; I don't know and I don't much care, but it needs to be stopped." He paused a moment, squaring everything in the balance. "There's a hint my father may be involved, so I'm going after them hard. I need you to pull whatever strings you have left at the Department of Defense and help me this time."

Humphreys took a long moment. "That does sound serious. And your father? If you're right about any of this, the Department will take action. There's something you should know before we proceed any further, however."

Wren snorted. "What, they fired you? Who do I call to-"

"Not exactly. You're not going to like this, Christopher. Rather than bumping me down, they promoted me." A pause. "They made me Director."

It took a second. Wren had to turn the word around once in his head before it hit him. "Overall Director? Not just Director of Special Activities?"

"Director," Humphreys confirmed.

Wren laughed. Was there anyone less fitting to be the top dog in charge of the CIA? "You're kidding me."

"I can guarantee this is not a joke. Check it online."

Wren did; opened his phone and checked the news. It was all there. After the previous Director had been asked to step down for her failures against the Blue Fairy, the baton had been handed to Humphreys for his perceived success.

"You took the credit," Wren said.

"No," Humphreys answered sharply, "I did not. I gave it to you and Rogers, to everyone who lost their lives in the operation, but you've squandered that. You could've come in a hero, but you're too wedded to your purist vigilante morality!"

Only one thing to say to that. "So be purer."

"Be purer?" Humphreys fumed. "Do you really think I liked having the

526

Blue Fairy harness between my teeth? It was disgusting, repugnant, but sometimes..."

Wren tuned him out. He didn't need a moralizing lecture from Gerald Humphreys of all people, whether he was Director or not. There was only one thing he'd said so far that mattered.

"Sally Rogers is hunting me?" Wren interrupted.

It took Humphreys a second to climb down from his high horse. "Yes. She's been arguing for you at every stage, but you're committing murders." Some of the heat faded from his voice. "She's been asking for leniency, but she's dogged. She will find you."

Wren considered. Gazed out into the driving snow, where the Dhruv helicopter was just a white mound now, secrets buried beneath the surface.

Sally Rogers. Getting hunted by her was only going to make this harder. He didn't want to think about how things would go, if it came down to him and her in the dark, guns pointing at each other.

"Call her off. No more catch/kill order."

Humphreys laughed. "Are you being serious? You're public enemy number one. I can't just call that off. What are you going to give me in return?"

Wren gritted his teeth. Everything had a price.

"I'm going after my father. If I happen to save your billionaires into the bargain, even put down these anti-rich idiots before they cause real damage, that's to your benefit. You want me inside the tent for this, Gerald, not on the outside pissing in." He took a breath, kept on before the other man could speak. "This thing could go bigger than the Blue Fairy, and if my father is involved? We all need to start singing from the same hymn sheet, sharpish."

Humphreys took his time. "Perhaps there's a deal to be done here. It depends-"

"How long have they been missing for?" Wren interrupted. Take the deal as read and start at the beginning. "The billionaires."

Humphreys took his time. Getting on the same page, sweeping the past aside, for now at least. "Three weeks. That's the longest of them. Merriot Raine, he was taken first. He had minimal security forces at the time; they were all killed. The others have been taken in stages, three a night, with warnings to the FBI not to publicize them." Wren heard keys clattering.

Humphreys starting the ball rolling. "You said Handel Quanse is dead. You mentioned 'anti-rich'. Do you know why they killed him?"

"Some nonsense about claiming reparations in blood. It's grim stuff, high production values, a video designed to go viral by pitting the rich against the poor. They voted for him to die, it seems. And their ultimate goal? I've got no idea. It's-" Wren stopped as a ping chimed on his phone. The spider coming back with something. He clicked the link through to the streaming app WeScreen, where a new video had just started to play. It began with the spiraling shot of a familiar golden arena, seen from the top down, with the gameshow voting box in the top right. Wren copied the link and sent it to Humphreys.

"The video's just been uploaded. See for yourself."

11

QUESTIONS

Questions churned in Wren's mind as he tore back through the storm on his stolen snowmobile. Four dead Pinocchios and a snuff film featuring a billionaire Foundation member, all laid out for him to see first. There had to be a reason why these 'Reparations' wanted him involved in their schemes, but he had no idea what it was.

He'd never been rich. Other than Joes, he didn't know any rich people. He wasn't a natural target, and neither was his family. Living in a duplex in Delaware with some guy who installed surround sound speaker systems for a living, nobody was going to target them.

So why try to drag him into this? Why include Damalin Joes? Why reference his father?

The snowmobile revved hard. There was almost zero visibility in the storm, and Wren steered with his thighs more than the handles, feeling the verve and flow of the snowcapped land as it punched up through the skids. Flurries of snow crusted over the goggles, an endless curtain of white that kept on unpeeling to nowhere. At least the lay of the land beneath the machine didn't lie.

Or maybe it did.

This whole thing felt like that, a snow screen masking some deeper plot.

He'd checked Theeravit's house over one last time before he left, a fifteen-minute final sweep, but the killers had done a clean job. The Reparations. He even rode out to the jetty to check they hadn't left a trail, but there was no evidence. Not only of their passage through those spaces, but of Theeravit's too. No sign of the cryptography laptop he'd shipped up here. No hard drives at all. No notes, no papers, no clear onward steps left, as if they wanted Wren to have only one lead to follow.

The video.

The snowmobile jolted then hit a downward slope, pulling Wren's attention back to the present. His speed increased, no way to know it from the empty surroundings, but he felt it in the wild revving of the engine. Dangerously fast, the handles hammering into his palms. Any second he could hit the stump of a desiccated tree, the flank of a wandering polar bear, the Jurassic blade of some ancient crag shooting up through the ice.

Hit and be sent flying. Soar through the air then strike Earth head-first, crumple his neck, shatter his collarbones, maybe tear his arms and legs off like poor old Handel Quanse, left as a red spot in the snow soon to be covered over.

Fear raced through his heart and out into his arteries and veins, telling him to slow down. Protect yourself.

Wren pushed the pedal harder and leaned into it.

Faster.

Harder.

The wind ripped at his face. Snow blinded him. His feet went numb with the thumping vibrations punching up from below as the snowmobile bounced like a skier over moguls, faster and faster.

Fear would only hurt you and make you small; that knowledge was branded onto his soul. Uncertainty was a rock to founder on. Faith and self-confidence were everything.

Wren pushed the engine to the max and leaned into the storm. There was no better defense than an overwhelming offense, every time. He'd watched Damalin Joes come to the same realization, sitting atop his horse and listening to the cries of the dying Quanse. You either killed or got killed, and he had no intention of getting killed. If that meant getting used as a cog in some diabolical plot, Wren figured he could ride that horse just as far as he needed to before wrestling it to the ground.

No other thing for it but leap first, plan the landing later.
Fine by Wren. He'd have it no other way.

12

EXTRA-LEGAL

Wren stopped at the depot, checking in on his dead friends. Nobody had moved them. Simon was still there, Hartright laid out beside him, the unnamed second cop lying flat on his back, like he was sleeping off a five-day drunk.

Wren stood in the doorway with his back to them, looking out over the frozen lake. The storm was ebbing now, like a tidal movement draining from an estuary. That was good. Hopefully he could catch the dawn flight out, get a jump on his investigation of the Reparations. He still had a couple of hours until then.

He brought up his phone, powered it on and was inundated with a rush of chimes as notifications poured in. Top of the screen were the latest; reports from the spider algorithm he'd set up to search for fresh instances of the snuff film. In the last hour it looked like hundreds of new versions had gone up.

They were everywhere.

He'd predicted as much to Humphreys. The video was going viral, and he understood why viewers were sharing it. It was horrific viewing, but people liked that kind of thing. They stopped to rubberneck at a car crash, they searched for video of the aid worker who'd had his head cut off by jihadis, they couldn't help themselves.

It helped that this guy, Handel Quanse, was near-universally despised.

Wren only had to scan a few headlines on major news sites to see how they were reporting his death. There was outrage at the murder, but there was also an undercurrent of glee. Why else would they list in the first or second paragraph all the reasons people had to hate him?

Handel Quanse's predatory investment activities had put tens of thousands of people out of work, apparently. Then to add insult to injury, he'd gone on talking head shows to call it tough love. Trickle-down economics, he'd said, only works if you're willing to work as hard as me. Slack off and you deserve to starve by the side of the road.

Comments were already trending toward sympathy with the Reparations. How could they be bad, people were saying, when they took trash like Joes to task? A fair point.

Wren checked into his darknet, where his hackers and the inner Foundation team were putting together lists of potential suspects, beginning with protest groups focused on income inequality: the 99%, Anti-Ca, SST. Wren knew a little about them from the mainstream media, but there wasn't much to know; they were all loose conglomerations of reformers, socialists and marginal communists.

The 99% were named after the percentage of people in society who owned less than 10% of the wealth. Anti-Ca was short for Anti-Capitalist. SST took their name from the Latin phrase favored by John Wilkes Booth, 'Sic Semper Tyrannis', meaning 'Thus Always to Tyrants.' According to the research, some of these groups had greater financing, some less, but none had perpetrated any protest action nearly as massive or as brazen as the Reparations video. None were considered a terrorist threat by Homeland Security, and Wren had received no briefings about any of them. At worst, all they did was turn up at rallies and try to throw red paint on the 'symbols of capitalism', like coffee shop chains and fast-food joints.

Wren scrolled through some photos of past protests the various groups had attended. Mostly they were family-friendly crowds, parents with little kids in tow holding up signs like:

YOUR YACHT OUR DEBT

MONEY COSTS TOO MUCH

COULD YOU PASS THROUGH THE EYE OF THE NEEDLE?

A few members wore black tactical gear with helmets and masks, tried to start fights with the police, but they never achieved the critical mass they were hoping for. The families never joined them in punching through the windows of sneaker shops and designer gyms.

Ani-rich rage. Income inequality. Maybe there was plenty of injustice there, but nothing acute enough for Wren to get involved with. That was for the lawmakers to resolve, not a black-ops operator.

That left him nothing much to go on. He checked his mailbox, found a message from Hellion, his genius hacker.

THE VIDEO IS GUARANTEED NOT DEEPFAKE, CHRISTOPHER. NO METADATA SIGNATURES IN THE VIDEO APPEAR, HOWEVER, NOTHING WE CAN TRACK. WE ARE SEARCHING FOR MANY LINKS: GEOGRAPHICAL, FINANCIAL, DEMOGRAPHIC, BUT NOTHING YET. RECOMMEND YOU EXTRACT INFORMATION FROM SOCIAL MEDIA COMPANIES, WHERE THIS FILM IS POSTED. WE CANNOT HACK THEM FROM HERE. THEY WILL HAVE BETTER METADATA.

Wren grunted. Extract information from social media companies? He didn't pay too close an eye to tech news, but even he knew Internet content companies like WeStream, NameCheck and Iota were locked in battle with the US government over issues of content moderation. The companies wanted the advertising money that disinformation and violent content generated, and the government was tiptoeing around that just trying not to trip over freedom of speech issues.

Inserting himself into the middle of that didn't sound feasible or productive, but maybe it was the best lead he had.

The phone started chiming again as more notifications came in from the spider, and Wren squeezed it silent. Across the way an old guy in a yellow parka walked along the road, pulling a sled loaded with low wooden crates. Wren raised a hand in greeting. The guy waved back.

"The wife calling you?" he shouted.

"You got me," Wren answered with a neighborly grin. "Out all night."

The guy gave him a thumbs up. "Depot open then?"

"Fixing it up," Wren shouted back. "Gas leak. It'll take a few hours."

"Good man," the guy answered, and turned his attention back to pulling his sled.

Wren checked the time. Still two hours to the next flight out. He had to get out of here. Better use that time productively, so he placed the call he'd been putting off. It took minutes, and Wren listened and watched as the old guy trudged on, pulling his load toward the wilderness. Wren wondered what he had in those crates. He was two hundred yards away when the phone finally clicked.

"Agent Rogers."

It was Sally Rogers' voice, but it came through flat and emotionless like he'd never heard it before.

"It's me, Sally," he said. "Have you seen the billionaire video?"

She said nothing. A moment passed and Wren stepped back into the depot and out of the wind, pressing the phone tight to his ear. Sally Rogers had been with him at every stage in their battle against the Blue Fairy. He'd handpicked her to lead his digital team months before that, an ambitious and brilliant analyst looking to move into field operations. Together they'd mutinied against Humphreys, leading to her helping him execute a tanker full of Pinocchios off the New Jersey coast. Making her complicit in all those deaths.

Where did that leave her now? Angry, he figured.

"Turn yourself in, Christopher."

There it was. She did sound angry. Burning cold with anger, in fact.

"I'm sorry, Sally. For how things went. For how that might have affected you. But I think my father's involved with the death of Handel Quanse." He paused a moment. "At least somebody wants me to think that he is. The Reparations, I'm calling them. I need your help to-"

"I don't work for you anymore," she interrupted. "And I can't make any promises, if you force me to hunt you down. I don't want to kill you, but I will."

That was a little stronger than he'd expected. "Let's avoid that outcome, agreed. So can we call a truce? Humphreys is on board if you are. Stop the hunt." A pause. "Even help me."

The wind rushed by sharp and stinging. Rogers breathed low on the other end.

"Killing Pinocchios on the tanker was one thing," she said. "I didn't know about it at the time, but I understand it, I thought maybe it was the right thing. But this? CIA don't even act within the Continental US, Wren. We certainly don't execute citizens without a trial. You're on the hook for all of that, and that means I am too, because I'm an accomplice. So come in. The law has to apply to you too, or none of this is worth anything."

Wren grunted. She was right, he did owe her for that. It surprised him how easily his answer came.

"Fine. When this is done, I'll come in. Peacefully."

He felt a mental milestone ticking over. Once in Rogers' hands, he might go to jail for the rest of his life. He wouldn't see his kids, his wife, his Foundation again. Caught in the moment with the Apex in the wind, though, none of that mattered. Better that he never saw them again, but they were safe, than any other outcome.

"Deal," she said swiftly. "What do you need?"

"I need you to corral the social media companies. The search engines. We need to find out who planted this video. Crack them open with subpoenas, smash in their doors in a dawn raid, censure the CEOs or repossess their infrastructure, I don't care. Get that data and use it to track the Reparations back."

She barely let a beat go by before answering. "Not possible, Christopher."

"Why not?"

She sighed. "You've been out of the loop. We went through all this after the Blue Fairy. The government suspended free speech and censored the press, social media, much of the Internet? We had that power then, but now it's long gone. The big companies have slipped the leash, incorporating overseas, placing their decisions outside the remit of American law. It'll take a year before any of it comes up before the Supreme Court. We can't shut these companies down even if we raid their offices on American soil. Ask your hackers if you don't believe me. We'd have to slap a firewall around the coasts and a dome across the sky to prevent information getting though, and that's an isolationism we can't afford, not after the damage we took from the Blue Fairy." She took a breath. "The world hates us right now. For our excesses, our selfishness, our cruelty. This video capitalizes on that hate perfectly."

Wren cursed under his breath. Of course, she was right. If billionaires were a symbol of anything, it was America. Rags to riches. Make your fortune. Capitalism on speed.

He started pacing in front of the depot, each footstep a crunch through snow, thinking it through. "They're not American companies anymore," he said. "Outside your jurisdiction."

"Exactly," Sally confirmed. "They're colonizers in a new Wild West, the global information landscape, and there are no laws out there, while we're hamstrung by the Constitution. It gives them all the power with none of the accountability, so they do what they want, and what's best for their bottom line."

All that made sense. Wren spun the issue. "It's free to ask. Persuade them helping us is better than siding with these Reparations."

Rogers snorted. "We're asking. We ask all day, Christopher, every day. But they're corporations, their only loyalty is to their bottom line, which means serving exactly what their users want. If their users want disinformation and violence, so be it. So what do you think their answer is, when we ask nicely for their help to shut down and investigate their biggest current revenue stream?"

Wren took that on board and dialed the lens back a step. Big picture. "OK. So give me your read. My hackers say I need metadata on the video from the big companies; how do I get that if the government can't help and the companies won't volunteer it?"

"No legally-mandated force can compel what you're asking," Rogers said. Sounded like she was carefully choosing her words. And did she emphasize 'legally'? Maybe. "That's all she wrote."

Wren took a second, reading between the lines. "Nothing you can do legally. But extra-legally?"

He heard the hint of a smile in her voice. A little of the old Rogers shining through. "What can I say? People break the law all the time."

There it was. A hole in the State apparatus through which he could slip. "People do. But people would never get in if the government had eyes on these companies. Do you have any federal overwatch in place?"

She was right there with him. "Why would we?"

And that was the rest of it. Everything he needed to know. An assault on the Internet companies wasn't going to bring down an immediate federal response. If he was going to jail already, may as well add a few more crimes to the list.

"I'll be in touch," he said, killed the call, then started walking away from the depot, back to where his Jeep was waiting.

13

DASH 8

A t 07:32 Wren boarded a passenger turboprop plane out of Deadhorse, capacity thirty-seven, occupancy twelve, all pallid pipeline workers drained of color and life by their stint in the far north. In three hours he hit Anchorage International, where he took a runway shuttle to a private HA-420 HondaJet, capacity six, occupancy one. Flight time to San Francisco International Airport was five hours, scheduled to touch down by 16:14.

He drank coffee, ate a microwave meal of Kobe beef brisket and asparagus, and dug into the Internet.

It frothed with celebration and condemnation both. On streaming site WeScreen there were already hundreds of video responses to Handel Quanse's death: shock-faced teens making O-faces; comedy trolls running play-by-plays like they were commentating a sporting event; talking heads snipped out of network newscasts saying how this was the dawn of some dark new Internet age: post-law, post-decency, heading toward an era of politics by gladiatorial combat.

No one lamented his death. Handel Quanse was a hated man, and as far as most were concerned, these were the just desserts he'd earned. Pegged against that, the Reparations came off as a modern-day kind of Robin Hood.

On social media site NameCheck a spray of hashtags were battling for dominance: #splittherich, #99rising, #stormthebastille, #handelthat! and the clear winner, #REPARATIONS. Trending feeds ticked over constantly in swells of alternating excitement and fear. A little-known Congressman went on record saying it was perhaps a a necessary reckoning. A mega church preacher claimed it was the onset of the Revelation. Video re-mixers on WeScreen auto tuned their comments and turned them into rap battles laid over the scene of Handel Quanse's death.

With every passing hour in the air, Wren watched the tone darken like a scab hardening around a wound, making the message real by reflecting, digesting and amplifying it. Billionaires were not untouchable. The rich could be brought down. The masses liked what they were seeing, and they wanted more.

YOU ARE OWED REPARATIONS

CLAIM THEM IN BLOOD

Already there were instances of real-life mimicry. Sometime around noon the copycat videos began. They started off soft, with a twenty-second clip of kids in ski masks spray-painting WHERE ARE OUR REPARATIONS? on the drive of a wealthy neighbor. That video went viral under the hashtag #REPARATIONS, and opened the floodgates for more.

A fast-food worker in a drive-thru made a fire-in-the-hole video, tossing a full milkshake into the waiting open window of a Ferrari, mostly hitting the driver's young daughter. Another group of teens, this time in mustached Anonymous masks, walked along a marina firing red paintball pellets at the hulls of yachts. #REPARATIONS again. A pool cleaner filmed a fluffy Pomeranian repeatedly trying to climb out of a marble swimming pool, and laughing. #REPARATIONS.

It was beginning with minor property damage and pranks, but those were catalysts only. With the people already on edge, and social media providing virality to videos that offered dopamine satisfaction for strikes back at the wealthy, Wren believed it'd soon lead to real violence. Call it mass self-radicalization on an accelerated timescale. He'd seen it happen in the Pyramid, a thousand people stampeding themselves toward self-immolation. Without anyone able to stop it, the anger would only build.

Wren didn't care. Mobs always did. Made up of people who thought they were righteously redressing some injustice; they became an echo chamber that drove their members to commit fresh and worse injustices.

Injustices to what end? Wren didn't care.

What mattered was digging through their anti-rich bullshit to the core. If that meant destroying the mob before it could mobilize, he would. With an online mob that meant shutting down their Internet access, and it just so happened Wren already had the social media companies in his sights for their metadata on the video.

Two birds with one stone.

He'd already selected his prime target. Housed in an expansive campus along the south coast of San Francisco Bay, the beating heart of Silicon Valley. NameCheck, the biggest social media behemoth and owner of WeScreen, the largest video streaming site. Between the two NameCheck had a near monopoly on the Internet eyeballs of America. They were the prime vector by which this video was spreading.

"It cannot be done," his elite hacker Hellion said, on the jet headed south toward San Francisco, after he'd explained the plan. "No, Christopher, impossible."

Her accent sounded unusually harsh through the scratchy connection; Wren mid-air on the satellite phone, Hellion answering from a convoy somewhere in the ex-Soviet sphere, probably Moldova or Ukraine, two of her favorite haunts.

Hellion was a twenty-one-year-old genius, a Bulgarian wunderkind who'd taken up hacking as a fun thing to do after conquering the world of real-time strategy game StarCraft. Her incredible APM, or Actions Per Minute ratio, meant she could execute up to 400 meaningful keystrokes every sixty seconds, which was faster than most concert pianists.

She'd leveraged that awesome speed into taking down one of the biggest black hat hackers in the world, known only as B4cksl4cker. Now her partner-in-crime, his specialism was corralling vast 'botnets' of remotely slaved computers to do his bidding, whether that was to build deepfake videos, hack into bank vaults or bring down government infrastructure via Trojan-like 'cryptoworms'.

For the past two years they'd been working for Wren through the Foundation, his rehab group for ex-cons, disgraced soldiers and white-collar criminals. For the past three months they'd been hunting Wren's father using the Blue Fairy's stolen infrastructure, a kind of 'second skin' on the Internet, and getting nowhere.

"Why not?" he answered.

Hellion let out a long sigh. "Christopher. Where do I begin? Let me guess, you think this company, NameCheck, it is playground, yes? Children's slide in office, theme park rooms, ping pong in break room? It will be easy to infiltrate and find CEO, you think, force him to help you, correct?"

Wren shrugged. She couldn't see it, but that didn't matter. "I'm sure they've got security. I just need you to hack it and buy me a way through."

Another sigh. "There is no way to 'hack' them, Christopher. These corporate campuses are digitally air-gapped. Do you know what this means?"

"I can guess."

"Do not guess, please, you will hurt yourself."

Wren smiled. A little bit of Hellion was refreshing. "Enlighten me."

"It means there is no outside Internet line leading into security, personnel, anything," she went on. "Air gap, like digital moat. There is no way to remotely create ID or fake 'fast pass' to CEO's office. And it is CEO you wish to see, correct?"

She was correct. Wren was after Lars Mecklarin, the late-twenties inventor and CEO of NameCheck, famous for still wearing one brand of cheap red sneakers despite being the third-richest person on the planet.

"So phish me an identity. Socially hack him. You have-" Wren checked the time. Already it was past midday, and there were three hours left in the flight. "Four hours until I'm at their door. Find a worker, steal his ID, give it to me."

Hellion chuckled. "You are sweet. NameCheck has impressive biometric analysis, such as retinal scans, fingerprint scans, and so on. Let me send you illustration."

His phone chimed, and images popped up. Maps of the NameCheck campus as seen from above, overlaid with security notation. A cursor appeared and moved to highlight certain parts of the map.

"Look here, only two or three entrances to this campus, guarded by dual guard posts. B4cksl4cker is running background observation for intel. B4cksl4cker?"

A moment passed, then the big Armenian came on the line, his voice husky like a bear. "Christopher, yes, Hellion is correct. I see four elite security force members running biometric ID pass approval. I have leads on screening, also. There is automated detection CCTV on all approach roads, linked to best facial recognition and gait analysis algorithms in existence. You know this, gait recognition?"

"I wouldn't want to guess and hurt myself," Wren countered.

Now B4cksl4cker sighed. Wren's smile broadened. His hackers were always so put-upon. "This means the way you walk, Christopher. It is unique, like fingerprint. If you, Christopher Wren, walk up to their gate with your face and your walk, they will know. You are not in records. You will not pass."

Wren took a moment. "OK. So we're onto forceful insertion. I won't need a pass, then."

B4cksl4cker was ready for that. "Come in by vehicle, try to ram through security gates, they are ready. Hidden blast barricades everywhere. These will rise instantly if you leave the road, capable of stopping military vehicle. Security teams from special forces will meet you, with permission to fire. If you somehow breach past them, there are multiple panic rooms in missile-proof bunkers underground, capable to fit entire command team." He took a breath. "You will never get near CEO."

Wren nodded along. All that certainly limited his attack paths. He couldn't hope to mount any kind of brute-force assault. A parachute drop onto the roof would be spotted by CCTV and lead to campus lockdown. Entry on foot with a paramilitary team would have the same result. Neither could he attempt a covert digital insertion; there were no ways to mount a hack across an air gap.

He was going to have to get creative. He had Hellion and B4cksl4cker, after all, as well as a guy in LA who could fly in to help out, and a wider Foundation filled with all kinds of skillsets.

He explained the plan as it came to him, looking down through the clouds to the land far below. Maybe beginning to see the shape of things.

"Not possible," Hellion insisted, after he finished. "You are talking about 'God Mode', Christopher. This is dream. Impossible coordination. Many moving parts. We do not have time. I have tried this before, and never succeeded."

Wren just smiled. 'God Mode' was a nice name for what he was suggesting. "You never tried it with me."

14

GRUBER

The jet soared in over San Francisco around 4 p.m., and as it banked Wren saw the NameCheck campus lying below like a brightly colored theme park. Large adult trampolines, a full volleyball court, whimsical designs written out in various pathways through the green inner courtyard.

The jet landed within minutes at San Francisco Airport and taxied to a private stair car, where Wren was shuttled to the customs building and ushered through at pace.

As planned, his LA Foundation member had flown in ahead and was now waiting for him in short-stay parking. Steven Gruber was a slim, tousle-headed 33-year-old NSA analyst, dressed in board shorts and a Hawaiian shirt, sitting in a rented yellow Prius. Wren gave him a nod and strode over, carrying no baggage, and climbed into the back like it was a taxi.

"Good to see you, Steven. Let's drive."

"Man says drive," Gruber said and pulled away, into the spaghetti network of feeder roads out of the airport. "Man says fly up from LA, I get it done. Everything you need's in back."

Wren grunted thanks, unzipping the Day-Glo pink and green backpack on the seat beside him. Steven Gruber had this curious habit of starting his sentences about Wren as 'Man says-' or 'Man does-'. Maybe they'd address it in a coin meeting sometime soon; issues with authority, probably. When had their last coin meeting been?

The Prius cleared the overhanging access roads and rolled onto the open 101. Gruber rolled the windows down and warm, salty air rushed in; a relief after being cooped up on planes for nine hours. Wren took a moment to just breathe. It was a beautiful afternoon in the Bay Area, an azure sky streaked with hair-thin cirrus clouds like a balding old man's well-combed head. Hot, low 90s. A total shift after the snowstorm in Deadhorse, and he shrugged off his woolen jacket.

"Sixteen months," Gruber said, conversationally, like they didn't know each other all that well and Wren hadn't once broken into a mass orgy with him at the center, sweaty and pink-assed, "since I heard direct from you."

"That's my bad," Wren said, turning his attention to the backpack. "I've been busy."

"I know that," Gruber said, smiling and glancing at Wren in the rearview. "Taking out the Saints. The Pinocchios. You're a national hero."

Wren tipped out the backpack. Pink short shorts came first. That was ridiculous. He pushed them to one side. A yellow string vest followed. What the…? He looked up at Gruber. Dressed like a normal person. He looked at the pink and yellow outfit.

"You said light and bright," Gruber said, watching Wren in the mirror. "I didn't have time to keep looking; that's what they had."

"Were you in a strip club?" Wren retorted.

"The airport. A sports clothing store, that's what they had."

Wren held up the yellow vest. 'Skimpy', was one way to describe it. "There wasn't a GAP?"

"Man said come fast. I came fast. And it wasn't the only thing on your shopping list. Does it really matter?"

Wren sighed. No, he supposed it didn't. He'd certainly look non-threatening, dressed in the shorts and vest, and that was the point. He rummaged through the rest of the backpack's contents while the Prius weaved gently through traffic, with the Bay peeling and unpeeling to his left behind layers of industrial buildings, housing, parks.

4:25, time rushing by.

There was the earpiece he'd asked for, and a clippable bodycam to wear on his chest. It was light enough, but looking at the flimsy yellow shirt he figured it wouldn't hold up the weight. A camera wasn't much good that drooped to the floor.

"There's a strap, shoulder-holster thing," Gruber said, trying to point while driving.

"Look at the road," Wren said. "I'm not getting pulled over."

"Yeah," Gruber said, then continued softly to himself, "man says look at the road, look at the road."

Wren found the strap.

"You wear it like a Go-Pro," Gruber said encouragingly. "Life-streaming, the kids are calling it."

Wren looked at the strap, an elasticized band in hot pink. He was going to look like a clown. "Which kids?"

"In the shop. They showed me some clips. It's the new big thing. Life-streaming with commentary, the only way to vlog."

Vlog? Of course, that's what these #REPARATION posts were about. Wren sighed and kept looking through Gruber's shopping. Big sunglasses, check. At least these were black. Blue flip-flops, because why not add blue to the mix? A burner cell phone: he booted it. There was a welcome message from Hellion and B4cksl4cker waiting for him, along with twin icons. The first he pushed, and it synced the phone with the earpiece and the bodycam; footage of the car seat began streaming on the screen. He inserted the earpiece and heard a low testing hum, then Hellion's voice.

"Getting signal," she said. "Lift me up."

Wren lifted the bodycam.

"Good," Hellion said. "Checking levels. Precision. Contours. Excellent, your boy bought nice lens." There was a pause, then, "Christopher, are you wearing that?"

He put the bodycam back down. She'd seen the shorts and top laid out on the seat. "Not your department."

"You have figure for this, I am sure, but-"

Wren tapped the earpiece and her voice cut out. Everything was here, except…

"Where's the board?" he asked Gruber.

"In the trunk," Gruber said enthusiastically. "You're going to love it. I got you the top model, glides smooth as a lunar rover."

Wren frowned. Was that an expression? "All right."

"Man says all right," Gruber muttered.

Wren opened his mouth to address the 'Man says…', briefly thought better of it, then went ahead anyway. "You realize I can hear you, every time you say, 'Man says' something?"

"Hmm?" Gruber asked, looking at Wren in the mirror.

"I'm saying, when you repeat what I said and add 'Man says' before it, there's no need."

Gruber looked puzzled, like he had no idea what Wren was talking about. "How's that?"

Wren opened his mouth to continue, then gave up. "Never mind."

"Man says never mind," Gruber muttered to himself.

Wren let it go, and pulled his shirt off, shrugged on the yellow vest. It had to be several sizes too small for him: tight to his broad shoulders, snug on his ripped stomach. The tattoos on his chest were showing; his wife's name, Loralei, his kids Quinn and Jake.

"Suits you," said Gruber.

Wren ignored him and swapped his pants for the pink short shorts. They were really short. He hadn't dressed like this since, well, his Pyramid days? Running in the desert, a few minutes of stolen fun from all the cultish pain and nonsensical BS.

He snapped back to attention. His heavy-duty boots came off, replaced with the flip-flops. The bodycam clipped onto his chest and the harness went around his shoulder. He tapped the earpiece again, bringing Hellion back online.

She sounded amused. "I'm not saying anything."

"What?" Wren asked.

"B4cksl4cker says this is good look for you. I'm waiting to see effect when you stand."

Wren frowned down at the bodycam. How had she-?

"Traffic cams," Hellion said. "Hacked. We are tracking you, with good angles through windows. You arrive in five minutes. Get out in four. You will need to approach via board; this is common practice. All feeds show NameCheck CEO is in position, we think building three, but campus also has underground facilities, these may link many buildings. He may not be there-"

"He's there," Wren said.

"Are you talking to me?" Gruber asked, confused.

Wren ignored him, looking now at his pink pants. There wasn't even a pocket to put the cell phone in. He'd just have to hold it.

"There's an arm strap," Gruber said, pointing helpfully.

Wren found it. Orange; he'd mistaken it for part of the backpack. He was going to look like Jackson Pollack had vomited up a rainbow. He tucked the cell phone into the strap and cinched it around his left bicep; it barely fit.

"Christopher," Gruber said from up front. Wren looked up. In the mirror, it looked like uncertain emotions were playing across his face. "I know this is not the time, and like you said, you've been busy, but I could really use a coin meeting. Not now of course, but I mean, just…"

He trailed off.

Wren nodded. This was his fault; sixteen months was too long without a check-in. Losing his family, then hunting down the Saints and the Blue Fairy had distracted him, but that was no excuse. He had a responsibility to his members, and maybe Gruber had already fallen off the wagon. Gone back to the orgies that had been his addiction. There wasn't anything necessarily wrong with 'free love', but Gruber was an addict and couldn't handle it, plus the groups and cults who ran the events were generally self-destructive.

He softened his voice. "You're right, Steven, we're overdue. We'll do it as soon as this is finished, I promise. Thank you again for coming today. I couldn't do this without you."

That puffed Gruber up a little.

"And I'm sorry I haven't been there. The coin system's a promise and I've been breaking it. I'll do better." Gruber nodded along. Wren thought he saw the glimmer of tears forming in the young man's eyes. "But for these clothes, I think I have to penalize you a coin."

Gruber laughed. The moment broke. Wren smiled too. This was what it was all about, why he had hunted down the Blue Fairy, why all this mattered. Not just his family, but the Foundation too. That brought the thought of Damalin Joes III to mind, out there somewhere facing a gruesome death, and the smile faded from his face.

They approached NameCheck.

Wren pictured Hellion and B4cksl4cker poised like spiders over their computers, half a world away. His other Foundation members somewhere out there, crunching video on the biggest servers B4cksl4cker could steal. Hunting for leads. It all came down to this.

"Here is your spot," came Hellion's voice in his ear. "Outside surveillance range. Get out."

Wren tapped Gruber's shoulder, and he pulled off the freeway onto a quiet side road with a big palm tree and a view over parked cars to the calm green-blue waters of the Bay. The NameCheck campus was less than a mile away. Wren got out, leaving the backpack and his old clothes behind. The Bay breeze blew a warm wind around his bare legs.

Would he pass? Probably. With no bag, not even any pockets, he wouldn't look like anyone's idea of a threat. A big guy still, bearded and tattooed, but beards and tattoos were commonplace in Silicon Valley. And pièce de résistance? He popped the trunk and took out his hoverboard. 4:32. Time to get moving.

15

NAMECHECK

Wren had never ridden a hoverboard before. It was small, sturdy, white and felt like a motorized bathroom scale; just enough space to fit his feet then a five-inch wheel either side. Like a Segway, it responded to the way he balanced his bodyweight; slightly forward, slightly backward, left to right, steering as he leaned.

He leaned forward and it picked up some speed. He whipped past a few pedestrians, leaving them in his dust. It was quite exhilarating, more so even than riding a snowmobile with a flashing blue light; something about the power of just 'leaning' ever so slightly and having the world respond accordingly.

He whipped past the end of the parking lot then was out onto an exposed strip by the Bay; winds buffeted him and made for their own challenges. Easily 15mph now, half of the 100m record sprint speed, like a superhero gliding in for a dramatic landing. One bump in the sidewalk would send him flying, almost naked, without any of the protective leathers a motorcyclist would wear.

God Mode.

He whizzed onto Veterans Boulevard and slid off the sidewalk into a cycle lane. New-build residential lots flew by either side. Soon the warehouse bulk of the NameCheck campus rose up ahead like a cluster of colorful cruise liners.

He drew in.

"They have eyes on the road from here," Hellion said in his ear. "You're already in their early warning system, so don't step off the hoverboard here. Remember, gait analysis of the way you walk. Also, do not take off your sunglasses. Facial analysis."

Wren grunted. In moments he'd be there, hopefully categorized under the security algorithms as a STATUS UNKNOWN. Hellion had been emphatic about the importance of achieving that status. By withholding his facial and gait data, the NameCheck system wouldn't have enough data to categorize him as either AUTHORISED or UNAUTHORISED, and would therefore kick him over to the gate security team to run a direct ID check on.

Wren slowed as he passed the familiar NameCheck logo, a twenty-foot sign on the campus' grassy corner, rising out of a bed of plastic flowers. The buildings were angular and modernist, off-setting the fortress-like look of their construction with playful colors and plasticky flair. His target was the north end access road, a broad avenue with a low gate.

A steady stream of millennials was trickling out through the gate. Closing time. There were two guard-boxes made up to look like ice-cream vendors, left and right.

"Left," Hellion said as Wren rolled up, scanning the scene through the bodycam. Wren veered over then Hellion corrected with a snappy, "No, right!"

He played it off as a trick. Almost threw himself off the hoverboard, then spun up to the desk. A glass window, two guards behind it, neither looking so cheerful. Decals in the window of different ice creams. It made a mockery of their job, really. How often did punk kids come up asking for a Mister Softee, raspberry sauce, thinking it was some great joke?

"Angle up," Hellion said, and Wren leaned back slightly, giving the bodycam the view it needed of the guards' faces. "Now buy us a minute."

"You see that, brah?" Wren asked the guard, adopting a California surfer accent. "Sick twists. You ride?"

The security guard eyed him dispassionately. Probably Wren's age, mid-thirties, half-jealous at how much money Wren must make, half-dismayed at what a dumbass he looked on his hoverboard in his stripper costume.

"The system can't log you when you ride up," the guard said tiredly. His colleague in back looked on. "You have to walk. The memos have gone out many times."

"Ah, sorry brother," Wren said, "I'm just an addict, you know? I can't get enough of the air, shooting down the boulevard riding the wind, there's nothing like the lean, do you-"

"Pass," the guard said, holding out a hand.

"Fifty seconds yet," Hellion said, keys clacking wildly through the earpiece.

"Pass, I feel that," said Wren smoothly, "I got it right here." He went for his pockets, then made a show of discovering he had none. He patted his hips. Patted his shirt. "Shoot."

"Forty seconds," Hellion said.

The guard's expression locked. 'You're all children,' that expression said. Wren leaned into it.

"I forgot," he said.

"So go home and get it," the guard said. "Ride the wind."

Hellion laughed.

"Nah, I think I got it here," Wren said, and went for his phone. "Got a special leave."

The guard sighed.

"Longer," Hellion said.

Wren unzipped his shoulder holster and took out his phone, then fumbled it on purpose. It hit the cement walk-up and he leaned over to get it. The hoverboard responded to his shift in weight, banging against the guard post's cement plinth. Wren rocked back and turned, then bent over again.

"Step down, sir," the guard said, with the infinite patience of a parent with a toddler.

Wren looked up at him, playing confused.

"Off the board. To get your phone."

Wren smiled and laughed "Right on."

"Don't walk," Hellion said. "One step. Almost there."

Wren put one foot down, fished for the phone with the other.

"Twenty seconds," Hellion said.

The guards were waiting. Starting to lose the edge of patience, maybe getting suspicious.

"Here you go, brah," Wren said, and held out the phone. The guy took it and sighed.

"It's locked. PIN."

"Ready," Hellion said.

Wren took the phone, tapped in the PIN and handed it back.

The guard squinted. If everything had gone well, Hellion had near-field hacked the guard's computer, built Wren a pass by overwriting a legitimate employee, then backloaded it onto Wren's phone.

The guard squinted. The moment stretched out. If something went wrong here, that was it. NameCheck security would be alerted, and he'd never get close to the CEO. The guard turned to his colleague, pointed at the screen, and the guy looked, smiled, looked up at Wren.

"You really like the hoverboard, huh?" he asked.

Wren didn't know what that was about. "Sure do, brah."

The front guard handed the phone back. "In you go, Mr. Rider. Like the wind."

Wren grinned like an idiot and rolled away from the guard booth, through the gate, looking at his phone. There was a pass with his photo, time-slotted for that hour, but it wasn't under his name. Where his name was supposed to be, it now read AIR RIDER.

"You're kidding me," he muttered. "Hellion."

"What?" she answered, clearly restraining her laughter. "This is good strong American name."

"Hardly God Mode as I envisioned it."

That made her burst out laughing.

"You are in," B4cksl4cker reasoned. "This is very good cover. Now, proceed to building 3, Christopher."

He knew better than to argue it in the moment. In the aftermath, it'd just be too ridiculous. Better to roll with the punches.

"That's Mr. Rider to you."

They both laughed as he rolled into the campus.

16

GOD MODE

Wren rolled along a rubberized red asphalt path through an inner green space of spruce trees and grass, workers out picnicking on the grass. On the right lay a trampoline pod with two teenagers, no doubt coding prodigies, bouncing merrily. The interior building façades were coated in shades of garish neon orange, yellow and pink that matched Wren's clothes.

"Building 3 is to your left," Hellion said.

Wren veered left, passing the sculpture of a dinosaur, twenty feet high. It had giant rainbow feathers and a placard scrawled at its feet: RETHINK THE PAST. A pod of employees passed him, playing some kind of Augmented Reality Game that saw them swiping at invisible enemies in the air.

"Here," Hellion said. "Left at Narnia."

The path forked whimsically at a lamppost jeweled with fake snow, and Wren followed it. His pass scanned at the entrance to building 3, a violet affair with diagonally slanted windows. Finally he dismounted the hoverboard, took his first step into the building, where the gait analysis cameras should no longer be filming.

A security guard inside gave him a wave, and Wren headed up stairs decorated with child-like artwork on the walls, along a corridor beside a sports hall where people wearing giant inflatable plastic ball-suits were trying to play soccer, bouncing off each other.

Lars Mecklarin, CEO of NameCheck, was in his office on the third floor running a meeting around a standing conference desk. Wren strode up alongside the room's all-glass wall, surveying the five people inside: two in suits, three in colorful shorts and T-shirts boasting punk hairstyles, extreme body modification, tattoos. The atmosphere seemed intense.

Wren opened the glass door and stepped in. All eyes turned to him.

"Who the hell are you?" a guy asked, short-sleeve suit jacket, wireframe spectacles and a topknot with shaved sides. Not Lars. Lars wasn't even looking at them, focused on something on a tablet before him.

"Rider," Hellion said dramatically in Wren's ear. "Air Rider." He ignored her.

"My name is Christopher Wren," he said calmly and confidently, projecting strength. These people before him were not weak. Each ran a division that dwarfed his Foundation, each managed budgets that made his slush fund look like the dregs in a beggar's cup, each influenced the daily thoughts of millions, far more than the reach of his Megaphone app. Next to them Wren was just an ant stumbling into a magpie's nest. "I'm here about the Reparations videos." He let that hang. "About what you're going to do about them."

The topknot guy frowned. "Are you even supposed to be here? What's your clearance level?"

"I'm new," Wren said. "Lars Mecklarin, it's about the Reparations videos. You'll want to hear what I've got to say."

Lars looked up.

Next to the others, he appeared normal. Wren had seen him on magazine covers: lily-white, slender, nondescript T-shirt and cargo pants, large nose and limpid eyes with a shaving rash on his throat; just another billionaire, though he hadn't made the Reparations cut. Yet there was an intense focus in those pale, wet eyes to match any stone-cold killer Wren had met. You didn't get to where he'd risen without crushing plenty of people along the way.

He gazed at Wren for a moment, and his wet eyes shifted. Now there was curiosity alongside the intensity, maybe even something close to excitement. "It's OK. You can go, Alec."

The topknot guy, Alec, frowned. "Are you for real, Lars? This guy's a nobody. I'm calling sec-"

"Don't call security," Lars said firmly, and Alec froze. "I know who he is. It'll be all right."

Alec looked confused.

"Go, all of you," Lars said. "We'll pick this up later."

It took a few seconds for the others to register it. They obviously had questions. They'd ask each other as soon as they stepped out. Probably one of them would call security anyway. It didn't matter. Wren had reached the inner sanctum.

They shuffled out.

A few seconds passed as Lars Mecklarin studied him.

"Christopher Wren," he said at last. Like he was amused. "You're famous. I heard the FBI are hunting you?" He let that hang. It made sense to Wren. The head of a globe-spanning corporation would get security briefings direct from the government. "I didn't recognize you, dressed like that."

"I'm undercover," Wren answered, not missing a beat. "This is what your employees wear."

Lars almost cracked a smile. They stared at each other.

"A call just went out to the police," Hellion said in his ear. "I couldn't block it. Do this quickly."

There was no such thing as quickly. Wren just stood. The message had already been delivered; his presence here alone said it all, and Lars was smart enough to receive it.

"You're making a point," he said. "That you can break into my company? Get in a room with me. I don't know how you did it; I'm told our security is triple-layered and uncrackable, best in the world. But here you are."

"I've got some of the best hackers in the world. You'd be amazed what a hoverboard and sunglasses can achieve."

Lars' eyes narrowed, parsing that out. "So you're here. It won't make a difference. I can imagine what you want: for me to block the Reparations videos. Am I right?"

Wren just stared. Lars looked like a nice enough guy, as far as billionaires went. Better than Handel Quanse, that was for sure. Don't be evil, all that. An idealist, after a fashion, but unwilling to take responsibility for the dangers his tool of mass communication could cause.

"Think of it as an opportunity," Wren said. "Not a setback."

Lars angled his head slightly. "Before you make your pitch, let me give you the answer. It's no. Under no circumstances, as I said to the CIA, the FBI, the President herself. We fought them all off already, after they suspended habeas corpus with the Blue Fairy. That was you too, correct?" A long pause. "I understand your fears, but you don't know what this place is. NameCheck. It's more than just a company; it's the next stage in human connection. Nothing you can say, nothing you can do, is going to change that. I won't put hard locks on the Reparations videos. Free speech is at stake, and that's just the start."

Wren didn't break eye contact. "Now can I make the pitch?"

Lars laughed. "By all means."

"The campus is going into lockdown," Hellion said in Wren's ear. "Satellite feeds show security sweeping the grounds. There's an armed squad coming your way; police cars scrambling down 101. They'll be outside the office in minutes."

He ignored her. "Two sides to the pitch, Lars. First side, you're going to get great press if you cooperate with me. Open your servers and let us find the origin of the execution video, there may be metadata attached that'll leapfrog me to the source. You think I took risks to get in here? I'll do anything to find the people who made this video. Anything." He took a breath. "Thus far, wins all around. The public will love you for arresting the slide into violence. So we move onto the flip side, and this is just gravy now, you shut down the copycats. We both know these videos are not in the public interest. You flip your model right now, start human vetting of every new uploaded video, it shuts this thing down before it gets too dangerous."

A moment passed.

"We have vetting procedures already," Mecklarin said. "The execution video clearly contravenes our standards, and it comes down every time it's re-posted. As for the copycats, who are you to say they're not in the public interest? Plus what you suggest, human vetting on this kind of scale, is an impossible task."

"Not impossible," Wren countered. He was no expert, but he'd had a thorough briefing from his hackers. "Outsource human judgment for pennies per video, set up a system of trusted vendors who require less frequent oversight, you'll cut down the BS massively within minutes of setting it up. It'll dig into your profits, but that's the cost of doing business."

Mecklarin snorted. "Outsourced human judgment for every video? Even with a trusted vendor scheme, that'll take months to set up."

"So get started now. Now what about server access, the video metadata? That's what I want most."

"Absolute non-starter," Mecklarin said. Face flat and implacable. "I'm sorry, but it's impossible. If we believe in privacy, which we do, I can't just hand data over to you whenever you ask."

He stared at Wren. Wren stared back.

"You want to hear the third side of the pitch?" Wren asked.

Mecklarin smiled. "Is it a threat?"

Wren took a step forward, held up his phone so Lars could see a video just beginning to roll. "Let's find out."

17

DEEPFAKE

It was a familiar video, but altered.

Hellion ran the new feed and Lars Mecklarin watched. In seconds he realized what he was seeing and leaned in. After ten seconds he looked up at Wren.

"You think that's going to compel me? Nobody's going to believe it."

Wren killed the video. There were hundreds of copycat Reparations videos now. People vandalizing the property of the wealthy, spitting in their faces, running them out of restaurants. It was an easy thing to digitally cut out the faces of the attackers and put Lars Mecklarin's face in their place. Deepfake technology had come a long way. The way Hellion and B4cksl4cker had rigged it, it looked real. Lars Mecklarin tearing the brand name sneakers off a child's feet. Lars Mecklarin punching an old man in the chest, then relieving him of his watch.

"This is a proof of concept," Wren said. "Exposing the flaws of the NameCheck system. I upload this video, or something like it but very much worse, and it goes live right away, right? There's no advance moderation across your whole network. How long will it be up there, drawing views, before you get around to bringing it down?"

Lars snorted. "Not up for long. As I said, we have moderation. And very much worse, like what?"

Wren leaned in, spoke more quietly. "You know I took down the Blue

Fairy. You'll also know what kind of footage those sick men were collecting. That I now have. I could put your face into a thousand videos like that in seconds. Would that get your attention?"

It did. Lars visibly winced, as if he'd been punched in the gut. Starting to imagine what that could mean, spread across his social media empire. Videos that were poison, even if they only surfaced briefly, could do irreparable damage to his brand. To his company.

"You wouldn't do that."

Wren smiled. "Wouldn't I? Who's to say I haven't already? Who's to say the first video of many isn't cued up and ready to go out right now?"

Lars' eyes widened, his skin paling further. Wren recognized the onset of shock, heart racing, breath shortening. "It won't matter. People will know it's not me. And in any case, that kind of video already contravenes our standards. It'll be crushed swiftly. The algorithms will flag it, dial it down and nobody will ever see it."

"Nobody," Wren said, considering. "Hours. Shall we put that to the test?"

Lars paled harder. "No. Don't-"

"It's already done." In the background Hellion worked her keyboard. "Use that tablet. Bring up your page."

Lars licked his lips. Wren knew the pattern of fear well: dry mouth, shortness of breath, clenched jaw. You couldn't prevent automatic responses no matter how hardened you were. "My page?"

"On NameCheck. A billion friends, that's you, right? Never mind, I'll do it for you."

Wren leaned over, tapped Mecklarin's tablet and brought up the NameCheck site. A simple search revealed Mecklarin's front page. Oddly, he hadn't posted anything for years.

"Security response are entering the building," Hellion said in Wren's ear. Mecklarin scrolled, hit refresh, then the video was there. Now there was footage of a group of men led by a deepfaked version of Lars Mecklarin, hounding a young woman carrying a Versace bag.

"This is nothing," he said.

"Keep watching," Wren advised.

"Security are right behind you," Hellion said. Mecklarin's eyes briefly darted to the side, confirming it. Wren turned. An armed private security squad stood beyond the glass wall, five figures with rifles trained on him.

Wren turned back to Lars. "You better hope they don't shoot me."

Lars nodded, held out a hand to ward the squad team off. Watching the video on his feed.

"B4cksl4cker is amplifying now," Hellion said.

"There," said Wren, pointing.

Lars eyes widened as the share count on the video suddenly rocketed. In seconds it was past a thousand, two thousand, three thousand. For a second the count froze, then jumped to ten thousand and climbing.

"We can do this with any footage," Wren said. "Force virality. Share it again and again, too fast for you to respond. Millions of people will see what we want them to see, splashed all over your front page. We will do that, if you don't help me. I'm asking only for server access to track that video back. Advance human moderation of all uploads will go a long way as a gesture of goodwill, also."

Lars looked up at Wren. This was a man abruptly on the edge, seeing an end he'd never envisioned closing in. "How are you doing this?"

Wren shrugged. "It's easy enough, the same way the Reparations videos are doing it. A few botnets to drive up shares and force it to go viral. Gaming your system as it currently exists, Lars. Look at the trending table."

Twenty thousand shares in less than a minute, and the video had already hit the top of the trending table on the right. All the fight went out of Lars at once, like he'd been knocked out standing up. Seeing control of his life's work snatched out of his hands.

"You can't do this with pornographic material. Not with my face. You wouldn't."

"I'm already doing it," Wren answered firmly. "As long as you're letting the copycat videos through, you'll be letting whatever deepfake videos I put up through as well. A hundred every second, as soon as I say the word. Horrific stuff, Lars. Nobody should ever see it, spread across your network, using your tools. So do something to stop it."

Lars looked distraught. "I-"

"The digital Wild West is over, Lars. Think of me as the sheriff riding into town. You follow a law of common decency or I will destroy you personally, using your network as the weapon. Tell me you'll give me what I need."

Lars stared, running through the ramifications. The same face Damalin Joes had made on horseback, right before he led the execution of Handel

Quanse. Already thinking of ways to turn this to his benefit and get the first-mover advantage in a new era of ethical communication. You didn't become a billionaire without being able to take advantage of a crisis.

"Lars," Wren barked.

"I'll do it," the man answered. "It'll cost billions. Backlog the entire Internet. But we'll do it."

"Then make the calls. Get me that video ready." Wren pointed through the glass. "And wave them off, too. I'm leaving now. You'll hear from my team; we'll want everything you've got. Get it ready. Goodbye, Lars. Be grateful it's not you in one of the Reparations' cages."

Lars squared his shoulders. There was that visionary resilience coming through now. He picked up his phone and met Wren's eyes, then waved off the squad behind the glass.

Wren walked out. The squad tracked him with their muzzles but made no move to intercept. Down the stairs Wren went, past the bobble-bodied soccer game and out into the balmy afternoon light. Sirens screeched closer.

"That is fast," said Hellion in his ear. "It is happening already."

"They provided the video?"

"Yes, also all video on NameCheck is going dark. Their child companies too; WeScreen is showing a blank! It looks like every single one. We begin analysis of original video for metadata, Christopher. This is great win."

She hooted. Another record-setting hack.

It was a beginning.

18

BFFS

Wren rode off on his hoverboard. More security rushed past him. Who would think a near-naked man on a hoverboard was a threat? Running ahead of the descriptions. Wren gritted his teeth and leaned forward, speeding up. By the exit his legs were trembling.

"What is wrong, Christopher?" Hellion asked. "Your heart is racing."

He tapped the earpiece to mute it, pocketed the bodycam and rode through the exit barrier. Police were rushing up. A yellow Prius pulled up at the sidewalk and Wren jumped off the hoverboard, opened the backseat and tumbled in.

"Christopher," Steven Gruber said.

"Drive," Wren said. "Back North."

"Drive," said Gruber, not bothering with the 'Man says' this time, and pulled into traffic.

Wren opened the window wide and leaned out into the breeze, feeling the pop of sweat evaporating off his forehead. God Mode came with its own stresses.

"Water," Gruber said, holding out a bottle. Wren took a long pull, turned to watch the sirens outside Namecheck recede, then looked ahead to where Gruber was watching him worriedly in the rearview mirror. Time to pull himself together.

"Lars Mecklarin liked my outfit," he said.

Gruber just stared.

"I got comments on the hoverboard too. Vintage, they said."

"It is a classic," Gruber answered, off-balance. "So did you-?"

Wren nodded. "We have the video. In the meantime, all video feeds are coming down across NameCheck and WeScreen."

"Wow," Gruber whispered. "How much data is that?"

"I don't know," Wren said. "A few hundred exabytes. Uncountable, probably. It'll get better."

Gruber whistled low. "Remind me never to get on your bad side."

"Never going to happen," Wren said. "We're BFFs."

Gruber beamed happily. Best Friends Forever. Wren looked out the window, then tapped the earpiece and heard Hellion's concerned voice.

"Christopher, what happened?"

"Post-God Mode jitters," he said. "Better done without a voice in my head."

She snorted. "Do you regret this, now? It is difficult, yes?"

"You told me so," Wren answered. "But we managed. Now, where are we up to with the metadata?"

Keys clattered from her end. "Working. We have NameCheck access now, B4cksl4cker is reconstructing the upload path for the execution video."

Wren sat up straight. "You have access?"

"Yes, Mecklarin opened data port for us. His system is very poorly organized, Christopher. He is like a hoarder."

He laughed. Of course she would criticize Lars Mecklarin. "So what have you got?"

"Nothing yet. This will take time, building matrix for analysis, enforcing structure, managing 'Big Data'. Good immediate news is, I sent your bodycam footage to other social media companies. Their videos are coming down. Moderation will begin."

Wren grunted. "We slowed the copycats down."

"It would appear so. This is good, yes?" She paused a moment. "Christopher, I have monitor on your heart rate, and it is erratic. This is not normal for you."

He grunted. Contemplated switching off the earpiece again, but that

563

would only rile her up worse. Besides, she wasn't wrong. His pulse was a reedy, too-fast thrum in his temples. Riding the knife edge of exhaustion.

"I haven't been sleeping so well."

"When did you last sleep?"

He ran a quick calculation. "Properly? Four days ago."

In the background came B4cksl4cker's baritone laugh. His voice joined the line. "This is close to my record. Christopher, when I was hacking Northern Korea Republic, I did not sleep for one-hundred and fourteen hours. This is long time, yes? Long enough for hallucinations."

"I'm not hallucinating. I caught a few hours here and there."

"Few hours is not sleep, Christopher. You must sleep now. Hellion and I will extract data from NameCheck database. Trust us with this."

Wren looked out the window. San Francisco Bay whipped by to the side, but filmed with a gray fuzz, now that the adrenaline high was pulling back. It left a throb in his head and a strange lightness to the world around him. Looking down he saw faint red stains on his palms.

The same blood he'd shown to Hartright, way up in the Arctic ice of Deadhorse. He was dead now, along with so many Pinocchios.

"I do trust you," he said. "And I'll sleep soon. For now I've got something else in mind."

"What?" Hellion asked.

Wren didn't say anything for a long moment. Always plunging into the past. He looked ahead to Gruber.

"Steven, you're on the line with Hellion and B4cksl4cker?"

"Yes, Christopher. I, uh, honestly I think they're right." He chanced a look around. "You don't look so great."

"I don't feel so great, but I can leverage that, where we're going. There's more in San Francisco than Silicon Valley." He took a breath, considering if this was a path he really wanted to take. Of course, there was no avoiding it. Call it karma. Not all data existed within the silos of the social media companies. "Take us to San Quentin."

Nobody said anything for a moment, until Gruber broke the silence. "San Quentin Prison?"

"The very same. Keep heading north, cross the Golden Gate Bridge, you can't miss it."

Gruber chuckled uncomfortably. "Are we, uh, going in?"

"I am. Hellion, get me Rogers or Humphreys, whoever answers first. We need a visitor pass for a very particular inmate."

A moment passed before she answered. "This does not sound wise, Christopher. What are you seeking?"

"Something to round out our profile of the Reparations. Unless you're confident the metadata will give us everything we need?"

There was a silence. "Metadata will be useful. It is one data point."

"Exactly. More data is always better. I think Shakespeare himself said that."

Hellion said nothing.

"We'll be there in an hour."

19

SAN QUENTIN

San Quentin State Prison lay on a stubby, snout-like promontory stretching a mile and a half into the blue-green waters San Rafael Bay. Wren and Gruber pulled around on the John T. Knox Freeway in the mellow early-evening light, warm winds blowing through the open windows. At the Richmond-San Rafael Bridge, stretching six miles low and level across the water, they turned right onto the prison road.

It ran half a mile along a row of handsome wooden residences, each with incredible bay views and excellent prison visitation opportunities. Wren adjusted his shirt, tight as a Twaron vest against his skin, as they drew into San Quentin's small visitor lot. On the right stood a US Post Office in gleaming white stucco, on the left was a shuttered HANDICRAFT SHOP, where the prisoners could sell their wares.

Wren briefly admired the many clumps of abstract-shaped clay on shelves in the window, a series of brightly colored busts, some watercolors in back. Arts programs were some of the most popular in any prison, he knew. They offered an escape from the gray reality.

The Prius rocked to a gentle halt a few yards from the black grille gate, manned by two armed guards. Wren had been to San Quentin several times before and knew the layout well: the four main blocks watched over by the large white and red lighthouse-looking gun tower; condemned men to the north, with east, south and west for gen. pop.; the open grass yard, the six closed concrete yards, the long warehouse-like 'factories' where prisoners were put to work dry-cleaning sheets for local businesses.

Giving back to their new community, at incredibly cheap hourly rates.

Steven Gruber cleared his throat, was looking back at him. "Do I, uh, let you out here?"

"Here's good," Wren said, and opened the door. Standing too fast made him briefly dizzy, and he held briefly to the Prius' frame.

"Um, do I wait here?" Gruber asked.

"Visitor parking," Wren said, and pointed to the side. "This shouldn't take long."

He walked toward the gate. There were familiar signs describing prohibited apparel, their colors faded behind glass in the relentless California sun. Nothing that the guards or the prisoners might wear was allowed: not the blue jeans or shirts of the inmates, not the tan shirts and forest green khakis of the guards, not the orange jumpsuits of prisoners in transit. Nothing metal, no stud buttons, no underwire bras. Wren couldn't help a smile as he approached the black grille gate. Still wearing his skimpy NameCheck gear, there was no way they could find fault.

Laugh, maybe.

The guard at the gate stared at him like he was an alien exiting the dropship. The guy had a barrel chest with porkchop arms and wore a black beanie with the prison's gold star brand on his head, pulled low so the brim blocked the sun.

"Help you, Sir?"

He didn't sound like he wanted to help.

"I'm in the system," Wren said. "Christopher Wren. It should be marked expedited."

His call to Director Humphreys thirty minutes back had been combative but effective. Humphreys had agreed to pull some strings, gaining urgent visitation rights if Wren 'promised to behave himself'.

"You owe me one for NameCheck," Wren had said, as the Prius had glided across the red glory of the Golden Gate Bridge. "You've been trying to crack that data lockbox for a decade."

"And we'll pay for that access," Humphreys had countered. "You just opened up a Pandora's Box of First Amendment chaos. But I won't argue the toss with you now. Rogers tells me you're coming in when all this is done. I'm going to hold you to that."

The guard appraised Wren like he didn't believe he could possibly have expedited status. Not in that outfit. He held up a finger slowly, said, "One moment," then headed into the guard box, leaving his colleague to watch Wren and smirk. It took a few minutes, Wren squinting against the sun.

"What's with the get-up?" the other guard asked, gesturing with his rifle. A slim guy with a thousand-yard stare.

"I'm on vacation," Wren answered.

Barrel chest came back out, and now his demeanor had changed significantly. On the ball, doing things by the book. Wren didn't know for sure, but he assumed his visitation request had been marked with a level red anti-terrorism flag. Nobody wanted to get in the way of that.

"I'll need some identification, Sir."

"Got it here," Wren said, and pulled his Agent Without Portfolio CIA ID from the hot pink shoulder band he'd used for the Go Pro, held it up for the guard to inspect. The guy leaned in, nodded once then signaled for the gate. It opened and he led Wren through.

Visitor parking lay to the left, behind a tall wire fence. Wren glimpsed Steven Gruber gazing through the wires at him, looking as lost as Merriot Raine. Wren gave him a reassuring wink then looked ahead, thinking about the man he'd come to see.

Rick Cherney, brother of Terry Cherney, who together had led the Sons of SAM in the early aughties. The Sons of Sam were a pseudoscientific finance cult that looked to set up a private fiefdom on a series of pleasure yachts moored off the California coast. Both brothers had been Wall Street bankers for a time, had lived wild and crazy lives in New York running investment scams on penny dollar stocks and pyramid trades, all while building up a network of Success-And-Money groupies, or SAMs for short.

Wren had been brought in early in his CIA career, as a cult expert on secondment to the FBI. The Cherneys had metastasized by then, turning their SAM followers, worshippers of all-things money, loose on any vulnerable people in their lives. On orders from Rick and Terry, the SAMs had drained numerous life savings accounts into their yacht-fund coffers, often on pain of death. Their reign of homicidal fraud only drew to a close when a couple of retirees managed to hit a silent panic button before getting executed in their Malibu beach house for refusing to open their private safe to a pair of success-addled SAM acolytes.

Wren was brought in for late-stage interrogations. The Cherney brothers had effectively taken a Manson defense, updated for the 21st Century. They claimed to have no knowledge that their followers were breaking laws to make the kind of money they'd brought in; certainly not that they were killing people for their cash. They'd never ordered any of it. All they'd done was inspire their SAMs to embrace the American dream. How could they be held responsible for what they'd done to achieve it?

They didn't crack under questioning. Wren was brought in as a last resort.

He entered the interrogation room armed only with a manila briefcase that contained three photographs, which one-by-one he laid out. Three of their SAMs who'd never been arraigned. That the FBI didn't even know about. That Wren had found on his own, through the Foundation. Three killers who'd helped jumpstart the brothers' rush to illegal acquisition.

They were posed in ashes. Laid on scrap heaps with junk yard backdrops. Burned down to the bone everywhere except their faces.

Rick had looked at the pictures and swiftly looked away. Clearly, he recognized the bodies. The younger of the two brothers, he followed his brother's lead in all things. Terry though was cocky, thick-lipped and full of New York swagger, clearly certain he was going to get away with it all.

"Whatever these are, they're over-exposed," he'd said, appraising the photos with a faint sneer. "Next time use a light meter."

Wren was unphased. Didn't matter that the photographs were deepfake mockups, created by a Hollywood creative Wren had just brought into the Foundation. They were convincing fakes.

"You think the system is the prison," Wren had said, gesturing around at the white walls of their interrogation room in a downtown LA jail. "Boys, you are dead wrong. Truth is, as of this moment, the system is the only place you're safe from me. The day you walk out of court free as birds, that's the day you put on an invisible orange jumpsuit you'll never take off again." He paused a moment, watching their reaction. There was none. "Every day you'll spend waiting for another set of SAM photos to come in the mail. I'll pose them real nice next time, get the lighting just so." He looked at Rick. "Might be Terry in the ashes, first. Might be you, Rick. Would you like that?" Terry snorted. "Might not come for a few months, even a year, but you'll know that any day, any moment, it will come. I'm not big on mercy, boys."

He leaned back in the chair. Terry sat there like a log, unperturbed. Rick though was starting to doubt. Eyes flickering to the photos, to his brother, maybe imagining what he'd look like burned up like the rest.

"You can't do that," Rick said.

"Look at those pictures and tell me what I can't do."

"It's bullshit," Terry said. "Those are fakes. Don't listen to him."

Wren had Rick separated out. Worked on him alone in a confession booth, watching closely as his eyes roved like he was looking for a way out. Wren afforded none. Kept talking about how it would look to see Terry all burned up. Offering a cushy life behind bars, maybe out on appeal after ten years, if he just cooperated. It was better than certain death at Wren's hands.

Within an hour he cracked. Gave the FBI everything they needed to put him and his brother safely behind the bars of San Quentin.

Now the Visitor Center loomed large before Wren in the evening light. It had a crenelated top like some medieval castle, and towered over him three stories tall, with rifle-armed guards patrolling the roof. Long opaque glass strips ran up the structure's sides like elongated church windows, matched by off-yellow shallow buttresses, striping the building like architectural bars.

Brutalist. Eloquent.

An old building. An old history. California's first prison, and only Death Row site.

The guard led him into the cool shadow of the Visitors Entrance, where he stepped through the metal detector, nothing to detect, and they led him right toward the visitation area. Down a long corridor past vending machines boasting jello cups, hot chocolate and packets of chips, until the space opened up in a row of six barred-off pods. No glass here; visitors could sit across from each other, reach through the bars, even be alone in the cage with the prisoner, if they wanted to.

Terry Cherney was waiting. Run to fat since his heyday, bloated like a pig and swelling out of his blue-on-blue outfit. Narrow pebble glasses on his head, a shock of gray hair that looked like a terrible wig, thick cheeks puffing then eyes widening as he saw Wren, as he recognized him.

"No," he said, standing up. Started shaking his head. "Not a chance. No way I'm talking to him."

Wren wasn't surprised.

Two months after the brothers had been locked up, Rick had tried to kill himself by driving plastic ball pens into both of his eyes. The shame of flipping on his brother, was how they told it. He'd survived, but blinded and with permanent brain damage. They still kept him in San Quentin, where Wren had heard he often wailed late into the night. Awaiting a death he'd tried to hasten, and failed.

"Terry," Wren said, as the fat man climbed to his feet, staring with mounting alarm.

"I've got nothing to say to this fool," Terry shouted at the guard. "Don't let him in!"

The guard opened the cell gate and admitted Wren, then locked the door after him and walked away. A cage barely seven feet on a side.

Wren studied Terry. He didn't look good. A decade of listening to your brother wail through the nights would do that to you. "It's your lucky day, Terry. I'm here to break you out."

20

SAMS

Terry Cherney just stared, gimlet eyes intent like a bug, searching for whatever trick Wren was going to pull. "You're going to get me out of San Quentin?"

Wren just smiled. Sat down. "There's no getting out of San Quentin. Nobody in the world's got the pull to do that. But there are other prisons, and other ways to escape." He tapped his temple.

"You're a whack job," Terry said. "I'm not listening to this. Guard."

The guard was on the other side of the room.

"Last night a billionaire died in a televised execution," Wren said, taking his time. "In an arena, before millions of viewers. Did you hear about that?"

Terry stared at him like Wren's mouth was a nest and the words spilling out were poisonous spiders.

"I'll guess you did. The victim was Handel Quanse, one of your contemporaries. Heyday of conspicuous consumption, greed is good, all that, though he turned a corner in recent years. They strapped his limbs up to nine horses, then pulled him apart." Wren let that hang. "That's one heck of a margin call, right? I'm here because I think you know something about it. I know you're still in touch with your SAMs. If anyone's got their ear to the ground on financial extremism, it's you."

Terry looked away. "Guard."

"I can help you, Terry," Wren pressed. "Tell me what you know, I make things better for you here."

"Better?" Terry scoffed. "Like you made things better for my brother?"

Wren was ready for that. "Let's talk about your brother. The way I understand it, you hear from him plenty. He wails through the night, they say. Now, maybe that's just the brain damage talking, or maybe he's in real pain. Physical, sure, it can't feel good to have busted eyes, no tear ducts left after they took them out, but I'd guess it's more than that. The spiritual cost, Terry. It's gotta claw at him. Knowing he let you down. Thought he was protecting you from me, thought his death would get rid of the shame, but none of it worked."

"Shut up," Terry said.

"You ever try calling that out to him, in the night? Maybe soothe him at first, until you get sick of the wailing, and you just tell him to shut up?"

Terry was getting hot. "You did that to him. You made that happen."

Wren shook his head. "Not me. I'd say it was your choices, Terry, all the way down the line. You damned your own brother when you started exploiting people to death. You carried him with you on that journey. I just held you both accountable. Though I'm pretty sure this is hell for him. Every day, every night." Wren paused a moment. "Now I'm offering him a way out."

Terry's throat pulsed visibly; his jaw tight. "I'll crush you."

"Don't talk nonsense. If you could do that, you'd have done it ten years back, and-"

Terry chose that moment to charge. Thick ham legs shooting him into a two-step stampede, which Wren turned like a matador turns a bull. On his feet and off-line before Terry had taken his first step, giving him a little shove on the way by. The big man's grasping hands shot through the bars and did nothing to halt his momentum, so he hit the cage wall full tilt down the left side of his face and bounced.

Back he went, staggering into the bars on the other side, and Wren was there to catch him. Kicked the man's feet out so he couldn't get them under him, sliding him down the bars fast and gentle to the ground.

Then he stood back. Sat down again like nothing had happened.

"We can do this all night, Terry. You won't lay a hand on me. Talk, though, and I'll open the door, set both you and Rick free."

Terry swore, rocking to get back to his feet, to the seat. Panting. A long vertical welt showed up down his face. Maybe he was thinking about mounting another charge, but this time thought better of it.

"What have you got to offer me, you psycho?"

"Arts and crafts classes."

Terry laughed. The first peal came like a cannon blasting off, the others followed like a fusillade off the bow, echoing loud and long.

"Your brother's blind," Wren plowed on, "but he can feel clay. I checked up on the facilities here; they've got potter's wheels, kilns, the capacity to fire anything between a thimble and a full-size toilet, should he want to. Something to do, Terry, other than think about killing himself. A way out."

"You call that a way out? You really are a psycho."

"The therapeutic benefits of pottery have been well-researched. It'll help with-"

"Rick hates art," Terry said. "With a passion. I guess you didn't do your research very well, or you'd remember he once burned an original Matisse just because he could. And you think pottery might be an *escape* for him? He broke his brain trying to kill himself, and I've lived with what's left of him for ten years now. Wailing, you call it?" He leaned in. "It's one wail. Two words. 'Kill me', he says. Again and again. And you think pottery's going to solve that?"

Wren set his jaw. "So you won't give me anything for pottery classes?"

Terry gave a brittle birdshot laugh. "Not a single dime. Handel Quanse is dead? Good. Kill them all."

Wren nodded. There was always a back up plan.

"All right. Second option, I get him removed from the prison on compassionate grounds. I've got it pre-approved. Put him in a secure psych ward somewhere, they'll keep him sedated, give him some counseling, try to ease his pain. How does that sound?"

Terry stood up. "You don't get it. Rick wants to die. That's it. Not some drug-addled coma. Not arts and crafts. He wants to die, and it's your fault. I will never help you. Never."

Wren took a breath. Saw in Terry the same stubbornness he'd seen before. Back then he'd used Rick to get justice, take the Cherney brothers out of circulation before they could hurt other people. That didn't mean there wasn't a cost. Justice often came with its own pain, even for the one administering it.

574

In a smooth movement, Wren unzipped the pocket in his armband and pulled out a plastic blister pack of pills. They were full-strength generic opioids, enough for permanent blast-off. No problem getting through the prison's metal detector. No need for a pat down, given his CIA credentials. A single stop-off on the 101 north at a pharmacy, using a doctor's scrip hacked through the remote ordering system.

Terry's eyes flashed wide.

"Third option," Wren said. "A final way out of the prison. Easy overdose, he'll go out in his sleep. It's a way out for you, too. Peace, at nights."

Terry's eyes sharpened. "You f-"

"Limited time deal," Wren interjected. "Once in a lifetime, and it's coming at you this minute, Terry. You give me everything you've heard from your SAMs, help me hunt down these Reparations, and I take this pack to Rick right now. I'll sit there and wait. Hell, I'll even hold his hand, say a prayer. No man deserves to be tied to this life when all he wants is to leave, am I right?"

Terry's eyes blazed. Fury blending with a strange kind of hope. "What are you doing? Who the hell do you think you are?"

Wren smiled, sad. "I'm not a monster, Terry. The man wants to die, and he's wanted it for a decade." He leaned back. "If clay's no good, and a mental health ward's no good, then this is what I've got." He paused. "You just say the word. His fate's in your hands."

Terry stared. In that moment he looked for all the world like Damalin Joes, the moment before he gee'd his horse on. Wren saw the decision click over.

"What do you want to know?"

Twenty minutes later, getting into Rick's cell was easy enough. Wren's status gave him the run of the place. By then the warden was involved, but Wren brushed him off, refused to see the injured Cherney brother in visitation, so they escorted him to the cell. On Wren's orders, the guard walked away.

Rick Cherney was sitting on his bed, vacant eyes staring at the wall. A gaunt, sallow version of his brother, like a dark mirror. Wren knew Rick heard his approach, but he didn't so much as flinch as the cell doors clanked shut. Hands flat on his lap like a good Catholic boy, just staring into the darkness.

"Terry sent me," Wren said.

At that Rick turned. Whatever was left of his brain after the pens had done their vicious work recognized that name.

"I hear you've been calling for him. Every night, right? He's come through."

Wren pulled out the blister pack, popped the pills one by one, then folded them into Rick's hands. His palms were pale as milk. Apparently, he never went out in the yard. Just sat on his bed day in and day out, staring through the wall like it might any minute open up and admit him through.

Rick's fingers sifted the pills. Slowly at first, then getting faster. His blind eyes looked to Wren.

"Terry says he loves you," Wren said. "He'll see you on the other side. The rest is up to you."

Rick took a second longer, then put the pills in his mouth and dry-swallowed. It took a few gulps. Wren waited as the pills took effect. He held Rick's hand, as the weight he'd been carrying for years began to lift. As he sagged to the side. He even said a prayer, as promised.

It didn't take long for Rick to slip under. The overdose came fast and silent. When his pulse stopped, Wren lifted his legs tenderly, laid his thin, wasted body out on the cot.

"Goodbye, Rick," he said, and brushed his empty eyelids closed.

21

ANTI-CA

The walk out from the Visitor Center felt like Wren was lumbering along the bottom of the sea. Exhausted. Maybe finally hallucinating. Feeling sick.

"Did you get what you wanted?" the warden asked eagerly, a watercolor smear somewhere to Wren's side.

Wren just nodded mutely. Didn't trust himself to speak. It felt like the words would come out inflected by Rick Cherney, a keening in his throat rising to a wail...

The sun was bright outside still, filtering down through dapples of seaweed-like cirrus clouds. A man was dead, and he couldn't call that anything but a mercy, but the death weighed him down. Coming on the heels of Handel Quanse, it left him wrung out.

Steven Gruber was waiting for him in the visitor lot outside. Standing outside the bright yellow Prius, both of them like facets from a forgotten world.

"Everything OK, Christopher?"

"I'll be OK," he said, sounded like a drunk in his own ears. "Let's go."

Wren fell into the back seat. Gruber started the soundless electric engine. They pulled out of the lot, bay on the right, fancy houses on the right.

"Where are we going?"

Wren blinked up, already drifting under. He couldn't sleep yet. "East," he said, "take the bridge." He fumbled against the seat until he found the earpiece, tapped it securely in, and dialed through to Hellion and B4cksl4cker.

"Christopher." Hellion's voice jolted him up above the surface one more time. He blinked, saw they were halfway across the San Rafael Bridge, so low to the water it felt like they were skimming right over the placid surface.

"Hellion," he said, taking a second to sync up his thoughts with everything he'd learned. "I got a lot from Terry Cherney. He has dozens of SAMs out there, all of them active in various financial pseudo-cults, some anti-rich, some pro."

He floated for a moment, lining up what was to come next.

"Yes?" Hellion prompted.

"He thinks Anti-Ca are our best target. He's heard about incredible dark money flows in the last two years, pouring into their coffers. A concerted effort to build out their infrastructure, setting up secret training compounds around the country." He paused, swallowed, went on. "He didn't know what for, but he knew they were buying in weapons, bomb-making gear, maybe potassium-cyanide."

There was silence for a moment. "Potassium-cyanide, this is suicide drug, yes?"

"Yes," Wren confirmed. "Same as they used at Jonestown. One of Cherney's SAMs is an Anti-Ca member, and she's been writing to him about that, whether she should stay or go." His head spun and he took a few careful breaths. "Apparently every one of their compounds has standing suicide orders, should it ever come to the end. Should federal forces attempt a raid, should the end of days come about, you know how it goes. Fight back as far as they can, then take all life to erase the record. Whoosh their way to heaven."

"Whoosh?" Hellion asked, her keys clacking distantly.

Wren was having trouble focusing.

"Where are compounds, Christopher?" came B4cksl4cker's bass voice.

"Cherney only knew about one compound. Northern Nevada somewhere, not even the SAM knew the exact location. They took her out blindfolded. She said there were families there, children, all kinds. She saw the gallon jugs of potassium-cyanide."

"Yes," came Hellion's voice again. "We will find this place. If there is synchrony with NameCheck metadata, this will help narrow a location."

Wren gulped agreement. "It could be the arena site. Set up the, uh…" He couldn't find the word.

"Search algorithms," B4cksl4cker supplied.

"Exactly. Top down, satellite, drone. Find the sand. Find the arena, the compound. Um." He was drifting now, caught himself swaying in the seat. Hellion said something but he didn't catch it. "I think we're going to have to hit it fast and hard," he went on, pushing the words out as fast as he could, barely outrunning the mounting waves of gray lapping at his thoughts. "I'll need a strike team, but discreet. Fast and hard enough to prevent a mass suicide."

"Strike team. You wish me to prepare this?"

"As best you can. Foundation operators only." He thought of something more. "And Rogers. We're going to need her help with this, if only to keep the feds out long enough to make sense of it. I'd call her, but I'm…"

He drifted.

"Christopher. You have done enough. You must sleep now, yes?"

The world was gray. He saw Rick Cherney's body lying there like Somchai Theeravit's back in Deadhorse. Cherney was a killer too, but it hadn't felt like that, in his last moments. Justice took a toll on everyone.

"Yeah," he said, "thanks," then took the earpiece out, closed his eyes and fell into darkness immediately.

22

SUICIDE ORDER

Wren was back in the Pyramid. It was the last day again, and all around him lay smoking bodies. A thousand dead, burned alive in the Apex's suicide order. Wren's friends, his family, the people he'd known all his young life. There was a terrible stench, and a heat, and he realized that in one hand he held a lit match, burning down to his fingers. In the other he held a paintbrush, sopping with acrid-smelling napalm.

He'd burned them all.

Wren jerked awake, panting hard. He looked around and the world swirled. Dizziness like a bad hangover filled his head. It was dark but bright white lights arced by, like the off wash of headlights from a highway. He tried to control himself, turn the fear to anger or something he could use, but control didn't come easily.

He rolled, fell off the seat into the footwell of a vehicle. The Prius? He pushed himself up, ignoring the mounting nausea, and scrabbled for the door handle. He had to get out. Away from the dream, away from the past. At last his hand found the lever, the door swung outward and he flung himself through.

The sandy roadside shale was chill beneath his bare arms. Still wearing his scanty NameCheck gear. He pushed himself to his feet and turned, taking in the unfamiliar surroundings.

Off to his left a highway spun like the CERN Hadron collider, shooting cars like atoms through the darkness. An Interstate highway. To the right was some kind of unmanned gas station; pumps but no shop to pay at, a canopy roof but no sign showing the price at the pump. A few lights shone from tall poles, marking an island of white in the darkness, beyond which lay gravel, scrub reeds rising out of desert sand, then darkness. There was a faint humming in the air.

Wren felt his pulse settling, the nightmare pulling away. He worked on his breathing. He hadn't had that dream in years. The end days of the Pyramid. It took him back to the interrogation cell with Terry Cherney, listening to the big man talk about suicide orders in Anti-Ca cells. Gallon jugs of potassium-cyanide. A suicide order ready to roll down, crushing families beneath it. Friends. Children, just like all of Wren's brothers and sisters who'd died for the Apex's mad dreams.

He took hold of the Prius' roof, breathing deep and even, and counted the pumps. There were six in total. Each of them was occupied by a vehicle, and all of them were unusual, which helped banish the dream further. One was tiny, barely nine feet long, like a roofed chair on wheels. There was a glossy sedan, and some kind of low-slung supercar, then a bizarre gray truck thing with six wheels that was all harsh angles and looked like a cyber tank, and there, cherry on the cake, was a NameCheck-branded mapping vehicle. Wren blinked, checking he wasn't hallucinating. A tall pole stuck out of its roof like a lollipop, gumball red at the top and equipped with multiple dark camera eyes, used for making street-level 3D maps of the real world.

What was going on?

Wren circled the Prius, saw the charging cable leading from its battery cap and back to one of the six pumps, just like the five other cables. He put the pieces together. A fast-charging station for electric vehicles. But there were no drivers in sight. Which meant…

There was a clank nearby as the trunk of the supercar slammed down, then Gruber appeared. He did a double take when he saw Wren. "You're awake?"

"I am. What's going on here?"

"Oh," said Gruber, looking around at the vehicles. "A lot, I guess. Um…" He paused a minute. "Do you want water?" He didn't wait for an answer, instead hurried over and leaned into the Prius' front seat, coming back with a bottle. "Here."

Wren drained the bottle in one go, head back and looking to the stars. A full sky of them. Past midnight, he figured, by Orion's position. He'd slept for around seven hours; far more than he'd intended. A hunger pang suddenly bit at his stomach. He scrunched the bottle and dropped it into the footwell.

"Tell me."

"Sure, but, uh…" He tilted his head to one side, the way people who weren't accustomed to an in-ear device often did, as if it would give them some distance from the voice abruptly in their head. "I'm talking to Hellion. Well, listening is more accurate." His eyes defocused. "OK, yes. I got it." He refocused. "She wants to speak to you."

Wren held out a hand.

"First she says you eat, though," Gruber said, and leaned back into the Prius, came back with a strawberry milkshake and a ham and cheese sandwich. He put them in Wren's hand.

"Give me the earpiece," Wren said.

"Eat first, Hellion says," said Gruber. He looked uncomfortable. "I'm not sure what the hierarchy is here, but she's right. You haven't eaten in most of a day. You should."

Wren glowered but opened up the sandwich's plastic bag and took a bite. The soft white bread filled his dry mouth like a stodgy, comforting blanket. He took a glug of the milkshake, and the sweetness lit up his palate. When *had* he last eaten? Too long. Gradually the swirling in his head began to recede.

"Hand her over," Wren said, around a mouthful of sandwich. "No debating the hierarchy."

Gruber nodded sharply, then tilted his head and banged on the side like he was trying to shake out water after swimming, catching the earpiece when it dropped free. He gave it a rough rub down and handed it over. Wren took it and looked at it for a moment.

"Thanks."

"De nada," Gruber said. "I'll take a nap now too, I think. I'm shattered."

He wandered off. Where? Wren had no idea. He gave the earpiece another rub then inserted it, and swiftly heard Hellion's familiar tones. Not only Hellion: she was talking quietly with B4cksl4cker in Russian.

"I'm here," he said. "I need a full sit-rep."

"Christopher!" B4cksl4cker said, like he was welcoming him late to a party. "It is good you are alive."

Wren snorted.

"We thought it was best to let you sleep," Hellion said. "There is a lot to process right now, both good news and bad."

"Tell me there's been no suicide order."

That took her a moment. "Of Anti-Ca? Why would there be?"

Wren had no good answer for that. Because he'd seen it in a dream? His pulse pounded noisily in his temples. "Because that's what Cherney said. They've drilled for it. If they think we're coming for them, I believe they'll carry it out. Women, children, whether they want it or not. I can't allow that to happen."

"Then this is also good news," Hellion said. "There is no suicide order we can detect. We are on their communications. We have location for this strike."

That woke him up. "Where? And how did you get it?"

"How is by combination of Cherney eyewitness and Namecheck metadata. This is Anti-Ca compound, dark money, North Nevada, on edge of Duck Valley Reservation," Hellion took a breath. "One hundred miles north of place called Battle Mountain. Do you know this place?"

Wren racked his memory. "The reservation, not the town."

"It is remote. Wild everywhere. Except for compound."

Wren's mind began spinning. Thinking about children holding cups full of poison cut with grape-flavored soda. Thinking about the young Christopher Wren, then known only as Pequeño 3, forced to burn everyone he knew alive. "Is the arena there, too?"

"Not that we can see. We have scanned all surrounding land for several thousand square miles. If it was there, it is not there now."

Wren played that out. "Then how certain are we this place is connected to the Reparations? What's the link?"

"Metadata from NameCheck confirms video upload first came from this compound," B4cksl4cker said. "Secret Anti-Ca facility. Many weapons stockpiled, bombmaking equipment. This is just beginning for them, we think."

Wren considered. Thinking about past raids on cults that had gone bad, like Waco. He had to be sure, and do it right. "You have eyes on the compound?"

"Yes," said Hellion, and Wren's phone pinged from inside the Prius. He had to lean in through the back window to fish it out. An image had autoloaded, looked to be the heat map of a large compound.

"This is infrared image of Anti-Ca from drone we have circling," Hellion said. "Look at top right."

At the top of the map a couple dozen individual heat signatures were pressed in a building closely together, looked like a bunker of some kind.

"We believe this is holding cell. Many ages in this room; perhaps waiting for suicide."

Wren studied the map. "You think they have a sense we're coming?"

"Social media is down, Christopher, because of you. There is footage of you on hoverboard, Mr. Air Rider, on nightly news. Everybody knows you are coming."

He grunted, looked down at his pink and yellow outfit. Not his most elegant debut on the national media. "Anything else? If we hit this place hard, people are going to die. We need to be sure."

"We are sure," Hellion said. "There is more, from Foundation research. Anti-Ca belief system has changed sharply in last two years."

Wren looked out at the dark sky, finished the milkshake with a big glug. "Changed how?"

"Two years ago they had one. Reparations, they wanted. Redistribution of wealth from rich to poor. Nobody was listening. Then two years ago they went silent. We can see dark money flows coming in. This is like incubation period, yes? Now there is arena video, and calls for Reparation in blood."

"They've radicalized. Become extreme."

"Yes. Perhaps under guiding hand of one man with very particular set of skills."

Wren frowned. That was one way to reference his father. He looked over to the road.

"How far out are we?"

"Currently one hour from Duck Valley. We have been driving you this direction for last seven hours. Rogers took flight, she is there now, waiting in desert. We also picked up things along the way. Some vehicles."

Wren looked at the pumps. "I count five. Who's driving them?"

A beat passed. "Steven Gruber is driving the Prius."

That was half an answer at best. "And the others?"

"I am driving the others."

For a moment Wren thought he'd misheard. Then he realized he hadn't. Of course. That explained how strange the vehicles looked. Each one was a prototype for a new range. "These are self-driving cars?"

"Remotely enabled," Hellion said. "It is simple hack to control via wireless protocol."

Wren held in a sigh. This is what you got when you fell asleep and left the hackers in charge. "You're driving five cars at once?"

"This is easy matter. In gaming I would control hundreds."

"This is not a game."

She just laughed.

"Where did you get them?"

"You were in San Francisco, Christopher. Silicon Valley, there are many such cars with road approval. I only hacked five. I could have taken many more."

Wren looked out over the desert. Hackers were like children with toys. "Why?"

"There is very practical application. For fast strike on Anti-Ca compound. It is reinforced heavily, metal walls. These vehicles will be foot soldiers for our assault. Battering ram, cannon fodder for absorb incoming fire. Many uses."

Wren sighed. So they had several remote-controlled vehicles to play with. That was good, he guessed. It only took them halfway, though.

"Who's on my strike team?"

"Yes. Let me see." Keys clacked. "We have an ex-Qotl cartel member you took across the border, Alejandro. He is very nice man, a Scorpio I think, but dark past. Many drug mule crossings across Mexico border, before he changed mind. There is also Doona, she was child soldier in South Sudan before you rescued her, eighteen but excellent shot with AK-47, she says. Last, there is Chuck Metzler. I do not really know much about Chuck, but he was very interested, and he says he was in Afghanistan, so…"

Wren tilted his head slightly, not sure if he was hearing correctly. Alejandro and Doona were trained operatives, each trustworthy and capable. Alejandro was a solid, squat Mexican who'd changed his life dramatically since joining the Foundation, starting a non-profit to help addicts turn their lives around. Doona had been handling weapons since she was twelve years old, had killed her first man at thirteen, and Wren wasn't keen to throw her into combat again. He'd send her back home, if she would go. As for Chuck?

Chuck was a pathological liar. Just putting himself forward for this expedition was enough to get him coin zeroed. He'd have to be sent back for sure; as far as Wren knew he'd never even fired a gun. Wren had caught him swindling old folks out of their social security checks in an elaborate, circular Ponzi scheme in the Florida Panhandle. It had been a holiday for Wren, with his family to see the alligators. Chuck had been working the coaches. Fast-talking hadn't saved him from Wren; a new member joined up within twenty minutes.

"You put an open call out on the boards? And Chuck answered?"

"Yes. Your Foundation members exist behind firewall from each other, Christopher. Your purposeful design, yes? We do not know these people; they do not know each other. This makes them difficult to vet. Why do you ask?"

"Chuck's a conman. Maybe he has a death wish? More likely he just wants to go where the 'fun' is." He sighed. At least there was Rogers and Alejandro, Doona at a push. "OK. Are they all in position?"

"Five miles out from compound. Waiting for you."

"All right." He took a breath. Getting everything lined up, tracking back along their conversation. "So what's the bad news?"

There was a brief silence before Hellion spoke again. "There has been another Reparations video."

23

HATCHET

W ren brought up his phone, and as before the video full-screened to darkness. On the right hung the gameshow-like box with the names of all nine remaining billionaires, vote tallies spinning beside them like slot machine wheels. Millions of votes and growing fast. Now trust-fund inheritor Merriot Raine was at the top, with billionaire financier Damalin Joes in second.

"This happened live four hours ago," Hellion said in Wren's ear. "The vote counts reflect real votes cast through websites and apps via the darknet."

"Why didn't you wake me?"

"What would you have done, Christopher? On three hours sleep, in transit to strike location? You would not sleep again, after seeing this. It is better we let you rest."

Wren was about to grumble, point out that he didn't need much sleep, then a strobe lit the darkness on his phone's screen. Electric-blue lights flashed like scalpel blades through the black, briefly revealing the same long, narrow cages as before. Dead ahead on the concrete floor, naked and pale, lay Damalin Joes, just now shuddering awake.

The flashes sped up, freezing images of the big man like stop-motion animation. Joes rubbing his face. Rolling up to a seated position. Fingers touching some kind of thick collar around his neck. Wren squinted closer to try and pick it out, but it was dark and Joes kept moving, then gasped as he saw something ahead of him. The camera panned slightly as Joes scrabbled backward, heels hammering on the floor until his back struck a pole in the fencing. A haz-mat figure was standing some ten paces away, near the entrance of his cage.

The strobe lights flashed faster. The figure looked like a butcher in a slaughterhouse apron, splattered red. A large camera rested on his shoulder, a bulbous microphone projecting like a distended forehead above its one dark eye, red light blinking.

The feed cut to that camera, on a level with and close up to Damalin Joes.

"What do you want?" Joes asked, pressed back against the cage wall. He was clearly straining for bass, to sound powerful and commanding, but it came through reedy.

The camera inclined slightly to the side, focusing on a rough wooden block a few feet from Joes, with a wicked-looking hatchet buried in the middle. Joes's eyes bugged. The sleek silver blade glinted in the flashing light. The camera refocused on Joes, who looked at the blade, the camera, then beyond to the cell gate. The camera swiveled to follow his gaze.

The gate stood ajar.

By the time the camera swung back, Joes had gotten to his feet and was reaching for the hatchet. The second his fingers closed around the grip, a chime sounded through the cells and a light flashed on the strange collar around his neck.

Joes let go of the hatchet at once and reached up to his neck as if stung. The camera zoomed in as Joes ran his fingers over the device hesitantly. He tugged on it several times, worked it between his fingers, but failed to find a release catch. A thick band of metal, looked to be barely room to get one finger between it and his skin. Cautiously he tried to bend the metal, but it didn't flex. For a long moment his eyes fixed on the hatchet, putting the pieces together.

As if to help him along, the strobes began flashing brighter, illuminating all the cages. To his right the eight remaining occupants of the Forbes list were starting to rouse. They each had a collar around their necks and a haz-mat camera operator standing over them. No one else had a hatchet, though.

Looking into Joes' eyes, Wren saw the decision happen; another moment just like the death of Handel Quanse. Maybe one of a long string of such decisions Damalin Joes III had taken all his life, to exploit the opportunity before him. When life handed you lemons…

Joes took hold of the hatchet once more. Again there was a chime, a flash from his neck, and now also a display on the side of the blade that lit up bright red. Joes pried the blade from the wooden block and held it up to study the display; the camera pushed in alongside him. There was some kind of digital LED readout slotted into the blade itself, displaying a single name in block capitals.

RAINE

Wren glanced at the voting tally. Raine's name was at the top by a close margin, with Cem Babak the arms dealer just below him. Raine's name was also on the hatchet. It seemed pretty clear.

Joes wasted no time thinking through the morals of it. He strode past his camera operator and out of the cell, swishing the hatchet experimentally through the air. Flashing strobes illuminated his path. Merriot Raine was in the cell next door. The gate hung open. Joes stepped in.

Raine was already on his knees, wide eyes flickering from Joes' face to the blade.

"No," he said. "Please, Damalin, don't. I can pay you. Whatever you want. I can pay."

Joes lifted one finger to his lips, strode closer and pulled back the blade. Raine started to scream. It was all happening so fast. Joes brought the hatchet down.

The blow didn't land. What happened instead was intense and stunning: a blinding light filled the cells, Joes' collar lit up an electric blue and he jerked, unable to finish the downward sweep. Raine screamed and Joes lurched to the side, barely catching himself on the chain-link cell wall.

Wren recognized the sudden shift. Joes had just been hit by an incredible electric shock, presumably delivered by the collar around his neck. Like the cattle prods they'd used to level Handel Quanse. As if to confirm it, Joes' left hand shot up to the collar, his breaths came in a painful wheeze, but he didn't waste time recovering. Instead he took a shaky step over to the screaming Merriot Raine, lifted the hatchet again and tried to bring it down a second time.

This time Wren's phone screen turned wholly white, so dazzling he had to look away, before returning to darkness lit by occasional strobes. Now Damalin Joes lay slumped across the body of Merriot Raine, who was crying out for help and struggling to get free. The hatchet lay on the floor beside them both, the display screen glowing red.

"What's going on?" Wren muttered.

"The vote changed," Hellion explained in Wren's ear. "See the side tally?"

Wren looked at the vote bar on the right, where the number one slot had shifted. Now Cem Babak's name was at the top. As if to confirm it, the camera focused in on the blade of the hatchet, where the same name was highlighted in red.

BABAK

"It's updated live," Wren said. "Nominated by the popular vote?"

"Exactly," Hellion said. "Millions of people were voting when this went live."

Wren nodded along. "So Joes gets punished if he tries to use the hatchet against the wrong man?"

"Precisely. It is ingenious, yes? Like video game without tutorial, where you..."

Wren tuned her out and focused on the footage. The image of Joes atop the wriggling Raine cut away, replaced by a shot of social-media-sellout turned green-energy-ecowarrior Inigo De Luca running down the side passage, also wearing a thick shock collar. He looked like he'd been chiseled from marble, muscular and so pale he was vampiric in the flashing lights.

De Luca entered Raine's cell, smoothly swept up the hatchet, swung it above his head without once looking at the display and brought it down-

His shock came synced to another long flash. Wren turned away until the screen resolved back to darkness broken only by the strobe. Now two bodies lay slumped atop Merriot Raine, and Raine was still wriggling frantically to get free. The hatchet lay off to the side, the blade display shifting rapidly name as the vote tallies spun.

RAINE

BABAK

JOES

"They are slow learners," Hellion said.

Wren grunted, watching as other dim bodies closed in like ghosts from

the dark, coming toward Joes and De Luca on the floor. Merriot Raine finally escaped past them. Cem Babak the arms dealer stood at the entrance to Raine's cell now, thick and solid with the swollen trapezoids of a powerlifter, eyeing the hatchet until a foot suddenly lashed out into his knee. Damalin Joes had regained consciousness. There was a yelp and Babak went down.

Joes rose swiftly to his feet, sent a sharp heel kick into Babak's face. Seemed like he'd had some fight training; was pretty handy with his limbs. Voices clamored in the bristling dark, calling for Joes to stop and think, but he was clearly beyond that now. The camera caught the mad flare in his red eyes; probably half-blind from the flashes of light and half-mad from the shocks, driven now by animal instinct alone.

Babak and De Luca both lay on the ground. The hatchet lay to the side. Joes lunged over and swept it up, raised the weapon high to strike Babak and-

-stopped.

"Finally he understands," Hellion said.

Wren glanced at the vote tallies, his own heart thumping. This wasn't live right now, but still he felt the surging excitement, the illicit thrill of watching something real. Like gladiatorial combat in the days of Ancient Rome. At least one of these billionaires was going to die, and it was hard not to pick a favorite and root behind them.

Merriot Raine topped the ranking again. A man who'd never done nothing with his inherited money but squander it on himself. An easy man to hate, and a coward to boot. His vote totals had shot up again, after he'd fled and left the hatchet behind.

Now the hatchet display showed his name.

RAINE

Joes strode out of the cell, over Babak's unconscious body, and broke into a run. The screen split into two to show Joes charging on the left, Merriot cowering on the right in some other cell. Joes reached the end of the row of cages in seconds and plunged through the open cell gate. Raine had dropped to his knees in the corner, arms up and begging.

"Please, Damalin!" he shouted, raising his arms as Joes raised the hatchet back. "I can make it worth your while, everything I have I can-"

"It's not about the money, Raine," Joes replied, then brought the blade arcing down. There was no flash this time, no electric shock. The hatchet blade cleaved through Merriot Raine's soft palm like a cord of wood, slicing deep into his wrist. He screamed, blood sprayed out over Damalin Joes, but he just raised the hatchet and brought it down again, this time into Merriot Raine's skull.

Now he fell silent. His body dropped. His name fell off the listing.

Damalin Joes stood in the cell, chest heaving, vote tallies spiraling up, the name on his hatchet shifting rapidly. Out in the darkness, the other billionaires clustered and stared. Wren anticipated the feed cutting away, the game ending, but it didn't. Perhaps Joes had expected the same thing, but after a minute or two, he seemed to realize, and brought the blade up slowly to his eyes.

BABAK, read the display.

"It goes on like this," Hellion interrupted. "Another five minutes. One more dies."

Wren watched it through to the end, when the action faded to black with the same stark end titles as before.

YOU ARE OWED REPARATIONS

CLAIM THEM IN BLOOD

For a long moment Wren stood leaning against the Prius, trying to come to grips with what he'd just seen. Afterglow from the flashes in that sick prison still spotted his retinas.

He didn't want to watch any more videos like it. Who would? At the same time, it was no more gory than mainstream movies and TV shows. It had been filmed like them; high production levels somehow made the violence more palatable, as if you could watch and pretend it was just another piece of bingeable entertainment.

It made you root for the billionaires to die.

Through it the Reparations were training their audience to cheer on real deaths. It helped that these were some of the most despised men on the planet, but not all deservedly so. Damalin Joes III had been turning himself around. Inigo De Luca, Geert Fothers, a handful of others had ramped up their charitable giving to incredible levels.

Killing them was no answer to the fear and anger people were feeling, after the Saints and the Blue Fairy. Though in the heat of the moment, Wren knew it would feel like it. Violence was a contagion. Show people the way and they'd follow.

Then something struck him.

"How did this get out," he asked. "We killed social media. We added moderation on all videos going live. How is anyone seeing this or voting on it without NameCheck and the rest to distribute it?"

Hellion took a breath. "Yes. You are not going to like this, Christopher. It looks like they played us from beginning. Played you, really. You see…"

24

HOW?

Wren stamped away from the road and into the nearby desert, fury burning through his veins and Hellion's words reverberating in his ears.

"First execution film had tiny piece of code attached, virus," Hellion explained. "This virus installed new app on every device. Phone, computer, tablet, whatever. App replaces NameCheck, Iota, WeStream, all Internet companies. Reparations video plays through new app, and app allows all content. No moderation." She took a breath then piled on. "There are many copycat videos, now. Such video uploads passed one per second one hour ago, and it is not just children damaging property. It is worse. Hatchets, Christopher. People are being assaulted. Some are dying."

Wren kicked up dust and clenched his knuckles, staring out at the stars then the flashing cars racing by on the highway.

"Reason this has worked so well, Christopher," Hellion went on, "there is no other streaming site. No other place to upload, watch video. No entertainment except Reparations." A pause. "We did this."

Wren frowned. Felt understanding coming on but wasn't ready for it. "What do you mean?"

"We shut down many companies after WeStream. These companies followed some rules. Now there is nothing. True Wild West, Christopher.

No law at all. Worse, video through this app is untraceable. We cannot hack them. This is game, and they win."

They win. The words rang in Wren's head and chimed with the message carved in the flash drive, wrapped around Somchai Theeravit's neck.

I THINK YOU'LL ENJOY THIS ONE, PEQUEÑO 3.

Like some kind of game.

"This is why they wanted me," he said softly.

"What?"

Now the pieces were coming together. Finally starting to see the land beneath the thick layer of snow. Pythagoras strung up and waiting for his attention. Damalin Joes III staring at the cameras. He'd known back in Deadhorse that there was some reason the Reparations wanted him personally involved.

Here it was.

"They set me up," he said. "They knew I'd go after social media. Knew I'd break laws to clear cut the Internet in ways nobody else could."

Hellion had sucked in a breath. "Yes, this may be true. You are wrecking ball."

Wren snorted. Wrecking ball was putting it lightly. He'd always leaped before he looked. But Rogers had made it very clear how difficult the Internet companies were to rein in. Nothing could control them, not government laws, not military force, not hackers on the darknet. The change had to come from within, and getting within organizations and bringing them down was Wren's specialty.

Hellion was right. He'd been played.

"No other video sources to watch," he murmured. "No way to bring them down."

"Yes. App is now only supplier of unmoderated video content." A pause. "No competition. Reparations own eyes of the world."

Wren shook his head, trying to kickstart a lead. "How many people have the app?"

A second passed as keys clacked. "Hard to be certain, but at least one hundred million subscribers."

That was an immense number. One hundred million people feeding off this darkness. Feeding into it. Uploading videos in this new violence economy. Killing people for kicks and fame, with Damalin Joes' life on the line.

All Wren's responsibility.

"How many dead, in the copycat attacks?"

"Best guess? Dozen, perhaps. Hatchet attacks, Christopher. Very messy."

Wren stamped a tight arc around the recharging station's white glow, feeling the world flipping around him. When laws cracked with no accountability, new permissions were granted; not just to him but to everyone. People would watch the app like an addiction. Not all, but many. Some would be sick already, wouldn't need much to push them over the edge. Others needed a few more shoves.

There were seven billionaires left. Enough material for six more 'episodes', assuming one death per episode and a single winner. All with the goal of ripping the US apart. Wren's mind raced. The government couldn't move fast enough to stop this thing. His hackers hadn't even seen it coming. That left only one path.

Swift, unrelenting justice.

He stopped in his tracks. They'd wanted it personal. Now it was.

"Hellion?"

"Yes, Christopher."

"Tell the Foundation to hunt the killer copycats," he said through gritted teeth. "Use clues from the videos to locate them. All of them."

A moment passed. "We can do this. Hunt them and hen do what, Christopher?"

The words catch/kill floated through his head. The same order Humphreys had laid against him, but the first half of that equation wasn't going to get the job done, and the Foundation didn't have the resources to imprison people anyway. When you were in the Wild West, justice came at the barrel of a gun.

"Kill them."

There was silence for a moment.

"Are you sure?"

"I'm sure. Relay the order. Kill them and film it. We need to put up some warning flags. Enforce some accountability." He paused, spinning the next few hours forward. "This movement has to die at all costs. We'll all pay our reparations when it's over."

25

ROGERS

The convoy went dark five miles out from the Anti-Ca compound, silent electric engines whirring. Wren's pulse rate rose, sixty to seventy, in anticipation.

A phone alarm went off, and it took him a minute to realize what it was. Not Hellion or the Foundation, but the alarm he'd set every night for the past three months. Time to call his wife back in Delaware.

Gruber was asleep in the passenger seat, now, with Wren driving. The phone was in back, and he let the alarm ring until it gave out.

"Here," Hellion said, on a rise a mile out.

The convoy pulled over ahead, shaping up like an odd low wall in the darkness. Wren parked at the front, looked at Gruber with his head lolled against the window, and decided to let him sleep through. He was intelligence, not combat. Better not to give him the choice.

He opened the door and strode out. The desert air hummed with night life: brown bats swooping on buzzing insects; kit foxes rustling down prey-trails; chuckwalla lizards and woodrats burrowing up from their dens. A dusty wind carried the lush scent of dry sage and the rain-smell of creosote bushes. Off to the left he could just pick out the outline of the compound by moonlight, low on an open brush savannah. A dark ring in the night, no lights.

To his right was Rogers. Standing alone in the dark, alone, half her face lit by the moon, blond hair pulled back tight. Jaw set, eyes gleaming with things unsaid. Beyond her stood his 'team': the slim silhouette of Doona, the short and stocky Alejandro, the office-worker frame of Chuck. They didn't advance to greet him; waiting to let the Wren-Rogers fracas play out.

"There you are," Rogers said. Not loud, but her voice carried in the quiet. "I've been looking for you."

Wren took a few steps closer. For some reason her voice made him sad. Nostalgia for their brief cooperation against the Blue Fairy, maybe; a vision of himself that couldn't last. "Here I am."

Seconds passed. An owl hooted far off. "Our deal stands," she said. "When this is over, you come in."

"That's right. Humphreys knows you're here?"

"In theory, but not specifically. We never found the Blue Fairy mole, so if your father had one then, he still has one now." A pause. It was strange to hear her talking with such certainty about his father. "So I'm off portfolio. Humphreys has given me latitude."

Wren nodded. He knew about going off portfolio. To bring down a cult you had to bend all the rules.

"I'll pay for my part in this, too, when it's done," she added. "Not quite like you, but for my conduct. I've cut corners."

Wren grunted. That was probably on him.

"My team are in Deadhorse," she went on. "They found the bodies in the depot. Bad guys. Lots of evidence in Somchai Theeravit's bunker linking them to abuse. Not a whisper about his activities anywhere."

"He was a shipping magnate. When you're a millionaire, people look the other way."

Rogers stared. Judging. "That's really the issue now, isn't it? Wealth and privilege."

"Wealth and privilege," Wren agreed. "They're no protections now."

A moment passed. "I met your team. One of them is a copier salesman."

Wren took that on board. Chuck. His new job? That was embarrassing. "He's undercover."

"As a copier salesman? To break open the infamous dark paper cabal?"

Wren said nothing. It didn't seem like jokes between them were possible now.

"He asked me where the safety was on his Glock 17," Rogers said. "His own gun, Christopher."

Wren grimaced; glad Rogers wouldn't see it in the darkness. Glocks didn't have a safety; they had a trigger lock. Everyone knew that.

"He's in training. Don't worry about him, he's here to observe only. Or Doona. It'll be you, me and Alejandro with the cavalry, we'll be good."

Rogers glared, eye whites catching the silvery light. "Cavalry. Call them stolen vehicles. Who's going to pay for that?"

There were some criticisms he wasn't going to entertain right now. "Add them to my tab. Let it go, Rogers. We've got bigger things to deal with right now."

She stared. She let it go. "I've run the circumference." She pointed, beyond the line of silent vehicles to the dusty savannah bowl. "I don't see anything. No lights, nothing. Your hacker's been in touch, her thermal drone confirms they're still in guard positions on the rooftops, with women and children huddled in the main building."

"They know a hit's coming. Or they fear it."

Rogers shrugged. There was plenty of fear to go around. "After you crushed their Internet presence, I'd be surprised if every Anti-Ca compound wasn't on high alert."

It was a good point. "No word on the suicide order?"

"Just that they have the supplies. Potassium-cyanide. Orders smuggled and laundered through various small-time labs in neighboring states. But no death order in the air."

Wren nodded. At least they had that, though it all depended on how far gone the Anti-Ca people were. If they received the order and were willing, they could all be dead within minutes.

"How many?"

"Census says zero. In government records this place doesn't exist. From the drone though, looks like sixty-three."

Wren whistled low. Sixty-three against him, Rogers and Alejandro. Even with three remote-driven vehicles, they weren't good odds. "Armaments?"

"Looks like some heavy munitions. Rifles, a handful of autocannons, grenades, potentially bombs."

Wren grunted. "Entrenched security?"

"There's a wall around the compound, many buildings butting against it. Tin sheeting, it looks like, but still."

"Likely reinforced. Do reports say they're laying in for a siege?"

Rogers just glared. "No. They've got lots of orange juice, though."

It took Wren a second to register that. Hellion hadn't mentioned it; probably she hadn't realized the significance. He flashed on the chemical reactions that accompanied potassium-cyanide when swallowed. Fruit juice sped the fatal reaction. It was how they'd taken their cyanide in Jonestown.

A third of the deaths at Jonestown had been children. Seventy people had received the poison unwillingly, via syringe. Rogers' eyes glowed with that same knowledge.

"How many children?" Wren asked. His throat was tight.

"A dozen, best guess, from the thermal imaging. Gathered in the central bunker."

He saw red. "The drone shows they're alive?"

"Sixty-three are alive. If others are dead, we wouldn't see that."

Wren's mouth went dry. They'd be cold; invisible to infra-red. Ready to be buried in their pits. It was hard not to feel the shadow of his father overhanging the dark compound; Apex of the largest suicide cult in American history. Getting people to kill themselves because the power felt good.

"Sentries?"

Rogers held up a tablet, the screen dim but live. Wren took it and scanned the infrared footage from Hellion's drone. There were hot red figures spread around the faint outline of the compound's circular wall. Some proned out like snipers, some clustered tight together, likely behind barricades, perhaps manning the autocannons.

At the center was the main bunker, one room brightly lit with multiple heat signatures. Some small and fragile looking; the children. Kept in a cell. Wren's jaw set. If anyone was going to spill whatever they knew, it was the people in that room. The doubters, who needed to be locked away with the kids.

Wren picked out a route through several of the sniper emplacements, fastest path to the bunker.

He held up the map for Rogers to see. "I'll go right. You go left. Our goal is the bunker."

"To save the kids," she said.

"And dig out what they know."

"Couldn't have said it better myself."

Wren committed the outline to memory. "We go now," he said, felt the urgency shooting adrenaline into his system. "Where's my gear?"

"In the truck."

"Two minutes. I talk to my team and we'll roll."

"Have at it."

He strode past her. His 'team' were waiting. Alejandro was squat and solid, dark wifebeater over dark gang tattoos, tear drops down his cheeks. Doona was as black as jet, only the whites of her eyes gleaming in the night, hair cropped close and clutching a rifle. Chuck did look like a copier salesman in the desert; timid, trying to be brave, way out of place.

"Chuck, you stay here," Wren said in a firm voice, giving no room for argument. "Alejandro, you're mid-convoy, I suggest the mapping car; shoot only if they're shooting at you. Doona, I don't want you in this. You're barely through immediate PTSD."

Doona racked the slide of her AR:15. "I ride with you, or I run there myself. Either way, I am fighting."

Wren considered that, made allowances. She was eighteen, after all. "We do need you. Mid-convoy then, the car behind Alejandro, the saloon. Same directive. Study this outline." He held out the tablet, pointed to the central courtyard area inside the compound walls, in front of the bunker. "I want you both in the middle right here, stirring up as much trouble as possible. Your vehicles will remain in motion at all times. Hellion?"

"Yes," Hellion responded. "I will do this."

Wren refocused on his team. "You keep them busy with noise and fury. Rogers and I will break for the bunker at the center. Any questions?"

Alejandro and Doona stared back at him. Wren nodded.

"What about me?" Chuck asked.

"You shouldn't even be here," Wren said and strode away.

"Are you wearing that?" Doona called after him.

Wren had forgotten his clothes. Still the skimpy gym outfit. "It's tactical," he called over his shoulder. "Get in your vehicles."

Rogers stood at the trailer bed of her Ford pickup, gesturing to the supply cache of boxes inside, lit by the Ford's dim running lights. "You like Twaron armor? Fill your boots."

Looked like she'd brought an armory. Wren opened boxes and grabbed a pair of sturdy combat pants, a tough canvas jacket and proper boots, pulled them on in the dark. A Twaron para-aramid bulletproof vest and thigh-plates came next, then a shoulder-holster for a Colt M1911 with left thigh ammo belt, a Benelli M2 3-gun tactical shotgun with a 24-shell chest bandolier. He sighted down the shotgun, dry-fired it, then twisted it in his right hand to check the loading port, plucking four shells from the bandolier in a quad formation in his left hand. With a clean sweeping movement he speed-loaded two of the shells, two more then spun the shotgun upright again.

"Smooth," Rogers said.

"I've been practicing. Now, shall we?"

"We shall."

Wren strode back to the Prius.

"Ready for this, Hellion?" he asked.

"As ever, Christopher," she answered in his ear. "We take them by surprise. I will punch hole with tank truck. Draw fire. Trust me, I have raided compounds like this thousand times before."

Wren throttled a laugh. "In video games."

"Is same thing. Just do not get shot."

"Amen to that."

He opened the Prius' door, woke Gruber and asked the man to step out.

"Huh?" Gruber asked groggily. "Are we there?"

"Just step out a second," Wren said. "I'll explain."

He stepped out. Wren got in, hit the gas and peeled out with a rush of dirt.

"Taking lead," Hellion said in his ear. "Good luck, Christopher. B4cksl4cker will be your voice operator. I will be occupied with running vehicles."

The convoy woke behind him. The cyber truck pulled into the lead, with Wren, Rogers, Alejandro and Doona following on behind, chased by the tiny silver chair car. Across the desert savannah the vehicle train accelerated to ramming speed.

26

COMPOUND

Three minutes of darkness and dust followed, the Prius rocking and jolting over hummocks in the hardpan desert, then the first crash came from ahead as the huge cyber truck hit the tin sheeting and ruptured a hole straight through.

"No response yet," B4cksl4cker said in his ear, "hit in four."

Three seconds, two, one then the Prius hit the gap, scraping sparks down its bodywork off reinforced joists backing the tin wall. Wren burst through into an interior that was now flooded with a sudden storm of high beams; Hellion's attack truck already starting a spin like Damalin Joes' horse in the Reparations video, headlights blaring. The Prius banked hard to join its mad spiral, and Wren surveyed the compound's interior as they spun around at forty miles an hour.

Tin outer walls, wooden buildings like the Pyramid's fake town in Arizona, now four vehicles spinning tight donuts in the center, wheels spinning, with the final two crashing through in seconds to enter the furious dance.

"Rooftops," B4cksl4cker said sharply. "Snipers are activating, I see ten, no, eleven on infrared, all around you; they are sniping us, aiming for engine blocks and windshields."

Wren couldn't hear the incoming fire through the roaring of vehicles, couldn't see the snipers through the riotous spill of light.

"Give me a target!" Wren barked as the Prius circled wildly, taking an incoming high caliber round that crumped in through the back window and out through the chassis.

"Main building is heavily guarded, Christopher! I recommend best access is over rooftops; large building due south has two snipers, large wooden bay doors, clear route to main building."

Wren yanked the Prius hard over, cutting through the dance and rerouting Hellion's slaved vehicles, in seconds barreling thirty miles an hour straight into the barred wooden front of what looked to be a motor pit. The Prius hit and the doors ripped off their hinges to fly ahead like a desperately flapping butterfly.

The Prius skidded into a dark interior of vehicle elevators, stacked tires and stripped-back pickups. Wren killed his lights before the butterfly doors landed and flung himself out the door. The car sped on to crash through metal shelving and beyond while Wren rolled into cover behind a tire stack.

From outside the sound of electric vehicles tearing over dirt chewed into the air, pierced now by the deep cracking reports of armor-piercing rounds slotting through metal.

"Two on the walkway ten o'clock," came B4cksl4cker's voice; swift analysis of Wren's body-cam footage. "Rifles trained on the door. Another two possibly three on floor with you, to your-" pause, "-two o'clock, behind shelves. Could be grenade, one of them had arm back and-"

Wren heard the dull skittery clink of metal on the concrete flooring, ringing scant feet to his left, where the roving headlights from Hellion's dance troupe flashed out an epileptic's nightmare.

Grenade. Wren lurched up at once, drawing instant rifle fire that sprayed rubber chunks off the tires and blasted chips from the wooden walls beyond, then dived. A second and a half later the grenade blew.

Light washed out, the percussive bark followed and a blast wind caught the soles of his feet as he flew beyond the edge of the tire stack. The tires erupted and buried him in torn and burning vulcanized rubber.

"Cover me!" he managed to shout, before a second clink landed nearby then thumped up against the blanket of carbon black tire shreds. Wren scrabbled to get under the chunky blanket then the second grenade erupted.

The blast rang out like a wet firework, shredding tires and spraying rubber fragments across his left hip, chest and thigh, pummeling his ears and showering him with a secondary rain of burning black confetti. More clinks landed nearby, then a thud to match them as one grenade landed amongst the tires, and Wren had half a second to shout, "Hellion!" and half a second longer to contemplate his imminent disintegration, when two things happened at once.

The grenades erupted like a string of firecrackers, each blast tremendous and devastating, hurling tires through the air, gouging craters into the concrete floor, sending shrapnel whistling out through the walls and spattering Wren. Shrapnel also ripped through the side panels, dented the chassis, burst the tires, imploded the glass and bent the A and B columns of the cyber tank truck now skidding to a stop directly over Wren's prone body.

Saving his life.

"Cover," came B4cksl4cker's voice, barely audible over the tinnitus ring of the blasts. "Literally. Now get up."

Wren wasn't going to waste the opportunity it presented, while just tossed more grenades. He rolled through burning tire scraps and out from under the scarred truck as several more blasts rang out nearby, answered now by incoming fire and the roaring of engines.

He raised his head by the driver side door to see a hellish scene of fire, light, smoke and tracer rounds; the sleek red supercar shot across the wreckage-strewn mechanic's pit to collide with a desk by the wall, drawing screams. The snipers above trained their fire on a secondary vehicle incoming, the mapping car with Alejandro leaning out the window and firing up into the gantry, now pulling squealing, smoking donuts through the rubble.

"Every building is rigged like this," B4cksl4cker said, "Hellion is regrouping for another charge."

Wren was already running, taking advantage of the confusion and ignoring the stinging pain down his left side. He vaulted a spray of shattered crates, reached the crumpled desk as the supercar revved its wheels into a hard reverse, then rolled over the top, dropping flush in beside two bearded men with startled faces. They brandished rifles and wore a bandolier of grenades each, even now trying to bring their weapons to bear.

Wren fired twice with the shotgun; twin contact shots, one each in the chest at point blank range. Two shell-loads of bismuth pellet slugs blasted through their bodies like wet cardboard, the immense volley of sound lost within the chaos of squealing wheels and sniper fire.

Two down.

Sniper fire pinged the countertop. Wren slid out flat on his back, aiming upward to put two tightly grouped shots through the underside of the walkway corner; the slugs tore through metal and into the men above, drawing fresh screams.

"Take the rooftops," B4cksl4cker said. "Hellion is coming in again but snipers are finding our range. If they take out vehicles, all fire will turn on you."

Wren strode three steps over the shotgunned bodies, speed-loaded four more shells and raced up the metal ladder to the gantry. From behind more gunfire came; he spun, saw Alejandro surfing atop the mapping car like a pole dancer now, firing across the burning space at the two injured snipers above. Seemed he had it covered.

Wren reached the gantry and kept climbing, five more rungs to an open chute to the roof, where for a second he paused.

"Get me a distraction," he ordered.

"Ten seconds," Hellion answered, and Wren heard it coming; the roaring of his convoy charging toward the motor pit, probably enough mass and velocity to take out the support walls and bring the whole thing down.

Just as the first vehicle struck below, he surged up the last few rungs into moonlight and the roar of battle.

27

ROOFTOPS

The roof itself lurched a clear foot down with the impact below; the whole corner support blown out with a resounding crunch. Wren felt the backwash wind of a bullet brush his temple then he lurched sideways into a shoulder-punishing roll.

Another shot tore up the tarpaper as he rose to his feet, catching glimpses of twin shooters at the roof's northwest and southeast corners, each silhouetted against the charging headlights of Hellion's dwindling cavalry as they raced a distraction derby below, plowing into more buildings' supports.

A second crunch jolted the roof as Hellion hit it again, a fault line opened down the middle and the structure began to tip. Wren scrambled up the steepening surface chased by gunfire until a third impact came and dropped the southeast corner of the building completely away.

The sniper's scream ended in a thud as he landed below. Wren leveled the shotgun and charged at the northwest corner, speed-firing four slugs in a second flat. Two punched into the roof, one zinged away through the air and the fourth pinged the sniper dead on.

Wren didn't slow, reached the trembling roof at a full sprint and leaped. One second he sailed through the air, vehicles stampeding twenty feet below like the running of the bulls, then his chest slammed into the next roof over. His left foot caught his weight against the wall, the shotgun clattered away to the dirt below, then he was up again and zigzagging, Colt in his hand and picking out targets.

"Take out their supports along my route," he shouted into the night.

"Hellion's on it," B4cksl4cker responded instantly, and five steps along Wren felt the hit come below. The jolt dislodged another sniper and Wren fired three rounds into his center mass, then hit the edge and was airborne again. Alejandro surfed by on his mapping car below, firing calmly. Wren hit the next roof smoothly and ran at two figures in a machine-gun nest circled with sandbags.

One yanked at the oversized weapon, spinning it off its pre-sighted tripod aimed at the courtyard, but took a shoulder and rolled back. The second grasped for the trigger but was thrown off-balance by the tiny silver chair car thudding into the building below.

Wren fired two shots through the guy's chest, heard B4cksl4cker's cry of surprise, then was leaping again. "Report!" he barked.

"Two more and you're there," B4cksl4cker snapped, "central hub is reinforced with concrete, ram proof; they are retreating toward it. I see seven snipers remain, eight down; Alejandro and Doona are picking them off, Rogers is circling to meet you. Only three vehicles left in commission."

Wren jumped another roof, fired on two guys Doona had pinned down, and got his first clear look at the main hub. It had a low rolled aluminum roof, a radio antenna lit up by stray flashes of light, concrete walls and a metal blast door, with two snipers hunkered in a recessed guard tower.

"Suicide order has gone out!" B4cksl4cker shouted abruptly.

He had to get inside that building.

"On my signal hit the wall below the guard tower with everything you've got," Wren answered, unloaded his last two bullets into a lone figure then ducked behind the rain barrel cover he'd been using. He reloaded the Colt with a smooth slam into the handgrip, took a second to breathe while incoming fire fragged musically off the barrel's wooden staves.

"Doona's hit," B4cksl4cker narrated as the prickly sound of gunfire ran out across the compound. Wren peeked over his shoulder; Hellion's three remaining vehicles were pulling into a tight spiral again, spinning up speed like a centrifuge. "Alejandro's securing her."

"Send me the map car and hit the building," Wren answered, working the angles. It would be ugly, but...

"Pick up?" Hellion chimed in.

"Exactly, give me the count."

"Coming in three, two-"

Wren spun out of cover; the map truck was right there and sweeping toward him. The timing was perfect; he leaped and took the elevated camera bulb in his gut, hunched over it with his elbows locking him in position, the Colt out and firing.

"Go!"

Hellion broke the convoy's spiral like a carpet unrolling, unleashing their stored force in a line direct to the hub. Wren clung onto the map car and charged like a medieval knight jousting. The east guard tower unleashed their fire on him, strafing off the camera as they tried to pick him off. He hit one, took a dart of shrapnel off his right elbow, then dropped away the second before collision.

The convoy crashed dead into the concrete hub and momentum rocked it forward; the camera globe dinged the roof of the guard shelter while Wren slapped meatily off the wall and fell to the dust. He saw stars and breathed cordite, too dizzy to think, feeling it through his back as the two remaining vehicles crashed into the reinforced wall.

Then someone was shouting in his ear, pulling him to his feet.

Alejandro. He pressed Wren flat against the wall as bullets sparked off the map car's mangled metalwork.

"Ay, Dios mío, pendejo, what happened to your face?"

Wren ran a hand up to his cheek and felt hot blood. "I'm fine."

"This way," Alejandro shouted, and turned to run for the bunker door, but something zinged in and spun him.

Wren darted in and grabbed him, pulled him into shallow cover behind the map car just as the supercar pulled up. Most of its glass was starred or missing from incoming fire, the bodywork was pocked with hundreds of bullet holes. Lucky the battery was under the chassis, or they would've killed the drive by sheer chance by now. Wren tugged the rear door open, saw Doona laid sprawled and pale in the backseat, but she inched up to make room for Alejandro beside her.

"Get them out of here," he ordered, and the supercar reversed hard across the courtyard toward the hole in the wall, drawing heavy fire. "Get a doctor on the line, talk Chuck through treatment for them both."

"On it," B4ckslacker answered, "end this, Christopher."

He grunted, spun to see Rogers by his side. She gave him a nod, and he pointed to the hub's outer concrete shell. It had broken like an egg under the vehicle's impacts; the concrete walls shearing out of the too-shallow foundations and opening a slim vertical crack.

"Cover me," Wren shouted, then fed himself through the crack into darkness.

28

HUB

L ights sputtered fitfully inside, faintly illuminating dozens of faces spread before him.

Old people. Children. A young pregnant woman, a man in a wheelchair, all staring up at him from the edges of a ten by twelve room. Like a scene from the Pyramid: desperate people driven to an extreme, but still devoted to whatever their cult leader ordained.

Not a fortress. Not a room full of dead bodies yet, reeking with the burned almond fog of potassium cyanide. Just terrified souls staring back at him. He raised his palms and spoke in a calm, authoritative voice.

"I'm not here to hurt you. What I need to know is-"

A large figure lurched suddenly up on the right, leveling a gun, and Wren flung himself to the side. There was a vicious bang, the room lit up for a split second like the Reparation's strobing cells, then Wren was scrabbling on all fours over arms and legs in the darkness, unwilling to take an answering shot and risk innocents with the ricochet.

For five seconds the room was wild with screams, then Wren surged; his shoulder struck the thickset figure in the midriff, the gun discharged behind Wren's back, and they thumped down together amongst squealing bodies. Wren let his momentum propel a crushing elbow into the figure's face.

Teeth cracked. The big guy went limp, and Wren snatched up the weapon; another Colt by the feel and weight, an LW Commander.

"They're alive," came a voice at his back and he whirled, both Colts trained on a figure by the crack in the wall. Rogers. She wasn't even looking at him; she was focused on the people huddled in the flickering shadows.

"These ones are," Wren called over them. "The suicide order went out, and I'll wager their most devoted are already heaped up in the back. I'll dig in; you find out what these people know."

Rogers nodded. The light of gunfire flashes and wheeling headlights washed through the jagged crack beside her like Taser strikes.

"And watch your six. Anyone comes in, shoot them."

He turned without waiting for a response. Answers had to lie deeper inside. He scanned the dark room, saw only one door and he strode toward it, holding his hand to the earpiece.

"Get the vehicles out of here, we'll need them intact for extraction."

"Relaying," B4cksl4cker said.

Wren laid one hand on the door handle and pulled, taking a sharp step to the side.

Light spilled in and gunfire erupted through the opening. Chips spat off the far wall, drawing fresh cries. Rogers shouted something but Wren ignored it, counting bullets. Three weapons, one semi-automatic. The hail of bullets halted for a moment, and Wren dropped low and bobbed around the door, sighted on two shapes leaning at the end of a bright corridor, and fired.

Twin hits.

Wren didn't wait, charging into the corridor full speed. A rifle muzzle appeared around an open door to the left and he fired to pin it down. It fired in return, blind shots stitching a line across the far wall and up the ceiling, taking out one of the lights in a spray of sparks and glass. Wren hit the opposite wall, ran low and fast under the angle of spray to whip a big right hook through the open door frame.

His fist hit a soft throat and the rifle dropped. The figure groaned and Wren snatched up the weapon, stepped through and launched a headbutt into the sagging guy's forehead. He dropped.

Intermittent fire came from the end of the corridor, and Wren leaned out of the door, shot out the two remaining lights in sprays of glass, then moved. One of the two figures at the end of the corridor was sagged against the corner, gun propped across her chest. Wren fired first, caught her in the shoulder and sent her reeling. The other lay still, flat on his back whispering last words nobody would hear.

"Wren?" Rogers called.

"I have them," he answered, and dropped to retrieve the weapon from the woman and check her pulse. It was erratic, she was breathing weakly now, likely not long left.

"Where is he?" Wren asked.

The woman's eyes stared back in confusion. She'd never died before, didn't know what it meant, what anything meant anymore. Her mouth opened and she tried to frame words, but nothing came out.

"Is he here?" Wren pressed. "The Apex?"

If anything, her last expression was one of puzzlement. Her face froze like that. Wren stood.

Rogers was calling him.

"I'm fine," he said, choking the words out, "three down."

"They're rallying out there, Christopher! B4cksl4cker says we're far outnumbered. We need to get out of here now."

"Soon," he answered, and strode deeper into the dark.

DEEPER

L ights guttered throughout the compound. Wren strode on, Colt at the ready and heart racing as he turned every sputtering corner, but no more shots rang out. There were no more people to shoot. No leader, at least not in here.

In a room decked out with burned down candles, he found bodies. Old people. A few children. Sprawled in their death throes already. He kneeled; they were warm still, with bubbly froth on their lips like shaving foam. There were cups scattered on the floor and the bitter stink of almonds in the air, cut with the sweet zest of orange juice.

Potassium cyanide.

The order had come down. It looked like he'd disturbed them at the beginning of their work, though these didn't look like the most devoted. The most devoted were out on the rooftops fighting. These were the ones who'd had to be compelled. Who weren't able to fight, and couldn't be trusted to take the medicine themselves.

His anger blurred with disgust. Kill the weak first. He had scattershot memories of his long slaughter through the fake town, painting napalm onto unwilling bodies at the Apex's command...

A deep thudding reverberated up through Wren's belly, pulling him back to the present. He looked around. "What's that sound?"

"They are ramming main doors," came B4cksl4cker's scratchy voice in his ear, high and distant. "I think they will hold for now, but. Ah. They are attaching lines to door. Bringing vehicles into position. It will be like Handel Quanse. You have minutes only, Christopher."

Wren left the suicide room with its stink and its memories and hurried on. To his left a long office room had been stripped, the contents of three metal filing cabinets torched in situ, computers pummeled by sledgehammers, nothing that could help him now. In a kitchen he found unmarked chemical kegs stinking of potassium cyanide, alongside half-full cartons of orange juice. In a dormitory hall he rifled through drawers, cabinets, under beds, in desks, but there was nothing: no flash drives, no cameras, no trapdoor leading down to a dungeon holding the billionaires.

This was the right place, but there was nothing he could use. Somewhere far off shots tinkled musically.

"Sun is coming up," Hellion barked in his ear. Wren blinked, realized he was looking at his own face in a bathroom mirror. He looked like a zombie afflicted with a flesh-eating virus. The grenades had spattered fragments of rubber across his cheek and neck, turning him a mottled black. The pain from that was really settling in. His whole body felt hammered.

He moved. The FBI would be here soon to clean up this mess. The site would lock down in a siege. There had to be something of value, and he had to find it now, but what? He staggered back to the corridor where he'd begun. At the end of a blood trail lay the dead woman, she'd managed to drag herself along maybe ten feet.

"Alejandro is in trouble," came Hellion's voice in his ear. "He needs medical attention now."

"Trouble," Wren echoed. Racking his mind for the next move.

"We are waiting for you," she sped on. "Christopher, we have to get out, they are pulling blast doors now. Fourteen men, three vehicles. You cannot fight them."

Wren grunted. Everybody was outside, except for the ones in the cell. The reluctant ones. It gave him an idea. He ran to the kitchen, mixed up a fresh cocktail, then sped back into the cell. A few dozen pairs of eyes widened on him. It was dark and it stank of fear.

"You look like death," Rogers said, white eyes wide as he approached, nodding at the cup in his hand. "What's that you've got?"

Wren ignored her, surveyed these remnants of Anti-Ca. The man whose teeth he'd busted now lay slumped against the wall, his face pale. The rest were a few old folks, the pregnant girl who could barely be twenty years old, the guy in a wheelchair and some kids. To them he had to look like the devil.

Time to stamp that home.

He held out the plastic. Pilfered from the kitchen, now filled to the brim with orange liquid.

"To your health," he said, and held the cup up like a toast.

They stared. An indictment. Every one of them knew what it meant, and Wren trapped that knowledge with a hard stare, looking into their eyes one by one and seeking out the softest touches, those least strong in their faith.

He saw what he was looking for in the pregnant girl's eyes.

He'd seen it a million times before. Shock and awe. A soul carried along by the tide of her cult, not strong enough to break free, each time taking the next step because all her friends and family were too.

Wren held the cup out toward her. She flinched, though he was ten feet away.

"How about you, sister?" he asked. "Will you toast our good health?"

Her eyes peeled wide, trying to press herself back into the wall. Wren strode toward her. She was blond and string-thin apart from the swell of her belly. Eight months along perhaps, risking her baby just by being here, but what was risk when you expected to die by your own hand?

He dropped to one knee before her, holding the brimming cup right in front of her face. "You want to die for the movement? So die."

Her eyes danced from Wren to Rogers. She didn't understand. She didn't want to drink, but Wren had her isolated, forced to think for herself.

"Don't listen to a word-" someone shouted, and Wren spun, drew his Colt and fired. The bullet hit the wall next to an elderly woman's head. She looked like she'd swallowed her tongue.

He holstered the weapon like nothing had happened. The girl was bug-eyed now.

"Don't be afraid," Wren said hypnotically. "I've been here before. I've done this before. I know you're ready to die and take your baby along with you. Your cause here is just. So prove it."

He pushed the cup against her lips. She tried to pull away but there was nowhere to go. Orange liquid spilled down her chin. "Drink."

"I-I-" she stammered.

"What's the matter? Lost your faith?"

No one spoke. Rogers sucked in a breath.

"That's what I thought," Wren said. "So tell me where the Apex is, or I'll hold your nose and pour this down your throat."

She sucked air in a sharp gasp, eyes dancing side to side, looking for help. None came.

"For God's sake, tell him what you know!" Rogers shouted. "Where are the Reparations? For your baby's sake, tell us!"

Wren ignored her. Nothing needed to be explained. Everything came down to him, this woman, and justice in a cup full of bitter liquid. He tipped the cup further, so the liquid wetted her lips.

"Where's the arena?" Rogers shouted. "Where are the billionaires? Tell us where they are!"

Wren tipped more. The acrid orange liquid poured over the girl's chin and streamed into the hollow of her throat. She shook her head to spray it away, so Wren took hold of her jaw in one hand and squeezed until her mouth popped open.

"Drink," he commanded, and poured the liquid into her mouth.

Something hit Wren from the side, hard enough to send the liquid sloshing to the floor and Wren tumbling. He hit the deck, rolled and came up on his knees, Colt drawn and extended.

Rogers stood there; her own gun trained in on him.

Wren felt the world twisting.

"What the hell are you doing, Chris?" Rogers shouted.

He knew that look in her wild eyes. Always going too far, it said. Permission denied. But you had to go far. If there was one thing he'd learned in the Pyramid, it was that you had to be willing to go right up to the edge, sometimes even jump over.

He turned back to the spluttering girl. She was trying to retch out the liquid. She couldn't know it wasn't potassium cyanide, rather a bitter mix of orange juice and apple cider vinegar. All they'd had in the kitchen.

"Where is he?" Wren asked. "I have the antidote. You need it, or you're going to die a slow and painful death. Tell me. Where is the Apex?"

"Who?" the girl cried, wiping her mouth frantically, spitting and gagging. She was beyond terror now; pale skin, sweat trails running down her cheeks, eyes flared and shaking. She thought she was seconds from death.

"Give her the antidote!" Rogers barked. He looked at her. The gun was still trained on his chest. It gave him the rest of the play. The edge he wasn't supposed to cross; the way to show these people how serious he was.

"She knows something, Rogers."

"Bullshit she does! I put up with you killing the Pinocchios on Pleasure Island, with all your crazy tactics, but this is too far. You're not going to get answers by killing her. Give her the damn antidote!"

She took a step toward him, her weapon trained on his chest, her blond hair pulled loose from its tight bun and clinging to her cheeks. Grit, grime, furious blue eyes. She looked beautiful, really. Standing up for what was right.

"Stand down, Agent Rogers. The bullet will go right through you."

"So let it!" she countered. "I won't let you execute another innocent."

"She's not innocent," he growled. "The Pinocchios weren't innocent. All these people are part of it."

"Part of what, your father's cult?" Rogers eyes were wide with disbelief. "He died twenty-five years ago! Let it go, Chris."

He shook his head.

"That's it. I'm accelerating our timeline. I'm taking you in right now."

Her finger squeezed the trigger. Wren felt it more than he saw it. Reaching boiling point.

He fired first.

Hit her left of center mass.

She was punched back. Colt M1911 at close range, standard issue .45 ACP full metal jacket rounds in the chamber, 230 grain and traveling at a muzzle velocity of 830 feet per second; a relatively large slug, relatively slow out of the barrel, famously ineffective against body armor.

The Twaron vest should take the brunt of it. He hoped so. Either way, Rogers spun and went down.

Screams followed.

Always there was screaming at a transformation. Wren didn't need to see them; their horrified eyes, but this was part of it. To truly break the hold of a cult you had to break its link to the past, go beyond its sense of rules. The Reparations understood that. Take away any semblance of control and drop a nuclear bomb where it had been.

Rogers hit the floor. A voice called in his ear, warning the blast doors were about to breach. Wren spun back to the girl. She was spitting still, wiping her tongue on her sleeve. There were so many things to say, but now he didn't need to say any of them. Actions spoke louder.

He leveled the gun at her face.

"I was there!" she cried abruptly.

There it was. He felt the moment teetering. What did it matter that her people were coming in through the blast doors any second? Wren was here right now.

"I don't know about this 'Apex', but at the arena when they killed the billionaire? I was there! We didn't even think it was real." Tears raced down her cheeks. "I swear, we didn't know. I'll tell you everything, if you-"

There was an almighty crash that resounded through the building. The wall shook and the crack sheared wider.

"They are in, Christopher," B4cksl4cker shouted. "Ten seconds to exfiltration. There is one chance."

Sound rushed back in like air filling a vacuum. Wren heard the remnants of the convoy ripping through the defenses outside, rattled by gunfire. He heard the stamping of feet racing through the building, coming for him. In. Out. Ahead was the girl; pregnant. By his side lay Rogers, unconscious. Life was made of choices.

He chose both. Holstered the Colt and took the girl by the arm, grabbed Rogers by the wrist, and dragged them both up to the crack. Rogers went first, like posting a deadweight sack through a vertical letterbox, then Wren pulled the girl through after him.

She flopped to the earth just as figures stormed the cell in back. Rogers' Ford pickup was waiting for them outside, rocking with stalled momentum, taking bullets off its A-columns and bodywork, all the glass already gone. Gruber was in the driver's seat, looking wild-eyed and terrified. Doona was in the passenger seat, bandaged and returning fire.

She pushed the back door open and Wren bundled the girl in ahead, dragged Rogers after him, and Gruber hit reverse with a jerk. They revved backward through the courtyard of wreckage, away from the hail of gunfire past scattered flames and fallen bodies, to scrape sparks off the gouge in the compound wall and out into the night.

30
_____

COME IN, CHRISTOPHER

Wren woke in a moving vehicle, head fogged with a range of thoughts seeking some kind of completion. He remembered Rogers crumpled on a dark floor, and a girl sobbing, and the blurry, misremembered face of the Apex, and couldn't understand what they meant.

The vehicle jogged side to side. An ambulance? He was lying flat on a gurney, drip bags spooling blood into him, one at his wrist, another leading up to his throat.

"Don't touch that," came a stern voice. He looked and his vision swirled. Rogers?

"You're supposed to be anesthetized. You don't want to be conscious for this."

"Unhh," he managed to say.

"Trust me. That's a lot of tissue damage to your face. Unless you want to lose these good looks, I need you out for this, Christopher. There's a good boy, put your head down."

She was familiar. He couldn't quite grasp who she was. Not Rogers. Matronly. Tough. For some reason the words Munchausen Syndrome-by-proxy came into his mind. Was that...? He smiled, yes, remembering a case. Marissa, the surgical nurse who kept her patients sick for longer than she should. Only a little at first, only a few days, but then lengthening it, enjoying the power, the attention, their neediness.

Who knew, in time, if she would have graduated to killing them? With kindness, with constant care? Attend the funeral, sob along with the rest, enjoy the silent thrill of absolute power. He remembered picking her out by chance from datasets during a hospital opioid drug sting, a side project he'd taken on when the recovery times of patients didn't stack up. He remembered the moment he'd confronted her in the underground parking lot. Put her on a coin.

"Coin... zero..." he managed.

She snorted. Short, sharp. "You're in no state to make threats, young man. Now get back under, you're in my care here. Count down from five."

He laughed, barely a breath, though it wasn't funny. He managed the five, then...

When he woke next the movement had stopped; he wasn't in a vehicle anymore. It was a bedroom. The curtains were drawn, but light glowed through them warm and orange, revealing walls painted pale green, a full-length mirror, pine wardrobes reaching close to the ceiling.

He twisted but it hurt to move. He remembered taking rubber shrapnel from several grenades. Flashes of his own face in a mirror somewhere, black and mottled, came back to him. Names played in his head: Rogers. Gruber. Doona.

He climbed from the bed. Someone had taken his pink shorts off and replaced them with a pair of Hawaiian swimming trunks, red and black with embroidered skulls. Hardly better. His head pulsed and his mouth felt as dry as beef jerky.

With careful fingers he stroked the bandages on his left side. They began at the tip of his elbow and ran along his triceps, filled out his armpit but absent down his ribcage, where the Twaron vest had caught the grenade's spray. They picked up again over his hip then stopped where the thigh plate had been. He touched his jaw tentatively, then his cheek. Bandages too. There was that sensation of numbness that signaled a bad injury, temporarily masked by strong painkillers. Soon they'd wear off, and it wasn't going to be pretty. For now though, he was golden.

He leaned over and drew the curtain.

Light flooded in, momentarily blinding him. He blinked as his eyes teared up and adjusted. A cornfield came into focus outside; fields of green and gold plants standing proud like thousands of soldiers awaiting the sheafer. A red clay yard covered the gap, with a few tattered old pick-ups parked neatly. A barn stood to the right, faded red. It was mid-afternoon, judging by the high sun in the blue sky, around 3 p.m.

The exfiltration from the compound came back to him in flashes, as the Ford had pulled up to where Chuck was waiting in the dark. He'd checked Rogers; her Twaron vest had stopped the bullet, which proved a relief. Alejandro was out cold on the side of the road with a through-and-through shoulder wound, Chuck was dithering, Doona had taken shrapnel in her right thigh, and Gruber was trying to dab at Wren's face.

He'd told Hellion to activate their medical backup. Marissa Brey, his 'Angel of Death' Foundation member, on standby nearby.

They'd lit out. He remembered the thin stream of lights pouring out of the compound, coming for them. The pregnant girl was babbling by then, weepy and terrified. He held her face and looked in her eyes. "It wasn't poison," he said. "Orange juice and apple cider vinegar, that's all. You and your baby are fine."

She'd tried to slap him. He rolled most of it, then they were away. The girl handcuffed in the Ford, Alejandro curled into the pickup bed alongside Rogers, Gruber in the driver's seat, Doona riding shotgun. He sat by the girl and tried to interrogate her, but blood-loss and wooziness got the better of him, making his thoughts wander.

From there it was brief highlights only: the handover to the medical team as they pulled up for a mid-desert meet; him insisting Rogers, Alejandro and Doona all had treatment before him; traveling while Marissa put in stitches, the minibus clanging and jolting; finally his turn on the operating bench, and the anesthetic to put him under…

Then he was here.

Maybe ten hours gone. Half a day, and no time to waste.

A white T-shirt lay on a chair, and he pulled it on. His shoulder and side tightened, but the pain remained muted. Out the door he went, down wooden stairs to a hall hanging heavy with the smell of cinnamon and caramelizing butter, like someone had been baking cookies. There was a sunken den, a dining room, and an open-plan kitchen with a granite-topped island. A beautiful Midwestern farmhouse, right out of a furniture catalog.

"Hello?" he called.

No answer came. He patted his pockets, but his phone was gone. He went to the faucet and poured out a tall glass of lukewarm water, drained it, repeated that three times. Popped the fridge, found a quart of milk and drained half. Took five still-warm cookies from the cooling rack and started eating as he limped out, swinging the screen door onto the front porch. They were delicious.

Outside there was red dirt, balmy air, sharp sun in his eyes. He held up a hand to shield the light and headed for the barn. The corn rustled in the wind. Reedy cirrus clouds drifted like washed-out blood smears. He passed a large tractor then reached the barn doors. They creaked loudly as he pulled, announcing his entrance.

He wasn't at all ready for what lay on the other side.

Eyes turned his way, a dozen? People seated around a cluster of tool-bitten workbenches on the hay-strewn floor, watching some kind of PowerPoint presentation on a rigged-up projector screen. Vehicles crowded around them in the barn's wings; an ambulance, the bullet-scarred Ford, others.

Wren stared. He couldn't make sense of it. Some kind of business meeting, in a barn, in, where? Iowa?

Then he recognized one of them. In the hot dark, sitting at the center of the group, the first one to rise was-

Wren almost took a step back. Not possible.

Chicago Teddy?

He wasn't big like he'd once been, before an assassin for the Order of the Saints had put a bullet in his skull nine months earlier. Last time Wren had seen him he'd been in a coma with no hope of waking any time soon. Extensive risk of brain damage, the doctors had said. Wren had arranged for the best possible care on the Foundation's tab, but feared the worst.

Now he was here. Half-bald on one side where they'd jacked open his skull, buzz cut for the rest. He had a tight goatee beard shot through liberally with gray on a Hollywood-square jaw. He looked like an oversized skeleton wearing Teddy's skin, making him more angular and somehow infused with purpose.

Wren's jaw opened, closed.

Teddy and Cheryl had led a cult of play-acting 'vampires' in Chicago's S&M scene for years, before Wren came along and put a stop to all the fun. Nobody had died by then, as they'd taken it in turns to 'bleed' each other, but that date hadn't been far off.

623

Wren's eyes roamed, and yes, there was Cheryl too, seated at Teddy's left like Mary Magdalene at the last supper. Steven Gruber was on the other side, looking unhappy. Doona was there in bandages, even Chuck too, Alejandro in a wheelchair, along with many others: Alli the scrapyard worker from Wyoming, who'd helped him bring down the Order of the Saints; his Montlake professor of film, Raymond Craik, looking severe in a Mandarin-collared shirt; his mpeg analyst, Sonny Leland, out of Houston; Marissa Brey, his Munchausen Syndrome by Proxy surgeon; then two more that were both the cherry and cream on the cake.

Hellion and B4cksl4cker. Wren blinked in disbelief. Right there at the edge, but not actually in person, as he'd first thought. Rather twin large-screen TVs had been set up atop giant cable spools, streaming live video footage of them from the waist up. The effect was uncannily impressive, like they were in the barn.

Altogether, it felt like a dream; one of those teenaged dreams he'd heard about, where you're suddenly naked in school and everybody's looking and laughing. Of course, all his dreams at high school had been nightmares about the Pyramid, but he'd seen enough TV to know the trope.

Except this was real. The sun was hot on his back. The clay was cool underfoot.

"Come in, Christopher," Teddy said, his voice a deep grind. "We're ready for you."

31

BARN

Wren entered. In the gloom he picked out more faces, more names. Members of the Foundation, gathered together. Now he saw the single chair set before them, alone, like the defendant in a kangaroo court.

"Take a seat, Christopher," Teddy said.

Wren stood by the chair. He didn't know what to feel. Anger, maybe. Perhaps pride.

"You're looking better, Teddy," he said, and let that hang for a moment. They were all staring at him. Waiting to see what he would do. Their leader, Christopher Wren, as unpredictable as ever. "Thinner, at least."

"A coma will do that to you," Teddy said. "Please, sit down."

Christopher looked at the chair, back up at his jury. "I'm not sure we have time for this. Whatever this is."

"We insist. Please take a seat."

"I prefer to stand."

Teddy looked a little put out. Wren gazed calmly at him, at the others. Putting the pieces together. Teddy opened his mouth to speak, but Wren beat him to it.

"It's an intervention. I get that, and it makes sense you'd head it up, Teddy. You always wanted a cult of your own."

Teddy looked uncomfortable. "It's not that, Christopher, it's-"

"It's what? You don't like my methods, or you're worried about my mental state?" He paused a moment, thinking both through. "You wouldn't be the first on either. I'm right there with you. I just shot Sally Rogers." He took a breath, remembering the awful moment. It didn't sit well. "That's bad, I agree. I need to pay for it, I agree. But right now, punishment can wait. Damalin Joes' life is at risk. America is at risk. My father is out there, pulling the strings." He took a breath, looking into their eyes. "I need to talk to the girl. Hunt down the Reparations and cut off their head. What else is there to discuss right now?"

Teddy looked more embarrassed than chastised. He glanced side to side; at Cheryl in her leathers, at Alli in her denim dungarees, at the hackers on their screens atop their cable spool like it was the kids' table. None offered him any support, but he didn't let that slow him down. "You *did* shoot Agent Sally Rogers. The Foundation *is* worried about your mental state. We're gathered here less as an intervention and more as a…" Teddy shifted uncomfortably. "Vote of no confidence."

Wren almost laughed. Held it in.

"Vote of no confidence. In my own Foundation?"

"Is it your Foundation, Christopher?" Teddy countered. "You don't communicate, except to make demands. You don't run coin meetings anymore. You just kill without compunction. You shot Sally Rogers." He paused. "Is this who we are? What the Foundation is for?"

Wren let that wash over him. Took a sidetrack. "Is Rogers OK?"

Teddy shifted in his seat. "When last we saw her? Yes."

"What do you mean?"

"You dropped her at a hospital five hours back." A pause. "We couldn't bring her here."

Wren looked around the barn. Farming equipment. Some old bales of cornstalks, maybe useful for composting. Tired old hoes, rakes and shovels. "Because heaven forbid she should see this place. The incredible tech you've got, I can't imagine the secrets she'd uncover."

"Christopher," Hellion said abruptly, her Slavic accent coming loud through the speakers and cutting the cozy barn vibe. "Take this seriously, yes?"

She looked bored, like she had a million better things to be doing.

"So get serious. I'm listening."

She shrugged and gestured half-heartedly off her screen. "We voted. This is Theodore's job. Listen to him."

He turned to Teddy, and Teddy took a moment, then took a breath, puffing his skeletal frame up. "We did take a vote, Christopher. About you. About your role in the Foundation."

That was worth another laugh. He'd built the Foundation with his bare hands. But he didn't laugh. He just waited for Teddy to go on.

"You see, all this began with Dr. Ferat."

That was hardly a surprise. Dr. Grayson Ferat had been one of Wren's earliest members, a professor with a penchant for exploiting the work and life experience of his students, turning them into examples in his many research papers. Wren had refocused his attentions on the Foundation fifteen years back, put him on a coin, and just three months ago Ferat had gone to his death against the Blue Fairy. He was a hero.

"Ferat's dead," he said.

"He is," Teddy allowed. "But you are aware he was rewriting the Foundation? Setting up committees, hierarchies, buddy programs, buying up properties and formalizing the coin system?"

Wren grunted. Distantly, he was aware of all that. He'd been too busy killing Pinocchios and hunting his father's trail to pay much attention.

"What you're seeing here is a natural outgrowth of that work. You remain the Foundation's head, obviously. The CEO, if you like. Charismatic leader, a man we all owe loyalty to, some of us our lives, but…" he paused. "I'm afraid that's not enough anymore."

"So what do you want?" Wren asked. He'd be more amused than angry, if it weren't for the ticking Reparations clock. "To be off the coins again?"

Teddy blinked. "Off the coins? No! Of course not."

Wren weighed Teddy's loyalty in the balance. He'd always wanted to be free of the Foundation's system of accountability, the coins. Maybe that was even fair, now. Several members of the Foundation had paid with their lives. Teddy and Cheryl had almost died, likewise Doona and Chuck. Dr. Ferat was dead. Abdul was dead. Wren had pressed many of his members into the Foundation, but he didn't want to press them to die.

It didn't leave him with much. Take it with grace, maybe.

"Then what?" he asked,

"Nobody wants off the coin system, Christopher," Teddy said, leaning forward now. "If anything, we want deeper in."

That surprised him. "What do you mean, deeper in?"

"We need training," Teddy said. "We need resources. We need to work together better if we're going to do this properly." His voice swelled. "I don't regret getting shot for you, Christopher. I'm proud of it and I'd do it again. But I want to be better prepared the next time, so I don't need to get shot. I want your skills. We all want them. We want you to train us. We want a school. We want the Foundation to have a thousand members, ten thousand members on different continents, all around the world. We want to take this thing you've built and make it bigger. You can't do that alone. You go it alone, or with untrained members," he glanced briefly toward Chuck, "and Rogers gets shot. People get hurt who shouldn't. We want to avoid that."

Wren took a breath, trying to absorb that. Deeper in. He hadn't expected any of this and didn't know what to think. To make matters worse, his side was beginning to tingle; first sign that the painkiller was wearing off.

"We also want a code of conduct. A moral system to better underlie the coins and everything we do. One that binds you as much as it binds us, because without you the Foundation falls apart." Teddy paused, "We don't want that. This group has the capacity to be a truly beautiful thing. Rehabilitation. A second chance. A way to meaningfully contribute. We simply want higher standards, for us as well as for yourself. Everyone in this barn is ready to fight, even die for this cause, if you can show us it's truly worth dying for."

Wren listened to Teddy, wondering at how fast things could change. Teddy himself was a different man than the lost, desperate soul he'd been in Chicago, living in the past and unable to see any future. Wren was changing too; he could feel it. The hunt for his father had transformed him. The loss of his family. Just moments ago he'd thought the Foundation was falling apart. Now he might be deeper in than ever.

"You want to take the Foundation bigger," he said. "And you want me to be accountable."

Teddy nodded, looking slightly relieved. "Yes, exactly that."

"And you want training," Wren summarized. "Maybe more facilities like this?" he gestured around at the barn.

Teddy smiled encouragingly. In for a penny, in for a pound, Wren figured. It was true that in the last year he'd used the Foundation in ways he'd never really anticipated. It was only fair the Foundation should change too, to accommodate that. That he should change in turn.

"OK," he said, thinking it through as he spoke. "I agree. And let's go further. You've all gathered here already, so let's formalize that by instituting a Board of Directors. Everyone here is now a member. Yes, even Chuck." He looked at Chuck, who instantly reddened. There was the slightest chuckle. "After this it can be a vote system to decide leadership, with contribution weighted by coin status." Wren focused in on the thin, shaven-headed man at the center. "Teddy, they've already elevated you, so why don't you head it up? COO, Chief Operations Officer. I can be President, partially a figurehead role, but with authority in a crisis. That's non-negotiable. I built this thing and I can't let it slip completely. As for the rest, Dr. Ferat's expansion, joint coin meetings, the buddy system? I like your ideas. Work on them."

Teddy had his palms flat on the trestle table now, as if he had to stabilize himself. Probably this was going far better than he'd expected. Maybe worried it was all a dream.

"And the camps?" he asked.

Wren considered. He'd kept a loose eye on Dr. Ferat's purchases. Eight months ago the good doctor had started buying up large, obscure properties across the States using Foundation money. Farms, mostly, but some sections of unplumbed wilderness, still scattered with dinosaur bones left untouched for millennia. They were meant to be training camps, places to learn paramilitary tactics, hacking, Neuro-Linguistic Programming, cult de-indoctrination and whatever else it took to be a good Foundation member.

Wren didn't much like it, another step taking his Foundation further into the real world, but he'd been pushing for his members to take those steps anyway. His calls to action had put them on the radar of numerous intelligence agencies. Fully establishing the physical properties would be the biggest step yet, giving the FBI a nexus to assault in the future, just like Wren had hit the Anti-Ca compound.

But still...

"Keep them," Wren said. You had to compromise. He needed to train, prep and outfit the Foundation core better if he wanted to keep calling on them. And if their expansion plans came about, taking the Foundation to a thousand members, God forbid as high as ten thousand someday, they would need a physical presence. "But keep them absolutely secret and absolutely above board. We will never have cause for a face-off with the authorities. Hellion, B4cksl4cker," he turned to them, "that's on you. Protect Dr. Ferat's legacy."

"And the coins?"

That was Chuck. Wren looked back at him. The man shouldn't even be here. But he was here. Wren looked at Teddy, playing it all out.

"You want to put me on a coin?"

Teddy glared back at him undeterred. "Coin zero, Christopher. For shooting Sally Rogers. At the edge of our tether."

Wren grimaced. Nodded.

"Coin zero. OK. But we're still in a crisis. Formalization of all these new rules and systems can wait until the immediate threat is over. Does anyone disagree?"

Wren looked around. Nobody spoke. He didn't know what he'd do if they did. Go it alone, maybe. Split the Foundation down the middle, between those loyal to him and those loyal to Teddy. Happily, no one spoke or raised their hand.

Coin zero, then, in his own organization. Wren could live with that.

Time to get back on the clock.

"Now, where's the girl from the compound?"

32

DUCKS IN A ROW

Steven Gruber was first up, handed Wren an earpiece then led him out of the barn.

"I can't believe you're even standing," he said, walking alongside as they stepped out into the swirling, dry air. Wren inserted the earpiece, heard the beep as it paired him through to Hellion and B4cksl4cker. "The doctor said-"

"Doctors are babies," Wren said, which impressed Gruber into silence but drew a snort from Hellion in his ear.

"You are baby," Hellion said. "You cannot even walk properly. Like aliens in human bodies. What movie is this, B4cksl4cker?"

"Bodysnatchers," came B4cksl4cker's voice without skipping a beat.

"Exactly, like you do not know how to use your own legs."

Wren didn't bother to answer. Rather he found himself smiling. Pain was just weakness leaving the body, after all.

"And your face, Christopher," Hellion went on, "it is hideous. Leatherface. Mr. Hyde. Yes. You will need cosmetic surgery, if you wish to be beautiful again."

"Again?" B4cksl4cker asked.

Wren tuned them out. Focused on walking through the gathering pain. Getting his ducks in a row. "Tell me how Rogers is."

"Yes, Agent Rogers," Hellion said. "We are watching her hospital. She will be fine. Soon she will be looking for you again."

Wren grunted. Of course she would. "Doona and Alejandro, are they OK?"

"Yes. Both are healthy. Alejandro lost much blood and is resting now. Doona also."

Wren thought that through. His strike team were out of action, and Rogers was off the game board for now. That brought positives as well as negatives. Director Humphreys would have to send someone else after him; somebody less effective. It bought him latitude.

"And the Reparations?"

Hellion's voice sank. "This is ugly."

He made the leap. "There's been another video, already?"

"One. It is strange. Damalin Joes having angry sex with a woman, but she is pixelated. We cannot see any details. The leader, we suspect. She calls it a reward for what he did."

Wren hadn't expected that. A reward.

"Additional, copycat videos have increased by factor of ten, on Reparations app." Keys clattered. "Highlights are, this morning four high school lacrosse players tied up their coach and pulled him apart in school parking lot. Four SUV vehicles to do this work. Apparently, coach abused two of them years ago. Claiming reparations in blood, Christopher. They filmed this, of course. They are heroes in the app now." She took a breath. "Also, there have been three mass shootings, two on country clubs that killed a dozen total, one that did not make it past lobby of Fortune 500 company. Add this to handful of hatchet attacks, and day is only half over for you. All claim for Reparations."

"Death count?" Wren growled.

"Rising toward one hundred. Your borders are closing. One man in Los Angeles Airport killed five Haitian tourists before guards shot him down, shouting about foreigners. Bomb threats are closing schools and train stations, reports of armed gangs roaming streets, some video. Police are activated but avoiding full pitch battle."

"People are going crazy," Gruber contributed from by Wren's side. "Like hell just opened up."

"America's on the boil," Wren said softly.

"Old crimes," B4cksl4cker said in his ear. "Hashtag Reparations. Up-

632

votes for videos on this app hit ten million within minutes. People around all world are enjoying this and cheering. It is best entertainment yet, 'great Satan' America finally consuming itself."

Wren stepped up onto the porch deck, thinking hard. He'd set a lot of plates spinning before heading into the Anti-Ca compound: likely Hellion had kept on top of the results.

"Anything on a location for the arena?"

"Nothing definitive," she answered. "We are constructing data ghosts. Models of potentials, but this is all guesswork. We need more hard details."

Wren worked the possibilities. Data ghosts and details. "How many prospective targets have you got?"

"Based on an oval space, tiered seating, filled with sand? Almost zero, Christopher. Two that we have found, by algorithm searching satellite map data. One, a private volleyball court. Two, a rich man's reconstruction of a Roman colosseum. But it is not these. There have been no movements near them for many months. We have live satellite data."

Wren grunted. "What about hacking the app?"

"We are working on it, but it is embedded deeply. FBI chatter says US President is considering total shutdown of all communications; Internet, phone, television, while Army and National Guard flood in and secure streets, institute lockdown and daylight curfew."

"They are panicking," said B4cksl4cker.

Wren thought it sounded like a good move. It was what he would say to Humphreys, if Humphreys would take his call now. Absolute quarantine. Take the poison out of people's hands. Without this app driving them on, the heat would abate. But with Rogers removed from the loop, he knew Humphreys would never listen to him. There'd be no 'catch' anymore. Only 'kill'.

It all came down to needing more data. It came down to the girl.

Gruber held the fly screen open. "She's upstairs," he said, "but she's refusing to say a word."

Wren pushed through the door. Just like the Pinocchios before her, she'd speak for him.

33

JESSICA

Climbing the stairs made Wren's whole side ache. At the top Gruber led him to a bedroom door with a crudely screwed-in bolt-bar.

"She's angry," he warned, slotting a key into the padlock. "Last time she tried to club me with a bed slat."

"She succeeded," Hellion corrected in Wren's ear.

"Open it," Wren said. Gruber did, looking unhappy. Now Wren saw the welt on his forehead.

She came at him like a jack-in-the-box. Must've been waiting there all along. As soon as the door swung inward, she lunged through with a sharp length of wood held out like a spear.

Wren slapped the wood away and scooped her up like a puppy. She screamed. Wren carried her back into a room that had been thoroughly wrecked; bed stripped, walls scored, furniture smashed. He deposited her on the edge of the bed and kneeled before her, holding her wrists firmly and shackling her legs with his elbows.

"Cut that nonsense out," he said softly. "We've been through this already." She tried to bite his face. "And that. You'll hurt the baby."

She went to headbutt him, then cursed long and loud as he leaned just out of reach.

"What are you, eight months along?" he asked calmly. Her eyes flashed. "You're ready to pop any minute. Tell me, have you picked out a name?"

The cursing slowed. She hadn't expected that.

"It's a girl, right?" Wren pressed on, keeping her off balance. Her eyes froze a second, and Wren corrected. "No, a boy. I've got one of each myself. I don't get to see them much. It's a tragedy, but I'm learning to take responsibility." He gazed calmly into her eyes, seeing a lifetime's worth of anger coming hard on the shame of her earlier admission. The best way to get through that was to slip around the side.

"That's the first thing you feel when you become a parent," he said, "the weight of responsibility. You can't imagine it until it comes, then, bam, it's all on you. This tiny life in your hands. All her prospects, all her hopes, they begin with you on day one and they never stop." He paused a moment, looking at her. There was fear in her eyes now, driving the rage. "If you start being responsible now, maybe you can steer this child to make better choices. She needn't end up in a suicide cult gargling a potassium-cyanide cocktail."

She strained against him again but was unable to budge in his firm grip.

"Now, we're going to talk. Last night you told me you were present at the arena. I need you calm and talking about that right now. I need it all. Short me and I'll know. You won't like what happens next."

She spat in his face. Not pleasant, but a waste of time. He wiped his face on her shoulder once more. "So think about this. I shot my own partner to get you out of there. You think I'll be nicer to you?"

"I'm not helping you," she snapped.

Better. At least now she was talking. "You already are. So let's come at it from this angle. Your compound, Anti-Ca, you all went to the Reparations arena. You already told me that; you were the audience. Was it by bus or plane?" She just stared. "OK. We'll work up to it. What interests me now is the cyanide. The orange juice. You knew about the order to commit group suicide. I'm even thinking you might've placed a call for help, soon as you heard about it. Was that you?" He saw the guilt flash across her eyes. Bingo. He'd picked the right person in the chaos of that safe room. "OK, you did. But you stayed anyway. Why?"

She went abruptly still. Wren felt the difference in his gut, like she was a suicide bomber about to pull the pin. The shame of her battlefield confession was shutting her down and her eyes were emptying out, like she'd just become a ghost.

He pulled back, not enough room to launch another headbutt attack, but room to breathe. Took ten seconds then carried on. "What's your name?"

She stared blankly back at him. Wren turned to Gruber.

"Jessica," he said.

"Jessica," Wren repeated, running those dizzy moments in the Anti-Ca compound through his mind again. A room full of dead bodies. The others just waiting for their turn. "That suicide order was about me, Jessica. You know that, right? They told you to die because they knew I was coming, and they wanted you dead, so all the evidence was cleaned up." She flinched slightly. "Your own leaders wanted you to die just to shut me down, and you wouldn't be the first. I think that's disgusting. They valued you and your baby less than their mission. Why don't you think about that for a minute?"

Her eyes widened slightly. Wren plunged on.

"Think about what that says about them, and about me. I would never tell you to kill yourself. I'd never tell you to kill your own baby." Her eyes began to shine with tears. Anger, confusion, shock. "They're playing a game here, Jessica, and to them you're a pawn, easy to sacrifice. Help me stop them before too many other pawns die." He gazed steadily into her eyes. "I know you believe in your message. The rich need to pay for their crimes, I'm one hundred percent behind that, but this is something else. For the people behind these videos, your movement is just a tool. They're not trying to save America; they're trying to destroy it."

A tear spilled down her cheek. He could feel the emotions burning inside her.

"But you made that telephone call, asking for help. You didn't drink the poison when I told you to. It's because you want to live, and you want your baby to live. So live, Jessica. Tell me how I can stop them. Tell me where the arena is."

In one smooth movement he let go and backed away, leaving her bowed protectively over her belly on the edge of the bed. Teary and red-eyed, staring at the sharp slat that lay on the floor.

"Wren," Gruber cautioned.

Wren ignored him.

"Jessica," he said. "It's a beautiful name. It comes from the Hebrew,

636

'Yiskah', which means foresight. Now it's time to live up to your name, Jessica. Show me what you really are."

He waited. For long moments she didn't budge. Deep processes turning inside. Maybe five minutes passed before she looked up, her eyes still red but intent.

"So ask your questions."

34

QUESTIONS

Wren dropped to one knee, closer to her eye level. "I need to know where that arena is, Jessica. I need to know anyone you saw there."

"I don't know where it is," she answered. "They put us on a bus from the compound, told us we were going to make history, but we had to wear blindfolds."

"Blindfolds? For how long?"

"For the whole trip. It was really uncomfortable. I think I fell asleep, at one point. So I don't know how long it took."

That didn't help any. A duration of travel would at least give Wren a search radius. Still, there were other ways of telling time. "So tell me what you know. Was it light when you left? Dark when you arrived?"

She thought for a second, eyes rolling up and to the left, accessing memory. "We left around noon, after lunch. I don't know if it was dark when we arrived. We wore the blindfolds even when we got off, until we were indoors."

"OK. We'll come back to that, but let's stick with the bus for now. Did they feed you while you were traveling? Were you hungry when you got off?"

She thought for a moment. "They didn't feed us on the bus. I was hungry, yes."

"How hungry?"

"Really bad. It woke me up."

"Painful? Like a knife in your stomach?"

She countered fast, like a tennis game. "Not that bad. Just hungry."

Wren estimated the hours. Less than sixteen, when hunger pangs really kicked in. More than eight, enough to wake you up. It gave a rough range of six hundred to one thousand five hundred miles, traveling at an average of sixty miles per hour. He had to narrow that range down.

"Did your legs hurt afterward? Pins and needles when you got off?"

She smiled, like she'd caught him out. "They hurt all the time. I'm eight months pregnant. Answer me this: how will you get me to a hospital, here?"

Wren countered just as fast. "We have a doctor here, better than whatever you had in that compound, I promise. Now." He started down a different track. "Tell me about faces. Who did you see?"

"I didn't see anyone. Not once. They all wore those white suits, like in the videos."

"Even when you arrived at the compound?"

"I didn't see them until we were in the arena. Only our leader actually talked to them."

"Where's your leader now?"

She barked a single laugh. "You broke his jaw. In the safe room."

Wren remembered. One elbow in the chin. He hadn't really seemed like leadership material, but you never knew.

"OK. So give me numbers; how many of them did you see up close?"

"I don't know. In the arena? Maybe two came close."

"Voices? Men or women?"

"They barely spoke. I don't remember."

"How many total then? In the video it looked like a dozen, plus perhaps a dozen more in various production roles."

"I don't know." She rubbed her belly. "Yes, maybe."

"OK. So walk me through the process from the bus to the arena. Were you outdoors when you got off the bus?"

She frowned. "I don't think so. It was cold, and echoey. Like an underground parking lot? There was the sound of a metal door coming down, like they were sealing us in."

"A loading bay," Wren murmured. "OK. What next?"

"They led us to a waiting room."

"Still in your blindfolds?"

"Yes."

"A long distance? All indoors?"

"What does that matter?"

"I'm trying to get a handle on the size of this place. So they take you to a waiting room. How big is it, how many people, and how long are you there?"

Her eyes narrowed. "Big. Like, a football field? It looked like a warehouse, bare walls, concrete. Um, there were a lot of people. You saw the video. They kept bringing more people in. We guessed it was other Anti-Ca cells, more coaches coming. Thousands, I think. I, uh…"

"This is all good. Good details, Jessica. Keep going. How long were you there?"

She gave a shy smile. First sign of trust. "Well, I don't know. There was no clock. They did feed us."

"Feed you what? How many times?"

"There was a buffet. I went up twice, I think. Also, I slept."

Wren tallied the facts. "So you're in one long hall. Did you see other halls?"

"I don't think so. But I don't know for sure."

Wren smiled. "I know you don't. Don't worry about that, I'm not trying to test you on things you don't know. Let's stick to your experience. Talk to me about transit to the arena from the hall. How did that happen?"

"They told us to put our blindfolds back on."

That was curious. "Oh? Why? Did they take you outside?"

"I don't know why. I don't think we went outside until the arena. Just, walking along corridors."

"How was it, cold, hot?" Wren tried to put himself in her shoes. "Did you feel the sun on your skin? Did the sound change as you walked along, like wood, or concrete? How did it feel underfoot?"

"I don't, uh… Hmm." Her tongue poked between her lips. "It was hard floors all the time, like concrete. Echoey, even when we were in the arena. I didn't feel the sun, at least, not until later."

"So the hall was connected to the arena," Wren confirmed. "This sounds like a large building. Especially if there were other holding halls. Describe the arena to me. Going in."

"I didn't see it going in. They didn't let us take off our blindfolds for a while."

"For how long?"

"I don't know. Maybe twenty minutes? They were directing us to empty seats. It was hot, but stuffy, you know."

"It was stuffy?"

"Right. Humid. They gave several warnings about the blindfolds. One guy took his off, they weren't happy about that. I think they escorted him out."

Wren considered. "Why do you think that was? You were already in the arena. What was the big deal?"

"I don't know." A pause. "Maybe they just wanted to keep the surprise."

Wren chewed his lip. "So then you took the blindfold off."

"Right," she began, then paused, and briefly a smile played on her face. "It was so strange. We were in this kind of Roman arena, but there was popcorn being handed out, beer, even hotdogs. The atmosphere was great, like we were at a ball game. There were people in the haz-mat suits coming up and down the tiers, handing us stuff. They even gave me a beer."

"They wanted you relaxed. A better response to the show. Did you drink?"

She laughed. "I'm not an idiot. I had a hotdog. Someone gave me a big foam hand."

"Dressing the set," Wren murmured. "So they've got you set up. Getting drunk, eating, like a ball game."

"Yes. But first there was another announcement; something about keeping all this a secret. How important for the cause it was. We were lucky, we were going to see the start of a new revolution. Get ready for amazing special effects, they said."

That caught Wren's attention. "Special effects?"

"Right," said Jessica. "About what came next."

Wren said nothing, just looked at her. What came next was the brutal murder of a man, followed by cheering. Perhaps she saw some of that suspicion in his eyes, because her expression soured.

"Wait. You think we thought it was real?"

Wren said nothing, didn't need to, just waited as her sour expression lapsed into anger. "No, of course we didn't! They told us it was a show, a special effects extravaganza, why would we not believe that?"

641

Wren just watched her. This was straining credibility. "Special effects."

"Yes!"

There was no point lingering on it. Either she'd known it was a man dying or she hadn't. "OK. So did you see anything else? Any buildings or mountains on the horizon?"

Jessica wasn't done. "Wait a second, you really thought we wanted that man to die? You thought we were cheering that he actually died?"

Wren eyed her. "We watched the video, Jessica, and we saw crowds cheering. Thousands of people. Of course we believed it."

"Right, but they lied to us! They just tried to make us kill ourselves. Don't you believe me now?"

He looked in her eyes, and the outrage seemed real. "I do. So let's figure this out. Could you see anything outside the arena?"

It took her a second, swallowing her anger. "No. I just saw the arena. It was so bright. It was breezy. The sky was blue, no clouds, and the sun was hot. People were everywhere. The walls were all stone, you know that from the video, and there was all that sand at the bottom. It pretty much started after that."

"The brought the billionaires out?"

"Yes. It all happened fast. Minutes only. We didn't even know who they were at first, just naked men, until the big screens started showing close-ups. I figured they were lookalikes, but it still felt good to see them laid low, humiliated. It made for a carnival atmosphere, like we were already celebrating a victory."

"So it happened fast. Soon they're on the sand, they're circling up."

"Right, then they hammered the big guy. It was horrible; but people near me were laughing. I just figured, yeah, it's not real. Special effects. This is the show, so go along with it. I even started to cheer."

Wren nodded. Helping her shed the guilt, as it would only get in the way. "You couldn't know it was real. You didn't know what was coming."

She stared back at him. "I didn't. None of us did. I may hate the one percent, but I'm not an animal."

"So they kill him. Then…?"

She swallowed. 'So they kill him' glossed over a lot, but Wren saw nothing to gain in digging in deeper. "Then that was it. Blindfolds back on, we were out of there in minutes. The event was over. They escorted us to the holding area, then the bus back."

Wren rocked back on his knee, one hand on his chin and picking through the story. There were clues, but not enough. Lots of buses arriving at different times from different Anti-Ca compounds. A large complex anywhere between eight to sixteen hours' drive away, directly connected to an open-air arena.

Except the arena couldn't be open-air. B4cksl4cker had said as much. Even a movie set arena would take time to assemble. That much sand, that scale of tiered seating, all that fake stone; even if it was just polystyrene sprayed gray, it would take at least a day to build, maybe more. You couldn't fake sand. Satellite overwatch updated constantly and would have seen it.

Wren spun back through Jessica's answers. The Reparations video was long, but much of that was the buildup and editing tricks. Actual raw footage of the arena in daylight, with the crowd roaring? Less than fifteen minutes. Easily short enough to evade crisscrossing satellites above. Timed, perhaps, to perfectly avoid being seen…

"Jessica," he said, leaning in, "this is important. You said 'breezier' earlier, after you took the blindfold off. Before that you said the arena was stuffy. What did you mean?"

She looked at him for a long moment. Thinking. "Stuffy, like a car parked in the sun."

"Hot. Like contained heat."

"Right. And then, yes. It was just breezier. I don't know. Maybe they turned the fans on."

Wren was on it now. Bigger than he'd considered. The scale of planning. "Did you hear fans?"

"Uh, I don't think so. No."

There it was. The key to unlock the data ghost. Only one way to explain it.

He stood. "You've been very helpful. Thank you, Jessica. The others will take care of you. Welcome to the Foundation, if you want it, coin one."

Striding down the stairs and out over the dusty clay, Wren's heart thumped hard. Rage rushed through him at what they'd done to Jessica, twisting a pregnant woman's mind so she'd come this close to killing herself. There were no words for how disgusting it was. He looked up and after-images of the Anti-Ca's dead children flashed across the baking sky, bubbles at their lips, forced to drink poison, and for what?

For some half-baked, anarchist vision of reparations. For what could only be the Apex's mad design, luxuriating in bringing America down. Just another psychotic game for his father to play with innocent lives.

By the time he stamped into the barn his limbs were trembling with fury. His new 'Board' were spread around the shadows, working on laptops or phones, but all eyes flashed up as he stormed into their midst.

"The arena was not open to the air," he announced, his head spinning through the possibilities. "I'm thinking they built it under a huge tarpaulin, in a large, roofless structure, then pulled the cover back just long enough to evade satellite overwatch." A pause, and his eyes beaded on them one by one. "How many completely flat roofs of that size went up in the last few months, within a six-hundred to fifteen-hundred-mile radius of the Anti-Ca compound? We're looking for at least two large adjoining halls, one with loading bay doors. Maybe a derelict factory or warehouse. They built their arena inside it like a cuckoo's egg in the nest. Do whatever it takes, use whatever assets you need, but find me that arena!"

The Foundation stared back at him. He touched one hand to his earpiece.

"Hellion, B4cksl4cker?"

"Yes, Christopher," Hellion answered.

"We're going to fight fire with fire. I want a line into the Reparations' app, and the means to make a video go viral. Can you do that?"

A second passed. "Yes, this is possible. We cannot shut it down, but we can manipulate it. What video?"

Wren was already ten moves ahead. "Our own. We're going to livestream my attack on the arena. The people want reparations for past crimes? I'm going to show them what real justice looks like. We'll need cameras, drones, hundreds of thousands of eyeballs prepped and watching. Can you get our feed into the Reparations app, boost it viral so their whole audience sees it?"

The sound of keys clattering came from Hellion's end. "This is possible. We will do it."

"And get me through to Humphreys at the CIA. He won't want to take the call, not after Rogers, but force it. I'm going to need his help to pull this off. If we fail to stop these videos, he needs to be ready to kill-switch the Internet. Turn it off at the source, shut down the Internet Service Providers and clamp the trans-oceanic pipelines, or just snatch peoples' phones out of their hands. Whatever it takes."

"Understood. Working, Christopher."

He took a breath. Hopped up on the surging pain and rage. He focused in on Teddy, standing thin as a grim reaper at the center of the barn. One more order he could give, since this was an accelerating crisis.

"I want Foundation members across the country ready to mobilize, if all else fails. Set up stings on the biggest Internet Providers, take out cell towers, masts, server arrays, as many as we can. If we can't stop this infection cold, then we slow it down." He took a breath, looking around at his team. His Foundation core. "This is everything. You asked for responsibility and a larger role, so here it is. I trust you with my life. Now fire me at these bastards as hard as you can. We're going to hammer them into the damn sand."

35

FOURTH

The fourth Reparations video came while Wren was in the air, an Eclipse 550 microjet after hopping a Bell 429-7 helicopter pick-up from the farm. Forty-thousand feet high and heading south-east at four hundred miles-per-hour, tracking the best intel Hellion and B4cksl4cker had yet produced on the arena.

Wren hunched over his phone in the expansive jet's seat, light flooding in through the window, he held up his phone. With only a blister pack of over-the-counter painkillers for company, he hit play and watched the video began.

It began with a raised stage festooned with American flags. The seven remaining billionaires stood in designer suits at seven lecterns, like this was some kind of political debate. Damalin Joes III stood at the center, a vast man in a tailored suit that made him look powerful, sharp and rugged at the same time.

The other billionaires flanked him like spokes in a wheel, Geert Fothers the oilman, Cem Babak the arms trader, Inigo De Luca and the rest. A voice was speaking, describing the format for the 'debate'. Each of the men would be given five minutes to make their case why they should be allowed to survive, and why the others should die.

At the end of the brief announcements, a wooden cart was brought out by haz-mats, cloaked with black velvet fabric. Its wheels squeaked noisily as they pulled it up a ramp to the stage. They left it in the center, every billionaire straining to see, then pulled off the velvet.

Beneath lay the price of failure. A large wooden block with a curved dip in one edge. A long-handled axe. A black hood. All the equipment you needed for an execution by decapitation.

Wren's mouth went dry. It was outrageous but compelling, and fully visible to everybody watching. Like a high-stakes political debate for the Presidency, twisted to some kind of Russian roulette. In response, the vote tallies began to spin like the dials on a casino slot machine.

Wren checked the viewership count. Hundreds of millions and rising. The billionaires' names danced in the ranking box like a stream of shells ejected from an autocannon, Joes then Babak then De Luca then Joes again.

The debate began. Opening arguments, it seemed, five minutes each. The billionaires took it in violent, raucous turn to rip each other to shreds, calling out hypocrisy after hypocrisy as reasons the others should die and they should live: murders they'd spent millions to cover up; countless rapes and abuses they'd buried with lawyers and NDAs; thousands of innocents crushed underfoot; thousands of careers destroyed out of spite, of rival companies decimated, of wars begun and ended in the name of personal profit.

The wages of corporate capitalism flowing unchecked.

It was sick, unmissable viewing. At various points tears erupted in self-pity, in anger, in attempts to elicit sympathy. Soon they moved from opening arguments to questions tossed by some unseen female moderator, focused variously on their contributions to humanity, their value to friends and family, their plans on how to use their billions for the betterment of America.

The billionaires wrung themselves out, turning red-faced to make promises and vie for trust, while still getting punches in on their competitors wherever they could. It was a verbal bloodbath. A fistfight broke out at one point, only broken by haz-mats with cattle prods, leaving two men with bloodied faces and rumpled ties. The onslaught of questions and answers went on regardless, guilty men roaring out vile accusations and proclaiming lie-filled promises, only to have vile accusations leveled their way in turn, with greater lies promised at each turn.

Only Damalin Joes III somehow managed to stay above the fray, as he had every time before. It was incredible to behold, as he held the center by diving into the filth and embracing it. He was indeed vile, he boasted proudly in his five-minute speech. A grotesque man. Yes, he'd done all the things they were accusing him of. He was proud of it. But that was the American way. The strong survive. The weak die. Forget decency, forget kindness, forget being 'polite'. He was not his brother's keeper. Human nature was red in tooth and claw, and if you wanted to succeed, you had to prove you were worth it. If you wanted to succeed, you had to be strong like him.

It wasn't the Damalin Joes Wren had come to know on his superyacht, during their week of interrogations en route back to the US. That Damalin Joes had been a ruthless man, but not blind to the negative impact of his choices, not trying to convince others they were the true American way. It certainly wasn't the man Joes had been in the process of becoming, with the coin system propelling him toward charitable actions to benefit his fellow man.

This was a new Damalin Joes III. A Joes who radiated power, a man who'd blossomed within a very different system to the coins, one that catered only to strength. In this system violence was survival, and Joes had been an adaptive chameleon all his life. This was just his latest iteration, like a brand-new smartphone with a killer new app.

The people loved it.

The vote counters swung his way hard by the end of the debate. His unapologetic stance and powerful demeanor spoke volumes, where the others crawled and apologized desperately, abasing themselves in their own shame.

Damalin Joes stood cool and calm. When the time elapsed, and the vote counting ended, it hardly seemed important who had actually lost the 'debate'. Rather all eyes were on Joes' massive bulk, his swarthy face, waiting for their new winner to proclaim the loser. Longing for more billionaire blood.

Like the judge on a reality show sending one contestant home, Joes extended one long arm slowly, riding the wave of anticipation, until it could no longer be in doubt who he'd selected.

Cem Babak.

It wasn't the popular choice. The voting tallies had selected Inigo De Luca, but in the moment it didn't matter.

Babak realized it and ran.

De Luca was first to give chase. The rest fell over themselves to follow, and the cameras raced after them; shoulder-mounts held by jogging hazmat operators, crane-cam gliding smoothly in, boom-operators racing to keep pace through the wires and detritus of the set's backstage. Crosscuts captured every detail in crystal-clear 4K with stereo sound, as five billionaires ran down one of their own.

Babak fell to a flying tackle from De Luca. He rolled and briefly tried to fight back, then the others descended and the destruction began, beating one of their own with all their strength, too terrified for their lives to do any less. The cameras and microphones caught every thud and cry.

Joes alone waited on the stage, holding court like a king.

"Enough," he boomed at last, a thundering bass that carried impressively through Wren's phone, and the beating ended. Babak lay still, just about dead already. "Bring him."

They dragged him like a dead dog. Joes stood still as a statue as they came, executioner's axe in hand. The cameras pushed in as Babak's eyes flickered faintly, capturing his recognition of what was about to happen. He made fleeting efforts to resist, but he was weak. They laid him before the wooden block, where he flattened to the stage like a deflated balloon.

"Hold him up," Joes commanded.

Again De Luca was first, lifting Babak and forcing his head onto the block. Geert Fothers the oilman helped. Joes took up position. He solemnly pulled on the executioner's hood then raised the axe. The studio went absolutely silent. Every eye craned forward. The cameras flowed right up to the stage, as desperate as the millions around the world to truly see.

"For your crimes," Joes said, and brought the axe down.

It was a clean stroke. Babak's head rocketed clear and tumbled noisily off the stage. His body went limp. The screen flashed to black.

YOU ARE OWED REPARATIONS

CLAIM THEM TONIGHT

The Internet went crazy after that.

Wren was left in shock. The impact was so stunning he watched the tail end of the video a second time, and still felt like he'd been sucker punched in the gut. As a work of populism it was incredible. He'd never seen anything like it. The power of it was entrancing. The effect it would have...

The familiar chill grip of fear rushed up his spine. Turn the billionaires against their own. Debase their humanity until they were nothing but animals scrabbling for survival. Turn the rewards of capitalism on their head, make raw might seem more moral rather than reason, and give permission to any and every worst instinct the people had.

It was genius, and Damalin Joes III was their perfect avatar. In all, it was incredibly destructive.

Wren intended to respond in kind. He switched off the video and made the necessary call.

36

HUMPHREYS

"I'm going to kill you, Wren."

Gerald Humphreys, newly minted Director of the CIA, sounded nothing like the man Wren had known. In the echoing cabin of the Eclipse jet it sounded as if he too had been transformed by Damalin Joes' performance. The Reparations were working their alchemy on the minds of everyone in the country, turning neighbor against neighbor, ally against ally.

"Tell me you're going to take their phones," Wren said, ignoring the threat and diving right in. Hellion and B4cksl4cker had been working for hours to get the CIA Director on the line, and Wren didn't intend to waste a second. "Every phone, every house, every apartment in every city, you need to cut the flow of this poison before nightfall. It's going to be a bloodbath."

Nothing had come for a moment other than heavy breathing.

"I read your file again," Humphreys said, his rage transmuting to ice. "It's all there, every sign of this megalomania, narcissism, trumped-up self-righteousness. James Tandrews spoke up for you, but he was a fool, like I've been a fool too. Thinking maybe we could wield you like some blunt weapon; our own pet cult leader, fight fire with fire." A pause. "We were arrogant fools. I don't care anymore if you're on our side or not. You're as much a poison as these videos. You're broken, Wren, and you cannot be fixed. I hate you for it."

"I-"

"You shot Agent Rogers. You dumped her at some country hospital. It was-"

"I'll pay for that. Arrest me when it's over. Right now it brought us a lead."

Humphreys barked a laugh; disbelief. "Arrest you when it's over? How much damage will you cause before you decide it's over? And it bought you a lead? In what world, you mad fool, is it acceptable to shoot your partner to get a 'lead'? She was the only person arguing for you! The only thing keeping us from unleashing every contract killer and mercenary in the world to hunt you down. And you shot her!"

Wren took a breath. This wasn't helping him or Humphreys. The Director was going to hyperventilate if he climbed any higher.

"The bill comes due at the end, Humphreys. We are all going to pay, myself included. Now stop grandstanding like you're a man of moral fiber and listen. This last video, it puts a clock on the Reparations. America explodes tonight if you don't take immediate steps to shut this app down. You need to activate every agent, officer, soldier, militia member you can. We need an overwhelming flood of bodies out there, switching off Internet lines and taking phones and computers right now. Do this or face total anarchy."

Humphreys' laughed sounded crazed. "Take every phone? Shut down the ISPs? Have you any idea how massive a logistical task that is? You're mad, Christopher. Really, I admire it."

"You didn't listen to me about the Blue Fairy. Listen to me now."

"It's impossible!" Humphreys crowed. "You're talking about hundreds of millions of phones alone, billions of SIM cards, and all the computers too? There are Internet-capable devices everywhere! You may as well ask me to go strip every American naked at once. It can't be done!"

"Then you better get started right now," Wren said, uncompromising. "You saw the debate video. It's a kind of propaganda attack we are not equipped for. There is no antidote but to crush it completely."

The laughter turned darker now. "Oh, Christopher Wren. You've done this to me. First Agent Rogers, now me. I just became Director. You're going to cost me everything."

"It's not me doing this. Start activating teams right now. I'm tracking the Reparations; I have a lead and I'm heading now to stop the flow of footage, but you need to be ready in case I fail. The copycats are the real threat."

Humphreys' tone changed abruptly at that, like a sailor glimpsing land through the storm. "You've found them?"

"I've found something. Maybe the arena."

"Where is it?"

"I'll let you know." A pause then as he ran calculations, deciding how much to share. "New Mexico. My team did some analyses on satellite data. I need boots on the ground, but they'll have to follow my command without question. A helicopter strike squad, six Marines minimum, on standby in El Paso. Can you do that?"

Humphreys was bewildered. "Wait, now you're actually asking me for a team?"

"Get me a team or I go in alone, and we'll see how that shakes out. Probably you should have missiles on standby, a couple of Patriots out of White Sands base should do it. I'll release the coordinates when I'm on-site; blow me up if you like." A pause. "Don't overthink this, Humphreys. Order me the team, set the missiles and focus on building an army to quarantine this app." He checked the time until nightfall. "Can you be ready in seven hours?"

It took Humphreys five gaping seconds to get his feet back under him. "You really think it's coming apart tonight?"

"I think it's coming apart right now. Nightfall is the deadline when there's no going back. Take all that we've seen so far and ten-x it. Multiply it by a hundred. We're facing an all-out purge, the poor against the rich, and I don't think anyone's going to pull their punches after seeing that video. They want what they think's their due, and they won't stop until they have satisfaction. We have to make them stop." He took a breath. "Now focus. We're at the sharp end of an exponential curve here; things are only going to speed up from this moment, and you have to be ready."

A silence.

"I'll put it to the President."

"Not enough," Wren snapped. "You head the CIA. Send the order right now. Lead by example and get your people moving, that's a hundred thousand agents and support staff, plenty to begin with. The other agencies will follow."

"But I-"

"Forget about holding onto your Directorship if you don't get this right. The country will be in revolutionary pieces, nothing left to Direct. Now get me that team."

He killed the line, sat for a moment staring out the jet's oval window as intermittent chimes rang from his phone; notifications about fresh #Reparations atrocities. Far below, three hundred thirty million petty rages were transmuting to action. The Reparations videos blazed a trail around logic, reason and any sense of proportion, allowing blind animal rage to roar through the gaps. Building the chaos his father had always thrived on.

It would feel good. Reparations for so many crimes. Wren willed the jet on faster.

37

FACTORY

In two hours Wren was there, a silicon chip factory.

Abandoned in the late nineties, busted down and dilapidated, circled by a half-hearted barb wire fence. Wren stood on the sand a mile out, southwest corner of New Mexico near the town of Antelope Wells, barely across the border.

The air was bitterly dry and hot like an oven, enough to gum your eyelids to your eyes. His rental Jeep ticked at his side as the radiator tried to cool the engine and failed; the air had no room to vent the heat. Baked yellow sand skirled by his feet; no rainfall here for a generation, it felt. Barely any cacti, pampas grass, scrub. A no-man's-land, nothing alive, perfect for the hermetically sealed environment required to manufacture precision-grade silicon chips.

This was the place, no doubt.

The factory lay ahead like a wrecked ship's hulk. Decrepit, twenty years out of business and showing its age in tarnish, rust and sun bleach. The parking lot was coated with sand; a few burned-out vehicles dotted here and there beneath defunct security lamps. 5 p.m. in the afternoon and not a hint of movement but for white blinds shifting in a low wind through the broken office windows.

The structures Jessica had described were all there: a huge warehouse with three elevated loading bays, each sealed shut; a huge roofless factory structure, called a 'fab' according to B4cksl4cker, five hundred yards of windowless metal siding stretching into the desert, big enough to fit the arena within it; a low office building that linked the two, corporate logo reduced to plastic shards on the ground, double door entryway devoid of glass.

Hellion spoke in his ear, and Wren half-listened. Apparently records showed the factory had shut its doors years ago, thanks to competition from China. Globalization. Outsourcing. Automation. The age-old enemies of the average working Joe, together with billionaires making up the four horsemen of the apocalypse for small-town middle America.

It made sense.

"This plan is reckless," Hellion said in his ear.

Wren said nothing. No way to be subtle with only five hours left on the countdown clock he'd given Humphreys, before the United States turned on its own people and started snatching up computers and phones.

Going reckless was the plan.

He brought up a pair of 10x42 USCAMEL binoculars, and a twinge of pain ran down his left side, threatening to drop him flat. He grunted, consciously slowed down his movements. This was nerve damage from the grenade shrapnel, he figured. Some surgery and a few hours in bed wouldn't fix something like that.

Instead he blinked and shook his head, trying to clear it. The pain was bad, walking was just getting harder and generic painkillers wouldn't cut it anymore. With every step stitches pulled tight down his left side, bleeding in pinprick stars through a new black shirt. When he opened his mouth, his left cheek sweated blood. He'd hoped to do this cold turkey and clear-headed, but that didn't seem possible anymore. Pretty soon he'd struggle just to walk.

He reached into the Jeep for medication and came back with two prescription bottles. From the first he popped a white oxycodone pill, swigged water, swallowed, then chased it with a tabs of methylphenidate; basically crystal meth, but the same thing they used as a stimulant for ADHD kids.

And they said the country had a drug problem. He slammed another swallow of water, and the hit came quickly: pain relief, a sharpening of the senses and a parting of the fog, plus some mild euphoria. Basically the same stuff they'd given to soldiers in Vietnam: wired for the kill. Add some antipsychotic chlorpromazine for the stress and guilt and he'd have the full GI cocktail.

The effects kicked in swiftly. The pain washed back; an intense sense of focus rolled in. He steadied himself and raised the binoculars again to his eyes.

"This is only clear match," B4cksl4cker had said hours earlier, back when he'd been on the helicopter off the farm. "Nothing else on radar similar."

"Talk me through it."

"It is simple satellite image search," B4cksl4cker answered. "Same as we searched for golden eye of sand, the arena. I program algorithm to search for roofs of certain size, all one color, on flat angle."

"You can program for the angle?"

"It is shadows, Christopher. Flat roofs have certain shadow. Inclined roofs have different one. Our tarpaulin will be flat, as walls of arena are same height."

Wren grunted.

"After that it is comparisons. There are many large flat roofs in your country: warehouses, offices, malls, fulfillment centers. It is not as distinctive as sand arena, but how many buildings like this were built in last few months?"

"Within fifteen hundred miles? Dozens, I expect."

"Correct. How many in isolated areas, on top of old factories?"

"Not many."

"Just one," B4cksl4cker said. "It fits our proportions."

He walked Wren through the factory's closure, the 'clean' fabrication rooms left behind that were easily large enough to accommodate the arena, and the white suits workers had to wear. "They are called 'bunny suits', Christopher, for ultra-clean environment."

Wren had grunted. Full-body white 'bunny suits' that looked just like hazardous materials disposal uniforms. The clues had been right there from the start. The haz-mat suits weren't a coincidence.

Somebody was trying to make a point

"What have you got on this factory?"

"Schematics. Looks like kids got into large fabrication room, or 'fab', after factory was abandoned, and burned it in the early 2000s. There was no roof after this."

"Surrounding buildings?"

"Two. One, large warehouse with underground levels to keep chips cool. Much concrete flooring, connected to the fab through office block. No need to go outside, plus several loading bay doors; everything the Anti-Ca girl described."

"Jessica."

"Yes."

"And the woman? The one Damalin Joes was having sex with in video three? You said she seemed to be the leader."

"Yes. We are still scrubbing our databases. It is like digging fossil out of rock; you start with jackhammers and dynamite then graduate to toothbrush. There is not much to see on in sex video, pixilated. The Foundation has collected long lists of rejects from film-school, dropouts with canceled streaming accounts, some Anti-Ca propagandists. Coming from the other angle, there were many techs on staff at chip factory with daughters; some would have been teens when the place shuttered."

"That's a prime age for radicalization," Wren said.

"Yes. We are cross-referencing records."

"Good. And mass movements of buses to this place?"

"We are winding back satellite record. We already know the Reparations are good at evading overwatch. As far as we can see, not one vehicle has gone near this place in last six months. One day two months back black tarpaulin roof went up, but nothing since. No people, no movement."

Nothing since.

Wren dialed the binoculars on the factory. Three buildings, pretty much what he'd expected. He tracked the path Jessica and the others must have taken from the left to the right. Pull into the warehouse on the bus while the sky was clear of satellites. Stay in its concrete depths for a time while other buses arrived, completely sealed-in with a buffet table for food, then blindfolds back on for the trek through the offices in the middle. Last they went into the arena, built inside the walls of the fab.

The billionaire prisoners were probably kept in the fab too, their long cells tucked underneath the arena's tiered seats. The second video had been filmed there. As for the third and fourth videos, the sex scene and the debate, they could've been shot anywhere: a re-purposed part of the fab, or the warehouse, or somewhere completely different.

The debate had closed out just hours ago. Maybe they were all here still.

"Where's my strike team?" Wren asked the empty air.

"In the air twenty minutes out of El Paso," came Hellion's crisp response. "Cheyenne gunship with eight-man Marine squad, all cammed up for livestreaming, as you asked. You have five minutes and they'll hit."

"And our feed?"

"Fifty thousand viewers so far. Reparations have secured their app against take-down attack, but they cannot prevent our piggyback. We are a go."

Wren grinned. Since the farmhouse Hellion and B4cksl4cker had led a massive botnet in hacking cell phones with the Reparation app; not enough to shut it down, but enough to force a new video to go viral. All the pieces were in place now to exploit the Reparations' soft infrastructure from within, using their own tactics against them.

"Set to livestream?"

"All feeds are ready. I have camera drones above, your bodycam, dashcam, chopper, troops also."

Wren spun the assault forward in his head. Using the power of viral videos to drop a justice bomb into the mass psyche. If you couldn't beat them, join them.

"Four minutes, Christopher."

He felt himself settling into a sense of calm. Eye of the storm. It happened sometimes on the battlefield, charging into the unknown, about to put his fate in the hands of the almighty.

He climbed into the Jeep. Started the engine. Put his hands on the wheel. With the windows down, he listened to the sand rustling by outside, his heart thumping blood up and down his left side, straining until he caught it: the faint sound of helicopter blades chopping closer.

"Three minutes," Hellion said, "your uplink is live to the Reparation app. Now is the time."

Wren swiveled the dash cam to point at his face.

"My name is Christopher Wren," he said gruffly. "I took down the Saints and the Blue Fairy, I took down NameCheck and WeScreen, now I'm coming for the Reparations, and maybe for you." He paused a second, staring long enough to let that settle in. "Anyone who picked up a hatchet, who put on a white suit, who strung cables from their car and ripped a person apart, believe that I am coming for you. Nothing comes for free. You will all pay reparations for the crimes you chose to commit. There will be an accounting for us all. Now watch; it's what you do best."

He spun the camera back around so it pointed out through the glass.

"Short and sweet," Hellion chimed in.

Wren laughed, hit the gas and revved the engine loud. Eyeing the dilapidated structure ahead. "What do you think about that office wall? Can I go through it?"

She laughed in turn. "I think we will find out."

He slammed the stick into first, punched the gas and the Jeep roared away.

38

FAB

The Jeep's tires chewed hard through crusted sand as Wren cranked up through second to third then fourth gear like a bullet down the barrel of a gun.

"Pushing your feed viral," Hellion said. "Chopper inbound. Make sure the camera sees it."

Wren just laughed and hit fifth gear, inclining the dash cam upward. Fifty miles an hour and eating up the distance, less than a minute out when the Cheyenne gunship roared in low overhead. Tactical black and massive, Wren saw its gun turrets, the Marines leaning out the open bay doors, and laughed harder.

The Jeep shot off a rise and caught air into the parking lot, spewing sand out back as it approached sixty, fishtailing toward the double-doors of the broken office structure with only seconds left then burst through the opening like a Tomahawk missile.

The truck pulverized the flimsy doorframe and cheap plasterboard walls, spraying inward like confetti, barely dropping any momentum. Beyond lay a completely empty cement expanse, an office space stripped of carpets, desks, light fittings, and Wren skidded into it, cranking the handbrake and spinning the wheel hard to the right.

A voice came in his ears, screaming out wild yahoos. His own. The windows were down, hot stuffy air pumped in.

"A hundred thousand watching now, Cheyenne dropping rappel lines to the tarpaulin roof!"

The tires squealed, cornering at forty and burning rubber, seeking traction until the treads caught a few yards before he pinballed off the rear wall.

Wren wrenched the wheel straight and started a head-on run toward the fab's entrance, hung with anti-static plastic strips.

"Pray it is clear," Hellion shouted over the roar of his engine, "or you will crumple on airlock; this is tons of reinforced air filtering equipment."

Wren just laughed and slammed the pedal down.

"Lights on!" Hellion shouted, then the Jeep hit the strips and whooshed through into darkness.

Almost at once the Jeep made contact, metal poles that whipped up and away with high pranging sounds as he smashed blindly into some kind of scaffold support network; likely holding up the arena seating above. The Jeep's engine screamed, Wren kicked on the flood lamps and saw the forest of poles lying ahead.

The Jeep hammered through and Wren spun the wheel left into a corner, chopping out support poles with his B column side-on, so sharp he had to swing the wheel back right just to keep his back end from spinning out, racing around the outside of the arena like it was an F1 track.

The sound of poles ripping from their supports and ricocheting away became an uproarious cacophony, demolition derby style. To his left Wren tracked the sheer wall of the roughly built arena in gray cinder blocks, to his right raced the plain concrete fab wall, and then-

The long cage cells lay dead ahead. Empty.

Wren yanked the Jeep straight and ran it like a ten-pin ball directly toward the wire mesh. There were no cameras here now but his own, no haz-mat operators, with the stage walls pulled away; a film set deconstructed. As the Jeep hit the cell dividers, they ripped out of their stapled foundations like pulled teeth, chicken wire spooling up and wrenching off his wing mirrors.

The Jeep slowed and he downshifted to increase torque, third gear and surging through the seventh, eighth, ninth cells and then he was clear and accelerating back into the wild turn, taking out more support poles down the far side of the arena.

"Virality is rocketing," came Hellion's voice in his ear.

Let them all see what would happen to the Reparations.

The sound of scaffolds tumbling like skittles became a tremendous, thunderous roar. Wren completed his first circuit and charged on faster, swerving to take out poles he'd missed the first time. The front of the Jeep was smoking now, and he pressed it faster, until through the crashing of poles and the engine's scream he heard the first huge crack as the structure above began to come apart.

By the red glow of his taillights in the rear view he saw a portion of seating come crashing down, beginning a domino effect. Dust filled the once-clean fab as the tiered seats collapsed behind him, destroying this monument to the lowest depths of humanity.

Wren stormed on until he was running up on rubble and light spilled in from above; the tarpaulin roof had cut loose and peeled away in the chaos, was now flapping in the wind like a giant kite. The strike team's Cheyenne hovered black and sudden as a tank in the sky beyond it, eight Marines already rappelling through the gap.

"Now, Christopher," came another voice in his ear.

"B4cksl4cker!" he called as he smashed a path through rows of plastic seating littered with cement dust.

"There are people in the arena. Try not to kill them."

"I'll do my best."

He pulled the wheel hard left, powering a four-wheel-drive run-up that smashed the truck into the cinder block arena wall and crunched it right through.

The windshield burst inward, and the lower ranks of the arena seating exploded outward, spraying across sunlit sand. The Jeep skidded through the gap, tires tearing on wreckage, to screech to a halt at the arena's edge. Overhead the tarpaulin lashed like a giant whip, like the sky itself was coming unstuck as its last mooring points pinged free, finally unveiling the Reparations' sickness to the light.

His Marines were on the sand already, circled up like the billionaires. Wren kicked the Jeep's door open, snatched up a tactical shotgun from the passenger foot well and lunged out. In the center of the arena, circled by five haz-mat suit-wearing camera operators, stood an Asian woman in a dark jumpsuit, staring back at him.

39

ARENA

"This is her," said Hellion in his ear as he strode forward, "the leader, one hundred percent."

"Don't shoot," Wren called to the Marine squad as they closed in like a noose. His voice barely carried above the beating rotors of the Cheyenne.

The woman was beautiful; slender, tan, dark hair hanging in wet-look tresses, chiseled features, mid-thirties. A model if she wanted, a CEO, a Hollywood actress. She watched him unafraid, as if she'd planned all of this. Her camera operators circled warily, filming her, him, the Marines, the helicopter, the whipping tarpaulin until finally the last pinions ripped away with a machine-gun flurry of pops, like a giant bandage torn clear.

The Cheyenne banked away. The Marines held position in a circle, rifles level. The cameras on the operators' shoulders pointed right back, blinking red.

"Dueling livestreams," Hellion said. "Her video feed just came out of nowhere. You're both hitting a million plus viewers right now."

She had a plan. She'd been waiting for him. She wanted this too.

Twenty yards and closing. "Can you ID her?" he asked Hellion low.

"Yes, from image search, local records. She is Yumiko Harkness. Japanese mother, Texan father; laid off when factory closed. Home schooled, never uploaded single frame of footage as far as we can tell. She is social media void."

Wren grunted. From above the receding chop of the Cheyenne was replaced by the buzzing of Hellion's camera-mounted drone. All shot in vivid 4K, and Yumiko was ready for it. There could only be one reason she was here now; like him, she recognized they were coming to the end of the road. Four hours until nightfall; time for the season finale.

"That's far enough," she said when Wren reached ten yards out, and held up a device with a red button on the front, depressed by her thumb. A cartoonish dead man's switch, triggered the moment she released her grip. "The arena floor's set to blow. One more step and we're all vapor."

Wren stopped, smiling now. He didn't believe her; not for a second. She wasn't going to die like that.

"Take the camera operators," he said. "Non-lethal."

Five shots rang out from his Marines. Five cameras fell, military-grade Taser shots in their chests or backs. Five bodies hit the sand and jerked.

Yumiko didn't break eye contact. Neither did Wren. Dark eyes, dizzy depths. With so many assets, such a complex game, there was more at play here than just rage about outsourcing.

"You're the director of the Reparations," he said.

She smiled. It looked practiced: white teeth, a perfect reality-show grin splitting sleek contoured make-up. Her fifteen minutes of fame. "Director, producer, cinematographer-"

"I don't need your whole CV," Wren interrupted. "I don't give a damn about you, Yumiko: who hurt you, who sowed this 'darkness' in your heart." He did air-quotes. "What I want is my father, Apex of the Pyramid, Damalin Joes the third, alive and well, and the Reparation app's source code, in that order. Hand them over."

Her smile stretched. A delicate pink tongue, dancing as she spoke. "You more than most should know, the urge for reparation is widely distributed. It lives on in the hearts and minds of those who've known injustice."

Wren laughed. His left side throbbed in spite of the drugs. "Now that's some BS. Come on, girl, you and I both know you're in this for the thrills. It's fun to stick the boot in some other guy's face, right? Tear down the system that tore down your pops. I can't even begrudge you your anger or your desire for reparation. I've spent my life seeking justice for secret crimes, but there's one difference between us. I never threw my lot in with the psychopathic leader of the country's most famous death cult. Justice is a scalpel, not a bludgeon."

Harkness smiled. "Spoken as a man who works within the system, for the system, upon the system's orders. You could never-"

"Let's get real," Wren interrupted, no interest in her excuses. "The ride's coming to an end, even you must see that. I guarantee we'll find Joes and the others three hours out, on the run, wearing wigs and sunglasses while they hide out in some gas station restroom. The dragnet is closing in, Yumiko. As for the app, well, after we get done here, you think your billionaires are going to keep playing along? And about my father? You used him to suck me in. Handing him over's non-negotiable. All must pay for their crimes, am I right?"

Her eyes flared a little. Some fire there. Wren set himself to fan it hotter, but she spoke first.

"The crimes of your father are not mine. They belong to you as much as anyone."

Wren frowned. "That sounds like some grade-A victim blaming there, Yumiko. What do you even know about the Pyramid?"

Her smile widened. Not so easily drawn. "I know you are a killer like the Pyramid's Apex, Mr. Wren. How many men have you executed over the years? How many Pinocchios have you executed in the last three months, chasing your father's ghost?"

"I can always kill more."

She laughed sharply. "Of course. You claim we're different, but we are not. Both acting out against the crimes of our childhood. You are barely even in the CIA anymore. Nothing you do is sanctioned or legal, they are in fact on the verge of turning their weapons on you, but still you act on their behalf. These men," she gestured to the Marines, "they are just mercenary extras in the Christopher Wren show."

He snorted. "If it's all just a show, then your cast is looking a little thin." He nodded at her camera operators, still writhing on the sand, then gestured around the ruined arena. "Your set's getting worse for wear, too."

"My set?" She laughed in a long high trill. "This is your inheritance, Mr. Wren. You know what we call you?" She waited only a half-second. "The ungrateful son. Your father gave you so much and you squandered it. So many gifts." She trailed off, sounding sad.

That spiked something into Wren. A hint of a buried memory, maybe.

"Enough, Yumiko. You stayed behind for a reason. If you wanted to kill me, you would've done it. I don't believe there's explosives underfoot. So let's find out."

He took a step forward.

"He spoke so well of you," Yumiko said, like she was reading from a script now, except her eyes genuinely glistened with tears. A better actress than he'd taken her for. "His Pequeño 3."

There it was, another hammer on the spike in his chest. Pequeño 3. The same old fear. The same old shortened breath, tunnel vision, crawling fear. Like she really knew his father.

"Steady, Christopher," came Hellion's voice, "your pulse is racing."

"I got your message in Deadhorse," he countered, playing for the cameras too. "What a pleasant gift, another Pinocchio wrapped up for me. I should have expressed my gratitude earlier."

Yumiko looked sad. "It won't save you, you know, this fake bravado. You can't bluff anarchy. In the end all your clever talk won't mean a thing. When you kneel before him once more, Apex of the Pyramid, and beg forgiveness for your many crimes, what do you think he'll say?"

There it was. His greatest fear of them all. Being at his father's mercies and whims like he'd been as a child. He'd tasted it in Somchai's mansion, when the name 'Pequeño 3' alone had sent chills of fear down his spine, coloring the world red and making the walls close tighter in. Fight or flight lapsing into fear...

"Christopher, you are going to have embolism like this," Hellion said in his ear, so very far away. "Control yourself!"

He took a shaky step closer, seven yards distant. "So you read my Wikipedia page. The Apex is an old bogeyman, long dead. Do better research, Yumiko. I've moved on."

It wasn't his best comeback. As if to show that she knew it, Yumiko took a step toward him, the dead man's switch held out.

"You really are a wonder to behold, Ungrateful Son. I have been looking forward to this moment. The last survivor of the Pyramid's rapture, in the flesh. I wondered what kind of man you would be. Could you defy my expectations?"

Another step, five yards, and now Wren caught a dizzy scent on the air; something familiar, acerbic and bitter, biting at his nasal passages. Her hair was clumped together and damp like she'd just taken a shower.

"How do I measure up?"

"You are a disappointment. So simple, like a clockwork toy following the same tired pattern every time. They bring a knife; you bring a gun. They bring a gun; you bring a squad of Marines." She gestured at the men around them. "Simple escalation every time. It makes you as blind as the child you were. Don't you get tired of running on the spot?" She took another step and the scent grew even stronger, billowing off her in a fog, making his eyes water.

"Christopher," Hellion said. "Something is strange here. I am sending in Marines."

He knew it. Couldn't put his finger on it. Yumiko's eyes were everything now, swallowing up his world. He felt lost in them. There was something there he had to understand. Something on the tip of his tongue, but he couldn't get out the words.

"Your every reaction, we knew it before you did," Yumiko went on. "From the Saints to the Blue Fairy to now, you have been utterly predictable." Four yards. "Ungrateful Son, ask yourself this: why did we want you involved at all? Why start this trail with Somchai Theeravit in Deadhorse?" She gave a smaller, secret smile. Like a lover. Three paces now, moving languidly, sensuously. Her jumpsuit dripped clear liquid to the sand. "And that message? They told me not to write anything, but I couldn't resist."

He flashed back to the flash drive. I THINK YOU'LL ENJOY THIS ONE, PEQUEÑO 3. That was her doing. He was struggling to follow along, and now she was only two yards away. The chemical stench was unbearable, burning into his nose and throat, some liquid clinging to her skin in a thin, shiny film. Her eyes were red, not from tears but from the fumes. Her jumpsuit was soaked. Wren felt seconds away from understanding, the revelation just inches away, but he couldn't quite reach it.

She leaned into the gap between them and whispered. "I am *your* director, Ungrateful Son. *Your* writer. *Your* choreographer. I delivered the script and you have been my lead actor ever since, reading your lines to the letter. Call this your last reparation; an original sin that will be made right today, as it should have been so long ago."

One yard. She was so close now, almost touching. All Wren felt was her breath on his face. All he saw were her red eyes, like the pull of some heavenly body sucking him in. She leaned closer still, so close his shotgun barrel pressed against her stomach, barely breathing the words.

"He told you what to do all those years ago, and you didn't do it. You defied him, Pequeño 3. Again and again, you defied him. You appreciated nothing, and now this is your punishment."

Wren opened his mouth to say something, but Yumiko Harkness closed his lips with a sudden kiss, sealing them with the burning chemical tang.

"From me to you, brother," she whispered, "a final gift."

Then she took a step back and raised the dead man's switch. Looking into Wren's eyes, ignoring the Marines circling close, she released the button.

There was no explosion.

Only a single flame. A lighter igniting. For a moment Wren felt relief. A misfire? But of course not. It all came crashing back. That stench overpowering him for hours as he'd painted person after person through the desert streets of the Pyramid's fake town.

Napalm.

Yumiko gave a last, secret smile then pressed the naked flame to her throat.

The napalm caught and she became an instant fireball. A blast wave of heat struck Wren as the flames engulfed her, thick and searing, angry orange and red. The inferno chewed into her skin, consumed her hair in a single greedy swallow, lapped down to her feet and sucked away the surrounding oxygen.

Wren lurched away, fell. On his back on the sand like Handel Quanse, he stared up at her. Still standing, still burning, so glorious that-

He didn't-

He couldn't-

He was back in the fake town, holding the paintbrush dripping napalm, by his father's side and doing the good work all the way until the end. A thousand people had died just like this, on the Apex's command, at Christopher Wren's hand.

Call it a thousand and one.

40

BROKEN

At some point he must have stood up.

The Marines let him go.

Walking in the desert, he felt blind, deaf and dumb. He felt the heat on his face still. Smelled the napalm. Equal parts petroleum and a thickening agent, to make the brew gelatinous and cling: aluminum salts of naphthenic and palmitic acids. Na-palm. Burn you down to the bone, burn you underwater, kill you in seconds.

She'd just disappeared before his eyes. Yumiko Harkness, gone.

He should have recognized the smell sooner. He'd been there at the mixing the first time in Arizona. The worst memory of his life, right there for the taking.

Punishment from the Apex. Reward. They were the same thing.

He limped. The pain was coming on hard. His mind felt slow and thick. Who the hell was he to just stand by and watch it happen all over again?

How could that happen again?

He shuddered. He felt cold, like all those nights left with the children in their cages, with the believers in their pits, thinking he was just proving his resilience against his father's endless experimentations. Only survive, that had always been the key.

Then the last day. The barrel of napalm. The paintbrush.

He dropped to his knees and gagged.

Yumiko Harkness was right: everything that had followed was a reaction to that incredible atrocity. Becoming the 'Executioner' for the CIA had made him feel part of something good. Like he was paying off an old debt, for people he'd killed a long time ago. From going undercover with cults and cartels for Uncle Sam right up to killing Pinocchios in the hunt for his father, it was all the same thing.

Seeking justice. Seeking to pay down old debts.

He tripped, didn't see it coming, landed flush on his chest, smacked his cheek on the sand. His whole body shuddered, lying there on the desert scrub, panting hard while some awful kind of panic attack coursed through his system. Paralyzed by the stress, the truth, the past.

He couldn't get in enough air. That was another effect of napalm. In Vietnam they'd dropped it on whole villages; terrorist camps, was the euphemism. Those who didn't burn up suffocated as the potent mixture blazed through all the oxygen.

She'd just lit up. Yumiko Harkness, beautiful, could have been a CEO, and this was her choice, a message from his father that got through unfiltered.

I'm alive, Pequeño 3. I'm out here, waiting.

It leveled him. For so long he'd hunted, suspected, but to have it confirmed like this?

His father was alive.

It felt like twenty-five years of his life had been erased. His accomplishments didn't mean a thing. His Foundation. His family. He didn't even have to close his eyes to see them all again, lining up for the napalm brush, except now it wasn't Pequeño 3 dipping the brush and painting the townsfolk; it was Christopher Wren painting his wife, his children, painting all the members of the Foundation one after the other.

And why wouldn't he? What was to stop him? He'd done it before.

"I am so proud of you, Pequeño 3," the Apex had said.

He'd said it again and again as each one burned, carving the words into Wren's mind. Making him worse than complicit, worse than co-opted; making him proud too. That all-consuming glory in Yumiko Harkness' eyes, to be making the Apex proud. He'd felt that exact same emotion himself.

He'd come to yearn for it. He'd missed it ever since.

On his knees he came back to himself, SIG .45 in his hand, safety clicked clear, gun pressed to his temple. He didn't have any napalm, but yes, this was right. Better than watching himself do it all over again, better than becoming the Apex's Pequeño 3 once more.

He pulled the trigger.

41

CALL

T he boom rang out.

He couldn't think. The all-consuming sound stuffed his memories back into a bundle in the depths of his brain, a cellar he'd locked beneath his own Foundation. The rot had always been there.

He blinked, ears ringing. Blue sky. He could breathe again.

The SIG .45 was pointed up at the sky. He hadn't realized. Hadn't even done it consciously.

He held the gun barrel before his eyes, cordite smoke drifting in pale wisps. It wasn't a miss. On some level he'd made the decision not to fall for the Apex's tricks again; not to do what his father wanted.

That felt like progress.

The guilt was useless. The rot of the past couldn't be ignored, and maybe he'd never be fully free of what he'd done, but the future could be different.

It would be different. With the acrid stink of napalm still in his nostrils, he knew the fight was still on. He needed to find his father, needed to shut down the Reparations once and for all. The cellar beneath him was opening, and in the darkness within he glimpsed all the horrors he might yet become, but he wasn't going to go back to that, though.

It was time for a new path.

The gun discharged again into the sky. He hadn't even realized he'd pulled the trigger, but the sound and recoil helped ground him in the moment. It felt like a clear, sharp dividing line between his past and his future, putting the shutter back on the cellar just long enough to-

He fired again and lurched to his feet, starting away at a ragged run. The pain dropped him after five yards; fire up his whole left side, along with the memories rising in time with his straining pulse, with him back in the Arizona desert with his father right there, saying-

He fired all but his last round into the air. The silicon chip factory lay ahead like an island in orange sea. He ran until his left leg gave out and he fell. He squeezed the trigger hard, firing the last round into the sky.

"Sir, please stop shooting!"

He blinked.

The voice gave him a momentary reset. He spun, casting around the desert sand until he saw a man in tactical black drawing in. One of the Cheyenne Marines.

"Sir," the man said, edging closer. He held something in his hand. It was hard to hear, like his voice was coming from the far end of a long corridor. "There's a call for you."

Wren laughed. A call? He even knew who it was, who it had to be. How fitting. So it came down to this, no bullets left before his world turned upside down, and he'd finally complete Dr. Ferat's dying advice.

Talk to your family. Not just your wife and kids; your whole family.

On his feet, he reached out one hand. The Marine put the phone in it carefully and backed away, eyes on the SIG .45. Wren looked at the phone in one hand, the gun in the other. He lifted the phone to one ear, holstered the SIG, and prepared himself for what was about to happen.

"Christopher," came the voice on the other end. Deep, authoritative, the once-adoptive father he'd avoided for twenty years. James Tandrews.

42

TANDREWS

Agent James Tandrews.

In 1995 he'd been Commander of the FBI's Gold tactical Hostage Rescue Team. Two years after the Waco debacle, he'd been first on the scene at the smoking ruin of the Pyramid in their fake town in Arizona, to find one thousand dead and only one survivor.

A twelve-year-old boy with no name. Barely able to speak. Covered in burns and wearing blackened clothing, stinking of gasoline, dehydrated and wandering amongst the dead bodies.

Maybe it was guilt that drove him to take the boy in; for failing to stop the Pyramid, for the deaths at Waco. Maybe he was lonely. He was forty-two then; marriage dissolved by the job, children grown and flown with their mother, no longer the center of anybody's world, on the way out at the FBI after his twin cult failures.

He took on the child known only as Pequeño 3, and for five years molded him, channeling the boy's rage, pain and PTSD into action. He'd kept him away from other children for those early years, from school and the mall and the county fair until he was ready, and plunged him into a constant flood of fresh challenges. There were no friends for him back then, no family, only the two of them stalking the midnight forests of Maine, far from the deserts of his earliest years, learning to live off the land for weeks at a time. For long days and nights they barely spoke, just experienced the raw and brutal reality of nature.

It had rooted him in something different and real. He'd come to trust Tandrews; the man never buried him in a pit, never drowned him in a vat, never made him beg for more time in the cage. He only taught him how to use the natural skills of his body and mind; to ground himself in observable reality. Fighting. Shooting. Shelter. Family.

In time, high school had come. Wren got to experience a 'normal' life for a few years; make friends, have a girlfriend, until on his seventeenth birthday, there was the adoption.

Tandrews had waited until Wren was seventeen, when legal adoption would not carry the weight of control. It didn't mean much in the eyes of the law, especially after they'd already filed Wren's papers of emancipation. But it meant something still, a symbol of their connection. A certain respect. The young man once named Pequeño 3 had agreed. He'd been happy. Then the night before they signed the papers, a panic attack had hit like he'd never experienced before.

A sense of being trapped, like he was right back in the Pyramid. It wasn't logical but it consumed him completely. It burned up all his ideas of college, his high school life, his friends and his girl. It rooted him back in the Pyramid, in that fear, which he knew he would have to spend the rest of his life fighting.

He'd fled Tandrews in the middle of the night and never gone back. Signed up for the Marines the next day.

Now Tandrews sounded the same. Older, maybe. There was a lot of pain in that voice.

Wren couldn't speak. He just held the phone to one ear, held the gun to the other like a vise around his head.

"I know you're there," Tandrews said. "Christopher. I can see you on the drone feed now."

Wren turned. There was the drone, hovering. He hadn't heard it.

"Don't speak, if you're not ready," Tandrews went on. "Just listen. Dr. Ferat put me in touch with your hackers six months ago. I know you didn't want to see me then, and I understood, just like I did twenty years ago. You had your own reasons." He took a breath. "Christopher, twenty years ago I asked Dr. Ferat to watch over you for me. I thought he was just your lecturer, but when he confessed you'd asked him to join your Foundation I was-" he trailed off. "I didn't know what to think. I-" another pause. "I kept that hidden from the FBI. They would have seen you building your Foundation, and I stopped that from happening. I always believed, Christopher. You were my son. I know, we never signed the papers, but I don't let go. I never will. You are my responsibility."

Wren just stood. Wavering. He felt shame beating back the darkness of the cellar. It felt good. Some things you should feel shame for; that was a pain to hug close.

"I saw what happened in the arena," Tandrews said. "The woman, the napalm. I know what it means for you. I know what you're thinking right now, and why you keep firing that gun."

Wren felt separated from his own body. It wasn't even him listening. It was someone else; this boy who'd chosen to call himself Christopher Wren, named after the great architect of London. Even that felt like a foreign ambition, to design great structures built out of people, a child-like desire to surpass his father, the Apex.

Now he was a child again, still charred from the fires.

"I know what you're feeling. The fears. I woke up with you screaming enough times. I heard about what happened with your family in New York, and I'm sorry. Life was never going to be easy for you, but there is one thing I am absolutely certain of. You are a good man, Christopher. The Apex twisted you the way he twisted everyone, the way he twisted that woman, but you never broke. Maybe that's why he let you live; a curiosity. In any case, you are not a little boy anymore, and your country needs you now more than ever."

Wren breathed hard. The dark cellar receded slightly. Tandrews' presence blocked it out. Who could have predicted that?

"This proves he is out there, Christopher. I know you've been hunting him. I never stopped hunting either. He's doing this to us, and now he wants you at the center; the only person alive who really knows him. The Apex. That makes you our greatest weapon against him. Do not let him break you like this. You were a child then. You're not a child now."

Wren felt like the barriers he'd spent so many years building coming down. He'd built a wall against Tandrews for the crime of trying to be close to him. At seventeen formal adoption was a symbol only, a gesture of love, but he hadn't been able to accept it.

"I-" he managed, his voice a croak. The cellar was there, but no longer so terrifying.

"I love you, Christopher. I have since I saw you in that godforsaken town. I loved that you were alive at all. It inspired me, as you have done every day since. Your capacity to heal was astounding. You kept fighting. You made me a better man, and I am still proud to think of myself as your father. Not him. You will always be my brave, wild son, and that is what's real."

A tear spilled down Wren's cheek. So this is what Dr. Ferat wanted. It felt so hard, had been coming for so long. It turned him inside out.

"I-"

"Don't say anything," Tandrews said, his voice gruff. "You don't owe me an explanation, an apology, not a damn thing. I'm just proud of the man you've become."

Wren's breathing came easier now, the panic attack easing, and he pressed the phone tighter against his ear, trying to catch every last breath.

"I hope one day we see each other again," Tandrews said. "Man to man, when you're ready. I hope you'll trust me that much. Until then, I know you'll do what's right. You'll close this chapter and move on to the next, and you'll hunt that rat-bastard down. He's a loser, Christopher, and that's all. Only losers do this, and one day we'll piss on his grave. You always had the strength to bring him down. I know he saw it, and I see it now more than ever."

The words entered Wren like a balm, far better than oxycodone and methylphenidate. That he wasn't broken. That his past didn't have to be a weakness, but could be a strength.

He had to speak, had to get the words out fast before the moment slipped and he missed it. "You saved my life," he managed. "Then and now. Thank you, Tandrews. I'll fix this, I promise."

He killed the call, let the phone drop by his side.

The sun beat down, lowering over the horizon. Time marched relentlessly on, toward nightfall.

He felt different.

The Marine still stood there, silhouetted against the sky, like the ferryman between heaven and hell. Watching Wren curiously through his helmet visor, hands on his rifle. Probably confused about what he was seeing. This man covered in blood, who only seconds ago was staggering and shooting and crazed. Now he stood erect, transformed.

Wren felt it too, a flush of new strength.

Part of it came from the foundation he'd built in the forests of Maine with Tandrews, but that wasn't all. Part came from the pits of the Pyramid, too, buried beneath the sand in the wilderness of Arizona. His life with the Apex right alongside everything that came after. Both underpinned his own foundations. Both made him what he was. Moral. Ruthless. Able to walk the line between the two.

Now he would embrace them both.

Like an explosion, new routes spun out ahead of him. Now he finally saw the whole plan, clicking into place like the last pieces of a jigsaw. What Yumiko Harkness had said about him; always escalating. His reliable MO, and how they'd used him to further their own aims. He understood what she'd meant by calling him her lead actor, how every move of his was so predictable.

And she might be dead, but the show wasn't over. The final curtain call was coming, and she'd left him a part to play there too.

He knew what he had to do.

"Bring the helicopter down," he said to the Marine. Even his voice sounded stronger. The pain in his left side was beaten back. "We've got a mission to complete."

43

LIVESTREAM

W ren strode back toward the factory, phone squeezed tight in his hand.

FIND DAMALIN JOES he typed on his Megaphone app to the whole Foundation. THIS ENDS WITH HIM. DO WHATEVER IT TAKES. AND GET ME HUMPHREYS.

He shoved the phone in his pocket and the Marine jogged alongside him, a glorified escort. The limp was coming through on his left side, but he felt unstoppable, heading perfectly straight like a targeting laser guiding in an air strike, cutting through walls and bodies and bunkers.

All the fear from before was gone, burned up in this blazing laser beam of purpose. He had the monster inside him, after all. The Apex and Tandrews were twin pillars of his personal foundations. Pequeño 3. Christopher Wren. He was a product of his twin pasts, like naphthenic and palmitic acids brewed into napalm, becoming something terrible together.

The Apex didn't know what kind of monster he'd made.

He stamped into the stripped office, past his Jeep's twin burnt rubber trails on the flat gray concrete, past a red stain on the concrete and through the plastic curtains and out over the rubble of seating into the arena.

The air hung with greasy smoke and the drifting smell of exhausted napalm. Yumiko Harkness was a blackened charcoal patch in the center, circled by the hog-tied bodies of her operators. Three Marines guarded them with their rifles at the ready. The Cheyenne helicopter loomed over them, rotor blades still and wilting.

He tapped his earpiece. "Are you seeing this, Hellion?"

Her voice came through clear, the first time he'd really tuned into her since before the burning. Maybe she'd been there in his ear throughout, but he hadn't heard a word. "I am here, Christopher. I see you."

Time to ramp things up a notch. "Bodycams live? The drone feed?"

"There are many cameras, yes, but we are blocking all feeds. You do not look well, Christopher."

He grunted. That had to be an understatement. "Put the livestream back up."

"What?" blurted B4cksl4cker.

"Do it now. Show them I'm alive and I'm coming. Put the fear into them."

"Are you sure this is good idea? I do not-"

"Hellion," he said, calm and intense. "Trust me. This is the right thing to do."

Keys clattered down the line. "Done. All cameras are up."

"On me," Wren said.

"I have drone incoming."

Wren watched it come in a surging buzz of rotors, falling like a rock to catch itself in a hover at head-height two yards away from Wren, camera pointed dead at his face.

"You are live," Hellion said. "There are still some hundred thousand left watching, even after we cut the feed."

Wren stared into the lens, feeling more ready than ever. Everything he said and did now would be heard by the wider world, but that was all right. He was done covering up the past. Time to let all his demons out. "I know you filmed me breaking down in the desert," he said, gazing into the lens but talking to Hellion. "I want you to add that to the feed. Everyone should see."

There was a pause punctuated by the chop of the drone's blades. "Christopher, this is-"

"The right thing to do. Please, Hellion."

More clicking keys. "It is done."

The drone lens was right there. He felt like a laser boring through it straight to his father. "You thought you could destroy me." His voice came out resonant and intense. "You thought I'd be ashamed, afraid, a broken man when I saw the depths of that poor woman's madness." He pointed to the cinders of Yumiko Harkness and the drone spun to take her in. "But you were wrong. It's true that I was part of the Pyramid suicide cult as a child, but I was only a child. Sick people twist children every day." He took a breath. "People are cruel. Fate is not kind. The pain mounts up and the cruelty circles on until at some point, we all want justice, but what the Reparations are offering is not justice. It is blind, aimless vengeance." He paused a moment, letting the momentum build. "The Reparations do not care who your revenge is against. They simply want the circle to spin faster. More pain. More violence. More chaos. More death. But it has to stop. There cannot always be the justice your heart craves."

He paused. Staring. Thinking. The pain down his side was coming on fast, brought on by the adrenaline burst, and he had to stay ahead of it.

"As of this moment, I'm declaring an amnesty." His voice boomed around the ruin of the arena. "All minor crimes committed during the reign of the Reparations are hereby forgiven. I don't care what you did. I will not come for you. But if you committed serious crimes? If you hurt people, killed people, tortured or tormented people? If you plan to commit those crimes tonight, then I swear, I will find you, and there will be justice. Do not run from this. Accept it and seek to pay your own reparations, before I come for blood."

"View count is a stampede," Hellion said in his ear, her voice flushed with a rare excitement. "This is going very viral, Christopher. Tens of thousands joining every second." She paused a moment, breathless. "The people want this!"

"Back from the dead," chimed in B4cksl4cker, deep voice rumbling. "I set up twin streams so they can watch you in desert while they watch you now. Both are topping all rankings."

Wren went on. "The first step in your reparations is to halt the cycle of violence immediately. The app you are viewing this video feed on is a crime. All your shares, your likes, your copycat videos condemn you." He felt like he was staring into the soul of America. "So delete them all. Delete your videos. Delete your shares. Delete the app. It's time for the bloodletting to stop, and this is the only time I will warn you." He took a raspy breath. "We are all the victims of the greatest act of brainwashing in history. Our pain has been co-opted. Our hurt has been weaponized. But the

682

Reparations will not help us heal. Delete the app and let the real healing begin."

He was panting now, almost toppling over as his left leg trembled. Maybe a minute left.

"If you don't do that, then I will come for you." He pointed again at the corpse of Yumiko Harkness. "I was twelve years old when one thousand souls in the Pyramid cult burned alive. You may know I was the sole known survivor. What you don't know is that I burned those people myself. My father drove me on, but I was the one who painted napalm onto the skin of those thousand people. I was the one who lit the spark on each and every one."

Wren felt a stunned silence stretching out, through the cameras and on into the world. Not the Apex. Him. He'd never told a soul. He hadn't even known it himself until recently.

"What is this, Christopher?" whispered Hellion.

"We just hit one billion viewers," B4cksl4cker said. "That is large part of global population."

"I burned a thousand people alive, and I will do it again, if I have to," Wren said. "I will find you, I will soak you, and I will burn you to the ground. So turn off your feed now, there is nothing left to see."

For a long moment his fierce gaze blazed down the drone's lens, then he said, "Kill it," to Hellion, and the red light on the drone cut out.

At once Wren dropped to one knee, no longer able to hold himself up. What he'd just done felt like a seismic shift. The truth was out there for once and all, who he was and whom he'd killed. There was no turning back now.

"It is happening," B4ckscl4cker said, sounding stunned. "They are cutting out. View count dropping.

Hellion laughed in his ear. Magic. He felt like laughing himself. He had both in him. The cult leader. The cult survivor. The Apex's gift. Tandrews' gift. He was transmuting now like lead to gold into something new.

Wren 2.0

A Marine appeared at his side, placed one hand tentatively on his elbow. "Sir?"

"There's drugs in the car," Wren managed. His throat felt on fire, moments away from passing out. "Get them for me, please."

The man ran. Wren dropped to both knees, grateful just to be alive.

44

NOT ALL

"Sir," came a voice.

Wren looked up and saw the Marine right there. Holding out two pill bottles, concern on his face.

"Thanks," said Wren, and tried to take them. His hand missed the target, swiping uselessly at the air. "I-"

"Shall I?" the guy asked. Not embarrassed. A battle-hardened Marine, he'd seen worse than this before.

Wren managed a grunt. The adrenaline rush that had been holding him up was gone. He tried to stand but the pain in his side leveled him. He'd pushed himself too far, too fast. His body flashed hot and cold. Where was his laser guidance now?

He spluttered a laugh.

"Here."

The Marine was holding out a gloved palm, twin pills nestled there neatly. Wren managed to pick them, put them in his mouth. The Marine had a water bottle ready. Wren took it, drank and swallowed.

Wait for the kick. Hellion and B4cksl4cker gradually came into focus, twittering in his ear like far off birds. Steadily the world came back: shapes took on solidity, he felt the sun on his arms, smelled the Cheyenne's kerosene fuel. The tunnel vision receded, and his erratic pulse steadied out.

"You're back?" the Marine asked.

"Getting there," Wren said, and craned his neck to look around the wrecked arena, sand mounded now over the heaps of fallen seating, blown by the Cheyenne's downdraft. The Marine gave him a hand and Wren pulled himself back to his feet. His left side was weak still, but he could stand. "Hellion, report."

"Copycat videos are bottoming out," she said. "Users are deleting the app in the millions. Pings confirm it."

Wren breathed a cautious sigh of relief.

"About half of all video content has been pulled down. Shares and likes coming down too, but not all. We have analytics running, behavioral projections say ninety percent will delete the app and erase their presence."

Ninety percent was an excellent number. Not enough, though. Ten percent could still precipitate outright chaos in the streets. "What about the ten?"

"Our target demographic. I am tagging them all. B4cksl4cker and I have long memories."

Wren smiled. At best he'd won a moment to breathe in. The country still stood on a knife edge, and Yumiko Harkness had known it. She'd even called him out, a windup clockwork toy, she'd said, always escalating: knife to gun; gun to Marine strike team. His MO was always to go all-in and escalate, and it made him predictable.

She'd been right.

The smile faded from his lips. Now he saw it all, clear and stretching away into the night. She had predicted him to a tee. His MO. His next steps, to escalate again. She'd known her suicide would throw him over the edge, and already laid out the script for him to follow.

Crush the contagion. He'd set events in motion already, telling Humphreys to send out an army of federal officers to raid every single American home and snatch the phones directly from peoples' hands. He'd told his Foundation to prepare for it as well.

She couldn't have dreamed up a more damaging visual if she'd tried.

Federal officers storming a million homes around the country, forcefully snatching private property from people's hands. Cutting off their free access to information by killing the Internet. It would be the biggest government incursion into the private lives of the citizenry in history, busting through about half the Constitution and most of the Amendments.

He laughed as all the potential repercussions fell into place. Yumiko

Harkness had baited him, and he'd leaped in without looking. All she had to do then was set cameras to watch it. With just enough people left over to watch those videos, she'd flip her popular uprising against the rich into a revolution against the state itself. The government. Every authority figure Wren could muster.

It was brilliant. Genius really. It pushed Wren's search for his father far into the background. Hunting the Apex down to keep Wren's family safe wouldn't mean a thing if they didn't have a country left over to live in after it was done.

He couldn't let things go that far.

"We have to find Damalin Joes," he said to Hellion, spinning the gears in his head hard. "He's going to be at the center of what's coming. He must be nearby. You're running satellite sweeps?"

"We are."

"They'll be evading overwatch. Search for bands of geography outside our satellite coverage, patches where they could get through unseen, and sync those blank spots to their schedule."

"This is vast range." Hellion's keys were already clacking frantically. "Number of blind corridors through satellite overwatch is large and shifting. Can you narrow it, Christopher? Departure time would help, plus means of transport, some idea of their final destination."

Wren's mind buzzed like a drone. He ran it all backward and forward, working through the Reparations' track record, their actions, their MO. Always prepared, that was one. Within an hour of Wren signaling an interest in the Anti-Ca compound, they'd passed down a suicide order to wipe out the evidence, activating a store of potassium-cyanide and orange juice.

They'd been ready for him. Within a day, Yumiko Harkness had accelerated her billionaires' execution timeline to political speeches. Wren had to imagine she'd taken ten of them for a reason, intending to knock them out one-by-one like the stages in a reality show. Six more shows, that meant, but all cut now. He'd moved fast and they'd adapted; getting the penultimate video out before Wren could nail them in the silicon chip factory.

"They must have had vehicles here," he said, "prepped for an emergency evac."

"Yes?"

Wren looked up at his Marine, the methylphenidate driving him on. "What's your name, Marine?"

"Acton, Sir."

"OK, Acton. I need you to go check the warehouse." He thought a second. "Run searchlights over the ground near the loading bay doors. You're looking for drops of gasoline, anything that glistens." He thought more, piecing it out. "The vehicles wouldn't have been fully fueled, not with six kill videos left to go, which means they fueled them in the last few hours. I'm thinking you'll find spots; soak some up with gauze. If it's clear, that's regular motor gas, meaning they left by road. If it's blue or green, those are dyes added to aviation grade gasoline, which means light helicopters. Go."

Acton started away at a run.

"Light helicopters in the warehouse?" Hellion asked.

Wren worked the math. "The loading bay doors are wide enough for a semi-trailer. You could park two Vertical Hummingbirds on it nose-to-tail. Two trailers, that's four Hummingbirds, a sixteen-seat passenger capacity total, enough to get all the billionaires and crew out. Way faster than anything by land. It's what I'd do for imminent bug-out."

"Lining that up for search algorithm. We will pull in local radar data; four helicopters will stand out, help narrow radius." Wren heard keys flying madly. "Next is when, and where?"

Wren rewound again, stripping his memory for clues. There'd been something in the entrance to the empty office, like a puddle of mud right before the Jeep's burned rubber slug-trails began. Except it hadn't been mud.

He reached out and grabbed another Marine. "In the middle of the office there's a red stain, maybe blood. Go find it."

The man ran. Wren laid a hand on the Cheyenne, holding himself steady as his left side throbbed, thinking hard and breathing harder. In less than a minute the Marine came in through the radio. "I see it. It's blood."

Wren nodded, playing the scene through in his head; a pack of homicidal billionaires being shepherded out of captivity. Accidents happened. Arrogant men who'd been wound up to fight would be capable of extreme violence.

Somebody had been beaten there, maybe died. One of the haz-mats, most likely, he figured. They'd taken the body with them, too much evidence to leave behind, but there'd been no time to sop up the blood.

"Describe the color," Wren said.

"You ran through the patch with the Jeep," the Marine said. "Brown around the edge, still red at the center."

Wren ran the numbers. When blood left the body, it began evaporating water immediately, ultimately leaving behind only a reddish-brown crust. This was basically rust, made primarily of iron. It took time, of course; you could date a sample with some precision by how much it had evaporated its water content.

Still red at the center, the Marine said. Still wet, which made the death more recent. In a hot environment like this, with a dry wind blowing through, he figured the death had happened within hours. Call it two max. Any longer and the evaporation would be complete.

"Departure between one and two hours ago," he said to Hellion. "No sooner than one, they wouldn't cut it that close."

"Better," Hellion said, and the keys flew. "Finally, where are they going?"

Wren spooled Yumiko Harkness' script forward. She wanted to turn his nationwide phone raid into a mass revolution, synced to nightfall. Wren checked the sky, saw the sun was below the wall of the fab. Coming up in an hour or so. Footage of that would blow through the app in minutes and prime resistance. A gross violation of American liberty, a scenario from every Second Amendment supporter's worst nightmare; the government coming into their homes and taking what was theirs by force.

The action was clear, the script, but what would the setting be? She could choose any stage set she wanted, to maximize the impact. What environment would be most likely to offend Middle America the most? His mind raced. It couldn't just be a set, either, couldn't look contained or fake in any way. It had to look real. It had to be real.

"A small-town suburb," he said swiftly, as the words came to him. "Picture perfect. Nice green yards, neat roads, white picket fences, porch swings, pure Americana." He played it further, like she'd handed him a copy of the script and he was reading the directions right out. "I think the billionaires will be waiting inside a regular house. Like the fab, it'll be a purchase within the last six months, maybe a year. Waiting for our strike forces to hit." He stopped, thought again. "Scratch that. No."

He played the idea forward and back. Yumiko wouldn't take the chance of waiting for the actual Federal strikes to come. No way to know for sure where the Feds would hit first, or when, and no way to control for that outcome. If the actual strike came too late, raids across the country would already have snatched millions of phones by the time their feed went live; nobody would see it. That meant...

"They're waiting, but not for us," he sped on. "Look for a cluster of federal-marked vehicles. ATF, FBI, whatever, probably under cover now somewhere near a small town or suburb." He put the last pieces together. "The whole thing's going to be fake. Actors dressed as police rushing in for the phone-snatch." He kept on calculating. "It'll happen soon, so they can get their video of successful resistance out and prime the people before the real raids come. They'll fight them off. The billionaires will win, at least Damalin Joes will. It'll show the people the government can be beaten. Just like they did with Damali Joes!"

The weight and scale of it about floored him. It made perfect sense. It was like clockwork. He checked it, turned it and saw no flaws. Every raid after that would be met with hardened resistance. It would be Waco all over again, all across the United States. The people would turn against their government.

"Winding back through overwatch, looking for emergency vehicles converging on a small town or suburb," Hellion said, typing furiously.

Nearby a speaker crackled and Acton's voice came through clear.

"I found the drops, Sir. The gasoline's blue."

Wren perked up. "Hellion?"

"Heard it, light helicopters. Search algorithm programmed and going live."

Wren looked to the Marines around him. Still feeling weak. The drugs whizzing around his system were the only thing holding him up. He looked at the step up into the Cheyenne, and knew it was too much.

"Get me on this helicopter right now."

45

PHENOMENAL INTUITION

The Cheyenne lifted off; the sound of rotors elevated to an eardrum-splitting storm. Wren sat slumped flat on a seat taking every second of rest he could get.

Odd thoughts danced in his mind. His son, Jake, loved helicopters. Every time one had passed by overhead, whether a traffic copter, a police unit or an Air Force transport heading to or from Fort Hamilton, he'd wanted to rush out and watch it.

Quinn, his daughter, hated the racket they made. She preferred trains. Every time they took the subway, she'd glue her face to the window and watch carriages rattling by in neighboring tunnels, seemingly awestruck. Wren could understand that. Different people on different tracks, briefly brought into alignment side-by-side before pulling apart again, in different directions.

Yumiko Harkness was like that. She'd called him brother.

He missed his family. All of this was supposed to be for them. To find his father and make the world safe, but he wasn't sure if he was achieving it. Wasn't sure what he was achieving but more vengeance. The exact same thing he'd accused Yumiko Harkness of.

"Christopher," came Hellion's voice in his ear, dragging him back to the present.

"Have you got me Humphreys?" he asked on throat-mic.

"Working on it," Hellion answered. "Seems he's busy."

Wren snorted, let his head rock to the side. Through the half-glass of the Cheyenne's door he watched the silicon chip factory recede. With no tarpaulin roof and no sand in the arena it didn't look like anything special at all; just another abandoned structure in America's crumbling industrial core, left to rot. Soon it was gone, swallowed by the desert.

"Where are we going?"

"North," Hellion answered, "unless you think they'll film in Mexico."

"Four helicopters over the border," Wren said, then paused to catch his breath. "Too conspicuous on radar."

"We agree. And you said perfect Americana, picket fences, green yards? This is not Mexico. There are few in New Mexico also; image search exhausted these in seconds. There are many picket fences in nearby towns: Antelope Wells, Hachita, Playas, Anima, but none of these have green yards. It is all desert."

Wren second-guessed himself. It seemed a lot to bank on a hunch. Maybe the Reparations didn't care about green yards. But then, yes, they did. Image was everything, when it was all you had. The power of propaganda lay in the imagery. It had to be right.

"Anything more?"

"Not yet. Look out though, here is Humphreys. He sounds angry."

When did he not? "Put him on."

His earpiece clicked.

"Humphreys, we need to-"

"I always knew you were a killer, Christopher," Humphreys fumed. "I didn't know you'd killed a thousand people when you were twelve."

That took Wren by surprise. For a moment he'd forgotten about his confession. It had played its part, laying out a credible threat to the bulk of people still amenable to coercion. And what did it mean beyond that; what was Humphreys going to do differently, hunt him down harder? Line up outstanding warrants for the thousand dead, brought forward twenty-four years? Stacked atop the Pinocchio executions, it would put him away for a thousand life sentences.

"It's true," Wren said. "But now-"

"I'm sorry," Humphreys interrupted. He sounded different, like his anger wasn't at Wren anymore, but at some joint enemy. Finally. "I didn't know. It's easy to forget what you went through when you're out murdering

Pinocchios every day. So listen to me now. Earlier I said we wanted you as a blunt weapon, our own pet 'cultist', and that was true, but it's not the whole truth." He took a fortifying breath. "We always knew you were a genius. Temperamental, dangerous, but on the Emotional Quotient scale you were like nothing we'd seen before. The intuitive leaps you made at seventeen? They were phenomenal. And the things you do now, Christopher, the way your mind works…"

Wren didn't know what to say. It sounded like an apology. He wasn't sure.

"I needed to say that," Humphreys added. "It doesn't let you off the hook for what you've done. There is the possibility you may have been licensed for the Pinocchio executions. It'll be the President's call."

Wren almost laughed. Licensed by the President, to kill? He cleared his throat. "Humphreys, we need to-"

"Let me enjoy the quiet for one second more," Humphreys said. "The great Christopher Wren struck dumb, basking in the glow of my praise, not immediately just telling me what to do."

Wren gave him a second. Several, in fact.

"OK," said Humphreys. "Go ahead."

"You need to cancel the strikes to grab phones. All of them, right now."

There was a long, painful silence.

"You're joking. Ha ha, Christopher. Very funny."

Wren took a deep breath, pressed on. "I'm not. It's not funny. I'm for real."

"Unh."

Wren imagined Humphreys face-palming.

"Think of all the money you'll save."

Humphreys groaned. "Christopher! Why do you do this to me? Money we'll save, are you serious? We've spent billions already. Have you got any idea how much it costs to mobilize millions of people across different sectors, train them, equip them, arrange logistics to transport them, not to mention the analytics required to split America into sectors for a simultaneous strike?"

"I don't know. A lot." A pause. "I'm sorry."

A long sigh. "A lot. Well, at least you're sorry. I can dine out on that when Congress hauls me up for gross incompetence."

Wren saw a gap opening up. Humphreys had shifted. This wasn't the man he'd spoken to earlier: burning cold with anger, blaming Wren for everything. This was a man who'd re-balanced his perspective.

"I'll use my Emotional Quotient," Wren tried. "Phenomenal intuition, wasn't it? Maybe I can pull some strings with the President."

Steel crept back into Humphreys' voice. "Don't push it. We've got you on dozens of murder charges."

Wren almost laughed. Not back the way it always was, but better than before.

"Fine. Either way, the Reparations are counting on those strikes. They've been using me as a foil. They knew I'd escalate at every provocation, because that's what I do. They push me with their app, and I push for the strikes. They're going to use it as a call for revolution. An over-reaching government; it's the great American fear. We can't give them that."

Humphreys took a moment, then cursed loud and inventively.

"Right. I'm not such a genius now."

Humphreys laughed; it sounded almost like a sob. "So call off all the strikes?"

"Not quite all. Hellion's sent you the analytics? People are deleting the app themselves. We've got ten percent projected to stay on and try to keep the revolution rolling. You need to focus your best on them. Don't raid them, give no provocation, just watch them and let them see you're watching. Let them see it's futile. We'll arrest the worst of them later, when the heat's gone out of this thing."

"What about your amnesty?"

Wren chuckled. "I was wondering when you'd mention that."

"I must say, I am glad you carved out some room for us, when you made that announcement. Gave us permission to make arrests for murderers and such. Thank you."

Wren knew he was mocking him, but took it seriously still. "I don't want them to fear you. You're not the enemy of the people. I want them to fear me."

Humphreys just laughed. "They will definitely kick me out of the CIA for this."

"Maybe make you VP."

"Ugh. All right. I have to go face the music." He paused and Wren almost killed the call, but Humphreys had one more thing to say. "Oh, and thank you for the chance to meet your hackers. Hellion, I think it was? She called me a 'pussy wearing a dick-suit'."

Wren tried and failed to stifle a laugh. Probably that was the hydrocodone.

"I'm glad it amuses you. That's ten years, for maligning an officer in pursuit of his duty."

"Well, you always had the best suits," Wren said. "Now I have to go kill some bad guys. Good luck."

"See you in jail, Christopher."

The line went dead.

"He is pussy in a dick-suit," Hellion said flatly.

Wren laughed. It didn't hurt that much. Somehow, he felt good. So what if he went to jail? He'd just been preaching the importance of making atonement, of paying down your debts. He had so many to pay. Families of the Pyramid deceased he owed apologies to, a thousand now and counting, debts he'd never even realized were his. Members of his Foundation that he hadn't been able to properly help. He just had to take out his father, try and make things right with his kids, and then jail would come as a relief. It'd give him time to set up a payment plan on those debts. Ten steps for ten coins. Get into writing letters.

He blinked. The drugs were playing havoc with his head.

"Do we have a destination yet?"

"Tentative," Hellion said. "There are few towns in light helicopter range, with matching gaps in oversight and green yards and flood of blue light vehicles coming in. What I am seeing, either these are Reparations or this is criminal convention. Many ghost movements, changes between satellite overwatch cycles."

"Where?"

"Twenty minutes north of you, a little place called Pie Town on other side of Gila National Forest. And get there fast Christopher, the Reparations app is warming up new livestream now. It is still shot of your Constitution. Viewing numbers are climbing."

The Constitution. Wren had been ready to run it underfoot, and he cursed silently. This was a lesson.

"Yeah," he said, and looked out of the glass again. The sun was sinking low to the west, nightfall was coming fast. His giddiness burned away. The Cheyenne tore on. It all came down to this.

694

46

PIE TOWN

The Cheyenne swooped in over trailer park homes interspersed by yellowing yards and dark green Douglas Firs. Wren should have known it; Americana but leaning poor, like the majority of the country, the people with the most to be angry about. There were picket fences, but the effect of downward social mobility was everywhere. A few had fresh coats of paint, but not nearly enough.

The place felt like defeat.

Blue lights flashed ahead. Wren pushed himself upright and nearly tipped off his seat as the Cheyenne banked tightly over dirt roads and scrub.

"Sir," said Acton at his side, catching Wren by the shoulders and steadying him. "Are you sure you're fit to engage?"

"Just be there if I fall, son," Wren said. He was maybe only ten years this Marine's senior, but whatever; it gave him the privilege to call him son.

"Yes, sir. Now, we've got AR-15s, more shells for your shotgun, magazines for the SIG .45, or you can-"

"Don't need them," Wren said, holding up his hands. "All I want are these." He made fists, but they didn't feel tight, the knuckles barely whitening. He was as weak as a six-year-old. "Just keep me alive."

"Sir," the guy barked.

"And whatever you do, try not to kill the billionaires."

Acton's brows pushed slightly closer together. "Sir? Aren't they considered hostiles by now?"

Wren looked around at his team; eight Marines in tactical black, armed to the teeth. "They are, but I repeat, do everything you can not to kill them. This is a special operation, with far more at stake than immediate life and death." He took a breath, saw the doubt on his squad's faces. "You know Stockholm Syndrome? Consider these men hostages who've been co-opted. Forget about what they've done, that was all under duress. They've been brainwashed. If we kill them, and those deaths are caught on the livestream, we may win the battle, but we will lose the war." He sucked air. Speaking so much winded him. "Am I understood?"

They'd surely had few directions like that before. Most propaganda wars weren't actually fought in the streets.

"Oo-rah," they replied.

"Coming in," shouted the pilot.

The Cheyenne swung hard right barely ten yards above the roof line. A cluster of emergency vehicles was parked at the head of a blacktop road, clearly recently tarred and painted with fresh yellow lines. More set dressing, thanks to some unnamed benefactor to the county council. It beat out the dirt roads that linked the rest of the tiny burg and completed the picture-perfect image.

Just your average American suburb.

The Cheyenne stopped sharp in back of a neighboring house, then the doors kicked open and the first two Marines jumped out on rappel lines.

Gunfire began; outgoing and incoming. To Wren it was all a lot of noise.

"I'm tethering you to me," Acton said, and clipped onto Wren's jump harness with a karabiner. "You can't make this jump alone."

Wren just grunted and rose to his feet. His head spun with the sudden surge of blood, making him dizzy. "Go," he said and stepped out into air. Acton was already ahead of him and paying out line for their rapid descent. Wren fell, was caught in the harness then closed the last few yards under Acton's smooth control; Wren just watching the yellowing grass spin up toward him.

They hit the ground together. Wren's left leg gave out and he dropped to his knees, beyond dizzy already. Automatic gunfire ripped on all sides. Acton hoisted him back to his feet.

"Go," he barked.

"Go," Acton amplified, and the team moved; eight-strong with Wren at the center. It took five fast steps, punctuated by gunfire with the trees and faded white siding a blur. Acton held one hand to Wren's harness as they ran, holding him steadier.

They ran around toward the front of the house, where a haz-mat camera operator swung to film them with a look of shock on his face. Ahead lay the carnage of a fake gunfight in the street, haz-mats and billionaires in the house fending off the over-reaching arm of the State.

One of the Marines cold-cocked the haz-mat as they hunkered briefly beside the front porch. Wren stared at the manic battle in the street. Up close it didn't look fake. It looked real. Bodies lay scattered and bleeding. Bullets sparked convincingly off the bodywork of patrol cars. A woman in a police uniform lay on the blacktop, bleeding from a vicious head wound. You couldn't fake that kind of injury with makeup.

The Marines split and fired: one squad flanked left around the fake emergency forces, dropping them in a spray of lower leg shots; the other mounted the porch, Acton helping Wren with the ascent. A flashbang grenade went off nearby and stunned him; smoke billowed out through an open window. His team were rolling in, black-clad bodies streaming into smoke with goggles on and firing. There were screams. Wren tried to run after them, but Acton held him back.

"Wait, sir," he said.

They waited. Smoke enveloped them. Covering fire kept the forces on the street at bay, the few of them who were still standing. Haz-mat camera operators moved through the firefight like it wasn't even there.

"Now," said Acton, hoisted half of Wren's weight and ran in.

Smoke was everywhere, biting at Wren's eyes. He could barely see a thing; dark shadows moving in the gray, Marines firing disabling shots, throwing blows, leaving...

Wren saw his target.

"Let me go," he said to Acton.

The man melted away. Wren almost fell at once, but managed to lock out his left leg and just keep his feet. Through the bitter smoke, there he was. Bare-chested and enormous, his prodigious weight powered by muscles as big as watermelons, arms wide, pale skin sprayed with blood, wounded bodies quivering at his feet.

697

Damalin Joes III. The people's billionaire. Lips pulled back tight and eyes wide with the fire of some newfound righteousness. In both hands he held hatchets. Wren smiled. Of course. Haz-mats spun around them, capturing it all. A hell of a finale. Wren steadied his legs, took a stance, and raised his fists.

Damalin Joes saw him and laughed. "Christopher Wren," he boomed, "you barely look like a half a man anymore," then flew in with the hatchets arcing back.

47

DAMALIN JOES III

The right hatchet came in first, a haymaking chop from above, powerful enough to split Wren right down the middle. He barely sidestepped it, but Joes redirected his vast momentum with a nimbleness incredible for a man of his size, spinning out a hooking left strike.

Wren staggered three steps backward to evade it. On the fourth step his heels hit something, a body maybe, and he fell, rolled, then came up on his knees by instinct.

Damalin Joes III stood massive before him in the clearing smoke, a too-wide grin on his face, like clown makeup, clearly enjoying this.

"Not so fast as before," Joes said appraisingly. "Try that choking trick now."

Wren pushed himself to his feet, and Joes danced two lightning steps forward to swing both hatchets at once, a pincering blow that would lop Wren's head off like a dandelion. He barely flung himself away in time, feeling the rush of the blades passing near, then thumped into a wall.

The wind slammed from his lungs. This time Joes didn't press forward immediately. Instead he just watched, like he was studying a bug with its wings removed, struggling to fly.

"I saw your speech," he boomed through the smoke. "In the arena, after Harkness died. I thought it was so sad. An alpha surrendering."

Wren's mind spun, slowly straightening up. Damalin was a different man, there would be no reasoning with him. Kill a couple men in an arena, and your personality could change like a summer flood. Wren just needed to find the angle.

"Better than a beta rolling over on their whole life," he countered, hoping an adrenaline dump would come soon and speed up his sluggish reactions. His whole body felt out of sync and disoriented. "Are you a billionaire titan, Joes, or are you Yumiko Harkness' wind-up toy?"

Joes laughed, a deep rumble. "You can ask Cem Babak about that." He darted in again, right hatchet sweeping down hard. There was no time, nowhere to go, so Wren threw up a hand like Merriot Raine had, fingers splayed, but as the blade flew in he shoved off the wall, managed to slip the metal head and snag the handle.

It felt like catching the pumping piston of a steam train. The tendons in his wrist wrenched back, only just halting the hatchet's metal head within an inch of his scalp. Joes didn't hesitate and sent his left hatchet in a tight scythe toward Wren's extended arm, but Wren was already kicking off the wall. The momentum sent him barreling straight into Joes' chest.

He hit, Joes staggered a step then together they went down, hatchets clanking on the hard wood floor. Wren rolled away fast, eyes streaming with the smoke, maybe feeling a trickle of adrenaline pushing through, enough for one or two more concerted efforts.

On his feet, fists up again, for the first time he got a real sense of the room as the smoke cleared. It was a den, but devastated, littered with the dead and dying. Police, FBI, SWAT; bodies like props in their terminal performance. There was blood sprayed on the ceiling, there were wounds. All real. Joes had been in here for minutes only before Wren's Marines arrived, and he'd worked a whirlwind of devastation. The man was as powerful as a bull.

Nearby black-clad Marines surged through the smoke, battling the billionaires hand-to-hand. Wren caught flashes of weaponry, but no gunshots rang out, in line with his orders. Everything was tracked by the Reparations' camera operators, four of them weaving smoothly around the action in their red-stained white haz-mats suits, streaming video to the ten percent.

The message was all that mattered now. No help was coming from the Marines. Wren was on his own.

He turned back to Damalin Joes. The huge man was on his feet. A thin trickle of blood rolled down his jaw, but he was grinning still. Wren knew he couldn't take the man hand-to-hand, not even with the adrenaline, not in his current state.

"She's using you, Damalin," he said, and felt his father's firebrand voice ring out from his throat, stronger than expected. "You're the poster boy for a vengeance you don't even understand."

Damalin Joes just laughed, advancing as Wren circled around a toppled coffee table. "Like you used me? And do you think I care?"

He came in fast, this time leading with a big front kick. Wren rolled it with his left forearm, spun and bounced a backhand off Joes' head. Joes barely noticed, spinning tight to slam his right-hand hatchet into Wren's injured side.

The Twaron vest blocked the edge but still the force carried through, thumping the wind out of Wren's lungs for a second time and sending shooting pains deep into his spine. Wren acted through the pain: with his left hand he trapped the hatchet-head against his ribs, with his right he hooked Joes' upper arm and for a second they looked into each other's eyes, locked in an embrace so close they could kiss. Then Wren put a stinging head-butt into the bridge of Joe's nose.

The big man broke away, hatchets flailing for balance. Wren himself staggered and almost fell. Hard to breathe after that, head spinning. Ignoring pain was one thing, but you couldn't ignore damage. He had minutes left before that blow in the side took him down; the shrapnel wounds re-opened, maybe some internal bleeding if he was unlucky. He had to make it happen now.

Damalin Joes caught his balance and stamped back, lips awash with blood pouring from his broken nose. He spat blood at Wren, red on the Twaron, and whirled his hatchets.

"Try that again," he said, and lunged.

Wren barely slipped the left swipe, dropped and rolled under the right. It took it out of him; he came up slow and wheezing.

"You're tired," Joes said, advancing. "You've had a hard day, half man. Lie down and rest."

Another swing, another duck. Wren managed to bat a follow-up strike clear, but it was close, just barely deflecting off his thigh armor plate and almost burying in the meat of his leg.

Joes kept advancing as Wren limped backward across the den. "This is all you've got? It's so sad. I can do this all day, but you?"

Another powerful swing: Wren backed into the sofa and rolled over it awkwardly, calves smacking down hard on a fallen chair, arms slipping off a wet body. Joes stalked him like a predator.

"To see the mighty so fallen. I know all about your 'Foundation' now, little man. It's pathetic. To think I ever let you guilt trip me? You should have fired that gun early, ended things in the desert."

Wren had only seconds left, maybe one good play left before one of Joes' hatchets landed. His body was exhausted but his mind wasn't, and he'd done this countless times before. Deprogramming cult members. It took days, weeks, a lifetime sometimes, but these were extreme conditions, coming on the back of an extreme conversion, and extremity helped move the needle.

"How does it feel," Wren asked, barely lurching out of range of another haymaker behind the sofa, "knowing that all this was for me?"

Joes sprang over the sofa and came at Wren direct, hatchets high. "What are you babbling about? You're a footnote."

Now Wren laughed, hobbling behind the dining table and clutching his side, managing to bark out a few more words. "You were a reality show contestant, Damalin!" He skipped back from a chop that smashed splinters out of the table. "A billionaire reduced to nothing more than an actor on a stage, recruited solely to capture *my* attention." Another wild slash. "This doesn't lead to anything for you, and you must know that. I survived Harkness' attack. The Reparations app is gone. There's nothing left for you to do. Even if you win here, what do you think you'll get?"

Joes grinned, bright blood outlining each of his perfect white teeth. "Have you heard of mindfulness, Christopher? It's all the rage. I didn't really know what it was until a few days ago. Now I understand."

Wren laughed. "You think killing is mindful?"

"It's the only thing that is." Joes lunged forward and Wren staggered back. "The way it feels when you look a dying man in the eyes. I think you more than anyone know what I mean. You killed a thousand, didn't you?"

Wren tried to catch his breath, limping and reeling. So Joes had watched the video. He had only a couple chances left. "I did. I saw that look in their eyes and it broke me, Damalin. There's always a cost. The rush of power comes right along with the shame. But you get to choose how far you twist yourself inside to deny the existence of either."

"Pretty words," Joes hissed and flung out a downward swipe.

Wren barely sidestepped and pressed on. "Words are everything! Yumiko Harkness used them to brainwash you. Just like I was brainwashed. We're both victims, Damalin. Right now I know it seems as if the whole world has shifted and permission has been granted, but the world hasn't changed, Damalin." He spread his arms wide. "There is no permission for this."

"You're making excuses," Joes said, twirling his blades so blood flicked like sparks from a Catherine wheel. "It's what weak men do right before they die. It's what Merriot Raine did. He begged me. He kept on begging as I brought the hatchet down."

"What about when you ripped Handel Quanse apart, Damalin? Was it the same then?"

That froze Joes for a second, standing between the coffee table and sofa. A strange mixture of emotions played across his face. Maybe uncertainty. Taking him back to the first moment of indoctrination and exposing the illogic; a standard deprogramming tool.

"He was weak."

Wren laughed. "Handel Quanse was weak? He was as strong as any of you. Your cellmate. So he had to go." Wren circled into the kitchen, cameras following tightly. "Were you were happy to lead that charge? Rip him up before he even had a chance?"

"That wasn't me!" Joes spat immediately, words out of his mouth before he could stop them. "I didn't want that."

Now Wren smiled. An opening. "Didn't you? Then who did? Was it Yumiko Harkness, should I be talking to her, your boss? Except she's dead, leaving you holding the bag."

Joes' glare darkened. The exultation was fading, replaced by defensive rage. Wren knew that feeling well. It was the ugly face men showed to avoid feeling shame. "You don't know what you're talking about."

"Don't I?" Wren edged around the granite-topped island, half a retreat, half an advance. "I've seen the videos. I've been to that arena. Hell, son, I just got done tearing it down. The cages, the stage, all of it. That was a silicon chip factory, Joes. It was rich assholes like you who killed it; outsourced the work, automated it away, and your boss, Yumiko Harkness?

Her father worked there! He lost his job, so she went bananas. It's as simple as that. You're just the instrument of her revenge." He paused as he circled, watching Joes' expression. "A smart woman. She thought she knew who I was too. She directed me step-by-step, just like she directed you with that electroshock collar, like a dog running to the command of a bell. She thought I'd over-react when she burned herself alive, double down on shutting down free speech, but she had me wrong. I think she has you wrong too."

Joes' face remained dark and angry, but Wren felt the uncertainty building in him like an explosion. Recognizing your own failures could feel like an act of self-destruction.

"Because you were weak," Joes said.

Again Wren laughed. Not mocking now, mournful. "Listen to what you just said, Damalin! I didn't destroy freedom of speech, one of the pillars of this nation, because I was weak? It was strength that got me through. Like you on that horse, yanking Handel Quanse behind you. You didn't want to do that, no matter what she told you afterward. You did what you had to to survive. But there's nobody here pulling your strings anymore." Wren gestured to the smoky, bloody room. "You can let it go; show your real strength and get back to the old version of Damalin Joes."

Joes stood perfectly still now, like a suicide bomber with his finger on the trigger. "The old version's a fool."

"The old version's a billionaire!" Wren snapped back. "*You* achieved that. Sure, maybe you started with a loaded deck, a nice inheritance, but what you built was still extraordinary, far more impressive than killing a few men with your bare hands, especially when every single death was fake!" He sucked in a breath. "Think about it, Damalin! The arena, the slaughter in the cages, even the stage; she wrote your role for you! She put you in a set with a script and a well-rehearsed cast and watched you recite your lines like a good little boy."

Wren was close to shouting now, about all the energy he had left. "And as a reward, she screwed you. Explain all this some other way." He gestured at the bodies lying on the floor. "You must know that these people are all just extras in costumes ready to die for her cause. People she brainwashed too. What does it even mean to kill them, when their deaths were scripted before this thing began?" He paused, reading Joes' breathing, the flicker of his pulse in his temple. "You're wearing the costume she

704

picked out, playing your part in her grand production. Maybe the lead role, but you think you're in charge? Don't make me laugh. She wrote the whole damn movie!"

Joes' breathing grew faster. Wren could feel the fight-flight state building to climax. Like Simon back in Deadhorse. One step either way and everything would change. Part of him would only want to chop Wren to bits, to revel in the thrill and kill his doubts. Another part would want to hear more, was crying out to be saved.

Finishing touches.

"You're a victim here, Joes. Like Merriot Raine, like Handel Quanse, like me. We're all just clockwork toys waiting to be wound up and set loose, used by our emotions, abused by our past until we do crazy things just to stay alive, just to get approval; things we would never normally do, and then we think we're strong for it? That's not strong! That's just survival. What's strong is you think for yourself, you look at what you're doing and what you've done and make a choice about who you want to be." He panted, exhausted. Could hardly talk any more. "You were a Rhodes scholar, Damalin! You clerked for the Supreme Court, you came up hard, bloodied a few noses along the way, but you were not afraid to face the truth. You made billions, and now you're ashamed of that? Think again. Just think."

Joes stared. Worlds turned inside his eyes. Permissions being granted, being revoked. It was a lot to swallow; what he'd done, what had been done to him. It would take years, but it always began with one step.

His arms twitched. Imagining using the hatchets. Maybe the onset of an attack. Wren steeled himself. He couldn't dodge any more. Take a few more hits on his Twaron, maybe, but then...

Then he'd be dead.

"Tell them to shoot."

It was Hellion's voice in his ear. She had his bodycam. She saw everything he saw, first-person perspective, and thought she knew better.

He ignored her.

"I'll tell them," she said.

From the corner of his eye Wren saw one of the Marines lift his rifle, listening to Hellion's orders. The billionaires were down and the guns were on Damalin Joes, but Wren couldn't turn away now. Couldn't say another word, had to trust the Marines would trust him more than her. Damalin Joes

III was frozen in indecision, eyes shining, hatchet blades trembling in the air.

One more idea to push the moment as far as he could.

"Nothing you've done so far condemns you, Damalin. You can come out of this stronger. Plead insanity; it's the truth, and it doesn't make you weak, only human. You were kidnapped from the safety of your home, man! Drugged, stripped naked, dehumanized, treated worse than an animal. The tactics they used on you will be studied for years to come; advanced psychological warfare, enough to crack the strongest minds we have. No person could have held up against the onslaught, and that was the point. That's why it worked; if the best amongst us can be turned against their own interests, then nothing matters, nothing means anything anymore." Wren gasped for breath, silver lights flashing before his eyes. "But our actions do matter, Damalin! What we say and do has meaning, and the balance lies in your hands. Turn away now, I guarantee you will be a hero. You resisted, your better angels won out, you're a case study for a new model of humanity. Push through though, you get to be king of the ashes. You get to kill me, but is that really the limit of your ambition? All addicts know the drug is bad for them. Few addicts become billionaires. I don't think you're the one bad penny to break that mold. Tell me I'm wrong."

Hellion shouted orders in the background.

His own pulse raced. Marines held their weapons high. At any second the whole thing could implode.

Then Joes let go.

Wren saw it first in his eyes, the opposite of that first decision on the arena's sand. Next the hatchets fell from his hands. He transformed in a heartbeat, back to the man he'd been before. Imperfect, yes, cruel, even vengeful, but not a murderer.

"I don't-" he began, but nothing more came.

Marines rushed in. They handled Joes gently, onto his knees, putting on cuffs like this was a police matter. No black bag over his head, and that was good. Wren turned to the haz-mat operators, half of them watching Joes, half watching him. He stared down their lenses.

"He's the last," he said. "No more forgiveness after this."

Then he walked out.

He didn't make it far. Out the door and onto the porch, looking over the scene of blood and wreckage. The Cheyenne had touched down in a neighboring yard, rotor blades still spinning. There were bodies everywhere, cars shredded by automatic weapons' fire, broken glass.

On the yellow grass he fell to his knees. Too exhausted. He had nothing left. Hellion was talking. More forces were inbound. Humphreys had the location now. A team was winging its way closer.

Then there were hands hoisting him up. It was hard to see, with his vision blurring. He saw the contours of a familiar face.

"Man says mobilize, I mobilize."

"Wha-?" Wren managed.

"Teddy sent us," Gruber answered, getting under Wren's arm, holding him up along with someone else. Was it Doona? "You'll be OK."

"Man says OK," Wren managed.

48

MAN ON THE INSIDE

A nother bed, another building. Drip cables fed into Wren's wrist. There was a window and a dresser with a mirror, flowery wallpaper looking a little worse for wear, a medical chart within reach on a side table. He took it.

'Medically-induced coma', it said. Three days. Ruptured left kidney. Displaced vertebra. Early-onset sepsis. Internal bleeding.

Wren felt hungry. His face hurt, and his back, and his side. He reached one hand up, touched his cheek. Stippled with scar tissue from the Anti-Ca grenades. Even with the best plastic surgery money could buy, he'd carry some remnant of these scars. His children might not recognize him when he saw them next.

He pushed the blanket away. It was thin cotton, but even that much exertion left him sweating and faint. His bare chest was yellowy with bruising, emanating from a dark purple blot above his left hip, as big around as a dinner plate. The scarring wasn't so bad here, thanks to the Twaron vest; it seemed his arm and face had taken the worst of it.

He swung his legs out and stood, barely holding himself up.

"Lie down," came a voice through a croaky speaker. Wren looked around slowly; it hurt to turn fast. Not a speaker in sight, but a teddy bear nannycam sat on the chest of drawers, dark glass eyes watching.

"I can see you," the voice went on. "I've called security."

"Hellion?" he asked, then, "security?"

The door opened. In came Steven Gruber, NSA Analyst. He looked pale and drawn. His face showed a lot of emotions. Happiness, yes, but also a kind of expectant concern, like he was very worried about what Wren would say or do next.

"You're up," he said cautiously, "ahead of schedule."

"And you're security?" Wren asked.

Gruber shrugged awkwardly. "Hellion likes playing games." Like that explained everything.

Wren looked at him, around the room. Just the two of them. "You've been looking after me?"

"I volunteered." Gruber took a step further in. "It only seemed right, given how we started this thing together."

Wren nodded. That was true. Breaking NameCheck felt like a very long time ago.

"Are we in the Oregon farm?"

"No," said Gruber. "A different one. Teddy set it all up. We're all busy now. A lot of private jets, doing surveys, 'resource investigation', he calls it. I've got a role there, but I wanted to do this first. To make sure."

"He's been doing everything," Hellion's voice came through the nannycam, mocking. "Sponge baths, comb your hair, brush your teeth, little goodnight kiss…"

Gruber reddened. "I didn't-"

Wren sighed. You couldn't stop the kids from being kids. "That teddy bear is starting to freak me out. Can you turn it off?"

Gruber looked surprised. "I, uh. Teddy, I mean, I know that's a kind of in-joke, Hellion's joke I think, but Teddy wanted-"

"Is Teddy here?"

A pause. Maybe Gruber was fighting the urge to look around and be sure. "Uh, no, he's-"

"So turn it off."

Gruber took a few hesitant steps.

"Do not terminate this device," Hellion's voice came through firmly, "it is condition of Christopher's new parole status, one-coin negative that-"

Gruber reached the bear, looked to Wren who nodded, then pushed the power button.

There was a silence.

"I'm one-coin negative?"

Gruber reddened further. "I… uh, I mean. I think they're trying it out. A lot of new ideas, you know?"

Wren fixed him with a glare. "Trying it out on me?"

"Uh."

Wren cursed under his breath. If Teddy couldn't steal the Foundation, he'd end up changing it so much it was unrecognizable. But Wren had left him in charge, and this is what he got.

"I think there's a Board meeting scheduled for the day you wake up," Gruber said, trying to be helpful. "The room's all set for it, I can-"

"Hold on."

Gruber stopped talking.

There were a lot of things to ask. To say. Three days in a coma, things would change. There were things that really mattered. There was no question what mattered most, though.

"How's Rogers?"

Gruber looked at his feet. "I think we should set up the meeting, get the full debrief, because-"

"Steven."

Gruber looked up, clearly at war inside himself, but making the decision fast. "I don't know. FBI took her from the hospital, and we haven't heard anything since. We think she's OK, but we don't know…" He paused a moment, then went on more brightly. "FBI swept the Anti-Ca compound too, right after your last transmission. There were surrenders, I heard, looks like they didn't go the suicide route, so that's good, isn't it?"

He smiled encouragingly.

"And the Reparations?"

"The app's dead. Most of them have gone silent. We have many of their IP addresses, the ones who wouldn't delete it. Most of them did, after Pie Town. It was…" Gruber seemed lost for words. "Inspired. The way you turned it around."

"I was half high on oxycodone," Wren said. "The whole time. Let's not read too much into it."

"Of course," said Gruber, though he clearly didn't think so. "Well then."

"And copycats?"

"Stopped cold. On TV they've been debating your amnesty. Pundits, talk shows, late night." A pause. "You're a major topic, too. You're famous now, your story is out there. People are coming down on all sides." He stopped, maybe reading the disapproving look on Wren's face before hurrying on. "But the amnesty, Congress is considering some kind of legislation. I doubt they'll get anything real through, but there seems to be a sense that people want to do something about inequality. It makes sense, right? If we weren't so unequal, this thing never would've gotten so crazy." He paused, thought a moment. "Following on from that, it seems nobody wants to hunt down the thousands of citizens who committed lesser crimes. graffiti, public disorder, property damage and so on."

"And the major crimes?"

"Arrests are ongoing. The billionaires, Damalin Joes foremost, are asking for insanity pleas, just like you said. It looks like they'll get them, if public opinion is anything to go by. They're not popular men, but there's a certain kind of understanding, right now? They've been talking about the experience on chat shows, about how it overwhelmed them, and nobody can really argue with that."

Wren nodded. "We all had a weaponized dose of manipulation. Make sure Teddy pushes that narrative. If it's good enough to get the billionaires off, it should get others off too."

Gruber stared. "Uh, you mean, I should tell him?"

"You're on the Board, aren't you?"

"Um, yes? I suppose so."

"So raise it. You're my man on the inside." Wren winked.

Gruber just stared. Probably he was wondering what he'd let himself in for. "I, uh, thank you?"

"Don't mention it."

They looked at each other. Wren smiled. He felt good somehow. There was the pain, it would be there for weeks now as he healed, but still he felt better. His father had done this, and he'd lost. Wren had come out of it stronger than before. He could think back on his past in a new way now. He'd even spoken to Tandrews. It felt like a dream, but it was real. Dr. Ferat would be proud.

Gruber shifted uncomfortably. "So, was there something I could get for you, or…"

"What's a guy gotta do to get some food in this place?"

"Oh, yeah," said Gruber, so relieved he laughed. "Of course, I'll get some. Hash browns, bacon, beans. Pancakes if you like, eggs too. It's around breakfast time."

Wren grinned sunnily. "Sounds perfect."

49

REPARATION

Five days later, Wren arrived in the little town of Frederica, Delaware not knowing what to expect. Deep black skies and a watery white moon. The past seemed very far away. The future too. He no longer had his phone set to a 4 a.m. alarm, because there was no need. He was planning to see his family soon.

The new family duplex had a grass yard, picket fences, just like Pie Town. He pulled up fifty yards away under the streetlamps, then sat with his heart pounding like crazy, hoping just to catch a glimpse of them when they woke. To see Jake rushing out to try out his BMX. To see Quinn pacing thoughtfully around the yard, checking on her plants. To know they were OK.

At sun-up he'd get out, go over and knock, try to explain things to Loralei as best he could. Try to get back in their lives, even a little bit...

Then the voice came.

"You're getting slow."

It came from behind him, through the open window. He turned and recognized the figure standing in the darkness, splashed by the streetlights. Just behind the C-column of his truck, holding a gun trained on him, with more figures in the shadows drawing near. Rifles, body armor, creeping up.

He watched her in the wing mirror, thinking that maybe this was always how it was going to go. Family was a weakness; he'd known that since he was a child. At least, seeing her came as something of a relief.

"Agent Rogers. You're alive."

"No thanks to you." A pause. "You promised me you'd come in."

There was a lot of hurt in her eyes. Anger. Leave it too long, and there'd just be nothing.

"I hoped I could see them first."

"The answer's no." Another pause, freighted with the past. "You shot me, Wren."

He gave a sad half-smile. She'd never called him Wren before. There was a lot he could say, but even in his head it all sounded like excuses: that she'd been wearing a bulletproof vest, that he'd been packing slow-velocity bullets, that she'd lost faith and pulled a gun on him first. All pointless, because in the moment he'd made the choice and put her at risk.

"I'm sorry, Sally."

Rogers said nothing. Wren looked ahead at the lights of the duplex. The truth was staring him in the face even now. It had been for hours, and maybe he just hadn't wanted to see. A light on in the living room window. He'd seen the curtains twitch a few hours back and ignored it.

"She called you, didn't she?"

He heard Rogers take a step closer. Unclasping handcuffs from her belt, sliding her fingers into the door handle. "You should've checked in with me, saved yourself a trip. Your family's been under my protection since you started slaughtering Pinocchios."

He couldn't smile through that. Didn't know what to feel. That Loralei was afraid of him. That his kids might be afraid. He turned in the seat, looking back at her. "Can I at least see them? That's all I want. Before you put me under."

Rogers tilted her head, and a stray wash of yellow lamplight caught her, cast through tree branches. She looked well, as solid as ever, blond hair tied back, no longer red-eyed and exhausted.

"You know the answer's no. They don't want to see you, and I couldn't allow it anyway. You're still on a catch/kill order."

That hit like a punch in the gut. Catch/kill. He'd allowed himself to dream, that the forgiveness extended for minor Reparation crimes might extend to him. Might extend to the past.

"Humphreys said I could be licensed for the Pinocchio deaths."

Rogers snorted. Her team moved up closer. "You should've known that was BS. He's a professional liar."

Of course. You didn't become Director of the CIA without telling your share of lies along the way.

"My father's out there, Rogers. I know it. This isn't over."

"We'll finish it for you."

Not much to say to that. They couldn't. Not against the Apex. But he'd let himself be cornered. "Catch/kill," he said softly. "Which are you betting on?"

"Neither," she answered. "A third option."

"Cooperation?"

She leaned in closer to the window. He'd always admired that about Rogers; she acted even when she was most afraid. "That, or something very much like it."

Wren smiled sadly. It was moments like these where you made decisions that forever affected your life. Who you were going to be. He had promised to come in, after all. Maybe his family would come see him in prison.

"Cooperation," he repeated, and just sat there, in the shadowy driver's seat while her team moved in front, rifles pointing right at him through the windshield. He wondered how much they were even following Rogers' orders, and how much this was on Humphreys. "He wants the Foundation."

"Above my pay grade," Rogers answered.

Wren squeezed the wheel. Felt any hopes he'd nurtured for the future crumbling. Realized that all along this was what he'd been dreaming of. Get himself straight. Clean up the threat to his family and maybe, just maybe, his wife would forgive him.

Not everyone forgave.

"I'll never cooperate," he said. "Not like that. I won't hand them over."

"Tell that to your interrogators," Rogers answered, "I don't care anymore. Now put your hands out through the door, Christopher, palms up."

He looked ahead, to the duplex and the yard, to the lit living room window where a silhouette now stood, looking back. Loralei.

A dozen plans played through his mind: steal Rogers' gun and turn it against her, take out the guys dead ahead, get the truck started and ram through the rest, spin out of Frederica and back out into the darkness. It wasn't impossible. He'd done it before. His Foundation would support him. He had doctors to extract bullets. He had the darknet to cover his tracks. They'd never come near him again.

Then there was Rogers, and her eyes. Hard eyes. Angry too. Angry at him, at what he was thinking even now. It felt like she could see right into his soul, like she knew what he was planning. What had he come all this way for, after all?

The cycle had to stop somewhere. Nothing came for free. The bill always came due at the end. His family were gone, and that stung more than anything else, and maybe it was exactly what he deserved.

He put his hands through the window, let her cuff him. She opened the door and pulled him out onto his knees. He could withstand their interrogations. Maybe Humphreys would come through with the license. Maybe not. What else did he have to offer, now?

"Reparation," he said.

Rogers opened a black bag, brought it down. In the second before it covered his eyes, he glimpsed a second silhouette at the living room window, standing behind Loralei and holding a hatchet high.

Then the bag came down, cinched around his neck and nothing he said mattered after that.

THE NEXT CHRIS WREN SERIES BOX SET

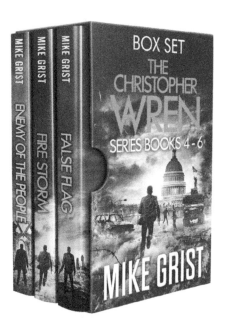

They made him their enemy. They'll regret it.

False Flag - Someone's framed Chris Wren for murder.
He'll kill to clear his name.

Firestorm - A woman burns herself alive online, and others follow.
There'll be no shelter from the firestorm to come.

Enemy of the People - The masses battle in the streets over hellfire and
lies.
Only Chris Wren can bring the truth to light.

AVAILABLE IN EBOOK & PAPERBACK

geni.us/HDixt

HAVE YOU READ EVERY CHRIS WREN THRILLER?

Saint Justice

They stole his truck. Big mistake.

No Mercy

Hackers came for his kids. There can be no mercy.

Make Them Pay

The latest reality TV show: execute the rich.

False Flag

They framed him for murder. He'll kill to clear his name.

Firestorm

Wren's father is back. The storm is coming.

Enemy of the People

Lies are drowning America. Can the country survive?

Backlash

He just wanted to go home. They got in the way...

Never Forgive

His home in ashes. Vengeance never forgives.

War of Choice

They came for his team. This time it's war.

Learn more at www.shotgunbooks.com

HAVE YOU READ EVERY GIRL 0 THRILLER?

Girl Zero
They stole her little sister. Now they'll pay.

Zero Day
The criminal world is out for revenge. So is she.

Learn more at www.shotgunbooks.com

HAVE YOU READ THE LAST MAYOR THRILLERS?

The Last Mayor series - Books 1-9

When the zombie apocalypse devastates the world overnight, Amo is the last man left alive.

Or is he?

Learn more at www.shotgunbooks.com

JOIN THE FOUNDATION!

Join Chris Wren's Foundation, and get your first coin - alongside Wren's top-secret CIA profile!

You'll also be first to hear when the next Chris Wren thriller is coming.

www.subscribepage.com/christopher-wren

Made in the USA
Monee, IL
10 August 2023

40783141R10426